Sharon Ellery was born and raised in London, and still resides there. This is her first novel.

To Robert & Julia

I hope you like the book.

Take Care

Sharon Ellery.

I would like to dedicate this book to the children of the world, who have suffered abuse and come through it, and sadly for the ones who didn't.

Sharon Ellery

SIBLINGS

AUSTIN MACAULEY PUBLISHERS™

LONDON • CAMBRIDGE • NEW YORK • SHARJAH

A CIP catalogue record for this title is available from the British Library.

ISBN 9781398437227 (Paperback)
ISBN 9781398437234 (ePub e-book)

www.austinmacauley.com

First Published 2022
Austin Macauley Publishers Ltd®
1 Canada Square
Canary Wharf
London
E14 5AA

I would like to thank Glynis, Susan and Deb, who gave me encouragement along the way.

Also, to Perry, who read it first and stayed up all night to finish it.

Chapter 1

As Alison looked down at her new bundle of joy, she knew she had never been happier, and her life would never be the same again. She thought back to that day. A day that was as normal as any other; only it wasn't...

She had gotten up as normal. It was only 8 am and she went into the kitchen to get her breakfast. Her brother, Tom, was already sitting at the table eating his cornflakes whilst drinking his glass of milk. She sat at the table and started to pour the milk on her cereal. Mum was drinking her coffee and Dad was reading the paper, just like any other Monday morning. After she finished eating, she put her dish into the sink and went into the bathroom to get washed and ready for school. Tom followed her and got himself ready.

"Mum," he called, "I can't do my laces up, can you help me?"

Eileen went to her son to help him finish getting ready.

"John," Eileen called.

"Yes, what do you want? I'm busy," replied John.

"I just wanted to know what time you were leaving for work?" Eileen asked.

"I don't have to go into until later this morning, Eileen. Are you ready to take the children to school yet?" her husband asked.

"Yes, nearly there," she said.

"Bye Dad!" both children said.

"Yeah bye..." he replied as they shut the front door and headed off to school.

Eileen, Alison and Tom were walking to school. It wasn't far away. Tom was talking to himself about the cars at school he wanted to play with. Alison was talking to her mum about some painting she was doing in class for her. They were all walking, happily holding hands, until they got to the school gates. Eileen kissed and waved the children off to their classroom and then she bumped into another of the mums who wanted to know about the school trip the children were going on. After about 10 minutes, Eileen said her goodbyes and walked back home.

When she got in, John was nowhere to be seen. She thought it odd as he'd told her he wasn't going in to work until later that morning. She thought they could have a coffee and a chat before he headed off.

John then reappeared with a brown bag in his hand.

"What's that, John love?" Eileen asked, observing the bag.

"Never mind. Have you got the kettle on?" John replied.

Eileen got up and went into the kitchen to put the kettle on.

John and his family didn't live in a house, but in a little flat at the top of a building with a shop underneath. John went to the cupboard where he kept his tools and pulled out an electric screwdriver. He then took out the two little suitcases he had packed whilst Eileen and the children had left for school.

Eileen hadn't seen the suitcases, but she had seen the lock and bolts that John was attaching to Alison and Tom's bedroom.

"John, whatever are you doing with those locks?" Eileen asked as she handed him his cup of coffee.

He ignored her, got out the screws he had in his hand, put them in the door frame and pulled out the electric screwdriver. John started to screw the screws into the lock and door frame.

"John, what are you doing? Why are you locking the kid's bedrooms?"

John, who had completely ignored Eileen, spoke.

"Those kids are not coming back here. They don't live here anymore. They are going. They are going to a home, I don't want them anymore, they are going, and they aren't coming back."

"What? What are you talking about? Don't be so ridiculous! John, they are our kids, our children, we made them! I gave birth to them! You can't just get rid of them because you don't want them anymore!"

John turned to Eileen.

"Those children are not coming back here…they don't live here anymore. I'm going out in a little while. When I get back, I want every trace of them gone. Do you hear me? GONE! Put their things into the two black bags that are there, one each for the rest of their stuff."

Eileen didn't know what to do. These two lovely innocent children whom she loved so much; she couldn't let him take them away, he couldn't do that… He loved them; she knew he did.

John picked up the two suitcases and off he went down to the school. He knew he was right. He knew that they couldn't stay with them any longer. It was easier this way, they could have a new family. But not with him and Eileen. Not anymore.

Eileen stood in the hallway in shock. She couldn't do it. She couldn't put their things into a bag. The few toys they had…Tom's little cars, Alison's two dolls—one with blonde hair and the other, brown, with their matching clothes in pink and blue. Tom had his big yellow dump truck, the ones you see down at a quarry, picking up and dropping off sand, concrete, salt for when the roads need it, when it snowed. She couldn't just wipe them from their lives. There had to be something wrong with John. She had never seen him like this before. He must be under stress from work or something. Maybe he wasn't well, and he wasn't thinking straight?

John arrived at the school and asked to see the headmaster. He didn't have to wait too long.

Mr Thompson, the headmaster, soon arrived.

John dumped the suitcases at his feet.

"You can have them now."

John walked back down the corridor.

Mr Thompson stood there shocked as if he were a rabbit caught in the headlights.

"Mr Davis, what's wrong, Mr Davis? Surely we need to talk about this?"

John just ignored Mr Thompson and carried on out of the school gates and back home.

Mr Thompson, who was still standing holding the two little suitcases, didn't know what to do, except call for Mrs Wilkins Tom's teacher.

Back home, Eileen, who didn't know what was going on, was waiting for her husband to return, with the children's suitcases and to say it was all a big mistake. That he had woken up in a bad mood and this was how he was handling it.

John walked through the door, saw Eileen sitting down, the toys were on the floor and so were the empty black bags.

"What the hell is this, woman? I told you to have all their stuff in bags, not be sitting down drinking coffee!"

John took two strides over to Eileen and he grabbed her by the arm and pushed her down on the floor.

"You see this stuff, this rubbish, I want you to put it into those two bags, NOW!"

11

"But John!" Eileen cried. "These are Alison and Tom's toys, their things, I can't just put them into bags, they will want them when they come back."

"You stupid bitch! They aren't coming back! Someone else is going to be looking after them now!" John bellowed.

Eileen couldn't take it in. How come her babies weren't coming home? What had he done with them?

With that, John moved over towards Eileen and punched her violently in the back.

"Do you hear me, woman? Get those things in that bag now!" he screamed in Eileen's face. Despite the pain, she put their toys into the two black bags as quick as she could: one for Alison and one for Tom.

Eileen had never seen John like that before. She didn't know what else to do. John picked up the black bags and took them out of the flat and he was gone.

Eileen didn't know what to do. In the whole of their eight-year marriage, she had never seen her husband act like that before. He'd never laid a hand on her at all. She could just about get up off the floor, but her back hurt. She hadn't felt pain like that before.

***

At school, Alison was unaware of what was going on at home and she was happily playing in the water pit. She had finished her painting of her, her brother, her mum and dad, all happy at the seaside.

Once they'd had lunch at school, they were playing in the playground. Tom was in the nursery, so he was in a different part of the playground, playing with the outdoor toys.

Alison was playing snakes and ladders with her friend Emily. It was a lovely day and they were having lots of fun. Once playtime was over, they had to line up to go back to class. They were making fondant sweets in the afternoon. They all had some fondant and some mint flavourings and also colourings, so some were made in pink, some green and some blue. Alison had made a couple of green leaves for Mum, as green was her favourite colour.

Tom had blue and Alison managed to find some red for Dad's fondant sweets. By the time they had finished and washed their hands, it was nearly home time.

Mrs Sharp, the deputy head, came into class to talk to Alison's teacher, Miss Howe. They were talking quietly but looking at Alison whilst they spoke. When school ended, Alison made her way to Tom's class, as that was where Mum picked them up from.

They were waiting for ages and Mum still hadn't arrived to collect them. *I hope Mum's OK*, Alison thought to herself, *she's never been late before.*

Mrs Wilkins came and sat down beside Alison and Tom.

"There's been a change of plan in collecting you today, children."

"There's nothing wrong, is there, Mrs Wilkins?" Alison asked, feeling a little nervous. Mum always picked them up from school.

"Oh no dear, but the headmaster wants to talk to you now," she replied.

Mr Thompson came into Tom's classroom and sat down with the children.

"Alison, Tom, Mrs Wilkins is going to take you somewhere, as I'm afraid Mummy can't come and collect you at the moment."

"How come, Mr Thompson?" Alison asked. At nearly seven years old, Alison was a very bright little girl.

"We don't know at the moment, but if you go with Mrs Wilkins, she will take good care of you."

With that, Mr Thompson left the classroom.

Alison and Tom looked at one another in bemusement, not knowing what was going on.

"Come along, you two, let's get a move on." Mrs Wilkins said.

So off they went. Alison, Tom and Mrs Wilkins, with the children's suitcases, to Mrs Wilkins' car. It was a little car, but it was a red car and Tom liked red cars. They got into the car and put their seatbelts on.

***

Mrs Wilkins and the children turned up at the children's home, which was a big white building with lots of windows. Alison and Tom followed Mrs Wilkins up the stairs to the main reception.

"I have the Davis' children with me. We spoke on the phone to a lady called Christine Walters, she said she would meet me in reception," Mrs Wilkins told the receptionist.

"Just one moment please, I'll call her and let her know that you're here with the children."

13

A large woman in a crisp brown tweed suit came to the reception.

"Hello, I am Ms Walters, we spoke earlier, nice to meet you," she held out her hand for Mrs Wilkins to shake it.

Ms Walters called to one of her staff, Sandra.

"Sandra? Oh, there you are, Sandra, please could you show Alison and Tom to their rooms?"

"Certainly, Ms Walters. Come on, Alison and Tom, let's get you settled in."

They went up some stairs to the first floor, on the right and down three rooms. This was going to be Tom's room. He had a roommate called Freddie.

Freddie was a little older than Tom, he was nearly four. There were two beds in the room. The one on the right was taken, that was Freddie's. Tom had the bed on the left. The room was quite bright. It had blue wallpaper with aeroplanes on them, different ones, big ones, small ones, and some in different colours. The carpet was dark blue, there were two wardrobes and two chests of drawers. Tom had the white ones and Freddie had the wooden ones.

Tom sat on the bed to see how bouncy it was. He took his coat off and unpacked his little suitcase, with the help of George.

George worked on this floor with the little and big boys. George was quite a young man, in his late twenties. He had worked at the home for a couple of years now and he loved his job.

When George and Tom had emptied Tom's suitcase into the drawers and wardrobe, George took Tom to have a look around.

Whilst Tom and George were sorting out Tom's things, Sandra spoke to Alison.

"Shall we find where you're going to be?"

Alison nodded yes.

She felt a little shy and didn't understand what was going on. They said bye to Tom and George and went to find where Alison would be sleeping. They came out of the room and back down the corridor to the staircase and up another flight of stairs.

It was the same layout as the floor below but this time they went to the second room on the right, where there were three beds in the room. It was a much bigger room. It had lilac wallpaper with little yellow daisies on them.

The bed on the left-hand side and the bed across at the bottom had both been taken by two other little girls and the bed on the right was to be Alison's bed. There were three wardrobes and three small drawers, but enough to put all of their things away. Two little girls came in, who were the other bed's occupants, Josephine and Hilary.

They went straight up to Alison.

"Who are you and what are you doing in our bedroom?" One of the little girls asked.

Before Alison could reply with an answer, Sandra, who was putting Alison's clothes away in the wardrobe and was hidden from sight, came out.

"Josephine and Hilary, this is Alison and she will be sleeping in your room with you. Is that OK?" Sandra said.

"Oh, yes, of course. It's just that it's only been Josephine and me for the last few months. We didn't know we were getting another girl in here," replied Hilary.

She gave Alison a very dirty look before leaving the bedroom.

"Take no notice of those two, Alison. They have had this room to themselves for a while now. They will be fine…any problems then ask for me."

"Thank you, Sandra," Alison said, but she knew that if there were any problems, she wasn't going to ask anyone.

Once Alison and Sandra had finished putting away Alison's things, they left the room for Sandra to show Alison around the home.

"That's the kitchen, where all of the meals are cooked and then there's the serving hatch and the long tables where we eat in the dining room. To the left of the kitchen is the utility room where all of the clothes get washed, dried and ironed, as you can see, it's a big room…oh yes, and four ironing boards, when there are lots to do."

They then went into the sitting room.

There were a few comfy chairs and two large sofas that could easily seat six people and a couple of recliners. There was a huge television so everyone, children, and staff, would be able to sit down together in the evening to watch a film or the latest show on TV. The windows were covered with wooden Venetian blinds, with thick cream blackout curtains, with room in the corner for a Christmas tree. The walls were painted in a pebble grey colour, which helped the room feel cosy as well as welcoming and functional.

"So," Sandra said smiling, "would you like to go and wash your hands and face as it's nearly supper time? I'll see you in the dining room in a minute."

There were girls' and boys' bathrooms on all of the floors, so Alison took herself off to the girl's bathroom at the end of the corridor. She walked inside and there were Hilary and Josephine, talking rather quietly. They stopped talking when Alison walked in. She went straight to a sink and put her hands under the taps to wet them. She took the soap to wash her hands. Her face was clean, and she would be having a bath later on.

Hilary was the first to speak to her.

"When did you get here then, Alison? Do you have lots of toys and dolls and how long are you here for?" she asked.

Hilary was the louder of the two little girls; Josephine was quieter.

"I asked you a question, Alison," Hilary said.

Alison was engrossed in washing her hands, she looked up.

"I came here straight from school, as you know, because you saw me in the bedroom. I don't have many toys with me, just my two dollies, and I don't know how long we are going to be here for."

"We? Who's we?" Hilary asked.

"Me and my brother, Tom," Alison said.

"Oh, you have a brother. How old is he?" Hilary's eyes lit up asking this question.

"Tom is three. He'll be four next year."

Alison shook her hands then dried them on the towel. Hilary and Josephine waited for her to finish and let her leave before them. Alison left the bathroom and made her way to the dining room. She could hear hushed voices talking behind her, but she didn't care; she wanted to catch up with Tom before they ate, but it wasn't possible.

On arriving at the dining room, Tom was already seated.

"Hi, Alison, sit down here with me and Freddie," Alison's little brother smiled. They were both sitting waiting patiently for their dinner.

"OK," Alison said and asked them to scoot up so she could join both the boys.

George and Sandra were in charge of the dinner. It was shepherd's pie with peas, carrots, broccoli and thick gravy.

"Mm!" said Tom, echoed by Freddie.

All three children tucked into their dinner, which they were reminded was supper, not dinner. Alison and Tom had dinner at this time, but people called their dinner different things; some called it supper, some dinner and some tea. They all had a glass of milk with their dinner, or water if they preferred.

It was delicious. They had to take their dirty plates to the kitchen before they could have their desserts. Alison handed Sandra all three of their plates through the serving hatch and returned to her seat. They had all enjoyed their supper and were waiting for dessert, which was bananas and custard or apple pie and custard. All three children asked for bananas and custard. It came to the table and they tucked into their desserts with sheer delight. When they had finished their food and drinks, they left the table and were called back by George.

"Hey guys, where are you off to? We need to wipe down the tables after supper ready for breakfast in the morning."

Alison went back to the serving hatch to collect a cloth from George.

"Sorry, George, we didn't know."

"Not to worry. In future though, after every meal we have to clean the tables, otherwise they will be all sticky when we eat breakfast next morning," he replied.

Alison took the cloth and went to wipe the table down. Tom and Freddie were trying to put the chairs in so it would be easier for Alison to wipe. After the tables were clean, they could then leave the dining room and go into the sitting room and watch TV. Tom and Freddie did, but Alison wanted to go to her bedroom for a little while. She was confused as to why her mum hadn't picked them up from school and why they were here, eating their dinner in a strange place. Why was she in a new bedroom? She liked her old bedroom at her home.

When she got to her room, Alison's dolls were at the bottom of the bed, rather than on her pillow where she had left them when she went with Sandra for a look around the building. She looked over and both Hilary's and Josephine's teddy bears were on their pillows, where they had been when Alison was in the room last. She moved her two dollies back to the top of her pillow and went to her chest of drawers. The few things she had, had been rifled through. Someone had been going through her clothes, her underwear and night things drawer, and her clothes, as if someone were having a look at them, but they hadn't put them back correctly.

Just as Alison was about to get changed into her pyjamas, there was a knock on the door.

"Hello, can I come in?" It was Sandra.

"Yes," Alison called out.

"Are you OK, Alison, what's happened here?" Sandra asked, looking at the chest of drawers.

17

"I just came back from supper and my dollies were at the end of the bed, not on my pillow where I left them, and someone has been through my drawers," Alison said quietly.

"Oh dear, would you like me to help you put them back?" offered Sandra.

"No, it's OK. I was just going to put my pyjamas on, is that OK? I wanted to get comfy before I went down to watch TV."

"That's fine, Alison, would you like some help?" Sandra asked.

"No, I should be OK, I will be down in a few minutes," she replied.

Sandra left and said she would see Alison in a while. Alison got her pyjamas out and started to take off her clothes and put them in the dirty laundry bin by her wardrobe.

She got herself sorted out and headed out of the bedroom, with her slippers and dressing gown on.

When Alison got to the living room, Tom and Freddie weren't there. She asked George, where they were. He told Alison that Tom and Freddie were playing cars in their bedroom for a little while as they didn't want to watch TV.

"OK," Alison said.

She left the sitting room to see Tom and Freddie. Their floor was below Alison's and when she got there, they had cars all over the place, in the garage over the other side of the room, which was really an old cereal box. They also had three cars in a line to have a car wash, and they had put some old Yellow Pages in front of one another so they could have an overpass. They were having a great time.

"Hi, Alison!" Tom said. "We're playing cars, would you like to join me and Freddie?"

"Err, no thanks, I don't think I will. You both look like you're having fun," Alison replied. "I'm going to watch TV for a while before I go to bed."

"OK," Tom said and he carried on playing.

"Brrroooommm, broommm, broommm," he said as he was pushing a car towards Freddie's car.

Alison left the boys to play and she went back to the sitting room to watch TV. *Starsky and Hutch* was on the television. Sandra was watching it with some of the older kids.

"Can I come and watch this with you please, Sandra?"

"Yes, of course, you can. Why don't you sit up here with me?"

18

Sandra helped Alison to get onto the sofa. It was a bit high for her, but she managed it in the end. They sat through the whole programme and then watched the next one, which was *George and Mildred*. It was a sitcom about a married couple who had been together for many years. George, the husband, hadn't worked for a long time, then he got a job as a traffic warden. Mildred, his wife, was a housewife, which meant she would stay at home to keep the house clean, wash, iron and cook her and her husband's meals. George was a lazy man who liked to watch the TV rather than take his wife out for an evening. Even though they had their quarrels; they would get on well.

When the TV programmes had finished, Sandra told everyone it was time for bed.

"But Sandra, it's only 7.30 pm!" One of the older children protested.

"Yes, I know, but the little ones have to get up for school in the morning. You bigger kids can stay up a little longer," she said.

The bigger children, who were nearly ready for secondary school, stayed up to watch the next programme, *Quincy*…a programme about a medical examiner who worked in a hospital in America.

Sandra and Alison went back to her bedroom. As she opened the door, she could see Hilary and Josephine prancing around the bedroom as if they were ballet dancers.

"What are you doing?" asked Alison.

"We're practising. We're going to be ballerinas!" Hilary said. "But you can only do it if you're good. If you're rubbish, they won't let you in," she added.

Alison wasn't really interested in ballet dancing. She still liked playing with her dollies. She did see a teddy bear that she had liked and had mentioned to her mum about. Her mum.

She hadn't thought of her mum all day. So much had happened since she and Tom had left for school that morning and it was still only Monday.

As Alison climbed into her bed, she was going to ask Sandra in the morning about her mum. Did she know where she was and why she didn't come to collect her and Tom from school this afternoon? And why were they here, in this place? Why were they sleeping in different places? Mum must have gotten held up shopping or something. That's what it would be.

Alison closed her eyes and drifted off to sleep, dreaming about her mum and dad. They were very happy, they had just had Sunday lunch—chicken roast, potatoes, Yorkshire pudding, peas, carrots and gravy, her favourite roast dinner.

19

Followed by jelly and ice-cream. Tom and she were playing snakes and ladders. They both loved board games; they had so much fun.

***

The next morning, Eileen rose early. She had waited for him to get ready to go. She hadn't wanted him to see where she was going, but she didn't want to be late. He got up at his usual time, seven o'clock, but he was taking his time. She wanted him to hurry up, to get out of the door, before she took her chance.

He made them both a cup of tea, he was eating his toast. She wasn't hungry, she hadn't been since the day before...since they left. He was talking about something he was doing with Tony, one of the guys from work. He wanted to show him some new equipment they were getting for one of the new jobs that had come up.

"Are you listening to me. Eileen?" he shouted.

"Yes, of course. Tony wants you to go with him to look at this new equipment for the new job that has come in," she replied.

"So, you were listening then," he smirked. "Anyway, I'm not sure what time I will be home tonight, hopefully a little earlier than normal. Maybe 6.30-7 pm. If it's any later, I will call you. Have a good day, see you tonight," he said before kissing her on the top of the forehead. She shuddered at his touch.

It was 8.10 am when he finally left for work. He usually started by 8 am but never mind, that was it, she was already washed and dressed. She grabbed her bag and keys. She was out of the door. She looked around when she got out of the front door, he was nowhere to be seen, he had gone, she was safe.

She turned to walk down the high street, as quickly as she could. She didn't want to miss them. She had walked as fast as she could and was a little out of breath, but she would be fine. Her back was a little sore, but thankfully she had her dark sunglasses on. It wasn't a very nice day for a Tuesday, the weather was a little cold and wet, so she did stick out a little, but she didn't care.

Only two more roads to go down and then she was there. She found a big horse chestnut tree, that would be good to hide behind. She could see them from there without being seen. She had only about 10 minutes before they would be in sight. She hadn't really noticed the tree before, but it was a good place, she could get a good look from where she was.

Alison woke up relatively early, 7 am, as she heard the staff knocking on the doors of the bedrooms telling the children they have to get up because it was a school day. She thought she had better get up. Everyone else was getting up and she didn't want to be late. She pulled off her cover.

Sandra had popped her head around the door and said to leave her cover at the bottom of the bed, so it can air for the daytime. She did as she was told and went to get her wash things and headed off to the bathroom with the other little girls. Hilary and Josephine had already got to the bathroom and were washing themselves, so Alison got herself a sink and turned on the taps and started to wash. When she had finished and dried herself, she then went back to her bedroom to get dressed ready for school.

By the time she had finished, it was nearly 7.30. Once the children were dressed, they had to go down for breakfast. Alison sat herself down with Tom and Freddie. George said that it would be better for Alison to start sitting with the bigger children her own age, so she could make friends with them and they her.

"It's OK, Alison, I'm sitting with Freddie. You can make friends with the girls," Tom told her. Alison moved away to the other table two tables in front of Tom and Freddie's.

Cornflakes, toast and jam or marmalade, waffles, fresh fruit, orange juice, or milk to drink.

Alison chose toast with marmalade. They had orange or lemon and lime. She chose lemon and lime. She sat down with her breakfast and tucked in. Once she had her breakfast and juice, she headed off back to the bathroom to brush her teeth. Sandra then called to the children.

"We have to go in five minutes, so please make sure that you have all of your things with you."

Alison, along with the other children, made their way to the front door. The school wasn't very far away to walk, but they couldn't go on their own as there were too many roads to cross. There were six members of staff taking the children to school. There were three schools that the children had to go to, so two members of staff per school.

Sandra and George were taking Alison and Tom's group to school that morning. They left the building, said goodbye to Jane, the receptionist, and left the building. The children said goodbye to the children going to the other schools. Six children were going to Alison's school; her, and Tom, then there was Sarah-Jane, who was in the last year at primary school, also Johnny who was in the same class as Sarah-Jane. They were both 10, but it was coming up to Sarah-Jane's birthday. Timmy and George, who were twins, were in the year above Alison, so they were seven years old.

Alison and Tom held hands, they walked in twos. Timmy and George held hands, they were at the front of the children, and Sarah-Jane and Johnny were at the back of the children but didn't hold hands as they felt they weren't little kids anymore.

The children and staff were walking happily down the road. Sandra was at the front talking to Timmy and George about their school projects and George was walking behind Sarah Jane and Johnny, talking to Johnny about the football team at school. Johnny didn't want to be in the team even though he was good enough, he didn't have enough confidence. As they were busy in conversation, they still held hands with the younger children when crossing the road.

Stopping at the road, just before the end of the pavement, they looked right to see if there were any cars coming, then they looked left to see if any cars were coming, then they looked right again to see if there were cars coming. There were none, so they were safe to cross. When crossing, they continued to look left and right, just like the Green Cross Code Man had taught them, to make sure they were safe. This was the last road to cross to get to school, they only had a little way to go to get to the building, everyone was chatty as they went into school.

Sandra had turned to say something to George at the back when she noticed a lady on the other side of the road. She seemed to be staring at the group. She had dark glasses on, but that was all Sandra could see, with only a fleeting look. Sandra then turned through the gates, to take the children into school.

Sandra went with Alison to her class so she could talk to Miss Howe, Alison's teacher, and George went into Tom's class to talk to Mrs Wilkins, Tom's teacher.

Once they had spoken to the children's teachers, they then said goodbye to Alison and Tom and said they would pick them up later on at the end of school.

"Isn't our mum picking us up, Sandra?" Alison asked. Sandra just smiled at her.

"Bye George." Tom waved to George.

Sandra and George left the children and then left the building. They were out of the school gate just talking and were distracted enough not to see the lady at the tree leave when they were out of sight.

She saw Emily first, Alison's friend, with her mum. She moved slightly so she wouldn't be seen. Emily and her mum were chatting away, she couldn't hear their conversation but they both looked happy. Then she saw the other children with their mums or dads taking them to school from Alison and Tom's class. Then she saw a big group of children with only a couple of adults. *There they are! There they are*, she thought. She could see them! Her babies! They both looked happy enough. They weren't scared or upset, they seemed fine. Then they disappeared into the school gates. She waited. She was staring. She wanted to see them for a little longer, but they were gone into the building and up into their class.

Eileen had done it. She had seen her two little lambs. She thought she wouldn't make it, she thought he may have known…but he didn't. Then she saw the people they were with. They were out of the gates and up the road. She moved slightly as she didn't want to be seen by them. But she had seen them, she was so happy. She turned and walked back up the road and thought she had better make a move home just in case he decided to come back and check where she was.

Chapter 2

It was Saturday, which meant Alison and the other children at Craven House Children's Home didn't have to be up as early as in the week. They had to be up by 8.30 am for breakfast for 9 am and everyone had jobs to do; whether it was cleaning their bedrooms, making sure all of their dirty wash bins were empty to go down to the laundry room to get washed, dried and then ironed, ready to be put away.

On Saturday, all of the children's school uniforms were washed and dried in the airing cupboard, ready for ironing for the following Monday, ready for the start of the school week.

Sandra and George didn't work on the weekends, they had that time off. Michelle, Roger and Julie were in charge of the children, ensuring they did their different chores.

After breakfast of toast, jam and a glass of cold milk, the children were putting their dirty plates and glasses onto the serving hatch, for Julie to put in the dishwasher. Michelle and Roger were helping the other children to wipe down the tables and sweep the floor which had also to be washed.

Michelle had grown up in the children's home and she loved it there so much, that when she finished her exams after college, she applied for a job there, so she felt like she was still at home.

When the children had finished cleaning the dining room, Julie would then wipe the kitchen down and wash the floors.

Michelle called to Alison and Tom. Because they were nearly at the end of their first week, she asked them to follow her down to reception.

"Pocket money?" the receptionist asked, smiling at Michelle.

"That's right. This is Alison and Tom's first week, so they need to get their pocket money."

Alison and Tom looked at each other. They had never had pocket money before. Anything they had wanted; Mum had bought it for them. They were intrigued. Alison was given 50 pence and Tom, 35 pence.

Alison looked a little bewildered,

"How come I got more than Tom?" she asked.

"Tom is a little younger than you, so you get a little bit more than him," Michelle answered. Alison didn't think it was fair that because she was older, she got more pocket money.

"Oh no!" said Tom. "I don't have a pocket, I'll have to give mine back."

"No, you don't," Michelle laughed, "you don't give back pocket money just because you don't have a pocket. That's for you to spend," Michelle said.

"Spend?" Alison and Tom said together. They never spent money before.

"You can buy sweets, or you can save it if you want to buy something a little bigger. So, if you want to buy sweets today, you can go out to the shops with the others or you can stay behind and go next Saturday," Michelle said.

Alison and Tom looked at each other. They had been to the shops with Mum before, but not with their friends.

"You can go out at 12.00 with the others, providing your jobs or chores are done. If not, then you can't go," Michelle told them.

Alison and Tom raced upstairs to their bedrooms to make sure their jobs were done. Alison checked her dirty laundry bin and it was empty. Her bed had been stripped and new clean bedding had been put on and the dirty washing taken downstairs to the laundry room.

Once Alison had checked everything, she went downstairs to check on Tom to make sure he had everything done. He also had clean bedding on his bed and his dirty laundry bin had also been emptied. So yes, they could both go to the shops with the others.

Tom held onto his money so tightly, he thought he would never let go of it. Alison and Tom went down to reception to join the others. Freddie, Hilary and Josephine were there, getting pretty anxious as they wanted to go, they didn't want to wait any longer. When Hilary saw it was Alison and Tom coming down the stairs, she gave Alison a dirty look, she wanted to be gone before they got there and was annoyed that they had held up the shopping trip.

The children set off, holding hands in twos to keep them safe, just as they did when they went to school.

They went along the familiar road that they went down to school, but instead of turning off, they carried on. They went a long way around, or it just seemed like it. They passed a chemist, a butcher, a greengrocer, a bakery, a little convenience shop and a sweet shop.

Tom's eyes were like saucers when he saw all of the jars lining up on the shelves full of sweets. Alison just looked; she had never seen so many sweets.

"Off you go. Go and have a look at what's there and what you like the look of," Michelle encouraged the children.

Alison liked the cola bottles, they looked soft and squishy.

"Michelle, how do I buy them?" she asked.

"What do you mean?" Michelle asked.

"Well, do I buy them loose? Are they one penny each?"

"No, Alison. The ones in the jars are weighed out, so you can buy two ounces or a quarter of a pound. If you want to buy loose sweets, so you can have more choice, then it's these sweets over here. They are one penny each," Michelle replied.

Alison and Tom went over to the counter and looked at all of the sweets. They didn't know where to start. There were some lovely coloured ones; yellow bananas, chocolate-covered bananas, cola bottles, pineapple chunks, pink spearmint chews, sugared mice, blackjacks and fruit salads chews, flying saucers, which were rice paper with sherbet inside of them. Their eyes were everywhere, they didn't know what to get.

In the end, they chose a couple of most of them. Alison spent all of her money and gave Tom some of her sweets, so they roughly had the same amount. This did not go unnoticed by Hilary, who voiced her disapproval loudly to Michelle and Roger, saying that Alison had given Tom some of her sweets.

"If Alison wants to give her brother some of her sweets, Hilary, it's up to her and nobody else," Michelle said, smiling at Alison, thinking that was very kind of her to do that, as Tom didn't get as much money as Alison did.

When everyone had finished, Michelle called the children to come outside, counting them as they did so. They didn't want to leave anyone behind their way back home.

"Eight children, all present and correct," Michelle said.

Alison and Tom held hands on their way back, looking at all of the other shops. Alison had been to the shops with Mum before, but not these. They had lots of lovely things in the windows, except the butchers; they had dead chickens

26

in the window and when you walked past the door, you could see a dead pig hanging upside down.

She and Tom walked quickly past that shop, but they liked the bakery. It had lots of lovely cakes in the window; lots of bright colours, pink and chocolate doughnuts, white stringy cakes that were called cheesecakes and a bread pudding. There were fairy cakes, round cakes with white icing and currants in them and a cherry on the top, along with doughnuts with jam in them and doughnuts with sugar on them and a hole in the middle.

The children had wide eyes. Two of the children wanted to go in so Roger took them into the shop to buy what they wanted. The others waited outside. They weren't gone for very long and soon they were heading back home.

Whilst they were walking on the same side, Michelle noticed a woman standing still on the other side of the road. She looked a little anxious and nervous as if she were hiding and didn't want to be seen.

Michelle looked to what the woman was looking at and then looked at the children. Which one of them was watching? She looked over again at the woman and noticed she was looking at Alison and Tom. Michelle looked at Alison and then realised the woman was their mum. She was thankful that the children were engrossed in what they were doing and hadn't noticed her.

***

She had done it. She had managed to get out to buy some shopping. She didn't need a lot, she had already gotten her vegetables the day before, but she wanted to get a chicken for dinner for tomorrow. He still wanted his Sunday roast.

John was watching her like a hawk. Every time she wanted to go out, he wanted to know where she was going. She had to go to the dry cleaners to pick up his suit. It needed cleaning and he was going to go with her. She said that there was no need as it was only down the road.

"OK, I will be looking out of the window, so don't be long. I will be watching you," John had said.

Eileen had never been so nervous in her whole life. She was now living off her nerves. She couldn't go anywhere or do anything without him wanting to know what she was doing and where she was. It was like being a child again.

Eileen's childhood had been great. She had fantastic parents and two older brothers who loved her to bits. Nothing was ever impossible. If she needed anything they would help. If she needed money, there it was on the side. If she wanted new clothes, they would always give her a little extra, in case she wanted shoes to go with her outfit.

Now Eileen had this life with her husband. He was her life and her two children were her world. They all worked together. Dad went to work, Monday to Friday, she stayed at home to clean the flat, cook, do the washing, change the beds, and general stuff at home, just like every other family.

Alison and Tom went to school and at the weekends, they always had family time together. They would go swimming when the weather is nice, play board games, which helped with the children's spelling. They played snakes and ladders; that was Alison's favourite game; up the ladder and down the snake when you got on that square. Sunday mornings always started with a fry up and relaxing, listening to music on the radio until dinner time. Then it was a bath and then pyjamas, watch a bit of TV, before going to bed, because it was school the next morning.

Now it couldn't have been more different. It was as though the children didn't exist anymore. Eileen was forbidden from mentioning them. They didn't really have many friends, so nobody would call the flat. Eileen hadn't seen her family in years due to an argument and there was no reconciling as John had thought that her family had been in the wrong and wouldn't have her lower herself to talk to them again. Now Eileen was isolated from everything she had ever known—her own family, her own children. And all because of a man she thought was kind and caring, but in reality, was a cruel and selfish person.

John had given her £10 to buy the chicken and a dessert, but he wanted the change back and also receipts for both items. She was glad to get out of the house. He couldn't look out at the window for her this time because these shops were a little way from their home.

She was walking down the road wondering what she should do next when she just stopped suddenly. There they were! Oh, my goodness, what should she do? There was no tree she could hide behind this time. There were no parked cars. She was stuck. If they turned around, they would see her. Would they want to see her? What if they ran across the road to say hello to her?

Of course, she would love it. They were her babies, but she didn't want them to get hurt or run over in trying to get to her. She stared straight at them, but they were engrossed in their conversation and the little white bags they were both holding onto.

Eileen hadn't noticed the member of staff watching her, watching her children. They were still walking, but now they were getting out of sight. She saw them, she saw them! She could jump for joy. They both looked happy, not neglected, which was how she thought they would feel, because she thought she had let them down. She didn't want to put them into care. He did! And she didn't know what to do next.

Eileen took a breath and gulped some air. A lump had come to her throat and a tear had come to her eye. She thought, *if I come down to these shops on a Saturday, I may have a chance to see them again.* That was what she was going to do next week; she was going to leave her Sunday joint and dessert to get on a Saturday, she would tell him it would be fresher to do that. That was it, that was her plan.

Eileen went into the butchers to get a chicken. *£3.50, that's not bad,* she thought. Then she went into the bakery, she chose a lovely Victoria Sandwich, that would be nice with a bit of cream or custard…That was £2.00. Eileen left the parade of shops with a little spring in her step on the way home.

It didn't take her long to get home and John was happy that she got chicken, a Victoria sandwich; a cake is a cake, it didn't matter to him. He did notice she seemed a little happier when she returned, but he put it down to her getting some fresh air.

***

When Alison and Tom got back to the home, they both went up to Tom's bedroom with Freddie to compare what sweets they had bought. Freddie had bought a small bar of chocolate. He didn't like the little penny sweets, he said they got stuck in his teeth, but Alison and Tom tucked into their sweets and were very happy that they did. They hadn't had such lovely things to eat. Even though they were very sweet, they weren't used to that much sugar.

Alison said that she was going to her bedroom, as Freddie and Tom started to get their toy cars out and making ramps for them.

Alison headed back to her bedroom, which was empty. She lay down on her bed. All that sugar had made her sleepy. She had her two dollies lying next to her when the door swung open.

Hilary and Josephine walked in and jumped onto Alison's bed.

"Where are your sweets? I've finished mine and I wanted some of yours," Hilary demanded.

"They're all gone," Alison replied, "I ate them."

"But you gave Tom some," Hilary snapped.

"Yes, and he has eaten all of his too," Alison replied.

Hilary didn't like that. She wanted to eat what was left of Alison's sweets.

"But you had your own sweets, why would you want mine? That's just being greedy," Alison said, standing up for herself. "We all have the same amount of money, why would you want mine too?"

"Because I do!" replied Hilary.

Hilary didn't like the other girls questioning her, even if it was justified. She wanted Alison's sweets because she didn't like Alison. She didn't want her in her and Josephine's room. Hilary didn't like the other girls because they were pretty.

Alison had blonde hair and was petite, and Hilary was a little fatter than Alison and she had clumsy feet. She also had curly ginger hair and pale skin.

Josephine had mousy, straight hair. She was skinny but also a little on the tall side. Josephine was quieter than Hilary and just seemed to follow with what Hilary was doing, like a little puppy dog.

"Lunch!" Michelle called out from the bottom of the stairs.

All the children came running down the hallways, and down the stairs to the kitchen and dining room. On a Saturday, things were more relaxed. When entering the dining room there were plates and plates of sandwiches, ham, cheese, tuna and sweetcorn, salmon and cucumber and, Freddie and Tom's favourite, jam. Freddie and Tom pulled the massive plate of jam sandwiches towards them, they were going to have a right feast.

Alison liked the cheese and ham sandwiches, so she picked up one of each and sat down and started to eat her lunch. She noticed that Hilary and Josephine were watching her. She didn't know why, but as soon as Michelle came into the dining room, they put their heads down and paid more attention to their lunch. Eating in silence and drinking their orange squash.

After Tom's third jam sandwich, he looked like he couldn't eat another thing. His belly felt quite full, especially as he had eaten all of his sweets only a little while earlier. Alison had two of each sandwich and she felt quite full. She helped Michelle clear the tables. Hilary and Josephine were watching Alison again, until they saw Michelle come back from the kitchen. They then made their way into the living room.

Alison liked helping in the dining room. She felt that she was contributing to keeping it clean and tidy. She swept the floor, but Michelle wouldn't let her wash the floor, in case she slipped over.

"Alison?" Michelle asked.

Alison looked up from sweeping the floor.

"Why do Hilary and Josephine keep staring at you? I've noticed it on at least two occasions," Michelle asked.

"I don't know, but it is annoying," Alison said.

"Take no notice of them, Alison. They probably don't like sharing their room with anyone else. It has been them two for a very long time," Michelle said.

Alison wasn't bothered; as long as they left her and her stuff alone, she didn't care.

Once Alison had helped Michelle clean the dining room, she was able to go into the living room and watch some TV. There was a film on Genevieve. It was about a very old car in a trip down to Brighton and then back again. The car was a vintage car, which had a small motor engine and had only two seats and a funny steering wheel, which wasn't set into a dashboard but standing freely.

Alison sat on one of the armchairs, which felt so comfy. She put her feet up under her legs so she could get more comfortable.

After watching the film for a little while, Tom strolled in with Freddie.

"Hi, Alison!" he said. "What are you watching?"

"It's a film about a car being driven to Brighton with lots of other old cars," she replied.

"Oh, like a race?" he enquired.

"No, not really, just they are going there at the same time for the same thing," she replied.

"Would you like to come and play cars with Freddie and me?" Tom asked.

"I'm fine watching TV. You and Freddie go and play, have fun."

"OK, see you later."

Tom went skipping away with Freddie. They liked playing with their cars. They made ramps and jumps for the cars so when they pushed them along, they would fly in the air.

The film didn't last too long, and Alison wasn't sure what to do next. There were some comics on the table: Jackie, Mandy, Whizzer and Chips, Twinkle.

Twinkle, that was what Alison liked the look of. There was a little girl on the front with Twinkles of light around her. She took the comic and went back over to the comfy chair she was sitting on.

Michelle stuck her head around the door.

"Hi, what are you doing?" she asked.

"I'm just looking at this comic, I haven't seen it before…it looks quite good," Alison said.

"Do you want to come down to the shops with me? We need some milk and bread, as more was eaten and drunk at lunchtime than I realised," Michelle said.

"OK," Alison said, "let me get my coat. Is anyone else coming with us?"

"No, just us two, is that OK?" Michelle asked.

"Yes, that's fine. I thought there would be a lot of us going, that's all," Alison said.

"I'll meet you in reception, Alison, I won't be a moment," Michelle told her.

"OK," Alison replied.

Alison went up to her bedroom to collect her coat. Hilary and Josephine were sitting on Josephine's bed talking, but they soon stopped when Alison opened the door. She grabbed her coat and left the room.

"Hey, where are you going?" shouted Hilary.

Alison ignored her, putting her coat on as she left the room and went to meet Michelle in reception.

Michelle was waiting for her when she got there.

"Ready?" asked Michelle.

"Ready," Alison smiled.

Michelle took hold of Alison's hand and off they went. The shop was only a little while away, not as far as the parade of shops they went to earlier that day.

"Are you alright, Alison?" Michelle asked as they walked down the road.

"Yes fine," she replied.

They walked down the road chatting away about what was for dinner. It was spaghetti bolognaise tonight, but sometimes some of the bigger boys liked bread and butter with everything they ate.

They had their shopping bags ready to be filled with their shopping. Alison had one bag with milk and a loaf of bread, whilst Michelle had two other bags with more bread and milk.

They were only gone about half an hour, but on their return, Josephine was in reception waiting for them to come back.

"Michelle! Michelle! Hilary has hurt herself, she's on the floor in our bedroom," Josephine said. She looked quite upset and was shaking. Michelle dropped the bags of shopping with one of the kitchen staff and rushed up to Alison, Hilary and Josephine's room.

Hilary was on the floor crying. She had hurt her arm. She had been crying and Alison felt sorry for her.

"What has happened? What did you do to end up on the floor, Hilary?" Michelle asked.

"I…I was on top of my chest of drawers and I slipped onto the floor, but I landed on my arm. It hurts, Michelle, what have I done?" Hilary cried.

"Alison, go downstairs to the sitting room and see if you can find Roger, he will have to be told that Hilary has hurt her arm and needs to go to hospital," Michelle instructed.

Alison ran as quickly as she could to find Roger. He was in the sitting room with some of the boys watching the football results. Alison told him what had happened, and that Michelle wanted to see him.

Roger and some of the boys followed Alison. The boys didn't like Hilary much, but they wanted to see her, just in case her arm was all dangly, or bent backwards. Roger picked up Hilary very carefully and told Michelle that he would take her to hospital.

"She will probably need an x-ray to be sure nothing's broken," Roger said.

"Are you sure, Roger? Don't you think I should take her?" said Michelle.

"No, it will be fine. I can carry her. Have you called for a cab? I don't think she needs an ambulance," Roger said.

"I'll call one now. If you can help Hilary get ready, it should be here soon," Michelle said as she picked up the phone.

"Yes, I'd like a cab please. Yes, it's Craven House Children's Home. Yes, that's the one, on Cromwell Drive. Yes, five minutes, that would be great, thank you."

"Roger, the cab will be here in five minutes," Michelle told him.

They had Hilary dressed ready for the hospital, and Roger then picked her up again, so she wouldn't hurt her arm any more than she already had.

Once Roger and Hilary had left in the cab, Josephine burst into tears.

"It's OK, Josephine. Hilary will be fine once she gets to the hospital and they can fix her arm," Michelle comforted Josephine.

"But will they be able to fix her arm, Michelle? It was all bent up. I know she shouldn't have been on the chest of drawers, but she wanted to show me how good she was at ballet," Josephine continued. "She likes her ballet, and she forgot her dolly, she won't be able to sleep without her dolly," Josephine cried.

"Oh, I don't think she will be in hospital long. She should be back later on; it just depends on how busy the hospital is at this time of the day," Michelle said. "Let's just see what happens when she gets back."

Alison felt sorry for Josephine. It was like she had lost her master. She went over to sit with Josephine.

"Josephine, Hilary will be fine. The doctors will fix her up good and proper, you'll see," Alison said, feeling like she was a grown-up, giving a bit of advice to make someone feel better. Josephine gave Alison a big smile, thinking Alison wasn't so bad. *Maybe Hilary has got it all wrong.*

"Do you want to come and watch TV for a little while, Josephine? We can't do anything in here."

The two little girls went, and for a quick glance it looked like they held hands, just for a split second.

There wasn't much on the TV; the boys had finished watching the football results and *Blind Date* was on ITV, so they sat down to watch it. Michelle stuck her head around the door and asked the girls if they were fine.

"Yes, just watching *Blind Date*, Michelle. It's funny!" Josephine said.

"Dinner will be ready soon, so do you want to go and wash your hands? I will be ringing the dinner bell in a minute," Michelle said.

The girls went to the girl's bathroom to wash their hands and then they headed off down to the dining room for spaghetti bolognaise. Dinner on Saturday evening was always at 6 pm and finished by 7 pm, then baths, then off to bed and then lights off at 8 pm.

The girls sat down together, and Tom came over to Alison.

"Where's Hilary? She normally sits with Josephine, not you," he said confused.

"Hilary has had an accident, Tom, and she's had to go to hospital, she should be back soon though," Alison told him.

"Oh, OK," replied Tom. Satisfied with the answer, he went to sit with Freddie. Freddie and Tom sat next to each other all of the time, but they also played together. It was lovely that Tom had met someone who he connected with, but he was also very astute to notice that two little girls weren't very nice to his sister.

Now that someone had been hurt, she was being a good person to the other little girl. *Too caring is my sister, too caring for her own good*, Tom thought to himself.

He looked at his spaghetti bolognaise and wasn't too impressed with it.

"Michelle, how do I eat this, I don't have a knife, but a spoon and fork?"

Michelle looked over at Tom and realised. She forgot that he was only three, and even though he could feed himself, spaghetti bolognaise wasn't going to be an easy dish for him.

"Would you like me to cut it up for you, so it's easier to eat with the spoon?" Michelle asked.

"Yes please," Tom said.

Michelle cut up his spaghetti. The mince and spaghetti should be easier for him to eat with his spoon.

Alison enjoyed spaghetti bolognaise. She hadn't had it before she came to Craven House. She ate it with such gusto. Tom enjoyed it too, but he did keep dropping it off his spoon an onto his dish. Once the dishes and plates were cleared away to be washed, it was bananas and custard or ice-cream for dessert.

Alison and Josephine chose bananas and custard, and Tom and Freddie had bananas and ice-cream. The other children had what they wanted, and they also had juice or milk to drink. The desserts and dishes were cleared away and then some of the children helped to clean up and the rest ran off to the living room or their bedrooms before it was time to go to bed.

Alison helped Michelle with clearing and wiping over the tables. Josephine asked Michelle for a cloth, so she could help. Anything to keep her mind occupied and not to worry about Hilary. It didn't take long to wipe down the tables and sweep the floor.

Michelle thanked both of the girls and said that they could run along, so they went into the living room to see what was on TV. Alison and Josephine seemed to be getting along quite well, as Hilary wasn't there putting her two pence worth in.

There wasn't anything they wanted to watch on TV, so they left the living room and went up to their bedrooms, but first Alison wanted to check on Tom, to see if he was OK. Tom and Freddie were putting their pyjamas on, but Tom was struggling with his top, he couldn't get it over his head properly.

"Hang on a minute, Tom," Alison said, "I'll give you a hand."

"Thanks, Alison," Tom replied.

When he got his head through the neck of his pyjamas, Tom was shocked again to see Alison and Josephine together.

"Where are you two going?" he asked.

"We're going up to our room to get changed ready for bed; just like you have," Alison replied. "Night, Tom," she said as she kissed him on top of his forehead. "Night Freddie, sleep tight both of you," Alison said as she was leaving the room.

"Night." Freddie replied.

Both of the boys got into bed and settled down to sleep. Even though tomorrow was Sunday, they could have a little lie-in, but the staff liked to make sure the children got at least 10 hours sleep at night.

Alison and Josephine left the boys to it and headed off to their bedroom. They only had to go to the floor above, so it didn't take long. They got into their bedroom and picked up their clean nightwear.

Both girls had pyjamas and when Alison took hers out of the drawer, she pulled them up to her face and smelt them. They smelled clean, like fresh flowers and she liked that. Alison remembered that when she was at home, her pyjamas would smell like sunshine and clouds. She liked the laundry washing powder and fabric softener, it smelled so lovely.

She was missing home. She hadn't thought of it for a little while as she and Tom had settled in so well at the children's home. They had been so busy; school all week and going out for treats on Saturday. They had been there nearly a week, but it felt like they had been there for a lot longer.

"Alison?" Josephine called. "Are you OK? You went very quiet, as if into space. Were you thinking?"

"Oh sorry, yes I'm fine."

"What were you thinking about?"

"Oh, sorry Josephine, I was just thinking about home. I picked up my pyjamas and I could smell the fresh flowers from them, then I thought about my pyjamas at home, they smelled of the sunshine and fresh flowers," Alison said.

"Do you miss home then?" Josephine asked, looking at her new friend.

"I hadn't thought about it until now, I suppose it has been a busy week, but it just made me stop for a minute and reminded me of home. I don't understand why we're here. I miss my mum…"

With that, Alison burst into tears. She hadn't cried once since being put into Craven House, but this, this little thing had triggered something off. Maybe Hilary being hurt and taken to hospital had started it all. But it was the clean washing; that was what had set her off completely out of the blue. She didn't know what to do. She had started crying, but now she was sobbing, like a baby.

Michelle came along and knocked and opened the door. She saw Alison sobbing and put her arms around her. She sat on her bed and picked her up so she could comfort her.

Josephine just stood there staring. She didn't know what to do.

"Michelle, she looked at her pyjamas, smelt them and then started to cry. She said she was missing home and her mum and then she couldn't stop," Josephine told Michelle.

Alison was crying so much her shoulders were moving up and down uncontrollably. Michelle kept holding onto Alison until she stopped crying.

After about 10 minutes or so, Alison started to calm down. Her sobbing was getting less, and her body had stopped shaking. Now she was just crying. Then it stopped. She had her head buried in Michelle's chest, for a couple of minutes, then she lifted her head, her face red and tears stained on her face.

"Feel better?" Michelle asked.

Alison nodded.

"I am so sorry, Michelle. I didn't mean to make your clothes wet," Alison said.

"Don't worry about that, I'm more concerned about how you are feeling."

Alison was quiet for a little while.

"I haven't thought about home or Mum or anything, and it was the washing. I smelt the pyjamas. They looked so fresh, then I remembered about Mum's washing powder, then I knew I hadn't thought of Mum since we got here. I think that with Hilary hurting herself today and going to hospital, it must have just been too much. I am sorry," Alison said.

"Alison, it's perfectly natural. You haven't seen your mummy since last week. You came here on Monday and you have just had to adapt quickly into life here, but maybe at the bottom of it, you just bottled up your feelings and got on with it, which is why with the incidents that have happened it just became too much. It's lovely smelling fresh laundered washing, but smells can bring you back to memories, some good and some not so good. But this brought you back to a good smell, but it triggered off something that hasn't been addressed. Do you know what I mean? Do you understand that?" Michelle asked, hugging her tightly to her.

"Yes, I think I do. I haven't had to deal with anything here apart from some chores to do and getting on with things. Today has been different because it's Saturday and there's no school," Alison said, drying her eyes on her sleeve.

Michelle asked Alison if she wanted some help getting into her clean pyjamas.

"Yes please, I think it would help," she replied.

"Josephine, would you like some help with your pyjamas as well?" Michelle asked.

"Yes please, if that's OK?"

"Of course, we don't want you to struggle."

Michelle helped both the girls get changed. The girls had put their dirty clothes into their dirty laundry bins, to be emptied the following day. If the washing wasn't taken on Saturday to be washed, then it was done on Sunday. But as long as the children's uniforms for school were washed it didn't matter.

Both the girls jumped into bed.

"Do you want a story, girls, or do you just want to get off to sleep yourself?" Michelle asked.

They both looked at each other and said in unison,

"Can we go off to sleep on our own, without a story?"

They both wanted to think about what had happened that day. A lot of activity for both of them and they just wanted to rest and fall asleep naturally. Michelle said goodnight to the girls and turned off the main light in the bedroom and their night lights automatically turned on.

Alison and Josephine hadn't actually gotten off to sleep when the bedroom door flung open.

"Watch it, I don't want to hurt my arm any more than it is!" Hilary shouted.

Both Alison and Josephine sat up straight in their beds. Michelle came in after Roger and Hilary, who was being carried to her bed, which Alison thought didn't make sense because she didn't hurt her legs but her arm.

"Michelle, will help you Hilary with her night things, as I assume you're not going to be able to do it yourself," Roger said.

"Thank you, Roger, for taking me to the hospital and staying with me, I really appreciate it," Hilary replied coyly.

Hilary was watching Alison and then looked over at Josephine as if to say, *aren't you coming to see me as I have hurt myself today?*

Josephine crawled to the bottom of her bed to see Hilary.

"How are you feeling, Hilary? Are you any better? Did the doctors fix your arm? Did you break it?"

"Yes, I broke it. It had to be set and then put Plaster-of-Paris on to help keep it steady and straight so it will fix as good as new," Hilary boasted.

"That's good, Hilary, we were all very worried about you today," Alison said.

"Were you? I didn't think you were that bothered about me?" Hilary said nastily.

"Of course, we were! Everyone was. Josephine was very upset, so we kept her busy to help keep her mind off it," Alison replied. "But you're back now and you look really rosy in the cheeks. Do you have to stay in bed, or can you get up and about?"

"Of course, I can get up and about! I haven't broken my leg, just my arm." Hilary snapped. "I have to go back to the hospital in six weeks to see how it's healing," Hilary said.

So, they've been keeping Josephine busy to take her mind off me, have they? Hilary thought. *The cheek of it! Why would they want to do that? She's my friend and of course she should be worrying about me. I bet Alison and Josephine have been laughing at me today. Well, I will show them! I'm back now and they won't do that again. If Josephine is worrying about me, she should be left to worry about me, not take her mind off it.* Hilary was not happy with the situation one bit!

Chapter 3

It was a week. A week! She couldn't believe it. A week since he had taken their stuff to school and told them that he didn't want them home again. Eileen still couldn't believe it. What was wrong with him? What had gotten into him; why had he done this? Was he having a breakdown? Was he having a crisis? She just didn't know what was wrong with him or why he had done it. But now…now it was as if the children never existed.

"John, do you want sandwiches this morning?" Eileen asked. She was waiting for his response, but none came.

"John! Do you want sandwiches this morning?" Eileen shouted. John came flying out of the bathroom with shaving foam still around his face.

"Don't you dare shout at me! I'm shaving! You do not need to scream and shout at me, is that clear? Is it?' John screamed back at Eileen.

He raised his hand, pulled it back and with great force slapped her with a crack on the skin. It sounded like she had just been whipped across the face.

Eileen lost her footing when John slapped her, and she fell backwards.

"I'm sorry…I only asked you if you wanted sandwiches for this morning and when I didn't hear from you, I didn't think you heard me, which is why I—"

John had put his hand up to stop Eileen in mid-sentence.

"I'll get something at work. I don't want sandwiches. I want a hot meal and don't you dare back-answer me again," he said in a very brusque manner.

Eileen knew that she should have kept her mouth shut, and just get on with what she was doing before this all started. What was she doing? She couldn't remember now. Oh yes, she was making some tea and toast for herself. She picked up all of the ingredients for John's sandwiches and started putting them back into the fridge and the cupboard.

All week she had been walking on eggshells. She didn't know what to say to John. He wouldn't talk about the children, or why he had put them into care. She was lost. She didn't know where to turn.

Eileen didn't really have any friends. John went to work, and she kept the house clean, did the washing and ironing and the shopping. The shopping was good lately, she had managed to see the children on the Saturday just gone. She was so pleased, but she couldn't tell him. She couldn't let on what and who she had seen, when and where…he would make her change her shopping days or where she went. She didn't want him to know, so ignorance was bliss.

She was determined she would see them without him knowing. She had wanted to go to the school and talk to them. They had been around to the flat, but John was there when they knocked, and he forbade her to answer the door and had told her she had to keep quiet. They obviously thought she wasn't in, so they left.

He knew when she went shopping. He knew where she went. He would phone home to check she was still there. She felt like a prisoner. She didn't know where to turn or who to talk to. John had become so violent this last week. A black eye was coming up around her eye, and a bump was appearing on her head. She grabbed a spoon and placed it on the bump on her head. The coldness should help it go down. She would fix her eye when he left for work.

John grabbed his bag, said goodbye to Eileen and was out of the door for work. The flat next door was getting used to the shouting and screaming. They also got used to the quiet when John wasn't there. They noticed the absence of children. No laughing or playing games and the giggling that used to come from the flat.

Mr and Mrs Coombes from next door didn't want to get involved. They now knew John had a temper, but only recently since they hadn't seen any sign of the children. Mrs Coombes liked Eileen, and they got on, but they never got involved with each other's domestic problems.

Eileen pulled out her make-up bag. She wondered how she was going to cover this black eye up without anyone noticing it. She got her foundation.

"That's a start," she said aloud.

Then she got out, a little flat compact, that was a cream, that would go over the foundation.

"That's better, it's starting to cover up now," she said to herself.

She had a rummage through her bag. She couldn't find anything else that would help.

"Oh well, that's a bit better. No, it's a lot better," she smiled at her reflection in the big mirror in the sitting room.

She knew that she had done a good job. She stared at herself in the mirror. She couldn't believe how old the woman looking back at her looked. She hadn't ever looked that old! She was only 36 and she looked like she had aged 10 years.

Oh well, nothing I can do about it now. Hopefully, when this is all over, I will look young again, she thought.

Eileen made her tea and toast and sat down to eat it. I know, she thought. Where's my address book?

She put her tea on the coffee table and went to the sideboard. It was a three-door cupboard, with a drawer above each door. Eileen pulled out the first one. She had a look and a feel around. No, it's not in there.

She went onto the next drawer. Again, after looking and feeling about, it wasn't there. That's funny, she thought. She tried the next drawer. She put her hand in the drawer and there it was, just on the top.

I'm sure that was in the other end drawer, she thought quietly to herself.

She sat down, took a sip of tea and a bite of her toast, then started to look through it. She noticed that the address book didn't seem as thick as it used to be. *I am sure it was bigger than this, what's happened to it?*

On closer inspection, it looked like some of the pages were missing. Few at first, but as she looked in the book, the page with the school's number was missing. As was the number of the lady who cleaned at the school. The pages had been totally ripped out.

The more Eileen looked through the book, it seemed that any numbers of people connected to the children were no longer in the book. She went through the whole book and there were pages ripped out. What was going on with her husband? She wondered.

Eileen suddenly had an idea. She would see her doctor. She could ask without John knowing she had been there asking questions. She looked further in the book, then she saw the number, staring back at her. Could she? Would she take her call? She hadn't spoken to her in a such long while. John had seen to that.

Is that when this has all come from? When he had had words with her mum and brothers? Did he see them as a threat? She couldn't call from the flat in case he dialled it when he returned from work and he knew she would have called her. She didn't want another black eye to match the one he gave her this morning.

Could she find a pad and a pen? She could take the paper out of the pad, write the number on it, and then go to the phone box, down the road. He wouldn't know that she would have called her, and she may get away with it.

She rummaged again through the drawers and the cupboard. Yes, she found a pad of notepaper. It was one where the paper goes over the top, so it can be taken out without any knowledge of it happening. Pen, now she needed a pen. Yes, she found one…did it work? She would have to test it on the paper, but not on the pad, otherwise it will show through. That was the last thing she needed.

She doubled over the paper and she put it on her hand. It wasn't great, but it worked. Eileen took down the number. She was going to call her! Oh, did she have change for the phone box? Yes! She had enough to make a call and if possible, she could always get her to call back on the phone box number or reverse the charges.

She ate the rest of the toast and gulped the rest of her tea. *Oh dear, I had better put the book back where I found it. That way he won't notice that I have taken it out of the drawer*, she thought to herself.

Eileen grabbed her keys and took another look in the mirror. It will do. No one will notice. I don't think that I have a black eye and I'll sort out the bump on my head when I get back.

Off she went. She had her head down. She didn't really want to have any eye contact with anyone. That way they wouldn't notice her eye or that her face was starting to swell. It was only a short walk to the phone box. Just a few more steps then around the corner.

There it was in all its glory, a red telephone box. She opened the door. It didn't smell very nice, but she didn't care. She held her breath for a moment before picking up the receiver and dialling the number on the piece of paper in her shaking hand.

She put the money in and waited for the phone to be answered.

"Hello? Hello?" The voice on the other end answered.

Eileen pushed the money into the slot.

" Hello, Mum? Mum, it's me, it's Eileen," she said, silently praying that her mum wouldn't put the phone down on her.

"Oh, my goodness! Eileen, is that really you?" Her mother said on the other end of the phone.

"Yes Mum, it is!"

"Eileen, what's wrong? We haven't heard from you in such a long time. Are you OK? Are the children all right?" her mum said, panic in her voice.

Eileen suddenly burst into tears. She was trying to tell her mum what had been going on this last week, but she couldn't get the words out. She was

43

stuttering, trying to find the right words whilst also aware that she didn't have much change on her.

"Calm down, Eileen. Tell me slowly," her mum said.

Eileen started slowly telling her mum what had happened. What John had done. She couldn't get her head around it. He had been violent towards her. Never in their married life.

Once she explained everything to her mum, she started to calm down and her words were getting clearer.

She explained that he had ripped pages out of her address book out and scratched through any numbers that had anything to do with the children. Her mother listened and then spoke.

"Eileen, can you leave him? Do you have any money to get away from him and to get the children back?"

"No, Mum. I haven't got any money. John's controlling the money. I can't even leave the house; he calls every hour to make sure I'm still there…hang on, I'm going to have to go in a minute, to get back in time for him to call. If I don't answer the phone, he comes straight back and then demands to know where I have been."

"Eileen, you can't live like this. It's not right! What about the kiddies; do you know how they are?"

"Mum, I have to go! He will be ringing in a few minutes, and I have to run. But please, when I put the phone down, ring this number back. Then next time I can call you, you can call me back. I don't always have money. I found this at the back of the sofa. Mum, I have to go, I'll call you again soon…I love you," Eileen said.

She put the receiver down and felt so much lighter now that she had spoken to someone about it. Oh no! She had to run and quick! She had to be in for when he called. Eileen ran as quick as she could. His job wasn't far away, but she had to get in quickly.

It didn't take her long to get it. She had put her key in the door downstairs, and she could hear the phone ringing, but by the time she got to it, it had stopped. *I know*, she thought. She darted into the bathroom. She needed the loo and if he came in, she could be in the bathroom. That's exactly what she did. She had just sat down and her front door to the flat opened.

"Eileen! Eileen, where are you?"

Eileen flushed the loo and came out of the bathroom.

"Eileen, there you are, is that why you didn't answer the phone?"

"Sorry, John, had you been calling? I think I have a dicky tummy; that's the second time I've been in there this morning."

John looked annoyed, but also relieved. His wife was doing what she was told. He didn't trust her. He knew she would try and sneak out.

"Right," he said, "I'm going back off to work. I will see you later and don't forget, I will ring again in a while," he told her as he left.

Phew, she thought, *that was close. He would have killed me if he knew where I had gone and who I had spoken to.* Eileen knew at that point that she had to start keeping secrets from John. She couldn't let on what she was doing, but she was going to become as devious as she could, if it meant she could see her children and talk to her mother. She needed someone. She couldn't keep all of this bottled up.

For now, she had made some contact with her mum and her mum wanted to hear from her. All this from John saying that her mum had disowned her, and it wasn't true. As soon as she could get the chance of getting some help, she would then get her children back. For now, she would have to just be happy that she had seen them. And now she had an ally in her mum.

Eileen carried on that day with her housework. John called on the hour every hour to make sure she was at home. She wondered how on earth he was able to make so many calls from work and still be able to pop back when she wasn't answering the phone. But at the moment that didn't matter. She would take each day as it comes and each time, she saw her children, was a blessing.

She now had a little contact with the outside world apart from John. The fact that he wasn't aware of it had to stay like that. She had to be careful.

That's it now; he's not the only one who has secrets, Eileen thought to herself. *I have to be more devious than him, so he doesn't catch me out.*

***

John came home at his usual time. He went to the fridge for a can of beer while Eileen was making the dinner, beef stew and dumplings. He sat down at the table which Eileen had already laid for them. A chequered tablecloth, with two placemats and two glasses for their drinks, salt and pepper, napkins. John read his paper while Eileen dished up their dinner.

45

It had been a bizarre day. Lots had happened but she couldn't tell him any of it. She also knew she needed to get an appointment to go to the doctors.

"How's your tummy now? Are you still in and out of the bathroom all day?" John asked her.

"No, it's fine. It's settled down now, maybe just something I had eaten. If it happens again tomorrow, I will make an appointment for the doctors so hopefully he can give me something for it," she replied. "I'll see how I go."

"OK, let's eat now then. No more bathroom talk at the dinner table," John said.

"OK, love," Eileen replied.

After dinner, and once Eileen had washed up, she said to John that she wanted an early night, with her book. She went off to bed, leaving him watching something that wasn't very interesting.

***

John turned off the TV and went to bed. Eileen had already fallen asleep, her book was on the floor, shut tight. He got into his side of the bed and lay there for a little while. He couldn't sleep, he turned over onto his left side.

Why had she made him do it? He got so cross earlier this morning, he was shaving and she was screaming her head at him. He didn't want sandwiches for work, he wanted to go to the canteen. He liked going to the canteen. His friends all took sandwiches, but he wanted to see Rita.

Rita was the lady who worked behind the counter in the canteen. She was friendly enough. She wasn't married, he had checked that she didn't have a wedding ring on her finger when he first met her. She said she didn't have a boyfriend, and she didn't want any children. She just wanted a good time.

He had taken her out a week ago. He really liked Rita and he wanted to take her out again, but he didn't know when and where to take her. He thought she was a classy lady. He had put some money aside so he could do his own thing when he wanted to, like take her out. He didn't want to take Eileen out. She looked too old and tired, knackered. She didn't always look like that, but these days she had seemed to have lost her sparkle. Since they'd had the kids.

The kids. Everything always came back to the kids. He didn't know what else to do with them, but he didn't want them anymore. Eileen did. That's all she thought about. The kids, bloody kids! She didn't want to be bothered with him,

46

which is why when Rita started paying him attention, he liked it. Rita was so willing and obliging. Why wouldn't he want to take her out?

He did miss them a little bit, but not enough to get them back. As far as he was concerned, they were no longer in their life. Eileen would do as she was told, otherwise he would get rid of her too. Not kill her. But he would leave her for Rita. He just needed to know that's what Rita wanted too.

He had a nice time with Rita on their first date. They had gone to a wine bar over the other side of town. He hadn't been there before, Rita had suggested it, so he thought, why not? It was about time John had some fun and he wasn't going to get any fun with Eileen.

It was a nice lively place, so he could be there without really being noticed. Rita wore a red dress, with her bosom pushed right up. It was a sight that John hadn't seen before as Rita wore an overall then a tabard over the top of it for work. But this view, he liked very much! Rita had long blonde curls and bright blue eyes. she was a lady who liked the good life and liked enjoying herself. When she ordered a white wine spritzer, John had never heard of it before. He normally drank a pint of lager or beer, but he thought, I'm out to have fun, so he ordered two of those.

After a few white wine spritzers, John offered to take Rita for something to eat, but she declined. She did have to get up early the next day for work, so she asked John if he would take her home, which he did. She didn't live far away. They went a few streets, then a left and then a right, then they were there.

John was hoping to be asked in for a nightcap, but Rita was having none of it for now.

"Thank you, John, for a lovely evening. I'll see you on Monday," she leaned over and pecked him on the cheek, gave him a cheeky wink and then shut the door behind her.

John had never taken another woman out for an evening, let alone walk her home. Normally, he would have rushed off home, but he was in no hurry to get there. Eileen would be up watching the TV. He was just glad that Rita hadn't worn any perfume. That would have been difficult to get rid of the smell.

John soon drifted off to sleep, and Eileen had woken up, but she stayed on her right side, eyes wide open, but lying there in silence. She could hear him breathing. She didn't know what to think about her husband, but more importantly what was she going to do for her next move?

She wanted to see her mum but knew she couldn't get her to the flat. Even though John would ring throughout the day, sometimes when he was due to call, he would turn up at the flat five or ten minutes early, to try and catch Eileen out. She would have to try and come up with something…it was just…what?

***

Eileen woke early the next morning. She wanted to call the doctors so she could get an appointment as soon as possible.

"Hello, I was wondering if I could get an appointment for some time today? Yes, that's right. Yes, Doctor Hayes. Yes, 10 am, that's great, thank you, see you then, bye."

Eileen put the phone down and called her husband.

"John, John, I managed to get an appointment this morning for 10 am," Eileen said.

"What are you going on about at this time of the morning?" John replied.

"The doctors, I got an appointment for 10 am this morning, so I won't be in when you call me?"

"Oh, all right. I will leave it until 12.00, then you can let me know how you got on. I know how busy them surgeries can get and also very long with waiting times…good luck with it and I'll see you later," John said.

John had taken to eating in the canteen rather than have lunch made for him at home to take. He was gone out with a slice of toast in his mouth.

Oh well, Eileen thought, at least I have some breathing space. He won't be able to call me for at least two hours.

Eileen started to get ready. She made sure that she had her mum's number in her pocket. She kept repeating the number in her mind, so if she lost the piece of paper with the number on it, she could still call her.

Eileen checked that she had everything she needed; change for the phone, her keys, her handbag, yes that was it. Oh yes, she checked the mirror, just to make sure the make-up she had applied to her face had covered her bruises. Yes, they were covered. They were getting better now. More green and yellow rather than purple and blue. Yes, the last check. She snapped her handbag shut and she was off.

The doctor's surgery was only a couple of streets away. She did have to go past John's work, and it was only around the corner after that. She was about to cross the road when she thought she saw something, was that? It certainly looked like him. No, it couldn't be. Her John talking to a woman like that. She was smoking a cigarette; how common. She quickly looked away. She didn't want to be caught staring, at least by him. She went past the building, then turned left.

The surgery was about the sixth or seventh building on the same side of the street. She got in the door and went to the reception desk. It couldn't be. If that was her John, why would he be talking to a woman like that…I wonder how long he had known her? Eileen's mind was whirring as she waited in the reception area. Is that why he put the kids away? He didn't want this woman to know he had any children, was that it? John didn't wear a wedding band. It was all making sense now. Well, she couldn't let on, but she now had something to work with.

"Mrs Davis, Mrs Eileen Davis?" The receptionist called from her desk. "The doctor will see you now," she said.

"OK, thank you."

Eileen walked along the hallway and knocked on the door.

"Come in!" came the reply from inside the room.

"Hello Mrs Davis, how can I help you today?" asked the doctor.

Doctor Hayes was a lovely doctor and always had time for a little chat. She was warm and friendly, and you could talk to her about absolutely anything.

"Well," Eileen said, "I don't know where to start…"

"How about at the beginning?" replied Doctor Hayes.

"I need to have something for a dicky tummy," Eileen said.

"So, you have an upset tummy, Mrs Davis, well…oh my god!" Doctor Hayes put her hand to her mouth as she looked at Eileen's face.

"OK, it's like this, Doctor. I can trust you not to say anything to my husband, can't I?"

"But of course. It's under patient and doctor confidentially…I am not allowed to tell your husband anything about you and I can't tell you anything about your husband," she replied.

"Right, I have had to make up an excuse to see you, by saying I have had a dicky tummy, so I need to have a prescription for something for my tummy…" Before Eileen knew it, she had burst into tears.

It was all coming out—the children being put into care, his all of a sudden violent nature, ringing her every day to make sure she was still at home, coming back if she didn't answer the phone.

Doctor Hayes sat back in her chair.

"Mrs Davis, this isn't good. You are suffering from domestic violence from your husband. There are places you can go as a refuge for battered women."

"I'm not battered!" Eileen protested.

"Yes, you are, Mrs Davis…Eileen," Doctor Hayes took Eileen's hands, "Eileen, I am a doctor, I can see your bruises under your make-up, you're shaking when you're talking to me. You're scared and this man has one hell of a hold over you. Do you want to resolve this, or do you want to leave him?" she asked.

"I can't leave him. I have nowhere to go," Eileen said.

"What about family? What about your parents? Siblings?"

"I called my mum yesterday, which was difficult. I can't call out, John has put a padlock on the phone, so it only accepts calls, not able to make them," she told her.

"So how did you contact your mother then?" the doctor asked.

"I went to the phone box, but it was while I was there that John had called home and I wasn't there to answer, so I made up an excuse, saying that I was in the toilet as I had an upset tummy."

"Oh, I see, yes, it is difficult. I suppose you could try her again, but what if you're caught? What if he finds out, Eileen, what are you going to do?" Doctor Hayes looked concerned.

"I've seen the children on their way to school. They didn't see me and even though I miss them, they look clean and happy and they have friends. But I miss them so much and I don't know what to do, I can't get them back, Doctor. He's the head of the house and his say-so is final."

"Not necessarily, Eileen, but you have nowhere else to live and no way to support them at the moment. If you leave them where they are for the time being, then you can get yourself sorted out. Then go for them, but you may have to leave the area if you're not going to press charges against John," the doctor informed her.

"Yes, I have a lot to think about and a lot to do. It's knowing where to start," Eileen replied.

"Eileen, what if you go to the school? They may be able to help. It's only an idea, but it also may be upsetting and disrupting to the children if they see you at the moment. As you say, they have settled in, it may really be challenging for them."

Doctor Hayes took her pen from her white jacket.

"Let me give you this prescription. When you take it, take it into the bathroom, shut the door, take a 5ml spoon, put the medicine on the spoon, then tip it down the toilet, then do the same again, sit on the toilet, then flush it away. Try and have the medicine when John is around; that way, he won't be able to dispute it."

"Thank you, Doctor Hayes, I am sorry if I took up too much of your time," Eileen said.

"It's fine, Eileen. And please try and get some contact with your family. If I give you any leaflets or pamphlets, if John finds them, it will only make matters worse, but when you're ready, come back to me and I'll see what I can do."

Eileen left the doctors and felt much better than she had done in a long time. She looked at her watch and saw it was 11.10 am. She had been there for just under an hour. She had a little time to get home, so she thought she would phone her mum from the phone box, just along the street, before she had to head home.

What Eileen didn't realise was that John had seen her go into the phone box. He was looking out of the window at work. *I wonder who she's calling?* He thought to himself. He left the office. He didn't need his jacket; it was a warmish day.

"Mum, Mum! Hi, it's Eileen. How are you?"

"Oh, Eileen! It's good to hear from you, darling! How are you? Did you manage to get any money?" Eileen's mum asked.

"No Mum, I haven't managed to get any money. This is still some from yesterday. Mum, can I come and see you? Can I come and stay?" Eileen asked. It had been so long, and she wasn't sure if her mum would want to see her.

"Yes, of course, you can come and stay, but how can I get the money to you so you can get here? Your brother is here, he wants to know if he can come and collect you?" her mum said.

"Oh, I hadn't thought of that. Yes Mum, that would be great. Let me think about when I can get you to come for me. I have a lot to think about and I feel like I am in a whirlwind," Eileen said. "How have you been, Mum?" she enquired.

"Yes fine, but more worried about you," her mum replied.

"I'll be fine, Mum. I just need to sort this out. There's a lot to do. I will call you again soon, someone wants to use the phone. I have to go, that's the pips." Eileen put the receiver down and opened the door without looking up.

"Sorry Sir, I've finished now," Eileen said.

"Yes, you have, haven't you!" replied John, who was watching Eileen with such fury in his face; all of the colour went from Eileen's face. She was as white as a ghost. He walked her home in silence, never said a word to her. All Eileen was thinking was, *oh my god, what the hell am I going to do, he's going to kill me.*

It didn't take long to walk home. Normally, when something is going to happen the feeling of dread is in the pit of your stomach and all you want is for time to go so slowly and even stand still.

John opened the front door to the flat and pushed Eileen so hard that she fell straight onto the sofa on her front. He whipped her over onto her back and slapped her so hard around the face.

"Who the bloody hell were you talking to on the phone? Hey? Come on, answer me!" John bellowed.

"I...I called my mum. To...to see how she was," Eileen replied, in a very small voice.

"Now why would you be calling your mother when I forbade it? You're not allowed to talk to her!" John screamed at Eileen.

Eileen had had enough, she stood up, she had had a week of this. Just a week. A lot of women have this for years. She couldn't hold back any longer.

"My mother is my mother! You have no right to forbid me from seeing or speaking to my family! You are not in charge of me and you can't tell me who I can or can't speak to!" Eileen shouted back.

John moved his arm as far back as he could, and as if in slow motion, he slapped Eileen so hard it cracked on her face. He punched her in the side, breaking at least one or two of her ribs. She was doubled up in pain, on all fours. John continued to hit her. He punched her in the back and kicked her up the backside three times.

He walked over to the sideboard, took out the address book, put it into the tin bin in the kitchen and took out the matches by the cooker. Lighting the match, he dropped it on to Eileen's address book.

Eileen was on the floor in agony, she had no idea that the bin was on fire and it had caught onto the curtains by the kitchen window. The pain made Eileen fall unconscious and was oblivious to the flat now being on fire.

***

She could hear it, but it sounded in the distance, a long way away. She started coughing. Coughing a lot and then all of a sudden, she was wet. Getting really wet. Now getting soaked.

Where was that water coming from? She was getting soaked and coughing. What the hell was going on?

The next thing she saw a big man coming through the window. She screamed as loud as she could…then everything went black.

***

Eileen woke up in the hospital. She didn't know where she was or why she was there.

"Hello, how are you feeling?" A nurse spoke to her.

"Where am I?" Eileen asked, her head groggy.

"You're in hospital, my love. You've had a nasty accident. You were in a fire?"

Eileen thought for a moment. A fire? How come I was in a fire? She couldn't remember. She heard someone shout in the ward and then she jumped out of her skin.

She remembered…John…he had found her in the phone box, they had argued when they got in, he had slapped her across the face. Then he had punched her in the ribs. She put her hands down under the covers and felt bandages.

Oh no, she thought, he did…he hurt her. He'd really hurt her. Her back was hurting her also.

She lifted the covers to get out of bed and the friendly nurse came over.

"Sorry my love, you can't get out of bed yet. You've been badly hurt, what would you like? A cup of tea, perhaps?"

"Yes please," Eileen said.

The nurse went away to get her a cup of tea. When she came back, she asked the nurse what day it was. She said it was Wednesday.

"Wednesday? I thought it was Tuesday?" Eileen was confused.

"It was but you have slept for so long. You came in at 12.30 pm yesterday and you were unconscious then. You've only just woken up and it's 10 am," the nurse replied.

Oh, my goodness, thought Eileen, *24 hours ago I was with my doctor, now I'm in hospital.*

"Nurse, has anyone been to see me while I was asleep?" Eileen asked.

"I don't know, I will have to check as I have only been on for a little while. I'll be back in a minute," she said, then she rushed off.

She was back only a few moments later.

"Yes, Sister said that a man came in to see you last night, he said he was your husband, but we asked him not to stay for too long, then he left." The nurse, who said her name was Sally, told her.

Right, thought Eileen, *this is my chance! Do I tell them not to let him in to see me? At least I can call my mum and get them to collect me when I am due out of here. I need to be away from him…he could have killed me last night.*

Sally returned a little later.

"Mrs Davis, there's a gentleman here to see you."

"Who is it? Is it my husband?" Eileen began to panic.

"No, I think it's a policeman. They want to know what happened to you and your home? Do you want to talk to them? I can tell them that you're not up to it yet if you like?"

"Sally, would you mind? I need to get some rest and the last thing I want to do is to talk to police right now. Maybe tomorrow?"

Sally left Eileen and went along to tell the police to come back tomorrow and that Mrs Davis wasn't up to visitors just yet.

"Thank you, Sally. And my name is Eileen, you don't have to call me Mrs Davis. Sally, what time is visiting hours and how do I make a phone call from here?" Eileen asked.

"Well, visiting hours are 3-7 pm daily and there's a mobile telephone on wheels that can be plugged into the wall socket for the phone. Who did you want to call?"

"Sally, I don't even know where my handbag is? I don't think I took anything with me when I came here. I don't even have any money to make a call. Did I have a coat with me when I came in?" Eileen asked.

"I don't think you did, not even house keys," Sally said.

"Well, that would be a laugh, as I don't think I have a home anymore, so the keys aren't any good. I think it all went up. But as I haven't seen or heard from anyone, so I have no idea."

Later that day, Eileen had two visitors, the couple from next door, Mr and Mrs Coombes.

"Eileen! Oh, my goodness, how are you?" asked Mrs Coombes. "We were so worried!"

Eileen was quite relieved to see both of them.

"I'm OK, a bit battered and bruised…"

"Yes, we know all about the battered and bruised. We heard him going bananas at you before the flat caught alight. Has he been here at all?" They both quizzed.

"The nurse said he came last night, but I was asleep, and they wouldn't let him stay," Eileen told them. They were a nice couple and very considerate and kind.

"Eileen, we asked but we're not allowed into your flat to get you any of your things. The fire brigade said it's too unstable and unsafe, but is there anything that you need, that we can get for you?" Mrs Coombes asked.

"Erm, I'm not sure. I'll have one of these hospital gowns on for now. They aren't too bad, but if no-one can get into my flat, then there's nothing we can do," Eileen replied.

"I tell you what then, if we give you some money, you can make a couple of calls and someone can get you what you need. Would that be of help?" Mrs Coombes asked.

This couple was really just lovely!

"If you wouldn't mind, could you give me some change, just so I can call my mum. This is where this all started," Eileen mused.

"Not just today though, was it, dear?" Mrs Coombes said. "We could hear what he was saying through the walls. I'm so sorry we couldn't help you, but he forbade you to see or speak to your family. They are the ones you must call. They are the ones who can help you."

Mrs Coombes gave Eileen £5.00 in change so she could make the relevant calls to her family. Thankfully, Eileen had remembered her mum's number. Mr and Mrs Coombes also bought Eileen some cakes from the bakers and a couple of drinks.

"Eileen, we have to make a move now, we haven't seen the police as of yet, but we can tell them what happened if you want? Otherwise, we won't say anything if you don't want us to?" Mr Coombes said quietly.

"It's up to you if you want to tell the police. I think I am going to have to, otherwise I am going to have to go back to him when I get out of hospital and it's the last thing that I want to do. Pardon the pun, but over my dead body comes to mind." Eileen smiled.

"Bye Eileen and please take care of yourself. We can come again, to see you're OK."

"Thank you, to both of you. It means a lot to me. I won't forget what you have done for me," Eileen said, she waved them goodbye as she saw them leave the ward.

Chapter 4

"Come in, come in." The deputy head, Mrs Sharp, welcomed everyone into the meeting.

When everyone had taken their seats, Mrs Sharp made a start.

"So, this is a formal meeting. Can we please introduce ourselves, just so everyone knows who they are?"

Miss Howe, Alison's teacher; Mrs Wilkins, Tom's teacher; Ms Christine Walters, the Manager of Craven House Children's Home; Mr Simon Prowse, the children's social worker; and Mrs Sharp, deputy head, all introduced themselves.

"I didn't know that Alison and Tom had a social worker," Miss Howe said.

The other members of staff nodded in agreement.

"Because of recent events within the family, the police notified social services and now they have been allocated a social worker, hence Mr Prowse is here," Mrs Sharp said.

"What events are those?" asked Mrs Wilkins.

"Well, as you know and are aware, Mr Davis put his children into care in the middle of May this year. Nobody knew why, including his wife, the children's mother. And from what I understand from the staff at Craven House Children's home, we have noticed that there has been a lady hanging around by the school gates, but not in front of them. She's been seen hiding behind a tree. When the staff told me, we assumed it was the children's mother. Obviously not wanting to be seen by the children, but wanting to see them, which is only natural."

"As I said, we don't know the reasoning of this happening, but my concern now is how the children are. Have they been upset by this massive change in their lives? Have they settled into the children's home? So, let's start by asking Miss Howe; how has Alison been since this massive upheaval?"

Miss Howe sat up straight and started.

"Alison is a quiet, happy, little girl, who does every task to her best ability. I haven't really noticed a huge change in her behaviour, she just gets on with her work. Which is a great distraction I suppose to her change of address as of the last few weeks.

"She does go out to play when the weather is nice. She plays with her best friend, Emily. I have seen them talking, but it seems that Alison doesn't really talk about her home life to anyone."

Miss Howe continued, "Saying that, I have noticed when she's out in the playground, she does look for her little brother and she's quite protective towards him, and him her. I think in these last few weeks, they have gotten quite close, but again that's understandable. You would have to ask Mrs Wilkins about Tom, though." Miss Howe finished, waiting to hear from Mrs Wilkins.

Mrs Wilkins began.

"Tom is a little more reserved at school. He also does his tasks to the best of his ability. He does get stuck from time to time, but he has the confidence to ask for help if he needs it. He plays with a number of children in his class and is a popular little boy with the other children, which helps with this situation.

"Nothing really seems to bother Tom. He also looks for Alison at break time. I think they just like to check in with each other to make sure the other is OK and doing fine." Mrs Wilkins ended.

"OK, Ms Walters, could you tell us how the children have settled into Craven House?" Mrs Sharp asked.

"Well, I have a report from my staff, who have been working closely with both of the children. Sandra, who works with them in the week, has said that Alison and Tom have settled very well into Craven House. They both share bedrooms with other children. Tom has a roommate called Freddie who is a little older than Tom, but they play cars together, they eat together and generally have a jolly good time together.

"They both like each other's company and it's like they are brothers. Tom is aware that Alison has settled into the home, but he also sees that she's a bit of a loner. She shares her bedroom with two other little girls; one is a little bit bossy and the other is just like Alison, quiet." Mrs Walters looked at down her notes and continued.

"She has no problem with her appetite. In fact, they both have good appetites and often clear their plates after a meal. They also help, along with the other children: tidying up, clearing the plates away and putting them into the hatch that leads into the kitchen. They've both adapted very well into life at the home. You wouldn't know that they have only been there for a short time.

"They both like the weekends. They go out with the other children and staff on a Saturday, sometimes to get ingredients for cooking, and sometimes they go to the local shop to spend their pocket money on sweets or whatever they want. They enjoy the experience being out with the other children at the home.

"A couple of the older children have said to both Alison and Tom that if they have any trouble from the children in their class to ignore them. That's what they had to do. Sometimes at the weekend, they can make biscuits or cakes. They use the dining room to make up the ingredients for the projects, then a member of staff uses the cooker, as the children are not allowed to enter the kitchen under any circumstances."

Mrs Walters ended her report and closed her notebook.

"I don't know if any of you have any questions about it?" she asked, looking around the room. Nobody had any questions. She was a little disappointed as she wanted to show that the children were happy at Craven House. But they may ask some when everyone involved had their say.

"So, now we come to Mr Prowse, but I would like to say something first if that's alright?" Mrs Sharp said, looking around the staffroom for the staff to comment. But they just nodded their heads.

"Now Sergeant O'Brien contacted social services on Wednesday 26 May when Mrs Davis was admitted to hospital, due to the fact that her flat was set on fire and she had lost consciousness.

"It looks also that she had suffered from domestic violence. She had cracked ribs, concussion, smoke inhalation and bruises on her back. She also suffered a black eye that she had been covering up, from what the sergeant had said.

"It wasn't good. Thankfully, the children are not aware of any of this. We have no record ever of the children having been beaten at all or anything like that, so I think this is only a recent thing that has happened since the children were put into care," Mrs Sharp said.

"Oh, my goodness!" Mrs Wilkins gasped. "Who would have thought it? You never know with some people."

"My, my, poor Mrs Davis," Miss Howe said, shaking her head.

"May I bring Mr Prowse into this discussion now then?" Mrs Sharp looked in the direction of the children's social worker. "Mr Prowse, would you like to begin?"

"Yes, thank you, Mrs Sharp. Mrs Sharp said that she had heard as I did on Friday last week, that Mrs Davis had been a victim of domestic violence. We know this has happened pretty recently, and that there are no previous incidents that anyone is aware of."

"We are aware that Mrs Davis had had an altercation with her husband, resulting in him punching her in the side at least three times, which caused her to crack her ribs. We also understand that he slapped her face so hard that he knocked her off her feet, which was when she fell down, she hit her head and had a concussion. When Mr Davis left the flat, he had already set alight her address book in a bin which was on the work surface that had the curtains nearby had caught alight," Mr Prowse looked livid as he spoke.

"When Mrs Davis was knocked out, she was unaware of the flat being on fire. She has been in hospital for two weeks, and her mother has been in contact with her. On being discharged Mrs Davis left with her mother to go to her home."

"The father, Mr Davis, has disappeared. He turned up at the hospital later that night, when Mrs Davis was admitted, but he didn't stay. The police have been to his place of work many times but cannot find him. Mrs Davis has implied that he may have gone to Ireland as he has relatives living there. But at the moment, we, like the police, have no idea of his current whereabouts."

"Now, we don't think he will get in contact with the children or the school, as his wife had said that he had scribbled out anything to do with the school in her address book, including other parents and ripped pages out, prior to setting it alight. But our main concern is the children."

"They do not know what has happened to both of their parents and in my opinion and view, it's better that they do not know about it at this time. Nonetheless, that may change as things unfold."

Mrs Wilkins interrupted, "Erm, so the children, Alison and Tom, have been getting to and from school, by escort from the staff of Craven House. Is that to continue and do we have anything to worry about from Mr Davis? He was the one who left them at school to go into care. Who's to say he won't want to get the children back?"

Mrs Sharp answered the question, "Mrs Wilkins, as it was Mr Davis who brought the children's things into school, he doesn't know which care home they have gone into and I don't think he wants them. It will be more likely that Mrs Davis will want to take the children home."

"What home? The one they lived in is now not fit enough to live in, and if she, Mrs Davis, is that ill, she won't be able to look after them?" Mrs Wilkins asked with concern.

"I was coming to that, Mrs Wilkins. Mr Davis is the police's problem as such, they are the ones looking for him and yes, Mrs Davis would want to have the children back, providing her husband doesn't come back. Yes, she is staying with her own mother, but she isn't in a fit state to look after them. However, she may do later on. Mr Prowse, what do you think as a social worker?" Mrs Sharp asked.

"Well, in my professional opinion, yes, we would suggest that families stay together, which is why Alison and Tom are in the same care home, they could have been separated, but weren't. But in this instance the only thing is, Mr Davis, who is or was the head of the household, had signed the paperwork to say that he is relinquishing all responsibility for the children and they are now care of the State."

"So, I think, unless Mrs Davis has very good reason to get the children back, I'm afraid it won't happen," Mr Prowse exclaimed.

"That's not fair, the children should be with their mother, rather than in a home. I didn't like this from the beginning! I said, didn't I, they should be with their mother…not let the father make the decisions!" Mrs Wilkins snapped.

"Mrs Wilkins, we know it's a difficult situation, but we have to do what's best for the children," Mrs Sharp said, looking squarely at Mrs Wilkins.

"So, as it stands, Alison and Tom are to be in care for the foreseeable future. Their mother is still recovering from a horrific incident, which I think has been leading up to this situation. She is staying with relatives. She had no means of support and didn't work; more than likely due to her husband wanting her to stay at home and look after the children and the home.

"Mrs Davis has no home of her own now, so we have to abide by the system that's put in place for the children. Does anyone have any questions regarding what we have heard in this meeting?" Mrs Sharp asked.

"So, all of this, it's going into the children's files then?" Mrs Wilkins asked.

"Yes, it will," replied Mrs Sharp, "we have to have a record of all of it, just so everything is up to date. "So, are there any more questions? No? Then this meeting is over.

"Mr Prowse, will you keep me updated with what's going on at your end and vice versa If anything comes up? I doubt very much if Mr Davis will come to school or social services, but if Mrs Davis comes to the school, we will let all of the staff know what's happening, so, if she does come here, she can speak to either myself or the head, who is also aware of what's going on and we can take it from there.

"Thank you everyone, for your time this morning. I know it was a bit rushed, but with recent events, we couldn't leave it any longer to keep everyone in the loop."

As everyone left the staffroom, Mrs Sharp shook Mr Prowse and Ms Walters by the hand and showed them out of the building. Mr Prowse and Ms Walters walked up the road together until they got to the end of it and they both walked in different directions.

Miss Howe and Mrs Wilkins returned to their classrooms, just in time for the children to return from playtime, all hot and bothered.

Miss Howe had her staff set up painting, but not with brushes, the children were taking their shoes and socks off, there were going to walk into the paint, feel it squish between their toes. Then they were going to get out of the washing up bowl with the paint in and walk along the plain lining paper that was placed on the floor to print their footprints.

Red, blue, green and orange. As more children walked on the paper, the colours started to change. Alison had red paint on her feet, but when she walked onto the blue footprints, the paint changed colour to purple. *That was fun*, she thought. The paint felt squashy under her feet.

When the children had finished with their painted feet, they then walked along to another washing up bowl, with water and soap in it. Alison enjoyed school, she felt safe there. It wasn't difficult and she was enjoying it more and more with lessons like these.

Tom had just come in from playing outside and he was playing with the water tray. There were empty washing up liquid bottles, that had the bottom part of the lid on them, so it had a smaller hole in it. If you filled it up a bit, you could squeeze the bottle, and the water would spill out like a water pistol, but on a much bigger size.

Tom liked to play with the water, but he didn't always remember to roll up his sleeves, so they got a bit wet. Tom wasn't bothered about little things like that, he was having too much fun.

He would fill up the jug and pour the water into another bottle, making a bit of spillage on the way, but it was great fun and it made you feel good, pouring from one bottle to another jug. Tom would play for as long as he could with the water, but his teacher, Mrs Wilkins called him aside and said that his fingers were starting to wrinkle, as they had been in the water for too long. She took a towel and dried his hands and fingers for him. Carefully drying them. He had small hands, but he liked the softness of the towel.

"Mrs Wilkins, what can I do now?" Tom asked.

"Well, we were going to sit down in the story corner, and I was going to read you all a story. It's going to be lunchtime soon, so it is a nice way to relax before lunch," Mrs Wilkins replied.

"Oh OK, can I choose a book for you to read?"

"Yes, that's fine. What would you like me to read?"

"I like the Hungry Caterpillar because he can eat what he wants and he doesn't get fat, but he does change into a butterfly," Tom replied.

"OK, that's what I'll read then. Red Class, would you all please come and sit on the carpet in the reading corner, as I'm going to read a story before lunchtime," Mrs Wilkins called.

The other children all followed one another to find a space on the carpet to listen to their story. Mrs Wilkins opened the book and began reading.

***

On returning back to Craven House, Ms Walters called Sandra and John into the office. There wasn't anyone there, so they could talk privately. Ms Walters left the door ajar, just in case she was needed, and she didn't want it to look like she was telling her staff off.

"Well," she started, "it seems there have been some developments since Alison and Tom have come to Craven House. We don't really know or understand why they were sent here, but now I have information as to what's been going on prior to their arrival.

"It has emerged that their father, Mr Davis, has freaked out at the children's mother. This has only recently come to our attention."

"Pardon?" Sandra asked.

"Sandra, please let me continue, and you will understand, hopefully as much as I do. It seems that Mr Davis has, on the one occasion, beaten up Mrs Davis, where she was badly hurt. He had cracked her ribs, hurt her back. She fell over and hit her head and caused her home to be set on fire.

"Mrs Davis was unconscious when the flat was set alight, but then woke when she was being rescued by the fire brigade. She was taken to hospital, where, we believe, she did finally speak to the police and they are currently looking for her husband. Her mother is in contact with her now. Mr Davis had forbidden Mrs Davis to her to see her family and now she is with her mother; she is recuperating," Ms Walters continued.

"So now you know and are aware of the situation, but I don't think the children have a clue to what's going on with their parents, and I think for the time being, that's the best way. They've settled in well here, and this would just cause them both a lot of upset and that's not fair at this time."

Sandra and John stood there with their mouths wide open. Sandra thought she saw something out of the corner of her eye, but she may have been mistaken.

"So, I think if we just carry on as normal around Alison and Tom, they shouldn't be any the wiser," Ms Walters said.

"Ms Walters, can I ask you something?" Sandra asked.

"Yes, go ahead."

"Once Mrs Davis is back to normal health, will she be allowed to have the children back, once she's back on her feet?" Sandra enquired.

"Unfortunately, no, Sandra. Mrs Davis can't have the children back. Mr Davis has signed over the children to the State. Even if Mrs Davis had a new home, a job to support both her and the children and run and pay for a home, she still couldn't get them back. She would have to take the State to court and even that's not a guarantee that she could get them back and she would have a huge legal bill, even if she got legal aid. It's not going to be easy for her.

"Now, that is it for now. If you could continue with your duties, I would appreciate it. And don't forget, this is only for the staff ears, and not to be talked about during your breaks. This is very sensitive," Ms Walters added.

***

Sandra and John came out of the office and walked towards the kitchen. Sandra noticed a little pair of legs in a nightie running fast away down the corridor.

Oh no, she thought. *Please don't say we had little ears listening to all of that, or we all going to be in trouble.*

"John, John, can you come over here for a second?" Sandra asked.

"What's wrong, Sandra?" Asked John.

"John, I think we are going to have to be very careful about this," Sandra looked worried.

"I know," John replied, "Ms Walters just told us that."

"No, you don't understand. I think we were overheard, by a little person who is supposed to be in bed sick," she replied.

"Oh no, no, not her! This is going to be a nightmare! Should we tell Ms Walters? She may not say anything?" he said.

"What, Hilary? Keep something juicy like this to herself when she can use this against Alison? Of course, we must tell Ms Walters, just in case she does kick off and we don't get into trouble for not reporting it…it will be our jobs on the line," John said.

John and Sandra went back to see Ms Walters, who was on the telephone. They knocked and waited for her to call them.

"Yes, come in!" She beckoned. "What is it, you have only just left the office?" Ms Walters looked annoyed.

"We know Ms Walters, but we thought we ought to let you know something," Sandra said.

"Go on then."

Sandra took a big deep breath. "When we were in the office talking about the children, Alison and Tom…"

"Yes?" Ms Walters said.

"Well, we think we were overheard," Sandra said.

"But how could we be? There was nobody here but the staff?" Ms Walters looked puzzled, then her face jumped with shock. "Hilary! Hilary is off school today sick!" Ms Walters said. "Oh, my goodness, do you think she heard anything?"

"I don't know, she was running away quite fast down the corridor when we left. I thought I saw something out of the corner of my eye when we came in, but thought I was imagining things. Now I think it was her listening," Sandra said.

"What do we do? Do we mention it? Or say nothing, and hope she doesn't say anything to Alison or Tom, and just be ready to deal with the consequences when or if they happen?"

Ms Walters thought for a moment.

"Well, we have had a bit of trouble with Hilary in the past, but would she be this nasty? She is only a little girl?" Ms Walters said.

"Leave it with me for now, as I think we should see what happens. She may not say anything and if she does, we will take it from there."

Sandra and John left her office, shaking their heads. They both knew that Hilary could be a right little madam when she felt like it. This would be like gold dust with bells on for her to have a go at Alison and poor Alison would be devastated to know her mum had been put through so much.

***

Alison and Tom were walking home with Sandra and John and the other children. They had all come out of school roughly the same time, which meant it was nice to not hang around waiting, and the children could all relax and talk about their day at school.

Alison was telling Sandra about her footprint painting at school and how she liked the feel of the paint between her toes. Tom was telling John how he liked the story of the hungry caterpillar and wondered if he ate lots of food, would he turn into a caterpillar or a greedy pig? Everyone burst out laughing with this story.

Some of the children had big appetites and Tom was no different. Sandra and John kept glancing at each other and just thought that this information that they had learnt earlier that day would destroy both of these children.

They were near the main entrance to Craven House, they looked up towards the floor where the girl's rooms are and saw a little girl looking out of the window. *Uh oh*, Sandra thought. They were in for it this evening. Hilary would just love something this juicy to have a go at Alison for.

Right, that was it. She wasn't going to leave Alison alone with Hilary once this evening, she knew that she had to get her on her own to say something like this. So that was her plan, not to leave her alone tonight.

When they got in, Alison walked up the stairs.

"Hey Alison, where are you off to?" Sandra asked.

"Just to take my bag upstairs and get changed out of my uniform," Alison replied.

"Would you like some help?" Sandra offered.

"OK, if you want. That would be nice." she said.

Sandra took Alison by the hand and off they both went towards the girls' bedroom. They saw Hilary was sat up in bed with a big smirk on her face. She saw Sandra enter the room and the smirk disappeared into a small smile.

"Hello Sandra, I feel much better now than I did this morning, can I get up now?" Hilary asked.

Sandra thought she looked like butter wouldn't melt.

"Yes, Hilary. If you feel better, you can get up. Is there anything you want to do then?"

"Oh yes, I wanted to go down and watch TV in the sitting room, would that be OK?" Hilary replied sweetly.

"Yes, but you have to put your dressing gown on over your nightie and don't forget your slippers. Then you can go downstairs. Would you like some help?" Sandra asked.

"Oh no thank you, I can manage."

I bet you can, thought Sandra.

"See you downstairs, Sandra," Hilary said.

Hilary left the room and Sandra and Alison were alone.

"Are you OK today, Alison?" Sandra asked the little girl.

"Yes, just like most days," she said.

"Do you have anything bothering you, at all?"

"No," Alison replied.

"There, all done. Don't forget to put your uniform in the dirty washing bin, then it can be done at the end of the week," Sandra told Alison.

"Done."

Alison and Sandra left the girls' bedroom, and went downstairs to the dining area, to see if there was a snack the children could have. Sandra kept her eye on Alison, but also both eyes on Hilary.

There were sandwiches and crisps on the side on plates for the children to have, as dinner was still a couple of hours away. Tom came down and sat with Alison, Freddie plonked himself down next to Tom.

"Hi Alison, have you had a good day at school today?" Freddie asked.

"Yes, it was lovely, thank you," Alison said. She then went on to tell him about the painted footprints that she did at school today, and Tom piped up about the Hungry Caterpillar.

All three children were in great conversation, so Sandra knew she had nothing to worry about at the moment with Hilary and Alison. When the children had cleared their plates of sandwiches and crisps, they took them to the open hatch to the kitchen and piled them up on top of each other.

They were deciding what to do when Hilary walked into the kitchen looking for something to eat. Sandra gave her a plate of sandwiches and crisps and a drink and asked John if he could supervise Hilary in the dining area, as she was going to play outside with the children on the swings.

John did as he was asked and was talking to Hilary, asking her if she was feeling better.

"Oh yes, John. I feel much better, hopefully I can go back to school tomorrow," she said to John, with a rather big smile.

Sandra kept the children outside as long as she could. They were having a whale of a time on the swings and the slide. Thank goodness there were only three of them otherwise she would need another member of staff with her supervising.

The children had a couple more goes on the slide then decided they were getting a little cold and wanted to go in and watch TV. Sandra took them back in. Alison had noticed that Sandra was spending a lot more time with them than she normally did, but she was pleased to have an adult with them. It wasn't always much fun playing with the other children, but the fun perked up when an adult joined in.

They went into the sitting room to watch TV. Hilary was there, but so were some of the other bigger kids. Hilary knew she couldn't say anything to Alison with the grown-ups, or the bigger kids around. They would have a go at her, so she thought she would wait until she got Alison in the bedroom on her own. Josephine would back her up, as she was her little mouse, her little puppet.

Alison sat on one of the big comfy armchairs. Tom and Freddie, wanted to go upstairs and play cars, so off they went. Sandra came back in and saw the children watching TV. Hilary, some of the bigger boys and Alison on her own.

"What are you watching? Playschool? I used to love watching Playschool. My favourite was Big Ted," Sandra said.

"I like Hanbal," Hilary said. "Who do you like, Alison?"

"I like Big Ted and Little Ted. I think they are sweet together because they remind me of me and Tom," Alison replied.

Once the children had watched their programmes, it was nearly time to wash their hands and face and go down for dinner.

Tom and Alison always went down together. She would wait for him to get washed and Tom, Freddie and Alison would enter the dining room together. They never left Freddie out once.

John came and sat down at Alison and Tom's table. They ate fish fingers, chips and baked beans or peas. They all had milk or water with their meal, and they all ate heartily. The children's appetites had greatly improved since they came to Craven House, which all of the staff were pleased about, as they knew they were doing something right.

This meant that they were happy at Craven House and had settled in well, which is always what they want to achieve.

When dinner was finished and cleared away, Alison knew it was her bath night. Tom had his bath the night before, so Sandra asked her to collect her nightclothes so that when she'd had her bath, she could put them straight on.

Once Alison had her bath and washed her hair, was ready with her nightclothes on. She headed back to her bedroom to put her dirty clothes in the dirty wash bin. Allison had left the bathroom and Sandra was tidying up after emptying Alison's bathwater. Sandra was distracted and had forgotten to go with Alison back to her bedroom.

Alison opened the door and there, sat on her bed, was Hilary, with a huge smirk on her face.

"I have been waiting all day to talk to you," Hilary said.

Chapter 5

"What did you want to talk to me about? Because you don't normally want to talk to me," Alison asked.

"I've been here all day because I haven't been well. So earlier today, I wanted a drink of water, but couldn't find Sandra or Roger, so I went downstairs to the office to see if Ms Walters was there," Hilary started.

"She was in a meeting with Sandra and Roger and the door was left open, so I could hear. Your mummy has been hurt in a fire which your daddy did, and she has been in the hospital because he hurt her a lot," Hilary reported with a sly smile across her face.

"You're lying, Hilary! My mummy is fine at home, with my daddy. We are just here for the moment," Alison replied.

"Oh no, she's not, and you don't have a home anymore! It's been burnt down to the ground, so you are going to have to stay here forever. Your mummy can't see you anymore because your daddy gave you away," Hilary retorted, standing up very straight, with her arms folded.

Alison's head began to swim.

"You're lying, Hilary! Just because your mummy and daddy don't want you to live with them, you're saying nasty things about my mummy!" Alison raised her voice.

"I am not lying! I heard Ms Walters telling Sandra and Roger downstairs today!"

Alison couldn't take it in. Her mummy hurt in a fire and her daddy doesn't want them anymore? Before anyone in the room knew what had happened, Alison had swung back her arm and slapped Hilary hard in the face. She grabbed Hilary's hair and hung onto it very hard. Josephine, who was sitting on her bed, trying to take in what she was hearing and now what she was witnessing, started to scream.

The whole of the building heard the screams. Sandra, now realising that she had left Alison to go back to her room alone, ran as fast as she could to the girls' bedroom. On opening the door, she was met with quite a horrific scene.

Hilary was on the floor, with Alison sitting on top of her banging her head on the floor, whilst kicking her.

Sandra managed to prise Alison off Hilary, who was shaking with fear. No one had ever attacked her like that before.

"Sandra! Get that wild animal off me! She doesn't deserve to live here with nice girls!" Hilary shouted.

Alison was shaking with anger at what had happened and what she had heard.

"Sandra, it was all Hilary's fault! She told Alison things about her mummy and daddy that she shouldn't have done," Josephine said.

Hilary gave Josephine a real dirty look, as if to say, *you just wait until I have you on my own.*

Sandra removed Alison from the room and took her back along to the bathroom. Josephine went too.

"Stay there with Hilary, please Josephine. I want to talk to Alison on her own," Sandra said.

"Please, Sandra, let me come, just so I can be with Alison. She needs me more than Hilary does," pleaded Josephine.

"Is that OK, Alison?" asked Sandra.

Alison nodded.

Both little girls went along to the bathroom, while Hilary, who'd had a big shock, stayed in the girls' bedroom. She couldn't believe it! She didn't think that Alison would attack her! Yes, she wanted to hurt her, because Alison was so prim and proper, but she didn't expect her to react the way she did.

***

They opened the bathroom door and Sandra brought both of the girls in. There were a couple of wooden chairs in the bathroom and Sandra beckoned them to both sit down.

"So, what happened after you left the bathroom, Alison?" Sandra asked.

"Well, I walked into the bedroom with my washbag and Hilary said that she has wanted to talk to me all day since I got in from school. She told me that my mummy has been hurt in a fire and that my daddy did it and that Mummy was in hospital, and he really hurt her."

By now, Alison was tearing up and struggling to get the words out with what else Hilary had said to her. Josephine held Alison's hand and continued the story for Sandra. Sandra was pleased that she had let Josephine come with Alison.

Sandra couldn't believe what she was hearing. She had already heard most of the story that afternoon and she knew she had seen Hilary's nightie as she had run along the corridor. This little girl was very wicked, and she had to see Ms Walters about her. They couldn't continue having her here after the trouble she had caused.

Sandra picked up Alison and put her on her lap to give her a cuddle.

"Alison, I am really sorry that you have been treated badly like this. I knew that Hilary wasn't a happy little girl, but I didn't think she would do this," Sandra said.

"Why not, Sandra? Hilary hasn't ever been a nice little girl. She is always trying to start trouble for the other kids, but she has picked on Alison since she got here, hasn't she, Alison?" Josephine said.

Alison nodded her head.

"Why on earth didn't you say anything before, Josephine? Were you frightened of her?" asked Sandra.

"Yes, I was, Sandra, but when I saw what she did to Alison today and how nasty she could be about another little girl's mummy and daddy, that was it. I knew that I didn't want to be friends with her any longer. I know Alison shouldn't have hit her, but she's hurting, and Hilary's words were very unkind."

Once Alison had been consoled and she had calmed down, Sandra took both of them down to the living room to watch some TV. She then called to Amanda, one of the other staff, to keep an eye on both of the girls. They all sat together on one of the big comfy sofas.

Josephine picked up Alison's hand to hold it. She turned to Alison and gave her a big smile.

"It will be alright, Alison, you'll see," Josephine said. And Alison knew that she was right.

**

Sandra had gone to the office to see Ms Walters to explain the incident and what on earth were they going to do about it?

"Well Sandra, there is only one thing we can do. Hilary, as you know, is a disturbed little girl, who doesn't like nice little girls. I think for this evening, she will have to stay here, but I will make some calls and she can leave tomorrow to go to Denham House the other side of town and won't return. We do have a place for her over there. We can't tolerate this sort of behaviour. I'll inform the staff of how they will have to keep an eye on her.

"Do we have another room that Hilary can go into tonight, as I don't want those girls sharing, it will make matters much worse and I don't want a severe incident on my hands. Go and return to the girls in the living room and see if they want some cookies and milk and we can move Hilary while they're watching TV."

Sandra left Ms Walters' office so she could make the necessary phone calls to their other home across town. She popped her head around the living room door and asked Amanda if she could stay with the girls until she came back.

Amanda said that was fine and Sandra went back upstairs to where the girls' bedrooms were.

There was another room that some slightly older girls were using, but they did have an empty bed at the moment.

"Hi girls, you will be getting a new arrival, just for one evening, is that OK with you?" Sandra asked.

"Yes Sandra, that's fine, who is it?" one of the girls asked.

"Hilary," Sandra replied.

"Oh no! What have we done to deserve this?" the girl replied.

"Unfortunately, there has been an incident in her room with one of the other little girls and Ms Walters wants her to stay in here with you for the night. I know, but please don't give her a hard time. As I said, it's only for one night," Sandra smiled.

"OK, Sandra," the girls said in unison.

Sandra said thank you and left. She went down to the girls' bedroom to collect Hilary. She opened the door and Hilary was sitting on her bed, with a look of wonder on her face. She couldn't understand it.

Hilary looked up when she saw Sandra walk into the room.

"Hilary, what happened earlier? Why did you tell Alison those awful things?" Sandra asked.

73

"I thought Alison would be sad when she heard about her mummy and daddy, not angry! Why did she attack me?"

"Hilary, you overheard something that wasn't your place to tell Alison or Tom. That was confidential information. You should have come to me or Roger and say what you had heard, rather than tell Alison what you knew," Sandra said calmly.

"Now we know what happened with your mummy and daddy, but how would you have felt if someone had come along and told you what happened because they heard it from somewhere else? You wouldn't like it, would you?" Sandra asked.

"No, I wouldn't have. She would have been naughty if she had done that to me," Hilary retorted.

"But that's exactly what you did to Alison. It isn't fair and it isn't right. You wouldn't like someone being horrible to you for no reason, so why did you do it to her?"

Hilary shrugged and looked down at her feet.

"Hilary, you're going to be moved from this room this evening. We can't have you and Alison in the same room without an adult, so you're going to be sleeping with the older girls upstairs. Would you like some help with your things?" Sandra asked.

"Erm, yes please. I do have rather a lot of stuff," she replied, a little shocked that she was being moved when it was Alison who attacked her.

"Sandra, am I being moved because Alison attacked me? Is it for my safety?" Hilary asked.

"No, Hilary," replied Sandra, "it's for Alison's safety, in case you say anything to upset Alison again, and she then has another go at you."

"Oh," Hilary said quietly. She started collecting her belongings.

The door opened and two of the older girls came down to see if Hilary needed help with her stuff being moved.

"Yes, thank you," Sandra said, "that will be a great help."

The three girls and Sandra took Hilary's belongings to the room upstairs. That way they would only have to move her stuff just the once and it wouldn't give Hilary an excuse to come back into that room again.

***

74

Alison and Josephine were still eating their cookies when Sandra came back in.

"Thank you, Amanda," Sandra said.

Amanda nodded, and left the room and went back to her duties.

"Alison and Josephine, you'll be going back to your room in a few minutes," Sandra informed them. There was a look of horror on Josephine's face.

"But what about..."

Sandra held up her hand.

"Hilary has been moved to another bedroom for tonight, so it will just be you two in your room. Hilary's belongings have been moved, so she will not be back in your room again, is that OK? Do you both think that you will be able to sleep without any disruptions?" asked Sandra.

"That will be fine. Thank you, Sandra," Alison replied.

"Well, I will take you both upstairs, when you've finished your milk."

Both girls drained their milk in one go. They then wiped their mouths and put their glasses down on the coffee table.

Sandra walked them both up to their room, got them settled down and checked they were both OK. She said goodnight to both of them and then left the room.

Alison and Josephine didn't take long to fall asleep. They had both had a hectic day. Sandra went downstairs to Ms Walters office to see how she had got on with Denham House.

Sandra knocked on the door and she heard, "Come in."

"Sandra, there is a place at Denham House for Hilary to go tomorrow; where is she now?" asked Ms Walters.

"Hilary is now with three bigger girls, in the Lily room. Two of the girls came down to help Hilary with her belongings. That way she has no reason to return to that room. Josephine is appalled at what Hilary has done to Alison, so she no longer wants to be friends with her," Sandra said. "What time will Hilary be leaving tomorrow?"

"She'll leave for school as normal, but when she finishes school, she will be collected from school and taken straight to Denham House," Ms Walters said.

"What about breakfast in the morning? All three girls will be in the same room?" Sandra enquired.

"I've thought of that, and for once, we will let the two girls have breakfast in their room and then they can head off for school with the others as normal. We'll tell them in the morning about Hilary going. We don't want them to tell her, that's our job. As they are on different floors, getting washed in the morning, they will be in different bathrooms and as you said, the bigger girls will make sure Hilary doesn't step out of line. She will be told in the morning, by me, before she leaves for school," Ms Walters said.

Sandra sighed. That was a relief. Alison and Josephine could sleep peacefully, and tomorrow they would know that Hilary was leaving Craven House.

***

The next morning, Hilary was in the dining room. She hadn't seen Alison or Josephine this morning. She was in another bathroom and then she got dressed in the new bedroom, but she thought she might see both of them in the dining room for breakfast.

Before she had finished her breakfast, Amanda came up to her and told her she has to see Ms Walters in her office before she goes off to school. Hilary was going to ask Ms Walters what was going to happen to Alison.

Sandra came into the butterfly bedroom to see Alison and Josephine. They had already got washed and were getting dressed ready for school. Sandra asked both girls to come and sit down.

Josephine was having a little trouble with her school tie. Sandra adjusted it for her, Josephine said thank you and then Sandra spoke to both of them.

"How are you both this morning?" she said, concerned that they might be fearful of seeing Hilary again.

"Fine," they both said at the same time.

"Now, you know Hilary was moved to another room last night, well, she is down having breakfast in the dining room."

Josephine screwed up her face.

"Josephine, it's fine. You will both be having your breakfast up here for a change, and once breakfast is over and you have cleaned your teeth, you'll be heading off to school. Hilary is going to be leaving Craven House today. Once she has left for school, she will not be returning here after school, but going somewhere else," Sandra continued. "So, Alison, you and Hilary shouldn't cross paths again. Is that all right?"

"Sandra, how come Hilary is being moved after yesterday's incident? I know she wasn't very nice to me, but to move her, isn't that a bit…" Alison couldn't find the right word.

"Drastic?" said Sandra.

"Yes, drastic?" said Alison.

"No. Hilary has lots of problems and has had for a while, but this was the final straw. We cannot allow a child to bring so much disruption to another child in our care. It's not fair and I told Hilary that last night," Sandra stood up. "Anyway, I will bring your breakfast, what would you like? Boiled eggs and soldiers? Orange juice or milk?"

"Boiled eggs and soldiers and orange juice please," both girls replied together.

Sandra left the room returning shortly with their breakfast on trays.

"Now eat up, as you're going to have to leave for school soon. I will come back in a little while," Sandra said as she left the trays full of food for them.

"Yum!" the two girls said as they tucked into their eggs.

***

"Hilary, as you know, you were moved last night into the Lily room, but you won't be returning to there. You will go to school as usual, but you will be collected from school and taken to a new home, Denham House. Do you know why you're being moved to Denham House?" Ms Walters asked.

"Yes, because Alison attacked me, and it's for my safety," Hilary replied.

"No, that's not quite right, Hilary. That's not why you're being moved, Alison didn't attack you as you say for no reason, Hilary. You overheard a conversation that had some very delicate information about Alison, which you then used to hurt her." Ms Walters sighed. "You didn't inform a member of staff that you overheard this information. Instead, you ran away as quickly as you could."

"I didn't!" Hilary said.

"Do not interrupt when someone else is talking, Hilary. Yes, you did. You told Alison exactly what you overheard, which then resulted in her understandably getting upset and slapping you. What you did yesterday, Hilary, was unthinkable and downright nasty. This is the reason you're being moved

77

because Craven House is no longer suitable for you to live in," Ms Walters said. "Do you have anything to say on this matter, Hilary?"

"No!" Hilary looked at Ms Walters square in the eyes. "Can I go now then please? I don't want to be late for school."

"Yes, you may now leave. Take your school bag with you. When you go to Denham House, your belongings will be there waiting for you."

Hilary left the office and headed back to where everyone was waiting to go to school. Josephine was still with Alison, finishing off getting ready. They grabbed their school bags and headed out of their bedroom. They bounded down the stairs to where their group were getting ready to head off.

Hilary's group had already left for school, Tom and Alison were standing next to each other, and Josephine joined them. Even though Josephine was attending the same school as Hilary, a member of staff was going to walk Josephine further along to her school, so she didn't have to walk with Hilary. The children all went in a happy mood to school for the second day of the school week.

***

Things were getting back to some sort of reality now that Hilary had gone for good. Alison and Josephine were getting on really well and you would never know that Hilary had even been at the children's home.

Tom was getting on well with Freddie. Ever since Tom had walked through the door of the blue room with Airplanes on the wall, he knew he and Freddie would be good friends. The girls still attended different schools, but they caught up with each other after school and at the weekends.

Nobody knew what would happen in the school holidays. Josephine had only been at Craven House since the end of January, so she hadn't been there much longer really than Alison. On Friday, on their return from school, Sandra and John called all of the children together in the living room. They had an announcement that included them all.

"Right now, quiet please!" Sandra said as the children gathered in the living room.

"Can everyone settle down and can we have a little hush. We have something very important to tell you," Sandra began.

78

Three of the boys at the front were talking rather loudly about what it was going to be about.

"Come along, you three, we want to give you some good news, but we can't do that if you're all still talking," John said.

Suddenly, the room fell quiet.

"Now, as you all know, it's coming up to the summer holidays soon and many of you haven't been here through the summer, so we have organised two holidays to choose from. You can go to Margate or Eastbourne," Sandra said excitedly.

"What will happen is the children interested in going to Margate will go for the second week of the summer holidays and the children who want to go to Eastbourne will be going on the fourth week of the holidays. This means that everyone who wants to go on holiday will be able to go shopping for their holiday clothes. You will all get an allowance to purchase some clothes of your choosing, the week before their holiday," Sandra told them.

Some of the bigger children put up their hands, and Sandra picked one of the girls.

"Yes, Kim?"

"Sandra, what happens to the others who are left behind waiting for their trip or who have already gone on their trip?" Kim asked.

"Good question," John replied.

"If you're waiting to go on your trip, you can go shopping with one of us and then it'll be just like a usual Saturday. You can chill out watching TV, or go into the gardens, but we will also be arranging some activities throughout the whole of the holidays; day trips out and, weather permitting, some stuff locally."

"Do you like the sound of the holidays? What's in store for you? Any questions?" John asked.

Alison put up her hand to ask something.

"Yes, Alison," Sandra nodded to Alison.

"How do we know what holiday trip we can go on and what else can we bring apart from clothes?" Alison asked politely.

"Well, there are 22 of you altogether, so we were going to put a list on two pieces of paper, and you can write on which trip you would like to go on. So have a think about what one you would like to go on and put your names down. We have to know soon, as we will be booking it."

"John, where will we be staying? A hotel, a caravan?" Another child asked.

"We'll be staying in a bed and breakfast. There will be four staff coming with you and we'll be going by coach. Your rooms will be rooms just like here, and we will be checking on you, as well as taking you all out," John replied.

"Alison, Alison, what trip are you going on? Can Freddie and I go with you and Josephine on your trip, so we can all be together?" Tom asked Alison.

"Josephine, what trip did you want to go on? Freddie, what trip do you want to go on?" asked Alison.

"Well, I liked the look of the Margate trip," Josephine said. "Freddie, where do you want to go?"

"I want to go to Margate too!" Freddie replied.

"Tom, where—"

"Margate, please!" Tom replied before Alison could get the rest of the sentence out. Alison wanted to go to Margate as well.

"Sandra, can I put down our names for the Margate trip, please. I've asked Josephine and Freddie where they wanted to go first, as me and Tom would be happy with either, but both of them said they wanted to go to Margate. So that's four of us for Margate, is that OK?" asked Alison.

"Yes, that's fine. That's the first four names up. You will have to be quick, children, as the places are going to go quickly," John said.

Some of the other children put their names down for the Eastbourne trip. Kim and two of her friends also put their names down the Margate trip and so did the children who went to Alison and Tom's school.

"Did anyone else want the Margate trip, as the places are nearly all gone?" Sandra asked.

No, the rest of the children wanted to go on the Eastbourne trip.

***

The children's home was buzzing for the next couple of weeks. They only had three weeks left of school, then they could all start getting ready for the holidays. Tom was excited, he was going to be with the best people in his life, his big sister and her friend and his best friend Freddie.

Although it was coming up to Alison's seventh birthday, she hadn't said anything about it, as she didn't want a fuss. Last year they had a little party at home. Her mum and dad and Tom. This year she would forget her birthday as she was going to have a holiday with her favourite people. Tom, her brother, his friend Freddie, Josephine, Sandra, John, Celia and George.

Tom was counting down the days on his calendar in the kitchen. He put a red cross on each day as it had finished.

School had ended for the summer and the children were getting excited to go shopping. As they had no school for the week, they could go shopping in the week, rather than at the weekend. Sandra took the girls to the shops to buy what they needed for their holiday. Tom wanted to come, but Sandra said she would take the boys separately and Alison could come along to help him choose what he wanted.

Tom was happy with that, and Alison didn't feel too guilty that her little brother wasn't going with them.

Alison, along with the other girls, went with Sandra to town. There wasn't much in the way of choice of clothes for younger children, except Woolworths and Mothercare. They all went into Woolworths first. They had some lovely clothes in the store. The weather in England is always unpredictable, so Sandra told them it would be a good idea to take a bit of everything just in case.

Alison saw a lovely pink dress, that was a few pounds and also a couple of t-shirts and shorts and a pair of pale blue cotton trousers. She needed some new underwear as she was starting to grow out of hers. By the time she'd bought all that, her allowance was spent.

Josephine chose a mint green dress, a pair of pink cotton trousers, a few t-shirts and she needed some new socks, as her feet were getting bigger. Both girls were also bought a pair of sandals each.

The bigger girls chose a few t-shirts and some short skirts, which Sandra shook her head at, saying they were too young to be wearing such short skirts, but she found something a bit more suitable which they hadn't spotted but did like.

Kim chose a navy-blue polka dot flowing skirt, with a matching scarf to be worn around her neck. Sandra found a big straw hat and suggested that she tie the scarf around the bottom of the hat instead. Kim liked the idea of that, so her friends all chose something similar.

Once they had all finished, Sandra suggested that they go along to the local Wimpy bar and have something to eat and drink as a treat before they headed back to the home.

Alison's eyes lit up as she looked at the menu. She didn't know where to start! She chose a hamburger and chips, with a mint choc milkshake. Josephine had the same, but she preferred strawberry milkshake.

The girls had a great time, all sitting together, excited with their purchases and talking about their holiday. Sandra knew it was Alison's birthday tomorrow. The staff knew of all of the children's birthdays and they always made a big thing for them. They would have a party and they got given gifts and the other children would make a big effort for them too. Especially if it was their first birthday in the home without their families.

Sandra had already told the other girls about Alison's birthday the following day, so they could keep her out of the way while the other staff and children could wrap up her presents and make her cake for her birthday party.

When all of the girls had finished their meal and drinks, they headed back to the home. All of them were talking excitedly. They couldn't wait to get back home and try on their new things they had bought.

"Don't forget they are for your holiday and NOT to be worn before. By all means, try them on, but we don't want to see you in your new clothes until your holiday, OK?" Sandra said.

The girls all raced upstairs, when they got back home, to try on and put their new things away, as Sandra had instructed.

***

Alison had just put away her new clothes when Tom walked into her bedroom.

"Hi Alison, have you just got back from the shops? What did you buy?" Tom asked.

"I bought a couple of t-shirts, shorts, trousers, a pink dress and some new underwear," Alison told him.

"I can't wait for us to go shopping in the next couple of days, I can get some new things too. Alison, I am so excited for us to go on holiday, we haven't been on holiday before, have we?" he asked her.

"No, we haven't. We have been to the seaside for the day, but not for a holiday. I'm looking forward to it as well. Come on, let's go downstairs, it will be dinner time soon," Alison said to her little brother.

She shut the door to her wardrobe and off they went back down to the dining room for their dinner.

After dinner, they went into the living room to watch a little TV before washing themselves and brushing their teeth to get ready for bed.

"Goodnight Alison," Tom said as he kissed her on her cheek.

"See you in the morning."

"Night Tom, yes, see you in the morning," Alison smiled at her brother.

All of the children went up to bed. They'd all had a busy day around the shops and then off for a Wimpy meal. Alison and Josephine tucked themselves into bed, then there was a knock on the door, it was Sandra.

"Do you girls have everything done? Washed everywhere and teeth brushed?" She asked.

"Yes, we have, Sandra," both girls replied.

She checked they were tucked into bed. All of the covers over them so they wouldn't get cold.

"Night then, see you both in the morning," Sandra said, closing the door behind her.

Sandra checked on all of the girls before she went down to the living room, where John followed her not long afterwards.

"Is everything ready for tomorrow for Alison's birthday?" he asked her.

"Yes, everything is ready. Her cards and presents will be ready for her in the dining room so she can open them before she goes out with Tom and Freddie to get their clothes for the holiday, then you can get the children to help you decorate the sitting room for her party for when she gets back. I don't know if she has a party dress though. She would want one I suppose, her own one," Sandra thought for a moment. "We can get that tomorrow while we are out. That would be an extra treat. All of the children get an outfit for their birthday treat, it's part of what we do, John," Sandra exclaimed.

"Right then, I am off to bed. Is Celia on duty this evening to take care of things?" she asked John.

"Yes, also Roger is here tonight to check on the boys if needed," John replied.

"Night John," Sandra said.

"Night Sandra," John replied.

***

83

The next morning, Alison woke quite early. Even though the children were on their summer holidays, it was easy to still be on school getting up times. But today was special. She would have woken up early anyway. It was her birthday! She was seven today! She was a big girl and soon she would be going into the juniors when she went back to school.

Alison was happy. The sun was shining through the curtains, and she could hear Josephine stirring. She turned over but her eyes were still shut. Alison just lay there, enjoying not having to get straight up like she did most mornings. Since she and Tom had been there, they only had one school holiday and that was half term. That was only for a week. The summer holidays were for six weeks!

They were still only on the second week off and the girls loved lying in bed and being able to have a chat whilst still in bed, rather than running around the bedroom making sure they had everything for the day for school.

"Morning Alison, did you sleep well?" Josephine asked.

"Yes, I did; Josephine, did you?"

"Yes, I most certainly did. We had a busy day yesterday, so it helped me to get to sleep."

Both of the girls sighed at the same time.

"I suppose we had better get up. Sandra will be up soon, knocking on the doors," Alison said.

At that moment, there was a knock at the door.

"Up you get, girls, it's time to get up," Sandra said as she walked down the corridor knocking on each bedroom door.

"Come on, we had better get up, we don't want her to come in and chase us downstairs," said Josephine.

Both of the girls got up from their cosy beds, pushed the covers to the bottom of the bed so that they could air, and they grabbed their dressing gowns to put over their nightclothes. At the weekend and over the holidays it was a little more relaxed than school days. All of the children could go down to breakfast in their dressing gowns, but they had to get washed once they'd eaten their breakfast.

Alison and Josephine walked from their bedroom, down the corridor and stairs into the dining room. Alison and Josephine were the last ones to arrive for breakfast. It was pure silence, then all of a sudden, the whole of the dining room erupted into song:

"HAPPY BIRTHDAY TO YOU, HAPPY BIRTHDAY TO YOU, HAPPY BIRTHDAY TO ALISON, HAPPY BIRTHDAY TO YOU!"

Alison stood there in shock.

"I didn't know that you knew it was my birthday today," she said, then she beamed into a huge smile.

"Thank you so much!" She had tears in her eyes. She'd never had so many people sing Happy Birthday to her before, even in class, as her birthday was always in the summer holidays.

"Come and sit down, you have cards and presents to open unless you would like your breakfast first?" Sandra asked her.

"Can we have breakfast first, then I can open my presents and cards in the living room. Would that be all right?" Alison asked.

"Of course, it would. Roger, please could you take Alison's cards and presents into the sitting room where she can open them after breakfast?" Sandra asked.

"Anything for the birthday girl!" Roger replied.

Alison, and the other children, tucked into their breakfast, which today was pancakes, or waffles with maple syrup, or jam or honey, orange or pineapple juice. There was also fruit salad, so Alison, Josephine, Tom and Freddie all opted for the pancakes and maple syrup with a small bowl of fruit salad and orange juice.

Tom was watching Alison like a hawk. He was eager for her to open her presents. He had chosen a lovely gift; a little heart necklace. He'd saved up his pocket money for a little while and John and Roger gave him extra little jobs to earn some money for Alison's birthday present.

He saw it on one of their trips. He didn't really have enough, but John and Roger quietly chipped in the rest he needed as he was so intent on buying it for her. Tom never mentioned home or their mum and dad, not because he didn't miss them or love them, but he loved Alison more and he didn't want to upset her by talking about them.

Breakfast was all done. All of the plates and dishes were in the dishwasher getting washed and the tables were wiped down. The floors would be done whilst the children were getting ready with the banners for the party afterwards.

Alison walked into the living room with Josephine and everyone was sitting down on the big cosy chairs. Her gifts and cards were in the middle of the room with a chair there for her to sit on, whilst she opened her gifts.

Alison had never seen so many gifts for one person before. At home she would get a few gifts, but only from her mum and dad, not really anyone else. They didn't see many family.

"Come on Alison, sit down and open your gifts!" Tom said excitedly.

Alison took centre stage in the middle of the room and looked at the gifts and didn't know where to start.

Sandra sat down on the floor next to Alison.

"Where do you want to start Alison?"

"I have no idea! Just hand me one the gifts or the cards and take it from there."

Sandra nodded and handed over a card and gift. Alison opened the card and it said Happy birthday Alison, from the girls in the Lily Room. She unwrapped the lovely pink and white candy-striped paper. Inside was a pink and white Alice band with some pink and white hair clips.

"Thank you!" Alison said, looking in the direction of the girls from the Lily room. They had big smiles on their faces, they were pleased she liked their gifts. Then Sandra handed her another gift. This one was wrapped in yellow and white polka dot paper. The card read "Happy Birthday Alison, from the boys in the Train Room. Their gift was a big colouring book with colouring pencils. They also smiled. Alison loved their gifts. Boys never knew what to buy girls as gifts, so they made a good choice.

Alison kept opening cards and presents. She got a couple of reading books, a new doll, a hairbrush and comb set, a paper cut-out-doll, with the wardrobe of clothes that it came with, which went into an envelope. Alison kept opening gifts and cards. There must have been fifteen or twenty cards!

When everyone had given Alison her gifts, Tom held out his hand to give Alison her card and gift. His card said, Happy birthday to my special sister. Alison's eyes started to fill up with tears as he handed her his gift, which she carefully opened. It was a gold heart pendant on a chain.

"I chose it myself, Alison," Tom said very promptly. He was beaming as he said it.

Alison took it out of the box and Sandra opened the catch and put it on her. She was looking at it with pride. Everyone in the room eyes filled with tears, they hadn't seen such love between a brother and sister before.

"Right, who's going to get washed and dressed, we have some shopping to do today and it won't get done staying inside," Sandra said.

Then they all bounded out of the door and up the stairs to go to the bathrooms and get ready to go out.

"Alison, you're going with Tom and Freddie today to get their holiday clothes, is that right?"

"Yes, Sandra, is that alright still?" replied Alison.

"Of course. Now go and get ready then we can get down to the shops."

"OK, Sandra."

"We all ready? Good, let's go then," Sandra said a few moments later.

Tom, Freddie and Alison were on their way to go and buy Tom and Freddie's holiday clothes. Tom and Freddie were full of chat on the way down. Both were holding Alison's hands, one on each side. She didn't mind. Freddie was like a little brother as well.

It wasn't long before they got to the high street to Woolworths. Both boys held onto Alison. It was a big shop and it was quite daunting to little boys, who really wanted to go and look at the toys, but they had to buy their clothes today.

Sandra took them over to the boys' clothes area. There were t-shirts, shorts, cotton trousers, sandals. The boys liked the clothes but didn't know what to pick. Tom, with his skin tone and hair colour, chose Navy and red, tops, shorts, and navy-blue cotton trousers. He also bought a long-sleeved top, a pair of navy sandals and some underwear. Freddie went for the pastel colours, pale blue, mint green and yellow. He got some pale blue shorts and deeper blue cotton trousers, he also got sandals, but in a beige colour.

When the boys had paid for their items, they carried their bags out of the shop with big beaming smiles. Sandra knew that they had chosen well, and they were happy with what they bought.

"Right, we have another stop to make, if that's OK with both of you boys?" Sandra said.

"Yes, that's fine, Sandra," they said together.

Alison was a little confused, as they had bought everything that the boys had wanted. They hadn't been greedy but got what they needed.

"Ahh, here we are!" Sandra said as they stopped outside a little boutique that specialised in party dresses for little girls and bigger girls.

Alison's face was a picture! She was dumbstruck.

"Are we going in there, Sandra?" She asked.

"We sure are! I want you to have a good look around and see if there is anything you would like to try on," Sandra smiled.

"To try on?" Alison said quizzing.

"Well, every birthday girl has to have a birthday dress, don't they?" Sandra said.

Alison looked around the shop. Pink was her favourite colour, so she went straight to look at the pink dresses. Some had pink taffeta with white lace on them, some were made to look like satin with lace on them, some were made in cotton… but then she saw it! It was a lovely pale pink, cotton dress, with a delicate pink lace to match. It had a lovely little collar and cuff sleeves, that has lace at the bottom of them, which came up to her forearm. It had a sash around the middle that tied up at the back, which gave a little gather.

"Sandra, please can I try it on? It's beautiful!" asked Alison.

"Yes, of course, you can!"

Alison went into the changing room with Sandra. She asked the assistant to keep an eye on the boys. They were sitting on a chair waiting for Alison to come out of the changing room.

"Oh, my, Alison, you look just like a princess!" Tom said. His face had lit up.

Alison turned around to look at herself in the mirror. She loved it! It would be her party dress and she would love it forever.

"Sandra, can I have this one please, I love it?" Alison asked.

"Of course, Darling! It's for you for your birthday party," Sandra replied.

She took Alison back into the changing room and helped her take off the dress. Alison then changed back into her own clothes. Sandra left her so she could get dressed in private. She then paid for the dress, so when Alison came out of the changing room, her dress was all bagged up. What Alison didn't know was that Sandra had also bought her a pair of pale pink ballet slippers, but they were at the bottom of the bag, which she wouldn't know about until she opened it to put her dress on.

They all said goodbye to the sales assistant and all four of them left the dress shop and then headed down the high street.

"So, would you like to go for a Wimpy then, guys?" asked Sandra.

"But we only had a Wimpy yesterday, Sandra," Alison said.

"Wouldn't you like one now, then we can have a chat about what we bought today?" Sandra said.

"That sounds like a good idea!" Tom piped up.

So off they went into the Wimpy. Sandra wanted to make sure that they were out long enough for everyone to sort out the party preparations.

"What are you going to have?" asked Sandra.

"Chips!" said Tom and Freddie both together.

"Alison?" asked Sandra.

"Can I have a cheeseburger and chips and a milkshake, please?" Alison asked.

"Sure. Boys, what would you like to drink?"

"Coke? Is that all right, Sandra?"

"Yes, Tom and Freddie, it's fine. Just don't drink it too quickly or you'll be burping all day!" she laughed.

You would have thought that Tom and Freddie were brothers. They did everything together. They finished each other's sentences and spoke in unison a lot of the time.

They all sat down at a table. Tom and Freddie both asked Alison if she liked her dress. She said that she did. She never had a party dress before. Sandra asked the boys again if they liked their new clothes, and both boys answered together yes, they did.

Their food came and they all tucked into it. The boys like their coke and Alison had a chocolate milkshake this time, which she thoroughly enjoyed. Once they had finished their food, the boys said they felt stuffed and would need piggybacks all the way home!

Sandra made sure that the children had all of their bags and hadn't left anything behind. Sandra told them but they could take it a little slower if that made them feel a bit better, but she wasn't giving anyone a piggyback!

***

It didn't take too long to get back to the home and everyone was running around a little bit.

89

Tom, Freddie, and Alison went up to their rooms to put away their new things. Roger helped Tom and Freddie as John had the day off today. Alison went to her room to put her dress on the front of the wardrobe door. She then went back downstairs to see what was going on with everyone.

The girls who were normally up in their rooms, doing their hair or nails, were sitting on the sofas watching a film. They all seemed engrossed in it.

"Hi Alison! Did you enjoy your shopping trip with the boys and Sandra?" They asked her.

"Yes, it was lovely! The boys got what they wanted for their holiday and I got a party dress! I didn't know I needed a party dress," she told them.

"What colour is it?" One of the girls asked.

"Pink! It's lovely!"

"Can we see it later on; we are just watching this film?"

"OK, I'll show you later then," replied Alison.

The girls smiled. Alison didn't know she was having a party later on in the afternoon. Once the film had finished, the girls all got up and went upstairs to their bedrooms.

"Would you like to come, Alison?" They asked.

"What about...?"

"Josephine can come as well. We wouldn't leave her out!"

"Yes please, Kim!" Alison went to fetch Josephine.

She hadn't seen Josephine since she came back from the shops with the boys, so she went to look for her. She went into the dining room, she wasn't there. She went to the reception, she wasn't there. She went into the bathroom, she wasn't there, either. Then she went to their bedroom.

Josephine was sitting on her bed when she saw Alison come in.

"Hello Alison, have you just got back from your shopping trip?" Josephine asked her.

"No, I got back a little while ago, I was looking for you, but didn't know you would be in here. Are you OK?" Alison asked.

"Oh yes, I am fine. It's just I wanted to give this to you on your own." Josephine handed Alison an envelope and a little box, which was wrapped in pink tissue paper with a bow wrapped around it.

Alison looked shocked, she thought she'd already received a gift from Josephine,

"I didn't want to give it to you in front of anyone." Josephine said. Alison took the card and opened it…Happy Birthday to my special friend. Alison looked up at Josephine, and she hugged her.

"Open your present now!" said Josephine.

Alison carefully unwrapped the ribbon and then the tissue paper. There was a little blue box. She opened it up and inside was a pair of gold earrings, shaped like a teardrop. Alison looked up and she gave Josephine the biggest smile. She loved them! She gave Josephine another hug. She has such good friends. She didn't know that she was liked so much.

Sandra knocked on the door then and popped her head around it.

"Hi, are you both going to get changed for your birthday party, Alison?" Both girls nodded.

"Would you like some help with your dress then?" Sandra asked.

"Yes please, Sandra," Alison said.

"Josephine, do you have a dress to change into?" Sandra asked.

"Yes, I have my lilac dress, and I can wear my lilac ribbons if you could help me?" asked Josephine.

"No problem," replied Sandra. "Oh no! I forgot Kim and the others asked us to go to their rooms for a little while," said Alison, feeling awful that she forgot.

"I'm sure it's going to be fine, Alison," replied Sandra.

Sandra helped both of the girls get ready for the party. Alison looked lovely in her new pink dress, and she loved her new pink ballet slippers, which she got a big surprise when she saw them.

Josephine looked equally lovely with her lilac dress, white shoes, and lilac ribbons in her hair. They both looked like the belles of the ball.

Both girls walked down to the party in the living room to find everyone already there.

"Kim, I'm sorry, I forgot to come to your room with Josephine, as I couldn't find her at first," Alison apologised.

"Not to worry, Alison, there's always next time, anyway, we wanted to keep you out of the way for the surprise!" Kim laughed.

There were trays of food all laid out on platters, sausages on sticks, cheese and ham sandwiches, cheese and pineapple chunks, chicken drumsticks, ham/beef and chicken on platters, salad, rice, jelly and ice-cream and gateaux chocolate and black forest. There was also a big birthday cake with seven candles on it, for Alison to blow out.

There was orange and lemon squash, and everyone was dressed in their best party clothes. Once everyone had eaten, they started to play a few games, blinds man's buff, pin the tail on the donkey, musical statues.

Then they had a little disco, so everyone could have a little dance. A good time was had by all and everyone enjoyed themselves. Before they knew it, it was time for bed.

"Alison, have you had a good birthday today?" Asked Sandra.

"Yes Sandra, it was the best birthday I have ever had!"

"Come on, it's been an emotional day for you," Sandra hugged Alison to her.

"Yes Sandra, but it's also been the best birthday ever! Thank you for today," Alison replied, as she headed up to her bedroom with Josephine; they had both had a good day today.

Chapter 6

"Morning everyone! Come on, get up! We have a lot to do this morning before we leave for Margate," Sandra shouted up the corridor.

Alison and Josephine had not long gotten up anyway. They were both pulling their covers on their beds to the bottom of the bed. If they rolled it, it would be easier to pull back when they got back. But as they were going to be away for a week, the beds would be stripped later that morning for all of the bedding to be washed.

"Are you excited, Alison?" Josephine asked.

"Yes, I am. I haven't been on holiday before," she replied.

"Me either. I've been to the seaside for a day trip, but not on holiday, so it should be good fun," Josephine replied.

Sandra popped her head around the door.

"Just checking that you're both up, girls. We will be getting washed and dressed soon and then down for breakfast, then back up to your rooms to collect your suitcases. Have you both finished your packing?"

"Yes," they said in unison.

"Great, then off you go to the bathroom, we need to get moving," Sandra said.

Both of the girls grabbed their wash things and headed off to the bathroom. They were both skipping down the hall and were so excited about their trip.

Once the girls had both washed and got dressed—both girls wore white t-shirts and a pair of dungarees, with a white cardigan and pumps on their feet—they were ready to go down to breakfast.

Once they had their breakfast of toast with apricot jam and orange juice, they all handed their plates and cups to Michelle to put onto the hatch, so that the cook could wash them.

Michelle was staying behind with the other girls and John was staying with the boys. Sandra told all of the children to wait in the living room, so they could make sure everyone was there. They didn't want to leave anyone behind.

"Right, so now that breakfast is over, you can all go and brush your teeth. Could you then go to your bedrooms and collect your suitcases, and anything else your taking? Stand outside your doors, with your items, then we can come along and help you downstairs with them," Sandra instructed.

The staff had to go to three different floors to collect the children who were going away, that way, they wouldn't lose anybody. Sandra and Roger went to the top of the building to the girls' rooms, to collect the three of them. Then they headed down to the floor where Alison and Josephine were waiting patiently outside their room with their cases and carrier bags. They all followed on so they could collect the boys.

Tom and Freddie were waiting outside their bedroom with big beaming smiles on their faces. They then collected the other three boys as well. George and Celia were waiting down in reception to go with them. All of the luggage that the staff were taking was there also.

"We're just waiting for the coach to arrive, then we can head off," Sandra said.

Everyone was milling around waiting for the coach, then it turned up. It was huge! It was a big shiny white coach. All of the little ones ran up to the window to have a good look.

Roger went out to see the coach driver and then he returned a little while later.

"Are we set and ready to go?" he asked the group.

"Yes!" They all shouted excitedly.

Ms Walters came out of her office.

"Oh, my goodness! I wondered what all of the noise was! You're going on your holiday today, how exciting! Well, have a lovely time all of you and I look forward to seeing you next week on your return, all refreshed and ready to enjoy the rest of the school holidays," she said, waving them off and smiling.

Sandra and Roger helped the children with their suitcases.

"Now does anyone need to use the toilet before we leave. It's going to be a long journey on the coach."

A couple of the children put their hands up.

"Well, you know where to go. I'll wait for you here to board the coach when you get back," Roger said.

The rest of the children climbed onto the coach. Roger and George were helping the driver put the suitcases into the storage at the bottom of the coach, while Sandra and Celia were getting the children all settled into their seats. The children, who went to use the toilet, came back and Roger seated them onto the coach. George had a quick look around reception to make sure they hadn't left anything or anyone behind. No, that was it. They were off!

"Bye Ms Walters, see you next Saturday," George said.

Ms Walters and Michelle and John were on the steps waving them all off. The children on the coach were waving back just as excitedly. The coach pulled away from the building and the children and staff all cheered.

Roger asked Sandra if they had head counted.

"Yes, there are ten children and four staff and one coach driver," she laughed.

Freddie and Tom were sitting at the front, behind the driver and Josephine and Alison sat behind them. Sandra and Roger sat the other side to Freddie and Tom, George, and Celia sat nearer the back, with the other children. The coach itself sat about 21 seats, not including the driver. The children were on their way and they were giddy with excitement. The journey itself would take a couple of hours, so once they had gotten out of town, it wouldn't take too long on the motorway.

On the motorway, the children could see trees, and grass, fields, and animals. Sheep, horses, cows, they were loving the scenery as they went passed in the coach. Tom and Freddie were chatting happily away, as were Alison and Josephine, while the others in the back, were singing.

George and Celia started to sing a song that everyone could join in with…

"Oh, we do like to be beside the seaside, we do like to be beside the sea…" Everyone was singing. It was such a happy time. Everyone was enjoying themselves and they hadn't even got there yet.

By the time the sing-song had finished, after about six songs. They had arrived in Margate. They hadn't yet got to the sea, but they could see it in the distance. They could see and hear the seagulls flying away towards to sea.

It was very exciting to see the sea for the first time, and the children were lifting themselves out of their seats to have a good look.

Sandra got up out of her seat.

"Yes, we can see the sea, children, but please remain in your seats until the coach stops. Otherwise, if the driver has to stop quickly, you're more than likely to hurt yourselves," Sandra said.

The children got back into their seats. They didn't want to fall over.

After a couple of more roads, they pulled up to a house that had a sign saying, Whelk Combe on the door. The children cheered when they saw the house.

"Right, children! Roger and George will take the luggage out from the coach and put it out onto the street and then you can pick it up before we go into the guest house. So, if you can stay on the coach for a couple more minutes, but make sure you have everything you brought with you, and please take your rubbish with you. It's not the driver's job to dispose of it," Sandra instructed.

"Yes, Sandra," the children replied.

Once the luggage was on the pavement, they were all able to get off the coach and get their suitcases. Tom and Freddie were first off the coach. They were so happy.

Sandra called to everyone when they had their luggage.

"Right, follow me, everyone!" she said.

Everyone trudged up the few steps, behind Sandra, to the entrance of the guest house.

On entering the building, a rather large lady met the children, with grey/white hair and big rosy cheeks.

"Hello, everyone! I'm Rose and welcome to Whelk Combe. I hope your stay with us will be a happy one," Rose said.

Sandra went up to reception, greeted Rose and signed in so she could get the keys to the rooms for everyone.

"So, that's ten children and four adults," Rose confirmed, "we have two rooms for the staff and two rooms for both the girls and the boys, is that OK?" she asked.

"Yes, that's great, thank you, Rose," Sandra said.

"Right children, if you can get your luggage, we can make our way up to our rooms. Tom, Freddie, you have your own room, the other three boys have another room. Alison and Josephine, you have a room together, and the other girls have the other room," Sandra said.

The children took their luggage and went to their rooms. George and Roger went to put their luggage away and then helped the boys that needed it to unpack their suitcases. The older boys were OK, they could manage, but Tom and Freddie needed some help.

Sandra and Celia helped the girls to their rooms and then they took their luggage to unpack later on when everyone was sorted out.

Like the boys, the older girls were able to manage, but Alison and Josephine needed some help to unpack their things and put them away.

Once everyone was unpacked, they had arranged to meet downstairs in reception. Tom and Freddie were waiting patiently with Roger and George, whilst everyone else was making their way downstairs. Sandra asked if they had all sorted out their un-packing, it was all done, Yes, they had, they had done well.

Sandra told the children that they were going to have a look around the town and see what was about there. They would hand in the keys to reception and then collect them when they returned from town. All of the children nodded and watched Sandra hand the keys to Rose,

who had a beaming smile.

"See you later then, have a nice look around and don't forget dinner is at 6 pm," she said to them. They got up from their seats and off they went out of the building.

"Bye Rose, see you later," Tom and Freddie said. They were holding hands in pairs so they wouldn't get lost and the staff could keep a check on having all the children in one place at the same time.

"They seem a nice lot of children and staff looking after them, Henry. They have lovely manners and look well behaved," Rose said.

"Just wait until the end of the week, when you'll be glad to see the back of them. They will play up, just like every other kid we see here. After a couple of days, they start getting all stroppy because they can't have their own way," Henry replied.

"No, I don't think so with this bunch. These kids seem well behaved. Anyway, we have to get on, there are another two sets of families coming this afternoon. We need to make sure the rooms are finished," Rose said.

"OK, I will get cracking and get them sorted, see you in a little while, Rose," Henry replied.

***

The children walked along the main street towards the town. At the bed and breakfast, they would have their breakfast and evening meal, but they had to sort out their own lunch.

They were looking in the shops in the town. There was a Marks and Spencer, a British Home Stores, C&A. There were a couple of food shops, not like a supermarket, but little shops. There was also a couple of book shops and a massive Woolworths, where the children made a beeline for.

"Not at the moment children. We just want to have a look around and find our bearings. We have plenty of time to go shopping. Anyway, there's a Woolworths back at home which we can go to anytime we want. Let's look for some shops we haven't seen before," Sandra laughed.

They all saw the Wimpy bar.

"Sandra, look there's a Wimpy, like we have back at home!" said Kim.

"Yes, they do. Once we finish looking around, we can go and have something light to eat there," Sandra said.

They had a good look around the town and time was getting on a bit. It was nearly 4 pm.

"We have to get a move soon, as it will soon be dinner time back at the guest house. What if we get a bag of chips from the local chip shop, that we can have on our way back. What do you think guys?" Roger suggested.

"Yes!" The children said. That sounded like a good idea. That way they could take their time and still be back in time for dinner at 6 pm.

They trundled off to find a chip shop. It wasn't difficult, they seemed to have one every other two shops.

In they went: 10 small bags and four medium bags of chips. Some of the children put salt and vinegar on them, some nothing. There was nothing like having a bag of chips at the seaside, it was lovely.

As they tucked into their chips, there was silence, for the first time that day since they all got up, apart from the chewing. It was a lovely sight to see; all of the children tucking into something they all like to eat. Once they had finished and they rolled up their paper into balls they then threw them into the rubbish bins.

"Come on now, we have to make our way back to the guest house, so we can wash up, ready for dinner," said George.

"Oh, but we have just had chips!" said Billy, one of the bigger boys.

"So, you're telling me you don't want steak pie, mash potato and beans or peas for your dinner, which Rose has been cooking then, Billy?" George laughed.

"Oh, actually, that sounds delicious!" Billy replied. He then couldn't wait to get back. "Come on then everyone, let's hurry!" Billy shouted. All of a sudden, he was hungry.

"You wouldn't have thought he had just had a bag of chips." Celia laughed.

When they got back to the guest house, Sandra spoke to the children:

"Before we have dinner, children, we have to go and wash our hands and faces."

"Oh no, Sandra! I thought we were on holiday. I didn't think we would have to wash our hands all the time!" Billy said disappointedly.

"Just because we are on holiday, Billy, we don't stop doing our personal hygiene and keeping ourselves clean. That happens all year round, wherever we are," Sandra said.

All the children went up to their rooms to wash their hands and faces. When they had finished, they all returned to reception, where Henry pointed them downstairs to the dining room. They would have their breakfast and evening meal here.

The boys were a little enthusiastic coming down the stairs.

"Hey careful, boys, you will hurt yourselves or someone else for that matter," Henry said.

"I am sorry, it won't happen again," George replied. "Boys! You have to be careful where you go! There is enough room for everyone, but don't be in such a rush," George warned the boys.

"I agree!" Came a voice from over the other side of the dining room, "Hooligans, the lot of them!" said the voice.

Roger walked over to the table of the gentleman who had made the comments.

"Excuse me, Sir? Yes, these boys are a little overzealous, but they are certainly not hooligans! Good day to you."

Roger walked back over to his table and sat down with his group.

"OK, boys, now calm down, we don't want people like them to say that you don't know how to behave out in public," Roger said quietly.

The boys had settled down when Rose came out with their dinner. As at the home, the children had waited until everyone had their food before they started eating. Once everyone had their full plates in front of them, Roger nodded and said they could start. They all tucked in at the same time. Rose had noticed how the children had all listened to their caregivers. They seemed like good kids; not like some of the children who had frequented her establishment in the past.

Once they had had their steak pie and vegetables, then there was dessert. They could choose from either apple pie and custard, or jelly and ice-cream. Some had jelly and the rest had apple pie and custard. Once the children had finished their food and drinks, they gathered up their plates so they could take them to the kitchen. Rose explained that they didn't have to do that. It was her job to clear the table and take them to the kitchen.

"We like to make them a little independent," said Sandra.

"It makes sense, but they are on their holidays," Rose replied.

Rose came along with her tray a few minutes later and she took away the plates and then came back for the rest of the crockery and cutlery. Once the table was cleared, the children didn't have to wipe the table down as it had a tablecloth on it, so, they sat there until they were told they could leave the table.

"Breakfast is between 8 am and 9.30 am, so don't be late or you will miss it. You know where to go now for your meals. Have a lovely evening, children," Rose smiled at all the children.

"Thank you, Rose; you too!" The children said.

Rose was very impressed with the children. They had good manners and they weren't like other children she had seen.

Now that dinner was over, it was the same as at home. The children could go in to the lounge to watch TV or get bathed before they went to bed. It was now nearly 8 pm.

"I think it would be a good idea if we all had an early night. We have done a lot today and travelling can make you tired, especially with this sea air," George said.

"Yes, I agree. Children, if you get sorted out for bed, just because it's been a hectic day today and I think the early night will help everyone settle down," Sandra advised.

The children all went up to their rooms.

Tom and Freddie had had a great day and they were shattered, so they just took off their dirty clothes, put on their pyjamas, and crawled into bed. Both boys were fast asleep within minutes of their heads touching the pillows.

Roger popped his head around their door once he had knocked, and they were both spark out asleep.

Alison and Josephine weren't too far behind the boys. The older children had changed into their bed things but were still up. They all had a TV in their rooms, but they were told not to have it on too loud and that lights had to be out at 9 pm. Which both the boys and girls took notice of.

"Well, that was a success today and all of them are tucked into their beds. We have to go into the boys' and girls' rooms at nine this evening to turn off their TVs," Said Sandra.

"I think we need to take our own advice; I am shattered!" George replied.

"I agree. Who's going to stay up for a while to check on the kids?" asked Roger.

"I will for a little while. I'll check on the boys. Celia, can you check on the girls in a while?" asked George.

"Yes, that's fine," replied Celia, "I'm bushed too, but I can hold on for a little while longer."

"Excellent, that's sorted. Do you two want to head off to your bedrooms, at least the boys are between both us; same for the girls, so we can hear them if they wake up or get up." Celia added.

Sandra and Roger headed off to their bedrooms and George and Celia stayed up a little longer to check on the children, just as they did in the home. When all of the checks had been done, the staff went to their bedrooms. Their colleagues were both asleep. They said goodnight and they shut their doors, until the morning when it would start all over again.

***

The children were up and about very early the next morning.

"There's something about the sea air that really gets into your lungs," Henry said, when the children and staff all came down for breakfast. It was already 8.30 am and they couldn't wait to start eating.

"Cereal, orange juice, toast and a fry up, OK for everyone?" Rose asked.

"Yes please, Rose," they all replied.

Henry told them where the cereal was and how much choice there was, so Sandra went over to the cereal and see what the children would eat.

"Rice Crispies, Corn Flakes, Weetabix, Special K, Sugar Puffs and Frosties. Do you want to come up and chose your cereal, children?" Sandra called to the children.

Celia and George helped the younger ones with their cereal, but the bigger children were helping themselves.

Tom and Freddie had Rice Crispies, so they could put their heads to the bowl once the milk was in and hear them go snap, crackle and pop. Josephine and Alison had Sugar Puffs, which George helped them with.

They took their full bowls back down to the table to put the milk on them. Rose had bought in their orange juices and tea for the staff, in small teapots, one cup and a bit per pot.

"The cooked breakfasts won't be long; Henry is just finishing them off for you," said Rose.

"Erm, what about my breakfast? I've been waiting for a long time, you know!" said Mr Grumpy over the other side of the room.

"I have just to bring your breakfast, Mr Snow. Henry is just finishing them now. Would you like another pot of tea while you're waiting?" asked Rose.

"No thank you, just the breakfast. I thought it was adults before children to be served?" he proclaimed.

"No, Sir, everyone is as important as each other here, so your breakfast will be out in a few moments," Rose replied.

Rose hurried back to the kitchen to see how Henry was getting on with the breakfasts.

"How are the breakfasts coming along, Henry? Old misery chops is having a moan again out there!" Rose said.

"All done!" He replied. "Take his out first so he doesn't go on. I don't want him upsetting those kiddies, they have done nothing wrong and he's out of order. Henry muttered.

"He said he thought the adults should be served before the children, I told him everyone is as important as each other here!" Rose said.

"That's my girl, you tell him! He's not very nice, especially to those kids. It's not their fault they live in a children's home. They are very polite, Rose, and they have good manners, so let me take old misery chops his food," Henry replied.

Henry left the kitchen with two trays with plates of food on them. He handed one of the plates to Mr Snow and then headed off to the other tables. Rose was putting the others on the trays to take to the children's table.

"This looks very nice, Rose," Billy said, admiring the food on his plate.

"Thank you, young sir," Rose laughed. She smiled to herself. She was taking a liking to these kids: they were just so nice!

When they had finished, Rose had cleared their plates and took them back to the kitchen. The children and staff then got up and went back to their bedrooms, so they could brush their teeth.

"Right, be back here in five minutes, so we can go down to the front and get some items from the shops," Roger said.

"What are we going to do then, Roger?" Billy asked.

"Well, we thought you might like to get some buckets and spades and fishing nets. Do you boys want to go crabbing with me and George?"

"Yes, please!" said Billy and the other boys. So off they went back up to their bedrooms and in five minutes they had all returned with fresh clean teeth.

"See you later, Rose." The children shouted.

"Breakfast was lovely, thank you," said Celia and George. They then waved her goodbye and off they went down to the seafront.

***

Everyone was in a chatty mood this morning. Tom and Freddie wanted to go crabbing but they also wanted to make sandcastles.

"What if we buy five buckets and spades and five fishing nets; that way you share and then you can chop and change when you want to, and there won't be any waste and you can take them back with you to Craven House and use them again next time we go out to the seaside or on holiday. What do you think?" George asked them. That sounded like a good option, so that's what they did.

"Now they have red, green, blue, yellow, pink, orange and purple buckets and spades, who wants what?" Roger said. They chose the colours they wanted; thankfully, they were all different. The same with the fishing nets. They chose the same colours as their buckets and spades.

"Right, so are we ready to go down to the beach?" asked George.

"Yes!" The boys cheered.

They headed off to the beach.

The children hadn't been down to the seafront yet, as they had only got there the day before. They could see all of the shops were open: gift shops, arcades, sweet shops, rock shops, more fish and chip shops; it was exciting at the seaside!

103

Everyone followed George who was at the front. The children walked in twos so that they didn't take up too much room and get in the way of others. They were soon down the path to the beach. Each of the children took either a bucket and spade or a fishing net.

The older girls wanted to collect shells; they thought they were pretty. Josephine and Alison were happy enough making sandcastles with their buckets and spades. Celia and Sandra stayed with the girls and George and Roger went along with the boys to a little cove just around the corner from the girls.

"Come on you lot, keep up!" Roger said.

Tom and Freddie were happy to be there. They were having a great time together.

"Roger, what are we looking for?" asked Tim.

"Well, do you see those little pools of water? The crabs should be in there. If you can't find them, they might be hiding underneath the rocks. These are called rock pools," Roger explained.

Tom and Freddie lifted a rock and they saw two big beady eyes staring back at them.

"Argh! George! There's a massive one here! He has huge eyes! Come and have a look!" Freddie said, a little nervous.

George and Roger came over and the rest of the boys followed. When they lifted the rock up, the crab with its pincers tried to snap at them. The older boys thought it was great, but Tom and Freddie were not as excited.

"Roger, have a look at the other rock pools over there and see if there are any smaller ones that they can look at," George said. "This one must be an adult, and he doesn't look too pleased at being woken up by the two boys," he added.

"Come on boys, let's have a look over here," Roger found another pool and they saw some smaller ones.

"Look at this one, Roger! He's a lot smaller than that big ugly one over there."

Billy held up a smaller crab by its claws.

"Be careful Billy, don't get it too close to your face, it may just claw you and we don't want you going back home with only one eye," Roger laughed.

Meanwhile, the girls were having fun making sandcastles. Most of them came out good; a couple not so good, where the sand hadn't gotten into the bucket and left a hole of the top of it.

"Josephine, if you want, we can make a lot of these sandcastles and make it a sort of royal kingdom or a village, or both! What do you think?" asked Alison.

"That would be great! We could make the royal kingdom, with a moat around it and then have the other smaller castles or houses or whatever at the bottom of it. What do you think?" she asked.

"What's a moat?" asked Josephine.

"Oh, a moat is a sort of river than runs around a castle to stop people attacking the castle. That way they can't get in," Celia explained.

"But how do the people get into the castle, then?" asked Josephine.

"Well, they have a drawbridge that is lowered so people, royalty, their family and servants can come in as necessary, but the drawbridge is raised most of the time. It's only let down for deliveries for provisions, like their food, and supplies needed," Celia said.

"That makes sense. To keep everyone safe inside and to keep all the bad guys outside. Just like Craven House, we all live inside, and the bad people live outside," said Josephine.

Celia and Sandra both looked at one another.

"What bad people are they, Josephine?" asked Sandra.

"You know, the ones that want to hurt you. The ones who don't want you with a family and tell you that you can't tell anyone, otherwise they will hurt you and nobody will believe you," said Josephine.

Celia and Sandra both looked at each other again.

"What man or lady has said that to you, Josephine? Is it someone you know? Have they said that to you?" asked Sandra.

Josephine put her head down and stopped filling the bucket with sand. She knew she had said too much, but it was too late now. They won't forget what she had just said.

"Come on Josephine, this town is getting really big now and I need your help with it please," Alison said.

Josephine put down her spade and left to go and help Alison.

"Well, I didn't see that coming, Celia. Is there anything on her file about abuse? Is that why she's at Craven House?" asked Sandra.

"I don't know, but I think we need to have a word with the men when we can. Later on, maybe? Just to give them the heads up when they return, out of earshot of the children though. Then see if we can get anything else out of her

105

before we go back home on Saturday. Then we'll need to have a word with Ms Walters."

Alison and Josephine returned to continue with their sandcastles. Josephine never mentioned another word about what she had said, she was just having a good time with Alison, having fun.

The boys returned with a couple of small crabs in their nets. The other girls returned with a huge bag filled with pretty shells. They also had found quite a big shell.

"Kim, Sally, did you know that if you put a shell up to your ear, you can hear the sea?" George asked.

"But the sea is right behind you, you can hear it and see it, look just turn around," Billy said.

"That's right, Billy, but if you put the shell by your ear when you get home, you'll be able to hear the sea again and you'll remember your holiday to the seaside," George explained.

All the children wanted to have a try, so they did, one by one.

"Alison, I love your sandcastles!" exclaimed Tom.

"They look great!" Freddie said. "What's this thing here?" he asked.

"That's a moat! It keeps bad people away from the castle so that the good people inside can't get hurt," replied Josephine, not looking up at from what she was doing.

Sandra and Celia looked at Roger and George, who both looked a little confused at them, but they had a look on their faces as if to tell them later on.

"Did you all have fun at the beach this morning?" asked George.

"Yes, George!" They all replied.

"Well, it's nearly lunchtime, do you want to get something to eat? We can come back here tomorrow if you want and the girls can do crabbing and fishing, while the boys can build sandcastles," Roger said.

"I don't want to make soppy castles like the girls do!" Billy protested.

"Well, would you rather make a fort then to keep the soldiers inside, ready to do battle instead then, Billy?" Asked Roger.

"Oh yes, that sounds a lot better! Yes, I think I'd like that!" replied Billy. The rest of the boys nodded.

"So, what do you fancy for lunch then?" George asked.

"Well, don't forget it's Sunday, so there may not be a lot of choice for lunch and don't forget, Rose will be cooking a roast dinner for this evening!" Celia reminded him.

"If we have a look along the promenade, we may find something nice. We did enjoy those chips yesterday," Sandra said.

They enjoyed looking at the different shops further up the road, which they hadn't seen yesterday. They went along and there wasn't very much in the way of food places, so they started to go up some side roads. They went down one and at the bottom of the rood, they came across a little café.

"This looks nice. We don't want anything too heavy for lunch as we will be having a big meal at Rose's later on," Roger said.

He and George had a look at the menu outside, on the front of the building by the entrance.

"What about an omelette, they do them with fries. That would do I'm sure until teatime. Is that OK with everyone?" Roger asked.

All the children nodded, so they all went into the café.

"Now choose tables that are all together, and don't make too much noise, we don't want to upset any other diners," said George.

Once all of the children were seated, they asked them what omelette they wanted.

"What do you mean, Roger? Aren't they all the same?" asked Billy.

"Yes, but do you want a cheese, ham, mushroom or a Spanish omelette?" Roger asked.

"What's a Spanish omelette?" asked Billy.

"A Spanish omelette is where it's a bit of everything," replied George.

"No, I don't think I like the sound of that. I think I'll have a cheese omelette if that's OK?" replied Billy.

Billy was the only child they knew that thought so much about his stomach, all the time.

"So, hands up who wants a cheese omelette?" Roger asked and counting the hands up in the air.

"Who wants a ham omelette?" George asked. Nobody put their hand up.

"And who wants a mushroom omelette?" Roger asked. Again, nobody put their hand up.

"Can I have a ham and mushroom omelette please, Roger?" Sandra asked. It looked like most of the children wanted a cheese omelette. Roger and George went up to order the food and got the children and the adults drinks.

Everyone was happy; they were chatting amongst themselves. Sandra checked they were all engaged in conversation before she tackled the men with what she and Celia had heard earlier that morning.

"Did you know about Josephine and abuse?" she whispered to George and Roger.

"No, I knew that she had been moved from her home and family, but I had no idea why? Do you think it would be in her file?" George asked.

"The only way to find out is to ask Ms Walters, but not before we get back. I had already called her yesterday to let her know we had arrived safely. But I don't think it's necessary until we return. Just be mindful to her and see if she lets anything slip again. But as she has already said this today, and not before. She may hold the reins back in with it, so don't worry if she doesn't say anything again."

"Josephine doesn't really open up about anything, especially her life before Craven House. She's on her holiday, she's is more relaxed, and she said something that she has probably not even thought about and this has just triggered it off. Just carry on like you haven't heard what she has said," Sandra advised.

The food and drinks had arrived, and everyone was tucking into it. They always did back home but Henry was right, the sea air does do something to your lungs. You're breathing in fresh seaside air, and their appetites had got slightly bigger and they all slept really well. This holiday lark was definitely something they had to do annually.

Once they had all finished their lunch, they hadn't really decided what to do for the afternoon. When they left the little café, they had a wander around to see what else they could do. The Crazy Golf was open. It was only 2 pm, so they had time to spare before they went back to the bed and breakfast.

"OK, let's go and play a round of Crazy Golf, shall we?" George said.

"What's Crazy Golf?" Tim asked.

"It's like the fun version of Golf! You have to hit the ball into the hole, but there may be fun things that stop you, so you may have to hit it more than once," Roger explained. "Do you want me to show you first?" he asked.

"Yes, please Roger, that way I think they have a better idea of it!" Celia laughed.

Roger asked if the attendant if he could show the children how to play the game before he paid to go in, if they liked it, they would all be playing.

Roger took his golf club and went to hole number one. It had a windmill at the bottom of the segment, with the hole just behind it. You had to get the ball underneath the windmill sails. With his golf club, he took a swing, making sure there was nobody in the way first, then hit the ball straight over the back. The children all cheered, but the ball didn't go in the hole. Roger tried again. This time the ball went in the hole!

The children all cheered and said they all wanted to have go at it. They paired into two's so that they could share the go's, otherwise they would have been there for another week!

Tom and Freddie paired up. Alison and Josephine paired up. Billy and Tim paired up, Kim and Sally paired up and that left Jennie and Patrick, who also paired up. George and Sandra paired up and Roger and Celia paired up.

That was it everyone was ready. It was a little hard for the younger ones, but they had a go. It was very funny! Even though they all had a golf ball, Tom and Freddie kept finding odd ones that had gone astray, but they still enjoyed themselves.

Once they had all finished their games and had told their stories of how and who whacked the ball in first time and how some had taken about twenty times before getting the ball in the hole, they started walking back to the guest house.

Roger chatted to the children and asked if they all liked the guest house, they were staying in.

"Oh yes! Rose does great food, real platefuls, so when I have finished, I feel happily full up!" Billy Said.

"Yes, we had noticed!" Roger laughed.

"Yes, I like Rose and Henry, they're very friendly and they feel very warm," Josephine added.

"Warm?" Billy said. "How do you know, you haven't cuddled them, so how do you know they're warm?"

"I meant they are lovely warm people. You can talk to them, and they're friendly," Josephine explained, "and no I haven't cuddled them, thank you Billy!" she added.

"OK, now we know they are friendly, and they have made us feel welcome and yes Josephine, they are warm people. Which means they are nice people to be around; to make you feel safe and cosy," George replied, "Is that what you mean, Josephine?"

"Yes, exactly!" replied Josephine.

"Anyway, it's time we were heading back," Roger said, "the girls can sort out their shells and we can put the buckets, spades and fishing nets away." They carried on back to Rose's chatting away until they got back.

"Hi Rose. Hi Henry." The children said when they got in.

"Did you enjoy your time at the beach then?" Rose asked.

"Yes, they had a great time and then we went to the Crazy Golf, where they had a great time hitting the golf balls, and I think some came away with a couple more than they should do!" George laughed, looking at Freddie and Tom.

Alison and Josephine went up to their bedroom to put away their buckets and spades, then the older girls came into their room.

"Hi girls, we were wondering if you wanted some of these seashells, they're very pretty and there are far too many here for us?" Kim said.

They emptied the bag of shells onto the bed. There were hundreds!

"You were very busy!" Alison said.

Alison and Josephine had a small bag full each. The girls sat on the beds chatting.

"Do you like it here, Alison?" Kim asked.

"Yes, I do. I've never been to the seaside for a holiday before and it's lovely and I do like Rose and Henry, they're very friendly," Alison replied.

"What about you, Josephine, are you enjoying yourself?"

"Yes, I am, thank you Kim. Like Alison, I haven't been to the seaside for a holiday before. I used to go to my nan's down in Devon, at holiday times," replied Josephine.

"That must have been nice, were you near the sea then?" Kim asked, "because that's a seaside too," she added.

"No, we used to go to a farm down the road from my nan's. There was a wood there too, which I used to like going to, but I haven't been there for a little while now," Josephine said.

"Oh, why's that? Didn't you like going there anymore?" quizzed Kim.

"Erm no. It's just my uncle used to take me there and he's now a long way away. Then I came to live at Craven House. I miss seeing my nan though, but it can't be helped. What about you, Kim, are you having a nice time here?" Josephine changed the subject.

"Yes, it's great! It's lovely to be by the sea. I used to go to Great Yarmouth in Norfolk. We used to love it there. Then things changed at home and I had to come and live at Craven House," she said.

"What changed at home, Kim? If you don't mind me asking?" Josephine asked.

"Well, my dad died due to a heart attack and my mum couldn't look after me and my brother, so we got sent here," she said.

"I didn't know you have a brother, Kim?" Alison said.

"No, you wouldn't have. He couldn't come here; he was too old, so he is at Denham House. We see each other as often as we can, and we get on great, but we don't see my mum anymore…she had a breakdown," Kim added.

"I am so sorry, Kim," Alison said, "I don't know what I would do if I didn't have Tom with me. Sorry, that doesn't sound too nice, especially as you don't see your brother every day. I hope I didn't upset you?"

"Alison, honestly it's fine. I see Jimmy every other week and our time is special so we both make the most of it. I think its lovely the way you and Tom get on so well."

"My uncle is called Jimmy," Josephine interrupted, "He used to take me into the woods in Devon and he used to hurt me. He used to touch me, where he shouldn't touch me…" Josephine trailed off.

Kim left the room immediately and went to find Sandra.

"Sandra! Josephine is saying some very weird stuff. She has opened up about someone not doing nice things to her. I thought I had better come and find you. Please can you come to their room?" Kim asked.

"OK, but if you could go back to your room with the other girls? I'll need to talk to Josephine on her own," Sandra said.

"Yes, that's fine."

"Thank you, Kim, and thank you for letting me know. Please don't speak of any of this to the boys, if you don't mind?" Sandra added.

***

Sandra knocked softly and went into the girl's bedroom. Josephine was still going on about the woods and what had happened, but by this time, she was saying it through her tears. Sandra asked the girls, including Alison, to go to another room. Josephine was oblivious to them going and Sandra coming in.

Celia saw the girls going to the other room. Kim had told her that Sandra was going to see Josephine. Celia followed the girls into their room, and they were all talking at once.

Sally said that when Kim had left the room, Josephine was really starting to go into some graphic stuff that had happened to her. It was like Josephine was a different child to the one they had known and had begun to love as a little sister. Sally was telling Celia what Josephine was saying so she could fill Sandra in later on. Just so they hadn't missed anything. Sandra came into the girls' room to talk to Celia.

"Celia, could you go downstairs to Rose and see if she wouldn't mind bringing up some sandwiches for the girls and some milk, also some for Josephine. This is going to take a while, and I think if she has something to eat, it may help her. I know it's not the done thing, but I am at a loss at the moment as what else to do. I know dinner is in an hour, but I am sure Rose will be fine with it. If we need to pay more money, then that's fine. Thank you, Celia, I had better get back to Josephine," Sandra said.

Celia went downstairs to speak to Rose and found her in the Kitchen with Henry preparing the vegetables for dinner.

"Rose, I'm really sorry, but I have a huge favour to ask?" Celia said.

"Go ahead, my love," Rose said.

"One of the girls is going through a bit of a rough time at the moment, and my colleague Sandra is with her. We wondered if it would be possible if we could have some milk and a few sandwiches for the little girl who's upset and the others to keep them occupied as they are aware of the situation. I know this may sound a bit of a cheek, but we don't know what else to do at this time. We can pay for the extra sandwiches," added Celia.

"Now don't you worry your pretty little head about it; we can make a few sandwiches and some milk. Can some of the girls help you take them up, as we're in the middle of making dinner? Will they still want dinner?" Rose asked.

"Oh yes, I'm sure of it! Their appetites have grown, which is saying something they all had big appetites before they got here! It must be the fresh sea air down here!" replied Celia.

"Pass me the bread there, Henry. Can you get the girls who are going to help, and they will be ready by the time you get back?" Rose said. She gave Celia a big warm smile. Celia hurried off back up to the rooms to get Kim, Sally and Jennie to help her.

Before she went back down to the kitchen, she went to find the men and briefly tell them what was going on. She then headed back to the kitchen to find the girls with their plates full of sandwiches and Celia took the milk.

"Thank you so much, Rose, you have done us a huge favour," Celia told her.

"Think nothing of it. If they could bring the empty plates and glasses back down with them, it would be much appreciated. Now we'd better get back to making dinner. Henry, are the potatoes nearly done?" Rose asked.

"Nearly!" Henry replied.

***

The girls went to their rooms with the sandwiches, and Celia put down the glasses. She picked up one of them and a plate of sandwiches.

"If you girls wouldn't mind staying in here for the time being, while I take this next door to Sandra and Josephine."

Celia knocked on the bedroom room.

Sandra came to the door, and Celia gave her the sandwiches and milk for Josephine, then spoke softly and shut the door.

Sandra handed Josephine her sandwiches and milk. She put the glass of milk onto her bedside cabinet, then she picked up her sandwich and took a bite of it.

She had been talking constantly to Sandra for an hour and was totally worn out. The sandwich did the trick. She perked up a bit but was still a bit tearful.

"Sandra, what happens now? Can I still go down for dinner or is this my dinner?" she asked.

"No, sweetheart. This is just something for you to eat and drink. You can still come down for dinner if you wish. You haven't done anything wrong," Sandra reassured her.

Josephine nodded. She had felt better; better than she had in a long time. She had never told anyone outside of the family before and being away on holiday and the fresh air and everyone having a wonderful time, something just happened, and she couldn't hold it in once she had let snippets out.

Josephine hadn't intended on telling anyone, but at the beach, a little bit of information slipped out and then another and then she just couldn't hold back.

"Josephine, do you want Alison or the others to come in and sit with you for a while, just before we go down to dinner?" Sandra asked.

"Can I see Alison for a little while as she is like my sister and we share a bedroom together?" Josephine said.

"OK, stay there, I won't be a moment," Sandra said and she left the room. She knocked on the door and Celia opened it.

"Alison, will you come with me, please?" Sandra asked.

Alison took Sandra's hand and they went back to their bedroom. Sandra opened the door and Josephine was sitting on her bed, looking a little of the worse for wear. But she looked better, like a huge weight load had been lifted from her.

"Hi Josephine, are you alright?" Alison asked.

"Yes, thank you Alison. A lot better than in a long time," Josephine replied.

Alison walked over to her friend and hugged her. Josephine hugged her back just as tightly. They both pulled away, with big smiles on their faces.

"Everything will be alright again, won't it?" Alison asked.

"Yes, it will. Back to normal," Josephine said.

"Right, girls, grab those plates and I will get the glass. Pop into next door and collect the plates the girls have and then we can go down to dinner," Sandra said.

The door of the bedroom occupied by the other girls opened and out came the girls with their empty plates, while Celia was holding their glasses. Kim came over to Josephine and hugged her.

"OK now?" Kim asked.

"Yes, very OK." Josephine smiled.

Celia and the other girls made their way to the dining room with their plates and Sandra followed, Alison behind her and then Josephine who closed the door of their bedroom behind her, on their way to dinner.

Chapter 7

The girls entered the dining room where everyone was already seated. Rose came in with their dinners: roast chicken, roast and mash potatoes, Yorkshire pudding, green beans, spinach, carrots and parsnips, with thick gravy.

"Oh, this looks lovely, Rose, thank you!" said Billy.

"Tuck in then, you don't want it to get cold. There is juice on its way," replied Rose.

"Err, what about my dinner, rather than dealing with these children?" Mr Snow said.

"Mr Snow, your dinner is coming, now please just wait a couple of minutes and it will be at your table," said Rose.

"It's a disgrace that I am being served after those children!" he replied.

"Those children, as you call them, are lovely children and you could take a leaf out of their book, with their manners," Said Rose.

Henry came over with Mr Snow's dinner.

"And about time!" said Mr Snow.

Henry just ignored him. He thought he was arrogant enough and he didn't want to get into an argument in front of the children and it wasn't really professional as a host.

The children all tucked into their food with lots of "Mms" and "Ahhss". They thoroughly enjoyed their dinners.

"Don't forget to put your cutlery together in the middle of your plate, that way Rose knows that you have finished," George said.

Tom and Freddie picked up their cutlery and put it in the middle of the plate.

"No, not like that, Tom. Put the cutlery at the bottom of the plate, but so it sits in the middle of the plate," Alison said.

Freddie copied Tom's plate and cutlery so his was the same. Josephine was looking at everyone. She had wondered if they were talking about her, as she had changed the dynamics of the afternoon for everyone. Nobody was taking any notice of anything apart from their plates and drinks.

Celia and Sandra told the men staff they had to talk to them, but it had to be later on in the day or even the evening when the children were in bed. Both men nodded, they understood.

Rose came out with dessert, Jam Roly Poly and custard or trifle? Some of the children put their hands up for trifle, but the rest put theirs up for Jam Roly Poly. They all enjoyed their food. Once everyone had finished, Sandra and Celia helped tidy up the table so it would be less work for Rose.

Mr Snow, as miserable as ever, cleared his food and tea, picked up his paper and left the dining room, grunting as he walked past the children's table.

"What's his problem, Rose?" asked Billy. "He's not a very nice man and he's always grumpy."

"No idea, lad, but it's not nice behaviour to be setting to you young un's. Everyone's not like that, so don't pay him any mind," Rose said.

"Rose is right, children. Some people have had hard lives, so they get a little grumpy when things don't go their way," replied Roger.

"So now it's coming up to 7.30 pm, I think it's time for baths," Roger added.

"Hmm…" the kids grumbled. "Can't we just have a wash and then have a bath tomorrow instead? We've had washes earlier when we returned from the beach," Billy said.

Roger relented.

"OK then, everyone upstairs, have a wash and get into your night things. Then maybe if no one's using the living room, Rose will let us use it and we can watch a film," George said.

Off the children went upstairs to get their wash things. Thankfully, all of the rooms had washing facilities.

"Rose, is anyone using the living room? We thought we could put the TV on, and the children can watch a film and not get in anyone's way?" Roger asked.

"Of course, most people want to stay in the bar for the evening. I'm sorry about Mr Snow, he's not normally like that, but for some reason the children rub him up the wrong way," said Rose. She was about to continue, but Roger tried to interrupt her. Rose put up her hand.

"I'm not saying the children are doing anything to annoy him, he's just got a problem with them and I don't understand it. The children are fine, they aren't upsetting anyone, they're just being children. So please don't worry, I'm not. They're great children," replied Rose.

Roger was quite relieved. He was worried that the children weren't behaving themselves. "Now off you go, I want to finish clearing up after dinner, and yes go into the living room when you're ready," Rose added.

"Thank you Rose, I am so glad we came here and so are the children," Roger replied.

Roger left the dining room and Rose continued to clear everything from dinner. As she took the last of the plates, she said to Henry, "Henry, love, what do you think is up with Mr Snow? He's getting really annoyed when the children are in the dining room. Everyone else who is here is fine with them, it's just him."

"No idea, but if he continues at mealtimes with them, I am going to have a word with him, as the other guests are noticing it too. I've already had some complaints about him with those children. It's not like they are unruly or anything. They have great staff working with them. Anyway, we shall just wait and see what occurs over the next day or so. The children are only on their second day, they have until Saturday. We can't have this all week until they go home," added Henry.

***

When the children were upstairs getting their night things on, Sandra checked on the girls, who were all ready to go down to the living room. Sandra checked on Josephine, who seemed to have perked up. Alison gave Sandra a smile and off they went.

When the children and staff all got to the living room, *Genevieve* was on the TV. It was just starting. Everyone got comfy on the chairs and sofas. The curtains were shut so it was nice and cosy. Rose popped her head around the door and Sandra came out.

"Ms Michaels?" Rose said.

"Sandra, please," Sandra replied.

"Sandra, is that little one OK from earlier? I just wondered if what we did with the sandwiches was enough?" Rose asked.

"Rose, it was more than enough. She had something on her mind that was bothering her and she got really upset, but when the other girls left the room and

117

you sent up sandwiches and drinks, it gave her something else to focus on, so she was able to open up more. I can't thank you enough, it was a great help," Sandra said.

"I am also sorry about that Mr Snow who keeps having a moan every time the children are given their food. We are going to try and keep him in check," Rose said.

"Oh, not to worry. I don't think they are really taking any notice of him but thank you for letting me know," said Sandra. "I had better return before they think I have been kidnapped!" Sandra laughed.

"Do you think they would like sandwiches for supper while they are watching their film?" asked Rose.

"Oh no, I think they have had enough, and I don't want them to be sick in the rooms. But thank you, Rose, for thinking of them, you really are sweet," Sandra said.

"Oh, don't be silly, it's nothing. I will let you get back to your film," Rose said.

Sandra returned to the living room.

***

The children all enjoyed watching *Genevieve*.

"I didn't realise that *Genevieve* was about a car that did the run from London to Brighton. It's an old car, isn't it, George?" Billy asked.

"Err, yes, it is, but it's a lovely story. The man in with Genevieve is a nice man, not like his pompous friend, Mr Claterhouse," Tom added.

"It's Mr Claverhouse, Tom, not Claterhouse!" Billy corrected him.

"Yes, and he's like Mr Snow. He's a bit like that, only grumpier." Freddie laughed. All the children laughed too.

"It's not funny, children, likening someone you meet to someone on the TV!" Celia said.

"I liked it when he started up the engine and all of the coffee went over the lady and the TV people came along and filmed them," Billy said.

"I'm glad you all enjoyed the film, but now I'm afraid it's time for bed. Time's getting on and you're already a little over your bedtime, so can you all say goodnight now and off you go," Roger said.

"Night, Night, Night." The children said at once.

Alison and Josephine went up together and so did Tom and Freddie.

"Night Alison, Night Josephine!" The boys called out.

"Night Tom and Night Freddie, see you in the morning," the girls replied.

Alison and Josephine pulled back their covers and got into bed. Sandra popped her head around the door.

"Just checking you're both in bed. Let me just tuck you in so you're as snug as bugs in a rug," Sandra said. "Are you all right now, sweetheart? You've had an eventful day."

"I am a lot better now, Sandra. Thank you for today. I-I hope I didn't upset you and everybody else, I didn't mean to," Josephine said.

"You didn't upset anyone, my love. Everyone is fine with you. You're part of our family, just as long as you're OK?" Sandra added.

Josephine gave her a big smile and Sandra said goodnight to both of the girls and left the room to check on the others.

***

Sandra had just sat down when Celia joined her with a cup of tea. She handed one to her and placed two other cups on the table for when the men came back from checking on the boys.

"It's been a hell of a day today, not what I was expecting either!" Sandra said.

"No, I bet not! It has been hard. How's Josephine doing? Did she settle down? She was quiet at dinner," Celia said.

"Well, yes, she was OK. I did ask her if she was all right, do you know what she said? She was more concerned that she had upset everyone today! I couldn't believe it, the poor little lamb."

"Trust her to think of the others first; it's no wonder we had no idea," Celia said.

"No idea about what?" Roger asked as he came into the room. "Oh, I see what you mean," he added.

"I was just telling Celia that she was more concerned about upsetting everyone else than herself," Sandra said.

Roger and George sat down, and Celia handed them their tea to them.

"Who's upset?" George asked.

119

"Oh, no one is upset. Josephine thought she had upset everyone this afternoon, that's all," Sandra said.

"Right, so what happened today? We know that some stuff happened on the beach and then back here, so what started it all off?" George asked.

Sandra started to fill the others in on what happened at the beach and what had kickstarted it all off. She told them about the moat and keeping people safe and then the name Jimmy, which is what Josephine's uncle is called. That was it. It was like opening the floodgates and it all came out.

The men were quite shocked. They didn't expect this to be what it was about.

"But when you got back and Kim came to get you, what happened when you went into their room and she started talking?" Roger asked.

"Well, the girls left the room so I could speak to Josephine. she was speaking incoherently through her tears, but we got the girls to go down and get sandwiches and milk from Rose so hopefully that would help her to focus and she eventually began to calm down," Sandra said. "And did it, did she calm down?" asked Roger.

"She did and what she said alarmed me! Did any of you know that Josephine was taken from her parents because she was abused by her uncle? This has happened many times to her by him."

"But how?" interrupted George.

"I was getting to that," Sandra said. "When she used to visit her nan in Devon, it was near a farm, but also near some woods. He would always make sure he was there at the same time as them, so he would take her out for a while. No one would think anything fishy about it, and they would go down to the woods, where it was quiet, and nobody ever went there. He grew up in Devon, so knew the woods very well. Anyway, they would be gone for an hour or so every time. To a child that is a long time, so she couldn't be too sure. Anyway, there was a little cabin in the woods, where he would take her and abuse her.

"It wasn't until her father came looking for them one day and he caught his brother in the middle of it and he attacked him. Josephine thought she had been bad and was in trouble. Her father nearly killed him. Social services were involved, and she was removed from the home.

"The mother was never the same since. She had a mental breakdown and kept blaming herself for it happening and also for not seeing it. When Josephine was taken to the police station, her mum and dad were behind the glass, having

120

to listen to what he had done. He went to prison for it, but she was already taken into care by then," Sandra explained the whole horrible story.

"Didn't Josephine ever tell anyone?" Celia asked.

"No, she was told that nobody would believe her and that he would go to prison if he got caught," Sandra told them.

"Well, he got that right, didn't he?" Roger said.

"Yes, but why would they take Josephine away from her family? Not let her live with her mum and dad?" Celia asked.

"I suppose once the state got involved, they probably thought they could keep a better eye on her than her family. Even though it didn't happen in the household, it still happened underneath their noses and they didn't recognise anything with their daughter," Sandra said.

"Poor little girl. We'll have to keep an eye on her while we are away, but I think not to mention any of this until we get back to Craven House and only amongst the staff when the children are out of the way. We don't want a repeat of the Hilary situation on our hands, do we?" Sandra said.

The staff drank their tea, which was getting cold, thinking about the day they had today.

Roger interrupted the silence.

"So, what are the plans for tomorrow then?"

"I thought we could take them down to the seafront and have a look at that funfair. Bembom Brothers, is that what it's called?" asked George.

"But if we go down there, it's unfair not to let them in and have a look around and have at least a couple of goes on some of the rides," Roger said.

"If we have a look around, at least we will know how much money we will need for Friday, the day before we go home. That way it's a nice way to end their holiday and we can let them use up the rest or what's left of the rest of their spending money," George said.

"Good thinking. What else are we going to do for the rest of the week? There isn't exactly a lot to do in Margate, not like I thought it was anyway," Roger said.

"Well, don't forget we have that trip to Leeds Castle on Tuesday, then on Thursday we're going to Canterbury Cathedral. So that just leaves Wednesday and Friday. Wednesday we can do the beach again. This time the girls can go crabbing and the boys can make forts, then on Friday we can let them go a bit wild and go on the funfair and get souvenirs or something. What do you think?" George said.

"Sounds like a plan. I forgot we were going on a couple of trips. What time's the coach coming to collect us?"

"9.30 am and we should be back before 6 pm, so after breakfast but back before dinner," Sandra added.

"So that's every day accounted for. The beach two days, at the funfair one and a bit days with just wandering around and then two trips. Don't forget we've all played Crazy Golf today and they may want to play again tomorrow or Wednesday. Let's just see how this pans out," Roger said.

They all finished their teas and set off to check on the children then head off to bed.

***

The next morning, the girls had felt refreshed after a good night's sleep. They woke up about the same time. Their room had lovely big windows with pastel coloured curtains, which let lots of sunlight through it. It was easy to wake early.

"Morning, Josephine," Alison said.

"Morning, Alison, what time is it?" Josephine asked.

Alison had the bedside clock by her bed.

"It's nearly 8.15. We'd better get up as breakfast will be served soon. Can you smell that bacon? It smells lovely!" Alison remarked.

Both girls got up, then Kim knocked on the door and stuck her head around it.

"Just checking you two are up…breakfast will be ready soon and we want to make sure Billy doesn't eat it all!"

They all laughed.

"Just getting ready now, Kim, thank you for checking on us," Alison said. They both pulled out their shorts and t-shirts for the day and also white ankle socks and their sandals.

They had got washed in their bathroom, but not cleaned their teeth, not until they had eaten their breakfast.

"There, ready!" They were both looking in the full-length mirror in the wardrobes.

Sandra knocked on their door.

"Oh, you're both ready, are you hungry?" She asked them. They both smiled.

"Yes, we are, can we go down now?" Josephine asked.

After yesterday's activities, Josephine was already very hungry. It had been an emotional day for her, but today was a new day.

"Come with me then, let me just call on the other girls," Sandra said as she opened the girl's door. The other girls were already waiting for her.

"Right then, let's go down to breakfast." Celia said.

The girls all made an orderly queue, they didn't want anyone to fall over or down the stairs.

When they had got to the table, the boys and men were already there patiently waiting for them.

"Sit down quickly, girls. Rose will be bringing out the cooked breakfasts soon," Celia said.

The girls had started to tuck into their cereal. They seemed to have the same thing every day, either cornflakes or sugar puffs. That's what they wanted to eat. The orange juice was already poured into their glasses.

Mr Snow was on the other side of the dining room, was reading his paper and drinking his tea, ignoring the children, until he heard Rose come out with the cooked breakfast. Henry was right behind her with his plate full of cooked food. Henry wasn't going to let this man upset these children with his childish antics and complaining.

"Mr Snow," Henry said, as he put down his plate, "be careful, the plate is hot."

"I should hope so too!" grunted Mr Snow.

The children were tucking into their breakfasts. Some of the other families who came down for breakfast said hello to the staff and the children. The children also returned the greetings. The staff were pleased. The children weren't annoying anyone. Mr Snow disagreed, but he was a crotchety old man, who probably didn't have anything else to do other than complain about everything.

Once the children had cleared their plates and put their cutlery to the middle of it, Rose came in to collect the plates.

"Where are you off to today then, children?" Rose asked.

"We're going down to the Front, to have a look at the shops and take it from there," Roger said, with a bit of a wink. He didn't want the children to know where they were going yet, as they didn't want to bring the house down with their cheers, especially as breakfast had been a quiet affair for once.

The children left the dining room, thanking Rose again for their delicious food and went back up to their rooms and clean their teeth before leaving to go out.

Rose and Henry had cleared all of the breakfast things away.

"Don't forget the Jackson family are checking out today, Henry. We have to clear out their room and air it ready to make up later on. We don't have another family in that room until tomorrow," Rose said.

"OK, how many pairs of hands do you think I have, missus? I'm not an octopus! I'll just finish washing up these cups, saucers and plates and then I'll make a start on the Jackson's room."

"Oh, you can't go up there yet, they aren't leaving until 10.30," Rose said.

"Rose, my darling, it's past that already!" Henry replied.

"Oh, dear! I had better check reception to see if they have signed out and handed in their keys. Sorry Henry, back in a mo."

When Rose had returned to the reception, the Jackson family was waiting there with their luggage.

"I am so sorry, my loves, I got distracted with the time. We hope you enjoyed yourselves while you were here in Margate, do you think you will return again sometime?" Rose asked.

"Well, yes, Rose. That's why we're are still here. We'd like to book up with you again for next year, for the May bank holiday, Whitsun, if that's OK with you?" Mr Jackson said.

"Yes, I'll just get my diary. Excuse me for a moment, it's here somewhere. There that's it. Now you said May Bank Holiday, Whitsun? That's the one at the end of May?" Rose flicked through the diary to the following year.

"Yes, that's right," Mr Jackson said.

"So that's the 23rd of May? For one week or just the weekend?" Rose asked.

"The whole week, please. 23rd May until 30th May," Mrs Jackson said.

"Right, that's in the diary for you, my dears. See you next year and have a safe journey home. We will send you a reminder nearer the time for your deposit. Is that OK?"

"Yes, that's fine Rose. See you then," Mr Jackson said. He picked up their luggage whilst Mrs Jackson spoke to Rose.

"Rose, I hope those children from the home have a great holiday. They're such lovely children and they have great manners. Anyway ta, ta!" she waved goodbye.

Mrs Jackson was right; they were lovely children and they had great manners. As Henry had said before, few of the children who came through their guesthouse were as well behaved as these little mites.

"Henry, that family, the Jacksons, are coming back next year. They've already booked it. And yes, I told them that we would send out a reminder nearer the time. They also said that they hope the children from the home have a lovely holiday. Isn't that nice? So, it's not just us who think they are lovely children. Do you know what I was just thinking about, you know Betty Linton down the road? She and her husband, Bruce, were trying for children for a long time, you know. These are the sort of children I think they would love," Rose said.

"Rose love, you can't just hand over children! There are procedures to go through to foster or even adopt before you can get one of those children. Don't be telling me you've been thinking of odd things now, Rose?" Henry said.

"No, of course not, and that's not what I mean. Betty has wanted a baby for years, but they haven't gotten lucky, but I was wondering if she and Bruce had even considered fostering or adopting an older child, like one of those? One from around here, not going to another town or city to do it. But I just wondered, that's all," Rose said.

"You are a great big softy, Rose Benton!" Henry laughed.

"No Henry, I just love children. Me and Ron weren't lucky enough to have any of our own and him dying in the war, well that was it for me. So, when I opened this place, it was like a second chance. Then you came along as my porter..." Rose said.

"But I'm not just your porter, now, am I?" Henry had a twinkle in his eye.

"Oh, be away with you!" Rose chuckled.

Rose and Henry had been together for a long time now. It was a silent partnership. Rose was still the boss and they had been happy together. It was hard work running a business like this, but so rewarding.

They went along to the room just vacated by the Jackson family.

"Come on Henry, this won't get done on its own. Let's crack on, then we can have a couple of hours to ourselves, watching the TV with our feet up. Everyone has gone out for the day," Rose said.

"OK then, let's get to it. I do like those kids, Rose. They do grow on you." Henry smiled.

***

125

"Hi guys, are you all ready yet?" Roger yelled.

He could hear all of the children coming down the stairs at once.

"It sounds like a herd of elephants are coming down the stairs!" George laughed.

"Everyone here?" Roger asked.

The children all shouted yes.

"Right, off we go," said Roger.

"Bye Rose, see you later on!" Sandra called out.

They all left the building and started walking down the road towards the beach. They were all in quite chatty moods this morning.

"Where are we off to then, Roger?" Billy asked.

"We are going down to the Front to have a look at the funfair and arcades as we haven't been there yet. We won't be staying too long because we can go and play crazy golf again."

"How come we can't stay too long at the funfair and arcades, Roger?" Billy asked.

"Well, if we go down there for a long time, we won't have any money left. So, we're going to have a look around and take it from there," Roger replied.

"That makes sense, doesn't it?" Billy said.

They went past the shops and the little boutiques, before long they were along the seafront.

"So, do you want to have a look at the funfair first or the arcades?" George asked.

"Well, it doesn't really matter what we do first, as we are going to be doing both," Celia said. "OK, let's have a look at the fair."

George took charge and went down the slope to see the attendant.

"Are you open yet, Sir?" George asked.

"No, not yet. We open at 12.00. If you could come back then, that would be great," The attendant said.

"Well, it looks like we are going to have a look around the arcades," Roger said.

Off they went.

There were only a couple of arcades, but the children didn't mind. They were mesmerised by the lights and the dings of the machines. There were the 2p machines that when you put your money in it and would zig zag down the back and fall onto the base, which then pushed the money to and fro. If you were lucky then some money would drop down into the slot and you collected it from the hole in the bottom with the little container that held the winnings for you.

There were some pinball machines and there was even slot bingo, which the kids looked a bit weird at.

"What's that?" Tim asked.

"That's slot bingo. You have a sheet with numbers on them and when the caller calls out your number, you then move your slot to the side, so it becomes black. When you have a line across you then win for that line. You then get a ticket for the prizes. Then they play for the house," Sandra explained.

"Whose house?" Tim asked.

"It's not anybody's house; it's just called house. When the whole sheet is covered with each slot, then you can win a prize, but you have to get a lot of houses before you can get any prizes from here," Sandra said, showing the children the cabinet full of prizes.

"You have to win a lot of houses to get anything from that glass cabinet Sandra, have you seen how high these numbers are?" Billy said.

They carried on looking at the machines in the arcade. Roger gave them all a couple of pounds that they could change up and have a couple of turns on the machines, which they did. Once they were on the machines he went around with the other staff checking that they were all OK.

When they had all finished and their money had run out, the children went back to the staff.

"Right then, shall we make a move towards the funfair now? It's nearly 12.00," Roger said. They left the arcade and headed back down towards the funfair.

"Yes sir, we're open now, what can I do for you?" The attendant smiled.

"We wanted to have a look around and see what rides there are for the children. Do we have to pay here, or can we just have a wander around?" George asked.

"Well, you normally have to pay here before you can enter the park, Sir, but if you just want to have a look around that should be OK. You won't be going on any rides, will you, Sir?" The attendant asked.

"No, we just wanted to see what you have here so the children can see."

"Oh, children as well, Sir? I'm sorry, I can't let you in if the children are with you. It would be against health and safety regulations, Sir. You're welcome to come back when you're planning on going on rides. Then I can let you in, good day, Sir," the attendant said.

George felt quite deflated.

"Sorry children, we can't go in until we pay," said George.

"Ahh, that's not fair!" Billy said.

"I'm afraid, rules are rules, Billy. We can come back on Friday instead though. Tell you what, let's head down for the Crazy Golf instead."

"The children enjoyed that, and it will take up some time. If we go for something to eat, then we can go for a walk or back to the guest house," Roger said.

They headed off for Crazy Golf and then for some lunch.

***

Once they had finished Crazy Golf and then lunch, they walked back to the guest house. They would see if they could watch a film or they bought colouring books and pencils for the children just in case they got bored.

Rose was in reception when they arrived back.

"Did you have a good time out and about?" Rose asked.

"Sure did!" Billy said. "But we couldn't go into the fair unless we paid, so we will go back on Friday to have a go on the rides. But I did beat Tim at crazy golf, Rose!" he said triumphantly. Rose smiled. She had really grown to love the children.

"Rose, is the living room free, we wanted to see if there was something on TV that the children could watch?" Sandra asked.

"Why, of course, I don't know what's on at this time, as we never get the time to watch TV in the day."

Rose went to put the TV on for the children.

Some of the boys didn't want to watch TV, so Roger offered them colouring books with pencils, so they did that.

"Can we do colouring in our rooms?" Tim asked.

"As long as you don't make a mess, and if you do make a mess, you have to clear it up. We don't need to give Rose and Henry more work than they already have," George said.

"OK George," Billy said.

The boys went up to their rooms, and the girls went in to watch TV where there was a Cliff Richard film on—*Summer Holiday*.

"Oh, I love Cliff Richard, he is soo dreamy!" Sally said.

The other girls looked at her as if to say *OK*.

They all settled down to watch the movie. Rose came in with some squash and biscuits for them, which the girls all said thank you for.

Sandra and Celia had both come in to watch *Summer Holiday* with the girls. Rose popped back with some tea for both of them.

"Thanks Rose, you are so thoughtful," Celia said.

Rose left the room and they settled down to watch the film.

Mr Snow popped his head around the door. He wanted to read his paper in peace and quiet and was quite annoyed that the girls had taken over the TV room.

"Bloody taking over in here now!" he said as he shut the door behind him.

Sandra and Celia both looked at each other.

"What is that man's problem? He never lets up about the children, you would think he was never a child!" Celia said.

"Yes, I know," whispered Sandra, as the girls were looking at them both as they were talking too loudly. They both grabbed their cups of tea and continued watching the film.

Before long, the film had finished, and it was nearly time to go and get washed for dinner. The girls went back upstairs to their rooms to get washed and Sandra popped her head around the door of the boy's bedroom. They were all colouring in their books and looked like they were having a nice peaceful time.

Roger got up to greet her.

"Are you packing up now, it's nearly time for dinner?" she asked.

"Oh crumbs, I didn't realise it was so late! The boys have been having a great time," Roger replied. "We'll be down in a few minutes. Come on now boys, it's nearly time for dinner," Roger said.

The boys packed away their stuff.

"See Roger, we didn't make any mess for you or Rose to clear up," Billy said, matter-of-factly.

"Cheeky devil!" Roger chuckled.

The boys washed their hands and faces and then made their way down to dinner. The girls were on their way down at the same time. They all sat down on their seats and they could hear Mr Snow grumbling away to himself. They just ignored it, like they were told to.

Alison, Tom, Freddie sat next to each other and Josephine sat next to Alison. All four of the children got on really well and they were all hungry. It was fish and chips for dinner with peas or beans if they wanted them.

"Fish and chips, please!" Billy said. He wasn't happy, until he saw his plate. The fish laid over the plate, the top and one end and the tail hanging over the plate on the other end. These children weren't eating off children's plates but full adult plates. The chips also covered the rest of the plate.

"Henry and Rose must have been cooking most of the early evening to get all of this lot out!" Billy said, with a mouth full of food.

"Billy, you know your manners; no talking while you have food in your mouth!" Roger said.

"Sorry, Roger," he said and chewed at the same time.

Roger just rolled his eyes and started tucking into his own food.

Henry took over Mr Snow's plate and he just grunted.

"Always the way now," Mr Snow muttered.

"Sorry, Mr Snow? Did you say something?"

Mr Snow ignored Henry and started to eat his food.

"I am getting really fed up with Mr Snow, Rose. Constantly passing comments every time those kids come in the dining room," Henry told her.

"I know, Sandra said that when the girls were watching TV, he came in, saw them in there, and said 'Bloody taking over in here now' then he shut the door and left. It's not on, Henry love. Why is he so horrible to those kids, they haven't done anything to him and he's just downright rude!"

"I have no idea, love, but it's not on. Something has to be done about him. I mean even one of the men staff went over to him in the beginning and told him they weren't being rude, but he just ignored him. We'll sort something out, Rose, these kids haven't had a great start to be put in a home, and they all seem to be enjoying themselves, especially the little ones. Have you seen those two little boys? You would think they were brothers, and those two little girls, you would think they were sisters, they seem devoted to each other," Henry said with a smile.

Rose went back into the dining room to see if everyone's food was OK. For the first time, Mr Snow wasn't complaining, he was just eating his food, but for how long?

"Everything's fine, Rose, thank you for asking," Roger said.

Once the children had finished their dinner, it was strawberries and cream or ice-cream for dessert, and Rose brought more squash for them to drink. It was quite a hot day. Mr Snow just wanted tea and to be left alone for a change.

They all put their dishes with their clean spoons on them and put their chairs back neatly. Then in an orderly fashion went back upstairs to their rooms.

The children got bathed and changed into their night things, and then into their beds, whilst the staff were sitting together talking about the day they just had. They all acknowledged that all of the children had really enjoyed themselves and had blossomed; especially the girls when they had that episode at the beach which continued into their evening at the guest house.

They all said their goodnights and went back to their bedrooms. They had very full reports that they had to give to Ms Walters when they returned, just so they knew how much or little the children enjoyed themselves.

**

The next morning the children were up with the lark. They got washed, dressed, and went down to breakfast. Rose had already put their juice on the table and their toast and cereal were there for them to start eating. Henry came in with their cooked breakfast as they just finished their toast. Their eyes were like saucers every time they had their breakfast brought to them.

So much on the plate, fried eggs, sausage, bacon, beans, tomatoes tinned or cooked, mushrooms and black pudding if they wanted it. Some of the staff would have everything, but some of the children didn't like mushrooms or black pudding. Everyone was enjoying their food, the children had juice and the staff had tea. Roger had coffee.

"Right, when everyone's finished and you've all cleaned your teeth, I want you all to go down to reception as we have to wait for the coach," George said.

"Where are we going again, George?" Billy asked.

"We're going to Leeds Castle today," George replied.

"Cor, we're going to be knackered going all the way to Leeds," Billy said.

"Leeds Castle is in Kent, not Leeds, Billy," George said.

"Why is Leeds Castle in Kent and not in Leeds?" Billy asked.

"Good question Billy, but I have no idea. We're going there today, so please finish up and be down in 10 minutes," Roger said.

"Good riddance to that lot today!" Mr Snow said.

"What was that, Mr Snow?" Henry asked.

Mr Snow ignored Henry and carried on with his tea and newspaper.

Henry glared at Mr Snow. He was getting quite annoyed with him, and the other guests were getting pretty fed up with his comments towards the children too.

Ten minutes later, all of the children, with newly fresh breath from cleaning their teeth, were in reception.

"Come on then, the coach is here," George said.

Everyone followed him out of the doors and onto the coach.

"Bye loves, have a great day out and enjoy Leeds Castle. It's lovely there!" Rose said, waving at them from the window.

Tom and Freddie sat next to each other and Alison and Josephine sat next to each other. They all looked forward to getting out and going somewhere else.

The coach ride wasn't too far away from the guest house, about an hour or so. The children had a lovely time exploring, the staff were having a nice time. Even though the weather was lovely, it was cool inside the building which they all appreciated.

They stayed at the castle for a while, then they had lunch there and did a tour in the afternoon. The staff took the children into the gift shop to have a look around.

"Look what I have found!" George said. "A tea-towel with Leeds Castle on it. I thought I would get that for Ms Walters as a souvenir, what do you think?"

The staff all nodded.

"It's OK, but there's not much in the way of souvenirs, is there?" Celia said.

None of the children wanted to buy any of the souvenirs. They didn't have to buy anything for their parents at all. Kim looked at a keyring for Jimmy.

"I think Jimmy would like this, he likes red. Yes, I'm going to buy it for him. He would love it here." Kim smiled, thinking of her brother.

Josephine was already outside, so she didn't hear Kim talking about Jimmy. She didn't want to upset Josephine by saying that name, so she would now just refer to him as her brother. The girls were really quite grown up even for their ages—eleven and twelve.

Celia bought a lighter for her boyfriend and a keyring for herself and then she too picked up a tea-towel for her mother.

"The coach will be here in a few minutes, can we please do a head count, just so we know we haven't left anyone behind?" Sandra said.

One, two three…yes, everyone was here. The coach pulled up and George stood at the entrance door of the coach just to make sure everyone got back on it. The children and staff all sat where they sat on the way there.

The doors were closed, and they were off back to the guest house. They hadn't had so much fresh air since they got there, so the staff knew that the children would eat well this evening and sleep even better.

***

The coach pulled up outside the guest house. They had a nice driver called Ted who said he would be back on Thursday to take them all to Canterbury Cathedral. Some of the children were walking off the steps, some of them jumping down the steps to get off the coach.

They all waved Ted off and went inside. They were a bit loud when they walked into the building and Mr Snow was in reception, reading his paper. He tutted.

"Children should be seen and not heard!" He muttered loudly.

Rose was behind the reception desk and with her mouth wide open with Mr Snow's remark, she quickly closed it.

"Come along now loves, let's see if there's anything you want to watch on the TV."

Rose was getting very annoyed at the way Mr Snow treated the children. She was going to talk to Henry when the young ones were out of earshot.

Rose went up to the TV room with the children and the staff. She pulled Sandra's arm just before she went into the room.

"Can I have a quick word please, Sandra?" she asked.

"Why, yes, of course? Is anything wrong, have the children been too noisy?" Sandra asked.

"No, not at all. I just wanted to apologise for Mr Snow's comments. He's very cantankerous, but his behaviour is just getting worse," Rose apologised.

"Oh Rose, please don't worry, we're used to this type of behaviour. We get it out and about a lot. We just try to steer the kids away, so they don't hear it," Sandra said, "but thank you, Rose, all the kids love it here and they love your cooking by the way," Sandra added.

"Thank you, Sandra. I'll let you get back to your TV."

133

Rose headed back down to the dining room. Henry had cleared all of the dinner things.

"Henry love, we have got to do something about Mr Snow. He's been so rude to those children again and I have just about enough of it. I've just spoken with Sandra and she said not to worry, they have to deal with it back home, but these kiddies are on their holidays, they need a break from it," Rose was getting quite upset.

Henry came over and kissed her on the forehead.

"I have had enough of Mr Snow. I know he's been a good customer, Rose, but I am taking things into hand now, this is not happening again!" Henry said.

"What are you going to do?" Rose asked.

"Now Rose, I know these are your premises, but sometimes I do have to step in when someone is out of line, and this is one of those times. So be a dear and let me deal with it." Henry smiled. "Now we still have some stuff to do before dinner is started, so if I can get on with that and did you say the landing lightbulb needs changing? I'll do that as well," he said, and off he went.

***

The children had a nice time watching TV. There wasn't much on, but they kept entertained. Soon it would be time to get ready for dinner. They could smell it coming up from the kitchen, so when they had washed their hands and faces, they all trundled down to the dining room.

Everyone was getting their seats. Mr Snow was already sitting down waiting for his dinner. Rose brought in the squash for their tables in jugs. They had lemon and orange squash. Then Henry bought in their dinners, beef stew and dumplings. All the children cheered, they loved beef stew. There were rolls and bread on the table.

Mr Snow was grumbling again, but the children were ignoring him as always. Once Henry had given the children their dinners, he came back into the room with a big suitcase and dumped it onto Mr Snow's table, where he was waiting for his dinner.

"What is the meaning of this? I'm waiting for my dinner and you hand me a suitcase?" demanded Mr Snow.

"First of all, Mr Snow, this is your suitcase already packed and this, my good man, is a cheque with a full refund which covers your stay with us," Henry said calmly.

"But I'm booked up until Saturday!" Mr Snow protested.

"Not anymore and please do not frequent this establishment again. Thank you, Sir. I will help you with your luggage to vacate these premises," Henry said.

"I have never been spoken to like that in my life!" Mr Snow looked shocked.

"Well, I'm very surprised with your attitude, Mr Snow!" Henry replied.

Henry took Mr Snow's suitcase up the stairs and out of the building. The whole dining room let out a big cheer.

"Now, now, children, that's not very nice," Sandra said.

"Don't you mean he wasn't very nice, Sandra?" Billy said.

"But he is an old man," she replied.

"Yes, but not all old men have to be that rude," Billy said.

"Well said, young man!" Henry said.

Everyone continued with their dinners and it was for a change a pleasant atmosphere during their meal.

Once dinner of beef stew and dumplings and trifle was over, everyone cleared their plates ready for Rose to clear the tables they left the dining room. The mood was a lot lighter now that Mr Snow had gone.

Once the children had got into their night things after their wash, they were chilling out. Rose knocked on the door wanting to know if they wanted to watch TV. Sandra and Celia said they would check on the men and boys and see if they wanted to join them.

***

The next couple of days went in a bit of a blur, as the children got to know Margate a little better and enjoyed themselves thoroughly. They had their trip to Canterbury Cathedral, which they all seemed to enjoy. The children had got used to being away from the city and were really settling in.

They hadn't had another episode since Sunday down at the beach. The children did go down to the beach and they had enjoyed doing the different activities than the last time they were there.

On Friday, everyone got up relatively early. They wanted to make the most of the last day of their holiday. Once they had breakfast, gone back upstairs to

135

clean teeth, then come back down again, they knew that they couldn't go into the funfair until later on. Sandra suggested that they go along to the shops in case the children want to buy things, gifts etc, then head over to the arcades before going to the funfair.

"That seems like a good plan and we could make it back here before dinner," George said.

"Actually, Rose wants to lay on a lunch for us today, as a farewell lunch," Sandra said.

"Oh, that is lovely! I think the children really have had an impact on Rose and Henry." Celia smiled.

"So that's what we will do. If we do the shopping stuff first, then the children can do the fun things before we go back. What time did Rose say to come back for lunch?" Celia asked.

"She said about 2 pm, that way they won't be too full for their dinner," Sandra replied.

"When have you ever known our children to be too full for dinner?" Roger laughed.

"Precisely!" George added.

The children were raring to go. They went to some shops in the town. Some of the girls wanted to buy a few bits and pieces to take back with them. They checked whether the boys wanted to do anything. They all really wanted to go to the arcades. Tom and Freddie were with the girls having a look, but there wasn't anything they had wanted.

Once they were finished, they went along to the arcades. Alison and Josephine had already looked around the shops and they had both picked up something they wanted. Alison picked up some lovely dolls clothes and Josephine chose some novelty note paper, that was scented. She didn't know what she wanted to do with it, but she thought it was pretty.

They didn't really want to play on the machines, so they just had a look around. They both still had some pennies left but didn't want to waste them on the machines. Alison had also picked up a blue and white truck for Tom, which he didn't know about. She wanted to surprise him when she got back, and Josephine picked up a green one for Freddie. They were both like her brothers, even though she was an only child.

***

It was time to go to the funfair! All of the children were excited about going.

George had gone to the ticket attendant; it was the same one he had met earlier that week.

"Can I have four adults please and 10 children? Thank you!" George said.

"Yes, Sir, that will be £20.00 please," the attendant said.

"£20.00, is that right?" George asked.

"Yes, Sir. There are 10 children and four adults. I could charge it separately and it will be over £40.00—£2.00 per child and £5.00 per adult, but if I charge you as two adults and four children twice, then it's only £10 per family," the attendant explained.

George couldn't believe it! They'd made a saving of £20.00 that was great!

"Thank you, Sir," George said.

"Thank you, have a wonderful time."

With their tickets, they were on their way. The children were so excited. They walked down the slope and out into the fresh air.

Wow! They could see so much—candy floss stalls, ice-cream stall, doughnut making stalls, then they saw the dart stalls, where you have to throw a dart at a number on a board to get a prize. There was hook a duck, and then they saw the rides! There was a water chute, which was a cart that went upwards on rails. It went around a bend and then, at very high speed, came crashing down into a lot of water—and you got soaked! The children liked the look of that one.

Then there was the ghost train, the big wheel, rides that went round and round and you went up in the air and then upside down. There were also the teacup rides, and lots of other rides. The children had big wide eyes like saucers as they looked at everything.

They didn't know where to start. The staff wanted all of the children to stay together, so no one would get lost. They chose a ride then whoever wanted to go on it, would go with at least one member of staff. The other children would wait until the ride stopped and then they would go to the next one and so on.

The children were in the funfair for nearly two hours and had great fun, but they were exhausted.

"Come on now everyone, you have been on everything twice, we have to head back now for lunch," Sandra said.

"Why are we heading back for lunch, we always eat outside for lunch?" Billy asked.

"As a special treat this lunchtime, Rose has made us a farewell lunch and I don't think it's polite to keep her waiting," Sandra said.

"I agree. Come on you lot, let's not keep Rose waiting," Billy said.

Billy knew that Rose cooked good food and lots of it. They were going to get a good lunch.

The staff looked at one another with their mouths open. It had been the only time Billy had been in a rush to go anywhere.

***

When they got back, Sandra told the children to put their things in their room and wash their hands and faces and then come back to the dining room.

When they arrived in the dining room, the table they usually sat on was pushed against the wall and it was covered in food. Sandwiches, pork pies, sausage rolls, salad, cocktail sausages, cheese and pineapple on sticks, and Rose had made jelly and ice-cream for the children and chocolate cake and Forest Gateau for the staff.

Billy made a beeline for the sandwiches and everyone tucked into the spread that Rose had laid on.

"Rose, thank you so much for this! We didn't expect anything like this. You truly have made these children's holiday. You are so patient, kind, warm and all of the children have really taken to you and Henry," Sandra said.

"I wanted to apologise really, because Mr Snow kept commenting on them all of the time and the other guests noticed it too, they also complained about him. He was awful to the children when he was here at mealtimes and just for being here. We didn't want them to think that everyone was like that here," Rose said.

"Rose, honestly, the children all thought he was a grumpy old man. A lot of these kids haven't had it easy, as you could tell at the beginning of the holiday, but they have developed a very thick skin. You've given them the most amazing time, especially Billy, who loves your cooking!" George said, looking over at Billy with his plate as full as his mouth.

The children had a glorious time at the lunch and then told everyone that they needed a little sleep, so they could be ready for the evening meal.

"See, I told you!" George laughed.

Sandra helped Rose clear the tables and put everything in the kitchen. The men moved the table back to where it should be and then the children went back up to their rooms to relax before dinner.

Sandra helped with the washing up. It was the least she could do. Celia was with the girls. It had been a great day, but once dinner was over, they had to check they had all of their packing done and to check they had taken all of their stuff from the wardrobes.

"It's chops for dinner tonight," Sandra said when she got back with the girls.

Alison and Josephine had already finished their packing. They just had their clothes they had worn that day and their night things to go into their bags and their toiletries.

It was soon dinner time and they came charging down like elephants. They were all seated. Henry came in with their squash and then Rose came in with their dinners, pork chops, new potatoes, green beans, peas, carrots, Yorkshire pudding, stuffing, and gravy. The children didn't know where to start, but they managed it.

When the staff and children alike tucked into their food and cleared the plates, Rose came out with a big bowl of instant whip and peaches or fruit cocktail with ice-cream.

The children thoroughly enjoyed their food while they were away. Once everyone had finished, they were the only ones left in the dining room. Rose and Henry bought in tea and coffee for Roger. They pulled up a couple of chairs and sat with them all.

Rose really was going to miss this group; she loved the kids and the staff were really lovely.

They were talking for a little while, but some of the boys were getting a little restless. George and Roger suggested that they return to their room for a little while, so Celia and Sandra could talk to Rose and Henry.

Rose asked about how you go about fostering one of the children.

Sandra told her that you have to contact social services and questioned if Rose and Henry thinking of fostering a child.

Rose told her about her friends, Betty, and Bruce, up the road. They had been trying for children for a few years. They weren't old; in their early 30's, but they just couldn't have any children.

Sandra told Rose to tell her friend to contact Social Services and they could hopefully help them. Rose thanked Sandra and then Sandra told the girls they should go upstairs and get ready for bed.

Sandra offered to help with the cleaning up, but Rose told her that was what Henry was there for. Rose gave Sandra a hug as she went upstairs with the girls to get ready for bed.

Once all of the children were washed and in their night things, the staff started to sort out their own packing, and make sure they hadn't left anything behind. They checked on the children to make sure they were in bed. They had a big day travelling back home and needed to get a good night's sleep.

Sandra and Celia came back from the kitchen with a mug of cocoa each so they would also get a good night's sleep.

"Courtesy of Rose," Celia said.

They all drank their drinks and reflected on their last week in Margate, how the children had really blossomed and got to know one another, and they all had realised new skills they had. It had definitely been worth going away with the kids and all of the staff said they would go with them again. Even back here to Margate.

***

"Come on everyone, it's breakfast time and we have to be ready to leave for 10 am as the coach will be here!" Sandra called out.

The children headed down for breakfast. Today there was boiled eggs, rather than cereal. They had toast, orange juice and a cooked breakfast, followed by tea for the staff. Everyone was glad it was time to eat, but sad as well that they were going home that morning.

The children didn't seem to want to rush their breakfast as they had done on other days in the week. Not that weren't looking forward to going home, but they were going to miss Rose and Henry.

Once they had finished breakfast, Rose came around with more juice for the children.

"I don't think they should have any more juice, as there isn't a toilet on the coach," George said.

"Good thinking, I hadn't thought of that, George," Sandra said. "We can though, have more tea I mean."

140

George chuckled. He poured himself another cup. Roger took the boys upstairs to make sure they had packed everything once their teeth were clean.

Meanwhile, Sandra and Celia took the girls up to make sure they had packed everything away once they had cleaned their teeth. They started to make their way downstairs with their suitcases, with help from George, and waited in reception.

Sandra and Celia gave a full sweep of their room and both of the girls' rooms. Every trace of them was gone. You wouldn't have known they were there.

George and Roger did the same thing.

Billy handed something to Rose in reception. It was a handmade thank you card, which read, "Thank you to Rose and Henry for our lovely time at your home and thank you for all of the lovely food xx."

Rose teared up as she read it, then she passed it on to Henry to have a read.

The coach pulled up and Roger and George went to double check all of the rooms to make sure nothing was left behind.

Rose had disappeared but returned with a big bag, full of sandwiches and snacks for the children and staff for their journey home. Sandra gave Rose a huge hug and then the children all piled in together to hug also and Henry wasn't left out; he got hugs too.

The coach driver tooted his horn, so everyone pulled away. Rose and Henry had tears in their eyes and so did the staff.

"Come along then everyone, time to go, we've already put your suitcases in the coach," George said.

Sandra and Celia both hugged Rose and Henry for a final time. The children were full of hugs and then waves of goodbye.

The staff were all out of the building now and so were Henry and Rose, they waved goodbye until their little arms were getting heavy. Rose and Henry were waving profusely. That was it; all the children were seated and counted. The driver turned on the engine and Rose and Henry were on the steps with tears rolling down their cheeks, as they waved until the coach was out of sight.

"Come on Rose, we have to clear out their rooms for cleaning." Henry hugged her.

Chapter 8

The coach driver tooted the horn as it pulled up in front of Craven House Children's Home.

"Right, children! We're home now, so let George and Roger unload the suitcases and take them up to reception then we can all get off the coach and collect our luggage," Sandra said.

The children were quite chatty as George and Roger unloaded the luggage.

"Bye, thank you for a good journey home, Ted!" The children shouted to the driver as they left the coach.

Ted got up to make sure nobody had left anything behind, then Celia jumped back onto the coach and check also if anything had been left behind. Yes, there had been a little blue rabbit that belonged to Freddie.

"Have to make sure Freddie has this, he won't be able to sleep otherwise," Celia said. "Thank you again, Ted, it was a great journey there and back. Are you taking the children next week to Eastbourne?" Celia asked.

"Yes, Miss. I'll take them there and bring them back," Ted replied.

"Thank you again and have a lovely day and weekend," Celia said.

Once Celia had returned to reception, the children were taking their luggage back up to their rooms. They were told to empty their suitcases onto the bed and put their dirty laundry into the laundry bin and the staff would take it back down to the kitchen to be washed, dried, and then ironed.

Alison and Josephine emptied theirs onto their beds. Thankfully, there wasn't any sand in them; not like the boys, whose luggage all had sand in them.

"Oh boys! We were supposed to leave the sand at the beach, not bring it back with us!" George said. "No, don't put it in your laundry bin, otherwise everything going in it will be covered in sand for months! I'll bring you some black bags, so we can put your holiday clothes into them, and it won't go everywhere."

Once Roger and George returned with the black bags, it was easier to transfer it to them than the laundry bins. Although it was Saturday, it was later in the day so the children who would have normally had their chores to do, were already done by the other children who had stayed behind.

It was agreed that when they were away, the children who had just returned had to do their jobs for the two Saturdays as well. That way, it was fair to all of them and they had learnt to share and take things in turns, just like you do in life.

Alison and Josephine went along to see how Tom and Freddie were getting on. They knocked on the door which as always was wide open.

Tom and Freddie were playing with their cars that they had left behind. You wouldn't have known that they had been away.

Sandra and Celia popped their heads into the boy's bedroom and told them that lunch was on its way and could they go down to the dining room once they had washed their hands and faces.

Once the children did that, they went along to the dining room. The tables were piled high with sandwiches—fish paste, ham, cheese, tuna, and egg mayonnaise. It was the first time in a week that all of the children were all back together and the air was filled with chatter and stories from their holiday. The children that had stayed behind were filling them in with what they had been doing for the past week.

"We went to the park and we went swimming. We also went to the cinema to see the early morning film, which was *The Return of the Pink Panther*, and we did some activities here," Adam said.

Once lunch was over, everyone went to the living room to see if there was anything on TV.

"Alison and Josephine, do you want to sort out these shells we got at the beach? We wondered if you wanted to make photo frames with us?" Kim asked.

"How do we make photo frames?" Josephine asked.

"Well, we get some plain ones, like these, then we glue them onto frames with help from Sandra and Celia," Kim explained. "Then when the photos we took get developed, we can all have a photo of our choice to put in the frame, what do you think?" Kim asked.

"I think it's a great idea, and once we have chosen our photo, we can put it by our bed!" Alison said.

Alison and Josephine went with Kim and the others to their bedroom to sort out the shells. "Oh, some of these are so pretty!" Josephine said.

"Yes, aren't they!" Alison said.

"Well, help yourself to which ones you like and once we have enough, we can see when we next go shopping if we can get a nice size frame each," Jennie said.

"Thank you, girls, they're so pretty!" Alison said.

When the girls thought they had enough shells and everyone had plenty, they said they had better go back downstairs with them. They took their shells back to their rooms to put them on their bedside cabinets. They were excited about decorating the photo frames.

Both girls lay on their beds, staring up at the ceiling. They couldn't believe their lovely holiday was over, but they were also glad to be back at home. And it was home, they had settled in well there and it felt like they had a big close family. All of the children had bonded whilst they were away, but so did the others who had stayed behind, so when they would go away the other children would be able to continue their bonding, but on their home ground.

***

"Ms Walters, Ms Walters?" Sandra called.

"Yes Sandra, how was the holiday? Did you all have a good time? I got your postcard. It looked a lovely place," Ms Walters said.

"Yes, we all had a great time, but there was something I wanted to ask you," Sandra said.

"Oh?" Ms Walters said.

"Yes Ms Walters, it's about Josephine."

"Oh, OK, please come into my office then and shut the door behind you, thank you, Sandra." Ms Walters showed Sandra into her office and Sandra closed the door.

"What can I do for you?" asked Ms Walters.

"Well, something happened on holiday and we were a little concerned. We went to the beach and the girls were playing sandcastles; well kingdoms really and Alison and Josephine were making a big royal castle and then Alison suggested building a moat, so we explained what a moat was and…well, it just went from there really," Sandra whispered.

"What went from there?" Ms Walters looked puzzled.

"Well, Josephine had said that she had been hurt by someone bad and a moat kept all of the bad people who can hurt you away. Then that evening, it all kicked off! Kim had mentioned her brother Jimmy, who is at Denham House, but Josephine heard the name Jimmy and was trying to tell the girls about Jimmy her uncle and Kim came looking for me, whilst Josephine was sobbing uncontrollably, but she couldn't get her words out.

"Once I got there, Celia took the other girls to the other bedroom, but then went downstairs to see Rose."

"Rose?" Ms Walters interrupted.

"Oh, Rose was our host at the bed and breakfast, it was her establishment. Anyway, she sent up milk and sandwiches which we thought may calm Josephine down, which it did. But it was a very emotional experience for her and the rest of the party of girls and Celia.

"The thing is, Ms Walters, why did none of us know anything about this before us taking her and the other children away? None of the staff was prepared for this and actually, I don't feel that's very fair," she added.

Ms Walters was quiet for a few minutes and then she spoke.

"Actually Sandra, I had meant to tell you about this, but with so much going on, it just simply slipped my mind," she replied.

"I am sorry, Ms Walters, but that isn't good enough. We had to deal with a situation none of us was prepared for and we dealt with it the best way we could. Also, Josephine now has the other girls knowing that she was removed from her family, which, you know as well as I do, we do not encourage for the children to talk about their backgrounds and the reasons of them coming to Craven House," Sandra added.

"Sandra, have you finished? I'm well aware of the rules at Craven House and the other houses as well. It was a mistake and I'm sorry. I didn't mean to keep you and the other staff in the dark, but it happened.

"If you could call on Celia, Roger and George to come to my office we can discuss this. There are still Michelle, John, Anita, and Joe who can look after the children. Then once we have discussed this, I will then tell the other members of staff, so they are all up to date on this situation," Ms Walters said.

"Sandra, I would like to remind you that you are still on a temporary contract and if you speak to me like that again with that tone of voice, you will be dismissed. Have I made myself clear?"

"Yes, you have made yourself crystal clear, Ms Walters!" Sandra said.

Sandra got up from Ms Walters desk and office and went to fetch the other members of staff. Sandra had also told the staff that Ms Walters had threatened her with the sack if she spoke out of turn again.

On arrival to Ms Walters office, Sandra knocked on the door.

Ms Walters was sitting at her desk with a file opened.

"Come in, come in, please sit down. Now, I have just heard from Sandra what happened over the holiday with Josephine. Firstly, I apologise for not telling you before, but I didn't think anything would crop up about it, but it did," Ms Walters started.

"Now, as you are aware, Josephine was brought to us just under a year ago. She was a quiet little girl as she still is. Her mum and dad didn't notice anything until the father caught his brother in the act, so to speak. Now, by the sounds of it, she has told you everything, but there is some information that Josephine doesn't have and that's it's not the first time her uncle was accused of doing this sort of thing. He had also been abusing a local girl and again he got caught, but there wasn't enough evidence to prosecute and he got away with it."

The four staff looked at each other, shocked.

"Also, Josephine doesn't know that when she came to us at Craven House, her mother was in the early stages of pregnancy and she now has a little brother, who is now six months old. Her family want her back, but the State has refused. They are keeping an eye on both of the parents and the baby boy."

"But that is not to say they will not continue trying to get her back. Now, Josephine has no idea about her brother, and you cannot tell her under any circumstances," Ms Walters said, looking directly at Sandra.

"It would only upset her and give her false hope. So, we have to keep it to ourselves. Does anyone have any questions?"

George put his hand up. "Yes I do, Ms Walters. Firstly, how long have you known this information and secondly, why were none of the staff informed?" George asked. He was quite annoyed by this new information.

"As the director of this home, I have been kept in the loop for a little while now, as I am with all of the children and what goes on with the outside part of their lives. I have been too busy to get all of this information together in time for your trip," she replied.

"I'm sorry, Ms Walters, but we all should have known about this from day one. Not because of a situation that arose whilst we were away—and I may add, the female staff dealt with this situation very delicately and professionally—

146

however, they may have been able to handle it differently if they had known what was going on before the trip," George said.

"And, I might add, as staff, that tells me that you don't trust us with delicate information. Which I am deeply upset by and feel that we have been let down by you. Is there anything else we need to know about this situation as I have work to do?" George snapped.

Ms Walters was shocked by George's outburst.

"No, that's all for now, thank you. If you could inform the other members of staff to come into my office and I will relay the same information to them, thank you," she added.

Sandra spoke to the other members of staff, telling them to go and see Ms Walters.

George, Roger, Sandra and Celia, all went along to the kitchen.

"Where are the children?" Sandra asked.

"They're all in their rooms, relaxing," Celia said.

"Well, I am bloody angry with what has just happened, aren't you also?" George said.

"I don't think she has a bloody clue about how to deal with us and these kids, she just wants to have all the information and tell us nothing until something occurs and then we have to deal with it. I'm not happy about it and I'm sorry but I'm reporting her. She doesn't deserve this job. We can do it with our bloody eyes shut and our hands tied behind our backs," he added.

"And how do you think the other staff will feel when they realise that SHE has been withholding information about the kids? They are going to be furious because this could have easily been them dealing with this if the children chose the other holiday," George was fuming.

"George is right, how dare she keep that information to herself! It's us who deal with the kids. We should know just as much as her. We deal with them on a day to day basis, she doesn't! She just sits in her office looking pretty," Roger said. "I think George has a point, I think she should be reported. If we all do it, then they have to take notice of it."

"She has already threatened me, saying that I am on a temporary contract and if I speak to her again as I did. All I did was tell her how it was, and she said she would dismiss me," Sandra said.

"Well, she can't, she doesn't have the final say, she may be the boss here, but not the boss of the Children's Homes; that's the council," Celia said.

"I thought she had the final say in everything?" Sandra asked.

"No, this is run by the council. She's just in charge of this home, thankfully, not the other three," George replied. "I'm going to put in a complaint about her first thing on Monday as it's shut over the weekend."

The others nodded in agreement, the three of them looked at Sandra, who then also nodded in agreement.

"Also, you can tell them that she threatened you with the sack, after all, you were only asking her what was going on and why didn't we have that information."

The four staff agreed and went staff went about their duties. Half an hour later, Michelle came looking for Sandra to see what went on.

"Ms Walters told us about Josephine and what happened on holiday and that she had forgotten to let you know what had happened to Josephine," Michelle said.

"Oh, she said a lot more than that, Michelle!" Sandra started. "She told me if I spoke to her like that again, she would dismiss me, reminding me that I was on a temporary contract," Sandra told her.

Michelle stood there with her mouth open.

"What did the others say?" Sandra asked.

"Well, we were all shocked, as you can imagine. We hadn't expected anything like that, but also, you had to deal with it, and she did praise you and Celia," Michelle said.

"Shame she didn't do that while we were in there getting a right telling off!" Sandra trailed off.

"The others want to report her, as they say she's incompetent for doing the job, withholding information that's crucial to the children," Sandra said.

"They're not wrong, Sandra. She's only got away with it because she's in charge. Will you put in a report or complaint about her?" Michelle asked.

"I'm not sure yet," Sandra said.

***

Sandra was sorting out the children's clean washing when Joe and John came up to her, they asked her about the meeting they had had with Ms Walters that afternoon, they also suggested she should put a complaint about her on Monday, because it looked as though she didn't trust her staff with delicate information.

148

On Sunday, the staff all put their complaints in writing. Ms Walters was going to be away in meetings that day anyway, which made it easier on the staff to get their letters in the post box on Monday. It wouldn't be any good doing it over the phone; they would need hard evidence and in writing.

The staff took it in turns to keep an eye on the children and get their letters written, so everyone had a chance to concentrate on both jobs. Thankfully, with the staff getting on with their work and letters, the children didn't seem to notice anything going on. It was a normal Sunday and once everyone had had breakfast, the children going to Eastbourne were starting their packing to go away in the morning.

Some of the older children who went away to Margate, offered a helping hand, as their holiday had been brought forward by a week due to overbooking. They wanted to make sure that the children took a jumper or a cardigan, as it could still get quite cold by the seaside. The other children were happy with the extra help and it meant that everyone was bonding once again over the holidays.

Michelle had checked on Sandra and Celia to see if they had completed their letters.

"Yes, just finished!" Sandra said.

"Do you think we can get these in the post box tonight before supper? That way Ms Walters won't be here until the morning and the evidence will already be gone," Michelle said.

"Good thinking, Batman!" George said.

George scooped up the rest of the letters, checking they all had stamps on them.

"Back in a few minutes," he said as he headed out of the front door.

George was back in no time, the staff had already left the office and headed off to the kitchen to check if lunch was nearly ready. It was nearly 2 pm, and yes, lunch was nearly ready, so they started to go up and call the children for lunch.

They started knocking on the doors of the children to let them know lunch was ready and to go and wash their hands and faces ready to come down for their meal. They all tucked into roast chicken with various vegetables. You wouldn't have known that these kids hadn't seen each other for a week.

The chatter was busy as the children going away the next day were excited that they were having a holiday.

Once lunch was over, Roger asked if any of the children who were going away had packed their suitcases? If they had, did they want him and George to collect them and put them in reception. The children who had packed, put up their hands. The staff helped the ones who hadn't packed.

Once all the suitcases were in the room behind the reception, the staff said that the children going away tomorrow would have to have early baths, so they could get in their night things and then watch TV. The children who had just come back would be able to bathe at roughly their normal time.

Once everyone was in night things and able to watch a bit of TV, time was moving on and before they knew it, it was time for bed. The children all went up to their bedrooms.

Alison and Josephine went up to their bedroom, quite pleased with themselves that they had helped the other little girls get their packing done for their adventure of a holiday.

***

Josephine and Alison woke to lots of noise in the hallway and running in and out of the rooms. It was like a herd of elephants going past! Both girls got up out of bed and opened their doors to see what was going on.

It was just the children going on holiday running around. They were excited and making much more noise than normal. Once everyone was having breakfast it started to settle down. Once breakfast was over and everyone going away was brushing teeth, the rest of the children stayed in the dining room so not to get in the way of everyone else.

Soon it was time for the children and staff going away on holiday to meet in reception to await Ted and his coach.

Ted sounded his horn.

"Right, come on, you lot, let's get on this coach!" John said.

The children started to move forward to get onto the coach. Roger and George helped with the luggage and the rest of the children and staff stood at the top of the steps and waved at the children on the coach.

"Good luck with the letters!" John whispered to Sandra.

"I don't think we will hear anything just yet, maybe when we get back?" John added.

Sandra nodded and hurried John onto the coach.

With a final wave to the coach, it disappeared around the corner. The remaining staff and children went back into the home and shut the door behind them.

***

Ms Walters wasn't there to see the children off, but the staff weren't too bothered as they felt a little uncomfortable with what they had done, and it was better that she wasn't there to see their guilty faces.

Ms Walters wasn't there actually for the next couple of days as she had back to back meetings with one thing and another, which the staff were grateful, as the tensions between the staff and their boss were at breaking point.

The children had been away for about three days before she made an appearance. As George had said earlier, they could do the jobs with their hands behind their backs. Everything was running as normal as always; apart from looking pretty to the bosses in charge, what was she actually there for?

The staff at Craven House received a postcard from the staff and children from their holiday saying they were having a fabulous time. The weather was great, and everyone was enjoying themselves. The week had gone really quick, the children who had stayed behind had a great week, doing stuff at the home, crafting activities and colouring in when the weather wasn't very nice.

With fewer people there, there wasn't as much to do, so the staff had lots of fun times with the children, like playing hide and seek, but only when Ms Walters wasn't there. They didn't want her complaining that they were too loud and making too much noise around the building.

Before they knew it, the children were back from their holiday. This time Ms Walters was back to welcome the children home.

"Hello children, hello children! Did you have a good time?" she asked.

The staff all looked at each other.

The children went into the building and John collared Roger and asked if they had heard anything yet from the council.

"Not yet John, but I don't think it will be long before we do," Roger replied.

"What makes you say that?" John asked.

"Well, yesterday she came in and shut the door to her office, she looked a little uncomfortable. Every time her phone went, she jumped!" Roger said.

"That means nothing," John replied.

"Wait and see next week," Roger said.

Roger had been right; Ms Walters had received a letter from the board of trustees saying that they wanted to meet with her urgently the following week, but they didn't give any information as to why, just that it was important.

Ms Walters had been wracking her brains all day and couldn't think why the board of trustees had wanted to see her urgently. They gave no inclination in their letter as to why.

No, it couldn't be about that, her staff wouldn't tell tales behind her back. She had already threatened Sandra, but she wouldn't have taken any notice about that. She didn't really mean it; she had just wanted to show Sandra who was the boss. Anyway, she would know soon enough. She was to be at the council on Tuesday morning. She just had to get the weekend out of the way and Monday, but Monday was an easy day, she just had a few phone calls to make about the supplies and orders. Then she could head straight to the council from home.

Once the children had dealt with their luggage and unpacking they headed downstairs to have their snacks, the dining room again was full of chatter about the past week away and what the children had done and how many crabs the boys had managed to catch.

"So, much going on here then?" John asked.

"Not really, just what I said earlier," Roger replied. "She had a letter on Friday and has been a bit weird, but that's all. I suppose we will know what's going on soon enough," Roger told John.

The children finished their food and cleared up after themselves and then left the dining room.

"Let's just get on with the job in hand and worry about the rest later on, OK?" Roger said as he was pushing his chair in under the table and then left the dining room.

Everyone got on with the normal stuff that they do at the weekend, so spirits were high amongst the children and staff as they carried on as usual. The staff knew that Ms Walters had a meeting on Tuesday but didn't know that it was to see the trustees as she had numerous meetings most weeks, so they weren't aware that she had already been called in to see them.

***

152

Once Sunday and Monday were over, Tuesday was now looming closer than ever and it seemed to get here as soon as possible.

Ms Walters got up early. She showered and pulled out a navy-blue suit, with a white frilly blouse. It wasn't the sort of thing she would normally wear for work or a meeting, but she felt that this was important, and she had to show a good impression.

It wasn't far to the council offices, but Ms Walters drove in her car. She didn't want to be late by going by public transport. She didn't have to be there until 10.30 am, so she gave herself plenty of time by leaving a little early.

There was little traffic and she pulled up outside the offices at 10.10 am. She locked her car door and made her way inside the building.

"Ms Christine Walters; I have an appointment with Mr Dunn at 10.30 am," she told the receptionist.

"OK, that's fine. If you would like to take a seat, Ms Walters, I will let Mr Dunn know that you're here," the receptionist said.

Christine Walters took her seat in the waiting area. It wasn't very busy at this time of the morning, so she didn't have long to wait.

"Ms Walters here to see you, Sir. Very well, I will tell her," the receptionist said into the phone. "Ms Walters, Mr Dunn knows you're here and will be with you shortly."

"Thank you," Ms Walters replied.

It felt like ages before Ms Walters was called, but at 10.30 am prompt, a lady came over to her.

"Ms Walters? I'm Miss Temple, Mr Dunn's secretary, would you follow me please?"

Ms Walters got up from her seat and followed Miss Temple along the corridor and waited patiently at the lift. When the lift came Miss Temple pressed two for the second floor.

When they got out of the lift, they turned left and then left again and Miss Temple knocked on a door on the right.

"Enter!" Came the reply from the other side of the door.

Miss Temple opened the door and ushered Ms Walters into the office.

It was quite a big room, and at the end of it was a long desk with four people sitting behind it. Ms Walters was shown a seat in front of the desk so she would be facing Mr Dunn, who seemed to be chairing the meeting.

"Good morning, Ms Walters, these are my colleagues, Thomas Tucker, Angela Maurice and James Pendle," Mr Dunn said.

"Please, call me Christine," Ms Walters replied.

"No, Ms Walters is better I think, don't you?" Mr Dunn said sternly, "as we are here on official business."

Ms Walters swallowed hard; now she realised what this was about.

"We have had several letters of complaint regarding a situation that happened on a recent trip with staff and one of your children at Craven House," Mr Dunn said, looking down at his notepad.

"We understand that the incident that had happened, on a trip to the beach, where a child started revealing information that not only the staff didn't know about, but now also the other children are sadly aware of. Now I would have thought, as the senior member of staff at Craven House, you would inform your staff of any events that had taken place before the trip. Had this been the case, your staff would have been aware of this information regarding this child," Mr Dunn looked over his glasses at Ms Walters, then continued.

"Thankfully, your staff handled the situation very delicately and sensitively and the children also were exemplary. Could you please give us your take on this situation, Ms Walters?" asked Mr Dunn.

"Firstly, I would like to apologise, my staff should have spoken to me regarding this situation and their concerns. I had spoken with them the day they returned from the Margate trip," Ms Walters said.

"And yet, you said to one member of staff that she was only on a temporary contract and if she spoke to you with insolence again, she would no longer be working in her current position; is that right, Ms Walters?" replied Mr Dunn.

"I never used those words, Mr Dunn."

"No, but you implied them with your authority," retorted Mr Dunn.

"I'm sorry, I didn't mean to do that. I had spoken with the staff on their return, where this incident was brought to my attention. I did have the information in the little girl's file, but I hadn't had the chance to share it with my staff," Ms Walters replied. She was getting nervous now. Not only had she abused her position by threatening a member of staff for insolence, she had withheld relevant information from her staff. Christine knew she was in for it now.

"Ms Walters, what do you think should happen now?"

"Erm, I'm afraid I don't really know. I have never been in this situation before."

"Right, I think we should have a break for fifteen minutes. If you would like to wait outside, Ms Walters, there is a coffee machine, and we will call you when we have discussed this matter further," Mr Dunn said.

Christine got up from her seat and she left the office. She got herself a cup and sat down. She was going over and over it in her mind. Why hadn't her staff come to her with their concerns with how she had dealt with this? But they had, right at the beginning, and she had used her authority to throw down Sandra's comments.

She hadn't dealt with this very well and her staff had gone over her head and really, who can blame them?

She thought she was better than them, she was in charge, she was the boss. But it wasn't true. Her staff could run that place with their eyes shut and she knew it. They had had to deal with a difficult situation with no knowledge of it. She was going to apologise to Sandra when she got back to the office today, she thought.

"Ms Walters, you can go back in now," Miss Temple said.

Christine stood up. She left the coffee on the table and smoothed down her skirt and followed Miss Temple inside the office.

Mr Dunn motioned for her to sit down again.

"Ms Walters, we have thought about this long and hard and we feel that there is only one way to deal with this and that is to remove you completely from Craven House. Nothing would be gained by letting you go back to work there, and as you have already had a complaint about using your authority over your staff, you will no longer have their respect in our care homes."

Christine felt the blood drain from her face.

"We need respect for the people in charge and the staff who work in our homes. Everyone from the cleaner, the kitchen staff to the executive manager, everyone is important and deserves respect," Mr Dunn said sternly. "I suggest if you have any belongings at your office, we can forward them onto your address."

Christine's head was in a spin! She couldn't believe what had just happened! She had been sacked! Lost her job of almost eight years as executive manager, and all because of withholding information.

"So, you're sacking me?" She stood up, incredulous at the thought. "I have worked for this council, for Craven House, for eight years and now because I have made one mistake, you're pushing me out? This isn't on!" Christine shouted.

"Yes Ms Walters, you're fired. You had privileged information of a highly sensitive nature that you withheld from the very people who were looking after a vulnerable child. Your staff were put in a very difficult position because of your arrogance and to feel your need of a higher authority. This situation could have ended very differently if the staff were armed with this information," Mr Dunn said.

"Thankfully, they could deal with it and very carefully I might add, but they wouldn't have had to, had you been honest with them in the first place. So, yes, I'm afraid to say, you are sacked. I do hope that you do not apply for any jobs in this field as I wouldn't like to refuse a reference. Your replacement will be at Craven House later on today. Thank you, and good day," Mr Dunn said as he tidied the letters on his desk into a neat pile.

Christine was furious! She thought she might get a slap on the knuckles or a warning, but to get sacked! Unbelievable! She was already standing outside her car, she put the key in and just sat there. What on earth was she going to do now? This was all she knew about, office work in the public sector.

***

At Craven House, Michelle had just taken a call at the office to say that Ms Walters would no longer be working at Craven House and her replacement, a Mr John Duffy, would be there later on that afternoon.

Michelle went along to the staff room to tell the staff.

"She's gone!" Michelle said.

"Who's gone?" Roger asked.

"Ms Walters, she's been sacked; her replacement Mr John Duffy will be here later on today!" They all sat there in shock.

"Well, she deserved it! You don't withhold information from the people you work with!" Sandra said.

Chapter 9

Mr Duffy settled in well at Craven House. It was like he had always worked there. He got on well with the staff. When he started and the children were at school, he called a meeting with the staff and to let them know that, even though he was new to Craven House, he wanted things to continue how they were. He wasn't going to make any new changes and that included the staff. They all had safe and secure jobs, but he would be open with his staff.

He had heard what had happened with his predecessor and he wasn't about to make the same mistake. He had been doing the job for too long. He had worked in a children's home at another end of the country and left with glowing references, but this was too good an opportunity to miss.

He did ask his staff if there were any suggestions they wanted to put forward, he would listen and look at them and see if it would be viable to make necessary changes, but this would only come from the staff.

Life ticked along nicely at Craven House and everyone was still happy enough the management had changed nothing else had. All the kids like Mr Duffy, so did the staff. He had a warm nature about him, and the staff said he was much more approachable than Ms Walters ever was. He didn't look down his nose at you.

Everyone was already back at school and looking forward to the half-term break, which was great because then it would be Halloween and then Bonfire Night the next week, then it was Christmas.

Alison and Tom used to love Christmas at home, but this was their first one away, but judging how they celebrated the kids' birthdays, they were excited about Christmas at Craven House.

***

Both of the other holidays had been and gone and now it was a countdown to Christmas. The staff had a meeting. They had been given quite a bit of money for the children for Christmas presents. The staff were writing their lists of gifts. Sandra and Roger had been looking. It was now time for them both to decide what to get Alison and Tom for Christmas.

Tom was really easy to buy for and Roger wrote Matchbox, Hot Wheels cars and an electric car racing set, down on his list. He would be able to play with Freddie and the staff. They also got him a Tonka truck and a cowboy outfit. They were getting Freddie an Indian outfit, so they could play dress up together. Freddie was also getting a Batman figure and the six-million-dollar man figure.

Tom and Freddie had just started watching it on TV and loved it. There were another few items on the boys' list, including a new teddy bear, also a couple of items of clothes and a pair of new pyjamas.

Now it was Alison's turn. They wrote down an Easy Bake Oven, a Barbie doll, a Spirograph, a pair of roller skates; even though she had never used them, they had so much space outside, she could learn. They added the Bionic Woman figure and its accessories, Gramma Rag Doll, some smaller toys and a new teddy bear.

Alison was also getting a couple of clothes and new pyjamas.

Every child who had their first Christmas at the home got a new teddy bear. They found that it could be very therapeutic to have something to cuddle up to in bed when they got upset and something they could tell all their troubles to.

"Right, that's my list complete for Alison, who's next on the list?" Sandra asked.

"Well, I have just finished Tom's and Freddie's, so it's now the bigger boys for me," Roger said.

"Well, I've now done Josephine's as well, so I think I may have a cup of tea, anyone want one?" asked Sandra.

A few people said yes. They were in the staffroom and the kids were at school, so they could talk freely about their gifts.

"Do you think Alison and Tom will be OK this Christmas?" Sandra asked.

"Yes, they will be fine. Have they mentioned anything about it or home at all?" asked Roger.

"No, they haven't said anything, but I don't think they will, they know us well enough now to talk to us if they need to," replied Sandra.

"The thing is, Roger, when we get all of these presents, where on earth are we going to hide them?" Sandra said.

It was now only four weeks to Christmas. June, who worked in the kitchen, was getting ready with ordering the turkeys from the butchers. She had to get six turkeys for the whole of Christmas. It may sound a lot, but there were thirty children and at least ten staff, that was a lot of mouths to feed for two days. Added to this, the shops weren't open between Christmas and New year, so they had to really stock up.

They always got the biggest turkeys though and cooked two for Christmas day, two for Boxing day and then the last two for New Year's day. Thankfully, June was able to get two of the men to help with the shopping. They went with the home's van. The men would push the trolleys around and June would put in what she needed. and they would help pack it up once it had been through the till at the other end.

Tesco's was down the high street, so they used to get a lot of it from there, but she liked getting the turkeys from the butcher's, telling Mr Duffy, they are fresher than in the shops. Mr Duffy didn't like to get on the wrong side of June, otherwise his dinner plate wouldn't be piled up, so he let her have a free reign over the shopping, especially as it was his first Christmas there too.

They stocked up on chocolates, After Eight Mints, Turkish Delight, a tin or four of roses chocolates. They would be home for a long time and if children weren't entertained, they would eat and eat. Not that anyone ever complained, but they didn't want to give the children rotten teeth! Soft drinks, including, Coke, lemonade, and fruit juices were all locked away in a cupboard in the kitchen and June had the key and wouldn't be parted from it.

The kids were also busy as school, rehearsing their Christmas plays. The school put on two plays on two consecutive evenings: one for the younger ones and the others for the older children. Alison was in the second evening, and as so many of the children went to that school anyway, two members of staff would go and watch them. That way the children felt that they were being supported, even though it was by the home and not their parents.

That was important to the staff at the home. They always wanted to make sure the children felt like they belonged there, not just tossed over on a heap. All of the children felt that they should be there, and it was great for bonding between the children.

The staff wanted to put up a Christmas tree in the corner of the dining room. June said it would be OK, as long as it wasn't in the way and the kids could decorate it.

"Yes, that would be great June, thank you," the children said, kissing her on the cheek.

"Get away with you now, I have things to make and bake." June laughed.

June was a fantastic cook. She made lovely apple pies, but also great chicken pies. There wasn't anything she couldn't turn her hand too.

So, they had an artificial tree in the dining room and a big real one in reception and a big real one in the living room. They couldn't fit all of the children's toys under the tree, or the dayroom or the living room, as there wasn't enough room. Someone suggested leaving them at the end of the children's beds, but on the floor, so they wouldn't be kicked off in the night or morning and broken.

***

The kids had had their plays at school, their Christmas dinner, and their parties, so their final day had come around so quickly.

They went shopping on Saturday after they had broken up for the Christmas holidays, so that they could all get one new outfit to wear on Christmas day.

The clothes they received for Christmas, could be a new jumper or skirt or jeans, something practical, but this shopping trip would be for something special.

They all lined up with Sandra and George, Roger and Celia and went along to the high street. Woolworths was always a great favourite. They always had nice clothes in there. All the children had nice shoes, so they would just get the outfit—dress or two pieces depending on what they liked.

Alison liked the dresses, but she wasn't too sure about the colour, it was green.

"But Alison, green and red are Christmas colours, so have a look at it up against you," Celia suggested.

She picked out her size with Celia's help and did just that in the mirror. Celia found her the red, but that made her look too washed out. Celia then handed her a darker red.

"Now that looks much better, Alison. Do you like it?"

160

She did. She had cream tights already and some shiny shoes that would look lovely with it.

"Yes, I do, Celia. Can I have that one please?" Alison asked. Celia took the dress from her and put it in the basket.

"Now, let's see what we can get Tom."

He already had a few shirts, that he didn't wear too often. Celia spotted a dark green tank top that he could wear with his shirt and there were some lovely corduroy trousers to go with it. Celia got his size out and put them up in the air to see how they would look. They looked really well together.

"Tom, come here a minute, I just want to see what these would look like for you?" She asked him.

Tom moved over to Celia and she put them up against him.

"Have a look in the mirror, do you like it?"

"Yes, it looks lovely, what do you think, Al?" Tom asked, looking for her approval.

"Tom, you look so handsome, I think you should get it," Alison said.

"Well, that was easy!" Celia said.

She looked around for Sandra, who was dealing with one of the other girls, who wanted a bit more expensive dress and shoes. Sandra told her no.

"It has to be a dress or a two-piece, no shoes as you all have enough."

The girl wasn't too happy, but she decided on a dress.

Sandra looked at her.

"Look Lucy, I am sorry, but we have our lists for everyone, and we have a lot of children to buy for, but if you're all good, we can for a Wimpy afterwards," Sandra smiled.

The rest of the shopping trip went quite smoothly after that. Thank goodness they were only taking this lot out for the morning and lunchtime. The other members of staff were doing the afternoon shopping.

Mr Duffy had given them their allotted money for the clothes trip, but added something else on, to get them lunch also. That was something Ms Walters never did. She was supposed to give the staff money to do things like this once in a while, as there was money available to spend on the children.

Sandra, Celia, Roger and George were scratching their heads about this. There was a lot more that Ms Walters hadn't done, now she was sacked they had found out how little she did do there, mainly sitting in her office but attending meetings that she had to turn up to at the council. The staff were unaware of what she actually did. They didn't think she stole the money, but she didn't think of using it for the children, she had just left it in the safe on the premises.

When Mr Duffy opened it up with the key, he was flabbergasted at to what he found. He called Sandra and Roger into the office. They had no idea it was there, but he had to report it to Mr Dunn, who was delighted that he had, because they never had any slips saying what the money had been spent on. Mr Dunn told them to spend it on the children whenever they saw fit and even if that included lunch on a shopping trip, so be it.

Mr Dunn had been in the job for years and loved what he did. He didn't like members of staff thinking they were above the job that they did, which is exactly what Christine Walters had done. Mr Dunn knew that by sacking her earlier in the year that he had done the right thing.

He had heard about John Duffy through one of his colleagues and knew he could be trusted to fulfil the position and do an excellent job. Whenever they needed anything Mr Dunn would always do what he could for the staff and more importantly the kids. It wasn't their faults that they had ended up there in these places, but he wanted to make sure they felt included, part of the family and if they had to go up to the schools to sort out a problem, they would go gladly. That is why Mr Dunn, was really annoyed when Ms Walters kept relevant information about a child away from the other staff. That's not how you have the trust of your team, your workforce, who are a surrogate family for these children, especially if they have had a bad start in life. Which to be honest, most of them had had.

***

The children left Woolworths and waited for everyone to gather. They always had to do a headcount whenever they went out, to make sure nobody was left behind. Nobody was. Celia and Roger had made sure they rounded everyone up.

They went along to Wimpy and went straight to the back where it was empty. Alison and Tom had had Wimpy before. Just before Alison's birthday. They were looking for something for Alison to wear and they wanted to kill some time so the others could decorate the room for a party.

They put their orders in for what they wanted to eat. Sandra and George sat with one group and Celia and Roger sat with the other. Everyone was starving.

They mainly ordered burgers and chips, with either a milkshake or a coke. Their drinks came and then their food and everyone tucked into it.

"Well, that's lunch taken care of," George said.

"Yes, well, June will be pleased; if everyone eats out, it means she can start sorting out dinner for tonight," George said.

"Oh, you mean thing, George! You make June sound like she is an ogre!" Sandra laughed.

"Not quite an ogre…but she does scare me sometimes," George replied.

"Why, what makes you say that?" asked Sandra.

"She can be a bit bossy, that's all," George said.

"No, she's not, George, she just likes her kitchen and store cupboards in order, that's all. She loves the kids. I haven't ever heard her say anything horrible to any of them, let alone shout at them," Sandra said, still sipping on her milkshake.

When everyone had finished their food, they went back out. It was rather cold, so they all wrapped up, pulled their coats in tighter. Thank goodness they hadn't had snow yet.

They got back to the home and bumped into the afternoon lot on their way back.

"Been to the Wimpy?" Michelle asked.

"Yes, it was lovely and empty in there," replied George.

They carried on. The other group were going to eat first, otherwise when they got back, dinner would be ready, and they would have already eaten.

Everyone stamped their feet on the mat when they got in. It had started to rain, so they walked upstairs, took their boots, and coats off at the top and their coats and put them on the hooks provided so they could dry.

They were all carrying their bags with their new things in them.

Alison and Josephine took theirs upstairs and hung them straight up. Alison was really pleased with her new dress. Jo had picked up a navy blue one, which looked beautiful on her.

They went to find Tom and Freddie. They were in their bedroom playing with their cars.

Thankfully, the staff picked up their Christmas presents for the kids and had them wrapped and hidden before they had all packed up for the holidays. Alison and Josephine went along to the living room to see what was on TV. Mary

Poppins had just started. With Christmas Eve only a couple of days away, the TV was better than normal.

Both girls got comfortable on one of the sofas and settled down to watch the movie. When something good was on the television, they would close the curtains and it would feel like being at the cinema. There were only two other girls watching the film with Alison and Josephine, but they enjoyed it just the same.

When it had finished it was nearly dinnertime and even though they had been to Wimpy that afternoon, they were still rather hungry. They called in on Tom and Freddie who weren't in their room, but already sitting in the dining room waiting for their food. This evening it was steak pie, chips and peas or beans, followed by jelly and custard for dessert. They all tucked into their dinner. Just before they started eating, the other group had just got back from shopping. They had to leg it upstairs and then back down again.

Once dinner was completely finished, and the tables were all cleared and clean, they all went upstairs, to get bathed, or get into their night things. Some bathed on a Saturday and some on a Sunday. Alison had already had a brief shower that morning, but Tom and Freddie had to be thrown in otherwise they would never get in there.

When they had finished their homework and chores, Tom and Freddie only ever played with their cars. Once they had changed into their nightclothes, they either stayed in their rooms or went to the living room to watch TV. Alison and Josephine stayed in their bedroom until they were tired.

***

The next day was Sunday and they didn't have to do much on a Sunday as most of it had already been done the day before.

Alison and Josephine had already bought their Christmas presents. The staff always told them that if they wanted to get any of their friends or substitute sisters or brothers gifts, they could, but not to buy the staff, otherwise it would get out of control. Christmas cards, yes, but not presents.

Sunday came and went and now it was Christmas Eve, which was a wonderful day, as the kids could help with some of the baking and decorating the Christmas cakes. June made lovely chocolate logs from chocolate Swiss roll and chocolate butter icing, then would sieve icing sugar over to make it look like snow.

The children liked getting involved with Christmas and decorating stuff. The tree had been decorated in the dayroom, the living room, reception and now a smaller one in the dining room.

Sandra and George took a couple of the kids out to pick up a couple of things that had been forgotten about like brandy sauce and custard, not all of the kids liked brandy sauce. Sandra picked up ten packets and two tubs of powdered custard, that way they should have enough. She also picked up some more mince pies. June already had lots of boxes, but you can never have enough.

Sandra and George were only out for a little while, it was going to be fish and chips for dinner, so they didn't want to be late back. The kids who were helping June had to be finished so everything was done, and the kitchen and dining room was completely clean.

Before they knew it, it was already five pm. June had started on cooking the fish and had the potatoes peeled and sliced. Michelle came and gave her a hand. Things were settling down and the kids were either still wrapping up their presents or watching TV. Tom and Freddie asked Roger for some help to wrap up their presents.

Alison and Josephine had wrapped theirs up the other night. They were both excited, as were Tom and Freddie. Half an hour later, Sandra all called the children down for dinner, but they weren't going to be eating off plates, but newspaper; how they used to years ago.

There were salt and vinegar on the table, but they also had pickled onions and gherkins as well. Just like a proper fish and chip shop.

If one of the staff had gone to the fish shop and got it for everyone, it would have been stone cold by the time they got it all back. This was the next best thing. Everyone was so excited. Every year they tried to do something different.

This year it was a fish and chip shop, some of the staff even made a 'June's Fish Shop' sign, which went down well with the kids.

When they had finished their dinners, they went upstairs to get bathed and showered. They all had a new pair of pyjamas to wear for Christmas eve and they watched It's a Wonderful Life; everyone enjoyed it. The living room was covered with people.

"Bodies everywhere!" Sandra said.

There was no room for anyone.

"Come on you lot, time's getting on. If you don't get to bed, a certain Father Christmas won't be coming if you don't go to bed to sleep, come on," George said.

The children knew that he was teasing them, but they did want him to put them all to bed.

Christmas morning was going to be a busy one. Everyone followed everyone else, and one by one they left the hallway.

"Sandra, can you hear that?" Roger asked.

"No, what?"

"Silence in the halls!" Roger laughed.

"Roger, you're nuts!" She laughed.

They went up and checked the children were all in bed, but not asleep yet, they were still talking and chatting. Within the next hour, the staff went around again and, apart from the odd child, they were all asleep.

Alison and Josephine were fast asleep, Tom and Freddie, also fast asleep. The staff went back downstairs to make a hot drink, they had needed this little break. It had been a busy day, well busy since the kids packed up from school. They hadn't stopped. They all opted for tea.

A little while later on, Alison and Josephine's bedroom door opened. A pile of gifts was put at the bottom of Alison and then Josephine's bed. Then the door closed and then on to the next room. It didn't take long to distribute gifts to all of the children's beds then the staff went to bed once they'd checked on everyone.

***

The next morning, Alison screamed with delight, waking Josephine up.

She could see something on the floor, by her bed, but she could see clearly at the bottom of Josephine's bed.

"Josephine, there are presents at the bottom of your bed and some on the floor."

"Yes, and there are some at the bottom of your bed too, Alison," Josephine replied.

"Oh!" They both said and jumped out of bed. These were the presents the children received from the home.

166

Alison started opening hers and Josephine started on hers. The bedroom door burst open.

"Happy Christmas, Alison and Josephine!" Tom shouted.

Tom and Freddie were so excited that they had a pile of presents to open.

They came into the girls' bedroom.

"Happy Christmas, Tom and Freddie!" Alison and Josephine both said.

"Did you get what you wanted, Tom?" Josephine asked.

"Yes, I did and more. Do you want to see what I couldn't carry with me, Josephine?" Tom said excitedly.

"Can I come and have a look when I've opened my presents?" Josephine said.

"Yes, we'll wait," Tom said.

They didn't take too long opening their gifts, they both 'oohhhed' and 'ahhhhed' at their gifts. They had both gotten what they had wanted and more.

Alison loved her teddy bear. It was light brown and really soft. She put it on top of her pillow.

Once they had both finished, they took the piles off the boys; they looked like their legs were buckling underneath the weight of them. They went back to their room and saw all of the paper all over the floor.

"Come on, let's tidy up this paper. Put it in the corner until someone comes with a black bag," Alison instructed.

The girls put the paper in the corner. Tom and Freddie had their presents on their beds. They were both so excited. They got similar presents but in different colours, so there could be no arguments.

"I'm surprised you're not hungry; you two?" Alison said.

"I knew there was something, Al. I thought I was hungry, but I'm too excited, I think," Tom said.

They all left the boys room and headed down towards the dining room. It was a fry up with toast or boiled egg and toast. Most of the children chose a fry up. The staff were happy with that too. June already had two turkeys in the oven and breakfast on the go at the same time. June was a whizz in the kitchen, and everyone tucked in. The staff enjoyed their tea and coffee too.

It was nearly 10 am already and most of the children had been up before eight. Once breakfast was over, the staff helped clear away the tables. The children were told to go upstairs for a change.

When the dining room was cleared away from breakfast, the staff stayed behind to dress the table for dinner. They put placemats, Christmas crackers, napkins on the table and a couple of centrepieces on each table; one at each end.

When they had finished, they gave June a hand with peeling the potatoes and sorting out the rest of the veg. The stuffing and Yorkshire pudding was made but had to go into the oven to cook properly. Once they had it all under control, the staff left June to it.

They went up to see what the children were doing. They had all washed and brushed their teeth and were all dressed in their new things that they had bought on Saturday. It was lovely having new clothes and an excuse to dress up.

Alison loved her new deep red dress and Josephine loved her navy blue one. They both had cream tights and patent shoes. They looked like they were going to a party or something.

The children were either in their rooms playing with their new toys or watching TV in the living room.

A Merry Morning was on the TV. A celebrity would visit a children's ward for children who were in hospital over Christmas and they would get gifts. In this episode, an entertainer called Leslie Crowther went around the wards giving out gifts, then sang a song.

The children's families would be there. It was a good programme, so between watching TV and playing with their toys, that would be their morning and early into the afternoon their busy time of the day.

"It's lunchtime, kids!" Sandra said.

George went upstairs to check if there were any children up in their room, but no, they had already gone downstairs. Playing with toys can make you hungry.

Michelle and Roger stood at the doors to the dining room. When they knew everyone was there, they opened the doors and all of the kids stood there for a moment. It looked lovely! Everything was decorated in Christmas red and green.

Once they had gotten over the shock of seeing the dining room all decorated for Christmas, they made their way to their seats and waited as normal to have their plates brought over to them. It took a while as there was so much more to go on their plates: stuffing, Yorkshire pudding, roast potatoes, plenty of veg and of course, turkey. As the children and staff tucked into their Christmas dinner, June sat herself next to one of the kids, she gave him a big smile,

"Is that nice, Christopher?" June asked. Christopher had a mouthful of food but nodded yes then gave her a thumbs up. June was pleased; she loved cooking and enjoyed that people, especially the kids, enjoyed her food. It made it all worth the while.

When the dinner was over, the staff cleared away the plates and cutlery. June went back in the kitchen, to start dishing up the dessert.

Sandra and Michelle started to load up the dishwasher; there's no way June could get all of this done quickly. It didn't take long; one scraped the food off and into the bin, the other put it in the dishwasher, which thankfully held a lot of plates and cutlery. Sandra switched it on. It wouldn't be finished by the time they had finished dessert, but they could wash the rest in the sink.

June passed Christmas pudding and custard or brandy sauce through the serving hatch.

Sandra and Michelle started handing out dessert with Roger and George helping out too.

They didn't want the food to get cold.

The pudding was a little too hot, so they started pulling their Christmas crackers. Some of the children struggled as they could be difficult to pull successfully. But they all got a gift and a paper hat and a joke inside. When they had told all of the jokes and stopped laughing, the pudding was warm enough to still eat it without burning their tongues or the roof of their mouths.

They finished their puddings and asked to be excused from the table. They couldn't walk as fast as they did into the dining room; they were all stuffed full of food.

They all went into the living room. *Miracle on 34th Street* was on ITV, but *Billy Smart's Circus* was on BBC1 and then *The Wizard of Oz* was on straight after, so that's what they all opted for.

When the staff came in to check on them, the room was silent, apart from the film on TV. They were so engrossed. When the film finished, it was nearly time for tea.

"Sandra, can we wait a little longer, we're still waiting for our food to go down." One of the older children said.

"Well, it's turkey sandwiches with pickle and pickled onions and June has made a huge chocolate cake if you don't want Christmas cake."

Tom was gone! He headed towards the dining room with Freddie hot on his heels. They both liked chocolate cake, but Christmas cake was a bit too rich for them. Everyone started to follow Tom and Freddie, they didn't want to miss any wonderful things like cakes.

When they had all had their fill of food and drinks, George had asked the kids if they wanted to play any games, but they said that they normally do that on Boxing day, so they went back up to the living room to watch TV.

The Two Ronnie's Christmas Special was on and they all howled with laughter watching it.

It was after nine o'clock when it had finished. It had been a long day. Even though they didn't have school the next day, they had all been up early, so the children who wanted to go to their rooms did so and the older ones were allowed to stay up for a little while longer.

Alison and Josephine walked up the stairs with Tom and Freddie. They said goodnight. They had both enjoyed their first Christmas there. The boys got into their pyjamas and as long as they didn't make too much noise they could stay up for a little while longer. Alison and Josephine said goodnight to the boys, then they made their way up to their bedroom and changed out of their Christmas outfits, put them in the laundry bin and put on their new pyjamas.

"Thanks, Josephine," Alison said.

"What for?" Josephine asked.

"My Christmas present, it was lovely!" Alison replied.

"You're welcome and thank you for mine, I love it!"

Alison had bought her some new hair clips and Alice bands. She had also picked up some new nail polish for her. Josephine had bought Alison a lovely photo frame and put a photo of her and Tom in it. She had had one done for herself too, because they were the nearest thing to siblings she had.

They had put them on their bedside cabinets.

Alison had loved what Tom and Freddie had bought her. She got a vanity set. It had a mirror, a brush, a combe in a lovely gift box. Freddie had bought her a china tea set, which her and Josephine would have plenty of time playing with.

Alison got into bed and was thinking about her day today. It was the first one without her mum and dad and she had hoped that they had a wonderful day as well as her and Tom.

***

Eileen had been staying with her mum since her husband had absconded after trying to kill her at home with the fire. She was still recovering from her injuries. She didn't think she had been injured as badly as she had been. She just hoped her little lambs had had an exciting time wherever they were and that they hadn't missed her too much.

She spent the day with her mum and brothers, who came over when they could. It had been a quiet day. Her mum had cooked, and she wanted to help, but she couldn't stand for too long. The phone had rung. Thinking it was family wishing them good wishes—but it wasn't.

"Eileen, is that you?" John asked on the other end of the line.

"Yes, it's me, John. What do you want?" Eileen asked.

"I just wondered how you were and to see if I could see you?" He asked her.

"No, I don't think that's a good idea, do you? And anyway, the police are still looking for you. Should I tell them that you called me again?" she said as she put the receiver down.

Eileen was sure she heard him call her a bitch.

Her mum came out into the hall.

"Eileen, are you OK? Who was that?"

"It was nobody, Mum. Nobody important," Eileen replied. Because that was how she had come to think of John as—nobody important to her anymore. After what he had done to her and her two little lambs, how could she think of ever seeing him or talking to him again.

Her babies were safe away from him. Even though she had lost them, she was grateful that they wouldn't hurt because of him. He no longer wanted them. She didn't understand why though. He had contacted her and hadn't once asked about the children. But that was the selfish man he was. They were all better off without him. She was trying to rebuild her life without him and sadly without them, but she would see them both one day, she just knew it.

Chapter 10

It had been two and a half years since Alison and Tom arrived at Craven House, and it was coming up to Tom's sixth birthday. The children had both settled in well and had made some great friendships. Their life before Craven House had become something of a blur now; they still remembered their mother and father, but they rarely talked about them.

Some staff had changed since they had started. Mr Duffy had replaced Ms Walters. John had left and had been replaced by Ian and Michelle had left and had been replaced with Rita. Otherwise, Craven House was plodding along nicely.

A few of the older children had left, but that was just to go onto the next step of their circumstances. Some had found flats of their own or had gone to other homes. Some of the children had been adopted. Children were usually fostered first and if it worked out between the family and the child, then they would become adopted. If once a foster placement went ahead and it didn't work out, then the child would come back to the home. In the whole time that Alison and Tom were there, no-one had even looked at them for foster care, let alone adoption. The children were in the care of the State, so if potential parents-to-be wanted to foster them they could.

It was a Monday afternoon, and the children had all just got back from school when Sandra came into talk to Alison. She wanted to know if she and Tom would come down to the sitting room before they washed for dinner.

"Why Sandra? Have we done something wrong?" Alison asked.

"No, no, of course not. I think we just need to have a little chat, that's all. I'll knock for Tom on my way down. Do you want to get changed out of your uniform?" Sandra asked.

"OK, I will be right down then," Alison said.

Alison changed out of her uniform and put on her after school clothes. She hung her uniform up and left her bedroom. Josephine was sitting on her bed

172

reading a comic. On entering the sitting room, Tom was already there sitting on one of the big comfy chairs. He could nearly touch the floor with his feet, but not yet.

"Good, now we can get started," Sandra said. "Now, you have lived here for two and a half years—"

There was a knock at the door.

"Sorry I'm late, Sandra, oh you have started," Roger said.

"Yes, only just," Sandra replied.

"As I was saying, you have been here now for two and a half years and we love you being here, you've settled in very well."

"Are you telling us to leave?" Tom interrupted.

"No, of course not, Tom," Roger said. "It's just that there is a couple who have a little girl and are looking to extend their family—"

"And they want us?" Tom interrupted.

"Erm well, sort of. They want a little boy and a little girl to add to their numbers," Sandra said.

"Well, why don't they have children the normal way?" Alison asked.

"They did have a little girl and there were complications, so they are no longer able to have any more children naturally, but they so much want to meet you both," Sandra said.

"I don't want a new family; I have a family here!" Tom said. "I love it here. Me and Freddie are like brothers and now we have Charlie in our room, I don't want to have a new family, and I already have a sister, Alison, so I don't want another one!" Tom shouted and ran out of the room.

Roger chased after Tom to help console him. Alison stayed with Sandra.

"So, what happens, Sandra, if we meet these people and we don't like them, or they don't like us? Or, what if we like them and they want to foster us and then adopt us? Will we be able to come back here?" She asked.

"That's a lot to take in now, but it will be small steps and we wouldn't do anything that you and Tom didn't want to. These people are nice; they have a daughter who's six years old; the same as Tom. They have a big house with a garden, you would both have your own rooms. I think you will love it," Sandra said with a smile.

"So, have you met them? Have you seen their home?" Alison asked.

"No, but others who have had a look said it's very presentable and they are lovely people. You can both meet them soon, even just for an afternoon; that's if you want to?" Sandra added.

Alison looked as if she was thinking. She and Tom had been so happy here, but maybe it was time they lived with a proper family?

"What are you thinking about, Alison?" Sandra asked.

"Maybe it is time that we moved on with a new family. We no longer have our own family, except the one here that everyone has made home for us both. I just want to get it right in my head to explain it to Tom. I think I need to go and talk to him," Alison said.

With that, Tom and Roger came back into the sitting room.

"Sorry Sandra, I didn't mean to run out, it's just a lot was said," Tom told her.

Sandra put her hand up.

"Tom, it's fine, I didn't mean to upset you, and I know it's a lot to take in. These people want to meet you both, they want to come here and have tea with you both, if that's OK with you?" Sandra added.

"What, with everyone else here?" Tom asked.

"No, they will have tea with you guys but earlier than normal, so there is some privacy away from the other children," Roger explained. "So, would that be OK with both of you? Maybe on Saturday, we can make the arrangements with the Coopers?"

"Coopers? Is that their name?" Tom interrupted again.

"Yes, their names are Harry and Ruth Cooper and their daughter is called Hannah. So, we can arrange for them to come over at four o'clock? Is that OK with both of you?" Roger asked.

Alison looked at Tom and he nodded.

"Yes, that would be fine, Sandra. Is there anything else we need to know about these people, the Coopers?" Alison asked.

"No, I don't think so at the moment, but we will find out what we need by Saturday, is that OK?" Sandra asked.

Sandra and Roger both looked at each other.

"Can we go now please?" Alison asked.

"Yes, Honey, off you go and don't forget to wash before dinner. Which is in about twenty minutes," Sandra replied.

Both of the children left, and Sandra and Roger looked at each other again. They were both very fond of both the children, they didn't expect this to happen. They thought they would be at Craven House until they moved onto the next step, but if they had a chance to live a happy life with a small family, it would make such a difference to them and to be out of the care system, which didn't always work well for later on.

Alison and Tom were walking back slowly to their rooms to mull over what they had just heard.

"Alison, do you want to leave Craven House? Do you want us to live with these people as a family?" Tom asked.

"I don't know, Tom. We have lived here a long time and we don't know what's ahead for us. We didn't when we came here, but Sandra, Roger, Rita, Ian, George, Celia, Anita, Colin and Joe and yes, Mr Duffy, would not let us see these people if they were bad. They're just trying to do their best for us and by us. We can meet them on Saturday and if we don't like them, then we stay here and don't see them ever again," Alison said wisely.

"Let's just see what happens on Saturday, yes?"

Alison left Tom at his room where Freddie and Charlie were playing cars on the floor, Freddie looked up.

"What's up, Tom?" Freddie asked.

"Nothing," Tom replied.

"It doesn't look like nothing on your face."

Charlie was playing with the cars to notice that anything was wrong with Tom.

"Me and Alison have just had a meeting with Sandra and Roger. They're some people who want to meet us on Saturday to see if we like them and if they like us. They might want to foster us," Tom said.

"No!" Freddie cried, "you can't leave Craven House! It's your home! It's our home and you're like my brother!"

"Freddie, we haven't met them yet, we may not like them. They may not like us. We'll know more on Saturday, but until then, we are brothers and we can play cars with Charlie too, so let's get ready for dinner; I think it's your favourite tonight, sausage and mash," Tom comforted Freddie.

Alison went back to her bedroom once she left Tom and Josephine was sitting on her bed, waiting for the news of what Sandra had wanted. Josephine gave Alison pretty much the same reaction as Freddie gave Tom. Alison also

175

explained that might not happen; let them get Saturday out of the way and then they would have a better idea of what might happen.

Both girls left the room to get washed up for dinner.

***

The week went unusually quick for a change. It was already Friday afternoon and all of the children had come back from school. They had put their school uniforms in their dirty laundry baskets and put on their after-school clothes and then sat down to do their homework, once they had eaten their snacks.

Dinner wasn't for a little while and they had time to do it in the dining room, so the dining room was packed full of kids doing their homework, with the staff supervising if they needed help with spellings or other things.

Alison and Tom had been a little distracted throughout the week and it was starting to show. They would be meeting the Coopers' the following day and they were both a little nervous. They finished their homework and went off to their bedrooms. Josephine was still doing her homework, so she stayed in the dining room. Freddie and Charlie didn't really have any, so they were in their bedrooms playing cars as usual.

Alison was sitting on her bed reading Josephine's comic when she came back into the bedroom. The comic was called Bunty, a nice girly magazine.

"Do you mind me reading your comic, Jo?" Alison asked,

"No, course not. I know you will put it back when you have finished with it." Josephine replied. Which is exactly what Alison did. They always shared their stuff, but always put it back when either one had finished using it or reading it. The girls had become like sisters and something was bothering Josephine.

"Alison?" Josephine asked.

"Humm?" Alison mumbled, not looking up from the comic. Then she did. Josephine had a puzzled look on her face.

"You OK, Jo?" Alison asked.

"No, not really. I know that you're meeting the Coopers' tomorrow, but I don't want you to go, Al. I know I shouldn't be saying this as you still have to meet them tomorrow, but I want you to stay here with me and Tom with Freddie and Charlie," she added.

"Jo, I'm not rushing into anything, we will meet these people tomorrow, but we may not like them, they may not like us. But can we really stay here forever? Probably not.

"But Sandra and Roger both said, if we don't like them, we don't have to do anything we don't want to. So, we will see what happens tomorrow and see from there. I promise I won't make any decision about any of it without letting you know first. You have to remember; Craven House has been our home for a long time I don't want to make the wrong choice. Also, do you think it's going to be easy leaving you behind?" Alison said, putting Josephine's mind at rest.

The girls both hugged.

"We had better get washed up for dinner, or the others will be knocking on our doors!" Alison laughed.

They went down for dinner, which was pie, mash, peas or beans, orange juice or water and then jam roly-poly and custard for dessert. The children left the dining room once it was cleared of all the remnants from dinner. Alison and Josephine went along to the sitting room to watch some TV. Tom, Freddie, and Charlie headed off to their bedrooms to play cars and trains.

Both Tom and Alison were nervous for the up and coming visit of their guests tomorrow. Tom didn't want Saturday to come around. Once the girls had left the sitting room to return to their bedrooms they lay on their beds and were talking about what they thought the new people would be like.

He would be average height, blonde, blue-eyed, very laid back, a happy disposition, a jolly chap. She would be of average height, long-brown-hair, brown eyes, a happy disposition, the same as her husband; a good all-round lady, who would be well kept. The daughter would probably look like the mother, long brown hair, big brown eyes, and smart, funny, and happy.

They would suit well together with this family. That's the conclusion the girls came to. When they finished their game of the imaginary family, they thought that Alison and Tom would go to, they went to the bathroom to get washed up to change into their night things to get ready for bed.

Both girls finished in the bathroom and headed back to their rooms. Alison dumped her wash bag on her bed, then put it away in her bedside cupboard before heading down to Tom's bedroom to say goodnight as she did every evening. She also kissed him on the forehead but also Freddie and Charlie too. She didn't have just Tom as a brother but two others as well.

She thought of that on her return to her bedroom.

Josephine was tucked up in her bed, which is where Alison was going next. Both girls went off to sleep very quickly. They'd a busy week and it had caught up with them. For the first time since she and Tom had come to Craven House Alison had dreamt of her mum. She was singing to her and cuddling her. And Alison felt so familiar, a feeling she hadn't had in a long time. Then her dream changed, her mum had turned into the figure that she and Josephine had imagined up what the lady who could be her mum, but she wasn't nice and cuddling her. She was scowling at her and pointing her finger in an accusing way, then it changed again, and it was the man who was her potential father. He was shouting and telling her off.

Alison woke up. Josephine was shaking her as Alison had shouted out, "No, No!" She was crying; tears streaming down her cheeks. Sandra came running, in. She was also in her nightclothes.

She held Alison and cradled her in her arms.

"What happened, Sweetheart? Hush now, it's OK, I'm here now," Sandra said as she comforted Alison.

"I was dreaming about my mum and then it changed, and it was horrible!" Alison said.

"Not to worry; now, let's try and get you back to sleep. Snuggle up under the covers and you will be fine," Sandra said.

Alison did, and this time, she slept more peacefully. This idea about the new family was upsetting Alison more than she was letting on. Sandra made a mental note to tell Mr Duffy about this and maybe the children weren't ready for this just yet.

***

The morning sun flowed into the bedrooms, and woke up the girls, Alison sat up in her bed. Josephine was already sitting up in bed.

"Are you OK?" Josephine asked.

"Yes, I'm fine," Alison said.

"Sure?"

"Yes sure, just a bad dream. Maybe I'm just nervous about today and it came out in my dream," Alison added.

Sandra knocked on the door, and then popped her head in.

"Morning girls, are you both OK?"

178

"Yes fine." Both the girls said in unison.

"Right, up you get, washed then breakfast, then teeth cleaned and then ready for the normal Saturday jobs. We need to get them done in record time today as we have visitors."

Mr Duffy was in today, so he could meet the Coopers on a professional level. When she was dressed and the children were having breakfast, Sandra popped along to his office to let her know of the last night's events with Alison. She knocked on the office door.

"Come in," came the reply from the office.

"Ah hello, Sandra, and what can I do for you?" Mr Duffy asked.

Sandra then reiterated the story from the night before.

"Thank you for bringing it to my attention, the Coopers aren't due to be here until 4 pm. I know it's your afternoon off, but would you mind staying until the Coopers' visit is over? I think if you're here, she may relax a little and the visit could go well, but if not you're here to help her, she might get upset. Would that be OK? And then maybe tomorrow have your afternoon off, would that be acceptable for you?" he asked.

"Yes Mr Duffy, that would be fine, it's just—"

"I know," he interrupted, "I know you're very fond of all of the children, but Tom and Alison do have a soft place in your affections."

"Yes, I would rather have my afternoon off tomorrow, to set my mind at rest also. Thank you for being so understanding, Mr Duffy," Sandra replied. "It's fine, I will be here today until the Coopers leave, I don't just want to be by standing, but more effectively involved with this situation as I am also fond of the children here at Craven House."

Sandra left Mr Duffy's office, feeling better about the situation. Mr Duffy was a soft warm person, who had a connection with these children. Not like his predecessor, who had the personality of a wet fish playing with a wet mop.

Sandra continued into the dining room, to check on the children. When they had finished eating and had brushed their teeth, it was job time. They would all be finished in time to still get ready for the arrival of the Coopers.

When the chores were completed, they went to the sitting room to watch TV. Most of the children were there or in their bedrooms. They could have all gone to the shops with their pocket money, but after being at the home for a while, the novelty of going to the shops had worn off and a lot of them would save their

179

money and they would go out maybe once a month. That way they had more money so could buy either bigger or more expensive items or buy more sweets.

Just after three o'clock, Sandra and Roger called Alison and Tom, to get changed into their smarter clothes. They could change back into the Saturday comfortable clothes when the Coopers had left.

Tom wore a pale blue shirt with a deep red tie, and a navy jacket, with beige trousers. Alison wore a pair of black pedal pushers, with a pink top, with white ankle socks and black, ballet pumps.

Alison had her blonde hair brushed, and as she wore plaits in the week, her hair had lovely blonde waves in them. Tom's hair had only been cut the week before, so it was brushed. Both children were inspected so they looked their best and they did. Sandra pulled the camera out of the cupboard in the staff room, so she could take a photograph of the two of them looking lovely. Once that was done and they were primping them up, there was a knock on the door, Roger popped his head around the door.

"The Coopers are here, are you both ready?" he asked.

Sandra took one final look at them both and nodded her head in Roger's direction.

Roger opened the door fully and both children followed him out, so did Sandra. The children were to go into reception to greet their visitors.

They walked along the corridor and down the stairs where the Coopers were being greeted by Mr Duffy, who was shaking their hands profusely.

Mr Cooper was a tall man with deep brown hair, which was starting to bald at the back of his head. His wife, Mrs Cooper, was a slight lady with blonde hair, that was curly and shoulder Length. Their daughter, Hannah, was a slight blonde-haired little girl, who seemed very shy. Sandra and Roger brought in Alison and Tom to greet Mr and Mrs Cooper.

"Ah, here they are with my staff, Sandra and Roger." He smiled.

Sandra and Roger both greeted the couple and their daughter.

"Come, let's go inside. It's a little cold down here from just coming in," Mr Duffy said as he escorted the family into the day room, where they had sandwiches, biscuits, and cakes also tea for the adults and squash for the children to drink.

The children all sat down. Hannah sat with her mother, whilst Mr Cooper sat down talking to Mr Duffy.

"Please call me Harry, Mr Cooper sounds so official and we are here to get to know one another," Harry Cooper said.

"So, did you have any problems finding us?" Mr Duffy asked.

"No, we used to live in the area years ago but moved out when I got a job near Brighton. We think the sea air would be good for the children. Do you like the seaside Alison and Tom?" Harry asked, looking at the children.

"Yes, we do, we've been many times, but not to Brighton," Alison replied.

Tom was a little quiet, but he was nervous.

"So, Tom what do you like to do for your leisure time?" Harry asked.

"Leisure time?" Tom paused, not sure what Harry meant.

"You know, time when you're not at school or doing your chores or jobs around the place."

"Oh, I see what you mean. I play cars with Freddie and Charlie; they are my brothers," Tom replied.

Harry looked at Mr Duffy.

"Two brothers? But I thought it was just Tom and his sister Alison?" Harry looked puzzled.

"Oh no, it is just Tom and Alison. It's just that Tom has known Freddie since the day he moved in here, so he naturally assumes that he's his brother," Mr Duffy explained. "The children all become quite close once they move in. They all look out for each other, especially if they go to the same schools."

Harry looked relieved; he thought he might have to have two more children.

Mrs Cooper started to talk to Alison.

"So, what do you do for Leisure time then, Alison?"

"Erm, well, once we have done our jobs that we are given, there's the sitting room where everyone watches TV. On a Saturday we sometimes go to the local shops, to spend our pocket money, either on sweets or if we save up and get maybe some new clothes," Alison said.

"New clothes?" Harry asked. "Don't they get an allowance from the State for what they need?"

"They do, Harry, but sometimes the girls save up their money, as they like to get some of the latest fashion, that is age-appropriate. The older girls normally go with them and staff members, so the older girls help the younger ones, with colours and that sort of thing," Mr Duffy said.

"Oh OK, that makes sense, also so they are not on their own then, safety first?" Harry said.

Alison had lost her train of thought once the conversation changed.

Mr Duffy looked uncomfortable with Mr Cooper asking these sorts of questions. Sandra got up and asked if Mrs Cooper wanted some tea, so she went to pour her some and brought the sandwiches too. Sandra offered Hannah, who took a ham sandwich and a glass of squash.

Roger offered Mr Duffy and Mr Cooper tea or coffee. Mr Cooper had tea, whilst Mr Duffy had coffee. Whilst everyone was eating and drinking, a silence fell over the room, apart from the slurping of drinks.

Roger left the room and came back with some board games, which he put on the table and opened up, so the children and the adults could play with them if they wished. The games were a welcome from the silence that Mr Duffy and the Coopers had engaged. They opened up Ludo and started to choose the colour of counter they wanted. It helped break the ice and got the Coopers and the children a bit more engaged with each other.

After several games they realised that they had been there for over two and a half hours, and the rest of the children had already had their dinners. Mr Cooper had thought that they had better start making tracks. They shook hands with Mr Duffy and Sandra and Roger and then turned their attentions to Alison and Tom, who had seemed to enjoy the visit and they liked little Hannah.

They shook both of the children's hands and asked if they could see the children again. Sandra and Roger took Alison and Tom back to their rooms, so they could change ready for their dinner, while Mr Duffy saw the Coopers out of the building. Mr Duffy said that he would talk to both of the children and they would take it from there.

He would contact the social worker in the next working day or so and let them know. Mr Cooper scooped up his daughter and his wife walked behind them; they looked back and waved to Mr Duffy.

Mr Duffy went back into the building where Sandra and Roger joined him.

"What did you think of that visit? It became a little uncomfortable when Mr Cooper started asking about the children's funds for new clothes, don't you think?" Mr Duffy asked.

"Yes, I think that it was definitely uncomfortable and that's a subject not for the children's ears either. I think we will have to wait and see if Alison and Tom want to see them again," Sandra said.

"I agree," Roger said.

"It did seem easier once everyone was playing the board games, thank you for that, Roger. Bringing the games in helped break the ice," Mr Duffy said.

Sandra made her excuses to leave, so she could check on both of the children. They were just putting their smart clothes back on their coat-hangers when Sandra knocked on the door and walked in.

"Hi, are you fit and ready for dinner?"

"Yes, all done now," Alison said.

"What did you think of the Coopers, Alison?" Sandra asked.

"They seem nice, they liked playing the games and Hannah is very sweet," Alison said.

"Do you think you would like to see them again?"

"Yes, I think it could be nice, but I'll see what Tom thinks first," Alison said.

"Ok, shall we go and see if he's ready for dinner then?" Sandra suggested.

They went to check on Tom. Once they had collected him from his room, they were walked to the dining room.

"I liked the Coopers, but I don't want to leave Craven House just yet!" he suddenly said.

"So, I take it you would like them to visit again?" Sandra asked.

"Yes please." They both said as they walked into the dining room.

Chapter 11

It had been two weeks since the Coopers were at Craven House. They were coming today, and it was also Tom's sixth birthday. He had been so excited about it for the last couple of weeks.

He had woken up early as he knew it was his special day. He had gone down to breakfast with Freddie, Charlie, Alison and Josephine, who was like his sister now. All of the children had become close over the years.

On entering the dining room, all of the children stood up and clapped Tom. They all sat down to a lovely breakfast of cereal, toast and boiled eggs to start, with orange juice or cereal toast and an English breakfast, fried or scrambled eggs, bacon, sausage, tomatoes, beans, black pudding, mushrooms, bubble and squeak.

The children's eyes lit up. It was a huge feast, especially on a Saturday. Some tucked into the full English whilst the others had boiled eggs, or if they preferred, they had porridge. Even after a breakfast like that, the children still had their jobs to do, which would have taken a little longer to do. But the staff didn't mind, as it was a special occasion.

Once the children had all cleared their plates and the tables had been wiped down, they could then leave the two children who were sweeping the floor and could continue with their own chores.

None of the children wanted to go to the shops today as there was a lot to do at the home, getting ready for Tom's birthday party, later on that day. They were to tidy up the sitting room, to put the decorations up, bunting, banners, balloons, decorate the tables in the dining room make sure his cake was properly finished, and put his birthday presents in the sitting room for him to open up after the party was over.

Everyone was busy. The party was to start at 2 pm and the Coopers were invited as well. They had shown much interest in the children, so it would be good for them to see both Alison and Tom at an occasion, as they had only seen them at Craven House for their first meeting and not watching them joining in with the other children and having fun.

***

Mr and Mrs Cooper arrived at Craven House at 2.30 pm, as they were stuck in traffic. They made their apologies to Sandra and George, who were working that day when they arrived.

George took Mr and Mrs Cooper's coats, and also little Hannah's. They were taken into the dining room, where the children were already tucking into their party lunch. Sandra offered to take Hannah to a seat near Tom and Alison, so she could also join in with the celebrations.

Hannah had been sat next to Alison and Josephine. There was a space made for her. Hannah was given a plate and told to help herself to whatever food she wanted. She looked over at her mother and father, who were in conversation with George, and her mother nodded her head so she could have some food.

Then she came over to Hannah, Alison, and Tom, and wished Tom a happy birthday and gave him a card with a present. Tom gave it to Sandra, so she could put it with the others. Tom thanked Mrs Cooper and continued with his food, which consisted of ham sandwiches, small sausages, sausage rolls and some crisps.

Party food came in all shapes and sizes and once the savoury food was eaten and everyone's plates were cleared, in came the jelly and ice-cream, which all the children cheered. Some of the jellies had fruit in it; fruit cocktail to be precise, and then the staff came around with the different flavour ice-creams. Tom chose strawberry jelly with strawberry ice-cream, while Alison had the peach flavour jelly with chocolate ice-cream. Tom was pleased he got two scoops of ice-cream.

The children were licking their lips with delight. Birthday parties were a big thing at Craven House. The staff thought that even though these children weren't living with their biological families, they should be treated just like any other child. They were just children like every other child in the district.

Once everyone had finished eating and drinking their juices, they all got up and left the room. They didn't need to tidy up after their food, as the kitchen staff would do it for them, so they all raced off.

Alison took hold of Hannah's hand so she wouldn't be left behind.

"Did you have enough to eat, Hannah?" Alison asked.

185

"Yes, thank you. I think I ate more than I thought I could!" Hannah replied.

They went upstairs to play hide and seek. It wasn't as energetic as some of the games they usually played, and the children had just eaten, so the staff didn't want them to get tummy aches or worse, be sick.

Alison, Hannah and Josephine went to hide upstairs. The boys would be looking for the girls and then the other way round. Their food should have been digested by then.

The girls hid in the cupboard in the girls' bathroom. they were in there for ages, but took to talking in a whisper, as they didn't want to get caught just yet. The bathroom door opened, and both Alison and Josephine put their index fingers to their lips. It was a long time before the boys found them and actually, they were the last ones to be caught.

Once the girls were caught, they stayed in the sitting room, and when everyone was found the girls would start the counting to fifty to give the boys a chance to hide.

When Alison, Josephine, and Hannah began counting, the boys bolted for the door and the girls started counting…one, two, three, four…and so on. Once they reached fifty, all of the girls got up and ran out of the room to start looking for the boys. Once caught, they had to return to the sitting room, whilst the girls were still on the hunt for the rest of the boys.

Alison, Josephine, and Hannah found Charlie in their bedroom, hiding on the top bunk. Goodness knows how he got there, as he was only small. Alison looked in the wardrobe and there was Freddie. Josephine looked under the beds and found Tom. All the boys caught in one hit, great! They headed off to the sitting room once Alison had been able to get Charlie down from the top bunk.

Hannah seemed to be enjoying the chase around the building. George and Michelle were with Mr and Mrs Cooper in the dining room until this game of hide and seek had finished, as there were children running around the whole of the building. Sometimes one of the children would come in, look under the tables and then run out again, apologising for the interruption.

"It's like a madhouse in here today, but that's a party for you!" George laughed.

"Is it always like this at parties?" Mr Cooper asked.

"Yes, we always make a fuss of the children because they are just that, children. Just because they live in a care home, they should be treated the same as other children," Michelle added.

Mr Cooper nodded his head in agreement.

Once the game had finished and all of the children had been caught, they decided to play musical statues, traffic lights and find the tuppence, which involved looking in a room for two penny pieces. The staff would be standing in all sorts of places in the room, but you would just have to look, there was money under vases, on window ledges, on shelves, behind the TV and all sorts of places.

Once the games had settled down, George and Sandra left the room only to come back a couple of minutes later. One of them had switched the light off, bringing in Tom's birthday cake with six candles on it.

Everyone sang Happy birthday to him. They had put the cake on the table and lifted Tom up so that he could blow out the candles.

"Make a wish!" Sandra said.

Tom took a huge breath and blew his candles out in one go, closing his eyes as he did so.

"Did you make a wish?" Sandra asked.

"Yes, I did." Tom smiled.

George turned the light back on and Sandra had the knife and plates ready so that everyone could have a slice of cake. With everyone having a slice of birthday cake, it was quite quiet in the room, except for the noise of chewing.

When everyone had finished their cake, Sandra had already bought juice in and cups, so everyone could have a drink after the cake. Then everyone was looking at Tom, then to Sandra and George, then Tom again, Sandra realised he hadn't opened his presents yet.

"Tom, do you want to open your presents in here now or later on in your bedroom?" Sandra asked him.

"Oh, in here, now please," Tom replied.

"OK, let's do it!" Sandra said.

George left the room and returned with a huge pile of gifts for Tom.

"Wow! Thank you, everybody!" Tom gasped at the huge pile of presents just for him.

Tom sat down on the floor with the gifts in front of him. Every one of the presents had a name tag on them. Tom started opening his presents from Freddie and Charlie. He received a new Tonka truck, in bright red.

"Thank you, Freddie and Charlie!"

Next was a set of matchbox cars from the bigger boys.

"Oh, thank you so much, guys!" Tom said.

Tom had opened lots of gifts, with colouring books and pencils and some practical presents, like some underwear, and a new hat and scarf set, but also some fun things like marbles, an aeroplane, a book on insects, a book on cars and trucks.

Tom opened Mr and Mrs Cooper's present. It was a big red car that had a remote control with it.

"Wow! Thank you, Mr and Mrs Cooper and Hannah!" Tom said, giving them all big smiles. He got up off the floor and went over to Mr and Mrs Cooper and hugged them both; Hannah got a hug too. She hugged him back.

"You're welcome, Tom, I am glad you like it."

Tom was getting through unwrapping his gifts. He received a new red jumper from Sandra, George, and the staff, and now he was getting to the gift Alison and Josephine had bought him. It was in a big box, and it was a new truck that would transport the other smaller cars along the road they had used in their bedrooms. It was bright yellow, and Tom loved it.

There was another box of Matchbox cars, but different to the ones he already got from the bigger boys. When Tom had finished opening his presents, he was aware to put his presents away from the ripped wrapping paper, so he didn't lose any of his gifts.

"Come on, Tom, let's take these up to your bedroom where you can have a proper look at them later on, when the party's over," George said.

"OK," Tom replied.

When the party was over, everyone went along to their own rooms or stayed in the sitting room to watch TV. Tom came back into the room to speak to the Coopers.

"Thank you for coming to my party and thank you for my present." He said and went over to hug them once again. He looked at Hannah.

"I'm happy you came today, and you looked like you had fun. I can't wait to see you again, bye!" he said and waved as he left the room with George and the boys.

Sandra shook Mr and Mrs Cooper's hands and knelt down to Hannah and repeated what Tom had said.

"Please come again to see the children. They loved having you here today," Sandra said.

"Yes," Mr Cooper replied, shaking her hand.

"Come along now, we have to head back home. Thank you again, Sandra, for the invitation today. The children did seem to enjoy themselves, and little Hannah too!" he said, touching Hannah's hair on her forehead.

"Thank you again, we will be in touch soon," Mr Cooper said.

Sandra ran up to Alison's room to see both of the girls, sitting on their beds.

"Alison, what do you think of the Coopers and little Hannah?" Sandra asked.

"They seem really nice and Hannah is lovely, but I think it's too early to make up our minds if we want to live with them yet, Sandra," Alison said.

"Well, there's no flies on you, is there Alison? Straight to the point!" Sandra laughed.

"But that's what you wanted to know, isn't it?" Alison looked confused.

"Well yes, it is. I just didn't expect you to say it before I had even really asked you about it, but yes, you're quite right, it's too early yet. Do you think Tom likes them as well?"

"I think he does, but he's also aware that it's still too early to make any decision. I know he's just turned six, Sandra, but he's ahead of himself," Alison said.

"Yes, the saying is he has an old head on young shoulders," Sandra replied, "you are right though, he is wise for his age."

"Now don't forget though, Honey, you don't have to go with them if you don't want to. Remember that. We won't be pushing you anywhere you don't want to go," Sandra told Alison.

"We know that too, Sandra," Alison replied.

"See you later on, I'm going back downstairs now," Sandra said. Both the girls said goodbye and Sandra shut the door as she left.

Sandra headed down to Tom's room. He was having the time of his life with Freddie, Charlie and George had stayed as well.

Sandra left them to it and went down to the kitchen and dining room, to see if she could help with dinner.

***

"So, what do you think? Do you think that Alison and Tom could fit into our family?" Mr Cooper, Ruth and Hannah, both looked at each other.

"Yes, I think they would be a great addition to our family," said Mrs Cooper.

189

"Hannah, what do you think? Do you think you could enjoy having a brother and an older sister in our family?" Mr Cooper asked.

"Yes Daddy, I like them. They're both fun and are remarkably close, I like that," Hannah replied.

"Yes, I had noticed that they were close," Mr Cooper said. He looked straight ahead out of the windscreen and continued driving.

The next two weeks went very quickly as the Coopers were visiting again that weekend. Alison and Tom were getting used to them popping over at the weekends, but not every weekend.

"Why do Mr and Mrs Cooper only come to see us at the weekends?" Tom asked Sandra.

"Because Mr Cooper has to work in the week and Hannah has to go to school," Sandra explained.

"What about Mrs Cooper? Does she work?"

"Mrs Cooper is a housewife so she will be staying at home to cook and clean the house ready for her husband and daughter to come in from their day to a nice clean house and dinner cooking ready to eat," Sandra said.

Before they knew where they were, it was already Saturday morning.

"What do you want to do today with Mr and Mrs Cooper? The last time they were here, it was Tom's birthday and the time before was the introductions. So, do you want to stay here today, or do you want to take them into town? Maybe grab a burger from the Wimpy? What do you think both of you?" Sandra asked.

"I think if we go to town and pop into Wimpy sounds a great idea and we can look at the shops. Maybe see what Hannah thinks too?" Alison said.

"Sounds good to me!" Tom added.

"Don't forget to do your jobs first though, Mr and Mrs Cooper will be here about 1 pm, depending on traffic," added Sandra.

The children both went off to do their jobs. They didn't want to let the side down, thinking they weren't pulling their weight. Once they had finished their jobs, they headed off to their bedrooms to get changed for their visitors. Alison wore a pair of dark denim dungarees with a pale blue polo neck jumper. It was the end of January and it was still cold, so she wore her boots and her navy duffle coat. Tom wore his brown corduroy trousers, with a deep red shirt and his hiker boots, he also wore his navy duffle coat.

Both of the children were ready to go and were waiting in reception with Sandra and Roger to greet the Coopers.' They didn't have to wait long. The

Coopers pulled up in their Blue Ford Cortina and Hannah was excited to see the children waiting for them. She waved furiously.

They all got out of the car, and Sandra, Roger, Alison, and Tom, came out to greet them.

"Hello Mr and Mrs Cooper," Tom said.

"Hello," Alison said.

"Hello you two," Mr Cooper said.

Mrs Cooper and Hannah greeted the children.

"The children wanted to take you around town so you could see where they go shopping and maybe have something to eat, if that's alright with you all?" Sandra asked.

"Yes, that's fine, it will be great to see your local town," Mrs Cooper said.

They all headed off down the road towards town. Hannah held onto Alison's hand. Hannah liked Alison and was looking forward to her being her big sister. Tom walked alongside the girls. Hannah also held onto her mother's hand, whilst Sandra was talking to her.

Mr Cooper and Roger were talking as they were walking. They talked about the latest cars and what would be the best one to get for a bigger family. Roger took note, but never said anything at the time.

They were then at the town. There were lots of shops, some boutiques and the main shops, Woolworths, Tesco, the local butchers, the ABC bakers, Wimpy, Co-op and also a massive toy shop. Even though they sold toys at Woolworths, there's nothing like a toy shop full of toys to amuse the children.

Hannah liked the clothes' boutiques and also the toy shop but loved Woolworths as it had a mix of everything. She especially liked the pick n mix sweets, where they didn't know where to look first—the toffees, the spearmint chews, the mini chocolates, the choice was too big. When they had had a good enough look, time was getting on and the children were getting hungry.

"Shall we go into the Wimpy and have something to eat and drink then?" Roger asked.

The Coopers looked at each other and nodded.

"Lovely, if we have something here, then we should be fine until we get home and have dinner," Mr Cooper said.

They all went into the Wimpy and found two booths next to each other. They looked at the menus and were still choosing when the waitress came over to see what they would like.

"Burger, chips and a strawberry milkshake, please," Tom asked.

"Burger, chips and a chocolate milkshake, please," Alison said.

"Hannah, do you think you could eat a burger and chips?" Her mother asked her.

"Yes, I can try," Hannah replied.

"And what do you want to drink? Would you like a milkshake too?"

"Yes, please. Can I have a mint-choc chip milkshake, please?" Hannah said.

"Do you think you will drink it all?" Her dad asked.

"Yes, if she drinks it slowly," Alison said.

Mr Cooper frowned then said his daughter could have one.

Roger gave the waitress their order and she took away their menus and put forward their order.

The adults had tea and Mr Cooper had coffee, with something light to eat. The children were chatting happily, and Hannah was really fitting in with both of them. She liked Alison as an older sister, but she also liked the chance of having a brother too, even though he was only a little younger than her. They were fun to be around. Mind you, it wasn't quite like that when they first went to Craven House. They were all a little shy. Tom fitted in quicker as if he hadn't lived anywhere else.

Their food and drinks arrived, and they tucked into it; talking in between mouthfuls. Thankfully, their mouths were empty at the time. The bill came and Roger took care of it, but Mr Cooper took it from him.

"Please let me pay for the lunch, I want to," Mr Cooper said.

Roger nodded.

"If you're sure?"

"Yes of course," Mr Cooper said.

Mr Cooper paid the bill and they left Wimpy.

"Cor, I feel stuffed now, Alison!" said Tom.

"Well, you would do. You ate all of your food and some of Hannah's!" Alison laughed. "And you finished the rest of her milkshake, I didn't know you like mint-flavoured milkshake?"

"Neither did I." Tom laughed. "I only normally have strawberry." Patting his tummy.

They walked back slowly and before they knew it, they were back at Craven House. They walked Mr and Mrs Cooper to their car. Alison and Tom both bent down to give Hannah a hug and she hugged them both back. She had a little tear in her eye.

"I had the best time today, we don't normally have Wimpy, thank you!"

Mr and Mrs Cooper bent down to give both of the children a hug and then opened the back door for Hannah to jump into the car. Mrs Cooper also bent down to hug the children, whilst Mr Cooper was holding the car door for her to get into the car.

"We will see you again soon, take care," she said.

"Sandra, Roger, thank you for a lovely afternoon, see you again in a couple of weeks," Mr Cooper said.

"Yes, see you again in a couple of weeks," They both said.

They waved the family off and Hannah waved back to them and soon they were out of sight.

"Come on, let's get you both inside, it's getting cold again," Roger said.

They all went into the building, taking their hats and coats off once they were inside.

Sandra took the children's coats and took them upstairs so they could take off their boots and put their slippers on. She put their coats on their hooks in their bedrooms and their boots in their wardrobes.

"Alison, do you like spending time with the Coopers? Hannah has really taken a shine to both of you," Sandra asked.

"Yes, she's very sweet. I think she enjoys our company, because at home she's on her own," Alison said.

"On her own?" Sandra looked puzzled. "What do you mean, on her own?"

"Well, Mr and Mrs Cooper are at work or at home, Hannah is at school all day and in the evening, she's on her own, she doesn't have anyone to play with. We have all of us, and yes, sometimes we get on each other's nerves, but we are all here and we play together, but poor Hannah has no-one to play with," Alison said.

These kids, they are so clued up, they have to grow up very quickly once they are in care, but these kids are amazing, Sandra thought.

Roger was asking Tom the same thing. His answer was similar to Alison's. They both liked Hannah, and the Coopers seemed nice, but it was too early to tell.

So, while the children were going to school and doing their normal regular things, the Coopers were coming down to see them every other weekend. They had been coming down for a few weekends now and it seemed that they wanted to see the children a bit more often.

"Hello, yes, Mr Cooper, Alison and Tom, yes, yes, I think that would be fine, yes, that's great. I'll let them know as soon as they come in from school, thank you. Yes, I think that would be fine. I'll call you and fine tune the details. Thank you, Mr Cooper, yes, and see you soon," Mr Duffy said as he put down the receiver.

He left his office and went looking for Sandra and Roger.

"Sandra, Roger, oh, good you're both together. I've just had a call from Mr Cooper. He wanted to know if the children would like to visit them this Saturday, so they can see where they live. But it would mean one of you driving down there and obviously staying with the children." Sandra put her hand up to interrupt, but Mr Duffy continued.

"Do you think you could both go this Saturday with Alison and Tom. Or rather, would you want to go with them?"

"Yes, of course we would love to go with them, at least we would be able to see them in their own habitat and see if the children like it down in Brighton," Sandra said. Roger nodded his head.

"But we have to run it past both of them when they get in. I can then contact Mr Cooper and confirm," Mr Duffy said.

Mr Duffy was a nice man. He was very thoughtful and always had the children's best interests at heart. The children were in Tom's bedroom when Sandra and Roger came looking for them, to talk to them about the up and coming visit this Saturday.

"So, this Saturday, instead of the Coopers coming down to see you, would you like to go and see them? They've invited you both down to see them in Brighton. Do you fancy going?" Roger asked.

"Erm, I think it would be fun," Tom said.

"Alison, what do you think?" Sandra asked.

"Yes, I agree with Tom, I think it would be fun and it would be nice to see Hannah's bedroom and what sort of things she has," Alison said, "see if I can add to them with some of the things I have kept, but no longer use," she added.

"So, that's a yes then?"

"Yes!" They both said in unison.

"Well we had better tell Mr Duffy to call Mr Cooper back then," Sandra said.

"Sandra, how are we going to get there?" Tom asked.

"Roger and I will drive down with you in the car," Sandra reassured him.

"Oh OK. What time will we be leaving?" Tom asked.

"I don't know yet, maybe about 10am, so you can get the best of the day down there," Roger replied.

"Right, I'll go down to Mr Duffy and confirm that the children want to go down for the day," Roger said to Sandra.

"OK, thank you, Roger."

The children went along to do their homework, talking about what sort of house they thought the Cooper's would look like. Before they knew it, Saturday was the following morning. The weeks were going really quickly. Both Alison and Tom finished their homework with tales of expectation of the Coopers home, but not thinking of their own bedroom's because even at this stage, it didn't cross their minds that the Cooper's want to foster or maybe adopt them.

After washing their hands and faces, they went down to the dining room with the others, to a busy dining room. Everyone was already seated. It was Friday, which meant fish and chips for dinner.

The children had all had busy weeks, and it was the Easter holidays in a couple of weeks. They had things they all wanted to do, but for now, it was dinner time and there was so much noise of chatter and tinkering of plates and cutlery.

Juice and water on were the tables, and everyone hungry. Once the food was in front of everyone, they started to eat. All you could hear was chomping, chewing, slurping of drinks and sounds of satisfaction of food and full tummies. Once everyone was fed and watered, they went upstairs for baths or showers, then changed into their nightclothes.

Tom and Alison were sitting in Alison's room with Josephine, talking about tomorrow.

"You have met them already, so you know what they are like, it's just going down there to see their lives, it will be great," Josephine said.

"I know, but it's not knowing really why we are going down there?" Alison said.

"Well, they've been here and seen us. Maybe they want us to see where they live, but why?" Tom asked.

"Are they going to be bringing Hannah to live here with us?"

"No," Alison said, "they want us to go down to them, not because they are being lazy, Tom, but because they might want us to live with them," Alison explained to her younger brother.

Alison thought, and all of a sudden it hit her, like a ton of bricks.

Josephine looked at both of them. Tom, who normally had it bang on, then had the lightbulb moment, he also realised what Alison was saying.

"Jo, how many children who come to Craven House, actually get fostered or adopted?" Alison asked.

"I don't know, because sometimes the kids move on, but I haven't met anyone who has been," Josephine replied.

"Yes, because they move on, but we don't know if they have been fostered or just gone onto another home. Listen Tom, we have just realised what's going on, so for now, we have to keep it quiet, not let on that we know now what's going on. Is that OK? We just have to be one step ahead. They don't know that we know. They may just think we don't realise. So, we will see how tomorrow goes and then we can make up our minds. What do you think?" Alison said.

"I think you're right. We know and that means Sandra and Roger know also, so we just keep this to ourselves and see what happens, right?" Tom said.

"Right!"

Both of the children knew what was coming. It would make a difference how this visit tomorrow would go, but until they got back tomorrow, then couldn't make any decisions.

"Roger will be looking for me in a while. I'd better go to bed, night Alison, night Jo," Tom said.

"Night, Tom." They both said together.

With that as Tom opened the door, Roger opened it from the other side.

"There you are! I was just looking for you. It's a big day tomorrow, you need to get some sleep," Roger said.

Tom waved to the girls, and they waved back. Roger said goodnight to the girls and shut the door.

"Alison, it will be OK, you know. Go and have a look tomorrow and see what you think. You don't have to do anything you don't want to. Sandra and Roger and all of the staff will not let you do anything that doesn't make you both happy. Anyway, get some sleep, you have a lot going on and need to get some rest," Josephine said.

Jo was wise, just as wise as Tom. She was like another sister to both of them, just as Freddie and Charlie were like little brothers to the girls. Both girls got into bed, then the door knocked, it was Sandra.

196

"Hi, just wanted to check you were both in bed. Good girls, sleep well and it's an early start in the morning for you, Alison. Get some sleep. Night!" Sandra said.

Both girls snuggled down under their covers and closed their eyes and fell asleep.

Chapter 12

The sun was shining straight through the windows; it was so bright, Alison turned over. She still wanted to sleep but the sunshine was shining on her face. She pulled the covers over her head and tried to continue to sleep.

"Alison?" Josephine asked.

"Hmmmm," Alison mumbled.

"Are you awake yet?" Jo asked.

"No, I'm still asleep. You should be too," Alison said.

"Al, come on! You have to get up. You're going down to the Coopers today. Just think how fun that will be!" Jo said excitedly.

"I don't want to go, I want to stay in bed, asleep…it was nice and peaceful!" Alison said.

There was a knock at the door.

"Morning girls, you're not up yet?" Sandra said. "Come on Alison, you're going down to visit the Coopers today," she added.

"You sound just like miss Jo over there! I want to stay in bed, asleep," Alison replied.

"Come on, Honey, this isn't like you," Sandra said, concerned.

"I know, I just want to stay in bed for a little longer. I'm tired," Alison replied.

"OK, 10 minutes, then I am coming to get both of you up, got it!" Sandra said with a smile.

Both girls got back under their covers. Before they knew it, Sandra was back in their bedroom. "Come on you two, up you get!" She said.

"OK, We're up!" Alison said.

"What's up, Sweetheart? Don't you want to go today?" Sandra asked.

"Yes, but I just wanted a little lie-in. It's Saturday and we don't have to get up for school and we still have jobs to do…I just wanted to stay in bed, that's all," Alison said.

"Oh, you won't be doing any jobs today. We have to leave early, which is why you have to get up a little earlier," Sandra said.

"No jobs today? Oh well, it has its advantages then!"

Alison stripped her bed and put her dirty bedding into the laundry bin. It would be made later on when she was out, but it could air for the day.

"Does that mean I have to do Alison's jobs then?" Josephine asked.

"No, it will be shared out by everyone, so just a little extra and as she has already stripped her bed, that will be made later on, just do your normal jobs. Michelle may ask for some help later with a couple of things, but otherwise, just carry on as normal," Sandra told Josephine.

"Do you want to go down to breakfast, then you can get washed and ready for leaving afterwards?" Sandra asked.

The two girls left the bedroom with Sandra behind them. Tom was already in the dining room with Freddie and Charlie tucking into scrambled egg on toast and orange juice.

"Morning Al, Morning Jo," Tom said, with his mouth half full of food.

"Tom," George said, "please close your mouth when you're eating and no speaking with your mouth full."

Tom swallowed his food and apologised.

Alison and Josephine sat down. Michelle bought over boiled eggs, toast and orange juice.

"Tuck in girls," she said, "what time are you leaving for this morning, Sandra?"

"About 10 am I think. We haven't been to Brighton before so need to take the A-Z so we don't get lost."

Once Alison and Tom had finished breakfast, they headed back upstairs to get washed and dressed. Sandra knocked on Alison's door.

"Are you ready yet, Alison?" She asked.

"Nearly!"

Alison had put on her navy and white polka dot dress with white socks and navy-blue shoes, with a white cardigan.

"Oh, you look lovely! Do you want me to plait your hair for you?" Sandra asked.

"No, I was going to leave it down, so it falls naturally, what do you think?" Alison asked.

"It looks lovely, have you brushed it yet?"

"No, I am about to do it. Jo let me have a splash of her perfume, behind my ears and on my wrists," Alison said, holding her wrist up to Sandra so she could smell it.

"Ooohh, that's lovely. What is it, Josephine?" Sandra asked.

"It's Charlie; I got it for my birthday. It has a lovely flowery smell," Josephine said.

"It's called Floral," Sandra said. "It's ever so nice, that was sweet of you, Josephine," she added.

"Well, we want Alison to smell nice when she sees the Cooper's, and she does look nice," Josephine said.

"There, done! All clean, scrubbed up and hair brushed," Alison said. Her blonde hair with bouncy curls was getting long now, but she liked it that way; very feminine.

"Great, let's go and see if Tom is ready, shall we?" Sandra said.

Josephine followed Alison and Sandra out of the bedroom down to see if Tom was ready. He had nearly was just doing the finishing touches to his brown hair. He looked all grown up now and he was getting tall. He wore burgundy trousers, with a white shirt and a burgundy tank top and navy-blue shoes.

My, how these two youngsters had grown in just over two years.

Roger came down the hallway.

"Are you both ready? Good, let's get your coats and head off, shall we? Are you both looking forward to today?" he asked.

The two children looked at each other and nodded.

"Yes, we are, it should be fun, and we get to see Hannah again!" Alison said.

The children picked up their coats, which were down by reception. They both wore navy-blue duffle coats, which they liked. Even though it was now March and spring was in the air, it was still a bit chilly.

"Have a good time, both of you," Josephine said, hugging Alison and Tom.

"Have fun, Tom, we will leave the cars set up for when you return this evening," Freddie and Charlie said.

The car was outside the home; a dark blue Ford Cortina, which was used as necessary for shopping and whatever else it was needed for. The children climbed into the back and Sandra got in the passenger seat and Roger the driver's seat.

Sandra had the A-Z in her hand and a road map just in case for a backup.

"Right, ready to go, see you later on," Roger said to Mr Duffy and the children who came to wave them off.

Roger looked behind him and put the car into first gear and off they went.

The children didn't really go out very often in the car, so this was a nice treat for them. They went through town and were both looking out of the windows. They watched as the buildings and shops passed by quickly. It didn't take them long to get near the motorway, but there was a bit of traffic.

"I didn't think it would be this busy as this time of the morning, Sandra," Roger said.

"Yes, but it's Saturday, maybe people are going down to the seaside."

"At this time of year? It's still cold out, why would people want to go to the seaside in this weather?" Tom asked.

"Well, we are, aren't we?" Sandra laughed.

"Are we?" Tom asked.

"Yes, the Coopers live in Brighton; that's a seaside town," Sandra explained.

"Oh wow, I didn't realise that!" Tom said. "It's still cold though, at least we're wrapped up!"

Most of the journey was quiet. The children were making the most of the scenery as they were driving past. They had been on the road for just over two hours when they turned off the motorway and were trying to find their way around Brighton. It was a good job that Sandra had the A-Z with her.

"Right, we need to find Pemberton Terrace," Roger said.

"Pemberton Terrace? Peddle Road? Peddle Street? Oh yes, I can see Pemberton Terrace, let me just get the page, yes page 61, that's it, actually Roger it's not far away now. Go straight down this road, yes, then turn left at the bottom…go straight down, turn right and then the first left, that's Pemberton Terrace," Sandra instructed.

"Yes, one, three…ah, there's number 15," Roger said.

"Look Sandra, there's Hannah at the window!" Tom said.

Roger pulled up and they all got out of the car.

"Tom, can you get out as the same side as Alison, please, as it's safer?" Sandra asked.

Tom did as he was told and shut the door when he was out of the car.

The front door opened, with Hannah at the front, followed by Mrs Cooper and Mr Cooper. They all had big beaming smiles on their faces.

"Hello, hello, please come in."

Sandra opened the gate and they walked to the front door. Mr and Mrs Cooper put their hands forward to shake them both by the hand. Mr Cooper stood back so that they could all come in.

"Hello Alison and Tom, welcome to our home," Mr Cooper said. "Please let me take your coats and in we go, there, straight into the living room."

Everyone followed Mrs Cooper into the living room, while Mr Cooper took everyone's coats.

"Would you like some tea? Maybe milk or juice for the children?" Mrs Cooper asked.

"Yes, thank you, that would be lovely," Roger said, "I'm sorry we're a little late; there was some traffic on the motorway, Mr Cooper."

"Oh, call me Harry. Oh well, you're here now, it's fine, and a little traffic happens quite a lot on the way to and from here, not to worry," Harry said.

"Mum, can I take Tom and Alison up to my bedroom, to show them my things?" Hannah asked.

Mrs Cooper looked at Mr Cooper, he nodded.

"Yes, off you go, and have fun," Mrs Cooper said.

Sandra had noticed that Mrs Cooper had asked with her eyes and expression to her husband for his approval rather than just say yes straight away. She didn't say anything but would talk to Roger later on.

Hannah took both of them up to her bedroom which was situated on the first floor. The staircase was quite big up to the first floor, but the staircase to the floor above was a little narrower. Hannah's bedroom was next to her parents. The door was open a little and Alison could see it was decorated with a green colour on the walls, a sage green with a green and white pattern on the duvet cover.

They went into Hannah's bedroom, which was decorated in a lovely pale pink, with lovely clouds painted near toward the ceiling. She had quite a big bedroom, with lots of fluffy teddy bears and when Alison looked a little nearer, every doll that you would find in a toy shop.

She had baby dolls, skinny dolls like Barbie and Sindy. Hannah also had all of the accessories that came with it. She had dolls with long hair, and she asked Alison if she wanted to brush one of the dolls' hair, which she said yes and was handed a doll and a dolls' hairbrush.

Hannah went over to a box under the window and handed it to Tom.

"Here you are, Tom. I got these for you to play with." Hannah said.

Tom opened the box and inside was half a dozen or so of Matchbox cars.

"Oh, wow! Thank you, Hannah!" Tom said.

"That's OK, I noticed yours when we came to visit. I hope they are OK? This is for you, Alison; just a little something for you to play with."

Hannah handed Alison a similar box, which she opened. Inside were some nail polishes.

"Thank you, Hannah!" Alison's eyes lit up.

"I'll leave them in my room for you, for when you visit again, is that OK?" Hannah said.

Both of the children looked up and nodded their heads.

"Hannah, Alison Tom, would you like to come down for some lunch?"

Mrs Cooper called upstairs. When the children had left the room to go with Hannah, the adults were talking mainly about the area…did Hannah like school? What are the local schools like? The three children came rushing down the stairs to have lunch.

Mrs Cooper had laid on a spread of sandwiches, crisps, biscuits, and cakes, very similar to what they had when they visited Craven House. The children sat at the table.

"Alison, if you sit this side of me and Tom the other, that way we all sit together," Hannah said.

The children did as Hannah asked. They weren't fussed where they were sitting, but they liked Hannah and she had made an effort for both of them. Everyone tucked in and the adults had tea while the children had orange or lemon squash.

Tom and Alison were eating their sandwiches, and Harry had suggested that they have a look around the garden. They had a big garden and Hannah liked to play outside.

When they had finished their food and drinks, they were excused to leave the table. Mrs Cooper and Sandra got up to clear away the table and take the dirty plates into the kitchen to wash up.

Hannah liked Alison and Tom and even though she was an only child she was quite happy, but very lonely.

"Hannah, does your mum and dad know that you had those things for us in your bedroom?" Alison asked.

"What makes you say that, Alison?" Hannah said.

"Well, you said that you would keep them in your bedroom for next time we visited but you didn't tell your mum and dad that we liked what you got us?" Alison replied.

"Well, I didn't know if you would like them and didn't want you to be disappointed and I didn't want to get told off. I got them with my pocket money," admitted Hannah.

"Oh, Hannah, that was so lovely of you. We won't say anything, but you shouldn't have used your pocket money, that was yours."

"But you were so nice to me when we came to visit you, I wanted to do something nice for you," Hannah added.

"Thank you, it was lovely and you're a sweet girl. We just don't want to get you into trouble, so we won't say anything, right Tom?"

"Right," Tom said.

"You will come again, won't you?" Hannah asked.

"Yes, are you coming to us again or are we coming here next?" Alison said.

"I don't know what the plans are, I think they are talking about it now, which is why we were told to look in the garden. Do you like the garden? The swing is good, but I want a slide. Maybe I'll get one for my birthday," Hannah said.

"What do you normally do when you're at home, Hannah? I mean when you're not at school?" Tom asked.

"We go to the park, I play outside here, I play in my room," Hannah said.

"Do you go anywhere with your friends at all? Do you have parties for your birthday and what do you do at Christmas?" Tom asked; he had a lot of questions.

"I see my friends at school, but I don't go to parties very often. Me and Mum go to the park, Dad's normally at work."

"Do you have to help around the house with jobs or chores?" Tom asked.

"No, Mum does that and sometimes we have a lady in to help. Do you want to see your rooms?" Hannah said.

"Rooms?" Alison and Tom both said together.

"Yes, your bedrooms for when you stay here, they're above mine. Come on, let's go inside and I'll take you up to them."

The children went inside, and Sandra and Mrs Cooper were just coming down the stairs.

"I have just given Sandra and Roger a tour of the house. Your father has just nipped out. Do you like the garden, children? Hannah has a swing out there and

204

we have the paddling pool when the weather is nice in the summer," Mrs Cooper said.

"Mum, can we go back up to my bedroom? I wanted to show Alison and Tom my books?" asked Hannah.

"Yes of course, do you want anything to drink?" Mrs Cooper asked.

"No, we're OK, thank you," Tom said.

Hannah, Alison and Tom went back upstairs to Hannah's room.

"Right, let's go quietly, and I'll show you," Hannah whispered.

They came out of the room like little mice and slowly went up to the next level.

There were two doors opposite each other and one in between.

"This is your room," Hannah whispered to Alison.

It was painted in a lilac colour, with a lilac and white floral pattern on the duvet.

Hannah quietly closed the door and went to the other door, beckoning the children over. She opened the door.

"This is your room, Tom."

It was decorated in a deep blue with a duvet cover that matched the walls with big trucks on it. Both rooms weren't nicely finished. Hannah closed the door and then opened up the door in the middle, to reveal a bathroom.

Hannah then closed the door, put her finger to her lips and ushered them back downstairs to her bedroom.

When they got back to her bedroom, they sat on the bed and Hannah sat on the floor.

"Hannah, why all the secrecy? Aren't we supposed to know that we are going to be staying here?" Alison asked. "Because that's what we thought would be happening?"

"You are meant to come for another visit, before you can stay overnight, then if you like it here, and us of course, you can then stay for good if you want to," Hannah said.

"That's what we thought would happen, as you have all come to see us so many times and now today," Alison said.

"Do you like it here? Do you like seeing me at your home now and me at mine, which could be yours soon?" Hannah asked.

Before either of the children could answer, Mr Cooper came up the stairs and asked the children to all come down again as they were going out for a little walk.

"Tell me when we get back," Hannah whispered and winked at both of them.

Alison and Tom got their coats on.

"If we have a wander about the place, you can get a feel for it and let us know what you think? That all right?" Harry asked.

Everyone nodded.

They all left the house. Roger and Harry were walking in front, then the three children, Hannah in the middle and Alison and Tom either side of her. Ruth and Sandra walked behind them.

"Yes, it's lovely here. It's a wonderful place to bring up children, as the beach is that way and there's the promenade. The schools are very good. Hannah loves school and has made lots of friends there," Mrs Cooper said.

Sandra thought that Hannah looked a lonely little girl the way she was holding tightly onto Alison and Tom's hands, but she dismissed the thought.

They went down towards the beach, so the children could see it, and then walked along to town.

"Do you like it here then, Sandra and Roger? What about Alison and Tom? Do you both like it here in Brighton?" Harry asked.

"Yes, it seems nice. It's a beautiful day, even if it is March," Alison said.

"Is there much to do here, I mean apart from the beach and promenade?" Roger asked.

"Yes, there's the swimming pool, down the road, and there's a roller-skating rink. Can either of you roller skate? Hannah is learning at the moment. She may need lessons, of course, as I can't stand on a pair of skates without falling over!" Harry laughed. The children burst out laughing at that thought.

Harry was relaying all of the other things that there was to do. Tom's eyes were wide at all that he was noticing, he was really enjoying himself.

Once they had been to town, time was getting on, they got back to the Cooper's home and Mr Cooper let everyone in. Sandra and Roger had suggested that they start to head back just in case they got caught in traffic. They wanted to get the children home before it got too late.

Mr Cooper asked if the children had left anything upstairs at all. Hannah, Tom, and Alison went to have a look, knowing that they hadn't.

"You will come back and see me, won't you? I love having you both around me. I feel good when I am with you both," Hannah said, hugging Alison. Alison hugged Hannah back.

"Of course, we will come back again," she said, looking at Tom.

"'Course we will!" Tom said and hugged Hannah.

The three children left the room.

"I left my gloves upstairs!" Alison suddenly said.

She knew they were in her pocket the whole time.

"So, what will happen next is that you will all come again to Craven House in a few weeks, and then a couple of weeks after that, Alison and Tom will come back and stay overnight, if that's OK with everyone?" Sandra asked.

"Will you be bringing us here next time?" Tom asked.

"No. Mr and Mrs Cooper; sorry, Harry, Ruth and Hannah will come and collect you, bring you here, you can have an overnight stay and come back on Sunday evening," Roger explained. "As you will be on your Easter holidays the next day, it doesn't matter if you're a little late back, as there will be no school the next day. Is that OK?"

"Oh, OK. Yes, that will be fine," Alison said, "We're looking forward to seeing you then in two weeks. Thank you for having us today, it was really lovely to see you at your home. It's a lovely home."

"We didn't get a chance to show you the entire house, but we will next time." Mrs Cooper said, bending down to hug the children.

Mr Cooper shook Tom's hand, but hugged Alison.

"See you in two weeks' at Craven House," Mr Cooper smiled.

Roger unlocked the car door and let the children in. Hannah ran up to them before they got in.

"Thank you for today, it was lovely seeing you both again," she hugged them both, before they got into the car. Roger started up the car, waved to the Coopers and so did Sandra. They all waved to each other until they were out of sight.

***

Mr and Mrs Cooper took Hannah in and shut the door behind them.

"Well, I think that was a success. What do you think, Ruth?" Harry asked his wife.

"Yes, it went very well. They seem to love Hannah and her them. I think they would make a great addition to this family," she replied to her husband.

"You like them too, don't you, Hannah?" Ruth asked her daughter.

"Yes, I really do! It will be nice to have a big brother and big sister," Hannah smiled.

Mr Cooper went upstairs to the top floor and opened the bedroom doors, to let them air, and the bathroom. He thought he chose the right colours for the bedrooms. Lilac for Alison and deep blue for Tom—all he needed to do now was put the locks on them.

***

"Did you enjoy your visit today, Alison, Tom?" Roger asked.

"Yes, it was good," Alison said. "I like the house, it's massive."

"I liked the garden, it's huge! And it has a swing, but Hannah wants a slide, she said, maybe she'll get one for her birthday," Tom said.

"Alison, did you enjoy yourself, Honey?" Sandra asked, concern in her voice.

"Yes, it was lovely, and Hannah is such a sweet girl," Alison replied.

The children sat in silence on the way home, looking out of the window mostly, apart from when one of them was asked a question.

It didn't take them long to get back home.

"Why does it seem quicker to get home, than it did to get there, Roger?" Tom asked.

"Sometimes that can happen, but thankfully, we didn't have a lot of traffic on the way home," Roger replied, pulling the car into the main entrance to Craven House.

Once they got out of the car, Alison asked if they could go to their bedrooms to put on their pyjamas as they didn't want to ruin their clothes. Sandra said that would be fine and they both went upstairs.

Tom went to go to his room, but Alison beckoned him to come upstairs to her room first.

"Why, Alison?" He asked.

"Because I want to talk to you, on our own," she whispered.

"But Jo will be there," he said.

"That's OK, but we need to talk," she added.

They walked along to Alison's room. Jo was there sitting on her bed.

"Did you both have a good time then?" Jo asked.

"Yes, it was OK, but there's something that's been bothering me," Alison said.

"What?" Jo asked, wide-eyed.

Alison sat at the top of her bed, Tom in the middle and Jo at the bottom of her bed, crossed legged.

"We had a good time getting there, admiring the view, looking at the buildings and when we got there, they were really pleased to see us, Hannah especially," Alison said.

"So, what's the problem?" Interrupted Jo.

Well, they had a lovely tea arranged for us, similar to what we had here. Hannah sat in between us and that was lovely. Before we had our tea, Hannah took us to her room to show us what toys she had—"

"What, to brag?" Jo interrupted again.

"No, I think she's quite lonely. Her mum said she has loads of friends at school, but she held on so tightly when we went for a walk…anyway, getting back to her bedroom. She has everything a kid could need, but she gave Tom a box with cars in it and me a box with nail varnishes in it. But she told us not to tell her mum and dad, as she had spent her pocket money on us. Which we said she shouldn't have done."

"Oh, that's lovely!" Jo said.

"Well, yes, it is, but why would she be worrying about what they would say? Also, I noticed that they didn't really talk to me and Tom that much, it was more to Sandra and Roger. They asked us what we like to do, can we roller skate, that sort of thing and sort of bombarding us with information," Alison continued.

"Anyway, there are two bedrooms painted out, one in blue for Tom and a lilac one for me, but there was something that didn't quite feel right. I can't put my finger on it. Anyway, we will have to see. They're coming over here again in two weeks and then I think we are going there for an overnight two weeks later on, just before the Easter Holidays," Alison said. "What do you think, Tom?"

"I think we just have to see what goes on the next time we visit. Hannah does think a lot of us, but she seems frightened to upset her parents. As you say, let's see what happens next time. Right, I am going to get changed. I'm hungry, we haven't eaten since tea. I am then going down for dinner, coming?" Tom said.

"Yes, we'll be down in a few minutes, when I get changed," Alison said.

Tom left the room.

"What do you really think of the Coopers and Hannah, Alison?" Jo said quietly.

"The Coopers, no idea at the moment, they seem nice enough. I think Hannah is lonelier than they are letting on about… Come on, let's get some dinner, I'm starving," Alison said.

Chapter 13

Two weeks later, the Coopers were due to come down on Saturday, but had to cancel because Hannah had the flu, so it was rearranged for the following fortnight, just to be on the safe side that she wasn't still contagious.

The family came the week before Easter, which Tom was quite glad about because he liked the Easter egg hunt they did at the home for all of the children. It was always a fun event because the eggs were left in all sorts of weird and wonderful places.

The Coopers came over as normal on a Saturday and stayed for a few hours and then left again. The children and staff were getting used to seeing them at Craven House, they were becoming a bit of a fixture there. They went to the park this time, rather than keep going to town, which Mr Cooper seemed happier with. They brought bread so they could feed the ducks which Hannah enjoyed. She loved the company of Alison and Tom.

They had brought sandwiches with them, well a picnic really which everyone enjoyed. Even though it was April, it was starting to warm up. Sandra and George brought a blanket so they could eat their food on the grass on a warm blanket. As always, their stay went so quickly. Everyone said their goodbyes and Tom and Alison hugged Hannah. She seemed to hold on a bit tighter than normal.

"Cor Hannah, you have a firm grip!" Tom laughed.

Hands were shaken and hugs were given, then the Coopers got into their car and they drove away, with Hannah in the back waving madly.

That little girl really enjoys Tom and Alison's time and attention, Sandra thought.

The children and staff went back inside. It was nearly dinner time and as always Tom always knew when it was mealtimes. He was a growing lad and loved his food.

Sandra and George were sitting down in the staff room for a few minutes.

"George?" Sandra said.

"Hmmm?" George replied.

"What do you think of the Coopers?" Sandra asked.

"What do you mean?"

"What do you think of them? Do you think they're genuine?" Sandra said.

"Yeah, they seem OK. They want the kids and Hannah seems to really love them already. Why do you ask?" George looked up from reading his paper.

"I don't really know. I can't put my finger on it…" Sandra said.

"You just don't want to let the kids go. I know you're fond of them both, Sandra, but this may be their chance to have a proper family life, you know, really be able to move on."

"Move on from what?" Sandra said.

"Well, you know, move on from Craven House, the care system. Don't forget they came to us from a loving home," George said.

"A loving home, where their father put them into care and handed them over to the State, because he could no longer be bothered with them. Oh, yes, they had a loving home," Sandra snapped.

"Well, their mother loved them, but once he put them in care, she had no chance to get them back let alone see them. I wonder how their mother is doing actually?" George asked.

"I wonder if we should contact her?" Sandra suggested.

"What? Are you serious? Sand, you can't open up that can of worms just because you're a little unsure about the Coopers. Their mother hasn't been in their life for over two and a half years. You can't go calling her now, even if you had a contact number for her. She may be just getting her life together. If you do this, which I don't think you can or are allowed to, you could be ruining her life all over again, do you really want to do that?" George advised.

"Come on, we have to get back to the kids. I think you need to keep your theories to yourself, Sandra. Remember what happened to Ms Walters because she held back information? You could be sacked for even contemplating contacting the children's mother. Let's get back to work," George said.

George wanted to change the subject. He also had reservations about the Coopers but was going to keep them to himself. He wanted to hold onto his job. But he also didn't want to let Sandra know he felt the same.

The Coopers were nice people and they had to give them a chance.

Sandra and George got back to their duties and forgot about the conversation they had in the staffroom. Sandra was worried about Alison and Tom, but George was right, she was so fond of them, she didn't want to let either of them go. Maybe this was all in her head. Maybe she was looking for a reason to not want to let them go. She carried on her work and dismissed her thoughts about the Coopers.

The kids were at home for another couple of weeks before they had to go again to visit the Coopers, and that really would be the tell-tale whether they wanted to continue with this foster placement or not.

***

The children had all now packed up for the Easter break, so the rules were slightly relaxed a bit. They still had to do their jobs at the weekend, but if there weren't any activities arranged, the kids would chill out in the TV room or they would play board games.

Easter came and went. The Easter egg hunt was a huge success, as it was every year, and it was getting nearer to the weekend when they had to stay overnight with the Coopers and little Hannah.

"Sandra, please could you help me with this bag, I can't get it zipped up properly?" Alison asked.

Sandra came into her room and looked at the bag.

"OK, let's have a go at this. If you can hold these two bits as closely as possible, while I try and manoeuvre the contents into these little spaces. No, it's not going. Let's open it up and start again."

They pulled out everything in the bag.

"Do you need to take all of these things with you, Alison? You're only there for one night," Sandra asked.

"Well, it's only clothes and my washbag, oh, and this little thing for Hannah," she pulled out a pink fluffy teddy bear.

"I picked it up in town in the week, when we went straight from school," Alison added.

"Ahh, this is lovely! That's very kind of you, Alison. Hannah is a very lucky girl to have you and Tom in her life," Sandra said.

"I thought she might like it. I know she has tons of soft cuddly toys, but this is from me, and I think Tom has picked her up a present too," Alison added.

"You two are just the sweetest children, very thoughtful," Sandra said to Alison.

Jo was sitting on her bed, watching her friend and the member of staff.

"Couldn't have Jo helped you with this?" Sandra asked.

"I did offer, Sandra, but Alison said she wanted your help," Jo said.

"I wanted to talk to you as well as your help, do you think my mum would be upset?" Alison asked.

"Upset?" Sandra said a bit puzzled.

"Yes, because we will be going to live with the Coopers, and not her?"

"Well, first of all, your mum won't know that you're going to the Coopers to live with them and secondly, your mum would want you both to be happy that you have found a family that want to have you as their children. Every mum wants their children to be happy, even in these circumstances," Sandra said.

Alison thought for a moment.

"I miss my mum. Do you think she misses me and Tom?"

"Yes of course, Sweetheart! She probably thinks of you both every day," Sandra replied.

Alison looked away for a moment. Her eyes were damp, and she reached down to grab a tissue from her box on the bedside cabinet.

"Oh, Sweetheart, I didn't mean to upset you!" Sandra said, grabbing hold of Alison to give her a hug.

"It's OK, you didn't. It's just I think of her often, and more so recently, because of meeting the Coopers and moving on. I feel like I'm betraying her," Alison confided.

Sandra held on tighter to Alison.

Alison wiped her eyes dry and Jo came over to sit on Alison's bed.

"Don't forget me, I'm going to miss you too," Josephine said.

The three of them sat on the bed hugging, when Tom came in.

"Hey, Alison are you ready yet?" Tom asked. "Hey what's wrong? Why are you all crying?"

"We're fine, Tom, just a little emotional. It's okay," Alison said. "Are you all packed and ready to go?"

"Yes, George helped me. What time are the Coopers coming to collect us?" Tom asked.

"Well, it's now nine-thirty, they will be here at ten, so have you got everything and washed everywhere? Alison tells me you got Hannah a little present, what did you get her?" Sandra asked.

"I got her a doll, I know she has lots, but this one is called 'Hannah'. It's her name, and I thought she would like it, as it's something from me."

"Right, are we ready, let's take these bags down to reception, and that way we can check we have everything," George said.

George picked up Alison's bag.

"Anything else?"

"No, just the bag, my coat is hanging up downstairs," Alison said.

"Do you guys have any money?" George asked.

"Erm, I think I have five pounds, I can get it, it's in my purse," Alison said.

"Just in case they want to get something, they have some money," George said to Sandra.

Alison returned with her Minnie Mouse purse she had gotten from Tom for Christmas.

"Here, I have five pounds exactly, I just checked," Alison said.

"If you want to put it in your coat pocket, that way it won't get lost," Sandra said.

Alison nodded.

George put the bags on one of the chairs in reception, and Alison put her purse in her coat pocket.

They still had ten minutes before the Coopers were due. Josephine and Freddie were in reception waiting with Sandra, George, Alison, and Tom. They were all talking, nobody noticed the Coopers' car pull up outside the main entrance.

"Hello Mr Cooper," George said, holding out his hand to shake Mr Cooper's.

"Where's Mrs Cooper?" Sandra asked.

"She stayed at home this morning, so she could do the finishing touches on the children's rooms and also get lunch ready in time for when we get back."

"Oh, okay," Sandra said.

Mr Cooper looked towards the children's bags.

"Are these their things? I'll put them in the car. Come along now, we have a long journey back home," Mr Cooper said.

The children followed Mr Cooper, but so did Sandra, George, Jo and Freddie.

Sandra and George hugged the children including Hannah. Jo and Freddie came over and gave both the children a hug. Hannah had already gotten into the car and the other two followed.

"Have a nice time you two, see you tomorrow evening," George said. "Are you sure you don't want us to pick them up tomorrow, Mr Cooper?"

"No, it's fine. Alison and Tom need to get used to me driving them about, thank you anyway, see you tomorrow. Bye."

George shut the passenger door and then waved.

There wasn't much talking at first in the car, as Mr Cooper was concentrating on getting out of the area. Hannah was sitting in the middle of both of the children with a huge smile on her face. Alison started talking to Hannah and Tom was looking out of the window.

"How was school this week, Hannah? Did you do anything nice?" Alison asked.

"Yes, I did drawing, and colouring, I've been learning math and writing," Hannah replied.

"Do you like writing?" Alison asked.

"Yes, she's getting there, she enjoys school," Mr Cooper said.

They got onto the motorway quite quickly.

"Let's play a game, shall we?" Hannah said.

"What sort of game can you play in a car?" Tom asked.

"Well, what if you count the cars?" Mr Cooper said.

"That will take ages, they move so fast!" Tom replied.

"How about if you just count all the Mini cars?" Mr Cooper suggested.

"What's a Mini car?" Tom Asked.

"There, that's a Mini, Tom!" Alison pointed to a red Mini.

"Oh, right! That's what a Mini looks like," said Tom.

"What cars can I count?" Alison asked.

"What about Beetle cars?" Mr Cooper suggested.

"Beetle cars?"

"Yes, like Herbie the beetle car," Mr Cooper said.

"I remember that film, yes that would be a good one, what about Hannah?"

"How about motorbikes?" suggested Mr Cooper.

"But it's not a car," Tom said.

"No, but you see how many motorbikes there are on the road," Mr Cooper said.

"One, two…Look Alison, there's a Beetle car!" Tom pointed out of the window.

"Thanks, Tom!" Alison said.

"Looks like there are more Mini's than Beetle cars, so just look out for your Mini's rather than Alison's Beetles, Tom," Mr Cooper said."

Alison was still looking. Tom looked a bit deflated. He and Alison always did things together.

Alison looked over towards Tom and gave him a smile.

"There's a Mini car, Tom!" Hannah said, trying to help Tom.

They were nearly ready to come off the motorway, Tom was still counting. He had counted up to fifty minis and Alison had only spotted about five Beetle cars, but she wasn't worried, it had made the time go quicker by counting cars.

The car was going around the roundabout, then it made twists and turns, just like it did when Alison and Tom came with Sandra and George. Finally, they pulled up outside the Coopers' home.

Mrs Cooper opened the door to greet them.

"Hello, hello! How are you, children?" she asked Tom, Hannah and Alison as they got out of the car.

Mr Cooper was taking Alison and Tom's bags out from the boot of his car.

"Come on in then, we don't want to be standing out here all day," he said with a smile on his face.

Hannah held Tom's hand.

"We did well, Ruth, not a lot of traffic. I got to Craven House bang on ten and now it's what?" He looked at his watch. "Eleven-thirty," he said, pleased with himself.

"Not bad if I say so myself. I'll take the bags up to the children's rooms. Actually, follow me you three then you can see where your bedrooms are," Mr Cooper instructed.

Alison and Tom followed behind Mr Cooper, and Hannah behind them, followed by Mrs Cooper. They went above the floor where Hannah's bedroom is.

"Alison, you're here on the left and there's the bathroom and then here, on the right is Tom's bedroom," Mr Cooper said, with a beaming smile. "Do you like your rooms?"

Alison looked wide-eyed.

"Yes, it's lovely, Mr Cooper," she replied.

"Now none of this Mr Cooper, it's Harry and Ruth, Mr and Mrs Cooper sounds so formal. We know each other now, so Harry and Ruth, okay?" Harry said.

"Yes, Harry," Alison and Tom replied.

Alison took her bag and put it on the chair in the bedroom. She had a massive window with lovely curtains that matched her bed linen.

"Now Tom, this is your bedroom. I know you like trucks and cars, we hoped you would like the colour and the trucks. We got you a couple of trucks to add to your collection, so when you come and live here with us, you could bring yours with you?" Harry said.

Tom nodded. He was awestruck! He loved his big bedroom, just for him. No more sharing and he also had a huge window, with curtains that also matched the bedding.

"Right, so do you want to unpack your things and we get the table ready for lunch?" Ruth asked.

"Come along Hannah, let them unpack."

Hannah did as she was told and left with her mother.

Alison sat on Tom's bed.

"Do you think we are going to like living here Tom?" Alison asked.

"Yes, I think it will be lovely, don't forget, Hannah showed us these rooms when we were last here, so we had an idea, but it's nicer now it's finished." Tom said.

"Yes, but Tom, you can't say that you have seen these rooms until today, don't forget Hannah wasn't supposed to show us. We have to just let them think this is the first time we have seen them. Come on we had better get unpacked, do you want some help?" Alison asked.

"No, I think I should be OK. When do you think we should give Hannah her presents?" tom asked.

"Maybe after lunch, and don't forget, we don't know what the rules are yet and what we can and can't do."

Alison left Tom's bedroom and went into her own to start unpacking. She opened up her bag, took out her clean clothes and hung them up in the wardrobe and put away her night things and underwear in the chest of drawers.

There were a couple of bottles of perfume and nail varnishes in there that she hadn't seen before. Once she had put away her things, she called on Tom, who had also just finished putting his own stuff away.

"Alison, Tom!" Ruth called.

"We're coming," Alison replied.

Harry, Hannah and Ruth were sitting down to lunch. There were sandwiches of tuna, ham, and cheese, with sausage rolls, scotch eggs, pork pies and cheesecake.

"All finished," Alison said.

"Come and sit down, there are napkins at your places. Tuck in, there's plenty to eat," Ruth said.

The children sat down and got comfortable, and went to tuck in, when Harry, told them, "If you could ask for the plates to be handed to you rather than just reach over each other, please.

"Like so; Ruth, could you please pass me the ham sandwiches, thank you," Harry said. Ruth passed the sandwiches over and Harry took what he wanted and gave them back to her.

"That way, there's no scrambling for the food and it's better table manners. When you have finished, please clear your plate away. Knife and fork are to be placed in the middle of the plate and then you ask if you may leave the table," Harry instructed.

Ruth kept very quiet while Harry was making his little speech.

Hannah then asked if she could have the tuna sandwiches, which she took and gave the plate back to her mother.

"See, it's very easy when you know how," Harry said.

Tom and Alison asked for the food that they wanted, and they all ate in silence. Tom usually had a very big appetite, but he didn't seem to want to eat much. They had no cutlery, so Tom put his napkin in the middle of the plate and asked to be excused.

"Alison, would you mind being a poppet and helping me in the kitchen with the washing up?" Ruth asked.

"Yes, of course, Ruth," Alison said.

Alison scooped up the plates and took them into the kitchen, then returned to get the plates with the food on them.

"Tom, Hannah, do you want to go and play in the garden, it looks so nice out there?" Ruth asked.

Tom and Hannah didn't have to be asked twice, they were out there so quickly. Hannah was straight on the swing.

"Tom, what's wrong?" Hannah asked.

"I didn't know we would have all of these rules," Tom said glumly. "We have them at home, but everyone mucks in together. Alison is doing it all on her own."

"It'll be fine, Tom, it's just getting used to the way we do things here. That's all. It will take time, but for now, will you push me on the swing?" Hannah asked.

"Yes, but not too high, you're still only little."

"You're the same size as me, Tom!" Hannah laughed.

Once the washing up and tidying had been done, Ruth told Alison that she could go into the garden with the others.

Dinner wouldn't be for a couple of hours or so. Hannah and Tom were sitting on the ground. "Hey, what are you two up to?" Alison asked.

"Not a lot, just talking, having fun while we can," Tom replied.

"What do you mean?" Alison asked.

"Well, all of these rules!" Tom exclaimed.

"We have rules at the home, Tom. It's what happens, so there's no chaos. Someone has to be in charge to keep order. It's the same whatever household you go into," Alison advised her brother.

The children all sat on the ground, soaking up the lovely weather.

"So, what happens now?" Tom asked.

"What do you mean?" Alison asked.

"Well today, tomorrow, once we get back. What happens next?"

"Well, as far as I know, once this visit is done, then there would be a meeting with Harry, Ruth, Mr Duffy, Mr Prowse, Sandra and George. Then once they had the meeting, they would all sign some paperwork and when everything was agreed then we would be moving here for good," Alison said.

"For good?" Tom looked confused.

"Yes, for good. Why do you think these visits have been happening, Tom?" Because Harry and Ruth want to make us part of their family," Alison explained.

"But that means we won't see Freddie, Charlie or Jo again!" Tom said, finally realising what this was all about.

"Yes, we can, we can write to them, we can go back and say hello and they can come here. And don't forget Brighton is a seaside town, so they can have holidays here and we can all meet up. Tom, it will be fine," Alison reassured her brother.

"I know, it's just I'm going to miss them. I like Harry and Ruth and I love Hannah, it's just that I will really miss Freddie, he's like a brother. I've known him for two and a half years," Tom said.

"Yes, but we will have a new family to love and love us, Tom. It really will be OK; you will be OK and so will I. This is just the next step in our life, our next chapter, we won't close the last chapter, we can keep it half open if you want?" Alison suggested.

"Alison! Could you come in here please and give me a hand with dishing up the dinner?" Ruth called out.

"OK, I'm just coming," Alison replied.

"Right, if dinner is nearly ready, we have to go and wash up, Tom," Hannah said. The two of them went inside to wash their hands and faces.

Hannah took Tom upstairs, she told him to carry on to the next floor so he can wash his hands and face in his bathroom.

"Can't I just use your bathroom to wash my hands and face, Hannah?" he asked.

"No Tom, that's why you have your own bathroom upstairs, by your bedroom. I share this one with Mum and Dad. You and Alison have your own bathroom between you," Hannah told him.

Tom went off to his bathroom. This all sounded quite weird to him. Yes, at the home, he and Alison used to use different bathrooms, because he was a boy and would wash with the boys and Alison would wash with the girls.

Tom went to his bathroom, washed his face and hands, and then used the towel to dry himself. There were two and pink ones and a blue one, he could guess which was which. There were also flannels and bigger towels in both pink and blue. Once he finished, he bumped into Alison coming into their bathroom to wash her hands and face.

Tom came downstairs, and then Alison.

"Were you both in the bathroom together at the same time?" Harry asked.

"No, Tom had just finished and was coming back downstairs then I reached the bathroom," Alison said.

"I don't want both of you in the bathroom at the same time, do you understand?" Harry bore his eyes into both of the children. "What do you say?" Harry said loudly.

"No Harry, we won't use the bathroom at the same time," Tom and Alison replied.

Everyone sat down at the table to eat. This time there was cutlery on the table, so once the food was dished out, they had to ask for what they wanted to eat. There was a jug of squash on the table for the children and Harry and Ruth both had coffee.

Once the children had finished their meal, Harry watched how they put their cutlery. Both of them put their cutlery in the middle of the plate, so they knew they had finished; Harry had a smile on his face.

They asked to be excused.

"Alison, what time do you normally go to bed in the evening?" Harry asked.

"On a school night, it's nine o'clock, but at the weekend, it's nine-thirty," Alison said.

"OK, well bedtime here is eight thirty on a school night and nine o'clock at the weekend. It's the sea air, you won't need to be up until late as it makes you tired," Harry said, looking up from his paper.

"Ruth, is it OK if we go up and put our night things on, that way we can be more comfortable?" Alison asked.

Ruth looked at her husband, he shook his head.

"We only get into our night things on when we are getting ready for bed. If you want, you can go and sit in your bedrooms. I think I have some magazines I got for you and some comics for Tom," Ruth said.

"Oh, what about Hannah?" Tom asked.

"Hannah?" Harry looked up.

"We got Hannah a couple of little presents, but haven't given them to her, can we do that now?" Tom asked, looking at Alison to then Harry and Ruth, then Hannah.

"Yes of course," Harry said, "but does it take both of you to collect your gifts?"

"Well, yes, as we both have them in our rooms, and we don't know where they both are. So, if we can get them?" Alison asked.

"Well, you go first then, Alison, and when you come back, then Tom can collect his gift," Harry told her.

Alison went up to her room and took Hannah's teddy from her bag, thankfully it was already wrapped. Then Tom went up and got his gift, which was also wrapped. Both of the children gave Hannah her gifts. Hannah looked at her mother and father and they both nodded, and she started to open them.

She loved both of them and gave both of them a big hug. She gave her mother the wrapping paper and then all three of them went upstairs.

"Don't forget Hannah, if you're playing, only on the landing outside your bedroom, please." Harry said.

"OK, Dad!" Hannah said she walked up the stairs.

"Why can't we play in your room, Hannah?" Tom asked.

"Because they don't like the bedrooms mixed up." Hannah said.

"Huh?" Tom said, confused.

"If we are playing on the landing on this floor, they can hear us, if we go into the bedrooms, they can't hear what we are doing and saying. So, we're only allowed to play in the garden, or on the landing, that's the only places." Hannah replied.

"So, we can't play in the bedrooms?" Alison said.

"No, and we can't go into Tom's room and he can't come into ours," Hannah told them.

"But we did when we visited you last time," Tom said.

"Yes, but now you will be living here, these are the rules."

Alison and Tom looked so confused.

"It will be fine. You'll like living here. Dad's out all day at work and Mum's home," Hannah said.

"Yes, but we'll be out too; we'll be at school," Alison said. "Hang on, I've just thought, we'll be going to a new school," Alison said.

"Oh no, I hadn't thought of that!" Tom said.

"Look, don't worry, Tom. Let's just see what happens. There's nothing we can do about it. When we move here, we can't go back and forward to our old school, we would be too tired, so we have to have a more local school," Alison said.

Alison looked at her watch, it said seven o'clock.

"It's getting late. Let's get ready for bed," Alison said.

"Yes, but it's only seven o'clock," Tom said.

"I know, but it's been a long day. Why don't we get ready for bed, then we can read our comics in bed and then just doze off when we're tired and to be honest, Tom, I'm really tired."

Alison went downstairs to talk to Ruth.

"Ruth, is it OK if I wash up, get ready for bed and then maybe just read a magazine in bed until I fall asleep?" Alison asked.

Ruth looked at her husband and he nodded.

"Yes, that's fine, Alison, do you have everything with you?" She asked.

"Yes, thank you, goodnight," Alison said.

Alison said she would tell Tom to do the same.

"But not at the same time!" Harry warned.

"No, we won't," Alison replied.

Alison left the room and went back upstairs and told Tom what they were doing. She would use the bathroom first and then he could use it.

The children had their washes got into their night things and they both headed off to bed.

They were both in bed for less than half an hour when they dosed off. They were both more tired than they realised.

***

Because their beds were facing the windows, the morning light streamed in very brightly, so they didn't get much chance of a lie-in. Alison and Tom were both up by 8.30am. They did get a good night's sleep.

Nobody had told them what they had to do in the morning, or whether they could go downstairs in their night things to have breakfast or if they had to get washed and dressed first.

"Alison, Tom, Hannah!" Ruth called out, "breakfast!"

"Alison, Tom!" Hannah called. She was on her floor, looking up for them. They both came out of their bedrooms. Tom's hair was sticking up on one side.

"Are you both coming down for breakfast?" Hannah asked.

"Just coming," Alison replied.

Alison and Tom made their way downstairs, meeting Hannah as they got to her landing, then all three of them went down together.

"Morning children." Harry said.

"Morning Harry, Dad," The children said.

They sat down at the table, and Ruth came in with plates of a fry up.

"There's toast on the table, jam, marmalade, butter and squash."

"Great!" Tom said.

"Thank you, Dear," Harry said to Ruth.

"Could you pass the toast, please Harry?" Tom asked.

"Of course, Tom," Harry replied.

Mealtimes were going to take forever if they were always like this! Alison thought.

When Ruth sat down with her breakfast, everyone started to eat theirs. There wasn't much noise at the table except for chewing and swallowing and then a gulp of food, also slurping of drinks.

Once again, once breakfast was finished, Ruth asked Alison to give her a hand. When that was done, all three children went upstairs to get washed and dressed, put their dirty laundry in their bags.

Even though it was Sunday, everyone was still dressed, but not going anywhere.

Alison had wondered if the Coopers ever seemed to relax. Tom, Alison and Hannah went outside in the garden to play. Ruth brought out some squash for them to drink, then went back inside.

"So how do you think it's going then?" Harry asked his wife.

"It seems to be OK. I mean it's going to take a while for them to get used to us and us to them. But they seem happy enough, Hannah likes them," Ruth said. "Do you think we're doing the right thing, Harry?"

"What do you mean, we have a big enough house, there's plenty of room. It's company for Hannah and we won't have to keep Mrs Fisher on. There's money coming in every week."

"But it's a big commitment, Harry. This is for the rest of their childhood and maybe into their adult lives," Ruth said.

"Who said it was going to be forever? This is only for six months, Ruth," Harry said.

"What?" Ruth said in shock.

"Once we agree to adopt them, we can get nearly eight hundred pounds a week for looking after those two. Even if we do it for five months, that's nearly twenty thousand pounds, Ruth! Just think what we can do with that!" Harry smiled smugly.

"But Harry, that money is to help to look after them!" Ruth said.

"No, it's not, Ruth. That is what we get for looking after them! There's also money that we can apply for to help clothe and feed them, and also don't forget, they get child benefit, that will help with what they need. We can get quite a lot out of this for not a lot to put in. We're going to be quids in and it won't cost us a penny, apart from collecting them and that's only a bit of petrol money. It will be fine," Harry said. "After the six months are up, we just say it didn't work out, move somewhere else and start again," confessed Harry.

"Harry, we can't do that to these kids! It's not fair!" Ruth said.

"Not fair? I'll tell you what's not fair, working all of the time, to just about manage, that's what's not fair, Ruth. This way we can get very rich, very quickly. And those kids get a bit of love and care in the process, then they go back to that home they seem to love," Harry said with a gleeful look on his face.

"I had better make a start on dinner, what time do we have to take the kids back?" Ruth asked.

"After lunch, so the earlier we have it, the earlier we can take them back," Harry said.

Chapter 14

The car pulled in, the engine turned off and the handbrake pulled up.

"Right, everyone out the car, that's us for now," Mr Cooper said.

Alison, Tom and Hannah all got out of the rear door of the car and Mr Cooper went around to the boot and took out their overnight bags. Mrs Cooper got out of the front passenger seat and closed the door.

Hannah ran up the stairs to the building of Craven House. Alison and Tom were shortly behind her and Mr Cooper handed their bags to Roger, who was waiting at reception with Sandra for them to arrive.

"Did you have a good time, Alison, Tom?" Sandra asked.

"Yes, it was good," Alison replied.

"Yes, it was OK," Tom said.

"Only OK?" Mr Cooper asked.

"I mean it was lovely being in your home," Tom corrected himself.

Mr Cooper smiled.

"Can we go upstairs with our things please, Sandra?" Tom asked.

"Yes, but be sure to come down again to say goodbye to Mr and Mrs Cooper," Roger said.

"We will!" They both replied.

"Hannah, are you coming?" Alison asked.

Hannah looked at her mother then her father.

"Go on, off you go, but don't be long," Mr Cooper said.

All three of the children went upstairs with the bags. Tom went off to his room.

"Alison, give me a knock when you're going back downstairs again to say goodbye to Harry and Ruth?" Tom asked.

"OK," Alison said as she made her way to her own room.

While the children had gone upstairs, this gave the opportunity for Mr and Mrs Cooper to finalise the meeting on Friday.

"So, if we get here for 11 am, is that OK?" Mr Cooper asked.

"Yes, that should be fine," Roger replied. "It shouldn't take too long and then when the children come home from school, they can get ready and head off with you. If it finishes early, you can always pop into town for some lunch or something?" Sandra added.

"Yes, yes, we can sort that out. Well, we will see you on Friday, then," Mr Cooper said.

"Alison, Tom, Hannah, are you ready?" Sandra called out, but the children were already downstairs.

"Mr and Mrs Cooper and Hannah are ready to go now," Roger said.

Mr and Mrs Cooper gave both Tom and Alison a hug each and said they would be back on Friday to collect them and both of them hugged Hannah. she didn't seem to hug them as tightly as she had done before, but they didn't say anything.

Mr and Mrs Cooper and Hannah went down the stairs of the building to their car and everyone waved them off.

They all went back into the building and Sandra called Alison and Tom.

"Hey, you two, how did it really go this weekend? Did you have a good time?" Sandra asked. Alison and Tom were heading back up to their rooms.

"Come on, let's go to Alison's room and we can talk there," Sandra said.

"What, me too?" Tom asked.

"Yes, you too?" Sandra said, looking confused at Tom's statement.

When they got to Alison's room, Jo was lying on her bed, feet at the top of the bed and head at the bottom. She was reading a magazine.

"Alison! Tom! How did it go this weekend?" Jo asked.

"It was OK—lots of rules though, Sandra," Tom said, pulling a face.

This is what Sandra had wanted to hear. She wanted to know what really went on.

"Rules? What sort of rules?" Sandra asked.

"Well, we can't go in each other's rooms at all. Not like here," Tom added.

"So, what are your rooms like?" Jo asked.

"They're nice. I have a lilac room with flowers on the bedding, and Tom has a blue room with trucks and cars on the bedding," Alison said.

"That sounds nice."

"Right, let's get back to these rules then?" Sandra asked.

"Well, as Tom said, were not allowed to go in each other's rooms at all. We can't use the bathroom together; one has to use it first, then the other. We're only allowed to play on the landing with toys or whatever—" Alison said.

Tom interrupted her...

"Yes, and we are on the top floor, Hannah's room is on the floor below the same as her mum and dad."

"So, there's only one bathroom and it's on the same floor as you both?" Sandra asked.

"No, there are two bathrooms: one on our floor and one on the floor below, the same as Hannah's bedroom." Tom said.

"OK, what else?" Jo asked.

"Well, we have to stay in clothes all day. There aren't any chill clothes and we can only go to our bedrooms and put our night things on when we are going to bed," Alison said. "Sandra, can I ask you something?" Alison asked.

"Yes, Sweetheart, of course you can."

"What did Mr Cooper mean when he said, 'See you on Friday'? I thought once this weekend had happened, we weren't going to see them for another two weeks?" Alison asked.

Sandra took a deep breath.

"OK, so what's going to happen is you're going to go to school on Tuesday, Wednesday, Thursday, and then on Friday, when you come home from school and you will be getting ready and you will then move down with the Coopers to live," Sandra said.

"Huh?" Tom said. "We'll be moving down to Brighton with the Coopers for good? But I don't want to live with the Coopers, I want to stay here with you, Alison, Jo, Freddie, and Charlie. I don't want to live down there with them!" Tom cried.

"I know, Sweetheart, but it's all arranged. It's just the signing of the paperwork to be done," Sandra said sadly.

"Tom, if it doesn't work out, you can always come back again. It's only for six months and as I said, you can always come back," Roger explained.

"So, if we don't like it there, we can come back, and I can still see Freddie and Charlie?" Tom said.

"Yes, this is a placement. Kind of like a trial basis and then if at the end of the six months the placement goes well, the family can apply to adopt you. If it doesn't go well, then you come back," Roger said.

"Can't we just stay here and not go?" Tom asked.

"Tom, if this is our chance to have a family, don't you want that? This could be our chance to move on, get out of the care system and have what other children at school have," Alison said.

Sandra looked away, a tear rolling down from her eye. She raised her hand to wipe it away. Her wards were growing up, they were moving on to pastures anew and she just had to accept it.

"Come on, you two, it will be an adventure!" Sandra put on a happy face.

"But what about school?" Tom asked.

"You will have a new school. I can ask about that on Friday if you want?" Sandra said.

"Yes please," Alison said.

"Right, where are your overnight bags? I need to get them washed. And you can both get into your chill-out clothes if you want and I will pop your clothes in the wash as well," Sandra said.

Tom left the room with Roger and Alison pulled out her chill-out clothes and started taking off her travelling clothes. Sandra left the room and said she would be back. She took the contents of the bag with her and returned a little later when Alison had changed.

***

"Alison, are you coming down, it's supper time and I am starving?" Tom asked.

"Yes, I'll be down in a minute," Alison said.

Tom left and Alison and Jo started talking.

"Alison, was it really OK down in Brighton?" Jo asked.

"I don't know, it's hard to tell but as Tom said there are lots of rules, apart from not allowed to go into each other's rooms and only playing on the landing. Tom is really going to miss Freddie and Charlie, they're like brothers to him. But as well as playing on the landing, there is the garden. Mind you, not that I got out there much, I was either washing up or drying up!" she said.

"What, the dishes? We don't even do that here!" Jo said.

"I know, as I said, we shall have to wait and see. Oh yes, all the food is out on big plates and you're not allowed to just help yourself, you have to ask to have this, ask to have that. Then the plate is handed to you, you take what you want, but they are watching you the whole time and then give the plate back," Alison told her.

"Wow…but as Roger said, if it doesn't work out then come back here," Jo said, giving Alison the biggest hug.

"Thanks Jo, come on, I'm starving too now!" Alison said.

***

The week went really quickly and before they knew it, it was Friday.

"Alison, do you have everything packed and ready?" Sandra asked.

"Yes, nearly done, just trying to shut my suitcase," Alison replied, "Jo, come and sit on this so I can zip it up please?" Alison asked.

Jo sat on top of the suitcase and Alison zipped it up.

"Ready!" Alison called out.

Sandra popped her head around the door.

"Oh good, all packed and ready to go?" Sandra asked.

"I don't know about that, Sandra," Alison replied.

"Do you have everything?" Sandra said, wishing this day wasn't happening.

"Yes, you wouldn't even know I had been here," Alison said.

Jo burst into tears. She didn't want Alison to leave, just as much as Alison didn't want to go, but they had to try and see if it would work. This was their big chance for a family life.

Sandra put her arms around Jo and Alison and hugged them both. She knew it was going to be hard. She wasn't going to be returning to this room when she came back, she was picking up her stuff from reception.

"I hope you get another girl who is nice to you Jo, you deserve it," Alison said. She thought she had said it in her mind, but the words came out of her mouth.

Jo hugged her tighter.

"We have to go to school yet, we aren't going until this afternoon," Alison added.

"Yes, but once you get back home from school you will be going straight away, and we won't get chance to say goodbye." Jo replied.

"I know, but better now than later on, otherwise we will all be in tears and won't be able to speak," she said.

"Anyway, come on, it's time for breakfast."

Alison went to pick up her case, but Sandra beat her to it.

"I'll take this and put it in the office until you need it later, OK?" Sandra suggested.

Alison took one last look around her bedroom. She had been in it for two and a half years. Shared it with Hilary at first, but then when she moved on, it was just her and Jo. She loved that bedroom. She was just making a last memory of her life at Craven House, as she said earlier, she wouldn't be coming back.

Alison and Jo headed down towards Tom's room, he was in the same sort of mood. Freddie and Charlie had all been crying, they didn't want Tom to leave either, but as Alison had explained it to them, this was their foster placement. If it didn't work out, they could both come back, she didn't dare tell them that if it worked well, they wouldn't see any of her family for the last two and a half years ever again.

"Ready?" Alison asked Tom.

"Ready?" Tom replied, puzzled.

"Yes, for breakfast, I know we have had a lot to do until now, but I would still like some breakfast before school, wouldn't you?" Alison asked.

"Yes, I do, I am rather hungry. Come on then," Tom replied.

All of the children went down to breakfast together and like Sandra, George took Tom's suitcase and bags down to reception, to be collected later on today.

When they walked into the dining room, all of the children stood up. They all looked dishevelled and sad that they were losing two of the loveliest children there.

"Come now everyone, sit down, breakfast will be over soon, and you will have to go to school on empty stomachs," George said.

Everyone took their seats. Their plates were brought to them, there was already juice on the table and toast and, both Alison and Tom didn't know what to eat this morning,

"Can I just have a couple of boiled eggs please?" Alison asked.

"Is that all you want, and toast into soldiers?" Sandra asked.

"Yes please, I don't feel like anything else," Alison replied.

"Can I have the same please, Sandra?" Tom asked.

"OK, if that's what you want. Elsie, are there any boiled eggs ready please?" enquired Sandra.

Sandra left the dining room and returned with boiled eggs and bread and butter and toast all cut into soldiers.

"Anyone else want boiled eggs and soldiers?" She asked, looking at Elsie. A couple of children put their hands up, so did Freddie, Charlie, and Jo.

"Yes please, Sandra," Jo said.

They wanted to have what Tom and Alison had for breakfast. That way there was a little bit more of a connection they could have before they left.

Once everyone had eaten, they went up to the bathrooms to brush their teeth.

"Alison, Tom?" Sandra called. "Can you come with me, please?"

Both of the children went with Sandra.

"Now I know that your stuff is already packed, but I got you both these so you could brush your teeth in this bathroom," Sandra explained.

"So, we are not with the others, you mean?" Alison asked.

"Sorry, Sweetheart, that's the rules. Just in case one of the other children decided to hide you in their bedrooms and not let you go," Sandra said with a smile. Because that's exactly what she wanted to do. She didn't want them to go either, and nor did the other staff. But they had to be professional about it, so she had to stick to the rules. She hadn't before and it had nearly cost her the job.

The children did what they were told and brushed their teeth and hair. Alison checked over Tom, to make sure he looked presentable.

"Yes, you'll do," she smiled. Alison checked herself in the mirror. She and Tom had come a long way since they walked into Craven House, and she couldn't believe that they were now leaving it.

They left the little bathroom, gathered their coats for school and waited downstairs in reception, as always, for the others to go to school. All of the children who went to their school were making their way downstairs and the others who went to a different school were on their way too.

Jo didn't go to the same school as Alison and Tom, she came over and hugged them both, as her group were going in a little while. She wiped a tear away from her eye when she thought Alison wasn't looking.

"Ready everyone?" Sandra asked.

"Yes!" The children replied.

She looked again at Alison and Tom one last time before they headed for school. A lump came to her throat. She gulped it back, opened the door and off they went.

***

"Good morning, children, that's it, sit down and find your spaces. Come on, we have a lot to get through this morning. That's it, now as you know we are losing two of our students today. Alison and Tom Davis, come on up, children." The headteacher, Mr Thompson, called Alison and Tom to the front of the hall.

"Alison and Tom are moving to Brighton so this will be their last assembly at school. I want you all to say goodbye to them. I know they are here for the day, but you may not all get the chance later on, when you have lessons," Mr Thompson said.

Alison and Tom stood up and went to the front of the hall.

"Goodbye, Alison and Tom!" The children said, sitting down on the floor, looking up at them. Alison and Tom waved; they didn't know what to say.

The headmaster thanked them for coming up and then told them to go and sit back down again for the rest of assembly.

Assembly didn't take long at all, about twenty minutes and once they had sung their hymns and said the Lord's prayer, the children got up in their classes and went back to their classrooms. Alison had art this morning and Tom had Mathematics and arithmetic, which he enjoyed.

***

It was nearly eleven and Sandra had made sure she had all of her paperwork and notes and questions she wanted to ask the Coopers. George was also going to be in the meeting. Mr Prowse had turned up early and was talking to Mr Duffy in his office.

Mr and Mrs Cooper came bounding through the door with Hannah trailing behind them.

"Sorry, are we late? A little traffic on the roads," Mr Cooper said.

"Mr Cooper, Mrs Cooper and Hannah," Mr Duffy said, shaking their hands on greeting them.

There were quite a few people for the meeting, so they decided to hold it in the room that they met the Coopers in when they first came. There was tea and coffee on one of the tables for afterwards.

"Right, so let's get started, shall we?" Mr Duffy said.

"Let's introduce ourselves…Oh, um before we start, Mr and Mrs Cooper, would it be OK if Celia took Hannah into the playroom, while we have this meeting?" Mr Duffy said, getting up his seat to open the door to Celia.

234

Mr and Mrs Cooper nodded.

"That way we can concentrate on what we need to sort out and Hannah won't get bored," Mr Duffy explained.

Hannah left the room with Celia, and they continued.

"Where were we?" Mr Duffy asked, looking down at his notes.

"Oh yes, for everyone to introduce themselves. Right, I'll start. I'm Mr John Duffy, the manager at Craven House," Mr Duffy said. He looked to his left.

"I'm Pamela Scott, Mr Duffy's secretary. I'll be taking the minutes of this meeting." Pamela said, looking to her left.

"I'm Sandra Michaels and I work here as a keyworker at Craven House," Sandra said, looking at George on her left.

"I'm George Wollaton and I am also a keyworker at Craven House," George said. He looked to Mr Cooper on his left.

"I'm Mr Cooper and a prospective foster carer," Mr Cooper said, looking to his left at his wife.

"I'm Mrs Cooper and a prospective foster parent."

Mrs Cooper looked to Mr Simon Prowse on her left.

"Hello, I'm Simon Prowse and I'm Alison and Tom's social worker," Mr Prowse said.

"Right, introductions over with, let's get down to business," Mr Duffy said.

"This meeting is to finalise a foster placement with Mr and Mrs Cooper and their young daughter, Hannah, to start as of today, once all of the paperwork is checked and signed. Does anyone have any questions?" asked Mr Duffy.

"Yes, I do, Mr Duffy," Sandra said. "Mr and Mrs Cooper, Alison and Tom are a little concerned that they don't have a school sorted out for when they come to live with you. Have you got them placed with a school as of yet?"

Mr Cooper cleared his throat.

"Erm yes we have, we applied for the local school, Balmsbary Peaks. They will both be able to start next Monday. They will need a uniform, but we can get that for them tomorrow."

Sandra made a note of the details. It was a question she wanted to answer to the children later on in the day before they got told from Mr and Mrs Cooper.

"As you know, Mr Duffy, Sandra and I went with the children a little while ago for a visit to Mr and Mrs Cooper and had a look at the area. It seems quite nice and it's very near to the seaside. As it says in my report, I wanted to know if there were any activities they would be doing once the school day is over?" George asked.

Mr Cooper cleared his throat again.

"At the moment, we want to get them both settled in at home and also at school, for the time being. But even though they will have homework to do, we haven't thought that far ahead, don't want to give them too much to load onto them."

Everyone was taking notes on what was said.

Mr Prowse then wanted to ask a question.

"Mr and Mrs Cooper, I have been in touch with your social worker, Mrs Hemsby," he said looking down at his notes. "She said that Hannah was happy at home and was looking forward to having siblings, as she is an only child. She has been to your home to make sure there is provision for both Tom and Alison. Your home is quite extensive. Do you think you would be looking to fostering other children at a later date?" Mr Prowse asked.

"Oh no, having three children is more than enough. We were looking for only one, but fell in love with both Alison and Tom, and separating them was out of the question. So, in answer to your question, no, we are happy as we are," Mr Cooper replied, matter-of-factly.

Mr Duffy looked pleasantly pleased with how things were going.

"Now, is there anything else anyone wants to ask?" he asked.

"Err, yes please, Mr Duffy," Sandra looked directly at Mr Cooper. "If either of the children were naughty, how would you punish them?"

Mr Cooper didn't clear his throat this time, he just replied, "I wouldn't hurt them, I would just stop them watching either their favourite programme or not let them have an activity they liked. But that would be it."

"You wouldn't send them to bed without their meal, would you?" Sandra asked.

"No, of course not! I wouldn't do that, children need their food, otherwise they wouldn't be able to grow in mind as well as body," Mr Cooper said, a little hurt that Sandra would ask such a question.

Mrs Cooper was shaking her head, while her husband was giving his answer. Mr Duffy looked slightly embarrassed, but he knew Sandra was asking the right questions, she was good at her job.

"Mr Cooper, I'm sorry, but we have to ask these things." Sandra smiled.

"I understand, you're only doing your job and your concern is for the children," Mr Cooper said. He gave Sandra a little smile, hoping that would suffice.

"So, any other questions?" Mr Duffy asked.

Everyone shook their heads.

"Right, let's get down to the final part and that's finances," Mr Duffy said. "You will receive the sum of £375.00 per child per week, starting as of next Friday. The monies will get sent straight to you in the form of a cheque, is that OK, Mr Cooper?" Mr Prowse asked.

Mr Cooper had his head down.

"Mr Cooper?"

"Yes?" Mr Cooper.

"Did you hear what I said? You will receive £375.00, once every week for each child. Would a cheque sent to you at home be OK?" Mr Prowse asked.

"Yes, that's fine," replied Mr Cooper.

"Now, that covers what the children will need, food, clothes, outings as such and there is also the child benefit form…Oh, but hang on, if you get child benefit for Hannah, it will be added to your claim. I would send it in anyway with a covering letter we will give you and that will sort out any problems that may occur. You will get all of this information sent to you with your first cheque this Friday, so please keep it safe as it's going to have all of the relevant information you will need for this placement," Mr Prowse explained.

"And as you know, if it doesn't work out within the six months, you will just have to let Mrs Hemsby, myself and Mr Duffy know, and we will come and collect the children. If it goes well and you all want to continue, you just have to let us all know, and we will finalise the paperwork with Mrs Hemsby and she will forward it onto us. Is that all clear?" Mr Prowse asked. The Coopers nodded.

"All we have to do now is sign on the dotted line," Mr Prowse said.

Mr Duffy left the room, so he could collect the paperwork from his office. He also had to sign the paperwork.

Mr Cooper was given all of the paperwork to sign.

"We have just signed for Alison and Tom to join our little family! We're going to be so happy together. Thank you, all of you, for making this happen. Our little dream is finally coming true," he said.

Sandra smiled tightly. She felt that something wasn't right but couldn't put her finger on it. She looked at the clock.

"It's only 12 o'clock, Alison and Tom won't be back just yet, so would you like to go out for some lunch or something? They arrive back at 3.20 pm."

"Yes, thank you Sandra, I think we should go and celebrate. We can take Hannah with us and then on the way back, collect Alison and Tom and then off we go back to Brighton," Mr Cooper said.

Celia came back into the room with Hannah.

"Hannah, we now have Alison and Tom in our family, isn't that great? We're going to get something to eat as Alison and Tom are still at school, is that OK with you?" Mr Cooper asked, picking Hannah up into his arms.

"Oh yes, Daddy, that's wonderful news! Yes, the quicker we go out, the quicker we can get back and pick them both up, that's a great idea!" Hannah said.

Mr Cooper shook Mr Prowse's hand, Mr Duffy's hand, along with Sandra and George's hands.

"We'll be back about 3 pm, is that alright?" Mr Cooper said.

Nobody had the chance to answer; Mr Cooper, Mrs Cooper and Hannah were already in the hallway ready to leave the building.

"You know what, George, that's the happiest I have ever seen that man? Maybe I have him all wrong?" Sandra said, but secretly, she was still unsure about Mr Cooper.

***

Alison and Tom had their school dinner and were in the playground. Their friends knew that they didn't want to go to a new home or a new school. The staff at school had done what the staff at Craven House had done and told them that it was a new start and a chance to be part of a proper family.

Alison thought she should try and have a better day on her last day there, so she picked up the skipping rope with her friends and they were playing. Tom was in a different playground and he was oblivious to what was going on with Alison. He was playing with his friends Dean and Michael, chasing each other around the playground playing tag. He was making the most of it without realising he was.

When it was time to go back into class, Alison sighed, it was English story time when she got In and she would have to write an essay. The teacher didn't give her a subject.

238

"Just write something that makes you happy." Her teacher, Mrs Wells told her.

Alison wrote about her time at Craven House, what she liked about it the sad times but also the fun times.

Before she knew it, it was nearly home time. Her teacher Mrs Wells, called the class to be quiet. She stood at the front of the class and called Alison up.

"Now, we know we haven't had a lot of notice of you leaving until Tuesday this week, but your classmates wanted to get you a little something to remember them by." Mrs Wells smiled at Alison and handed Alison a package wrapped in pretty paper.

"Can I open it now?" Alison asked.

"Of course, your friends want to see if you like it," Mrs Wells said.

Alison ripped open the paper, to find a box. Inside were some glass figurines. There was a dog like Snoopy; he had pink coloured ears though. Then there was a dolphin with a blue fin at the top and back, a fish that had orange on the tail and its fins. There was a cat with green ears and tail and a bear, with brown ears, nose, and paws. Alison loved it. It was something she hadn't ever seen before. The ornaments changed colour when the light caught them.

"Thank you everyone, this is lovely! I will treasure it always," Alison said, wiping away the tears that had just come. Mrs Wells hugged her and said it will be all right and if they were ever in the Brighton area, they would pop in. Alison nodded her head.

The bell rang and it was time to go home. Alison hugged her teacher again, said goodbye and left her classroom, taking one last look, just like she did at her bedroom at Craven House.

Alison caught up with Tom, who also looked like he had been crying. He also had a package. It was a truck and a car.

"Look Alison, what I got, do you like it?" he asked.

"Tom, it's lovely! I got a present too, from my classmates, look." Alison showed her brother her gift.

"Wow, they are cool, I like them, Alison."

"Now we have to wait for either George or Sandra. Look Tom, there's Sandra!" Alison pointed. Both of the children headed over to her.

"Hello you two, good day?" she asked.

"Yes, it was OK," Alison replied.

"Sandra, I got a truck and a car from my friends in my class," Tom said, pushing it into her face. "Sorry Sandra," he apologised.

"It's OK, Tom. I know you're excited!" Sandra laughed.

"How did it go today, Sandra? Did Mr and Mrs Cooper come to the meeting?" Alison asked as they waited for the other children to come out of class.

Tom's face dropped. He had had a good today and for a little while he had forgotten all about moving to Brighton.

"Yes, they came, and everything is sorted out. They should be back at Craven House when we get back," Sandra said with a heavy heart.

The rest of the children going back home were all here now.

"Everyone here? Right then, let's go home," she said, forgetting herself, it was a slip of the tongue, but it was where they were going. The children were chatting away as normal except for Alison and Tom; they walked back in silence.

Sandra had noticed but didn't say anything, the other children started to engage with them, as they didn't want their last journey home to be a sad one.

Tom was talking about his car and truck and Alison started talking to one of the other girls.

She had put her present into her school bag, which she would empty as soon as she got back to the home.

They had clothes ready to change into when they got back, so Sandra would take their dirty uniform and wash it.

**

Mr and Mrs Cooper were already at the home by the time the children got back home. They had been to town and had a Wimpy and walked around the town just to kill some time. They didn't fancy staying at Craven House unless they really had to.

"Hello everyone!" Mr Cooper said as the children came into the house.

"Hello." All the children.

"Shall we get your stuff for you then, Alison and Tom?" Mr Cooper asked impatiently.

"Well, they have to change into their other clothes, Mr Cooper, come inside and wait, maybe have a cup of tea?" Sandra suggested.

"No, I don't think we should have any tea. We have to be on the motorway and there isn't really anywhere to stop," Mr Cooper rolled his eyes as if it were an inconvenience that there were no services on the motorway.

"Can we wait down here?" Mrs Cooper asked.

"Yes, that's fine, we shouldn't be long," Sandra said.

Sandra and the children all went inside. She had the children's things in a bag ready for them. They got changed in the little bathroom. Jo, Freddie, and Charlie came down to reception along with George, Celia, Roger and Liz, all wanting to say goodbye and give hugs to the children.

"Oh, I forgot, you two! This is something each for you, a little parting gift from us at Craven House for you," George said.

They were both given a little box, and when they lifted up the lid, there was a gold St Christopher on a chain.

"It's for travelling. St Christopher will always watch over you and keep you safe," Sandra said, with tears welling up in her eyes.

George handed her a tissue.

"Take care, Alison. Take care, Tom. We will miss you both," George said.

It was quite an emotional time for everyone, and Jo, Freddie and Charlie were really crying now.

"I think it's best if me and George take you down to the car, with your stuff as I think the others will be too upset, is that OK?" Sandra asked.

The children hugged one last time and Celia took the others back upstairs. George collected the children's cases and Sandra took their bags. They opened the door of Craven House and took them down to their new foster parents and sister and gave Mr Cooper their bags and cases.

Mr Cooper put their belongings into the boot. Mrs Cooper shook Sandra and Georges hands and said thank you.

Mr Cooper came around and did the same then got into the car.

All three children were sitting in the back. Mr Cooper put his seatbelt on then turned the engine on.

"Are we ready? Then off we go."

The children looked out of the back window and waved. Mrs Cooper waved to Sandra and George, Mr Cooper stuck his hand out of the car and waved on the roof. Alison and Tom looked up and saw all of the children waving profusely at the windows, with Freddie, Charlie and Jo at the front.

241

Sandra and George waved until the car was out of sight and then went in. Both of them burst into tears, they were sad to see them go.

"Let's hope they have a happy life with the Coopers," Sandra said between tears.

She went back upstairs to see to the remaining children.

Chapter 15

The car pulled up to Number 15.

"Right, everyone out, let's get inside," Mr Cooper said.

Alison, Hannah and Tom got out of the car and Mr Cooper got their suitcases and luggage out of the boot.

Alison put her hand in her pocket, and she felt and found her purse she had brought with her a couple of weeks ago. She hadn't used her money as there really was nowhere to use it. She pulled her hand out of her pocket to grab her suitcase.

"No, no, it's fine, Alison, I'll take them inside, but you can take yours and Tom's upstairs to your bedroom, but just leave Tom's at the doorway," Mr Cooper said.

He shut the boot of the car and Mrs Cooper had already opened the front door. Hannah ran inside and straight upstairs. Alison had both her and Tom's suitcases and Tom tried to take their bags with him. He was struggling a bit, so left one behind and came back for once he had taken the other one up.

"Ruth, put the kettle on, I'm gasping for a cuppa!" Mr Cooper said.

Alison left her suitcase on the bed and took Tom's to the doorway; they both shrugged their shoulders and opened their luggage.

Ruth appeared in the doorway.

"Need any help, Alison?" She asked.

"No, I think I'm OK, Tom might do though," Alison replied.

"OK," Ruth said, "Need any help, Tom?"

"Erm, no I think I can manage. If I get stuck, I can call Alison," Tom replied.

"Actually, you can't, Tom. If you need some help, please would you call me, and I will come and help you, OK?" Ruth replied. "Come down when you're both ready and we can sort out what you want to do next."

Ruth headed back downstairs to make the tea.

Alison pulled out her clothes. There were hangers in the wardrobe, but only about ten. She opened the chest of drawers and started to put her underwear, socks and nightclothes in. She had a little dressing table, so she could put her nail polishes and bottle of perfume on top of it, along with her hairbrush. She looked around and there wasn't really anywhere to put her suitcase. She noticed a door at the bottom of the bed. Opening it, she found a place where she could put her suitcase, and nobody would know it was there.

When she had finished, she popped along to Tom's room and asked if he was OK.

"I've nearly finished, Al. I have to put this case away, but I don't know where to put it?" Tom said.

"Why don't you look at the bottom of the bed? Mine had a door and it led to a storage area. No one will know it's there. But you better hadn't let on I helped you," Alison said. Tom nodded.

They both left the room as tidy as it was before they got there. When they got downstairs, Harry was reading the paper, Ruth had just bought in the tea and Hannah was still in her room.

"Right, now tomorrow, we have to get your school uniforms for the local school and that's in town. So, if we can be ready for 10 am to head straight off, is that OK?" Harry asked.

"Yes, that's OK, Mr Cooper," Alison replied.

"Now, now, Alison, you can now call me Harry, and Ruth by her name. None of this Mr and Mrs Cooper, OK?" Harry said.

"OK, Harry," Alison replied.

"If you've both unpacked, Alison, could you please go into the kitchen and see if Ruth needs a hand with the dinner, there's a good girl? Tom, what are you going to do now?" Harry asked.

Tom had no idea what he was going to do. He would normally be playing with Freddie and Charlie in their bedroom with their cars and trucks.

"I don't know, can't I go and play with my trucks and cars?" Tom asked.

"Yes, as long as you play on the landing." Harry replied.

"Harry, where's Hannah?" Tom asked.

"She should be in her bedroom playing. She missed school today, so she's playing with her toys," Harry replied.

"How come Hannah is playing in her bedroom, but I have to play on the landing?" Tom asked. Harry wasn't too happy at being challenged by a six-year-old.

"Hannah is our daughter, Tom, and she can play in her bedroom so she won't be in Ruth's way and I will not be spoken to like that from a child, do you understand?" Harry snapped. "Well? I'm waiting?"

"Yes, Harry. Sorry Harry," Tom said as he left the room.

Tom headed back up to his bedroom to get his toys out of the cupboard. He pulled the red, blue and yellow trucks out, and also an assortment of Matchbox cars. He lined them up and put the cars in a big circle and was playing happily. Alison was still in the kitchen helping Ruth make dinner, it didn't take long.

"Alison, you can go back upstairs now, and I'll call you to come and give me a hand to dish up, if that's OK?" Ruth said with a smile.

"OK, Ruth."

She went back up to her bedroom. Tom was playing on the landing.

"You OK, Tom?" Alison asked.

"Yes," Tom replied, a little muffled.

"What's wrong?" Alison asked.

"Didn't you hear Harry have a go at me in the sitting room?" Tom asked.

"No, why did he have a go at you?"

"Because I asked why I have to play on the landing, but Hannah can play in her bedroom?" Tom said, with a sniff.

"What did he say?" Alison asked.

"He said that Hannah is his daughter and she can play in her room, so she doesn't get into Ruth's way whilst she is cooking dinner!" Tom replied.

"OK, Tom. First of all, I think we are going to have to adjust to living here. We're not at home now…well, we are at home, but not at the home now. We have to obey the rules and we have only just got here. Also, we are going to have to speak in hushed voices here, Tom, so they can hear us downstairs, OK?" Alison said.

"What's hushed voices mean?" Tom asked.

"It's like whispering," Alison said.

"OK, Alison," Tom said.

Tom always listened to what Alison said, because he knew she would always look out for him.

"Alison, could you come down here please and help me with dishing up dinner?" Ruth called out from the hallway.

"Coming!" Alison called back. "Just remember what I said, Tom, OK?" she whispered to Tom."

She left Tom upstairs while she went down to help Ruth dish up dinner. It was mashed potato, sausages and peas.

"Could you take the plates and put them on the table for me?" Ruth asked.

"Err, yes, but I don't know where anyone sits," Alison replied.

"Hannah, Tom, can you come down for dinner please?" Ruth shouted up the stairs.

Tom went to the bathroom first to wash his hands and face. Hannah came running down the stairs. By the time Tom got to the table, he was the last one to be seated.

"Tom, Ruth called you down a few minutes ago, why has it taken so long for you to come down?" Harry asked.

"Because I was washing my hands and face before a meal like we do at home," Tom said, with a big smile on his face.

"OK, but next time could you be a bit quicker? And this is your home now, and I would like you to follow the rules. Let's eat in peace," Harry said sternly.

They ate their meal in silence and there was squash on the table for the children.

"Oh, and in future, dinner is at 6 pm. Breakfast is at 8 am and lunch, when you're home from school, is at 1 pm. Hannah will help you if you get stuck," Harry said.

When dinner was eaten and the plates cleared, Ruth got up to take the plates in the kitchen. "Alison, could you bring the jug and the glasses please, not all at once, we don't want them breaking and you hurting yourself," Ruth said.

Alison did as she was told. Tom asked if he could leave the table and Harry ignored him at first. Tom asked again and Harry nodded. Tom went back upstairs to his bedroom. Alison was in the kitchen, helping Ruth wash and dry up the dinner things.

"Thank you, Alison. You can go back upstairs if you want to," Ruth said.

Alison went back up to her room and saw Tom sitting on the bed, he looked really miserable.

"Tom, what's up?" Alison asked. She had been in the kitchen and hadn't heard what had happened to Tom with Harry. Tom told her.

"Tom, it's all new here for us and for them," she said in hushed tones.

"Yes, but he really doesn't like me, Alison. I don't know what I've done. I don't like it here. I miss Freddie, and Charlie, and Sandra, and George, and Roger. They made our home feel like home, but this doesn't feel like home. It's not a loving family as we thought it was," Tom said through tears.

Alison hugged him and then Hannah came up the stairs.

"What's wrong, Tom?" Hannah asked.

"Nothing," Tom replied, wiping his eyes on his sleeve.

"So why is Alison cuddling you then?"

"Tom is just feeling a bit homesick, I think, Hannah," Alison said.

"But you have only just got here, you haven't given it a chance yet!" Hannah snapped.

Hannah was right, but it was really early days for things to start falling apart yet.

"I'll be all right, Hannah. As you said, we have only just got here. We have to get used to you all and you get used to us," Tom said, wiping his nose on his sleeve.

There was a clock on the hallway wall, but not in either of the bedrooms.

"Hannah, Alison and Tom, it's time to get your night clothes on! It's been a long day and I think it's time for bed," Ruth called up the stairs.

"Come on, we had better get changed for bed," Alison said.

"Oh, and the dirty laundry bin is in the bathroom. If you could put your dirty laundry in there, we can empty it in the morning." Ruth shouted again. "Did you hear me, children?"

"Yes Ruth!" They shouted back.

"You don't have to shout back at me, you can just call over the banister!" Ruth snapped.

They all did as they were told. Hannah went back down to her bedroom to get her night things on. Once they had changed, Alison put her dirty clothes in the laundry bin then Tom could go into the bathroom and do the same. Hannah had her own laundry bin in the bathroom downstairs that she shared with her parents.

Tom got into bed. Even though it wasn't that late, they had had a long day. School, the journey here, and then dinner. It didn't take him long to drift off to sleep, where he dreamt that he was still at Craven House with Freddie and Charlie.

Alison got into bed. Her curtains were still letting the light in. She would have to turn over onto her side so go to sleep.

"Please let us like living here and we haven't made a mistake," she whispered to herself.

She closed her eyes and also dreamt that she was still back at Craven House with Jo, Sandra and everyone else.

Ruth was tucking Hannah into bed.

"Mum, it is all right that Alison and Tom are here, isn't it? I mean, is it going to be like normal or are we going to have some fun in the house once again?" Hannah asked her mother.

Ruth sighed.

"I don't know, Sweetheart. We will just have to wait and see. I think it's going good so far," Ruth added.

"No, it's not, Mum. Tom was really upset earlier. Dad has already told him off twice," she added.

"OK love, I'll have a word with him, now don't you worry, it will all be fine, OK?" Ruth said. She tucked her daughter tightly in and then kissed her on the forehead. She turned on her nightlight and then turned off the main light.

She then went upstairs to check on Alison and Tom. Both were out like a light. She closed their doors and went back downstairs to Harry.

"Harry, what did you say to Tom since we got back?" Ruth asked.

"Apart from the dinner table. I never said anything," Harry said.

"Hannah said that Tom was upset because you said something to him," Ruth added.

"Oh that! Yes, he asked me why he had to play on the landing and Hannah could play in her room. I told him that Hannah was our daughter and she had missed school, so she played with her toys, and not to question me again, that's right, isn't it? I mean, he's a boy and I am an adult, he should have more respect," argued Harry.

"Yes, he is a boy, but he's just left the place he has called home for the last two and a half years, Harry. It's going to be difficult, especially with all of these rules you're imposing," Ruth said.

"They had rules at that home, and Hannah is our daughter, she should be treated differently, shouldn't she?" Harry asked. He wanted Ruth to support him, he was right on this.

"No Harry, they are our children now too, we are a big family now, not a little one anymore. These kids have had a hard time, which is why they ended up there in the first place. They need to feel part of something, part of a family, not disregarded because they aren't blood relatives," Ruth said. "Think how you would feel, Harry."

"OK, yes, I will," Harry said, looking back at his paper.

***

The sun was beaming in straight through to Alison, she turned over and saw the clock on her bedside cabinet: 7.45 am. Gosh she had better get up, breakfast was at 8 am and she didn't want to be late on her first morning in her new home.

She ran over to Tom's room and called him.

"Tom, come on, you have to get up, it's 7.45 am and we have to be downstairs in fifteen minutes," Alison called.

She darted into the bathroom to get washed. She shut the door and quickly washed herself, then went back to her room to quickly get dressed. Tom was going into the bathroom and he went as quick as he could. He then ran back into his bedroom to get his clean clothes. Alison looked in on him and grabbed his shoes and socks, so he could put them on. Then they both legged it downstairs to breakfast.

Harry was looking at his pocket watch. Eight on the dot. He snapped it shut and all of the children were at the table. There was toast in the toast rack and cereal in front of them. Ruth came in with a pot of tea and poured milk onto their cereal.

They all sat there in silence. When they had eaten all of their food, Alison was asked to help Ruth in the kitchen tidying up and cleaning and drying the dishes and cutlery. Tom went back upstairs to brush his teeth, then brush his hair.

He was admiring himself in the mirror when Alison came back upstairs to brush her teeth and hair. Once they were both done, it was only nine o'clock and they still had an hour. Alison went back downstairs, whilst Tom stayed upstairs.

"Erm Ruth, is there anything else you want me to do before we go out at ten to buy our new school uniform?" Alison asked. Ruth looked at Harry, he shook his head.

"No sweetheart, do you want to go back upstairs and play with Tom on the landing, but be mindful of the time, if you can both be back down here ready for ten to ten. Then we can head off to the uniform shop," Ruth replied. Alison went back upstairs but went to check on Hannah first.

"Hi Hannah, how are you this morning?" Alison asked.

"Oh, I'm fine, just sorting out this stuff to take to the jumble sale in the week," Hannah replied.

Alison could see she was sorting out teddy bears and dolls.

"Would you like a hand sorting them out?" She asked.

"No, I'm fine. I'm just checking which ones to keep and which ones to give away," Hannah replied.

Alison noticed that the doll that Tom had given her the first time they stayed was in the pile of toys to be given to the jumble sale.

"Hannah, this is the doll that Tom got you; don't you like it?" Alison asked.

"Yes, yes, I do, but Daddy said that I have to get rid of some of them, as there are too many and this was the one he wanted to put for the jumble sale," Hannah replied.

"Tom is going to be very upset, Hannah, can't you change your mind and put one of the other ones in instead?" Alison pleaded.

"Daddy said it has to go, so it has to go." Hannah shrugged.

Alison knew it would be no good to argue. She left Hannah to her own devices. She was upset with what Hannah had said, and things weren't going to be as rosy as she and everyone else had thought.

They had only been there for an evening and this was the next morning, but Alison was starting to think they had made a big mistake moving here.

"Come on everyone, it's time to go shopping!" Ruth shouted up the stairs.

Alison got her coat; she still had her five pounds in her purse in the pocket of her coat. She would bring it with her today just in case she saw something she wanted.

Tom had his coat on, but the buttons were done up wrong, so Alison helped him. They went downstairs. As she went passed Hannah's she noticed a black bag in the corner, which would have been full of stuff for the jumble. She carried on downstairs with Tom, everyone was waiting for them.

"Right, everyone ready, let's go then?" Harry said.

Harry opened the front door.

"We can walk up to town; it's a nice morning and it won't take long," Harry said.

Tom and Alison walked behind; Ruth was holding Hannah's hand and Harry was in front, saying which way to go and where they were. Alison and Tom were just following but had no idea where they were going.

It didn't take long to get to the uniform shop. They all walked in. Hannah was at the same school.

"Hello, can I help you?" The shop assistant asked.

"Hello yes. We need to get full uniform for these two," Harry said, pointing at Alison and Tom.

"What school are they going to?" The assistant asked.

"Balmsbary Peaks," Harry said.

"OK then, this way."

She walked over to where the school uniform for Balmsbary Peaks was. It was purple, yellow and grey. She got out her measuring tape.

"How old are you, young man?" She asked.

"I'm six," Tom replied.

"OK, so do you want jumpers or cardigans, or both?" The assistant asked.

"Erm, I don't know, maybe one of each?" Harry said.

She then measured Alison.

"And how old are you, young lady?" She asked.

"I'm nine, but nearly ten," Alison replied.

She felt a bit more grown-up now she was heading to double figures.

"Same, a jumper and cardigan?" The assistant asked.

Harry nodded. She put those items to one side.

"Now, shirts for you?" She asked, looking at Tom. "White or yellow?"

"White," Ruth said.

"How many?" The assistant asked, looking at Ruth. Ruth looked at Harry.

"Three," Harry replied.

"Blouses? Same?" The lady asked.

Harry nodded.

Next was skirts and trousers.

"We have pleated and straight skirts, do you have a preference?" The lady asked.

"Maybe one of each?" Ruth asked, looking at Harry for approval. He nodded.

"Trousers, now long or short?"

"Short trousers I think, please," Harry said.

The sales assistant put all of their items together.

251

"Anything else? PE Kit?"

"Yes, I nearly forgot about that," Ruth said.

"Now it's skirts or shorts for the girls," the lady said.

She disappeared for a little while and brought back one of each.

"Which do you prefer?" The lady asked.

"The shorts," Ruth said.

She put the skirt to one side and collected a pair of shorts for Tom.

"Now PE tops, they are yellow Airtex tops," she told them.

Harry noticed the price of them and thought that £8.00 was a lot for a top, especially when the white ones were only £5.00.

"Ruth, if we get the white ones?" he said. He put his hand up as she was going to interrupt him. "If we get the white ones, we can get two each and just dye them yellow. Woolworths sell dye. We can do them today, leave them overnight to take properly. Then rinse them off and let them dry out in the garden," Harry suggested. "What do you think?"

Ruth wasn't too bothered about the price, but she knew Harry would be.

"Whatever you think is best, Harry," she replied.

"Anything else?" asked the assistant.

"No, that's it now, thank you. Would you like some help taking this to the till?" Harry asked.

"No, that's fine, I can manage. I am just glad you got everything you need."

The sales assistant totted up the bill.

"That will be £132.00, please Sir."

Harry looked rather flushed. He got out the money and gave it to her. She pressed the button, put the money in the till and then gave him his change.

"Thank you, and see you again soon, Sir."

Harry said thank you and waved her goodbye.

"Right, now to get you both some school shoes, and plimsoles for PE," Harry said.

There was a shop just a bit further down.

"Clark's are the best for children," Harry said.

They went into the shoe shop, with their bags full of uniform, and took their seats. Harry started to look at the shoes.

The assistant came over said her hellos and was told what they needed.

"First I would like to measure the children's feet, that way we know what we have in stock and what they are comfortable with," The shop assistant said.

She came back with a measuring machine, that looked like it should be in a museum. She asked Alison to take off her shoe, put her foot into the machine, and put this measuring tape, which was attached, across her foot.

"Yes, this young lady is a size three, so have a look, little lady, at what is on the shelf and I will go and get them from the stockroom," The lady said.

Alison went along to the girls' shoes and saw some lovely black ones with a strap going across the middle of the shoe, which you did up with a buckle.

"I like these ones," she told Ruth.

"OK, young man, let's see what size you are then?" The lady said.

"Oh, it tickles!" Tom laughed.

Harry gave him a stern look, Tom looked down at his feet.

"A size eleven for this young man, would you also like to go and have a look at some shoes, and I will get them for you?" She asked.

Tom looked at the boys' shoes, there was a pair there that he liked. They had laces but he could fit his foot in without doing them up.

"I like these ones," he said, holding them up.

The lady disappeared into the stockroom and came back with two boxes of shoes.

Alison was up first to try them on. Hannah was also looking at the shoes. She wanted a new pair and didn't want to be left out.

When Alison had them on, the sales assistant checked to see where her big toe was and made sure the shoe fitted correctly and wasn't too spacious at the sides to cause the shoe to fall off. She checked the width.

"Perfect, now walk up and down and see how they feel," the lady said.

By then she was already undoing the shoes for Tom to try on. Alison liked these shoes and they were comfortable.

Tom tried his on and he liked them they fitted well, and his toes had plenty of room for when they grow a bit.

"If you can walk up and down, little fella and we can see how you feel in them?" The lady said. Tom got up as he was told to. He liked the shoes; they were also comfortable.

"Right, that's two pairs of shoes for two satisfied customers." The lady said, smiling at Harry. "Oh Miss, we also need a pair of plimsoles each for PE?" Harry remembered.

"OK, I'll just fetch them," she replied.

"Daddy, can I have a new pair of shoes as well?" Hannah asked.

"Well, we only came out to get some for Alison and Tom, but yes, have a look with your mother and see what you can get," Harry replied.

Hannah wasn't hanging around for her dad to change his mind. She grabbed her mum by the hand and looked at the shoes. The lady came back with the plimsolls.

"Err Miss, I don't want to be a nuisance, but could we get another pair of shoes?" Harry asked.

Alison and Tom looked at each other, then Harry pointed towards Hannah.

"Certainly, I should measure her feet first, is that OK?"

Hannah sat down as quick as lightning.

With her feet measured, Hannah had already chosen a pair of shoes, similar to Alison's. The lady returned with the other pair of shoes. Hannah tried them on. She was excited as they looked so nice. The lady then took all of the shoes and boxes to the till and totted up the bill to be £65.00. Harry took the money out of his wallet and paid for them, now all of the children had at least one bag each to carry with their new things in.

"Thank you and see you again," the sales assistant said.

Harry thanked the lady and waved goodbye.

"Right, the next stop is Woolworths," Harry said.

Alison and Tom's eyes lit up, maybe they were going to get a treat.

"We will wait out here while Ruth goes inside, it looks busy and we have lots of bags," Harry said.

Ruth came back about ten minutes later with a very small bag.

"Did you get it?" Harry asked.

"Yes, I got two packs just in case one isn't enough," Ruth replied.

"Ready to go back home now?" Harry said to his wife.

Alison and Tom were pleased they had new things, but they were uniform for school, not chill clothes, or playout clothes, but never mind, Alison was hopeful that was for next time. They all walked back in a chatty mood. Harry was pleased with what they had bought, it had cost more than he thought, but he was getting his cheque soon, so that could go back into his savings.

***

When they got back home, Ruth told the children to put their uniforms away on hangers. Alison had forgotten to put their dirty laundry into the basket in the bathroom, so she grabbed both hers and Tom's before they could come up and see.

Ruth took the Airtex tops out of the bags and got two big buckets, put the water and the dye in them and then the tops. By tomorrow, they should have gone a nice yellow colour. Alison hung up her uniform and put her shorts in the drawer just under her underwear.

Ruth came upstairs and checked if Tom needed help with his clothes. He did as he was struggling with the coat hanger and the jumper. Once it was done and everything was away Ruth asked the children to come down for lunch, as it was already one o'clock. They were having sandwiches, but they were already made and in the fridge.

Hannah had put her shoes away and came downstairs, whilst Tom and Alison were already there. They all sat down to their lunch again in silence. There were sandwiches, crisps and an apple or orange each. Once they had eaten, Tom had asked if they could have the TV on as there was always something good on a Saturday afternoon, like Starsky and Hutch. Harry told them that they only really watch TV in the evening, that way the day's jobs are to be done and not to be distracted by the TV.

Tom went back upstairs to his bedroom. He had had a comic he wanted to read. Alison also went back upstairs and started reading her comics. Again, she didn't get time to buy anything at the shop, so she left her five pounds in her coat pocket. Alison thought that Harry and Ruth would at least have gotten them some colouring pencils and some paper or a colouring book to stop the boredom, but it seemed that they had to do that for themselves. They hadn't had chance to go into Woolworths to have a look around.

Alison sat on her bed reading. Hannah seemed to be the only one who was ever playing. Before she knew it, it was time to start getting dinner ready. Once dinner was cooked and everyone was eating, Alison thought that all they seemed to do was cook, eat, clean up and then go back upstairs. They didn't seem to be having any fun.

She was starting to look forward to going to a new school. At least she could make new friends and be able to talk to Tom properly. It was now time to clean up again after dinner.

"Ruth, when I go back upstairs, would it be OK if I had a bath, and then get into my night things?" Alison asked.

"Yes, that would be OK. Do you need a hand with anything, like washing your hair or anything?" Ruth asked.

"No, I will be fine, but Tom will need help with washing his hair, I can do that if you like?" Alison suggested.

"No, I am sure I will be able to manage Tom with his hair," Ruth said very quickly as Harry was about to say something about it.

With the dinner things washed, dried and put away, Alison headed upstairs. She had some nice bubble bath that she was given at Christmas. She still had some left, so she grabbed her stuff and went into the bathroom.

The bath was lovely, not too hot, but very relaxing. She had washed her hair and had it up in a towel.

"Tom, I'm finished if you want to go in now. I've wiped around the bath for you. Do you have your Matey bubble bath?" Alison asked.

"Yes, I do, Alison. Ruth, can I have my bath now?" Tom shouted out from the top landing.

"Yes, you can," Ruth replied.

Tom grabbed his stuff and put the plug in.

"Tom, hold on, wait a minute." Ruth said, "I don't want you to put your hand in just in case it's hot water and you will get scalded."

She started to run the bath and put in Tom's matey under the tap. The water was just above warm.

"Here, put your hand in, how does that feel?" Ruth asked.

"That's lovely," Tom said, swishing the water around with his fingers.

"But Tom, you have to be careful, your hand can take hotter water than the rest of your body, so ease yourself in, just to make sure it's not too hot," Ruth said.

Ruth had a soft spot for Tom, she didn't want him to hurt himself and he did have a lovely nature about him. Once he got in, he said "Ahhh" and Ruth knew he found the water temperature at a good level.

"Now do you want me to wash your hair first and then your body, you do the front and I will do the back, then you can relax for a little while, does that sound alright?" Ruth asked.

"Yes, that's fine, then I can get out and dry myself," Tom said.

Tom really enjoyed his bath. By the time he got out, his fingers and toes had shrivelled up. He wasn't worried; that was how he knew he had a good bath. He got dried and then put on his pyjamas on and then got into bed. It was already gone 8.30 pm and they were all tired. They had had a busy day with the shopping and trying on of shoes. They were all glad to get to bed.

By the time Ruth had gone back downstairs, Harry had the TV on and was watching a drama.

Ruth went to the kitchen to make some tea.

"It went well today with the shopping, don't you think so, Harry?" Ruth said.

"Yes, it cost enough, but we will soon get that back and Hannah's shoes won't have cost us anything either," Harry said.

***

Sunday came and went like it did every week, but this one was as boring as the rest of the time at the Coopers. Alison and Tom couldn't wait to go to school on Monday. They were both up early excited at what the day would bring. Ruth took all three of them in, as Harry had gone on already to work.

The school wasn't far away, but they went in the car. Ruth said if they wanted to, they could walk home, but they would have to wait for Hannah too. It didn't take long to get to school and once they arrived, Hannah had already gone off to her class.

Ruth waited with Alison and Tom for the secretary to show them where they were going. Tom was going to be in Hannah's class, but being older, Alison was going into the third year of primary school, while Hannah and Tom were in the infants still.

Tom was dropped off first and he liked his new class. The teacher, Mr Armstrong, sat Tom down with another couple of boys, Lee, and Charles. They were doing things with plasticine and were having fun. Alison was happy to see Tom settle down straight away.

Ruth then went with Alison to her new classroom, where her teacher, Mrs Adams, introduced her to her classmates. She sat down with a couple of girls, Julie, and Kim. They were doing English essays, which Alison loved, so she got stuck in.

Ruth left the school knowing that all three of the children were settled.

She then made her way home. She had some things to do, but she was going to make the most of the peace and quiet, put her feet up with a cuppa and a chocolate biscuit or two.

Harry had left her a list of the things he wanted the kids to do: first of all, a chore/jobs list, that was going to be put up, in the hallway on their landing, with what they needed to do every day after school and at home on the weekends.

She had put the washing on and was slowly going through this list. Chores/jobs to do—check homework if any, clean upstairs, clean downstairs, entertain Hannah. That was enough for anyone to be going on with for now.

She finished her cup of tea and biscuits. She had some ironing to do, but not a lot. The kids had only been here a couple of days and only wearing one lot of clothes a day and then night things, there hadn't been much to do.

Alison and Tom loved their first day at school. Even though their breaks were at the same time, they were in different playgrounds, so Tom would go out with his friends, Hannah had her friends and so did Alison now. It was such a relief to talk to other girls her age.

Alison got on well with Julie and Kim. They lived down the road from her. Kim had two older sisters who had left school and already gone onto secondary school; Julie was an only child. It was nice getting to know the girls better and they were fine with her being in a foster placement.

Before they knew it, it was 3.30pm and time to go home.

Alison went to the main entrance to wait for Tom and Hannah. This was the only time that the three children could really talk away from home.

"Hannah, why is it so difficult to talk at home?" Alison asked.

"It's not difficult to talk at home, it's just Daddy likes peace and quiet, that's all," Hannah replied.

"But why can't we watch TV?" Tom asked.

"As I just said, Daddy likes peace and quiet, that's why we can only play on the landing and not in our bedrooms."

Hannah was getting a little annoyed. They knew the rules, so why do they have to keep asking?

They walked the rest of the way home in silence.

Alison thought, if "Daddy" likes peace and quiet, how come they can't play in their rooms? Surely it would be quieter than on the landing?

She didn't think about it anymore, it was just too weird.

Once they got home Ruth told them to go upstairs and take their uniforms off, put them back in their wardrobes and put on clean clothes. At the home, the children had a fresh uniform for every day. They would get in, take off their uniform and it would go straight into the wash basket. Here it just went back in the wardrobe. Never mind, they did as they were told.

On leaving her bedroom, Alison noticed the big sign in the hallway. How on earth could she have missed that? It was huge!

But she did, she walked over to it and started to read it:

After school, take your uniform off and put it back in the wardrobe unless been worn for two days running. Then put in the laundry basket in the bathroom to be washed.

Tidy up your bedrooms.

Make sure the bathroom is clean.

Hoover bedrooms, landing and bathroom on the top floor.

No food to be eaten in bedrooms under any excuse.

Alison couldn't believe what she was reading; that wasn't including what was to be done at the weekends and the holidays. But this was Monday, she wasn't going to worry about the weekend yet; that was still another four days away.

Tom hadn't seen the sign, but Alison beckoned him over and put her finger to her lips, so she would tell him quietly and not to make a sound.

***

The week had gone quite quickly considering. Apart from school and cleaning, the kids hadn't done really much. When the children got home on Friday afternoon, Harry was already home.

"Now, we have received a letter from Mrs Hemsby, she is the social worker at this end dealing with our and your placement here. She is coming over on Friday next week at 4 pm, so you both have to get back from school as quickly as you can," Harry said sternly to the children and Ruth. "Ruth, if you can make some sandwiches and lay out a bit of a tea?"

Ruth nodded her head.

"Good. Now if you lot want to go upstairs and get changed out of your uniforms, they should be put in the laundry bin today, so that Ruth can wash them and get them ready for Monday," Harry ordered.

The children nodded their heads.

"Sorry, what did you say?" Harry asked.

"Yes Harry, we will do it now," Alison said.

Alison and Tom headed upstairs, and Hannah followed behind. Tom had learned quickly not to say anything when they left the ground floor, they didn't know if Harry was listening and they didn't trust Hannah anymore. So much had happened in a week and it felt like a year.

When they got up to the top floor, Alison saw another big poster on the wall next to the first one for when they get in from school. This sign was titled 'The Weekend':

On the weekend, Saturday morning…

Roll your bedding towards the bottom of the bed to air it.

Dust and clean your surfaces, mirrors, chest of drawer tops, etc.

Hoover your floors. (Alison can clean Tom's bedroom as well, with Tom helping.)

Clean the bathroom, the sink, toilet and the bath, the shelving.

Sweep and then wash the floor.

Once the bathroom is cleaned and you have hoovered your bedroom floors, take off your bed linen and put it into the laundry basket in the bathroom.

Put on clean bedding.

Hoover all of the landing and then the stairs until you get to the first floor.

Unplug the hoover and wind the wire and plug around the back so nobody trips over it.

Alison couldn't believe it again. She had so much cleaning to do; she didn't have to do that at Craven House. She now understood how Tom felt about living here. She wondered if she would be able to speak to Mrs Hemsby about going back to Craven House, but she didn't dare say anything to Harry—he would explode.

She decided that she would see how things were next week. They would have been there for two weeks by then and see if things had settled down, but this new list didn't make it look promising.

Alison went into her room, took off her uniform and put on something else that was a bit more comfortable. Tomorrow was Saturday and she didn't know if she and Tom would be getting any pocket money, she wanted to save up some money just in case they wanted anything—they weren't going to get it from Harry and Ruth.

She appreciated she got clothes last week, well, school uniform really, and they did get new shoes, but they hadn't received any treats.

Alison checked in on Tom and he was getting undressed, he was struggling a bit. Alison looked over the banister and she could hear Harry and Ruth talking and Hannah was busy in her room.

Alison went in to give Tom a hand. She put her finger to her lips, Tom understood. They had become so close in the last week, they both realised very quickly that they weren't going to have the same sort of easy lifestyle that they had in Craven House. But for now, they had to just see what happened.

Alison put Tom's uniform in the laundry bin and tip-toed out of the bathroom and then went downstairs. Ruth seemed to always want her to help out with dinner when she got in from school.

Tom got out his cars that he wanted to play with and put them on the landing.

"Oh, there you are, darling, ready to give me a hand?" Ruth asked.

Alison nodded and helped Ruth with dinner.

Alison was peeling potatoes and dreading tomorrow but she wasn't about to question Ruth about the amount of work to be done on a Saturday. Both children had helped out and done their jobs at the home, but there were loads of people mucking in.

Here though, she would be doing the top floor on her own.

She carried on peeling potatoes in silence.

Alison knew that being at home after school and on the weekends were going to be no picnic and she couldn't wait for school the following Monday.

Before both of them knew it, it was Monday again. Ruth had done a good job on their uniforms and they were out of the door as quick as they could get, even with Hannah, they had learnt to walk quite fast.

They rarely had anything to do with Hannah at school, and only spoke to her on the way and back to and from school. She hardly had much to do with either of them once they moved in. But Alison was just happy to have Kim and Julie at school and Tom was delighted to have Lee and Charles. It was an outlet for both of them and to also feel like real children again, like they did at the home.

Everything always came back to the home, but it's what they felt. They both hadn't realised how much they loved it there, had fitted in with everything perfectly.

The rest of the week had flown by and now it was Friday. Harry hadn't gone to work as early as normal and before they all left for school, he said he wanted a word with them.

"Now, children, don't forget Mrs Hemsby will be coming here today at 4pm for a visit and I want you all to get home as quickly as possible so you can all get changed and ready for her. Don't forget Alison, Tom, she hasn't met either of you yet, but she has met Hannah. So, I expect you to be on your best behaviour," Harry said.

"What was that?" Harry put his hand to his ear.

"Yes Harry, we will be back as soon as possible," Alison replied.

"Don't forget!" Harry called after them.

Alison, Tom and Hannah walked up the road quickly so they wouldn't be late for school. Harry's pep talk had made them late leaving and they got in just before the bell went. They all darted off to their classes and took off their coats and bags.

As always, the days of the week were going quicker, and the evenings and weekends were going so slow. Alison was sure someone was speeding up the time at school and slowing down the time at home.

They had to wait a little time for Hannah to come out of class; she was talking to the teacher about something. Alison had already been waiting for ten minutes, Tom was with her, so she went back to his class to collect Hannah.

"Hannah, are you ready? We have to be home early today, remember?" Alison said. She wasn't very happy that Hannah was taking so long.

"Oh, sorry, yes, I had forgotten. I had to talk to my teacher about something." Hannah smiled sweetly.

"Hannah, we could have spoken about this on Monday, but never mind, have a lovely weekend and see you and Tom back on Monday," the teacher said.

So that was her game; she deliberately wanted to make them late back.

"Come on, we're going to have to run or we won't make it back," Alison said.

They did run back, but even though they got back just before 4 pm, Ruth opened the door and gave the children a look; they hadn't seen that look from Ruth before.

She let them in and they pushed past her, and could hear Harry talking to someone. Mrs Hemsby was already there, sitting down in the sitting room and being handed a cup of tea from Ruth.

"Hello Hannah. Hello Alison and Tom, it's lovely to meet you both." Mrs Hemsby smiled.

"Alison, Tom, Hannah, did you have a good day at school today?" Harry asked kindly.

"Yes, we did, thank you. Hannah was talking to her teacher about something, which is why we were late here, sorry." Alison smiled back"

She thought if she said something in front of Mrs Hemsby, they couldn't get into trouble.

"Not to worry, dears, these things happen, did you want to get a sandwich and a drink?" Mrs Hemsby asked.

"Erm, I think we had better change out of our uniform first, is that OK, Ruth?" Alison asked.

"That's fine, see you all in a few minutes," Ruth said.

All three of them bolted up the stairs and got changed as quick as they possibly could. They ran back downstairs. They sounded like a herd of elephants, but thankfully, even though Harry was very cross with them, he wouldn't show it in front of Mrs Hemsby.

He wanted her to think they were model parents and this placement was going fantastically well.

They sat down at the table, but Mrs Hemsby wanted to have a proper look at them, so she asked for them to come and sit down on the sofa with their food and drinks. Harry was feeling very nervous but kept it well hidden.

Alison and Tom did as they were asked. Hannah sat with her mother.

Mrs Hemsby wanted to know what it was like living at the seaside, did they like living with the Coopers? What was it like having another sister? Alison answered most of the questions; Tom didn't know what to say. He said that he liked living here and he enjoyed having a bedroom of his own, but he was stuck when asked what it was like to live at the seaside; they hadn't been or even seen the sea since they got here.

All of the children had a few sandwiches and a couple of fondant fancies cakes and juice. Mrs Hemsby seemed happy with how things were going on and how well the children were settling in with a big change like this.

"Well, that's me done then. I've assessed the children, and everything seems tickety boo, so, I will send in my report and Craven House will also receive one, as will Mr Prowse. I think everything is in order, so thank you, Mr Cooper, Mrs

Cooper, children. It was lovely to see you all," Mrs Hemsby said, shaking the Coopers' hands.

They walked her to the door and spoke for a few minutes, she got into her car and waved to them before she drove off.

"Hannah, upstairs to your room please and close the door behind you!" Harry ordered his daughter. "Ruth, go after her and make sure she closes the door, please," ordered Harry.

He waited for Hannah and Ruth to leave the room.

"How dare you disobey me by coming home late! I told you all to get back here as soon as possible after school!" Harry bellowed.

"But we were waiting for Hannah; she was talking to her teacher about something in class, Harry," Alison replied.

"Don't you dare blame Hannah for your incompetence! You were told to be here before 4 pm and you were late!" Harry shouted.

"But we were home before 4 pm, it's not our fault Mrs Hemsby was early," Alison said.

"Harry, Hannah did make us late. We had to go back to class to get her," Tom added.

Harry saw red.

"I have told you before, never, ever answer me back!" He screamed at Tom.

Harry grabbed hold of Tom by the arm turned him around and smacked him hard on the backside.

Tom was so shocked; he had never been smacked before.

"Harry, you can't smack Tom! He was telling you the truth!" Alison screamed.

With that, Harry grabbed hold of Alison and did exactly the same to her.

"Now both of you, get up to your bedrooms, get your pyjamas on! You won't be having any dinner tonight! Now go!" Harry bellowed at both of them.

The children ran upstairs in shock. They had never been smacked before by anyone. They ran past Ruth as she came out of Hannah's room.

"Harry, did you just smack both of them?" Ruth asked in shock.

"Yes, I did, and it was a long time coming!" Harry said. "That will stop their bloody ideas about being rude to me!"

"Harry, you can't smack them, they didn't do anything wrong!"

"Yes, I can! They live in my house and I make the rules! Me, not the bloody social workers. Me, Ruth! Do you hear?" He retorted to Ruth. "And don't you go up there, they need to learn a lesson! If you do, you'll get one as well!" Harry warned.

"Is that right, Harry? You're going to lump me one too, are you? You do that and I send those children straight back to Craven House, you got that? They may have a bloody better life there than they do here, so don't you forget it!" Ruth snapped.

She cleared the table and the tea things and went into the kitchen. She knew she had gone too far, but she was too mad and she didn't care.

***

When they got upstairs, Tom was crying, and Alison was nearly crying. They both walked over to the bathroom and started to whisper.

"Tom, I know it's hard, but we are going to have to be really good," Alison said.

"But I am good, Alison. I just spoke up to Harry, that's all," Tom replied.

"I know Tom, but we can't do that. We have to be really good and do as we are told. When we're not at school, we have to do our jobs and just stay up here, eat our meals in silence and if we're asked something, we answer but that is it, OK?" Alison wiped away his tears.

Tom nodded.

"Good, it's for our best interests. Until this placement is over, we have to stick it out, but one thing…" Alison said, "Hannah—we can't trust her, Tom. We can't be her friend. We have to do as we are told. If we have to speak to her at home, we do so. At school is another matter, we can go to and from school in silence, yeah?" Alison said.

Tom nodded again.

"Tom, I know it's early, but do you want to go to bed? You don't have to go to sleep unless you want to, but I think it's a good idea, that way we are out of the way, only get up if you need the toilet," Alison said.

"Yes, I think that's a good idea."

They both went to bed and only got up for the toilet. Alison's head was spinning around. She couldn't take in what had happened this afternoon. Harry was lovely when Mrs Hemsby was around, but as soon as she left, he changed. She turned over and slowly fell asleep.

Tom was exhausted; he started crying again when he got into bed and cried himself to sleep.

It was quite late when Ruth went up to check on both of them, they were sound asleep. What had she done; she shouldn't have let this placement go ahead. They were getting money to have these children and they were being treated awfully by her husband. It was no life for them whatsoever. She would see how things panned out over the next coming weeks and then she would take action if it didn't change.

***

Even with all of the extra work given at home, Alison got on with it. She didn't moan or complain. Tom stayed upstairs in his room or on the landing playing. After what had happened in the second week of them being there, they weren't about to give Harry an excuse to smack them again.

Before they knew it, they had been there for a month. They were both enjoying school, and both were excelling with their work. Their teachers were pleased with them, as they had joined the classes rather late in the year. It was only a couple of weeks away, then it was the six weeks summer holidays and both of the children were dreading it. Being at home with Ruth and Hannah; Harry had booked some time off work for the holidays.

Tom and Alison had hoped he would have worked through the holidays, so they wouldn't really see him, but he had arranged it before they had come to live with them.

Harry got quite cross a lot at home since they had moved in, and every time he shouted, both of the children jumped out of their skin.

Even though both of them were doing well at their lessons, their teachers had noticed a bit of a difference in them they hadn't spotted before, but they couldn't put their fingers on it.

Alison and Tom hadn't told anyone at school what had been going on, and Hannah wouldn't say anything about it either. They thought they would be in trouble and nobody would believe them or do anything about it. They were only children after all.

The next two weeks shot by. The children were all going up together the following year, so nobody had to say goodbye to each other. Tom, Alison and Hannah, all left school with their schoolwork. Alison and Tom didn't have much as they had only been there for a few weeks, but Hannah had quite a lot. Alison gave her a hand carrying it as there was rather a lot of big pictures and she couldn't manage it.

Ruth was supposed to collect them in the car but hadn't turned up. When they got home, Ruth was already there, she saw how much stuff they had and put her hands up to her mouth and apologised, she had forgotten to get them.

"I am sorry children, I had to do some shopping and I forgot the time. I've only just walked in the door before you," she said.

"Never mind, Ruth, we got back OK and here is some of Hannah's schoolwork she has brought home," Alison said.

Alison and Tom took their stuff upstairs and got changed out of their uniform. Harry came home early from work and saw Hannah's schoolwork.

"Hey Hannah, this is great, we can put this up on the wall in the kitchen, and maybe on your bedroom wall if you want?" he said, praising his daughter.

Hannah had a beaming smile on her face.

"Daddy, did you see Alison's drawing, it's wonderful!" Hannah said, showing her father the picture Alison had drawn.

"What, oh yes, that's nice," Harry said, not even looking up.

Alison took her picture upstairs. She was used to the idea that Harry wasn't interested in anything she or Tom did. It was all about Hannah.

Hannah popped up to the top floor.

"Alison, thank you for helping me with my schoolwork, I wouldn't have managed it on my own," she said.

"That's OK, it's done now," Alison said.

Alison wanted to be away from Hannah as quickly as possible. She didn't trust her, and she definitely didn't want to say anything in front of her. She had dropped her in it too many times already.

The next day, when they were having breakfast when Harry announced that he, Ruth, and Hannah were going to go out shopping and that they would be on their own for a little while. Alison was quite surprised at this news; they hadn't been left in the house on their own before since they had been there.

"But that doesn't mean you can get up to mischief, like running up and down the stairs. Mrs Baker next door doesn't want to hear you up and down the stairs like a herd of elephants!" Harry warned.

Alison helped with the washing up.

"Besides, you have enough jobs to do to keep you busy, Alison and I hope by the time we get back, you will have nearly finished." Harry said.

Once breakfast was over Alison took what cleaning materials she needed from the cupboard and went upstairs to make a start; their beds were already airing. She cleaned the bathroom next.

Alison heard the door close, and then locked. She continued with what she was doing. The good thing was that Tom could sit talking to her without worrying about getting into trouble and if he helped her, they could be finished soon.

"Maybe they are going out to get your birthday present, that's why they don't want you to go with them?" suggested Tom.

"Maybe, but I'm not holding my breath," Alison said. "Now let's get this done in peace and quiet," Alison said.

"Cor, you sounded like Harry then!" Tom laughed.

"Oi, shut up! Let's get this done," Alison laughed.

When they came back, the Coopers were all carrying bags, but nothing that looked like birthday presents. Alison had done all of her jobs and had left the hoover in a safe place on the first floor, as instructed. She took the dirty laundry basket downstairs and then went back upstairs. The rest of Saturday went as normal; dinner, tidying up afterwards and then bath and bed, by the time of the bath and bed, Alison was ready for it, she was exhausted. Never mind, she thought, it was her birthday in just over a week and she would be in double figures! Surely, they would get her something, she thought.

Alison turned over and fell asleep, dreaming about her last birthday at Craven House. It was wonderful. She had woken up early on her big day. Tom was singing "Happy Birthday" whilst trying to jump on her bed.

Then they had a lovely breakfast and lots and lots of fun, followed by a party later in the day.

***

The next day came and went. The same as every other Sunday, but this was different. It was the summer holidays, so at dinner, Alison asked what they will be doing over the summer holidays.

"Well, I have two weeks off and after that, there are activities all over town, we didn't have time to get you into playcentre over the holidays as it's fully booked. As I'm not at work, we are going to have some lazy days at the beach, but other than that, we haven't arranged a holiday or anything, just days at the beach," Harry said.

Alison was disappointed; they always did lots of stuff at Craven House, but she had better not say that; it would only annoy Harry. At least they were going to the beach for a lazy day, that sounded fun…no housework or cleaning. That would be something to look forward to.

Monday morning came and Ruth popped her head around the door.

"Morning Alison, we're heading out for a little while, can you get up please?" Ruth asked.

"Yes of course, where are we going?" Alison asked.

"Oh, you're not going anywhere. We're popping out to Hove to collect some things, so you and Tom will stay here, but you can play in the hallway with Tom," Ruth replied.

Alison couldn't believe her ears. They were staying home again while THEY went out.

Tom got out of bed, came over to Alison's doorway and asked what was going on. She quietly told him. Tom was glad, he didn't care they weren't going with them, they had the house to themselves and nobody telling them off for breathing.

Alison got ready and went downstairs and Tom followed after. When they got downstairs, breakfast was already made.

"You can clean up afterwards, can't you, Alison?" Ruth said.

She didn't have much choice.

"Yes, that's OK," Alison replied.

They left them behind and locked the door. Tom loved it! They could talk normally, no whispering. But the Coopers weren't out for long. They could only play, they couldn't turn the TV on, Harry would come straight in and put his hand on the back of it.

If it was cold, they hadn't touched it, but if it was warm, they had, and he would lose his temper. He had done it once. Tom had turned it on, and Harry hit the roof and shouted at them, but Tom had run up the stairs when Harry had chased him to smack him. Thankfully, with Tom being so small, he could run fast. He ran into the bathroom and locked the door behind him. No-one could prise him out for a few hours. He wasn't going to get another smack.

By then, Harry for once had calmed down. But he didn't look at Tom until the next day and only spoke to him if he needed to. So, neither of them touched the TV again. This going out without them was becoming a regular occurrence that Alison and Tom were getting used to.

***

The days were ticking by towards Alison's birthday. Tom had made her a card but couldn't buy her anything as he didn't have any money, but he knew Alison wouldn't mind. The day before her birthday, a card came through the letterbox, with the Craven House frank on it.

Tom knew where it had come from and so did everyone else. Ruth had gone out to the shop later that evening and didn't seem to come back with anything, but as Alison and Tom were upstairs looking out of the hallway window. They didn't see anything, but she had a card hidden inside her coat.

Alison and Tom had gone to bed. Alison was a little excited as she didn't know what her birthday would bring. She got off to sleep quite well. Usually, the day before her birthday she was too excited to sleep, but she was so tired with all of the work she was doing at home. She dropped off and was dreaming that she and Tom were running through a meadow full of pretty flowers and they were going towards the children and staff at Craven House.

It seemed like she had only been asleep for five minutes when Tom came bursting into her room, singing "Happy Birthday" to her. He had his card in his hand, he gave her a kiss on her cheek, and she opened her card.

"Thank you, Tom! It's lovely!" Alison said.

"Sorry I couldn't get you a present, I don't have any money this time," Tom added.

"Don't worry, I love the card," Alison replied. "Come on, we had better get up," she added.

Both of them got their clothes ready and went downstairs for breakfast.

"Morning Alison, morning Tom," Ruth said.

"Morning Ruth, it's Alison's birthday today!" Tom said.

"Oh, is it? Happy Birthday, Alison."

"Thank you, Ruth," Alison replied.

Harry was at the table reading his paper, he didn't even look up when the children sat at the table.

270

"Harry, it's Alison's birthday today. Harry?" Tom said, trying to get his attention.

"What? Oh, Happy birthday, Alison." Harry said, not looking up from his paper.

There were a couple of cards on the table, so obviously they knew anyway.

"Here you go, birthday girl," Ruth said, giving Alison her breakfast and handing her the birthday cards.

Alison started to open them. The first one was from Harry, Ruth and Hannah.

"Thank you for my card," Alison said. There wasn't any money and she hadn't noticed a gift at all.

Then she opened her next card. It was from the staff and children at Craven House. Harry's eyebrows perked up. Twenty pounds fell out of it.

"Ooh Alison, look what you've got!" Tom said, picking it up from the floor and handing it to her.

"It's been signed by everyone at Craven House! The staff and the kids, how lovely for them to remember me, and it even has a 10 on the front of the card," Alison said, quite overwhelmed with her card and money.

Hannah came down to the table and noticed the cards, she saw that they were for Alison. "Happy birthday, Alison," Hannah said.

"Thank you, Hannah," Alison replied.

When breakfast was over and Ruth had cleared up herself for a change, Alison looked at Ruth and Harry.

"Are we doing anything today?" Alison asked.

"No, not that I can think of," Harry replied.

"We could go into Town today, Harry, you know for Alison's birthday?" Ruth suggested.

"What? Oh, yes, we could do that later on," Harry said, looking back at his paper.

Alison and Tom went back upstairs to their bedrooms. Today was the first day that Tom and Alison were back to their normal selves before they came to live with the Coopers. Hopefully, Alison thought, this was going to be a new start and the time they had already been here was just teething problems.

Alison and Tom were on the landing talking about bits and pieces, nothing special when Ruth called them both downstairs and Hannah too.

"We're going out for lunch today to celebrate Alison's birthday, there is a nice little tea shop that do lovely cakes, so we will go in about half an hour. Do you want to all get yourselves ready?" She asked.

Alison and Tom didn't need asking twice. They raced up the stairs.

"Quietly please!" Harry said from the bottom of the stairs.

Alison pulled out her navy dress with shoes and a lightweight cardigan. It was July, after all. Tom had pulled out his light blue shirt and navy trousers. Ruth helped Hannah pick out a dress. She wore red; it matched her skin tone and her eyes shone bright when she wore bright colours.

Once they were all ready to leave, Harry came upstairs to make sure they had everything. Harry rarely went into the children's bedrooms. He had a quick look around and then went back downstairs again.

"Everyone ready? Then let's go!" he said, looking at his watch.

They went in the car, which was a real treat, as they had hardly gone in the car anywhere. They all climbed in and Ruth shut the back door of the car, then she climbed into the front. Harry started the engine, checked his mirror to make sure nothing was coming their way and then he drove off.

"Did you have to make a reservation for this place, Ruth?" Harry asked.

"No, we can just go in, it shouldn't be too busy," she replied.

It didn't take too long to get there.

Ruth entered 'Molly's Little Tea Shoppe' and everyone else followed. They were shown to their table.

"We're here for a birthday tea," Ruth said.

Molly stared at Hannah and said, "Happy Birthday, Little Lady!" Hannah beamed.

"No, it's Alison here. It's her birthday today," Ruth said.

"I beg your pardon, Happy Birthday, Young Lady," Molly said, correcting herself.

She gave Alison a huge smile and Alison smiled back.

Molly gave them all menus. They served a wide range of sandwiches and had scones with clotted cream and jam, also fairy cakes and Fondant Fancies. They had a set menu of a variety of different things to eat, which is what they decided on.

They also ordered squash for the children and a pot of tea for Ruth and Harry.

They started talking about the cakes and desserts and the fresh cream cakes on the trolley, Alison and Tom's eyes and mouths were watering.

Looking lovingly at them. Harry made a mental note of the cakes too.

Molly came back to the table with their drinks and then again with their sandwiches, which came on a three-tiered stand. None of the children had seen sandwiches that small all stacked neatly.

Ruth started offering the sandwiches out to the children first, Alison of course, then Tom and Hannah last. Harry, then took what he wanted, and everyone was eating their food, as always, in silence. Ruth poured the tea and the squash, so everyone had something to wash it down with.

When everyone had finished, Molly returned to clear the plates and took whatever was left of the sandwiches. She then returned with clean plates and cutlery. Her staff members brought over the cakes, also on a three-tiered cake stand. Harry had asked about the trolley of cream cakes, so Molly came back with those for him to choose from. Once Harry had chosen what he wanted and Ruth chose what she wanted, Molly went over to Alison, the birthday girl, to see what she had wanted.

"No, no, they can have these cakes that you have brought over already!" Harry said.

"But Sir, this cake for the birthday girl is free of charge for her, as it's her special day. We just would rather her choose for herself than us choose a cake and she doesn't like it," Molly said.

Harry didn't like the lady telling him what the children could have, but if he said anymore, it would make a scene and he didn't want that.

"Oh, right...lovely, thank you. Come on Alison, choose a cake, we don't want to keep the lady waiting," Harry said.

Alison chose a chocolate éclair; she hadn't had one before and it looked rather delicious.

Everyone was tucking into their cakes and Hannah kept looking at Alison every time she took a bite out of her éclair. She wasn't happy that she couldn't choose a cake off the trolley. She didn't care that Tom didn't have one, but she had wanted an éclair too.

When everyone had finished their cakes and drinks, Harry asked for the bill, which he was going through like a fine-tooth comb. Ruth looked at him as if to say, *Hurry up Harry, the staff are waiting*. Harry double checked that he was only paying for two fresh cream cakes and not three, but it wasn't on the bill, so he was relieved with that. He paid the bill and left a pound for a tip.

"Thank you and come again," Molly said, "and have a great birthday, Alison!"

"See you again soon, and thank you for a lovely tea and thank you for the cake, the éclair, it was lovely," Alison said.

They returned to the car.

"Well, that was a waste of time!" Harry said, loud enough for everyone to hear, including Alison.

She sat looking out of the window, Tom sat next to her and held her hand. She had a tear in her eye, but she wasn't going to let Harry see her cry.

When they got in, Harry asked Ruth to put the kettle on, and the children went upstairs. Harry followed them.

He went to Hannah's room to see if she was OK. She was fine, but a little disappointed she couldn't have an éclair like Alison.

"But Daddy, why couldn't I have a cake like Alison?" Hannah asked.

"Hannah, I didn't buy the cake and I couldn't make a fuss. Anyway, then I would have had to buy Tom one as well and he's greedy!" Harry said. "We can go again next time we go out on a Saturday on our own, would you like that?" Harry asked his daughter.

Hannah nodded, she would like that, she was getting used to going out with her mum and dad on her own.

Considering how she had seemed to get on with Tom and Alison before they moved here with them, she didn't like them anymore. Alison had heard what Harry had said about Tom, as she was standing on the landing by the banister and Hannah's door was open. Thankfully, Tom was oblivious to the conversation.

Alison was putting away her shoes when Harry knocked on her door.

"Can I come in, Alison?" Harry asked.

"Yes, of course," Alison replied.

Harry closed the door, but just left it ajar.

"Alison, I didn't realise that we would be going out for your birthday today as a treat, but at the moment, we really don't have the money for extras, so I was wondering if you could pay me back the money spent today at the tea shop. It was £17.20," Harry said.

Alison couldn't believe her ears.

"But Harry, I don't have any money," Alison said.

"Oh, but you do, you got twenty pounds in your card today from the staff and children at Craven House and I would like it please. We aren't made of money for treats. It costs a fortune to run a house this size and all of the extra food and clothes we have to buy you," Harry added, holding out his hand for the money.

Alison went to her bedside cabinet and took out the envelope with the twenty-pound note and gave it to Harry.

"Thank you," he said, and he left the room, leaving the door open wide.

Alison sat on her bed, absolutely dumbstruck by what had just happened. She didn't want to start crying in case Tom heard her and came to investigate. She didn't want Tom to know that Harry had just taken her birthday money from her.

Later that evening, Ruth made dinner and called the children down to eat. For once, Alison didn't have to help with anything. After dinner was over, Alison and Tom went upstairs, and Hannah stayed downstairs and sat on her dad's knee.

"Where's Alison and Tom, Harry?" Ruth asked. "I thought we would all be watching TV this evening?"

"They're probably upstairs in their bedrooms or on the landing," Harry said, not taking much notice. Ruth went to go upstairs to them, and Harry told her not to, to leave them upstairs.

"But it's Alison's birthday, they should be able to watch TV on her birthday, Harry," Ruth said.

"No, Ruth! Leave them where they are. We can watch TV as a family, for a change," Harry said.

"But Harry, they are our family as well, they shouldn't be left out," Ruth replied.

"Just leave them upstairs! I want some peace and quiet, Ruth!" Harry snapped.

"Did you enjoy your birthday, Alison?" Tom asked.

"Yes, I did Tom, thank you," Alison said.

"Did you enjoy the tea shop?" Alison asked.

"Too right I did, with old misery guts having a hissy fit because someone wanted to buy you a cake and that put Hannah's nose out of joint too," Tom giggled, "Let's just hope we aren't here for your next one!" Tom said.

"What do you mean, Tom?"

"I mean, let's hope we're back at Craven House or anywhere else, as long as it's not here!" Tom said.

275

They were still speaking in hushed tones, this house had its spies, mainly named Hannah, but they didn't want to get into trouble again.

"Come on, it's getting a bit late. Let's get ready for bed, it's been a long day and the quicker we get to bed, the quicker we can be in dreamland," Alison said. Tom nodded in agreement. He couldn't wait to get into bed.

***

A couple of days later, when Alison was helping in the kitchen making lunch, Harry was upstairs checking on Tom, who was sorting through his things. He wanted to rearrange his trucks and cars in his bedroom cupboard.

Harry then nipped into Alison's room; after seeing her collect that envelope from her bedside cabinet, he thought he would have a look around in her room and see what else she had there just in case she had more money than she had let on about. He pulled the bottom drawer out first and there were her toiletries and a manicure set she was given at Christmas. Nothing there he was bothered about. Then he pulled out the top drawer, he pulled it with such a force that one of her figurines she got from her classmates fell over and smashed on the floor. Harry kicked it out of the way. There was nothing there. He quickly shut it and went over to her chest of drawers, underwear, night things, tights, nothing there either.

"Hang on, what's this?" He thought. He found a little jewellery box and opened it up. Inside was a gold St Christopher necklace. He took it out of its box and put it in his pocket. He shut the drawers, opened up her wardrobe and had a quick look in, without disturbing anything. He then left her room.

Tom was busy doing stuff in his room, so he didn't see or hear Harry leave and he then crept down the stairs.

Ruth and Alison were busy preparing lunch and Ruth came in to call Harry, then went to the bottom of the stairs to call Tom and Hannah. They both came down a few minutes later after washing their hands and faces.

When everyone was seated, and they started eating as always in silence, the post dropped through the letterbox. Harry got up to collect it, he didn't want the children leaving the table while they were eating.

There were quite a few letters, one of which was from the council, where the children had lived. He went into the kitchen, everyone was wondering what he was doing, but they never questioned what he did. It wasn't worth the hassle. He was too hot-tempered and too unpredictable.

Meanwhile, Harry was in the kitchen with the kettle on steaming open the letter from the council. He'd prefer it if they had no more contact with him; he didn't want them questioning his methods on parenting.

It was just a letter asking them if the children were OK and happy and about his money. They wanted to know if they could start paying it directly into the bank, rather than send him a cheque each week. Harry was pleased with that. They already had his bank details with all of the paperwork he signed already.

He sealed the letter back up and left it on the kitchen windowsill so it would dry out. He returned to the table and continued eating his food.

Once everything was cleared away, the children returned to play on the landing.

Alison went into her bedroom, not realising the Harry had rifled through it only a little while earlier. She wanted something from her bedside cabinet and had taken off her slippers and socks so she could paint her toenails.

"Ouch!" Alison screamed.

Ruth came running up the stairs and so did Hannah and then Harry. Tom was the first one there but had to stay outside.

"Alison, what's wrong, why did you scream?" Tom asked.

Alison didn't know what had happened just that she stood on something sharp.

Ruth appeared at the door.

"Darling, what's wrong?" Ruth asked.

"I don't know. I think I stood on some glass, but I don't know where it came from," Alison said. "Oh, hang on! One of my figurines isn't there, it's all on the floor in pieces!" she cried.

"What? Hannah could have hurt herself with that glass!" Harry raged. "How could you be so irresponsible, you stupid girl!" Harry shouted,

Ruth went over to Alison and saw the blood and the piece of glass sticking out of her foot.

"Harry, why would Hannah be over here in Alison's room, she hardly ever ventures up here," Ruth said.

Harry was having none of it, he was fuming with what had happened. Hannah could have been hurt, which was all he could think about.

Ruth asked Tom to go into the kitchen and get some plasters, some Savlon and some cotton wool balls. Ruth didn't want to leave Alison to get it herself, she knew Harry and his temper.

Ruth removed the glass. It wasn't as big as she first thought, but it had still made Alison wince a little when it was taken out.

"Tom, please could you bring me up the dustpan and brush from the big kitchen cupboard, I want to clear up this glass before anyone else hurts themselves again," Ruth asked Tom nicely.

Tom did as he was told and was back as quick as he could. Alison was all cleaned up and a big square plaster was on her foot.

"Please put a pair of socks on, Alison, so you can keep the plaster on," Ruth said.

"Thank you, Ruth, for cleaning me up," Alison said, "I didn't knock over the figurine, I don't know how it happened," she added.

"Are you sure, Alison?" Ruth asked.

"I promise! I have no idea. I only came in, took off my slippers and socks, went over to get some nail polish and I stood on the glass," Alison said.

Ruth had already cleaned up the glass and felt her hand over the carpet just to make sure she hadn't missed any.

"Now, if you stay in here with your feet up, I'll bring you a drink," Ruth said.

"But we can't have drinks in our bedroom," Alison said.

"I'll make this an exception, but just this once." Ruth smiled. "Now get on your bed and take it easy on that foot."

Tom was still standing in her doorway.

"Are you OK, Alison?" Tom asked.

"Yes, I'm fine now, Tom, just it was a shock, that's all," Alison replied.

When Ruth came back, Tom was still waiting in the doorway.

"Alison, have you ever had a tetanus jab?" Ruth asked.

"I don't know, the home would know, I have had injections before, but I don't know if I had a tetanus…is that what you call it?" Alison asked.

"Yes, that's it. OK, not to worry, now rest that foot," Ruth said, leaving both of them.

Tom sat on the floor, while Alison was on her bed. He wanted to whisper, but he knew he wouldn't be able to, he would be too loud as she was a distance away.

"So how come that figurine got broken, Harry?" Ruth asked.

"I don't know, maybe Tom did it?" Harry said.

"But Tom isn't allowed in Alison's room, so do you think it was maybe Hannah then?" Ruth said.

"No, of course not, Hannah wouldn't go into someone's room without their knowledge!" Harry snapped.

"So, what was it that you were looking for, then Harry?" Ruth said.

"What?" Harry said, sheepishly.

"What were you looking for? Did you think Alison had loads of money stashed away and you wanted your hands on it?" Ruth answered.

She had gone too far this time, but the child had been hurt with his greed.

"Now you're on very thin ice, Ruth!" Harry glared at her.

"No Harry, I'm not, what were you looking for? They don't have anything." Ruth locked eyes with her husband.

"No, they don't, do they?" Harry said.

***

Two days later it was Saturday and Alison's foot was a bit better. Ruth had let her off the jobs to be done, but she, Harry and Hannah went out as normal, leaving both her and Tom on their own.

Tom had already realised that this didn't feel like home or how a home should be. He and Alison chilled out, which was a real treat. Hopefully, Harry would be back at work soon and it won't be so stressful when he isn't there.

When Tom had gone into the kitchen for the first aid stuff for Alison, he noticed a lot of post of the windowsill that looked like it hadn't been opened. He told Alison this, she wasn't interested, she didn't want to know about their business.

The weekend went quickly once Saturday was over, which pleased both Tom and Alison. This meant that Harry was going to be back at work. Considering they were supposed to go to the beach for lazy days, they hadn't gone anywhere or done anything except go out for Alison's birthday.

Harry had taken Ruth and Hannah out, but they had to stay at home, and not watch TV or do anything exciting.

Alison hadn't noticed before, but she thought Tom had lost a bit of weight. There wasn't much of him anyway, but he was looking thinner, he also looked paler than normal and his eyes looked a bit darker. With everything that had happened over the last few weeks, she hadn't spotted it.

She didn't say anything to him, he wouldn't understand anyway.

Harry had been back at work for a week now and the kids were enjoying a bit of peace when he wasn't there. Alison went upstairs to put away her clean clothes and she noticed Harry going through Tom's chest of drawers. She saw him pull out the jewellery box like that she had, he picked up the St. Christopher and put it in his pocket then put the box back. He then noticed he had been seen.

"What are you doing in Tom's room, Harry? And why did you take his St Christopher? I bet you took mine too, it's missing," Alison said calmly.

"Don't you dare accuse me of taking Tom's things or your things, you're a little liar!" Harry shouted.

"But you did, I just saw you," Alison said, trying to match Harry's tone so that Ruth would come upstairs, but she had gone to take the rubbish out.

"You dare say anything about this and I swear I will smack your backside so hard you won't be able to sit down for a week. Do you understand? Do you, Alison?" Harry said.

"Yes, I understand," Alison said.

Harry didn't ask her to repeat herself as he normally did. He had been caught red-handed and was going to lie through his teeth.

Alison had moved her purse from under the bed a few days ago, she went to check it was still there, and the money. Phew, yes it was. She and Tom had nothing and had to be so careful now. Alison didn't put it past Harry to set them up and say they had been stealing and stole those St Christopher.

Tomorrow was Saturday and they would be going out for a while, so she and Tom could have a little rest.

Later in the evening, once they had had dinner and Alison was helping with the washing up. Ruth came in.

"Harry, I left £5 on the side to pay for the milk in the morning, but I can't find it, have you seen it?" Ruth asked.

Harry put his paper down.

"No Ruth, are you sure you haven't moved it somewhere else?" Harry asked.

He went upstairs and came down a few minutes later with Alison's purse in his hand.

"Alison, can you come here please? I want a word with you?" Shouted Harry.

Alison came out of the kitchen.

"Sorry, what's wrong, I had the tap on full and didn't hear you," Alison said.

"Ruth said that she has mislaid five pounds, have you seen it?" Harry asked.

280

"No, why would I have? I've been in the kitchen for the last half an hour," Alison said.

"Don't you answer me back!" Harry retorted.

"I didn't, Harry. You asked me a question and I just answered your question. I haven't seen the five pounds that Ruth mislaid," Alison said again.

"Liar! What's this then?" Harry demanded, holding up Alison's purse with her five pounds in it.

"That's mine!" Alison said.

"What, the purse or the five pounds in it?" Harry demanded again.

"How do you know there's five pounds in it? I didn't tell you that!" Alison said.

She had been called a liar twice that day and that was her money, nobody else's.

"So young miss, where did you get it from if not from the kitchen?" Harry said sarcastically.

"I brought it down with me when we first came here for the overnight stay and I didn't spend it, I had forgotten I had it," Alison replied.

"Well, young miss, I don't believe you, you're a liar and a thief," Harry said, matter-of-factly.

With that, he raised his hand and slapped Alison straight across the face.

She was shocked, but she had nothing to lose.

"Why were you going through my things, Harry, it's not the first time. I saw you today, didn't I? Going through Tom's things and I saw you take his gold St Christopher, and you probably took mine as well," Alison shouted back.

She was fuming now. She had never really lost her temper before, and certainly not with an adult, but she had had it with this horrible man.

Hannah, Tom and Ruth all stood there with their mouths wide open at what they were hearing from Alison.

"Get up to your bedroom now and do not come back down this evening, go on both of you!" Harry shouted.

Alison had one hand on her face that was feeling quite swollen and the other she took Tom's hand. Tom started to speak, but Alison told him to shush. She'd had quite enough.

"Go on Hannah, you go upstairs too, please," Ruth said.

"Hannah, you can stay down here," Harry said.

"No Harry, she goes upstairs too," said Ruth, quite forcefully. "Now please tell me what Alison has said isn't true? Harry? Come on, I need the truth!" Ruth demanded.

"You have taken the money to have these children, you have treated them really poorly, and now you have taken their St Christopher's, why would you do that? They don't have anything, but you took what little they have and now you assume that Alison has taken five pounds that I, me, I have mislaid, which I have now found in the kitchen, it was under the coffee jar. You have accused that girl for nothing, because of your greed and your hypocrisy. I'm surprised at you, Harry I would never have thought you would hurt those two lovely children," Ruth snapped.

Ruth left Harry downstairs and went upstairs to see the children.

"Alison, Honey, are you OK? I am so sorry I didn't know what Harry had done," Ruth said, giving Alison her purse back with the money still inside it. "I found the five pounds that I had mislaid, but that's still no excuse for what Harry has done this evening. Did he really take the St Christopher's?" Ruth asked.

"Well, I saw him take Tom's and sadly assumed he took mine as well. They were a gift, you see, from the staff and children at Craven House as a going away gift, so that St Christopher would keep us safe," Alison said.

Tom looked really upset. Alison had never been hit before apart from Harry. This was the second time he had hit her in a matter of weeks.

"Look, let him cool down this evening, I will get them back for you; get to bed and I should have them in the morning, is that OK?" Ruth asked.

Alison nodded, so did Tom. Tom went back to his bedroom and got ready for bed. Alison couldn't believe what had happened today, so much drama in one day. She got ready for bed, turned off her light, said goodnight to Tom and went back to sleep.

Ruth popped her head around the door about an hour later, with Alison's St Christopher and left it on her chest of drawers. She did the same in Tom's room, then went down to check on Hannah, who was fast asleep.

The next morning, they got up as usual for breakfast for 8 am, and walked down the stairs in silence. Harry was already sitting at the table, and Ruth was in the kitchen, finishing off cooking breakfast. They all sat down and didn't speak to anyone.

Harry made no attempt to speak to anyone and continued reading his paper. Ruth bought in the breakfast and Harry put his paper down, he started to tuck into his breakfast. It was as if nothing had happened the night before.

Alison and Tom ate their breakfast in silence as always.

"Are we still going out this morning, Daddy?" Hannah asked.

"What, poppet? Going out, yes of course, I said, didn't I?" Harry replied.

He looked at Alison and Tom and they both ignored him. They didn't want to talk to him any more than they had to and this morning they didn't have to.

Ruth came in.

"What was that?" Ruth asked.

"Hannah asked if we were still going out this morning and I said yes we were," Harry replied.

Ruth looked at Alison and Tom and Harry shook his head. He was still angry about what happened last night, even though it was his fault and he was to blame, Harry was having none of it.

When breakfast was over, Alison helped Ruth in the kitchen clearing up. Alison didn't speak at all; she was still upset about the night before. Once that was done, Ruth came out of the kitchen, she called to Hannah to get her coat as they were going straight out.

Harry went upstairs to change his jacket. Ruth stuffed a twenty-pound note into Alison's hand, and mimed her to put it in the pocket of her jeans. Alison cottoned on and did so straight away. She gave her a hug, mimed for her to take some fruit and a drink each.

Alison understood, but she didn't know why.

Harry came back downstairs with his jacket, he called Hannah to get a move on. Ruth said to the children, to be good and then left closing the door behind her, but she came back.

"I left my reading glasses behind," she said to Alison, winking at her, she shut the door, but didn't lock it.

Alison now understood what Ruth was trying to tell her. She looked out of the window as she did every week they went out and watched them pull away. That was it, she ran to the kitchen, grabbed two tins of drink, a couple of apples and then ran upstairs.

"Alison, where are you going?" Tom asked.

"Come on Tom, get your coat?" Alison said. "Quickly!" she added.

"Why?" quizzed Tom.

"You will see!" Alison replied.

She jumped down the stairs, two at a time, thankfully she didn't hurt herself.

"I have your coat, I have put your St Christopher in your pocket same as mine, I have my purse. Now come on, we don't have much time," Alison said.

She put Tom's coat on him, grabbed the bag and ran towards the door, it opened. Alison and Tom shut the door quietly. She didn't want the neighbours to hear.

They went out of the gate.

"Now run!"

Chapter 16

Alison and Tom ran as fast as they could away from town. Occasionally, when Hannah hadn't managed to get to school a couple of times, they had tried different routes and found they could hide down the back streets, so they wouldn't be found so easily, so that's what they did.

They didn't have much food, but they did have a can of coke each, but they couldn't open it now if they wanted to keep running; it would explode everywhere.

The children ran down a couple of roads that looked familiar. They knew they were on the right track so far.

"Alison, please can we stop for a few minutes, I'm tired and I have a stitch. I'm not used to running this much!" Tom said.

"Tom, aren't you used to running in PE? We have to continue for a little while, so we can't be found by Harry and Ruth," Alison replied.

"Yes, I know, but at the moment, Alison, they don't know we're missing," Tom said, breathlessly.

"I know that, but we don't know which way they are going to come back. We have to be away from town, so they can't catch us," Alison said. "Look, if we go down this road, we are going further and further away from town and that's where they are going, so if we stick to the other direction, we should be OK," Alison said.

"Where are we going?" Tom asked.

"I have no idea yet, let's just get away from here as far away as possible. That way if they come looking, they won't find us yet. Come on now, Tom, we have to keep moving. We can stop again in a little while," Alison suggested.

They ran along quiet roads and stayed away from the main road, so they could hide if they needed to.

After about an hour, Tom and Alison saw a car the same as Harry's and bolted over a fence and hid behind a hedge. Tom looked shaken up, but Alison thought that they should carry on across the field they had just come across.

"If we go this way, then at least we are still on the right track. When we get to the other end of the field, we will see what's around and maybe have a little break and think about where we can go," Alison said.

At the end of the field, they found a big barn with some soft hay inside it. They climbed up on a bale and Alison opened the bag with the two pieces of fruit in it and open one of the cans of drink to share. They would save the other for later on.

"I think we should have a piece of fruit each and share a can of drink," Alison said.

"Why?" Tom asked.

"Because we don't know when we can get to a shop to buy anymore. We may need this for later on," Alison replied.

"Oh OK. I didn't think about that," Tom said. "So what are we going to do, Alison?"

"Well, I think if we can stay here for a little while, and then move on, and find…"

"Where are we going, Alison? We can't stay here in Brighton; they will find us and take us back. Where else can we go? Can we go back to Craven House?" Tom interrupted.

"Yes, that's my plan, but you have to remember we only came here and back in a car. We can't get one of those now, so we have to work out another way. Let's get some rest here and we can have a think of the best way to get back, OK?" Alison said.

"Yes, that's a good idea. I'm tired with all of that walking," Tom added.

The two of them settled down on the bale of hay, which was warm, soft and smelt so fresh. They closed their eyes and fell asleep.

***

The car pulled up and Ruth got out and let Hannah out of the back. Harry locked the front of the car and went to empty the boot. Ruth opened the front door in trepidation, hoping to have an empty house. It was.

286

"Put the kettle on, Ruth, where's them two, they normally come down after we get back," Harry said.

Hannah went upstairs with her shopping. She'd had a good shopping trip; two new dresses and shoes to match, some new underwear, a lovely lunch at Molly's and a chocolate éclair bigger than the one Alison had.

"Alison, would you like to come and see my new clothes that I got?" Hannah called out. "Alison, can you hear me?" Hannah called again.

She then went back downstairs.

"Daddy, I called Alison twice to see if she wants to see my new clothes and she hasn't answered me," Hannah sulked.

"I told you, Ruth, those children, they are so rude!" Harry said. "Alison, Tom, can you come down here please?" He called up the stairs. "Do I have to repeat myself!" he bellowed.

There was no answer.

Harry ran up the stairs, two at a time. He was down just as quickly.

"Ruth, they're gone!" Harry said in shock.

"What do you mean, gone?" Ruth asked, keeping the look of relief from her face.

"They aren't upstairs, I can't find them anywhere," Harry said, concerned now.

"Maybe they're playing hide and seek? Have you checked the cupboards and their wardrobes?" Ruth asked.

"No, I'll go back up and have a look."

Harry came back downstairs again.

"Ruth, Ruth, they aren't here." Harry was getting worried now.

"Do you think we should call the police?" Ruth asked.

"Err, no," Harry replied.

"What do you mean, no?"

"I think we need to pack, now! Everything we can take; our belongings, shoes, etc., as quickly as possible and get the hell away from here!" Harry was sweating profusely.

"What? Why? Harry, we need to call the police, we have no idea where they are!" Ruth shouted.

"No! We have to get away, now, Ruth! Come on. Pack everything you can manage into the suitcases and black bags, if need be, but we have to go in the next half an hour," Harry snapped.

"Don't be ridiculous, Harry! I can't pack up a whole house in half an hour!" Ruth said.

"Not the whole bloody house, you stupid woman! Our stuff: yours, mine and Hannah's, that way we can get most of it in the car," Harry said.

"But what about Alison and Tom's stuff?" Ruth said.

"We leave it behind. We can't take any of it with us. We need to make room for our things not theirs," said Harry. "Come on, quickly!

"Hannah, darling, could you get your most favourite dolls or teddies and put them in a big black bag, just the ones you really want? OK?" Harry said.

Hannah had no idea what was going on, but she nodded her head. Harry went upstairs to the cupboard on the landing and pulled out two massive suitcases. He took them to the floor below, so that Ruth could pack them as quick as possible. He emptied the drawers and threw the clothes off the hangers, then left Ruth to finish packing.

He had to get their paperwork together and also put the keys to the house in an envelope to be sent to the letting agent with a cheque. The lease was nearly up for this house, anyway. He went to his black box that he had in a cupboard in the sitting room. It had all their bank books, passports, and anything else they needed inside.

They had cash, but they could get the rest of it on Monday as the banks were already closed.

"Daddy, I have my teddy bears and dollies, but what about my clothes?" Hannah asked, showing her father a huge bag full of soft toys.

"Don't worry, Poppet, Mum is getting your case and we will take all of your clothes."

Harry went back into their bedroom to check how Ruth was getting on.

"That's our stuff packed. If you can lock the case, I'll do Hannah's now," Ruth said.

Ruth got Hannah's case out and started throwing her clothes into it.

"Mum, what's happening? Where are Alison and Tom?" Hannah asked.

"We're going on a little holiday and Alison and Tom aren't coming, as they have already gone on one, but they left us a little note, OK? So, let's get this stuff sorted together then we can leave," Ruth said.

Harry came back in the room. "All done?"

"Yes, can you take this lot downstairs? I'll take Hannah's toys; you take her case," Ruth said.

"I've already taken ours downstairs. Can I put the paperwork in your handbag?" Harry asked.

"Oh, Harry, there's a shopping bag in the kitchen. I can get that, and we can put whatever doesn't fit in that," replied Ruth.

"Err, good thinking," Harry said.

He had a quick look around. They had everything they needed.

"We need to post this as soon as we see a post box," Harry told Ruth, showing her the envelope for the letting agency. "Now, I'll put the cases in the car. We can put Hannah's toys with her in the backseat, OK?" Ruth nodded. She did as she was told.

Harry closed the front door. He was going to post the keys in a post-box but decided to push them through the letterbox—he didn't have time to mess about.

Harry wasn't aware that he had been seen by the next-door neighbour.

"How strange," she said to herself.

***

The minibus pulled up, alongside the house.

"You sure this is the right house, Sandra?" George asked.

"Yes of course it is. I would remember it anywhere. I just want to knock and say hello," Sandra said.

She knocked on the door and stood there for a few minutes. There was no answer.

"There's nobody in," she said, "maybe they've gone out for dinner or something?"

"There's no light on," George said. "Let's come back tomorrow, yeah?"

"Yes, we can do that," Sandra said.

"Let's head back to the caravan, then?" George suggested, "I want to go to the clubhouse with Lee and Scott, we need to finish that game of snooker, they beat me last time."

Josephine was a little upset. She would have loved to have seen Alison and Tom. But there was always tomorrow.

They were only in Brighton for a couple of days and she had jumped at the chance to come.

Freddie hadn't been well, otherwise he would have been there too.

***

Alison woke up to see it was now dark, they must have slept for a long time. She hadn't realised. She decided it was too dark to go anywhere now, so they would go back to sleep and wake up in the morning and then head off again.

The next morning, Tom woke up early.

"Alison, Alison, wake up, what time is it?" Tom whispered.

"Hmm?" Alison replied. "I don't know, hold on," she looked at her watch, it was 5.30.

"It's five-thirty in the morning," she replied, half asleep.

"What? We've been here all night?"

"Yes, I woke up last night and you were still fast asleep, so I let you sleep. Now we can't go anywhere at this time, nowhere is open, so we have to wait for a couple more hours, and don't forget, it's Sunday," Alison said.

Tom didn't realise he slept through most of yesterday. All this running away was tiring, which was why he had slept so long. They had to go back to sleep for a little while.

There wasn't anywhere they could wash, and they didn't take any clothes with them, so Alison said they had better stay where they were for now.

When they did get up, Tom was hungry. Alison said he could have his other piece of fruit and they would have to share their last drink. They hadn't eaten properly in about twenty-four hours, and even though their tummies rumbled, they knew they had to wait until they could get to a shop.

They got down from the hay bales, brushed themselves down and headed away from the field.

"Tom, I thought of where we can go so that we can get back to Craven House," Alison said.

"Where, Alison?"

"Do you remember a couple of years ago we went to Margate in Kent and we stayed there?"

"With Rose and Henry?"

"Yes, with Rose and Henry. We can try to get there, but I'm trying to work out how. Don't forget, we don't want to get caught by Harry and Ruth, so I think the best way, without hitch-hiking—"

"What's hitch-hiking?" Tom interrupted.

290

"It's when you stand on the side of the road and stick your thumb out on, which is a sign that you want a lift, but someone bad might pick us up," Alison said, "but, we could get a coach?"

"Oh yes, a coach seems a good idea, but what about a train?" Tom suggested.

"A train would be good, but we've run away, and they have guards on a train. We don't want them sending us back to Harry and Ruth," Alison said.

"A coach it is then!" Tom said. "Which way is the coach station then?"

"I have no idea, we can have a wander around and if we ask someone, we can tell them we are going to visit our nan, that sounds like a good idea and nobody should have any problem with that. Kids see their nans and grandads all the time," Alison said.

The children carried on past the barn the direction they thought was right.

***

"Sandra, please can we go and see Alison and Tom before lunch, that way we know they should be in? Please, please, please?" Jo begged.

"OK, we can go in the next twenty minutes, then we can have lunch in town before we head off back home."

"Come on, you lot, you have ten minutes to get your stuff together so we can head over to see Alison and Tom, as Jo keeps pestering me about it!" Sandra laughed.

They had only been there for a couple of days, but they all wanted to see how the kids were getting on with their placement.

"If you're not ready, we're going to leave you behind!" George said.

Everyone grabbed their bags and got on to the minibus. Sandra had a quick look around to make sure they hadn't left anything.

"Come on Sandra, we want to go now?" The four children shouted, excitedly.

Sandra shut the caravan door and jumped into the minibus.

It didn't take them long to get to Alison and Tom's road and they pulled up just outside this time.

Sandra got out of the minibus and knocked on the door, still no answer. She went over to the window and looked inside, there was no sign of life. It looked like they had just gone out again. She went back to the front door and rang the doorbell. Maybe they were out in the garden? They had a huge garden.

She looked through the letterbox and noticed a pile of letters. The back of them looked familiar. It was from the home; she recognised the frank mark on it.

Sandra banged hard on the door knocker.

The lady next door opened her curtains, then closed them again.

Sandra went to ask her if she had seen them, but she had gone. The neighbour's front door opened.

"Oh hello, I'm sorry to bother you, but do you know where your neighbours are? We came last night and knocked, but there was no answer and by the look of the post, they haven't been back today?" Sandra said.

"They've gone," The neighbour said.

"I'm sorry? Gone? Gone where?" Sandra asked.

"Gone yesterday, packed up, took the little girl and left." The neighbour shrugged.

"What do you mean, took the little girl? Didn't they have a little boy and another little girl with them?" Sandra asked, slightly confused.

"No, just the mum and dad and the little girl, I haven't seen the other two in a little while. I heard them being shouted at a lot though. The walls here aren't very thick," the woman replied.

Sandra felt herself go hot and cold at the same time.

"Did they say if they were coming back?"

"No, they didn't tell me anything, but I saw the man put some keys into an envelope and popped it through the letterbox, then they drove off."

"OK, thank you for your time," Sandra said.

"George! Oh God! Harry, Ruth and Hannah have all buggered and I don't know where Alison and Tom are!" Sandra said as she ran back to the minibus.

"What? Where are the kids?" George looked shocked.

"I have no idea, the neighbour said that she hasn't seen them in a while, but she did hear them being shouted at. Oh, George, where can they be?" Panic rose in Sandra's voice.

Sandra ran back to the neighbour's house.

"Excuse me, but do you have a phone I could use?" she asked.

"Yes, yes, of course," the neighbour said. "Sorry, but who are you?"

"Oh, I'm sorry, we're from the home where Alison and Tom came from to stay with the Coopers. I'm Sandra and that's George at the wheel, we came down with the children for their first visit," Sandra said.

"Come this way, Dear, the phone is in here, who are you calling?" The lady asked.

"The police. They may still be inside the house," Sandra said.

"Police, yes, I would like to report two children missing please, yes I am calling from…sorry, erm…yes, 13 Pemberton Terrace. Yes, I'm with the neighbour and there is another member of staff with me, if you could please come quickly, thank you," Sandra said.

She replaced the receiver.

"I'm really sorry about all of this. Sorry, what's your name, instead of me keep saying the lady?" Sandra asked.

"I'm Mrs Peabody, Gladys," The neighbour said.

"Gladys, I am just going to tell my colleague what's going on, but I need to keep it from the other children for the time being," Sandra said and she ran back to the minibus.

"George, I have called the police, it seems that nobody has seen the kids, but they could be inside needing help, so I am hoping the police will break down the door and we can have a look. Will you come with me? We can ask the police if one of their men can stay with the kids?" she whispered to George.

"What's happening, Sandra?" Scott asked.

"Nothing at the moment, Scott," Sandra replied.

"Why can't we see Alison and Tom?" Jo asked.

The police pulled up. There were two cars and six police officers got out.

"Erm, who's in charge here?" The first police officer asked.

"I am," Sandra replied.

This police officer seemed to be the one in charge. He opened his notebook and asked Sandra what had happened. Sandra told him what she knew, as did Gladys. They both had the same idea; that they could be still inside trapped not able to scream for help.

One, two, three…

A police officer swung the battering ram with full force, breaking the lock on the door.

Sandra and George ran in. They knew the property, so knew the layout.

The police followed and took charge.

"I think we had better go ahead first, just in case, they are here and need help," the officer said.

Sandra looked startled. It had only just really hit her. She nodded as the officers ran upstairs. Sandra and George had a look around the downstairs. They saw Alison's birthday cards on the mantelpiece.

"All clear up here, Sir." An officer shouted.

"May I go up, please, Officer?" Sandra asked.

"Yes, it's safe to. It doesn't look like the children are here."

George and Sandra ran upstairs to the next floor and saw that Hannah's room and Ruth and Harry's room had been stripped bare. Sandra ran up to the next level to Alison and Tom's room. Sandra opened Alison's wardrobe.

"George, come in here for a minute!"

"Found anything?" George said.

"No, but look!" Sandra said.

"What am I looking at, Sandra?" George looked puzzled.

"There's nothing missing. All her clothes are here. Quick, look in Tom's room."

George darted into Tom's room.

"Sandra, nothing has gone, all of Tom's cars and trucks are still here," George said.

A police officer came onto the landing.

"Excuse me Sir, but can we take these things back to the home with us? They're the children's belongings," Sandra asked.

"I don't see why not. It isn't a crime scene. It doesn't look as though the parents are coming back here." The police officer said.

"Hey, Sarge?" Another police officer called out.

"There's an envelope here…it's for Sandman Lettings."

"Is that important?" George asked.

"It could be." The officer ripped the envelope open, read it and handed it to his sergeant.

The sergeant took the letter and read it.

"Well, it seems that this house isn't owned but rented by a local letting agent not too far away," The sergeant said.

"George, I found Alison's suitcase!" Sandra called out.

"Whereabouts, Sandra?" George asked.

"Under the bed, look inside Tom's divan."

George found Tom's and also his bag. He put all of his trucks and cars into it.

"I can't find Alison's purse though," Sandra said.

"But that's good, that means they have some money on them," George said.

They took everything they could, Sandra checked she had everything they might need.

"Right, I think we have everything, I saw the envelope we sent her for her birthday, but the money is gone," Sandra said.

"But she may have it with her," George said.

"Now we have to get back and inform them at Craven House. Thank you, officers, for your help with this. What are you going to do about the front door?" Sandra asked.

"We'll leave a constable on the door, just in case they come back."

"The Coopers, you mean?"

"Well no, maybe the children, but just to be on the safe side and then we'll get a locksmith out to secure the house and get on to that letting agent in the morning. In the meantime, we will contact your local police to let them know what's going on and we'll put out an alert to all the stations in the area to look out for them. It's a shame we don't have a photo of them, but if you could give us a brief description." The sergeant asked.

"Officer! I have this in my purse!" Jo shouted and ran over to the sergeant.

She handed him a photo of Tom and Alison.

"You clever girl, how did you have it in your purse?" The sergeant asked.

"I kept it, so every time I got sad or missed them, I would take out the photo, have a look at it and then kiss it. I know it sounds silly, Sir but they're my family," Jo said.

"Come on Jo, let's get you back on the minibus," George said.

"We are like a big family, and all of the children missed them when they left," Sandra said.

"Thank you for this, Miss. We can copy it and circulate it on our system." The sergeant said.

Sandra thanked the officers for their help. Gladys came out with a flask and some soft drinks and sandwiches for their journey back.

"I have your number in case they come back, and I will tell the police if I see the Coopers again, have a safe journey home, my dears. I know they will come back to you; I can feel it in my waters. Take care," Gladys said.

"Thank you, Gladys, for all of your help. Without you, we would never have known anything was wrong. We have your number too, so we can let you know when we get the children back and thank you once again," Sandra said.

***

Alison and Tom had found a corner shop open. It sold newspapers, so it was open early. They both went in. Alison noticed that they had made rolls, ham, cheese, tuna, salmon, egg. She picked a couple up of each filling and grabbed a couple of fruit juices, a couple of bars of chocolates, six bags of assorted crisps and went to the till and paid for it.

Thank goodness Ruth had given her the twenty pounds back.

As they left the shop, Alison turned back.

"Excuse me, where can I get a coach to Margate?" She asked the lady behind the counter.

The lady looked at her quizzically.

"You need to go to the coach station back in Brighton, there isn't another one until you get to Hove and that's a long way away, dear," the lady said.

"Oh, OK, thank you," Alison said and left the shop rather quickly. She didn't want the lady asking her any more questions.

They went around the corner, to find somewhere to sit down and eat their food away from the shop.

"Tom, we have to go back to Brighton to get to the coach station," Alison said.

"But what if we run into Ruth and Harry?" Tom replied.

"If we go the way we came, including the barn and stay away for a little while, they won't think of looking for us in the coach station. Tom, I know it's not the best idea, but it's the only one I have. Don't worry, we'll be fine, you'll see," Alison said, trying to convince herself.

They were both tired from all of the walking, but at least they knew they could sleep back in that barn and get back to the station for Monday; the coaches would be running again then. They made their way back to the barn.

***

George stepped on the accelerator on the way back, they got back to Craven House in good time. Mr Duffy was there waiting to greet them. He told the children to go inside, there was a big lunch ready for them.

"So, you know then?" Sandra asked.

"Yes, the local police have been on the phone and have been here, wanting to know of anywhere they could have gone to. Celia helped me with information on the children's parents and they are following that up now. What's that you have there?" Mr Duffy asked.

"This is Alison and Tom's stuff from the house in Brighton, the police said it was OK to take it. It didn't look like the Coopers were going back there, and when the children do get back, at least they have their own stuff, because I can tell you now, those two never bought them a bloody thing."

Sandra was cross that she hadn't listened to that niggling voice in her head right from the start.

"So, what on earth did they do with the money that they were given from our end?" Mr Duffy asked.

"Who knows, but we will find out," Sandra said.

"At least if they take any money out of their account, the police will know about it. They will be telling their local branch to keep an eye out on the account, so it will be flagged up," Mr Duffy said.

***

Alison and Tom had wandered back the way they came. They took a slow walk and wanted to have some of the food left for later on that day, they still had a long way to go. They managed to get back to the barn before the sun went down. They covered themselves in hay and had the last of the rolls.

At least their tummies were full. Alison had bought just enough food. They still had a juice drink left each and were going to leave that for tomorrow. They wanted to be up early to catch an early coach to Margate. Tom was looking forward to seeing Rose and Henry again, then they would be going home.

"Tom, are you alright?" Alison asked.

"Yes, just looking forward to getting back home," Tom said, sleepily.

"Home?"

"Yes, Craven House, I can't wait to see Freddie and Charlie and everyone else, including Jo," Tom said.

Alison was looking forward to seeing everyone too. She didn't realise she was going to miss everyone, especially now and what they had been through.

They got themselves comfortable and settled down for the evening, watching the sun going down, it was very beautiful, they hadn't seen a sunset before.

"Night Alison, just think, tomorrow we will be on our way back home," Tom said.

"Night Tom, yes, we will, sleep tight," Alison said.

***

Bang! Bang!

"It's the Police!" A voice from the front door shouted. "Can you open up, please?"

"Police?" Mum said as she opened the door to see two large police officers standing on her doorstep.

"Eileen Davis?" The first police officer asked.

"Err, no...hang on a minute...sorry, please come in," Mum said.

"Eileen, can you come down please?" Eileen's mum called up the stairs.

Eileen rushed down the stairs.

"What's wrong? Oh my God! Is somebody dead?" Eileen asked.

"That good-for-nothing husband of hers, I hope!" Eileen's mother quipped.

"No, no it's nothing like that, Marm." The police officer said. "Mrs Davis, could you please tell me the last time you saw your two children?"

Eileen went white.

"Why, what's happened?" Eileen's mum asked.

"I haven't seen my children since my husband put them in care nearly three years ago and I haven't seen them since he tried to kill me. The local police couldn't find him when he absconded. I haven't heard from him since and I haven't seen my little ones since I watched them going to school not long after that. I've been living with my mother since I got out of hospital to recuperate. It's all in one of your files, you can contact the local office. Are they OK? My children?" Eileen asked.

The officer looked at his notes.

"It seems that your children have gone missing, Mrs Davis," the officer said.

"Missing? What do you mean missing? They loved where they were staying at the home."

"No, it isn't the home they have run away from, but a foster placement in Brighton," The officer said.

"Brighton? What the hell are they doing all the way down there?" Eileen said, furious that she hadn't been informed of where her children were living. "It's that bastard, he told them to send them away, so I wouldn't be able to see them again," she snapped.

"I have no idea about that, Marm. I think it was a placement, but it seems it didn't work out." The officer said, "So you haven't seen either of them recently?"

"No, she hasn't, not since that bastard put them away, and for no reason!" Eileen's mum said.

With that, Eileen bursts into tears.

"Oh Mum, where can they be?"

Eileen's mum consoled her daughter by cuddling her.

"Mrs Davis, if they turn up here or you hear from them, would you please let us know?" The officer asked Eileen nodded.

"When you find them, please could you let me know, I just want to know that they are safe," Eileen said.

The police officer nodded. He turned and they both left.

Eileen's tears turned into full-blown sobbing. Thankfully, she was with her mum who would give her comfort.

***

Alison woke up before Tom and she watched the sunrise. she lay there quietly listening to all of the noises. she knew a barn wouldn't just be there for no reason, so there must have been a farm nearby. She would give Tom half an hour more and then wake him up. They had a bit of a walk to get back to town and she wasn't too sure where the coach station was.

Once Tom had woken up, they had to make a start. They wanted to get a coach as soon as possible and it still took them at least two hours to find the coach station. They actually didn't live too far away from the station, but it was in the other direction.

Both of them were quite nervous; they didn't want to bump into Harry or Ruth. They were looking in all directions when they got to the station, but they couldn't see anyone they knew at all.

299

They went to the office to buy their tickets for the coach. It was going to cost £7.00 each. They had already used over six pounds on their food, so they just had enough. There was a coach leaving for Margate, in about an hour, so they had to wait and they sat on a bench just inside near the office.

They hadn't had a wash in over two days and were sure they didn't smell too friendly, especially sleeping on hay for two days running.

It was going to take about three hours to get to Margate as the coach diverted to different towns and then the seaside.

When it was time to board, Alison and Tom were the first ones on. They decided to sit at the back, so they wouldn't be as noticeable as anyone else. They also stuck to the story that they were going to see their nan. They had another of their rolls and a bag of crisps; that was the last of their food and they had one drink between them.

The driver closed the door, the engine started up and they were on their way.

***

The police went over to Craven House once they had been to Eileen's mum's house and they spoke to Sandra, George, Mr Duffy, and Celia. Everyone was worried sick as there had been no word of them or from them since the staff had found out that the Coopers had left, and the children were missing.

"It's a big world to be lost in," George said.

Sandra had wished he never said it.

Mr Duffy and the staff had had an emergency meeting last night when the children had gone to bed. They still had space for both Alison and Tom, that wasn't a problem. What they did have a problem with was what had happened to them in the last two months or so since they left Craven House. They would have to treat them with kids gloves as if they had just got there.

Mr Duffy was sorting out strategies for what they could do for them. At least it was the summer holidays so when they did get back, they had lots of time to relax and have some spoiling time.

Sandra and George had put the children's belongings back in their wardrobes and cupboards, so at least they would have their own things on their return.

***

The coach seemed to take a long time to get to Margate. With all of the stops, it was no wonder it took so long, but they pulled into Margate bus stop. Alison and Tom sighed a sigh of relief,

now all they had to do was find Rose and Henry.

They got off the coach last as they didn't want to attract any attention to themselves; not that there were many people who got on at the same time as them. When leaving the coach station, Alison found a map of the area. It showed places that she remembered from before, so they made their way towards them.

It took them quite a while to find the right road where the guesthouse was. They seemed to have been going round in circles for at least half an hour. Then they came across it.

They walked up the steps, pressed the doorbell and waited. They could hear footsteps and then a big lady with rosy cheeks opened the door to them. Alison and Tom collapsed in the doorway.

Chapter 17

Rose bent down to pick up Tom, Henry bent down to pick up Alison.

"Bruce, can you come here and hold the door open please?" Henry asked.

Bruce came running over and Betty was right behind him. Bruce held the door open, so they could bring the children in and put them on the sofas.

"How did they get here?" Bruce asked.

"No idea, Bruce, but they look absolutely shattered," Rose said.

Alison roused herself, but Tom was still asleep.

"Rose, Rose, is that you? Thank goodness we found you!" Alison said.

"Where have you come from, Alison? Where is everyone else?" Rose asked.

"We ran away," Alison replied.

"Ran away? From where?" Henry asked.

"The foster home!" Alison said.

"Come on love, let's get you up, are you hungry by any chance?" Rose asked.

"Starving, Rose!" Alison said.

"Come on, let's get you in the bath and then we can get you some food," Rose said.

With that, Tom opened his eyes.

"Did someone say food? I'm starving!" Tom said.

"Oh hello, you with us now, are you?" Henry asked.

"Henry! Rose! Alison, we made it!" Tom smiled.

"Yes, you sure did, both of you," Henry replied.

"Rose, let me put some food on and you can get them in the bath." Betty said.

"Oh, would you, Betty love? Thank you, that would be a great help. Henry, is room number three empty?" Rose asked.

"Yes. The Chapmans left this morning, only here for a few days," Henry replied.

"OK, let's get you two in the bath and then have something to eat, anything you fancy?" Rose asked.

"Anything, as long as it's hot please!" Tom said.

"Sure thing," Betty said.

While Rose took the two of them upstairs to the bathroom and ran them a lovely bubble bath. They stripped their clothes off.

"Would you like to get in together or would you like to have your own bathroom?" Rose asked.

"We can get in together, if that's OK, Rose?" Alison said. "We've had too many rules with bath times and that!"

"Do you mind if I wash these? I have some night things that are clean you can put on?" she asked.

Alison and Tom didn't really care, they hadn't had so much fun in the bath with all of the bubbles for a long time.

"Be careful, won't you, dears? We don't want you slipping and falling under now, do we?" Rose said.

She took their dirty clothes back downstairs to the kitchen and threw them in the washing machine. She checked in on Betty who was cooking them some food.

"Eggs, bacon, sausage, tomatoes, beans, mushrooms, fried bread or toast, Rose?" Betty asked.

"Toast, fried bread may be too heavy on their tums at this time of night," Rose suggested.

Rose went back upstairs to the landing cupboard to collect some clean night things for them. Pyjamas for both of them.

"So, how are you two getting on then?" Rose asked. "Would you like me to wash your hair?"

"Err yes, I think we should have it washed. We haven't had it washed for a few days, so we're probably a bit dirty," Alison said.

Rose handed her a flannel to cover her eyes with and put the jug under the tap to check that the water wasn't too hot. She washed it with a lovely smelling shampoo and gave it a good rub in with her fingertips.

"Ooh Rose, that's lovely," Alison said.

Once she had done it again, she asked if she would like conditioner, that would help make her hair nice and shiny and silky. Alison said yes, she would like that.

Now she was rinsed, Rose towel-dried her hair so it wouldn't drip everywhere. Then it was Tom's turn. He liked the water dripping down his body after his hair had been washed.

When their hair had been washed, Rose left them for a few minutes so they could wash the front of their bodies.

"I'll come back and wash your backs. Is that OK?" Rose asked. They both nodded.

She was back within minutes, bringing with her two of the biggest and fluffiest towels they had ever seen.

"Henry, could you come here a minute please?" Rose called.

"Yes, what's up?" Henry asked.

"Nothing, it's just I can't carry both of them out of the bath," Rose laughed, "would you take Tom for me please?"

Both of the children had towels wrapped around them and the water had nearly all gone down the plughole. Henry picked up Tom and carried him to room number three.

"You can both stay here tonight. It's a twin bedroom, so you can have one each," Rose asked. "We're just down the hall, so if you need anything, you can just shout," she added.

Rose got their pyjamas out, towel-dried their backs and left the room, so that they could finish getting ready.

"Alison, are you glad we came here?" Tom asked.

"Yes, I am, that way we know they will look after us until someone from Craven House comes to get us," Alison said.

The children put the pyjamas on. They were a little big for both of them, but it didn't matter. They were clean, had a lovely bath and now they were going to have some dinner or supper; they didn't even know what the time was.

"Ahh, you're both ready! Now, I don't have any slippers, but I have socks for you both. I don't want you to walk around in just bare feet," Rose said. She handed them the socks, which they put on straight away.

"Now downstairs for some supper, yes?" Rose smiled at them.

Tom beamed up at her. He was hungry, but he felt clean, so it didn't matter.

They sat down and Betty brought in their supper and a pot of tea, for the adults.

"What would you like to drink?" Rose asked, "I have milk or squash. It's a bit late for a fizzy drink or would you like a hot drink?" Rose asked.

"Milk, please?" Alison said. "For both of us. Thank you," Alison said.

"Now, you eat your food, we can talk later, and you have no need to thank us, we're just glad you made it here," Rose said.

Alison and Tom were tucking in when Rose got up and beckoned Henry.

"Henry, love, I think we need to contact the home. I'm just going to the office to look for the number, but don't tell the children just yet. Keep an eye on them for me!" Rose said.

"Of course, I will, don't be daft, go on go and find the number, they aren't going anywhere," Henry said.

Rose left the room and went to the office, which was really a large cupboard, but they had all of their paperwork and invoices and that there. She was looking through her address book for work, as she had all the contact numbers there, that way she wouldn't lose them.

"Ah yes, Craven House, let me see, yes Sandra Michaels," Rose said.

She dialled the number and the phone started ringing on the other end.

"Oh, hello, may I speak to Sandra Michaels, please? Yes, it's Rose, from Whelk Combe Guest House in Margate…yes, I'll wait, thank you," Rose said.

"Hello, this is Sandra Michaels, who's calling?" Sandra asked.

"Sandra, it's me Rose, Rose Benton from Whelk Combe in Margate," Rose said. Finally, Sandra knew who she was.

"I think I may have two little souls that you're looking for," Rose said.

"What? Alison and Tom?" Sandra gasped.

"Yes, they turned up at my place a couple of hours ago, I would have called you earlier, but we had to give them a bath and something to eat. It looks like they ran away from their foster home," Rose said.

Sandra didn't hear anymore; she just felt overwhelming relief flood through her. They had been found! They had made their way to Rose and Henry's.

"Sorry I didn't quite catch that, Rose, I'm still in shock! I'm so relieved that they made their way to you. Do you want us to come and get them now?" Sandra asked.

"No, I just wanted to let you know that they are here and they're safe. They've had a bath and are just having something to eat. We've made up two beds for them for tonight, but if you wanted to come tomorrow to get them. I'm not trying to get rid of them, but I think they want to go home with you guys," Rose said. "They might need a lie-in, so I thought about lunchtime?" Rose asked.

"Yes, yes, that's fine, Rose. And thank you so much! We'll be there as early as we can to lunchtime. I can't thank you enough," Sandra said.

"It's the least I can do. I'm just so glad they found their way here! I'll see you tomorrow then," Rose said.

Sandra clapped her hands.

"Could everyone please make their way to the dining room?" She said over the Tannoy. She ran upstairs along the hallway and then down the other stairs to the dining room. Everyone came running in. Sandra couldn't hold her excitement.

"Is everyone here?" She asked. She looked around the room. The staff were at the back of the dining room and the kids were all sitting down.

"I'm happy to report that Alison and Tom have been found!" Sandra shouted.

"Are you sure?" Roger asked.

"Yes. Do you remember Rose and Henry at Whelk Combe in Margate where we stayed?" Sandra said.

"We do!" Some of the children said.

"Well, Alison and Tom managed to make their way there. They got there a couple of hours ago. I just received a call from Rose, telling me they're there and they're safe," Sandra said.

"Why did she take so long to call, if they got there a couple of hours ago and only ringing now?" One of the children asked.

"Because when they got there, they were exhausted. Rose let them have a bath and are now tucking into something to eat. They have a bed made up for both of them and me and George can go and get them tomorrow. So, if we leave about 10 am, George we'll hopefully get there within about two hours, is that OK?" Sandra said.

"Of course it is," George said.

All of a sudden there was a huge cheer! Everyone was so happy that Alison and Tom had been found. Freddie and Charlie burst into tears.

"They really have been found?" Jo asked.

"Yes, Sweetheart and we are bringing them home tomorrow," Sandra hugged her to her. "Right, now I know you're all really excited, but it really is bedtime," George said, "so everyone back to your rooms and lights out in half an hour."

The children all cheered again.

The staff took the children back up to their rooms. Celia, Roger, and George stayed behind. "What else did Rose say, Sandra?" Roger asked.

"Just that they had found their way to her place and they were tired and hungry and to get there about lunchtime in case they slept in. Oh, and as we knew, they had run away from their foster home and they couldn't wait to get back here with us," she added.

The staff were pleased that they wanted to come back.

"Sandra don't forget to call the police and tell them they're safe, otherwise they may still be out looking for them," George said.

"Yes, I'll do it now."

Sandra dialled the number of the local police station.

"Hello, yes it's Sandra Michaels from Craven House. It's about the two missing children, Alison and Tom Davis?…They've been found, in Margate…Yes, we're going to collect them tomorrow…no, they're safe and with people we know there…they must have made their way there on their own. Please could you contact the police in Brighton for me and let them know? Yes, thank you for that. Yes, you will want to talk to the children when they get back, yes that should be OK once they've had a day or two to settle back in…OK, thank you again…Yes, you too." Sandra replaced the receiver.

***

Once they had finished their food, Alison got up to clear the table and take the plates into the kitchen, Rose didn't say anything but watched. She followed her into the kitchen. Alison put the dishes in the sink and put the water on and looked for the washing up liquid.

"Honey, what are you doing?" Rose asked.

"I was going to wash up our plates for you," Alison replied.

"There's no need, Alison. I'll do it later…well, Henry will." She laughed. "Come on, you come back in, would you like anything else to eat or drink?"

"No thank you, I think we should go to bed. We've only been sleeping on hay bales, so it will be great to get into a proper bed!" Alison said. "Come on Tom, let's go to bed, I'm tired now," Alison said.

"So am I!" Tom yawned.

"Henry, be a love, would you wash up what's in the sink?" Rose said, winking at Henry.

307

Rose went upstairs with Tom and Alison. She opened the door to number three and they both climbed into their beds. She tucked them both in. Tom reached out his arms and gave Rose a hug.

"Thank you, Rose," Tom said.

"You're very welcome, my love," Rose replied.

She then went over to Alison and tucked her into bed.

"Now, if you want anything, we are just down the hall, and the toilet is just through there, sleep tight you two," Rose said.

"You too," Alison said, nearly asleep.

They were both exhausted.

Rose closed the door but left it ajar. She returned back downstairs to the dining room. Henry came out from the kitchen.

"Would you like a cup of tea Rose?" Betty asked.

"Oh, yes please," Rose replied.

"Henry, I asked you to wash those dishes in the sink, because when I followed Alison into the kitchen, she was about to do them. Now when they were here, did you see her once go to the kitchen to wash dishes or dry them?" Rose asked.

Henry thought for a moment.

"No, I haven't actually. They never went to the kitchen once when they were here," Henry said.

"I think that little girl has been used as a skivvy. She didn't ask, she just did it automatically. We need to tell Sandra tomorrow when they come to collect them," Rose said.

"So, you got through then?" Henry asked.

Betty returned with tea for everyone.

"Yes, I spoke to Sandra, she was with them when they came here before. They were over the moon, by the sounds of it. They didn't know where they were. She was delighted to know that they were here though. I told her to come about lunchtime just in case they were still asleep. Alison has just told me that they have been sleeping on bales of hay, so goodness knows where they have been!" Rose said, quite alarmed.

"I'm just glad there got here without much trouble. Goodness knows if they had gotten help from the wrong type of person," Henry said.

308

"Right, come on Bruce, we had better go. Rose and Henry have enough on their plate this evening and tomorrow. Rose, I will see you tomorrow," Betty said.

Bye, love," Rose said.

Henry locked up and followed Rose up to their bedroom. They were only a couple of rooms away from Alison and Tom. They would be safe tonight.

Alison and Tom slept like logs; Rose was the one tossing and turning all night, wondering what the poor little lambs had been through. As Henry had said, she was so grateful that they hadn't fell into the wrong sort of people on their way to them. Mind you, it didn't sound like the family they had left were very nice to them either.

She had looked at the clock; it was 5.30am. Normally she would be getting up to make a start on checking the papers and getting ready, but they didn't have any guests for a day or so, so there was no need to get up.

Rose wasn't the only one tossing and turning. Sandra had been doing the same. She looked at the clock and it said 5.30am. She couldn't get up now; it was too early. Although, she could get up and make herself a hot drink. Yes, she thought, that would steady her. She grabbed her slippers and dressing gown and went down to the kitchen.

The cook was already there.

"Hi June, I was just going to make a hot drink, is that OK?" Sandra asked.

"Yes of course, I hear that Tom and Alison are coming back today, so you found them then?" June said.

Sandra making her cup of tea.

"Well, they found their way to a guest house we stayed at a couple of years ago and they called us. They were absolutely exhausted, so goodness knows how they got there, but thankfully they did. June, I know you're here early today, would it be possible to cook a roast dinner by any chance? I know it's a bit of a cheek as it's only Tuesday, but I don't think Alison and Tom have been eating very well. By the sound of it, they had a huge supper last night," Sandra asked.

"Of course, I can. I took out a couple of joints of beef yesterday. I had no idea why, but I do now. What about a trifle or two, do you think they would like that?" June asked.

"Yes, they would and so would the other children. June, you know the kids so well," Sandra said.

"Well, I've been here long enough, and it sounds like they have had a hard time of it. Right, I'd better get a move on," June said.

"June, would you have a quick cuppa with me first, if you don't mind? I haven't had the best sleep," Sandra said.

"Worrying about those poor kids, I suppose?"

"Yes," Sandra replied.

June poured herself a cup of tea and sat opposite Sandra.

"It's just not knowing what went on and why they didn't call us," Sandra said.

"Maybe they couldn't, Sandra. Maybe they didn't have the number or the use of a telephone. You won't know until they get back here."

"Yes, I told the police last night and they will want to talk to them when they get back, but if they aren't up to it, they will have to wait," Sandra said.

"But time is of the essence. If they leave it too long, they may not find them, and they have to, Sandra; what makes a child, or in this case, two children run away a couple of months of leaving here," June said.

"Right, I have to get on, thank you for the tea and the chat." June said.

"No, thank you, June, I hadn't thought of that," Sandra said, draining her cup.

It was now 6 am. She had better get back upstairs, at least she could have a shower before everyone got up.

***

Alison turned over, the clock said 8.30 am. She looked over at Tom who was fast asleep. She turned back over and lay there snuggled under the duvet. It was lovely and warm. She hadn't felt like this in a long time—happy.

Rose popped her head around the door.

"Would you like a cup of tea in bed?" She asked.

"Oh, yes please, this is a real treat!" Alison said.

"And how about breakfast in say in half an hour?" Rose asked.

"That would be great, Rose, thank you!" Alison said.

Alison picked up the teacup and saucer from the bedside cabinet once she settled herself upright in bed. This bed was so comfortable, she blew into her cup, she didn't want to burn her mouth. A cup of tea, first thing in the morning, she felt like a princess.

She enjoyed her cup of tea; life was going to be good again for her and Tom. Tom opened his eyes.

"Morning Alison, did you sleep well?" Tom asked her. "I did, I dreamt we were at Rose and Henry's," Tom said.

"We are, silly! Don't you remember coming here last night?" Alison laughed.

"Oh, I forgot!" Tom said, smiling.

"So where do you think we are now then?" Alison asked, looking around the room.

"I remember now, cor, I didn't realise we were still here," Tom said.

"Breakfast is at 8.30 am," Alison said.

"It's nearly that now, come on or we will miss it!" Tom said excitedly, scrambling out of bed.

Alison put down her cup and saucer, checked she had her socks on and pulled the duvet over the bed. She did the same to Tom's and then grabbed the cup and saucer.

"Come on Al, we will be late!" Tom said.

They pulled the door to, and then made their way to the dining room.

"Good morning you two!" Henry said.

"Morning Henry!" The children smiled.

They sat themselves down at the table.

"Now would you like toast and boiled eggs or a fry up or both?" Rose asked.

"Can I have boiled eggs and toast, orange juice and another cup of tea please?" Alison asked.

"Can I have the same please?" Tom said.

"Of course, you can, it won't be long, I'll just bring in the tea and orange juice," Rose said.

Rose returned a few minutes later with their breakfast. She had made herself and Henry a fry up, which they all tucked into their food. You couldn't hear anything except chewing and munching, all full tummies.

"Any more tea?" Rose asked. Everyone held up their cups.

When breakfast was over, Henry went into the kitchen to wash up, before Alison got there, but he was too late, she was already standing at the sink.

"Hey, that's my job, young lady," He laughed at Alison.

"Oh sorry, I just wanted to help," Alison said.

"You're a guest and that means you don't do washing up, right?" Henry said as he smiled at Alison.

Alison smiled back and said thank you.

Rose looked at Henry, and he continued with the washing up.

"Would you two like to go upstairs to the sitting room and I can put the TV on for you? I don't know what's on at this time of the morning, but I'm sure you will find something," Rose said.

"We can watch the TV?" Tom said, with great surprise.

"Yes, of course. You can treat the place like home. Our home is your home," Rose said.

"Not from where we just came from, it wasn't," Tom said.

Rose looked startled but said nothing. She took them upstairs to the living room, which was cosy. They both chose a lovely chair to sit in and Rose put on the TV. There wasn't much on as Rose had said but there were some children's TV programmes on; it was the summer holidays, after all.

Rose left them to it and returned downstairs.

"Henry, I think the place where the children were living wasn't very nice. They were surprised when I said they could watch TV. Maybe there weren't allowed at their foster home?" Rose said.

"What time is it? Oh, it's 10.30, Sandra and her colleague will have left by now, they should be here soon?"

"Are you trying to get rid of them, Rose?" Henry laughed.

"No, of course not, but I know how worried Sandra sounded on the phone. I just want them all to feel safe again," Rose said.

"Cooeey! It's only me!" Betty called out.

"We're down here, Bet. Do you want a cuppa?" Rose asked.

"Ooh, yes please! How did the kids sleep last night?" Betty asked.

"Like logs, the pair of them!" Rose replied.

"What are you up to at this time of the morning, Bet? We don't normally see you until gone 12?"

Henry said.

"Cheeky blighter!" Betty laughed. "I just wanted to see how the children are, that's all."

"He's only kidding. They're OK. They've had breakfast and are watching TV. Do you want to pop up and say hello?" Rose asked, "Here, you can take these up for them," Rose said, handing her a packet of biscuits and some squash.

312

Betty walked upstairs to the sitting room, knocked on the door and poked her head around the door. Both of the kids jumped out of their skins and screamed. Rose came running in.

"Alison, Tom, what's wrong?" Rose asked.

"Sorry Rose, this is your friend, she was here last night?" Alison said. "It's just the way she had her hair, we thought she was Ruth when she walked in," Alison said.

"Is that the lady who you lived with?" Rose asked.

"Yes, we thought she was here to take us back, sorry Miss. It's just you gave us such a fright, especially as we were engrossed in the TV," Alison said, rather embarrassed.

"Now don't you worry, my pet. I'm sorry, I didn't mean to startle you or frighten you. I just brought some biscuits and squash up for you from Rose and to say hello. I did see you last night, but you were both exhausted," Betty said.

"You cooked us our supper, didn't you?" Tom said.

"Yes, that's right," Bet replied.

"I'm Tom and this is Alison, my sister," Tom said.

"Well, it's nice to meet both of you." Bet said, holding out her hand to shake theirs.

"Come on Bet, let's go back downstairs and leave them to watch the TV," Rose said.

Alison and Tom turned their attention back to the TV.

"I didn't mean to frighten them, Rose," Bet said as she and Rose went back downstairs.

"Of course, you didn't, Bet. You know what it's like when you're watching something on the TV and someone comes in the room you don't know. Plus, they thought you were the lady who they had just left for whatever the reason. It would make them jump, don't worry about it. I've just made a pot of tea, come on sit down," Rose said.

Henry came into the sitting room and sat down on the sofa. Tom watched him sit down with his paper, he got up from sitting with Alison on the chair and asked Henry if he could sit next to him.

"Yes, that would be good, is it a good programme?" Henry asked.

"Yes, it's OK. I think it's more Alison's sort of thing than mine, but it's good to be allowed to watch telly." Tom said.

Henry smiled at Tom and Tom smiled back.

313

"Thank you Henry, for looking after me and Alison." Tom said.

Henry didn't know what to say, so he looked at his paper.

Tom continued to watch the TV as he sat next to Henry, with a beaming smile on his face.

***

The phone was ringing.

"Yes, I'm coming, hold on!" Eileen said.

She picked up the receiver.

"Hello?" She waited for a moment, but there was nothing on the other end of the line.

"Hello, can I help you?" Eileen said.

"Eileen? Is that you, Eileen?" The voice said on the other end of the phone.

"John? Oh my God! What are you doing calling me after all of this time?" Eileen asked terrified. She hadn't heard from her husband in nearly three years since he had tried to kill her.

"What do you want, John?"

"I wanted to talk to you, see how you are," John said.

"Why now? You haven't bothered with me for years, why now? Oh my God! You've got them, haven't you? You have my children!" Eileen screamed down the phone.

"Got who? What are you talking about?" John said.

"The kids, you took them, didn't you?" Eileen said.

There was a knock on the door.

"Who the bloody hell is that?" Eileen's mum said.

"It's the police!" The voice on the other side of the door said.

"You bloody bitch!" John shouted down the phone, then hung up.

Eileen stood there holding the receiver in her hand. Eileen's mum opened the front door and the police officer came in. Eileen put the phone down.

"Can I help you, officer?" Eileen asked.

"Morning, Mrs Davis, I just wanted to let you know that your children have been found. They're safe and well." The officer said.

"Oh, thank God for that!" Eileen's mum said as she sat down on the stairs.

"Where were they found then?" Eileen asked.

314

"They went to a guest house that they had been to a couple of years ago and they made their way there. But they are safe and sound and the staff at Craven House are going to collect them today." The officer said. "We did say, we would contact you if we heard anything and we didn't want to keep you in the dark."

"Thank you for that, officer. Have a good day," Eileen said.

Eileen saw them out and closed the door after them.

"Who was on the phone that you were screaming at, Eileen?" Her mum asked.

"You will never believe it, mum…it was John!" Eileen said.

"What, John your husband? Who bloody well tried to kill you?"

"Yes, but once he heard the police were here, he called me a bloody bitch and put the phone down," Eileen said.

"I always thought that man was weird. If he calls again, put the phone down. But write it down by the pad, the time and date he called and what he said," Eileen's mum said.

"Why?"

"Because we may not be able to trace him, but the police can and if he continues, it's harassment," Eileen's mum said.

***

The car pulled up outside the guest house and Sandra and George were relieved that they were finally here, and able to see the kids. They knocked on the door and Rose answered it, she told them to come in and she took them upstairs to the living room.

When she opened the door, Henry and the children were all sitting on the sofa watching TV. Rose moved out of the way and said she had a surprise for them. Alison and Tom looked in the direction of the door and both jumped up and ran to Sandra and George.

"Look at you two! How much you have grown in a short time!" Sandra said, tears escaping from her eyes.

"I'll go and make some tea, Henry, come and give me a hand," Rose said.

Sandra and George held onto the children as tight as they could.

"Let go, George, I can hardly breathe!" Tom laughed.

They both let go of the children and sat down on the sofa.

315

"How are you both? How is Charlie and Freddie George? Are they OK?" Tom had a million questions to ask.

"They're all fine; just worried about you!" George said.

"Worried about me?" Tom asked.

"Yes, because we knew you had left Brighton, but we didn't know where you were?" George said.

"How did you know we left Brighton?" Alison asked. "Nobody knew we had left Brighton, did they?"

"When did you leave Brighton then?" Sandra asked.

"Saturday morning, after Ruth, Harry and Hannah left to go out shopping," Alison said.

Tom shuddered at the mere mention of Ruth and Harry.

Rose returned with Henry, a tray of tea and some biscuits. Bet followed on behind.

"But we went to see you on Saturday evening and then again on Sunday lunchtime," Sandra said, "and it was only on Sunday that we knew you had gone."

"But how?" Alison asked. "Nobody knew we left on Saturday."

"Alison, when you and Tom left, Harry and Ruth got back from the shops. They realised you had left," Sandra said.

"So, they called the police?" Alison asked.

"No, they packed up their stuff and buggered, sorry, left with their suitcases," George said.

"How come?" Alison asked.

"What do you mean Alison?"

"Well, we left and went along the back and side roads. We thought we saw their car, so we jumped over a fence and hid under a hedge. Then thought it wasn't them, but continued across a field, and found a barn and fell asleep on some hay, longer than we hoped. So, when you were knocking at the door on Saturday, we were still in Brighton, we just didn't know it?" Alison said.

"Oh no! We had literally just missed you. What about Sunday? When we came back?" George asked.

"By then we had found that we had to go back to Brighton to get to the coach station, which we did on Monday morning," Alison said.

"Hang on Alison, how on earth did you get out in the first place?" George asked.

"Ruth had realised that Harry wasn't being very nice to us. She had pulled him up a few times, but when he called me a liar and a thief and then slapped me across the face, that was it," she said.

"What?" George said, spitting out his tea. "He slapped you across the face? Why?"

"Because he called me a liar and a thief and slapped me, it wasn't the first time either," Alison said.

"Yeah and it wasn't the first time and we went to bed without dinner also," Tom added.

Sandra, George, Rose, Henry and Bet couldn't believe their ears.

"Harry kept going through my things, he thought we had money, I only had that five pounds that I took down with me the first time, but I didn't spend it, it was still in my purse. I caught Harry going through Tom's things and he took his St. Christopher you gave him. Mine had already gone, he left the box though, but I caught him. He saw me watching him take it and put it in his pocket." Alison took a deep breath and continued.

"He told me I never saw anything. So, when Ruth said she had mislaid five pounds, he went up to my bedroom and found my purse with the money in it and I got the blame. But Ruth had found the money afterwards, he called me out of the kitchen. I was washing up and didn't hear him call me as the tap was loud. He had my purse in his hand, he called me a thief.

"When I told him where I got it from and he called me a liar, then he pulled his hand back and then slapped me across the face. I told him and Ruth that I had seen him in Tom's bedroom going through his things, and he took his St Christopher. He sent me and Tom upstairs. Hannah got sent upstairs by Ruth and she had it out with him. I was listening on the stairs. He wouldn't listen that he was in the wrong. It was all about money. They didn't want me and Tom, he wanted the money we bring," Alison said.

With that, both of the children burst into tears.

Sandra grabbed Alison and George grabbed Tom and held them close.

That's what those kids have missed, love from their family, Rose thought.

Rose and Bet had tears in their eyes.

Sandra asked something that was bothering her.

"Alison, how did Harry know you had money?"

"You know you sent me a card with everyone signing it? Well, Harry didn't like it. He didn't want any mention of anything to do with Craven House. Anyway, when I opened it, he saw the twenty pounds fly out," Alison said.

"So where is the twenty pounds now?" George asked.

"I had to pay Harry back for taking me out for tea on my birthday," Alison said.

"What did they get you for your birthday?" Rose asked.

"Nothing!" Alison replied.

"Nothing?" Sandra and George said.

"Nope," Alison shrugged. "They would go out every Saturday with Hannah and leave me and Tom in the house on our own."

"Alison had to do all the cleaning, and they wouldn't let us watch TV," Tom added.

"Harry would check the back of the TV to see if it was warm or not," Alison said.

"Alison, did this happen a lot?" Sandra asked.

"Not at first, but after Mrs Hemsby visited, we got told off for being late home. But she was early, and it was Hannah who made us late home. That day Tom got smacked for answering Henry back," Alison said, "and it just got worse from then on."

The grownups looked horrified.

"Now, children, would you like to come down with me to the kitchen and we can see if we have any cakes?" Bet said.

"Oh yes, please!" Tom said. Henry went with them.

"Sandra, I am sorry, we shouldn't have stayed to hear all of that," Rose said.

"Actually, Rose, I am glad you did. I can't believe what I have just heard, what about you George?" Sandra said.

"What? No, I can't believe it either, I hope the police bloody find those two," George said.

"Rose," Sandra said.

"Sandra, don't worry, we won't say anything, unless you need us to be witnesses, then we will speak up for them, they can't get away with what they did." Rose had tears in her eyes.

"Listen, I want you all to come back in a few weeks. I'll check my diary and see how busy we are, and we will sort something out for all of you, the staff and all the kids. I can't believe someone could be so evil towards children," Rose said.

"Oh Rose, I don't think we have the budget for it," Sandra said.

"Who said anything about budget? I want, we want, you to bring these children for a week and let them let their hair down. They've have had too much upset and it's not how children should be treated," Rose said.

"OK, we'll sort something out, and thank you, that's very kind of you," Sandra said.

Bet and Henry came back with the children and George looked a little puzzled.

"Alison, I still don't understand how you escaped?"

"Oh yes, sorry I forgot about that," Alison said.

Everyone sat back down again, and Rose returned, she sat down next to Henry.

"Well, the next morning was Saturday and we were at breakfast and Harry was reading his paper and acted as if nothing had happened. I helped with breakfast as usual and Hannah asked if they were going out again and Harry said they were. She wanted to go to Molly's to have a chocolate éclair. Anyway, Ruth asked quietly if we were going too and I saw Harry shake his head."

"Ruth beckoned me to the kitchen and stuffed twenty pounds in my hands and mimed for me to put it in my jeans pocket, then she pointed at the fruit and a bag on the side, also two tins of coke. Then Harry and Hannah came back down again, they got their stuff together, and left, but Ruth came back for her reading glasses, which she never uses, she winked at me and then shut the door, but she didn't lock it this time."

George went to say something, but Sandra punched him lightly in the stomach, she didn't want Alison to lose her train of thought.

"So, I went to the window as always, waved them off. Once they drove off, I waited a minute, then legged it upstairs. Ruth had put my purse in my coat, also our St Christopher's were on our dressers. I put them in our coats and ran back downstairs. We went out the front door and ran," Alison said completing her story.

"Alison, how did you feel when you got out of the house?" Henry asked.

"I didn't think, I just wanted to get away from there as quick as we could without being caught. I was more scared we would run straight into them, but we didn't, thank goodness," Alison said.

"Well, we are glad you came here, and now you can go home with Sandra and George," Rose said.

"But we'll always be here if you need us, OK?"

Alison flung her arms around Rose.

"Thank you for everything you have done for us, Rose, you too Henry and Bet. It was nice to see you, Bet," Alison said.

"Right, I think we had better think about getting some clothes on you two and making a move and give Rose and Henry some peace, what do you think?" Sandra asked.

"I think that's a great idea!" Alison said.

Alison and Tom went to their bedroom and Sandra gave them both a bag. It had new clothes; jeans and tee shirt for both of them. Rose collected their clean stuff that she had washed. Sandra put it them in the bag she just emptied.

"Oh Rose, can I use your phone quickly, I just want to let them know we are on our way back. Is that OK?" Sandra asked.

"Yes of course, it's just along the way there down the corridor," Rose said.

Sandra returned a couple of minutes later.

"Right, are we ready?" George asked.

Alison and Tom, both gave Rose a huge hug, they both felt so grateful and relived they got the help they needed.

"Don't forget Sandra, I'll be in touch in the next couple of days to arrange?" Rose said.

"OK, Rose, thank you and thank you for taking care of them," Sandra said.

They all got into the car, they belted up their seat belts and the kids looked around on the back seat and waved. Rose and Henry waved back.

They turned the corner and they were gone.

"Come on Henry, come and help me rearrange a week in a couple of weeks' time, I want them all back here, they all need a break after the stress they have been under lately."

They went back into the guest house and Henry did as he was told.

Chapter 18

George sat in the front to drive the car, whilst Sandra sat in between Tom and Alison in the backseat. They both held onto her hands quite tightly, and they were chatting happily. It was the most the children had chatted since they went to Brighton to live with the Coopers.

George and Sandra were both listening intently to them both, asking about everyone, how they were, was there still room for them at Craven House? Did anyone miss them at all and were they still able to go back to their schools when the summer holidays were over?

They wanted the children to come up for air but didn't dare say anything because they had been shut up for so long and now, they needed to express how they were feeling. Rose had given them drinks to take on the journey and some sandwiches, but now they weren't too far away, Sandra let them have their drinks.

Everyone at Craven House had been so worried since they heard that they had run away and had not known where they were.

"Not long now everyone, we should be there very soon," George said. He was glad that Sandra had asked that they both go and collect them. A few more roads away, the drinks had been finished and then they turned into the road where Craven House stood. Alison and Tom sat open mouthed; they thought they would never see it ever again or the people inside it.

George pulled up right outside the entrance and they could hear cheering. They got out of the car and the cheering got louder and louder. They looked up at the windows and saw the children waving to them. They looked so happy to see them. Alison and Tom felt overwhelmed by it all.

Mr Duffy came out and ran down the stairs. He grabbed hold of both of them and hugged them tightly.

"My goodness, we are so glad you have been found safe and sound," he said.

"Mr Duffy, you're squeezing me!" Tom said.

Mr Duffy pulled away from his hug and had tears in his eyes.

"Can we go in now then?" Tom asked.

They went up the stairs with Sandra and George, who also had tears in their eyes, this was definitely an emotional time. The main door was opened by the receptionist and they walked through it and made their way upstairs. By the time they got to the top of the stairs, it was full of children and staff, who started to clap.

They were so glad to see both of them. Tom and Alison couldn't hold back any longer, they both burst into tears. They couldn't believe everyone was so pleased to see them. On seeing both of them in tears, everyone started crying from the relief that they had been found.

They both looked like they needed feeding up, but that wouldn't be a problem. Once it settled down and everyone was coming to the end of their crying and tears were wiped, they all let out a huge cheer for George and Sandra for bringing them back.

"Right, you lot, who's hungry?" June asked.

They all left the hallway and went straight down to the dining room.

"Do you want to go down to dinner now or go to your room's first?" Sandra asked.

"Can we go to the dining room please, Sandra, I'm starving!" Tom said.

Alison nodded; they were both hungry.

They made their way down to the dining room and the children had left them their normal seats. Alison sat next to Jo, who also sat next to Tom, Freddie, and Charlie. When the boys got to see Tom and Alison properly, they just hugged them and didn't want to let go, they had more tears in their eyes.

"Freddie, Charlie and Jo, they're back now, safe and sound. You can let them go; they want to have their dinner," George said.

"No, we don't want to let them go ever again, George!" Freddie said.

The adults understood because that's how they felt—they didn't want them to go in the first place, but they didn't want them to miss out on a chance of a proper family life.

"Right now, who wants beef and all the trimmings?" June asked.

Everyone put up their hands.

Sandra and George left the children so they could go and help give out the dinners. Even though they had got Tom and Alison back, they still had their jobs to do. June took over two dinners to Alison and Tom first.

"I didn't make them too big as I knew you would want dessert, eh?" June said.

Tom gave June a huge smile.

"Yes please, June!" Tom said.

She looked at Alison.

"Yes please, June, thank you, this is delicious!" Alison replied.

Before long, everyone had their dinner in front of them. A couple of the children moved up so that Sandra and George could sit down with them. Everyone wanted to be near Alison and Tom, they felt so sorry what they had been through.

All you could hear was chewing, munching, and swallowing. There was juice on the table and Alison and Tom had a couple of glasses of each. It was like Christmas.

Once dinner was over, Alison got up as the rest of the children to clear the tables and wipe them down and then went to go to the kitchen. She got to the sink. Everyone in the dining room stopped what they were doing to watch her. She filled the sink and put washing up liquid in. June had turned around to look in the dining room and stopped to see where they were all looking. June walked over to Alison.

"Darling, you don't have to do that, it's my job. Do you want to collect the plates and put them just inside the hatch instead?" she asked.

Alison did as she was told, and everybody resumed what they were doing.

Once the kitchen was cleared and tables wiped down, everyone went up to their bedrooms.

They went up to Tom's room first. He got to his bed; it had fresh bed linen on it. Freddie held out his cars and trucks. Tom was astounded.

"Where did they come from?" Tom asked.

"When we went to Brighton to find you and the police were there, they let us bring your things home," George said.

"All of them? My clothes as well?" Tom asked.

Tom started looking for something, he pulled all of the cars and trucks out, throwing them all over the place.

"Hey Tom, what's wrong?" George asked, "Careful, you nearly hit Freddie with the car."

"I'm looking for...oh, I can't find it!" Tom said.

323

"What are you looking for, Tom? We have all of your cars and trucks here," George said.

"I'm looking for that red remote control car, the one they got me, for my birthday," Tom said.

"Oh, Tom, we didn't think you would want it, we threw it in the bin," George said.

"Did you? Did you? Thank goodness for that, thank you, thank you. I don't want it, I don't want anything from them, George," Tom said.

He hugged George.

"George, they can't come back and take us away again, can they?" Tom asked.

"No Tom, they can't take you back. You're staying with us now," George said.

"For good, George?"

"For good, Tom," George said.

Alison had headed back upstairs with Sandra and Jo. They walked into the very familiar room, which Alison thought she would never see again.

"Sandra, what will I do for clothes and nightwear? We left everything behind. I thought if we left, we would be safe, I didn't think for one moment to bring anything with us," Alison said.

"It's OK, love, we brought your stuff back with us," Sandra said.

"Huh, how come?" Alison asked.

"You know when we went to Brighton to see you and we had to call the police?" Sandra said.

"The police?" Alison said.

"Yes, Sweetheart, once we knew that the Coopers had gone with Hannah and not you two, we had to call them as you were then missing children. The police were very good. There were six of them and we had to get into the house."

"How?" Alison asked, a little confused.

"Well they have this big tool, that when it's banged really hard at a lock on a door, it breaks it, so we could get in," Sandra said.

"Yes! You should have seen it, Alison, it was brilliant!" Jo said.

"Wait? You were there too, Jo?" Alison asked.

"Yes, she was, and I am glad she was there, as Jo had a big clue," Sandra said.

"Did I?" Jo said.

324

"Yes, you had a photo of Alison, Tom, which she gave to the police officers so they could circulate it to other police stations all over the country. Just in case one of them found you and could bring you back here," Sandra said.

"You mean, if the police officers found us, would we have been in trouble?" Alison asked.

"No, it meant that they could bring you home here to us safely," Sandra said.

"So, what happened once the police broke the door?" Alison asked, a little puzzled.

Sandra explained what had happened in the house.

"The lady next door to you, Gladys? She was very helpful to the police, she said she didn't see either of you very much, but heard you being shouted at," Sandra said.

"No, we didn't really see anyone, but Harry shouted all the time," Alison said.

"What about Ruth? Did she shout at you?" Jo asked.

"No, Ruth was different, she was sort of softer. She knew what Harry would do and she would tell him off, but she then got told off. But the night before we left, she gave us our St. Christopher's back," Alison said.

Jo looked surprised but said nothing.

"She helped us get away. She knew Harry only wanted the money and not us at all. When they were here it was all for show."

My, how these two children had grown up in such a short time, Sandra thought.

Alison started to go through her things.

"Did you bring back my figurines with you Sandra?" Alison asked.

"Sorry no, Sweetheart, we couldn't. There were six of them, weren't there? We could only find five, but they had been smashed up. We couldn't have fixed them, but we will get you some more. I know they were from your classmates here, but we will replace them, I promise," Sandra said.

Alison hugged her. She knew Sandra would do her best to try and get another set.

"Alison, I'll leave you now, so you can sort yourself out. If you want to get into you night things you can, or not if you don't. But remember, we are all here for you if you want to talk or have a hug or just sit in silence," Sandra said.

"No silence, please! Me and Tom were told often enough not to speak. Even if it means we get sore throats, we're going to be talking!" Alison laughed.

Sandra smiled. She knew how much these kids had been through, but how they were feeling, that was going to take a long time.

Sandra left Alison and Jo in their room and went to find George, who was just leaving Tom, Freddie and Charlie.

"George, are you free for a few minutes?" Sandra asked.

"Sure," George said, closing the boys' bedroom door.

"Can we go to the staffroom? I think we need to find Mr Duffy as well," Sandra said.

"Good idea," George said.

Even though it was late, Mr Duffy was still in his office. It had been an eventful day today and he was just finishing up. Sandra knocked on the door.

"Come in!" Mr Duffy called.

"Ah, Sandra and George, please come in, sit down. How are you both after today's events?"

"Exhausted, to be honest, Mr Duffy," Sandra said.

Mr Duffy looked at George. George nodded.

"Mr Duffy, I'm not trying to tell you your job, but I think we need to have a meeting very soon about Alison and Tom. Not because they're back, but it's their behaviour since we saw them this morning," Sandra said.

"Go on?" Mr Duffy said.

"At dinner, when everyone had finished eating and drinking, everyone normally mucks in together to clear the plates, etc., wipe down the tables. Well, Alison went into the kitchen and started getting ready to wash up. Everyone stopped in their tracks at the shock of seeing her in the kitchen. AS you know, we don't allow the children in the kitchen for their own safety, with things on stoves and hot water and such. We think that from what Rose was saying this morning, that Alison was made to do lots of housework and cleaning.

"Now, we do some here, so that everyone learns how to do it, but not every day and on the weekend. She got quite sad, when I said that I couldn't bring back her figures from school as Harry, Mr Cooper, had smashed them up, but I said I would get her a replacement set," Sandra said.

Mr Duffy then looked at George.

"Tom had a bit of a meltdown when he saw his trucks and cars," George said. "He thought we brought back the one the Coopers got him for his birthday. We did bring it back with the others, but Freddie and Charlie told me which one it was when we were going through them and I threw it in the bin. I didn't know if

I should have done, but on seeing Tom a little while ago, I know I did the right thing," George said.

"I know one thing, I am so lucky to have the two of you working here, you're dedicated to your jobs and to the children. I think you're both right; we need a meeting. I also want Mr Prowse to come down as well and we need to talk to this Mrs Hemsby woman. Actually, we should have her report. I'll dig it out tomorrow and see if we can sort this out in the next day or two. Is that OK with you both?" Mr Duffy asked.

They both nodded.

"Now I know we still have a lot of staff here and other children, but I think you both need an early night. You have done some great work since the weekend and I am proud to have you on my team, but you both need sleep. I know in these situations, you can work on adrenaline, but they are both back safe and sound, so go and get some rest."

Sandra and George thanked Mr Duffy and said goodnight to him. They left his office, headed back up to the children and said goodnight to everyone.

***

The sun was beaming into Alison and Jo's room. Alison woke with a start. For a moment she forgot where she was and thought she was still in Brighton, with the Coopers. She looked around the room and saw Jo lying in bed, still asleep.

Alison let out a big sigh of relief. She was glad that whole nightmare was over and would soon to be forgotten.

Jo opened her eyes.

"Well, that's a sight for sore eyes!" Jo said.

"What is?" Alison asked.

"Seeing you in bed! It's something I didn't think I would see ever again. Al, I am so pleased that you and Tom are back home here with us, like one big happy family again." Jo smiled.

Jo and the other children were all pleased to see them back safe and sound, they still didn't know any details, they were just glad that no real damage had been done.

Sandra knocked on the door and popped her head around it.

"Morning, sleepyheads! How are you this morning?" Sandra asked.

"Fine, we haven't been awake for long." Jo said.

"Sandra, can I tell you something, but I don't want you to tell Tom. I don't want to hurt his feelings. You won't say anything will you? You either, Jo?" Alison whispered.

"No, of course not," Sandra and Jo said.

"When we were in Brighton, Hannah was sorting out a lot of toys, teddies, dolls and that, for the jumble sale, and Tom's doll that he bought Hannah was on top of the pile. I didn't tell him that, as I knew it would have hurt his feelings; it was a present, after all," Alison said.

"No, don't worry, I won't tell him," Sandra said.

Alison looked at Jo, she shook her head also.

"So, what's the other thing?" Sandra asked. She was glad it wasn't really anything serious, but considering what they had been through, she didn't want to say as much.

"Well, you know we went out for my birthday and Molly had given me a chocolate éclair as a treat, well Hannah was really unhappy about it, she wanted one too. But Harry wouldn't buy her one. Well, when we got home, she asked Harry why she wouldn't buy her a chocolate éclair, and do you know what he said, he said that if he bought her one, he would have to buy Tom one and they knew how greedy Tom was," Alison said. "Tom isn't greedy, is he, Sandra?" Alison asked.

"No, he is not greedy. He has a big appetite and for a growing child, that's a good thing, so you take no notice about what Harry said—he is the greedy one," replied Sandra. "Don't you worry any more about it. Come on now, time's getting on, let's go down for breakfast," Sandra said, pulling their duvets off and putting them down the bottom of the bed.

They left the bedroom and went downstairs. They bumped into Tom, Freddie and Charlie on their way down. George had been in to get them up for breakfast. The boys were chatting happily, and Tom seemed to be returning to his old self. They went into the dining room and all the children cheered again.

Once they were tucking in, Mr Duffy came in to speak briefly with Sandra and George, then left the dining room. When breakfast was over and cleared away, a few of the girls came over to Alison and Jo and started talking to them, asking if they wanted to go shopping later on that day, with Sandra and Celia.

Alison and Jo liked the idea of that. When Alison and Tom left to live in Brighton, the other girls took Jo under their wing, so they just continued with Alison as well, which Sandra and Celia were pleased with.

Once all of the cleaning up of the kitchen had been done, then all of the girls left the dining room to go up and get washed and dressed. Sandra and George went to Mr Duffy's office.

"Oh good, I'm glad you came as quickly as you could," Mr Duffy said.

Mr Duffy was a fair man. He got on with his job, notified the staff of any necessary changes and what was generally going on at Craven House. Unlike his predecessor, Christine Walters.

"Now, I've arranged with Mr Prowse to come over tomorrow for a meeting. I've also contacted the children's former school head, and she will be coming as well. Are you both free tomorrow? I'm hoping to get hold of Mrs Hemsby from Brighton Social Services today. I want her opinion, since her report she sent at the beginning of this placement. Is there anyone else we need to talk to about this? The reason I am asking you both is because I don't want to cock this up. There have been too many mistakes with this situation. Now, I'm not pinning any blame on anyone here, but we have to be very thorough," Mr Duffy said.

"No, not that I can think of, Mr Duffy. Have you heard anything from the police in Brighton?" Sandra asked.

"No, I am waiting for them to call me back this morning, but knowing the police, it could be a bit later than that, but I do need to talk to them today," Mr Duffy said. "Anyone else?"

"Well, not for the meeting, but I wanted to ask you something," Sandra said.

"OK, go ahead."

"You know we picked up Alison and Tom from Whelk Combe Guest House, well, the lady who owns it was so appalled at what she heard the other day, that she wanted to offer us all a week away for free. If she does, Mr Duffy, would it be OK for us to take her up on her offer? I think it would do the world of good for all of us," Sandra said.

"Let's see…did you say her name was Rose?" Mr Duffy asked. They both nodded.

"Let's see if Rose can sort it first. We don't want to be getting the children's hopes up. If she says she can then I think it's an excellent idea. You can all go and that will leave just me and the admin department; working hard, while you lot are having a whale of a time!" he laughed.

"Now if you can think of anyone else we might need for the meeting tomorrow, could you let me know before the end of the day, so I can make the relevant phone calls?" Mr Duffy said.

**

Sandra and George were both pleased with the results.

Sandra went up to find the girls and see how they were, and George went to check on the boys.

"Sandra, can we go with Emily, Julie and Susie up to town today?" Jo asked.

"I don't see why not, what time?" Sandra asked.

"Oh, they didn't say, but once we're ready, we can go and ask them?" Jo replied.

"I tell you what, what if I go now, while you two get dressed and whatever else, perfume? Nails? And then I can come back with the time. Can I come too?" Sandra asked.

"You don't need an invitation to come, Sandra!" Jo said.

Alison looked a little lost.

"Erm Sandra, I don't think I should go," Alison said.

"Why on earth not?" Sandra asked, a little puzzled.

"Well, you see I don't have any money, and I don't want to see something and I can't buy it," Alison said.

Sandra felt broken-hearted; how can a young girl feel like that? That she shouldn't go because she hasn't any money. Especially with what she has been through.

"Yes, I think you should go and don't worry about it, we will sort something out," Sandra said, leaving the room and legging it upstairs to the other girl's rooms.

"About 12, OK girls? See you downstairs in reception," Sandra said.

Sandra then popped downstairs to see if George was with the boys. He wasn't there, but she did find him in the staff room.

"George, can I have a quick word?" Sandra asked.

"Yeah, course, what's up?" George asked.

"Has Tom mentioned money to you at all?" Sandra enquired.

"No, he hasn't, don't forget, they only just got back. They won't have had any pocket money for a while," George said.

"Precisely!"

"Huh?" George replied.

"Come with me," Sandra said, pulling on George.

They went back downstairs to Mr Duffy's office and knocked on the door.

"Come in! Oh, it's you two again, what can I do for you?" Mr Duffy said.

"Well, it seems a bit of a strange one, but Alison and Tom, up to when they left, they had pocket money every week, but since staying with the Coopers, they received not one penny, so even though the Coopers were paid quite a lot of money, £750.00 per week for both of them, they didn't buy them anything, Mr Duffy," Sandra began. "I know we don't normally get involved with the money side of things Mr Duffy, but now they are back, but is there anything we can do?" Sandra pleaded with her boss.

Mr Duffy thought for a moment.

"Well, normally, they would get their pocket money on a Saturday, the same as everyone else, but this is a very different situation. Let me have a think about it and I can talk to my bosses and see what we can do, is that OK? Sorry Sandra, can I ask why you have asked about this now?" Mr Duffy asked.

"Well, it's just the older girls want to go into town this lunchtime and have asked Alison and Jo to come along. Only now Alison doesn't want to go, as she doesn't have any money. I don't blame her, but she has been through enough without her feeling worse because she has no money," Sandra said.

"OK Sandra, leave it with me. What time are they going out?"

"Twelve o'clock," Sandra replied.

Sandra and George left his office and went back upstairs.

"I understand now, they shouldn't feel bad because of what happened, Sandra," George said. "I know but when you are that age and your friends are buying things, there's nothing worse than having no money."

Ten minutes later, Mr Duffy's secretary came to the staff room, where Sandra and George were having a coffee.

"Sandra and George, can you come down to Mr Duffy's office please?" His secretary asked. They both got up and left the staffroom.

Mr Duffy's office door was open, he was on the phone again, but beckoned them both in and to sit down.

"OK, thank you, yes, talk again soon and thanks again, John," Mr Duffy finished his phone call. "I've just spoken with John Dunn from the council offices; actually, he's my boss. I've briefed him on the money situation and oh by the way, he's also attending tomorrow's meeting. Anyway, he said yes, the children can still have their pocket money as normal on a Saturday, but they have both been given an extra £100 for themselves. He's appalled at what has happened and wants to make sure that this sort of thing doesn't happen again. Anyway, he's told me to give it to you out of petty cash, to put a receipt in and he will bring a proper one with him tomorrow. Is that OK?"

"None of this is their fault, it was lucky that Alison had the head on her shoulders that she does, and they were able to get away to safety. Anyway, give me a few minutes and what do you normally do when they don't take all of their money with them?" Mr Duffy asked.

"They all have a locker each. It's not a safety deposit box but has any valuables of theirs inside it and their pocket money if they want to save it," George said.

"Oh, OK, come back in a minute and I'll have the money for you in an envelope for each of them," Mr Duffy said.

Sandra and George returned a few minutes later, collected the envelopes and then went upstairs.

"George, Tom hasn't said anything about going out just yet, so if you put his envelope in his box, I'll give Alison some of hers, see what she wants and then put the rest in her box. I don't think they will want to spend it all at once, but you never know. I think Alison needs this time with just the girls today, she needs to feel like a young person again, not a bloody skivvy," Sandra said.

Sandra bolted up to Alison and Jo's room.

"Sorry girls, I got a bit held up, the girls want to go out at midday, is that OK?" Sandra asked. It was already nearly 11.30 am.

"I don't think I will go, Sandra," Alison said.

"Is it because you don't have any money?" Sandra asked.

Alison nodded.

"Oh, but you do! I've just been down to the office to sort it out. You'll start to get pocket money on a Saturday, like you used to, but Mr Duffy has kindly sorted out some money that's owed to you," Sandra smiled.

"Money owed?" Alison asked.

"Yes, money that is owed to you, because you haven't had any pocket money since you left here, and we forget to stop it. It has accumulated to quite a bit. So that's money for you to spend and yes, Tom has the same as well," Sandra said.

Alison and Jo got themselves sorted out. Alison didn't know how much money to bring, but Sandra said she could hold on to it for her if she wanted. The other girls said they were only taking £20 each, so Sandra put the rest in her box for her.

Alison was chuffed to be going out with the girls, it seemed an eternity since she had done this with other girls her own age. On their way downstairs to reception, Alison and Jo looked in on Tom, Freddie, and Charlie. They were all playing cars, trucks, ramps, and wheelies. They were having a great time; it was like nothing had changed and no time had passed.

"Tom, we are going out in to town, did you want anything?" Alison asked.

"No, I'm fine, we're having fun with our trucks and cars and...oh, Charlie, that was a brilliant wheelie...have a good time, Al!" Tom said.

Tom was back to his normal self; you would never have known he had left and returned.

All the boys looked happy and were having so much fun. It pleased Alison and Jo to see the boys back together, having a great time.

Alison and Jo met up with the rest of the group in reception and Sandra signed them all out.

When they got to town, they headed straight for Woolworths. They had a good record section and the girls loved going there. All of them were choosing their favourite artists and Sandra was having fun just watching them all. It was so good to see Alison laughing with Jo.

Alison picked up a poster of Abba and Jo picked one up of the Bee Gees. They looked at the records. Alison was a huge Abba fun and picked up two of her favourites: *Angel Eyes* and *Voulez-Vous*. Jo, who was mad on the Bee Gees, picked out *If I Can't Have You* and *Tragedy*.

The two girls bought some pick n mix sweets. They didn't really want anything else.

The other girls picked up what records they wanted and a poster or two each. Everyone was into different music.

"But how are we going to play them?" Alison asked.

"Oh, we have a record player in our room now and Sandra said you can come and play them on a Friday evening and a Saturday evening, but not on a Sunday, as it's a school night," Julie said.

***

"Hello, hello, can I speak to Sandra Michaels please? Yes, it's Rose, Rose Benton from Whelk Combe…oh is she…OK, please could you get her to ring me when she gets back? Yes thank you, bye," Rose said into the phone.

"Henry, she's not there at the moment, she's out, but they'll get her to call me when she gets back."

***

"Come on you lot, we had better be heading back, it will be dinner time soon," Sandra said.

Everyone had enjoyed themselves and Alison was starting to look her normal self again. It didn't take long for them to walk back to Craven House. There were only five girls, so it wasn't difficult to keep up with them. They all bought what they wanted, had a bite for lunch in the Wimpy, looked around the boutiques but were pleased they settled on Woolworths in the end.

They walked up the steps and Mr Duffy called Sandra.

"You go on up and I will be with you in a few minutes," Sandra said.

"Sandra, a Rose Benton called you a little while ago and wants you to call her back when you get back," Mr Duffy said.

"Rose Benton? That's the lady who owns that guest house, I bet that's what it's about. Can I call her in reception?" Sandra asked.

"Use this phone and I can hear what's going on, if that's OK?" Mr Duffy said.

Sandra picked up the receiver and dialled the number. Rose answered the phone practically straight away.

"Hello, oh, hello Sandra, thank you for calling me back, I did ring a little while ago, but they said you were out…oh, taking the girls out for a shopping trip? I hope Alison enjoyed herself…Oh I am glad, put the rosiness on her cheeks again I bet? Now, I have had a look in the diary, and I can fit you all in on the 14th August for a week, is that OK?" Rose asked.

"14th for a week, and that will be for all of the children and staff?" Sandra asked.

"Yes, I just need to know how many that will be?" Rose asked.

"Well, there are thirty children and ten staff who can come, is that OK? Will you have enough room for all of us, Rose?" Sandra asked.

"Yes of course, we can accommodate all of you. Now, is a week long enough, or we can make it ten days?" Rose asked.

"No, no, a week is quite sufficient, Rose, now how much is this going to be?" Sandra asked.

"How much? Oh nothing, this is on us, now no arguments please, Sandra, we know those kiddies are good and we have seen Alison and Tom, so please, this week will be for free. Just bring yourselves, your luggage and spending money. Honestly, it's fine. Please let us do this for them and for you too," Rose said.

"I don't know what to say, Rose. You really are so kind and such a trooper. Now it's not going to be too much with all of us?" Sandra asked.

"No, don't worry about that. We've roped in our friends Betty and Bruce, you met Betty on Tuesday; she was there when Alison and Tom came, and they want to help," Rose said.

"OK, lovely then, see you on the 14th then. Take care and lots of love to the children," Rose said.

"So, I take it it's all arranged then?" Mr Duffy said, as Sandra replaced the receiver.

"Yes, all of the children, ten staff for a week, for free! She's got two friends who are going to help, but you know our children, we will keep them in check and some of them have already been away to Margate. All we have to do is get our coach, sort out the children's clothes and pack. We're going away in ten days' time!" Sandra said excitedly.

"When shall we tell the children?"

"What about after dinner this evening, it will give them something good to look forward to?" Mr Duffy suggested.

***

Alison and Jo went up to see Tom and the boys on their return from town.

"Hi Tom, Freddie and Charlie, are you having a good time? I know Tom said he didn't want anything from Town, but we got you some pick and mix, but for after your dinner's OK?" Alison said.

"Thanks Al, thanks Jo!" The boys said.

"It's alright, we're heading off back upstairs, see you at dinner." Jo said.

"Yeah, bye!" they replied.

They left the boys to it and went back upstairs to their bedroom. It was bliss being able to stay on their beds in the day. Even though it was the holidays, they did like to chill out. They didn't have activities booked for a couple of days, but then they were going to ice skating at the end of the week.

Sandra knocked, they told her to come in.

"Were you pleased with you got today?" Sandra asked.

"Oh, yes, Sandra! We were wondering if we can put up our posters?" Alison asked.

"Yes, but where would you like to put them and what are you putting them up with?" Sandra enquired.

"We were going to use Sellotape?" Jo suggested.

"Oh no, you had better not, it might pull the wallpaper off. Let me see if I can find you some Blu Tac; that will hold them up without pulling the wallpaper off when you go off them and want some big chunky hunk on them instead!" Sandra laughed.

Alison and Jo looked at each other and giggled.

"Never mind, there's plenty of time for that later on, be back in a minute," Sandra said."

She came back a short time later. In the meantime, Alison wanted to put her poster on one wall and Jo wanted to put hers on a different wall.

"What if we put them on the same wall but at each end, that way, Alison can see hers and Jo can see hers, without having to get out of your beds," Sandra suggested.

"Alison, did you want to put your coat in the cleaners? I have some other stuff to go," Sandra asked.

"Oh, yes please, thank you, Sandra. It hasn't been cleaned in a while," Alison said.

Sandra went through the pockets, just to make sure there wasn't anything in them, she didn't want her to lose anything.

"Alison, what do you want me to do with this?"

"What is it?" Alison asked.

"It's a coach ticket."

Alison whipped up her head as if by being struck.

"Do you want me to throw it away, Sweetheart?" Sandra said, knowing this was a sensitive subject.

"No, can I have it, please?" Alison said.

"Yes, but why, if you don't mind me asking?"

"Because it's a reminder that we got away from that awful family in that awful place, that's all," added Alison, her voice soft. "That we had the courage to get out the first chance we had. Can I put it in my shoebox please?" Alison asked.

"Of course. Actually, we were supposed to send them on to you, but completely forgot, isn't that great?" Sandra said.

Sandra took the coach ticket. She didn't need to write the date on it, it was already stamped on. She put it in Alison's shoebox that they kept for her. It was in another room away from their boxes with their money in it. They kept it separate just in case they got burgled. It hadn't happened before, but you never know. As it looked like a load of shoes, nobody would want to take them.

Sandra went back to the girl's room and then up to see the other girls and tell everyone it was time for dinner, so everyone made their way to the dining room.

All the staff were asked to come down from their breaks if they were on them as they had an announcement to make. Everyone was sitting down and the staff who couldn't find a seat stood. Mr Duffy came in and told everyone the news about the holiday that Sandra and George had sorted out. They were all going on holiday for a week, everyone together! The whole dining room went up in cheers. The staff were quite pleased too. Some hadn't been to that seaside.

Alison, Tom, Jo and Freddie were delighted they had been there before, and they were so happy to be going back to see Rose, Henry and Bet. They hadn't really met Bruce properly, but they wanted to thank them again for what they had done.

***

The next morning, the meeting was scheduled for 11 am. There were quite a few people attending, so Sandra and George wanted to get to the bottom of as much as possible.

They had been down to breakfast with the children and then they all got ready. The children were going to the park for a little while to feed the ducks and play on the swings. Celia and Roger had taken charge of what they were doing, as Sandra and George were going to be heading for the meeting.

With the amount of people going they weren't going to fit in Mr Duffy's office, so they went to the staffroom; it was the only room big enough to house everyone without being disturbed by the children.

Mr John Dunn, Mr Duffy's boss, was first to arrive, then Mr Prowse, the police sergeant from the local station, Mr Duffy, his secretary and then Sandra and George. There was no need for Alison and Tom to attend; they didn't want to upset them further. Sandra and George had filed a report, detailing what the children had been through since they had left.

They were to read it out at the meeting.

Once everyone was in the room, Mr Duffy closed the door. They had arranged the tables so they could put their paperwork on it, and it felt a bit more formal. Mr Duffy's secretary took the minutes and notes that were needed for later on. Everyone introduced themselves for the minutes.

"So, let's get down to business, shall we?" Mr Dunn started.

"Mr Duffy, would you like to start?" He asked.

"First of all, I would like to thank you all for attending this urgent meeting this morning, I think we need to give a quick outline of what happened when Alison and Tom first left Craven House," Mr Duffy said, looking at Sandra and George.

Sandra cleared her throat.

"So, Alison and Tom left Craven House on Friday 13th May. Once all of the relevant paperwork was all signed, we waved them off and they all seemed rather happy. Mrs Hemsby, the social worker from Brighton, assigned to the Coopers, saw the children exactly two weeks later. We have her report here and you each have a copy," Sandra said.

"Mrs Hemsby reported that the children seemed happy and had settled into their new environment with the Cooper family and she was happy with how well the transition had gone." Sandra took a sip of water.

"So as far as they were concerned, all was going well. Alison and Tom had said before they went to live with the Coopers, that there were rules, but we explained that every household had rules, otherwise it can't be run properly. But they said that they weren't allowed to play in their bedrooms; they could only play on the landing or in the garden. They ate their meal there in silence, but could choose their food, they came back happy enough after their first overnight visit, so we had no qualms on the foster placement to go ahead."

Sandra continued to explain what the first few weeks in the Cooper's household were like for Alison and Tom.

"Mr Cooper wouldn't allow them to watch TV and they started to leave the children at home so they could go out."

"Excuse me?" Mr Dunn looked up from his report. "They left the children alone at home?"

"Yes, Sir, they left Alison and Tom at home, and only took their daughter out. Alison was expected to clean the whole house. We know this to be true as we have witnessed this ourselves since she returned to Craven House."

Sandra was getting more cross the more she spoke.

"Mr Dunn, these children were happy when they left our home; they came back completely destroyed and damaged! Mr Cooper smacked Tom and Alison on the backside when he did nothing really bad and when Alison stuck up for Tom, she got slapped as well. Mr Cooper stole the little bit of money they had, and he broke some of Alison's figurines, and actually, she witnessed him going through Tom's things and removing a St Christopher on a chain that we at Craven House had bought them both."

Sandra continued to read out her report to the end.

Mr Duffy checked with his secretary to make sure she had all of this down on her notepad, which she nodded.

"How can you treat children like that?" Mr Dunn said, shaking his head.

Mr Dunn then asked Mr Prowse what he thought.

"Mr Dunn, Sandra, George, Mr Duffy, I am so sorry. I can assure you, we carried out all of the necessary checks. I was in contact with Mrs Hemsby from day one with this family, but since the placement has started, we had no need to get in touch with them, after Mrs Hemsby had filed her report. This should never have happened. How on earth did this family get awarded two vulnerable children to do what they wanted with!" Mr Prowse said.

"Mr Prowse, have you heard anything from Mrs Hemsby since the children have returned?" Mr Duffy asked.

Mr Prowse shook his head.

"The only thing I know is that since the children ran away, she has resigned, and her replacement hasn't been assigned yet. But there is no report on this either. I'll fill in a report after this meeting and send them a copy for urgent attention."

"The thing is to make sure this never happens again with any other family, Mr Dunn. I think we need to put new strategies in place. It may mean going back to the drawing board, but we can't have this happen again," Mr Prowse said.

"I'm not telling you how to do your job, but we cannot let another child go through this with very unscrupulous people. I feel that until we have done proper checks on these families, we are going to have to postpone any foster placements for the time being," Mr Prowse added.

"I agree," Mr Dunn said. "When we get back to the office, I have some things to do today, but I will get my secretary to reschedule and we have to tackle this now as an urgent matter."

"I have some information here from the Brighton Police Station, about what they know about the Coopers. It seems that they do not own the property in Pemberton Terrace, but had rented it for a year. So, it seems there were never going to extend the foster placement or go for adoption. It does appear that they were both only in it for the money," Mr Duffy said.

"A trace has been put on their bank account to flag up when and where they next use the account, but they haven't as yet. As to their whereabouts, we have no idea, I'm afraid. They have disappeared off the face of the earth."

"Oh, about that, before I forget, sorry John...we have stopped the money going to the Coopers since you called us on Monday. They won't be receiving any more. There may be some activity on the account on Friday if they are checking their account, so it might be a good idea to contact the local bank," Sandra said.

Mr Dunn nodded to the police officer.

"Yes sir, I can contact the Brighton police, they would be very interested to know that. As you said, there may be activity and we can jump straight onto it."

"Oh yes, I have managed to speak to the head at the children's school and they still have a place here for both of them to return in September. Anything else?" Mr Dunn asked.

"Mr Dunn, Rose from the guest house has sent in a report from when the children turned up on her doorstep, detailing how they were, apart from exhausted and malnourished. She and her partner looked after them really well. She wanted to put something in writing in case it would help their case. I have enclosed it in your pack if you would like to read it later on," George said.

"Oh, one thing that is bothering me, Sandra, how on earth did they get out and get to Margate from Brighton?" Mr Dunn asked.

"Mrs Cooper left the front door unlocked for them when she and her husband and child went out, Sir," Sandra said.

"How on earth did they know where to go?" The police officer asked.

"They didn't, they just took a chance to go in the opposite direction to the Coopers away from town and then went down the back streets. They're smart kids, I can tell you that!" Sandra said.

Everyone was sitting with their mouths opened. Mr Duffy's secretary started to cry.

"I am so sorry, but those poor, poor children. How could they do that to them?"

Mr Duffy handed her a tissue.

"Thank goodness they got away. What made them go, do you think?" The secretary asked.

"Alison is very protective of her brother. She knew if they stayed, their life would be hell," George said.

"Well, you have definitely given us food for thought this morning. We do need to change our strategies for these placements, and we need to be more thorough. If we can get all of the social workers together, Sandra, George, would you be able to come in for a meeting to help with this, as you have both seen it first hand, it would be very helpful?" Mr Dunn asked.

"Yes, they can do that, let me know when Mr Dunn, then I can arrange cover, would that be alright, Sandra, George?" Mr Duffy said.

"Mr Duffy, don't forget we won't be here from the 14th August for a week," George said.

"What's this?" Mr Dunn asked.

"Rose, the lady at the guest house, has offered a weeks' stay free for all of the children at Craven House, so they can have a holiday. She saw how dishevelled Alison and Tom were when they got there and wanted to do something for them," Sandra said.

"Well, that is a jolly nice thing for her to do. So, what I suggest is you have your break, we can brainstorm until you get back, but still hold any foster placements on postponement and then arrange a meeting. I will also give you £500 for the children and staff for the week away, I can sign that off on Monday and if someone can pick it up, that would be great," Mr Dunn said.

Everyone had smiles on their faces.

"It's a shame I can't come with you," Mr Dunn laughed.

"Actually, why don't you pop down for a day with Mr Duffy, we can show you the guest house? I know Rose won't mind and you can see the children, it can be done in one day," Sandra said.

"That's an excellent idea, let me know John what day you're free, I can get my secretary to sort out the travel," Mr Dunn said, smiling.

Mr Duffy thanked everyone for attending again.

Mr Prowse was going to work closely with Mr Dunn and his team to see what they could do to prevent this from happening again.

Chapter 19

"Is everyone ready, the coach will be here soon!" George asked. "Sandra, I'm going to check on upstairs, just to make sure we haven't left anyone behind."

Sandra was running around like a headless chicken; everyone had to be on the ground floor, because they wouldn't all fit in reception; it wasn't big enough.

"There should be 30 children and 10 staff," George said.

There was luggage everywhere, all piled on top of each other and most of the children were in the sitting room.

"This is going to be a mean feat, you know!" Mr Duffy said. "Do you think you'll all cope alright?" He added.

"Yes, it should be fine. Thankfully, some of us have been there before so we know what to expect," Roger said.

"That's everyone upstairs now down here. I've checked all of the rooms," George said.

"What about the bathrooms?" Celia asked.

"Yes, all checked!"

"Even the girls?" Celia laughed.

"Oops no, I'd better run back up," George said.

"Not to worry, George, I'll go; if there are any girls in the bathrooms, you'll make them jump. Back in a tick," Celia said, running back up the stairs.

Sandra returned.

"That's the downstairs sorted with June. She's going to give downstairs the once over, Mr Duffy. She will still be making lunch for you and the staff that are left, but she's going to clean the kitchen and dining room, so it's nice and sparkling for when the kids get back. She said she doesn't get a chance to do it properly with the children all here, but this week should be easy. I think she's going to miss them really and wants to keep her mind off them not being here really," Sandra said.

"So, Sandra, you're OK with me coming down with Mr Dunn on Wednesday? I think if we do it in the middle of the week; it breaks it up for us and the kids and it will be great to see them having some fun for a change," Mr Duffy said.

"Mr Duffy, whatever's best for you both will be fine with us," Sandra replied.

"Coach is here now, Sandra, shall we get the luggage in before calling the kids?" Roger asked. "You are joking! Of course, Roger. As soon as they see the coach they will be down here like a shot, making sure we haven't left their luggage behind," Sandra laughed.

Celia returned from upstairs.

"All clear, so are we ready yet?" Sandra asked Roger.

"All ready. The coach has just turned up, so let's get their stuff together, and then we get ours from the staff room. I'm so glad we got ours down here last night, that way no running around like headless chickens!" Roger said.

Sandra had been given a promotion to supervisor by Mr Duffy, because of the way she has handled all of the problems that have risen since he took over from Ms Walters.

George and Roger were loading the luggage onto the underbelly of the coach. It was like a production line. There was so much of it, it just kept coming.

"Right, you lot, are you ready to get on the coach, all of your luggage is now on?" Sandra asked. All the children got up and made sure they had their journey bags with them; just little things they wanted to do on the coach, like play cards or a book to read.

George and Roger went along to the staff room to get their stuff, Sandra and Celia went along to help and to check nothing had been left behind. When everything was all loaded and all of the children and staff were on board, Mr Duffy came out with June, the receptionist, and his secretary to wave them off.

The children waved furiously back at them.

This coach had a microphone in it, so Sandra and George, who were sitting at the front, could talk to everyone without shouting. They had already spoke to everyone on the coach and had counted heads to make sure they hadn't left anyone behind. Thankfully, they hadn't.

They were off, away from Craven House very quickly, everyone then settled down. Alison was sitting with Jo, Freddie and Charlie sat together and Tom sat behind them. It was the only way they could all sit together. A couple of the staff sat next to them.

"Al, are you looking forward to seeing Rose and Henry again so soon?" Tom asked.

"Yes, I am, because the last time we saw them, we had just come through a very rough time and now we are starting to get back to normal," Alison said.

"I can't wait to go back either," Jo said.

"I liked Margate, the beach is lovely, but just being by the seaside is so lovely!" Jo said, smiling at the thought of going back.

All of the children were engaged in chatting and watching the world go by through the big windows. This coach was much bigger than what they went in last time, but this time, they were all going, and everyone was excited.

They had headed off about 10 am and were making good time. The coach had a toilet on it, so they didn't have to keep making stops.

They got into Margate around midday. When they pulled in, Sandra pulled the microphone and turned it on and started to talk.

"Now children, as you know when we go anywhere, we have to be on our best behaviour. That means good table manners, bathroom manners and bedroom manners and when we are out, we have to stay together so we don't get lost. Is that understood? Anyone who doesn't do this won't be coming back with us when we come again. Is that clear?" Sandra said.

The whole coach erupted in cheers.

Rose opened the front door and Henry stood beside her.

"Right everyone, I know you're all very excited, but if you can just stay on the coach for a few minutes longer so that Roger and George can get your luggage from under the coach, then we can go inside," Sandra said.

George was already out of the coach and Roger had made his way to the front. Henry came down and helped them bring the luggage inside, so it wasn't standing in the way on the pavement.

Once they had taken it inside, Sandra spoke to Rose.

"Are you sure you want all of us for the week, there's a lot of us, Rose?"

"Of course, we do! Did you have a safe journey down?"

"Yes, it wasn't too bad."

"We can talk later; we have a lot to do now," Rose said.

"Everyone ready to get off now. If we take one side first," Sandra said, pointing to the side away from the driver. That was the side that Alison and Tom were sitting on. They were both excited to see Rose and couldn't wait to get off the coach.

They took their little bags with them and made their way to the front of the coach. When they got off, Rose was still at the door, she held out her arms and both of them hugged her. Jo, Freddie, and Charlie also came up for a hug. Rose remembered Jo and Freddie. Tom then introduced Charlie to Rose, and he received a big hug from her too.

"Come on now, we have to get you inside and show you to your rooms," Rose said, holding onto Tom and Alison.

George was ready to take the children's luggage up to their rooms. The girls had the room they had last time and Tom, Freddie and Charlie had a room to themselves. It was like they had never been away. They were in different rooms to the last time they were there just under two weeks before.

"I think we should unpack and then have some lunch," Sandra suggested.

Rose nodded.

"Henry will already be downstairs making a start on it," Rose laughed.

Bruce and Betty were there, helping some of the children with their suitcases. They saw Alison and Tom and waved, both children waved back.

They all unpacked their suitcases. The staff came in to check if they needed help. Some of the boys did as they were still small, but the girls managed to do it themselves. The older girls, Emily, Julie, and Susie were in the next room to Alison and Jo, which they were pleased with. They all got on well.

When everyone was unpacked and had put their clothes away, they made their way to the dining room. Sandra and George were already down there waiting for them.

Betty and Rose came in with squash for the children or milk if they wanted and tea and coffee for the staff. Betty, Bruce, Rose and Henry came in with plates piled high with sandwiches. There were big dishes full of crisps. There was a bowl of salad, if anyone wanted it and they were told to help themselves.

"Sandwiches!" One of the little boys, who hadn't been there before shouted, as he grabbed several from a plate.

"Hey John, that's enough," Roger said.

"Sorry Sandra," John apologised.

"That's OK, John. It's your first time here." Sandra smiled. "Rose is an excellent cook and so is Henry, but do you all really want a huge lunch with all of that travelling and also if we want to go out and explore later on. You don't want to feel full up, do you?"

John shook his head as he bit into a ham sandwich.

When they had all eaten enough and cleared their plates, Rose and Betty took them away and then returned from the kitchen and brought in dishes. Bruce and Henry came in with huge trifles, ice-cream, and jelly. The children's eyes were like saucers at the amount of food that kept on coming.

When lunch was over, Rose had a quick look at Alison. No, she didn't look like she was going to dart for the kitchen, she thought so she gave her and Jo a big smile. They all got up, pushed their chairs in under the table and made their way back up to their rooms to collect jackets and things.

Before Sandra and her group left, she went to see Rose.

"Rose, our manager and his boss are coming down on Wednesday, they want to see how the children are getting on and I suppose to see where you are and really to thank you for what you did for Alison and Tom, is that OK with you?" Sandra asked.

"Why, of course it is. Actually, I know all about it; Mr Duffy sent me a letter telling me. I don't blame them for wanting to come down here and check the place out after what happened to Alison and Tom. We are CRB checked; we wouldn't be able to run otherwise. Because it's a family place, we get checked every three years, so don't worry, I know all about it and our staff are all up to date," Rose said.

"Now you go off and have a lovely time with the children. Remember, dinner is at 6pm. I have to go now Sandra, got to get cracking for dinner; steak pie, mash and veg OK for dinner?"

"Oh yes! And thank you Rose, see you later," Sandra said.

Sandra took her group, and George came along too, they went down to the seafront. They had forgotten what it was like last time they were here, but it was for different reasons.

***

When they got back from their walk, they told all of the children to wash their hands and faces, just like they did at home, and then come down for dinner.

"Sandra? Alison and Tom both look like they did the first time we met them. They have their rosy cheeks back!" Rose said, smiling at the two children.

"Yes, it's been a slow process, but they're getting there. Tom started to wet the bed when he first came back; nervous, I suppose. A lot happened to them in such a short space of time," Sandra whispered.

347

Rose nodded, then left to go to the kitchen to get dinner.

Sandra was right, the food there was delicious and there were lots of it. These kids were definitely going to put on a little weight and in Tom and Alison's recent situation, that was a good thing.

After dinner, they all left the dining room.

Rose Henry, Betty and Bruce all cleared up and the children went to their rooms. Sandra and George had suggested an early night, because of all of the travelling and the sea air and tons of food already consumed. The children didn't argue and within an hour of going to their rooms, they were all tucked in and fast asleep.

Sandra and George wanted to have a word with Rose and Henry. They were in the dining room.

"Hello Rose, do you have a few minutes?" Sandra asked.

Rose Henry, Betty, and Bruce were all sitting down having a cup of tea.

"Oh, sorry, I didn't realise you were having a break," Sandra said.

"Sandra, George, it's fine, what can we do for you?" Henry asked.

"Well, we just wanted to have a chat really. The kids are all in bed and the staff are upstairs having a break too," Sandra said. "We just wanted to thank you for a start; for this week, for the children and to talk about Alison and Tom," Sandra said.

"There's no need to thank us, we wanted to do it, even Betty and Bruce wanted to help out. Mind you, if they didn't, we don't know if we could have managed it." Rose laughed. "And what about Alison and Tom?"

"Oh, and we wanted to thank you for submitting that report. That really helped a lot at the meeting," George added.

"Oh, it was nothing, we were glad to be of help," Henry said.

"No, actually it really was a big help; for the time being all foster placements are postponed. They're going to really go things with a fine-tooth-comb, they don't want anything like this to happen ever again," Sandra said.

"Oh, so it actually did make a difference then?" Henry asked.

"Yes, Henry it did. The social worker at the Brighton end has resigned," Sandra said.

"No!" Betty said, shocked.

"Well, I think that's as it should be. If she had done her job properly, this wouldn't have happened, and those kiddies wouldn't have suffered. It was like something out of a horror movie!" Betty said.

"Anyway, how are they both and how are you two?" Henry asked Sandra.

"Well they are both fine. I was telling Rose earlier, Alison is starting to come back to normal, and Tom sadly started to wet the bed, but it only lasted a few days. He's back to his normal pattern again now and us? We're just busy as ever!" Sandra said.

"Right, we are off, you've had a busy day and will have to be up early again, so, goodnight everyone,

and thank you again," George said.

"Who's on duty through the night?" Sandra asked.

"Rita and Roger," George said.

"Right then I am off to bed, George, night," Sandra said.

"Night, Sandra," George said.

Sandra left George on the stairs and went up to her room she was sharing with Celia.

"Rose, I don't know how you and Henry do it, it's knackering," Bruce said.

"You get used to it, Bruce. Are you enjoying yourselves?" Henry asked.

"Oh yes. Rose, do you remember a while ago me and Bruce were thinking about maybe fostering? Well, we were talking about it again recently, what do you think?" Betty asked.

Rose looked at both of them.

"I tell you what, ask me that again on Saturday afternoon when they have all gone and see if you still want to do it!" She laughed. "If you do, we can have a word with Sandra and George and ask them the procedure of how to go about it. Deal?"

"Deal!" Betty and Bruce said, at the same time.

"Right, can we go to bed now, missus? I'm tired and we do have an early start in the morning; over 40 mouths to feed!" Henry said.

"Over 40?" Rose said.

"Yes, we have to eat as well!" Henry laughed.

"Night, you two," Betty and Bruce said.

***

Before they knew it, it was Wednesday morning. The week was going so quickly! Mr Duffy and Mr Dunn were due around lunchtime, but the children were going to the funfair at lunchtime as a treat.

They had been good all week, done as they were told, tidied up when necessary and went to beach nearly every day; the sea air was definitely doing them all some good.

Once they had had their breakfast and went up and brushed their teeth, it was still early so some of the children had bought some gifts and souvenirs and were looking at what they bought.

Rose, Henry, Betty and Bruce had worked quite hard that week so far but had enjoyed having so many kids around. It was a first for the guest house; they normally had workers in, who were working locally, holidaymakers, families, and the elderly once in a while. To have just the kids and staff was a real treat.

Some of the children wanted to go out a bit early and have a walk down to the beach and then head off to Dreamland Fair, just down at the front. Sandra and George stayed behind, so that they could see Mr Duffy and Mr Dunn. They were due about 12.30 pm, but Betty thought that if they could have a chat first with Sandra and George before they got here, otherwise Sandra and George were constantly busy with the kids.

"Sandra, can we have a word with you please?" Betty asked.

"Yes of course, the children haven't done anything wrong, have they?" Sandra asked.

"Oh no, nothing like that, it's a bit more of a personal and professional matter really?" Betty replied.

Bruce had followed her in and so did George.

"What do you mean personal and professional?" Sandra asked.

"Well, it's like this; me and Bruce were thinking a long while ago about maybe fostering children. We got the information locally that we needed, but we wanted to know how difficult it would be? We'd like to try again, but this time put our names forward," Betty said, nervously.

"Well, what you would normally do, is speak to your local authority. Once you put your names down, there will be sufficient checks to make sure you don't have criminal records, you haven't been to prison for fraud or abuse or anything like that. Once you've done all of that, then if your successful you just have to wait until they find a suitable family for you. It could be one or two children, or a disabled child, or a child with emotional problems. It's a lot to sort out and deal with. You may be offered counselling too. It can take a long time and a long process, but you also have to be prepared to be turned down," Sandra said.

"As you know, Alison and Tom had had a horrendous time of it lately. The checks were done, but not followed through properly, and they slipped through the cracks and poor Alison and Tom were the ones to suffer. At the moment, our borough is not letting any foster placements go ahead until the powers that be want to make sure that they have been checked and double checked thoroughly and all references have been checked too.

They don't want something like this happening again to children, or even worse," George said.

"Can I ask you, how old are you both, because that makes a bit of a difference," Sandra asked.

"Yes, I'm 36 and Bruce is 38. We've tried for our own children, but no luck. We thought if we could give a child a happy home even for a little while, it may make a difference. This week so far has been great. Hard work, especially for you guys, but we have loved it. We just wanted to ask if we had a chance?" Betty asked.

"The thing is, Betty, foster care is always screaming out for foster carers, as there are so many children who need care. Sometimes when Mum has to go into hospital for a little while and not everyone has someone to look after them, so we offer a short-term time placement. It could be a few days, or a couple of weeks at the most. So, yes, I would say if you want to try to be foster carers or foster parents, go for it. You have nothing to lose, as long as the authorities can see your good people. You work hard, have a home to offer a child and lots of love, then you're all set," Sandra Said.

"I'll leave you some paperwork, but maybe wait until we leave because I don't think you're going to have a lot of time on your hands until then!" She laughed. "I will give you my number and if you get stuck you can always give me a call," Sandra said.

Betty sighed a sigh of relief.

"I was worried you were going to say we were too old," Betty said.

"Of course not, it's sometimes easier if you're a bit younger. Some of these kids have lots of energy and it's difficult to keep up," Sandra laughed.

***

The car pulled up and Mr Duffy looked up. Whelk Combe.

351

"We're at the right place, John. Let's see how the kids are getting on," Mr Dunn said.

Mr Duffy got out of the car and locked it and then went up to the front door and rang the doorbell.

Henry answered it and Sandra and George looked at their watches.

"That must be Mr Duffy and Mr Dunn," George said.

"Right we had better get back to work, thank you for the information Sandra, we will jump on it after the weekend, when we have slept a lot!" Betty said, laughing to herself.

Henry showed Mr Duffy and Mr Dunn to the dayroom and went to look for Sandra, George, and Rose. They wanted to have a word with her and Henry. Henry brought tea and biscuits in for them all.

"So how are the children? Where are the children? It's rather quiet!" Mr Duffy said.

"They've gone down to the beach for a walk before heading off to the funfair for a little while. They've been so good all week, so we said they could go there today. They shouldn't be too long. Did you have a good journey down?" Sandra asked.

"Yes, it's pretty quiet on the motorway. We are going to stay for a while today so we can see them all, have a bite of lunch and leave say this afternoon. Maybe take a look around town if that's OK with you?" Mr Dunn asked.

"Yes, whatever you want to do, Sir," Sandra replied.

"So, do you have things to do today, once we have finished?" Mr Dunn asked.

"We were going down to the funfair to see the children and then bring them back; the other staff have all gone down with them," Sandra said.

Rose and Henry then entered the dayroom and Mr Dunn looked at both of them. Sandra and George finished their tea said goodbye to Rose and Henry and left the room.

"What do you think that was about?" George asked.

"Who knows? Maybe they wanted to thank Rose and Henry for what they did for Alison and Tom. Come on we had better head down to the fair," Sandra said.

They grabbed their jackets and said goodbye to Betty and Bruce.

It didn't take long for them to get to the funfair. They paid their money to get in and went off hunting for the children and staff. They didn't have to wait long;

they found them at the Carousel. There wasn't enough room for everyone in one go, so they had to go in two sittings, but the children didn't mind. They loved watching the various horses and carriages they wanted to go on next time.

Then they wanted to go on the water chute. The kids had a great time there. Once they had been on all of the rides, some of the children wanted to stay. Sandra told them that they could come back on Friday just before they return home on Saturday; providing they had any money left. They had a quick count of heads before they returned to the guest house.

Once Sandra and George had left, Mr Dunn and Mr Duffy had wanted to talk to Henry and Rose.

"We haven't called at a busy time for you, have we?" Mr Dunn asked.

"Oh no Mr Dunn, we've done most of what we need to for the morning now, and we have our friends here Betty and Bruce helping us for the whole week. So, what is it you wanted to talk to us about?" Rose asked.

"Well, we know that you had arranged for all of the children and staff to come and stay this week, partly because of what had happened to Alison and Tom recently. But we wanted to ask you something?" Mr Dunn said.

Mr Dunn cleared his throat.

"We wanted to know if it would be possible for the children to come to you here every summer holiday?"

"All the children, for the whole summer?" Rose asked.

"Oh no, sorry I haven't explained myself properly. What we'd like to do is; we have four children's homes in our care Rose, and they don't always get the chance to go away. We know that Craven House came a couple of years ago and we do try to get them out and about and away whenever possible. If Alison and Tom hadn't come here, goodness knows where they would have ended up, they knew this as a place of safety," Mr Dunn said.

"So, what I am proposing is, over the summer holidays, we'd like to bring all the children from our different homes to you, for a week at a time. I know it's a lot to take in at the moment, but would you at least have a think about it? It would be all formal, a contract and if any breakages occurred, we would cover the cost. And if you decided that it wasn't possible any longer, as long as we had enough notice, we could end the contract and that would be it. As I said, have a think about it both of you and if it's a possibility then that would be great. I can leave you my number. I know you have Craven House's, but I'm based at the council offices. Would that be OK?" Mr Dunn asked.

Mr Dunn handed Rose a card with his office details, address and direct line.

"We'll have a think about it. Can we let you know in a few days?" Rose said.

"Yes of course, take as long as you need," Mr Dunn smiled. "And thank you both for what you have both done for our children."

***

The children had all walked back to the guest house. The front door was open in the day, so Sandra walked in and held the door open. By the time the rest of the children had walked in Mr Duffy and Mr Dunn had come down the stairs with Henry. Rose had gone onto the kitchen.

"Hello, children, how are you enjoying the seaside and Margate?" Mr Dunn asked.

"It's lovely here, Rose and Henry are so nice, and the food is excellent!" One of the older children said.

The children went upstairs, and Mr Duffy and Mr Dunn spoke with the staff for a few minutes, then said they were going to pop out for a little while. Rose had asked them if they were going to stay for dinner. Initially they'd said no, but on hearing how delicious her food was, they asked if they could stay.

"We can always make room, Mr Duffy," Rose said, "although you have to sit with the children." She laughed.

"Oh, that will be fine, but only if it's not an imposition," Mr Duffy said.

"Of course not; we always make room," Rose chuckled.

Dinner was rather busy that evening, and as Rose had said, they always made room. The sitting arrangements were a bit tight, but they all got in.

Mr Duffy sat on one table with the children and staff and Mr Dunn on another. They all enjoyed their time there and the children were right, the food was absolutely lovely.

Once they had dinner and then a hot drink each, Mr Dunn went to the kitchen to pay his compliments to the chef, who was Henry.

"See you on Saturday everyone!" Mr Duffy said to the children, as they finished off their desserts.

Some of the children left the dining room and returned to their rooms and some stayed in the dining room a little longer.

Freddie, Tom and Charlie stayed downstairs. They liked sitting down, waiting for Rose and Henry to come and join them. Alison and Jo sat down with the boys as well. They didn't go out in the evening. The staff wanted to keep track of the children and apart from pubs and beer gardens, unless you wanted to see a show at the theatre, there wasn't much else going on.

Rose and Henry, Betty and Bruce all came in with their hot drinks, asked the children how their day went and drank their teas. Alison, Jo, Tom, Freddie and Charlie all excused themselves and left the dining room. They knew the adults wanted to talk and Celia was on hand if they needed anything.

Tom, Freddie and Charlie wanted to go to their room and play cards and Alison and Jo wanted to chat in their room. Sandra and George said that they would leave Rose and Henry in peace, but if they wanted to talk about Mr Dunn's proposal, they were happy to answer any questions.

Rose said she wanted to have a think about it. This was hers and Henry's business for now, until they decided. If they did this, they would need to take on extra staff. Every summer holiday they were busy, but this would make them even busier.

Once they had cleared all up from dinner, Betty and Bruce left for the evening. Rose and Henry didn't really have much else to do so they turned in for the night; mainly to try and discuss what to do about the proposition.

"Do you think we should do it, Rose?" Henry asked. "It would be a guaranteed contract, meaning it would be like that every summer."

"I know, but it would be a lot of extra work, Henry," Rose said.

"Yes, but we could take on extra staff over the holidays."

"But what about our regulars?" Rose asked.

"We will still have them, but we'll have to just allocate the other two weeks to them, when the children aren't here," Henry said.

"Yes, but some of them might not want those dates, they may want to come when the kids are here. You remember the last time they came, and Mr Snow got all uppity?" Rose said. "I think we need to sleep on it for now, but also talk about it when the place is quieter; that way we can talk freely without anyone hearing or upsetting anyone?"

"Tell you what, when Saturday is over, we can talk about it. Do we have anyone in on Saturday afternoon?" Henry asked.

"No, we don't have anyone in until Monday," Rose said.

"Right let's get some sleep and we don't talk about it again until the weekend," Henry said.

They were both tired, and as Rose knew, they weren't getting any younger. Henry turned out the light and they were both off to sleep within minutes.

***

Saturday was soon here and there was so much noise! Trying to get everyone out of their rooms, and ready for the coach was a mammoth task. The staff checked all the rooms to make sure nothing had been left behind. Once the house was empty of the children and luggage, they were told to go and sit in the dayroom. Slowly it was filling up and the floors were emptying.

George was keeping an eye out for the coach. They couldn't believe how quick this week had gone. All of the luggage was in the bar and hallway, piled up ready to get on the coach. Sandra did a headcount in the dayroom.

George popped his head around the door for Roger. He was already on his way down with another suitcase and then followed George outside to put the luggage on board. Once that was done, George stuck his head around the door again.

"Coach is here, is everyone ready? Don't forget to say goodbye to Rose, Henry, Betty and Bruce," George said, as they were coming up from the kitchen.

All of a sudden, Rose was greeted by the children, she was in the middle of a huge circle, as they all hugged and thanked her.

Rose had tears in her eyes as they all boarded the coach. She had never known gratitude like it before. The staff thanked their hosts and hugged them all. They all knew the week couldn't have happened without them.

Rose, Henry, Betty and Bruce followed them out to the door. The children were all seated on the coach and waved at them all. All four of them waved back; Betty and Rose had tears in their eyes.

The coach driver closed the door, he turned on the engine, checked it was safe to pull away and drove off.

"I think we should do it, Henry," Rose said through tears.

Henry took one look at Rose's face and knew why.

"I agree," Henry said.

They went back inside to start stripping the beds. They had a lot of washing to do today.

***

The children had already been back a week and were going back to school on Monday. Sandra had told Alison and Tom that they were still able to go back to their old school. There were still places for them. As they were getting ready to go and start another school year, there was excitement in the air.

Rose had spoken with Mr Dunn, accepting his offer of four weeks of the year, the four children's homes would be attending for a week at a time, Acorn, Benson, Craven and Denham Houses.

Rose signed the contracts, and everyone was glad that they would be going there every year. Betty and Bruce had a few days off from working at Whelk Combe and they contacted their local council office to enquire about fostering children. When they had all of the updated paperwork, they would then send it back and wait and see what would happen next.

Alison and Tom were glad to be going back to their school. So much had happened since they had left in May. The classes were really pleased to see them back, but it did bring up a few questions. Their teachers didn't reflect on what had happened to Alison and Tom and the other children in the class just accepted that they were back.

Alison and Tom had now got back to normality. Their trip away had given them both rosy cheeks back and their happy personalities were almost back to normal. These children were very resilient and would bounce back quickly.

***

It took a while, but once all of the necessary checks were complete, Betty and Bruce had been accepted for fostering children.

They had spoken with their social services department, and they wanted to give it a try, so they had a chat with Rose and Henry, to see what they thought.

"It's up to you two," Rose said.

"We know who you both like and why don't you just ask and see what they say?" Henry winked.

"But they're not doing foster placements at the moment. They told us that when they were here last," Betty said.

"Now you have all of the paperwork, why don't you just give Sandra a call and see what they say? It can't hurt Bet, can it?" Rose said.

"When are the kids due again, Rose?" Bruce asked.

"Not until next summer, I'm afraid."

"Right then, we can't just wait until next year, what if we take small steps first, try out a short-term placement, just to get used to it first? That way, if we go for it later on, at least we have had some experience and it will be on our records, so they can see what we have done," Bruce said.

"But we need to be free for you next summer though, Rose," Betty said.

"You will be. Just try it out and see what happens," Henry said.

"Yes, you're right. I'll ring them when we get in, thanks Rose, Henry," Bet said.

They carried on drinking their tea and both of the women had smiles on their faces.

***

"Rose, Rose, it's me, Bet!" Bet said excitedly down the phone.

"We've been in touch with social services and they're coming around tomorrow, they want to talk to us about a foster placement! Isn't that great!"

"Oh, Bet! That's fantastic news! Congratulations to you and Bruce!" Rose was over the moon for them.

Things were going to be really great for them now.

They had their meeting the following day and it went really well. They were getting a little boy who was just three. It would only be for a couple of days while his mum was going into hospital. She had nobody to look after him, but he would be brought back home the day after.

He was a real treasure to look after. Bet was sad to see him go, but she was glad that she had the opportunity to see what it was like to foster a child. They had a call a couple of weeks later on and they were asked if they could look after a little five-year-old girl for a few days. There was a lot going on at home and her sibling had to go into hospital and mum and dad wanted to be with him.

Bet rose to the challenge of it and did really well. The little girl was nervous at first, but the short-term placement went well. It seemed that Betty and Bruce had a knack for this. They got on well with the children and occasionally met the families, who were always grateful for them looking after their loved ones.

Betty and Bruce had a few more short-term placements which took them to the early part of summer. The little boy they had at the moment was a little boy called David who had been with them for over three weeks. He was due to go back to his parents just before the summer season was going to start with the summer holidays and they were going to be with Rose and Henry for the next four weeks. It was perfect timing.

Both Bet and Bruce enjoyed fostering children, but they also liked helping out at the children's holiday for a month. David was due to leave them on Thursday and they were starting with Rose and Henry on Saturday morning.

Craven House were coming down on the second week of the holidays, but Denham House were coming down first. Denham House looked after the older children, who would be leaving the home soon and moving off onto their independent lives. As they were coming out of care, they had a good chance to a council or social housing property. They would transition over the course of about a year, so they could decide what they wanted to do; leave school, then either go to college or start an apprenticeship or even go for a job. They would be helped with application forms and interviews. Every young person got the help they needed.

This was a break for them to go before they took the plunge on the next chapter of their lives.

Betty and Bruce were looking forward to this week, but none of them had met the children.

Mr Dunn had taken a few of the staff down to meet Rose and Henry and the manager of their home, Mrs Frances Woods.

Mrs Woods had been with the home for many years and thought that this was such a good idea, for the children and the staff.

Bet and Bruce got to the guest house at 9am, so they could have a quick cuppa and then make a start. Before they knew it, the children had been there for a week and were about to leave. Betty and Bruce had seen a different side to the care sector; to what happened once they left their home. It wasn't anything they had really thought about before, but they would definitely look into this once the four weeks were over.

***

"Come on everyone, we need to get onto the coach, we have to leave soon. We don't want to hit a lot of traffic on the way down to Margate," Roger said.

Alison and Tom were looking forward to going down to the seaside again. They had had a busy year.

Alison had just left primary school and was starting secondary school in September, and they didn't have her new uniform just yet; they were going to wait until they had their holiday at the seaside.

Tom was growing up so much he was also a head taller than last year.

"Tom, are you ready yet?" Alison asked.

"Yes Al, just getting my bag. My case is here all packed and ready. I can't wait to see Rose and Henry, can you?" Tom asked.

"No, it's been a while, well, a year actually. I wish Jo was with us this year. Now she's moved onto Benson House, we won't see her there. But I think she's going for the last week of the holidays," Alison said, loud enough for Sandra to hear her.

"What's that, Alison?" Sandra asked.

"Jo is going down to Margate in the last week?" Alison asked.

"Yes, I think so. Denham House was there last week. I think they are leaving Margate today, but no, we won't see her," Sandra said. "Never mind, there's always when we come back next week. We can meet up with her, before she goes, what do you think?"

"That's a good idea, Tom's case is here, mine is just outside here," Alison said pointing to her case.

Jo had only been gone a couple of weeks and she still had to be allocated another girl to share her room, but no new children of her age had come to the home. Emily and Susie went with Jo to Benson House, so at least they all had someone they knew to go with.

Alison would be due to go to Benson House the following year, but the staff didn't really want to split her and Tom up, considering what they had been through the year before. They didn't know how Tom would cope without her, so they were leaving that information from them for the time being.

Everyone was getting on the coach. Alison sat at the back, Charlie, Freddie, and Tom sat on the back seat again. Tom knew that Alison was missing Jo already. He knew that she had taken it in her stride, but she wasn't used to being on her own.

It didn't take long to get down to Margate and once they had arrived Rose, Henry, Betty, and Bruce were there to welcome them there. Rose noticed that Jo wasn't there. Alison had told her she would be down in the last week as she had moved onto the next home. They were a little taken a back, but tried not to show it, they would still get to see her but not at the same time as the others. This was another change, they weren't expecting.

Again, this week flew by so quickly; it's as if they blinked and it had gone. The children were saying goodbye to Rose, Henry, Betty, and Bruce, and they made their way home.

It was the third week of the summer holidays and Craven House's coach had just gone. Betty and Bruce stripped the beds ready for the next lot to arrive. Thankfully, they had plenty of bedding to go around. It didn't take long. Betty took down what she could carry, so did Bruce, then Henry looked at the time.

"Right I'm going to make a start on the sandwiches, well buttering the bread at least. That OK, Rose?" Henry asked.

"Yes of course. We're going to put the next load of washing in the machine and bring down the rest. We've done well so far. Do you think we have time for a cuppa though?" Rose smiled. "I'll put the kettle on," Henry laughed, "bring down the last of the washing. Bruce said he will run the hoover around upstairs, then have tea, then do the first floor, then we're ready for the next lot of little darlings to arrive." Henry laughed.

"Do you know what Rose, I never realised how difficult these children's lives can be." Bet said.

"What do you mean, Bet?" Rose asked.

"Well, the kids to arrive first are the ones who now have to go off into the world on their own, after spending however much time in care. Once they get to a certain age they have to move onto another home, as we know there are four in this lot. It must be difficult for them, don't you think?" Bet said.

"I suppose it's the progression of the system, and if they don't move around there's no room for anyone new to come and as you know, that can happen very quickly. It's life, Bet. It evolves, and they have to adjust, just as we all do. It just means they have had a different hand of the deck given to them. But as we know, they are great kids, who for one reason or another had a tough time, but they get through it," Rose said.

"And unfortunately, not everyone sees their potential." Henry added, "Do you remember Mr Snow, Rose?"

"Oh, yes! He was really awful to the kids, but you know what, none of them really took any notice of him. It was us who felt sorry for them, but as Henry just said, they have had some hard knocks. Anyway, come on, drink up, we have to get cracking," Rose said.

Alison managed to meet up with Jo in the week before she left for Margate. They met up in town at the Wimpy. Sandra went with her. Freddie, Tom, and Charlie came along as they had also missed her. They wanted to tell her all about their time in Margate, as she was going on Saturday. Jo couldn't wait to see Rose and Henry, but she was going with different people this time.

They all had burger, chips and a lovely, thick milkshake.

"Are you picking up any new clothes to go with Jo?" Alison asked.

"I did that last week, while you were away. Susie and Emily came too, so it was fine, but I miss our trips into town," Jo said, looking sad.

***

Saturday came around rather quickly. The children from Acorn House were leaving just as Benson House were on their way.

Jo was really excited to be going to Margate, even though she wasn't going to be with Tom and Alison. She had Emily and Susie and they would have fun. All three girls had been before, so they knew what to expect.

When they pulled up and the children got off the coach, Rose, Henry, Betty, and Bruce were at the door waiting to welcome everyone. They were so excited to see Jo again; they'd missed her. The girls had the same bedroom that Jo and Alison had previously had, so Jo was happy about that.

Just like the past three weeks, the week went quickly by. Jo didn't really have much chance to talk to Rose and Henry as they were so busy, between cooking and cleaning. She did give them Alison and Tom's best wishes.

When it was time to leave, she gave them all a little longer hug. It would be a whole year before she saw them again. She got onto the coach and waved at them.

Rose, Henry, Betty, and Bruce went inside and flopped down on the comfortable chairs in the dayroom.

"Well, that was one hell of a ride, wouldn't you say, Bruce?" Henry said.

"I'm absolutely shattered!" Rose said.

"But it was worth it, wasn't it, Rose?" Bet asked.

"Yes, yes of course! It was great. Hard work, but we've done it now, so we can do it again for next year," Rose smiled.

"Right, I am going to put the kettle on, then we can go and strip the beds," Henry said.

Henry went into the kitchen to put the kettle on while the other three went upstairs to the bedrooms to strip the beds. On the departure day, if they didn't have anyone coming until later on, they would strip the beds and throw the bedding down the stairs, and the person at the bottom would pick it up and put it in the huge laundry basket.

***

The summer holidays were soon over, and Alison was ready to start her new school. Tom was excited to be back at school. He loved being away, but he liked being at home and school so him, Freddie and Charlie could have fun playing with the cars.

Betty and Bruce had a few days off once they had finished with Rose and Henry for the summer holidays. They had received a call from the social worker asking if they were free. They had a ten-year-old boy who needed a home for a little while. There were problems at home, and they were trying to get him into the local children's home, but they were waiting for a place for him.

Betty and Bruce took him in and even though he was a bit of a challenge, they did their best for him. It was just uncertainty for him. He didn't want to go into the home, but the father was being very heavy handed with his mother and social services didn't want him to stay at home while this was going on.

The placement lasted longer than normal; it turned into two months. Tim, the boy, wanted to get settled, but with the uncertainty of a vacancy at the home, he just had to wait a little longer. The parents were going through a tough time and it still wasn't suitable for him to return home.

Bet received a call one morning when Tim was at school saying that social services were coming today to collect him as they had found a place for him at the home. When he got in from school, the woman from Social Services was waiting for him. Betty helped him pack his things. He gave them both a big hug and said goodbye. He had tears in his eyes; he had never felt so loved, but he knew he couldn't stay. He would one day have to go back home, but for now, this was the next best thing.

When Tim had left, Betty and Bruce started to think about what they wanted out of this fostering.

"Bruce, do you want to go for a permanent placement rather than these small placements? I know Tim was longer, but what do you think?" Betty asked.

Bruce thought for a moment.

"Betty, love, we went into this because of what we saw at Rose and Henry's with Tom and Alison; how they were treated when they went to Brighton and stayed with those awful people. But now, I like having these children for a little while and we can free up time when we want. But we also do Rose and Henry's, to be honest they couldn't do it without us, but we all know that. If you want to go for a long term, then why not try?" Bruce said.

"You sure?" Bet asked.

"Yes, I think I am. It's nice seeing these children for a little while, but yes I think we would feel like a family, rather than foster people," Bruce said.

"Now all I need to do is talk to Rose and ask her what she thinks," Bet said.

"Rose? Why?"

"Because I want to see if we can get Alison and Tom," Bet replied.

"Alison and Tom? But they live at the home," Bruce said.

"Yes, but from what I have seen this summer, Alison will have to move on next year and I don't think Tom could cope without her. Oh Bruce, let's enquire about it? If we talk to their manager and Sandra and George, I'm sure they would be willing to help."

Bet was delighted that Bruce agreed to her idea. They loved Alison and Tom as much as Rose and Henry did. If they could get them, they would have their own family and they would love Alison and Tom as if they were their own children.

Chapter 20

"Hello Mr Duffy, it's Mrs Linton. I was just calling to confirm the meeting with you later on this week...yes, that's fine. OK, so it's still at 1pm? Great, I look forward to seeing you then...OK thank you, bye," Betty said and replaced the receiver.

"Well, Bruce, that's that done, we go up to Craven House on Thursday at 1pm. You're sure you're OK with this?"

"Of, course I'm OK with it. It's what we have both been wanting since we saw those two little loves collapse into Rose's." Bruce smiled at his wife.

"We'll go to the meeting. We have a good record of looking after foster children, so, it's not like it's new to us. Bet, please don't worry. Yes, we have lots of meetings coming up, but that's to be expected, especially with those two. Everything will work out," Bruce told her. He gave her a hug; she knew that he was right.

At the moment, they didn't have a placement, so they were able to give this their full attention to the matter. They had both talked about not doing any more fostering if they were allowed to have Alison and Tom staying with them. They wanted to give them a permanent home that would be filled with love and care. Proper care, not how they were treated by the Coopers.

"Bruce, I'm just popping along to see Rose for a few minutes," Bet said.

"OK, love, see you in a little while."

Bruce knew that she would be with Rose for a good while, so he thought he would put his feet up with a cuppa while he watched the racing on the TV.

***

"Yes, so we're going down on Thursday. I can't wait, Rose!" Bet said, trying to hold her excitement.

"You really want those two, don't you, Bet?" Rose smiled, already knowing the answer.

"Yes, I do! They are such great kids and seeing them when they come down here for a week, is great, even if we are all shattered to really see them properly. It's great to see them how they were before," Bet said.

"I know. It may be a long time before you get them though, you know that don't you?" Rose warned, not wanting to throw cold water on her excitement.

"I know, Rose, but it will be worth the wait, to have those two running around our house. We love kids and would have a house full of them if we could! We might even consider adding to our family!" Bet said.

Rose smiled, she knew the Bet loved kids and it was sad that she didn't have any of her own, but this was the next best thing.

"I had better get back and leave you to it, do you need a hand later on?" Bet asked.

"I don't know yet, but I'll give you a call, OK?" Rose said.

"Sure, just give me a ring," Bet said as she closed the door behind her.

The guest house didn't have many people in and rose and Henry could handle it well enough. When they got busier through the holidays, they needed help; it was getting a bit much for both of them. It kept them busy, but they were getting more tired the more they were doing.

***

Thursday morning had come around rather quickly. Betty and Bruce were up early. They wanted to make sure they had all of their paperwork with them. Mr Prowse had already been in contact with them and the social worker, in Kent, who dealt with fostering. He wasn't taking any chances.

"How do I look, Bruce?" Betty asked.

She had a navy suit on with a white blouse, cream tights and navy court shoes. She wanted to look as business-like as she could and make a good impression.

Bet brushed her hair again. She had a quick look at Bruce and nodded; they were ready.

With a huge file of paperwork, they closed and locked the door and got into their car. Rose was at the window and she waved at them.

They were chatting on the way down to Craven House. Both of them were nervous. Even though they had had these sort of meetings tons of times before, this one felt more important.

Betty and Bruce had hardly left Margate, so this was a real treat to go to another part of the country.

They arrived early and Bruce pulled up in a car space outside Craven House. Bet got out of the car and brushed herself down. Bruce locked the car and Bet arranged his tie for him; it was all crooked. Now it was straight.

"Perfect" She smiled.

They went up the stairs and pushed the door open. The receptionist said she would let Mr Duffy know they were there.

A few minutes later Mr Duffy appeared from his office. He greeted Bruce and Betty, shaking their hands, and led them into another room just next to his. Mr Prowse was already there, as were Sandra and George.

Once everyone was introduced, Mr Duffy spoke.

"Thank you for coming down today, Mr and Mrs Linton. We hope you don't mind Sandra and George attending this meeting?"

"No, of course not, that's fine," Betty said.

Mr Prowse was the first one who wanted to know a bit more about them, so he started asking questions.

"Mr and Mrs Linton, we know you have already met Alison and Tom when they visited Whelk Combe, in Margate?"

"Yes, that's right," Bruce said, "we met them briefly when they first came down for the week, then we saw them that awful night they ran away from their foster placement, and then two weeks later for a week. Then this summer again for another week," Bruce said.

"And you now foster children in your local area?" Mr Prowse said.

"Yes, we do. We've brought our CV with us, for you to read," Betty said.

"Oh, that's OK. As you can imagine, and in this case, I have already had a copy of it from your social worker, Jane Walker. I have to be very thorough I'm afraid, you do understand," Mr Prowse said.

"Yes of course, we understand. Those poor children had a terrible time," Bruce said.

"Your CV is very impressive, Mr and Mrs Linton. If you don't mind me asking, and as you have been very successful with your foster care, why do you want to take on Alison and Tom?" He asked.

"We do love looking after the children who are in our care. As we have met them a while ago and we know a bit of their history, only a little we want to give them a home full of love and care. I'm not saying that they don't get this here. I can see that with the staff and how the children are and how they are towards the other children. We saw all four of the homes this summer and you guys have your work cut out for you.

"We just want to give them a happy stable home. We know they won't be able to stay here forever, and I know they both love it here, but there will be a time when Alison will have to move on and Tom will be left behind until he has to move on. So, if we could get this all sorted before that happens, they won't have to be separated. Which I am sure will be very distressing and stressful for both of them," Betty said.

"Well, you definitely have thought about it very extensively, a lot of people wouldn't have even thought about that, Mrs Linton," Mr Prowse said.

"Mr Prowse, we know with these children and their circumstances. It's not going to be easy, that's why we know this is going to take a long time and we understand that you have lots of checks to do and we're prepared for that. We know Alison is twelve and Tom is coming up for nine, so we do have time, but also we know that it's not great to move a young person from their education when they are due to do exams," Betty added.

"You have definitely thought a lot about this," Mr Duffy said.

"Mr Duffy, we know it's going to take a long time if you agree for us to look after Alison and Tom, but we also know we have to really get to know them and you will want to come and see where they will be living, etc.," Betty said.

Betty did seem to be doing all of the talking, but she was really passionate about this; they could all see it.

"Does anyone have any questions?" Mr Duffy asked.

"I do," Sandra said. "Mr Duffy, Mr Prowse, if this is possible to go ahead for Mr and Mrs Linton with Alison and Tom, how long would it be before they could start the foster placement?"

"Erm, well, once the checks are complete, and the way this is looking with what you have done already and your social worker's report for you, it could be about six to nine months. As you know they used to take three to six months, but we have to double check everything and you have to see the children here, and then they go to your home for a day visit first, then overnight. But as you already know the children, I'm sure we can sort something out, but that has to also be with Alison and Tom's approval first, I'm afraid. We have to consider what they think. We didn't do that last time," Mr Duffy said.

Bet started to cry; she couldn't help it.

"I am so sorry," she said, looking in her handbag for a tissue.

"Are you OK, Mrs Linton?" Mr Duffy asked.

Bet wiped her eyes.

"Yes, I'm sorry, but it's so unfair that they didn't realise that they could have come back home," Bet said, "they must have been so frightened." Bet dabbed her eyes.

"I'm so sorry; I do get emotional when I hear about things happening to children. That's why we wanted to open up our home for children who, for whatever reason, needed a safe, warm home, even for a short time."

"Mrs Linton, we can see that on what you have done with your foster care at home. Your social worker gave a glowing report on your behalf. Look, we just have to fine tune the paperwork and have a meeting, but once we know what happens next, we can talk to the children, and once they are aware that this could be happening, we have to take it from then really. But we won't leave you dangling. We will let you know from there, is that OK?" Mr Duffy said.

He looked around the room.

"Any more questions, anyone?" He asked.

Everyone shook their heads. He stood up to shake the Lintons' hands. The meeting was over.

They all got up, said their goodbyes and Sandra showed them out.

"I think that went rather well, once they have their meeting, they should know the result, so, don't worry." Sandra saw that Betty looked a little nervous. "It will be fine, as Mr Duffy said, they have to fine tune everything and with what happened last time, they don't want to take any chances. It's not because of you, either of you, it's now the procedure. When this all happened, it gave the powers that be, a big kick up the behind, so now it's slightly different, but they won't hold out too long. It's just once you get the go ahead, it may take a little longer than it would have done, but it's fine. Look I have to go, take care, and speak soon. Oh, and say hello to Rose and Henry for me," Sandra said.

Betty said she would. She hugged Sandra and they both left the home. They got into the car and put the paperwork on the back seat.

"Let's go home now, Bet?" Bruce suggested.

"Yes, love. Do you want to stop off on the way home for a bite to eat, all of a sudden I'm hungry!" Bet laughed.

"I'm a bit peckish myself now!" Bruce said.

***

Sandra went back into the meeting.

"Sorry, they just wanted to say goodbye," she said.

"How do you think that went?" Mr Duffy asked.

"I think it went well. I know Mrs Linton got upset, but I think that's because she has empathy with these children and she doesn't like to think of them being hurt, which is understandable," Sandra said.

"Oh, don't worry, Sandra, we won't hold that against her. It shows she has compassion for the children she looks after and children in general," Mr Prowse said. "Their CV is very good. They're compassionate people, which goes in their favour, because of the children they have had to deal with recently. They haven't been fostering for very long, but they do a good job. I understand that some of the children have gone back to visit them once their placement has finished, with their parent or guardian, really to say thank you," Mr Prowse added.

"I think, if we have more time to let the children get to know them, that's if they want to, then we take it slowly, if you don't mind me asking, how many times did the Coopers see them before they went down to their home?"

"Eight times," George said.

"No George, it was six," Sandra said.

"Six? Are you sure, Sandra?" George looked shocked.

"Yes, don't you remember? They couldn't come a couple of times. Hannah was sick and they came a couple of weeks later," Sandra reminded him.

"Oh, yes, that's right! I forgot about that, that should have given us red flags, but you know what, it's done now. The kids will never forget it, but I think they have recovered well from it. Mind you, they both jump if anyone shouts, but that's to be expected," George said.

"Right, so, six times in all before they went to their home. Did the children come back here again before they stayed overnight?" Mr Duffy asked.

"Yes, I think they came one more time, then the next time a fortnight later. They stayed overnight, then they came back a couple of weeks later to sign the paperwork and then they were gone," George said.

Sandra was rather quiet.

"Sandra, George, none of this is any of our faults. Not the home, but us as individuals. The Coppers fooled us all, so please don't feel guilty. The children are back with us and are happy, but Mrs Linton is right; they won't be able to stay here forever, and the fact that they both want to get it sorted out before Alison is due to leave Craven House. And yes, I know Alison was supposed to go by now, but we can't do that. Tom would fall apart. He loves Freddie and Charlie, but Alison is his world and she's his."

"I think, if we all agree on this placement going ahead, first we talk to the children about it, then sort out a plan of a period for this to go ahead. So, if Alison has just turned twelve and Tom is coming up for nine, they need to go before Alison turns fifteen, so she can do her options for her GSE's. Then if she wants to do 'O' Levels as well, we want her settled for them. What do you all think?" Mr Duffy asked.

"I think you're right, Mr Duffy. I think if we talk to the children as soon as we can, perhaps within the next couple of days and see what they think about it. We don't want to keep the Lintons hanging around, that's not fair. I know they have set their hearts on having the children, but we have to be absolutely sure the children want to go this time," Mr Prowse said.

"Then maybe let them know next week, what do you think?" Mr Duffy said.

Sandra and George looked at each other and both nodded to Mr Duffy.

"When do you want to talk to the children?" Mr Duffy asked.

"Today? Tomorrow? I think as soon as, really, because we are going to have a lot to sort out over a long time, but the children have to decide what they think?" Sandra said. There was no way she was going to allow Alison and Tom to go anywhere they didn't feel welcome again.

"The thing is, as they already know Betty and Bruce. Do they really need to see them here? They've already seen them in their holiday setting. It might weird for both of them," she added.

"No, I think they need to see them here at least once, that way they can see them in their own home environment. They, as you say, have only seen them on holiday. It's different for everyday life," Mr Duffy said.

"I agree," Mr Prowse said.

"OK, it was just a thought, but again, we have to treat this like any other foster placement. I think everyone will be pleased with that. But talk to Alison and Tom when they get in from school," Sandra said.

371

"Everyone OK with that?" Mr Duffy asked. Everyone nodded. They all got up to leave.

"Oh, before we leave, can I ask something?" Sandra said.

"Of course," Mr Duffy said.

"What happens to the children that the Lintons were fostering, will they still be doing that? As it may be unsettling for Alison and Tom," Sandra asked.

"I have discussed that with them before today and they want to see if the children want to come and stay, but they have told their social worker they want to see how it goes, so they won't be available for fostering while they have the children unless Tom and Alison wish to have other children in the house. If they say yes, then they will continue to foster. If they don't want to, they will stop," Mr Duffy said.

"So, they really are putting Alison and Tom's needs before anyone else. Unless of course, it was Jo, Freddie, and Charlie. Tom may want them to come and live too!" George laughed. The thought of that gave them a warm smile and then their hearts sank. They didn't want to lose the other two just yet, they had already lost Jo recently.

***

When Alison and Tom came home from school, Sandra and George asked them both to come to Alison's room; they wanted to talk to them privately. Alison and Tom both looked rather worried.

"There's nothing wrong, kids, promise. Sandra said.

Both of them sat on Alison's bed and Sandra and George pulled up chairs so they could talk to them on the same level as them.

"Now, we wanted to ask you both something?" Sandra said, "do you remember Betty and Bruce who live down…"

"By Rose and Henry? Yes, we remember them, why?" Tom asked.

"Well, they have been fostering children since the year before last and they wanted to know if you both would like to try a short foster placement with them? It won't be happening for a while, but we wanted to ask you first. If you want to that's OK. If you don't want to, then that's OK too," Sandra said.

Alison looked a little bit shocked.

"Don't you want us here anymore then?"

Tom looked horrified.

"Oh no! Of course, we do, Sweetheart, but you won't be able to live here forever, you know that. We just wanted to get the ball rolling to see what you thought about it first. If you don't want to go to Mr and Mrs Linton, that's fine, but…I don't know how to put this," Sandra thought for a moment. "You know Craven House isn't just a children's home on its own; we have three others and some of the other children have all moved on to them at various times," Sandra explained.

"Like Jo has?" Tom asked.

"Yes, Tom, just like Jo has. As the children get older, they move onto the next place, until they become adults at eighteen, then they move out of the care system and hopefully into their own place or flat share or whatever they decide to do. So, what we wanted to know is, would you like to try this out?" George said.

Alison and Tom looked at each other, they didn't know what to say.

"So, when am I supposed to move on to another home?" Alison asked.

"You would have already gone with Jo, but we didn't want to split you and Tom up. We wouldn't know how you would be or how it would affect you," Sandra said.

"So, if I am supposed to have already gone, when would I be going next instead?" Alison asked.

"When you turn sixteen. You would go to Denham House, with the other older children," George explained.

"And Tom?" Alison asked.

"Tom would have to stay here until he was sixteen, then he would move on to Denham House, but you would have moved on to independent living, so you may have your own flat by then," George said.

"So, we have four years to get this sorted out?" Alison asked.

Tom was listening, but he hadn't realised that they were going to be separated, so he looked quite confused.

"OK, if me and Tom can talk about this, would that be alright?" Alison said.

"Yes of course, Sweetheart! We don't want you to go anywhere but stay here with us, but it's the system, you see," Sandra said.

"It's fine, Sandra, George. It's what has to happen, I suppose, but if we can sort this out before that and we can stay together?" Alison said.

"Yes, we have plenty of time. I tell you what, we'll leave you to have a think about it, and you can let us know later on, yes?" Sandra said.

Alison nodded her head and Sandra got up. George put the chairs back and left the room.

"Tom, did you understand all of that?" Alison asked.

"Yes, I think so. We will have to both be gone from Craven House by the time we're sixteen, but because you're three years older, you will move on before me. But if we decide to go with Betty and Bruce, we will live together, by the seaside. We'll also see Rose and Henry a lot more. Is that right?" Tom asked.

"That's exactly it! What do you think?" His sister said.

"We've met Betty and Bruce a lot of times and they are nice people, but we need to make sure Al. We can't go through what we went through before," Tom said.

Alison always knew Tom was older than his years, old head on young shoulders.

"No, we can't, but I don't think this will be like that, and they don't have a young daughter to get us into trouble," Alison said. They both laughed.

"Do you want to give it a try then, Tom? I know it was a couple of years ago, but how did you feel when we first met the Coopers, you know here at Craven House?" Alison asked.

"Well, they lied, didn't they? We thought they were nice, but they turned out to be horrible people! Al, I don't want to be separated from you. You're my big sister, and you have always looked out for me, and if this is the only chance we have to stay together, then we should do it. What about you?" tom asked.

"I think the same as you, Tom. If we give it a go and it doesn't work out, then we have to work by the system, and I don't really want to do that. I don't want to leave you. So, if we go and if it's great. We can ask if Freddie and Charlie can come and live with us as well?" Alison teased. "That's a good idea!" Tom laughed.

"Right, so shall we go and find Sandra and George?" Alison said.

"I think we should find out what else we can as well about it, how long it will take, how many times they want to see us and how many times do we have to go down there before we live there?" She added.

"That's a good idea, I think we do that before we say a yes," Tom said.

The two children left Alison's bedroom and went looking for Sandra and George, who were in the dining room.

"Sandra, George, is there any chance you could tell us a bit more about this placement with Betty and Bruce, before we decide what to do?" Alison asked.

"OK, well we wanted to find out first if you wanted to try it or not, because if you said no, then we would be telling Mr and Mrs Linton, Betty and Bruce, that it wasn't going to happen," Sandra said.

When she mentioned Mr and Mrs Linton, they looked confused, which was why she said their first names.

"Oh, they don't know if they've been accepted yet?" Alison said.

"That's right," George said.

"We wanted to know a bit more about it, because if we did go ahead and we didn't like it there, could we come back?" Alison asked.

"Yes, of course you could, but it would limit the amount of time of finding you both another placement," George said.

"Yes, we thought about that," Alison said, "if it didn't work out, we would just have to go by the system instead."

"Wow! How you two have grown up!" George said.

"So, if it's possible, how long would it be before we went down for the placement?" Alison said.

"We don't want to have to run away again; that was exhausting!" Tom said.

Sandra and George wanted to burst out laughing.

"No, we don't want you running away again! Also, we will make sure you always have some emergency money and you know the phone number for here and the address. And I don't think you will want to run away again. Betty and Bruce think a lot of you and you already know them. So, can we tell them that you're interested and then we can arrange for them to visit you here with us?" Sandra asked.

"But we know them, can't we just go down there?" Tom asked.

"No, Sweetheart. We have to go by the rules, and you have only seen them in Margate. They need to see you at your home, for everyday life," Sandra said, "but this is the first step. We can talk to Mr Duffy and he can let them know, and we see what happens from there."

"Sandra, George, when we have to go down there for a visit, will you come with us?" Tom asked.

"Yes, of course we will. You're like our own children and we want to see where you will sleep and what you're going to eat and all of that. We need to let them know what you like," Sandra said.

"Sandra, they know what we eat when we are at Rose's." Tom laughed.

Sandra and George had a little chuckle. Tom always brightened up their day and they were glad that what happened in the past hadn't really left a huge scar on him. He still had his personality. It came back, gradually, but he got there.

***

"So, Sandra, do you want to call them, or do you want me to do it?" Mr Duffy asked.

"Can I call them, please? I know they won't worry who calls them, but I think it may give that personal touch," Sandra replied.

She took the receiver from Mr Duffy and then dialled the number. It only rang a couple of times before Betty answered it.

"Hello, is that Mrs Linton…Betty?" Sandra said.

"Yes, it is. Hello Sandra, how are you?" Betty said, happy to hear her voice on the other end of the line.

Sandra explained that she had spoken to Alison and Tom and that they were very interested in living with Betty and Bruce.

"Oh, my goodness! That's fantastic!" Betty said, beckoning Bruce to come over to the telephone.

She put her fingers to her lips as she listened to Sandra.

"Yes, OK…so what happens next then? Of course, it does; all the training we have had, and I still have to ask, yes that's fine. So, when would you like us to come over?…Next Saturday? Yes, that's fine…what time…eleven thirty for twelve…that would be great, Sandra. Thank you so much and see you then," Betty said, replacing the receiver.

"I take it it's good news, Bet?" Bruce said.

"Yes, it is, Bruce! Tom and Alison have both said yes! They would love to see us more and they want to try a foster placement with us!" Bet said with a huge smile.

Bruce picked her up and swung her around.

"Oh, Bruce be careful, I feel dizzy now!" Bet said, laughing.

Bruce put her back down and hugged her tightly.

"So, when can we see them next?" Bruce asked.

"Next Saturday, around lunchtime. Now I want to go into town and pick those two little loves out something nice to take with us. But I'll see Rose first and tell her the good news, she'll be so happy for us," Bet said.

Betty opened the front door and popped down to see Rose and Henry. When she got there, she was beaming again.

"Rose, I have good news, no I have fantastic news!" Bet said.

"You've got them, haven't you?" Rose said.

"Well, we have the go ahead and the kids have both said they want to come down, but we have to see them at the home first and maybe a few times before it can be a reality for a full time placement," Bet explained.

She was so excited.

"Where are you off to now, then?" Rose asked.

"I want to go into town so I can pick them both up something to take down with us. Do you know if Tom still likes cars and trucks and what about Alison?" Bet asked.

"Why don't you just have a look around? You'll know when you see what you want for them," Rose suggested.

"That's a good idea, well I just wanted to let you know the good news, I'll see you later," Bet said, on her way out the front door.

"Bruce, are you coming with me?" Bet asked her husband.

"I wouldn't miss it for the world! I'm so happy, Bet! I can't wait. Do you know what you want to get them?" Bruce asked.

"No, Rose suggested that we just have a look around and we will know, so that's what I want to do."

They headed off in the car and took more time than normal to go around town, they had a look in some of the shops, but ended up in Woolworths. They had great stuff for the kids, toys, sweets, clothes, records for the teenagers, make-up for the girls. But where to start?

Bruce had wandered over to the boys' toys. He knew Tom was eight, so he thought to have a look at what was available in his age group. He found a number of cars that he thought Tom might like. He picked up a set of Matchbox cars, then found a blue lorry that had the space for cars to go on the top first, then underneath.

"I think Tom would like that," Bruce muttered to himself.

Bet came around the corner with a basket, also starting to fill up. She had picked up some toiletries and found Alison various colours of nail polish and remover. She also had a look at the records but had no idea what music she liked, so thought she would wait until the kids come over and they could take them shopping for them to choose such stuff.

She also bought her a jewellery box. It was a little wooden box in the shape of a house. When you lifted the roof, it played 'Edelweiss'. You could then lift the inside and it had a secret compartment for your treasures. She thought Alison would love that. She saw a lovely teddy bear. She knew that Alison may be a bit old for one, but this one was really soft. It was a light brown with a beautiful colour peach ribbon around its neck. That was it, she wasn't sure what else to get.

Bet found Bruce still looking at the boys' toys, and his basket was nearly full to the brim.

"Bet, I know that Tom likes cars and trucks, but I wondered if he would like trains as well? What do you think?" Bruce asked, excited and nervous at the same time.

"Bruce, if you think he would like them, then get them. I know you will have just as much fun with them as Tom, so get them," Bet said, with a loving smile at her husband.

They had been married for just over ten years and they were so happy.

When they finished their shopping, with both baskets as full as they can be, Bet had to put the sweets and other treats in her basket as they didn't fit in Bruce's. They went to the cashier at the till and Bruce paid for it all.

"Bet, do you fancy going for a bit of lunch somewhere?" Bruce asked.

"Yes, where do you fancy eating?"

"Well I was going to suggest that little tea shop down the road, but I think we had better eat in the Wimpy once in a while." He chuckled.

That's what they did. As he said, they would have to get used to it, but they didn't mind. If it made the kids happy and then it would make them happy. They went off to Wimpy, went inside, took their seats and the waitress came over and gave them both a menu.

"What do you want then, Bet?" Bruce asked, looking at the menu.

"I'll have a burger and chips, and a chocolate milkshake please," Bet said.

The waitress took their order and came back a few minutes with their milkshakes.

"Are you pleased with what you got Tom, then?" Bet asked.

"Yes, I am. I hope he likes them, I'm sure he will," Bruce said.

"If not Bruce, you could always play with them," Bet laughed.

"I can't wait for next Saturday!" Bruce said.

"No, me either. It will soon be here though," Betty said as the waitress delivered their food.

***

"Alison! Alison! They're here!" Tom shouted to his sister. He had been looking out of the upstairs window all morning and was waving furiously at Bet and Bruce. They looked up as they got out of the car and waved back at Tom just as excitedly.

"Tom, Alison, we are going to greet Betty and Bruce, do you want to come down as well?" Sandra asked.

"Yes please!" Tom said, pushing past Sandra.

Well, he wasn't like this before, Sandra laughed to herself, but she was really pleased he was excited. Of all the times the Coopers came, he was never this excited.

"Hello, come in!" Sandra opened the door to Betty and Bruce, who were carrying a few bags with them. Sandra shook both Betty and Bruce's hands and Tom and Alison came over. Betty had her arms open wide to greet both of them. She was so excited. Bruce bent down to Tom's level and hugged him as well, then Alison.

This was a very different experience to the last family.

"Come on up, we have tea made," Sandra said.

"Yes, and I helped Alison make some fairy cakes," Tom said.

Bruce held the door open for Tom; Alison was already walking with Bet and Sandra and George and showed them into the dayroom.

"May I take your coats?" George asked.

Both Bet and Bruce took off their coats and handed them to George, who left the room.

When George returned, some of the children had congregated outside and were peeking inside.

"Come on you lot, go outside and play," George laughed. "Sorry about that, the kids were checking you out, I'm afraid," he said to Bet and Bruce.

"That's fine, George, it's understandable," Bruce said.

"Would you like some tea, there are sandwiches and as Tom said some fairy cakes, that both of them made this morning," George said.

"That would be lovely, thank you. Erm, we have a couple of gifts for Tom and Alison, I hope that's OK?" Bet asked.

"You have gifts for us?" Tom's eyes lit up.

"Yes, of course," Sandra said.

Bruce gave Tom his presents and Bet gave Alison hers. Bruce got down on the floor with Tom, to see if he needed help. Tom was as excited as Bruce! Once he opened the cars, Tom's mouth opened wide.

"Oh look, Al! I have a lorry for the cars to go onto! I have a blue one and a yellow one!" Tom said excitedly. "Can you play cars with me, Bruce?" Tom asked.

Bruce's face lit up.

"Of course, I can, we can have hours of fun," Bruce laughed.

Alison opened her presents, nail polish and remover, and a musical jewellery box.

"Alison, I didn't know what else you would like, so when you next come down, we can go shopping and you can have a good look around Woolworths. They had records, but I didn't know what groups you liked," Bet said, a little nervous.

"Betty, it's fine. They're lovely, thank you, and yes, I would love to go shopping with you when we next get down to you in Margate," Alison replied, giving Betty a huge hug.

Bet felt so lovely, and so did Alison; it felt like she had come home.

Tom also moved over to Bruce and gave him a big hug too. Sandra and George didn't know what to do with themselves, they felt like they were intruding by being there.

Sandra got up and made tea. The children broke away from the adults.

"Sandwich anyone?" George asked.

George handed them all a side plate and the children sat down at the table, where Bruce and Betty joined them.

The first visit was a success. Everyone in the room could see this was going to be a great foster placement.

It was time for Betty and Bruce to leave, Tom and Alison got up to say goodbye to them.

"When can we see you again?" Tom asked.

"I'm not sure yet, Tom?" Bet replied, "I think it may be a couple of weeks."

"Can you come down in two weeks and then we can go out to town and you can see where we go shopping for our treats and stuff?" Sandra suggested.

"Yes, we would like that," Bruce said.

Alison and Tom gave them both a big hug and then they shook Sandra and George's hands.

"Don't you want to take the presents with you?" Tom asked.

"No, why?" Bruce said.

"Well, for your house," Tom added.

"Well, what if you keep them here with you, you can play with your friends and when you come down, you can bring them with you!" Bruce suggested.

"OK, thank you both," Tom said.

"Thank you, Tom, and you too, Alison, it's been a lovely visit and we'll see you in two weeks," Bet said.

They said their farewells again and Bet and Bruce left the building. Tom raced back upstairs to wave from the window. Bet looked up and then Bruce and waved furiously back at him and Alison joined him. Bet had tears in her eyes.

This was definitely one of the best days of her life and she knew in her heart this was going to be fantastic.

Sandra and George had a quiet word, out of earshot of the children.

"Oh, my goodness, George! This is going to work; I mean really work! Did you see how they all were when they hugged?" Sandra said.

"Yes, did you see Bruce get down to Tom's level? Mr Cooper never did that once, and they were so chuffed to see them and wanting to know when they can see them again. Both of them, not just the kids. I can really see this working out, Sandra, and about time too," remarked George.

"We had better get on, but I can't wait to tell Mr Duffy about this first visit," Sandra said. She was seeing him on Monday, so not long to wait.

Sandra went about her duties: she helped Tom and Alison take their new things up to their bedrooms. Tom was chatting to Freddie and Charlie and there were smiles everywhere. Freddie and Charlie couldn't wait to get their hands on Tom's new cars. They made loads of space, which meant when you went into the bedroom, you had to step over everything.

Alison put her jewellery box on her bedside cabinet with her figurines, which Sandra had managed to replace, and her nail polishes.

She wished she had Jo there to tell her all about the visit with Betty and Bruce. But she still had Sandra to talk to.

Sandra popped her head around the door to check on Alison.

"Are you OK, Sweetheart?" Sandra asked.

"Yes, I'm really happy, Sandra. That was a really good visit and Betty and Bruce are lovely. I love what they got us, and Tom's eyes were like saucers, did you see?" She chuckled.

"Yes, I did! Do you have any reservations about this placement at all or are you OK with it?" Sandra said.

"No, I think it will be fine. They were genuinely excited to be here with us. Bruce got down on the floor with Tom, which was brilliant, they had great eye contact. Did you see?" Alison asked. "Harry wouldn't have done that ever; he would have been frightened to get his trousers dirty," Alison said, bursting out laughing. "I'm looking forward to two weeks' time, when they come again. Sandra, do you know how many times they have to come here before we can go down there to see them?"

"I have no idea yet, Honey, but we will know soon enough," Sandra said.

"Come on, let's go down. It will dinner time in ten minutes," Sandra said.

Alison followed Sandra down the dining room, picking up Tom, Freddie, and Charlie, who were having a great time with the new toys.

***

The next two weeks went by really quickly and Tom and Alison were getting ready for Betty and Bruce's visit. They were going to going out this time.

Tom was waiting upstairs to look for their car to pull up. It was a bright red one. Tom loved red cars; they were so vibrant!

"They're here!" Tom shouted, as he ran downstairs.

Alison was already on the lower level. She had been helping to tidying up in the kitchen. She brushed herself down and made her way to reception. Tom had just got there. He was as excited this Saturday as he was the last one that they had come.

Bruce and Betty had bags with them again this time. They both had a new duvet cover each; a car one for Tom and a checked one for Alison. They were both delighted with their new things.

"We wanted something that you could use here, but could bring with you when you come down, is that alright, Sandra?" Bet asked.

"Absolutely fine, Bet. They can try them out here and then we can wash them so they can bring them back with you," Sandra smiled.

We got you both a rug for your bedrooms too, but maybe we should take them back home?" Bet said, looking at Sandra for approval.

"Do you want to show them first, then they can see what sort of thing they will have in their bedrooms?" Sandra suggested.

"That's a good idea," Bruce said.

Tom's rug had cars on it, and Alison's had flowers on it: lovely big peach ones, with light green leaves.

"Oh, they're lovely!" Tom and Alison said at the same time.

"Do you like the colours?" Bruce asked.

Tom's one was different colour trucks and cars, but the background colour was a lovely green. "Yes, they're lovely and I love the colour!" Tom said.

Alison nodded her head in agreement.

"Well, we will take them home and put them in your rooms for you, for when you visit," Bet said.

Bruce put the rugs back in the bags and Sandra asked if they were ready to go. Tom and Alison went upstairs to get their coats. It was October and was starting to get chilly now. They were back in no time, and they all left together.

Tom held Bruce's hand and Bet walked with Alison. Sandra and George lagged behind everyone. They went to town and looked in the boutiques for the latest fashions. There was a Woolworths and also a Wimpy.

Tom looked at Al, she smiled at him. Betty and Bruce took them inside Woolworths where Tom had a look at the trucks and cars. He had most of them, but there were a couple that he didn't have, but he had been given lots already, so he wasn't going to ask for any more.

The girls had a look at the perfume stand and had a smell of the testers. They then went to the record section.

Alison was looking at the posters, she already had one of Abba, Jo took her Bee Gees one when she went to Benson House. Bet made a mental note of what groups and bands Alison liked. She had thought of decorating her bedroom in a peach colour and Tom's in a lovely shade of green with other coloured accessories, lamp, rug, curtains near enough to match. She had lots she wanted to do for them when they came, but they would go shopping nearer home.

When they left Woolworths, Bruce and Bet headed towards Wimpy. Sandra and George had noticed how different this couple were to the last ones.

Bruce opened the door, and Alison and Tom chose where they wanted to sit. They chose a big booth, so they could all sit together.

Tom and Alison sat opposite each other, Bet and Bruce next to them, and then Sandra and George on the ends. They ordered what they wanted, and Bruce said he was paying for it today. The day passed very quickly and soon it was time for Betty and Bruce to go home again.

When Sandra had her meeting with Mr Duffy on the previous Monday, he said that if this visit was just as successful, the children could visit the Lintons if they wanted to.

When they all got back to Craven House, Betty and Bruce asked Sandra and George what was the next step?

"Well, if you want to, we can come down in two weeks and see you at home, if that's alright?" Sandra said.

Betty and Bruce were already happy, they looked like they wanted to jump for joy. Tom did! "That's great, so we can come down to you next time, so you don't have to get up so early!" Tom said.

"That's fantastic, we can see you at ours then in two weeks, about the same time, twelvish?" asked Bruce.

"Yes, that should be OK. George will be driving. Thankfully, we know where you are, and we can pop in to see Rose and Henry and say a quick hello," Sandra said.

Both Bet and Bruce nodded.

"Rose would love to see you both. Right, we had better make a move, thank you for today. Thank you, Tom, thank you, Alison," Betty said.

Bruce gave them both a hug and a kiss on the cheek, so did Bet, they were so excited they would see them again at their home in two weeks' time. They got into their car and pulled away.

"Sandra, I think we may be losing these kids a bit earlier than we anticipated!" George laughed.

Sandra had thought the same thing. This was going really well; she didn't have that niggly feeling she had last time with the Coopers. This felt really lovely and Betty was trying so hard to get it right for them. They both were.

***

Mr Prowse had asked Mr Duffy for a brief meeting once there had been two visits by the Lintons. He wanted to be kept up to date with the progress of the situation. Mr Duffy had asked Sandra and George to also attend. They were both happy with how it was going so far, they had really noticed a change in the children for the better and the atmosphere around the Lintons and the children were astounding.

They were very much promoting for this placement to go ahead, and the speed it was going was a little fast, but it felt more natural than any of the other placements they had ever had. Mr Duffy was keen to continue with it, providing everything was going by the book and everything was properly dealt with.

Mr Prowse still wanted to keep an eye on it. They didn't want another situation on their hands, but Sandra, George, and Mr Duffy, didn't think this was going to be the case. They said they would keep him informed with the progress and he was happy with that.

The day arrived and Sandra and George were taking Alison and Tom down to Margate. They left just after 10am and headed off in the car, waving goodbye to their friends.

"Are you two excited, then?" Sandra laughed.

"Yes, I can't wait to see Betty and Bruce! They are so lovely, and I think we have made the right choice this time, Sandra," Tom said.

They were all chatting happily on the journey down to Margate, and they didn't realise that they were already here. They had pulled up in front of Rose and Henry's instead though. George checked that he could park there and then they all got out of the car, locked it up and then went to knock on Betty and Bruce's front door.

Sandra had brought flowers for Betty and some cigars for Bruce. They knocked on the door and Betty opened it wide, Bruce was right behind her.

"Hello! Come in everyone!" Betty said.

Bruce walked into the sitting room, and George, Tom, Alison, and Sandra came in behind and Betty closed the front door after them.

"Can I take your coats?" Bruce asked.

They took their coats off and handed them to Bruce who took them to the hall and hung them up on the hooks.

"Please sit down, we have tea made and something light to eat, unless you want to go out?" Bet said.

"No, tea would be lovely, thank you," Sandra said, handing Tom the flowers to give to Bet, and the cigars to Alison to give to Bruce.

Tom handed the flowers to Bet, she was thrilled, and she gave him a kiss on his forehead.

"Thank you, Tom, Alison," Bet smiled.

Alison gave Bruce the cigars.

"Oh, thank you, Alison and Tom," Bruce said. He was chuffed to bits with the cigars.

Bet returned with tea and squash for the children. She had put the flowers in a lovely crystal vase and put them on the table. Everyone sat down and Bet poured out the tea and Bruce told everyone to tuck in there was plenty of food.

"Then when we have eaten, we can give you a tour of the house, if you want?" Bet beamed at the children. "I love to see children who have big appetites!" she added.

Once everyone had finished, betty invited them all to have a look around her home.

She loved her home. She and Bruce had made it so cosy and comfortable. The only thing missing was the children, but that was all going to change now.

Sandra went to clear the table.

"Oh, leave that, Sandra, I will do it when we come back downstairs, anyway I have more treats," Bet chuckled.

"Come on then, let's go upstairs," Bruce said.

They pushed their chairs in and followed Bet upstairs.

The building was on four floors. They were already on the ground and the next floor up was the first floor; that was where Betty and Bruce's bedroom was. They had a bathroom on that floor, as well as another bedroom.

They went up to another level where they had two more bedrooms and a bathroom. The rooms were basically the same as the Coopers. Bet opened the doors to both bedrooms.

"Now this will be one of your bedrooms and the other one opposite. So have a look and choose which one you want," Bet said. Alison looked at the one on the left, Tom looked at the one on the right, then they both chose the opposite rooms. Bet looked a bit confused but went with it anyway.

"So, Alison, if this is the room you want, that's fine, do you know what colour you would like it?" Bet asked.

"I can choose for myself?" Alison asked.

"Yes, of course, Honey! It's your room, you can have it any way you want. If you want to paint it all black with red curtains, then that's what you will have!" Bet said.

"Oh! OK. I hadn't thought about it. Can I let you know later on, before we go?" Alison said.

Bet nodded.

"Now, what about you, young man? What colour would you like for your room?" Bruce asked Tom.

"What about green, like the colour of the rug you brought down last time?" Tom suggested.

"That's a great idea, I love it!" Bruce said.

Alison walked into the room and had a good look around. It had lots of light in it. She thought for a moment.

"Betty, can I have peach, to go with the rug you got me?"

"What about peach and cream colours?" Bet asked.

Alison nodded.

"That sounds lovely, it's not too much trouble, is it?"

"No, not at all! We'll have it ready for when you both come down again, is that OK?" Bet said. "Right, let's go upstairs. Oh, before I forget, let me show you your bathroom," Bet said, opening the next door. It was a huge bathroom with lots of lovely fresh towels, loads of bubble bath and shelves full of toiletries.

"Who are they for?" Tom asked.

"They're for you two. We thought we would get you some toiletries, but if there's anything you prefer, just let me know," Bet said.

"No, they're great, thank you!" Alison said.

Betty continued with the tour of the house.

"Betty, why do you have more bedrooms up here?" Tom asked.

"Well, we hoped to have more children, and we didn't, so if you want to be up here instead, you can, but we thought you might like to be nearer us," Bet said.

"No, our rooms are lovely, I just wondered," Tom said.

They followed Betty up to the top floor.

"This is where we have another room and a toilet. We were thinking of turning this room into a study or something, a chill-out room," Bet said.

"A chill-out room?"

"Yes, well, what I was thinking. Perhaps have a desk in here, but also a sofa, so if you were studying for your tests or exams and needed some peace and quiet, then you could come up here. Also, maybe get a sofa bed, so if you had your friends over for a sleepover, then there would be room for them," Bet explained. "Mind you, I could always come up here, you know, for a break, if Bruce starts driving me crazy!" Bet laughed.

Bruce shook his head, but everyone else was laughing.

"So, do you like the house?"

"Yes, we love it, do you have a garden?" Tom asked.

"Yes, but we have to go right back downstairs, so let's go and have a look, shall we?" Bruce said.

They all trundled back downstairs and went to the back of the kitchen and Bet opened a door that led into a lovely sized back garden. They had some flowers growing and a little patio area, but only a little bit of grass that was rather patchy.

"I like to do gardening but haven't had the chance lately," Bruce said, "do you like gardening, Tom?"

"I have never tried it, but I am always willing to learn," Tom said.

The children loved the house and the garden. When they went back inside, Bet made another pot of tea and cleared the table and brought in the cakes she had made. Alison and Tom's eyes were like saucers, they haven't seen so much food on a table that size.

"So, you like the house then, children?" Bet asked.

"Yes, it's lovely, there is so much room, just for two people!" Tom said.

"Yes, but there will be four people soon!" Bet said.

Everyone was tucking into their sweet stuff.

"Would you like to go into town today or leave that for next time?" Bet asked.

"I would love to go today, but I'm totally stuffed, Betty," Alison said, "can we go next time?"

"Yes of course," Bet smiled.

"I know how she feels!" Sandra said. "I think we have eaten way too much!"

"Can we pop into the garden for a little while, Betty?" Tom asked.

"Yes of course, if you both want to go out there, Bruce will you get the chairs out of the shed; that way they don't have to sit on the grass. It's a little damp today."

Bruce took the children out into the garden via the garden shed.

"I think they want a little time on their own, probably to talk about things," Sandra said.

"Sandra, can I ask you something?" Bet said.

"Yes, of course."

"When we showed them the bedrooms, they both had a look and chose the opposite rooms to what they were looking at," Bet said.

"The layout of your house is very nice, but the rooms they had at the last place were the ones you chose for them today, so I think they wanted to choose the opposite, because if they woke up in the night, they may get a bit disorientated and think they were still there," Sandra explained. "Me and George had a look when they left, it was exactly the same, but the fact they want to stay on that floor is a good thing. They want to be near you both."

Bruce came in and wondered what he had walked into.

"Anything wrong? The children are sitting out there as if there were on holiday."

"No, nothing to worry about, Love," Bet said.

When the children came back in, Bet asked if they all wanted to pop along to see Rose and Henry. They all did. It was only a couple of doors away.

Bet took the keys and they went and knocked on the door.

Rose opened it up and had a big beaming smile on her face when she saw the children.

"Hello, my loves! How are you doing?" Rose asked. "Please come in, have a cup of tea!"

They all went downstairs to the dining room.

"Do you have a lot on at the moment, Rose?" Sandra asked.

"No, not at the moment. It's coming up to autumn, so there's not too much going on, but never mind, we like the break for about two or three weeks, then we get bored," Rose said.

"Did you enjoy yourselves in the summer when you were here?" Henry asked.

"Oh yes, we had a great time, you know Jo is now at Benson House?" Tom said.

"Yes, we saw her, she was missing you two a lot, but she did manage to have a great time," Rose said.

Sandra looked at the clock in the dining room, it said five-thirty.

"Oh, my goodness! We're going to have to make a move back, we won't be back until late otherwise and it starts getting dark soon."

Everyone said their goodbyes to Rose and Henry and then they went back to Betty and Bruce's.

"I'm sorry we have to go, but I didn't realise the time," Sandra said.

"Don't worry, Sandra, it's fine, we know how these things are. Now make sure you haven't left anything behind, got everything, good?" Betty asked.

They all gave Bet and Bruce hugs and they said to them that they should be able to come down in two weeks for an over-night stay if that was OK.

Bet and Bruce beamed.

"Yes, that would be great, so see you in two weeks!"

They gave the children a hug and kiss on the cheek and they all got into the car.

"Right, now then, Bruce, we've got two weeks to get the children's bedrooms done!" Bet said as they waved the children off.

***

Bruce and Bet were busy for the next two weeks getting everything ready for Alison and Tom's overnight stay, but this was more than just an overnight stay, this would be there home hopefully sooner rather than later.

Alison and Tom were getting excited. Sandra and George were taking them down and Bruce and Betty were taking them back on Sunday evening.

Sandra, George, Tom, and Alison got off as soon as they could that morning. They didn't want to hit the traffic. They had a straight run and arrived around eleven thirty. The children both had their overnight bags with them.

George pulled up outside the house. Bet and Bruce were soon at the door, really excited to see them all. They took the children's overnight bags and took them straight up to their rooms, which had been beautifully decorated to the children's colour scheme as they had asked.

Tom's room looked bigger. They both had huge wardrobes, chest of drawers and bedside cabinet, with a lamp on it and a lampshade on the ceiling to match and curtains the same.

"This is great, thank you both!" Tom said, tears welling up in his eyes. The room was decorated just how he had wanted.

"We didn't want to make the walls to dark as it would take out a lot of the light, so gave you lighter walls, but darker carpet. The curtains are blackout ones, so at the weekend if you want a lie in, it will be lovely and cosy," Bruce said.

Next, they went over to Alison's room. She burst open the door and was just awestruck. It was beautiful with lovely soft peach walls. Her wardrobes were cream as was the chest of drawers and bedside cabinet. They also got her a dressing table. The curtains, lamps, lampshade and rug all matched.

"Do you like it, Honey?" Bruce asked.

"I love it! It's special! I love the colours, they just all go together so well!" Alison said.

Bruce left Alison's overnight bag just inside her bedroom.

"Would you like a cuppa before you head off, just to keep out the cold?" Bruce asked Sandra and George.

"Oh, yes, that would be lovely, thank you. I must use the bathroom, if that's OK?" Sandra said.

Everyone went back downstairs. There was a hook in both of the bedrooms behind the door, with a dressing gown on each for them. Alison had pink and Tom had blue. They took their shoes off and followed everyone else downstairs.

Alison and Tom both looked happier than in a long time. They both had squash and the adults all had tea. Sandra and George didn't stay too long as they had to get back and get on with their duties.

They said their goodbyes and hugged both of the children. Alison and Tom stood in front of Bet and Bruce and waved goodbye to Sandra and George. Sandra undid the window and said that they would see them both the following day.

"We are doing the right thing this time, aren't we, George?" she asked.

"Are you joking? They're like little kids! I'm surprised they aren't playing pass the parcel!" George laughed.

Bet closed the door once Sandra and George had left.

"So, what would you like to do now then? Once you've unpacked your things and put them where you want to? It's still early, would you like to go to the cinema? *The Raiders of the Lost Ark* is on in town, then we could pop into the new tea shop, called Molly's," Bruce said.

"Molly's?" Alison said.

"Yes, we've been there a couple of times already, would you like to go?" Bet asked.

"Yes please, we have been to one before," Alison said. "You know, when we lived with the Coopers," Alison said.

It didn't take long for them to get to town. The children were getting more used to Margate now. Tom held onto Bruce's hand and Alison held onto Bet's arm they walked in such happy moods.

It was nearly time to go to the cinema.

"I don't know if the children should see this film, Bruce, it looks a bit violent," Bet said, looking at the film poster outside of the cinema.

"It will be fine, Bet, look it's more of an adventure film, and it's got Harrison Ford in it, you like him!" Bruce said.

Bruce went up to the counter, paid for the tickets, bought some popcorn and a few drinks and they went in.

The film was about two hours or so long and both of the children were mesmerised. They hadn't been to the cinema much, but when they did, they enjoyed themselves. They then headed towards Molly's Tea Shop, Alison and Tom were excited. They didn't know if it was the same Molly's as they had in Brighton.

They walked in the door and a little bell went off when they entered, a lady came over asked them how many and then showed them to a table in the window. She went away and then returned with some menus and then she noticed Alison.

"Alison? Is that you and Tom, yes, it is you?" Molly said.

Bet and Bruce were a little concerned.

"Do you remember me from Molly's in Brighton?" The lady asked.

"Oh, yes we do, how are you, Molly?" Alison said. Tom looked a little uncomfortable.

Bet and Bruce noticed how the children seemed to change.

"So, what are you doing here in Margate, then?" Molly asked.

Bet intervened.

"They are staying with us, just for the day and then going back home tomorrow," Bet said.

"Oh, back to Brighton?" Molly asked.

Alison and Tom looked really uncomfortable in their seats now.

"Err, can I have a word, miss, please?" Bet said, getting up from her seat. "Please could you show me the way to the ladies?" she asked quickly.

"Of course," Molly said, a little taken aback.

Molly moved away from the table and Bet followed her.

"This is the ladies, Ma'am," Molly said.

"Could you hold on for a moment please, Molly? So, you know Alison and Tom from Brighton? Alison did tell us of a lovely tea shop called Molly's. The thing is, Alison and Tom are staying here with us in Margate. They left Brighton and not on good circumstances; now I know you mean well, but it's taken us and the staff at the home they live in a lot of time, energy and a lot of encouragement to get the children back to some sort of normality. The only thing I would like to ask you is, have you ever seen the family they were with again?" Bet asked.

"No, I've only seen the children that time in the summer for Alison's birthday. The family did come in quite regularly, but not with Alison and Tom. I assumed they had gone away. I'm so sorry, I was just so thrilled to see both of them. I hadn't realised they had left on bad terms. Please forgive me?" Molly said.

"Oh, don't be silly. I was just wondering if you had seen their former foster parents. Tom and Alison had run away. I think Alison said that the family would have come to your place on the Saturday as the other little girl wanted to go back," Bet said.

"Yes, they did come back that day, but I didn't see them again," Molly said.

"No, that's because they disappeared later on that day. The police are looking for them at the moment. Thank you for remembering them," Bet said. "I had better get back to my seat before they think I have fallen down the toilet!"

She returned to her seat.

"Are you OK, Bet?" Bruce asked.

"Yes, just a little tummy ache, that's all, all better now though."

Bet looked at the menu, chose her food and waited with everyone else.

They were all talking about the film earlier when their food arrived. The children had both ordered milkshakes, Bet and Bruce had tea and sandwiches. When they had eaten, Molly came over with the menu for cakes. Bet asked her if she would bring the sweet trolley over instead, then they could all choose a cake or two.

Tom and Alison's eyes lit up. Alison had liked the chocolate éclair she had last time and she knew that Molly's cakes were lovely, so she chose one of those. Tom had a look, he thought he would have a piece of strawberry gateau or cheesecake, but he and Bruce both had a slice of strawberry gateau, which they thoroughly enjoyed. Bet also had a slice of gateau, but chocolate this time.

Alison looked at it.

"Would you like a slice as well. Alison?" Bet asked.

"No, I had better not," Alison said.

"Why? Because if you would like a slice, you can have one, you know," Bet smiled. She never wanted these children to ever feel they didn't deserve anything.

"Are you sure, Bet?"

"Yes of course, I think it would be lovely to have two," Bet said.

She asked for another slice for Alison.

Bruce asked for the bill and paid it, he didn't question it or moan, like Harry had, he just pulled out his wallet and paid the bill, with a tip for the staff.

"Come on, let's go home now. We can watch a bit of TV. If anyone has any space, we could always get fish and chips later on!" Bruce said.

These kids were never going to go hungry living with Bet and Bruce, thought Molly. They all said goodbye to Molly, and they made their way home, hoping for some of that food to go down before they got in.

They got in, saw the time, and Tom and Alison asked if they could put their pyjamas on.

"Of course, this is your home while you're here, we want you to do what you would do anyway," Bet said.

The children went upstairs to put on their night things, then came back down. Bruce was looking to see what was on TV. Tom sat next to him and Alison sat next to Bet.

"Thank you for today, Bet and Bruce. It was lovely to go out and do fun things, and it was lovely to see Molly again, she does have such lovely cakes," Alison said.

"Well, we can't go there too often, Alison, otherwise my waistline is going to get too big and I will burst!" Bruce laughed.

Alison and Tom had felt like they now had a proper family once and for all. They watched a couple of programmes and Bruce went and bought fish and chips. They thought they would all burst.

Alison and Tom asked if they could go to bed. It had been a long day. They kissed Bruce and Betty on the cheek and went off to bed.

"Goodnight!" They both called out.

"I will be up in a few minutes, just to tuck you in," Bet said.

Both of them walked up the stairs and into their bedrooms. They both got into their beds and snuggled up. Bet was up a few minutes later, she tucked them both in, made sure they had water if they needed it, kissed them on the cheek and left their rooms.

She had a night light on in the hall just in case they woke up in the night and forgot where the toilet was. She then left them and went back downstairs.

"They will be spark out within no time, Bruce, they are so tired!" Bet said.

"Yes, with what they have done here and the drive down, it's no surprise. Bet, what did you say to the lady in Molly's?" Bruce asked.

"I asked her not to mention Brighton again to them and told her about those horrible Cooper people. She said she hasn't seen them since. I think if anything, she was surprised to see them there with us and not the other family," Bet said, "Right, I am off to bed as I am shattered. Are you coming?"

"Yes, I am just going to lock up and then check on the kids and then bed," Bruce said.

***

The next day was full of fun.

"Bruce, be mindful of the time, love, we don't want them to get back too late. They have school tomorrow," Bet said.

They had all been playing board games, charades and having a jolly good time. When it was time to leave, the children had already had their Sunday lunch.

Bet went up to their rooms to make sure they hadn't left anything and grabbed their bags and put them in the boot of the car. They waved to Rose and Henry as they drove past and Bruce tooted the car horn. They made their way back to Craven House.

The journey back went too quickly, and they were soon pulling up outside. Sandra and George had been waiting at the window with Freddie and Charlie.

"They're back!" They shouted and raced downstairs to reception to greet them.

Sandra and George weren't too far behind them. Bruce opened up the boot and took out their bags and handed them to George. Bet didn't want to let go of their hands but did eventually. She got down to Tom's level and hugged him.

"We will see you again very soon, Tom. I hope you had a nice time with us?" Bet asked. She kissed him on the cheek and did the same thing with Alison.

"Thank you for having us this weekend, it's been lovely," Alison said. They then let them go before Bet changed her mind and offered the kids to get back in the car. They went in the door and waved.

Bet and Bruce spoke to Sandra and George. Before they left.

"We will be having a meeting in the week and will give you a call to let you know what's next, is that OK?" Sandra said.

They both nodded.

"That's fine, thank you, they were as good as gold and we can't wait to have them again," Bet said Bet.

"I know, Bet, it will be fine. Have a safe journey back you two and talk in the week."

Bet looked for the children who were now at the door waving frantically at them both.

"Did you both have a good time?" George asked.

"Yes, George, it was great. We went to the cinema, we saw *Raiders of the Lost Ark*, then we went to Molly's tea shop—"

"Molly's Tea Shop?" Sandra said.

"Oh yes, she now has a shop in Margate too!" Alison said, as she was walking up towards her room.

Tom, Freddie and Charlie had already gone up to their room, Tom was telling them all about the film they saw the day before. It was just another day at Craven House.

Chapter 21

"Right, everyone here? So, let's get started, shall we?" Mr Duffy said.

"So, how's the progress going with the Lintons and Alison and Tom?" Mr Prowse started.

"Mr Prowse, we can't believe how well it is going so quickly! The children love going down to Margate and spending time with them, and the Lintons are so happy to get them, even though it's a bit of a drive for them, they love it. Alison and Tom get rather excited when they know they are going down or they are coming up for them," Sandra said. "I was wondering if this continues, how long will it be before Alison and Tom can go down for their placement? I know things have changed in the system, but I don't know if I can speak for everyone else, I think it would be great if we could make it as soon as," Sandra added.

Mr Duffy looked at George.

"George, what do you think?" he asked.

"I agree with Sandra. I have never seen anything like it, they are all so happy, it's completely different from the last time," George said.

"What do you mean, George? Better or worse?" Mr Prowse asked.

"Oh, much better! 100% better! You wouldn't know that last placement had even taken place," George added.

"I just have to sort things out in Margate with Alan Taylor; the social worker assigned to this placement. I know it looks more positive than last time, but we can't take any chances again, can we?" Mr Prowse reminded them all.

They all looked at each other quite confidently.

"I have to speak to Mr Taylor later on today and then I can come back to you. Is that OK with you, Mr Duffy?" Mr Prowse asked.

"Yes, that's fine, Mr Prowse. When that's sorted out then we can arrange it all, but I do want Mr Taylor to do plenty of checks on the children after they go down there; just to be on the safe side, and if I have any qualms about it, I will go down for a visit myself just to double check," Mr Duffy said.

"Right, if that's all, then the meeting's closed." He added, tidying away his paperwork, "Thank you for all coming at short notice. Sandra, George, I'll see you later. Mr Prowse, I look forward to hearing from you later on today." Mr Duffy shook Mr Prowse's hand. Sandra and George left the office.

They waited until they were out of earshot and both punched the air.

"Yes! This time it's much better, George! We can all feel it. When they go down there and when they return, it's so positive. I don't want them to go, but this might be their last chance to stay together," Sandra said.

"Yes, I agree," George said, with a big smile on his face.

The two of them returned to their duties and hoped that Mr Duffy would call them both in later on to tell them of the decision that had been made. Sandra was changing one of the beds when Mr Duffy called her downstairs. One of the little girls had had an accident during the night and she had only just found out. She took the wet bedding down to the laundry room and then went to Mr Duffy's office.

"Ah Sandra, thank you for making the time to come down, I know you're rather busy. Mr Prowse has just called and it's a thumbs up! Alison and Tom can go to Margate with the Lintons. It will be the same procedure though; six months. When that's up if they would like to extend it, they can, but only once. If after that it doesn't work out, the children will come back, otherwise the Lintons can go for adoption," Mr Duffy said.

Sandra and George held out a hand and did a high five together.

"Err, so I take it that you're pleased?" He laughed.

"We are Mr Duffy! This is what those children need and deserve. May I ask you something?" Sandra asked.

"Yes of course!"

"What if the Lintons want to adopt Alison and Tom before the first six months are up, is that possible, or if they want to go for the adoption after the six months?" she asked.

"Well, if they want to go for the adoption once the six months is up, we still have to have the extension, otherwise everything is all in limbo. So, whether they go for it before or after the six months, it won't make any difference," Mr Duffy said.

"Oh well, it was a win-win situation then for all of them. So, is the process going to be like before? The kids will be notified before school and we'll have a meeting to sign everything off and then they go?" George asked.

"Well no, the protocol is a little different this time," Mr Duffy said. "Mr Prowse will, of course, be in correspondence with Mr Taylor and he will be going down there to check for himself this time. He doesn't trust the way the system was in place, not because he has any worries about Alison and Tom, he just wants to make sure they are being looked after and happy and getting everything they need. As you know, he has seen them here, without their knowledge and he was around when they came back from Brighton. Even though we did everything right last time, we were rather hoodwinked, weren't we? We can't take that chance again, especially as it's the same children, so there are extra measures in place. If it goes well and he's happy and Mr Dunn is happy, then there shouldn't be any problems," Mr Duffy said.

"Oh, OK," Sandra said.

"Oh, don't worry, you two will be going down as well at different times, just to check up," Mr Duffy assured her. "I told you, we aren't taking any chances."

Sandra and George had huge smiles on their faces.

"So, who's going to break the news to the children and the Lintons?" Sandra asked.

"I'll notify Betty and Bruce, but you two can tell the children once they get back from school, if you like? I'm setting up the meeting for Friday next week if you can both attend?"

"Of course!" Sandra and George said in unison.

***

"Mrs Linton? Hello, it's Mr Duffy from Craven House. It's about the foster placement for Alison and Tom. I'm thrilled to tell you it's all been approved. Is it possible for you and Mr Linton to attend a meeting here next Friday at 12.00? I know you have a long way to come, but it would mean that once all of the paperwork is signed and the children come back from school, they can go with you, if that's OK with you?" Mr Duffy said.

Bet's heart was racing.

"Yes, of course, that's OK with us, Mr Duffy. Yes, we'll be able to attend next Friday, and thank you so much! Yes, see you next Friday," Betty replied.

She put down the receiver and Bruce looked at her.

"Well?" he asked.

Bet paused for dramatic effect.

"It's a yes, Bruce! We have the children! We can get them next Friday after we have had a meeting to sign all of the paperwork! Bruce, we got them, we got them!" Bet was crying and jumping for joy. Bruce picked her up and spun her around.

Bet suddenly stopped.

"Bruce, is the top room going to be done on time? I said it would be decorated and then we could sort it out when they come down," Bet asked.

"Of course, it will! I will stay up day and night until it's finished, love. Just think, they will be with us next weekend, what will we do?" asked Bruce.

"What do you mean, Bruce?"

"Well, we can take them out shopping, if you want? What are we going to do about a school for both of them?" he asked with panic in his voice.

"Bruce, take a deep breath!" Bet laughed. "When they get here, we can ask them what they want to do and as it's the beginning of the school term, we will wait and see and take it a step at a time," Bet replied.

"But Bet, they need to go to school," Bruce said.

"Yes, I know that, but they are not going to go to any school just to get them a place. We'll talk to them and see where they want to go," Bet told him.

"Yes, you're right. I'm just a bit excited and terrified, I suppose," Bruce said.

"I know, love, but it will be fine. Oh, I just want to pop along to Rose and tell her," Bet said.

"Go on, I know you've been dying to tell her when it happened," Bruce laughed.

Bet had already left the house and hadn't heard him.

"Rose! Rose, Henry!" Bet called out.

"Just coming, Bet!" Rose said, "are you OK?"

"I'm more than OK, Rose!" Bet was smiling through tears.

Henry had just come into the room.

"Rose, Henry…we got them!" Bet screamed.

Rose and Henry looked at each other rather puzzled. Then the penny dropped.

"You got Alison and Tom?" Rose yelled.

"Yes, we just had the call. We have to go down next Friday lunchtime for the meeting then we get the kids once they finish school! Oh, Rose I can't believe it, I really can't!" Bet said.

"I am so pleased for both of you!" Rose laughed.

Bruce followed his wife in. Henry got up and shook him by the hand.

"I am so pleased for you, mate. At last you got what you wanted, and those children are great kids!" Henry added.

Rose and Bet hugged. They were crying now; it was just so wonderful. When they pulled away Henry went to the bar.

"This calls for a celebration!" He said.

"Oh, can we do it later please, Henry? I have tons to do now, what if we pop in this evening? Do you have anyone here?" Bet asked.

"No, not at the moment. Come back at 8pm we can have a celebratory dinner and a drink, then we will leave you alone to get everything ready for next week?" Rose said.

"Great, we must get on, see you later," Bet hugged Rose again.

They both left and Henry and Rose smiled at each other, they knew how much this meant to both of them and the kids too.

***

"Hello, you two, can I have a minute?" Sandra asked.

"Yes, Sandra, nothing wrong, is there?" Alison said.

Sandra grabbed hold of George and they all went up to Alison's bedroom.

Alison and Tom sat on the bed and Sandra and George pulled up the two chairs.

"Is there anything wrong, Sandra?" Alison asked.

"No, everything is fine, but we do have some good news for you both," Sandra said with a smile on her face.

Alison and Tom looked puzzled.

"We have had a call from Mr Prowse today, and the foster placement application has been accepted, which means you and Tom will be going to live with Betty and Bruce in Margate," Sandra said.

"Yes!" Alison and Tom said at the same time.

They were jumping all around the room and were so excited and happy. Alison stopped jumping for a second.

"But Sandra, when do we go?" She asked.

"Next Friday, Sweetheart, is that ok?"

"Yes, that's fine. It means we can say a proper goodbye to everyone, not like last time. It was very quick last time," Alison and Tom nodded in agreement.

401

"So, do we leave school next week then? And what about a new school?" Alison asked.

"Well, once Betty and Bruce come and have a meeting with us first, we can ask that for you, as it's coming to the end of October, there isn't much time left of school until Christmas, so we will see what we or they can do for you," Sandra replied.

"Are you pleased?" George asked.

"Silly question, George," Tom said, "of course, we're pleased! We're over the moon." He giggled.

"So, what happens now?" Alison asked.

"Well, we carry on as normal; well as normal as you can. Then we start preparing for you to move. We can have a proper leaving party for you as well. We need to talk to your schools again, but we can do that, you don't have to worry," Sandra said.

"So, get into your comfy clothes and we can do what we normally do in the week; chill out before dinner, or do you want to go and tell Freddie and Charlie?" George said.

"I think that would be good, then we can tell everyone at dinner, is that OK?" Tom asked.

"Yes, I think that would be great, it also gets everyone use to the idea," Sandra replied.

"And about this party, Sandra, George?" Tom said.

"We will sort it all out, don't worry, Tom," George laughed, ruffling Tom's hair up on their way out.

Tom and Alison went along to tell Freddie and Charlie.

At dinner all of the children were told about Alison and Tom's news and everyone agreed a party would be a good way for them to send them on their way to Margate.

"And just think," Freddie said, "we will still see you in the summer when we go on holiday!"

"Oh, yes, I forgot about that. You'll still see Alison and Tom again every year!" Sandra said.

***

The following week and a half went very quickly. Alison had done well at school and she was able to take her report with her. Her new school would only have to contact them to send any information they needed about her. Tom's school said the same. They hoped it worked out for them both this time.

They had the party on the Thursday before they were due to leave. They had packed up their stuff the afternoon, before and all the kids came home to help them. They really wanted to make sure that both of them were OK. They were, but they were glad the others were so caring about them.

Most of the children there knew what had happened before. A few new children had come to Craven House, who didn't know about Alison and Tom's earlier experience of foster care, but they all wanted to make sure they would be all right.

They all got ready for the party. Sandra said that she would put their party clothes in their overnight bags, so they could be washed when they got to Margate.

All of the children had a good time at the party. Tom was in deep conversation with Freddie and Charlie. Alison was talking to some of the older girls, who were just a little younger than her.

The staff had a surprise for Alison. They asked Tom and Alison to both close their eyes. Someone put their hands over Alison's eyes. She didn't recognise them, but when she opened them and turned around, it was Jo. They both hugged one another, then Tom, Freddie and Charlie all joined in.

"I am going to miss you two, you know that, don't you?" Jo said.

"Of, course, and we will miss you too, all of you! You have been such a happy family, and as Sandra said, at least we will all see you every year!" Alison said.

"Come on you lot, it's supposed to be a party, not a sad occasion," Sandra said. She also had tears in her eyes; this was going to be a sad time for all of them. Alison and Tom had been there six years, and this was going to be a big change for them.

"Come on, put some music on, let's have a dance!" George said, dancing without any music. Everyone fell about laughing.

"I've missed you lot!" Jo said.

"You've only been gone for a little while!" George said.

"You know what I mean!" jo laughed.

403

Someone put on some disco music and everyone started to dance. As it was a school night, the party couldn't end too late and they wanted to give Alison and Tom their presents.

"Presents?" Tom said, "but you got us presents last time, our St Christopher's for travelling."

"Yes, but we wanted to get you something else," Sandra said, "we are allowed, you know," she smiled.

They sat the children down and Sandra disappeared then reappeared with two huge boxes: one for each of them.

Tom looked at Alison and Alison looked at Tom. Tom opened his box first, there were three presents in his. He pulled them all out and moved the box out of the way. Alison copied. One of two of their gifts looked the same. They both picked up the bigger of the gifts first.

Tom had a big, mustard-coloured truck. Alison opened her bigger present. It was a bottle of Charlie perfume.

"Ooo!" The other girls said. It was a massive bottle.

They opened the one that looked the same. It was a Parker pen and pencil set.

"That's for when you write us postcards. Don't worry, we've put the address to Craven House inside your bags, and the phone number," Sandra said.

Then it was the smaller boxes.

They opened them at the same time.

"Oh!" Tom and Alison said.

"What? What did you get?" Jo asked.

Alison showed her. It was a gold necklace with the letter 'A' on it. Jo looked at Tom's one. He had a gold necklace with a tiny gold car on it, he was stunned.

"I know you may not want to wear them yet, but we want you to remember us, when you do wear them," Sandra said.

Everyone was filling up. They knew this would be the last time they would see them both at the home.

"Thank you everyone for our lovely presents, they are beautiful!" Alison said. Tom nodded.

"Come on, everyone, we will see them in Margate in the summer," Sandra said. But they were sad, but happy too. This was going to be a special time for the children.

Everyone came around the two of them and hugged them.

Sandra looked at the clock.

"Come on you lot, it's time for bed," she said. "Roger, can you drop Jo over to Benson House, please?"

"Yes, OK. Jo, are you ready?" Roger asked.

"I will be in a minute."

She went over to Tom and Alison gave them a final hug.

"I'll see you soon, you two take care, OK?" she said to them, giving them both a kiss on the cheek.

Jo left with Roger and everyone went upstairs to bed. Sandra and George helped them up with their new gifts. They took their gifts up to their bedrooms and George and Sandra put them in their overnight bags.

The best thing about leaving this room for Alison was it was just for her, as Jo had already gone, and it felt far too empty just for her on her own. She got undressed and into her night things. George helped Tom put his stuff away, and then he got ready for bed. Tomorrow was going to be a big day for all of them, but this time they hoped there would be a better outcome.

Once they were all in bed, George turned off the light, said his goodnights and made his way along the corridor, checking on all the other boys, to make sure they were all in bed.

George went along to the staff room. He was looking for Sandra who had just sat down.

"Tired?" He asked.

"Yes, a little, but we have a lot on tomorrow, so we should head off to bed," Sandra said.

She said goodnight to everyone, then made her way to her bedroom. The staff stayed overnight on a rota and Sandra wanted to stay for this week. Even though she should have gone home a few hours ago, she wanted to make sure this all went swimmingly for the children and the Lintons and everyone involved at Craven House.

She got into bed and closed her eyes, next thing she knew someone was knocking on her door.

"Go back to bed! It's still late!" Sandra called out.

"No, it's not, Sand! It's already morning, and we have to get up!" George laughed.

"Oh, sorry George, I thought you were one of the kids. I thought I had just gone to bed!"

"No worries, I did the same thing! As soon as my head hit the pillow, I was gone. See you in a few minutes downstairs, it's nearly breakfast time," George said.

"Nearly breakfast? Gosh, I did sleep in!" She said as she jumped out of bed and into the shower.

She darted in, then out again and got dressed. She had a big meeting at 12.00 that she just needed to get the paperwork in order. She had already prepared that the day before, but she wanted to check herself.

The kids all came down for breakfast, like a herd of elephants. Everyone was excited on a Friday. It was the last day of the week for school and once homework was done, they only had their jobs to do on a Saturday. It was more relaxed at the weekend.

Alison and Tom came in with a crowd of the others. Everyone wanted to sit next to them, which was impossible, as there wasn't enough room. They sat as close as they could. This was their last meal with everyone together.

When breakfast was over, they all ran back upstairs and brushed their teeth. Sandra went up with Alison and George went with Tom to check they had packed absolutely everything. All their cupboards and drawers were empty, and their dirty laundry was all kept together. Sandra picked up Alison's suitcase and bags and they left the room.

Alison took one final look around the room. This would be the last time she would be in it. She was sad to go. She and Jo had some great times in this room, but Jo was gone now. They were both starting new chapters in their lives. Alison then closed the door and walked behind Sandra.

George had put the suitcases and bags down in the staffroom for the time being, until the kids had gone off to school. The children were all lined up downstairs in reception waiting to go off to school. Some of the bigger children went together without a member of staff, but Tom still had Roger and George go with them.

Alison went with the other girls to school and Sandra went along with the younger ones like she did when she and Tom had come to Craven House. That was a long time ago now and she and Tom were going for their chance of a happy life with Betty and Bruce.

Once Sandra and George got back from the school run, Sandra gathered her paperwork to check it was all in order, and that there were copies for everyone in the meeting. She asked Mr Duffy, while she was photocopying, did he need anything copied for the meeting.

"No, thank you, Sandra, Jane did it for me earlier, but thank you for asking, see you just before 12.00, is that OK?" He asked.

"Yes, of course, George too?" She asked.

"George too," Mr Duffy said.

***

It was as if Sandra had blinked. It was nearly twelve o'clock. The morning had flown by and the Lintons would be here any minute. She and George knocked on Mr Duffy's door.

"Thank you both for coming in a bit early, sadly Mr Dunn can't make this meeting today, but he wanted us to all be here and Mr Prowse is just in the kitchen, so as soon as the Lintons get here, we can get started."

Mr Prowse came in to the office and shook both Sandra and George's hands.

"This is becoming quite a regular thing now, isn't it?" He laughed.

Sandra had all of her paperwork with her, and once Betty and Bruce arrived, she would give them a copy of everything. Jane, the receptionist, knocked Mr Duffy's office door and announced that Mr and Mrs Linton were waiting in reception.

Mr Duffy stood up and shook both of their hands and then offered them a seat. They then shook everyone else's hands too and then took their seats.

"So, shall we get started?" Mr Duffy asked.

"Yes, that's fine with us," Bet said.

Once everyone was introduced, Mr Duffy's secretary began taking the minutes.

Sandra handed them both her paperwork which they both took and mouthed "Thank you."

"Now, we are here today to finalise the paperwork on this foster placement, and as you already know the ropes about this Mr and Mrs Linton, is there anything you would like to ask or say?" Mr Duffy asked.

"Well, we know this is a six-month placement, but what if we would like to adopt Alison and Tom? Do we have to have an extension, or does it go automatically?" Bruce asked.

"Err no, Mr Linton," Mr Duffy said.

"Please call me Bruce."

"OK then, Bruce, what will happen is that, as you say, it's a six-month placement, but if you would like to adopt the children and they agree, and it's near the six-month period, we would have to go for an extension and put the paperwork in place. It all depends on how quick it goes through. But I can't see that being a problem. We can extend as often as needed until the adoption goes through," Mr Duffy said, smiling.

Bet looked like a weight had been lifted from her.

"Oh, that's good, Mr Duffy. We were worried that if we and the children want to go down that road, they would have to come back until it was sorted out," Bet said.

"No, once they are with you and if all want to go through the adoption process, we will obviously support you all until it goes through and afterwards," Mr Duffy replied.

"So, what happens once the children come home with us today? Will we see you again or just once a year when you come down to Margate, because your welcome to come down whenever you want, you will always be welcome," Bet said, looking at Sandra and George.

"Well, Mr Prowse will be down to see you sometime soon," Mr Duffy said.

"Yes, I will be coming down, just to check on their and your progress really. It's just with what happened before. Now, I'm not saying you're going to be like that with them, it's just we need to do everything we can to make sure this is a happy foster placement. I know you have done lots of fostering Mrs Linton, Mr Linton, but really this is just for our paperwork and procedure and nothing whatsoever to you both personally. I hope you can understand that?" Mr Prowse said.

"Of course, we can, Mr Prowse. Everything has to be done properly," Bruce said, looking at Bet.

She knew and understood that this was protocol to these situations.

"Sandra has handed you some paperwork to read at your leisure. I think that Sandra and George may have some questions for you?" Mr Duffy said, looking in Sandra's direction.

"Yes, Betty, Bruce, have you sorted out a school for the children to attend to yet?" Sandra asked.

"No, not yet, apart from getting everything ready for them to come. We do have all of the information of all of the local schools, but we wanted the children to choose for themselves. We would like them to be included in all of the decisions about them. Is that OK?" Bet asked.

"Yes, of course. You have to do what suits you best, as long as they get it sorted and they don't think they are on a permanent holiday, especially as you live at the seaside," Mr Duffy said.

"No, it's nothing like that, Mr Duffy, I can assure you. It's just with what happened last time with them, we want to take it slowly and make proper decisions rather than rush them and make a terrible mistake," Bruce said.

These two definitely had their heads screwed on.

"Now, we know from when they are at Rose and Henry's, they have good appetites, would you ever punish them with no dinner if they were naughty and send them straight up to bed?" Sandra asked. It was something she always asked about the children and their food.

Bet and Bruce looked shocked.

"No, we wouldn't ever do that! We would never, under any circumstances, not feed them," Bruce said.

Bruce knew they were only doing their job, but he thought that was unfair, then he realised what had happened to them before.

"I'm sorry, I know you have to ask these questions and I didn't mean anything by what I said, I don't agree in not giving children food. You have children, they need food, clothes, warmth, a roof over their heads, clothes on their back and shoes on their feet. You're doing them a disservice if you don't supply these things for them and that's just the basics," Bruce added.

"Bruce, it's OK. I'm not having a go at you, it's what I have to ask and I know both you and Bet love these children with a passion and won't let any harm come to them. And you have already answered my next question, so everything is fine. Please don't take it personally. It's just procedure," Sandra said.

Bruce smiled. They hadn't expected all of these questions, but he understood they had to be asked. He hoped he hadn't made things worse and they would change their minds about them having Alison and Tom.

"Mr Linton, I am so impressed with you and your wife and I think that all of us are delighted that you're having the children in your lives and living with you. I think we should be so happy that this placement is a positive one. Now, we have the paperwork for you to sign, if you would like a few minutes to read it through first, we can get a hot drink and come back if you want?" asked Mr Prowse.

"I am really sorry, I didn't mean to upset anyone, or sound rather brash. It's just we know they had a hard time and we want to make them a better life. Not that I am saying they aren't happy here, because we both know that they are. But we have to be realistic; they can't stay here forever, can they?" Bruce said.

"No, they can't, but they can have a happy life with you both. We'll be back in a few minutes. Tea or coffee?" Mr Duffy asked.

"Tea, please." They said together.

The rest of the group left the room, so they could read the paperwork.

"Oh Bruce, I thought you blew it then! I thought they were going to change their minds, why did you get so annoyed?" Bet asked.

"Because I thought they were looking down their noses to us, Bet. We're good people and want to make a life for Alison and Tom, these pen pushers think they know everything about people," Bruce said.

"You're wrong, Bruce, you have to remember what these two have been through not that long ago and because of that, they have to go through everything with a fine-tooth comb. That's all, you silly sod," Bet said.

"Now come on, we have to read this paperwork," she added.

***

"Oh, my goodness, did you see his face when you asked about sending them to bed without dinner, Sandra?" Mr Prowse said.

"Well, I guessed they would they do that, Mr Prowse. It's standard questions that I have to ask. The thing is, the Coopers said they wouldn't do it, and they were all smiles and happy when they replied. Bruce got annoyed because he's a genuine man. It's a natural reaction," Sandra said.

Once they had finished their talk, they then took their hot drinks back up to the office. They all took their seats again, and Bet cleared her throat.

"May I ask you something?" She asked.

"Yes of course, Betty," Mr Duffy said.

"It says here how much we will get for the children per week each and that's fine, but it doesn't say how much pocket money we can give them?" She asked.

Sandra and George burst out laughing, then composed themselves. Betty and Bruce looked astonished.

"Did I ask something I shouldn't't?" Bet asked.

410

"Betty, no you haven't, it's just we've never had anyone ask about how much pocket money to give the children. They normally take the money and we don't hear any more about it," George said.

"I'm sorry, we didn't mean to laugh," Sandra said.

"Well, if it's OK, we wanted to give them twenty pounds a week each?" Bet said.

Sandra and George's mouths fell open.

"Ten to spend and ten to save. We want them to open a savings account each, that only they can have for whatever they want. We thought it would help them with understanding money and how it has to be worked for, but also that savings would be a good thing for them as well, so they had something behind them if they didn't want to spend it on anything in particular," Bruce said.

Sandra burst into tears, she had never heard of a family wanting to help the children so much, George handed her a tissue and Bet looked a little puzzled, then went over to her.

"We just want to do our best by those children," she said.

"Can I come and live with you then?" Sandra laughed.

She smiled at Bet and then Bruce.

"Do you know what, I don't think we could have asked for better foster parents and prospective adoptive parents for those two. Thank you, both of you for coming into our and their lives," Sandra said, hugging Bet.

"Now, have you read everything, because if you have and you agree with it all, you both have to just sign the paperwork, as mentioned in the paperwork. The monies owed to you each week will be paid directly into your bank," Mr Duffy said.

"The bank? I thought we would have cheques?" Bruce said.

"We did, but it all got changed a little while ago," Mr Duffy said.

Betty and Bruce signed the paperwork and Bet burst into tears.

"They are ours now, Bruce! They can live with us full time! I still can't believe it. I can't wait until they come back from school!" Bet said, wiping the tears from her eyes.

Sandra went over and hugged the couple.

"What are you going to do now?" George asked.

"Wow! It's nearly two. Bruce, can we go into town and get something to eat? What time should we be back?" Bet asked.

411

"Well, the children usually get back about three, but as it's their last day, it may be a little later. Have something to eat and then come back when you're ready. The children may or may not be here, but you're welcome to wait," Sandra said.

Mr Duffy nodded. "Go and have some food and we will see you in a little while. By then, we will have your paperwork ready in a folder for you to take with you."

They left Mr Duffy's office and headed out of the building.

***

Bruce and Betty headed off to the Wimpy. They needed something to eat; they hadn't had anything since breakfast.

It was good to finally sit down and take in everything that had just happened. They couldn't wait for the children to come in from school. If they wanted to stay on for a little while and see their friends, that would be OK; they had no rush to get home.

They ordered their food from the waitress.

"You know what, Bet, I am getting used to eating in Wimpy, the food is lovely!" Bruce said.

"Yes, it is!" Bet laughed.

Their food arrived and they started to tuck in. It was nice to be able to reflect on the day's events.

***

Alison and Tom had returned from school and Betty and Bruce still hadn't returned to Craven House.

"Is everything OK, Sandra? I mean did Betty and Bruce sign the paperwork? Do they still want us to live with them?" Alison asked.

"Of course, they do! All the paperwork is signed. The meeting went on longer than expected and they hadn't eaten so they were going into town. They should be back soon," Sandra smiled.

"All of your stuff is still in the staffroom. Do you want to both go down to the dining room for a snack?"

Tom never said no to food.

"Come on, Al. They will be enjoying the last of their free time together, as they have us now!" He laughed.

With that Betty and Bruce came walking through the door.

"Hello, you two! Did you have a good day at school?" Bet asked.

"Yeah, it was OK. I said goodbye to my friends, and I got another truck, look Bruce, it's a big green one," Tom showed Bruce.

"Wow Tom! That's fantastic! So, what are you doing now?" Bruce asked.

"Well we were going to have a snack, but did you want to go straight away?" Tom said, a little sad that he would have to go in a few minutes, as Freddie and Charlie had just come into the dining room and he wanted to show them his new truck.

"We don't have to rush off. If you want to see your friends for a while, that's OK with me. OK with you, Bet?" Bruce asked.

"Yes, of course, that's fine, as long as we get off before it gets dark, we can stay a while," Bet said.

They couldn't believe it; the Coopers couldn't wait to get them out the door but Bet and Bruce were happy for them to be with their friends for a bit longer. Sandra suggested that they all go into the living room. They could bring some tea and the children could play for a little while.

They ended up staying for a couple of hours.

"Bet, I think we should go before they all have their dinner," Bruce said.

Bet took the tray down towards the dining room but bumped into Sandra before she got there.

"Sandra, I think we should go before you all have your dinner, we were going to get them fish and chips on the way home anyway, is that OK?" Bet asked.

"Bet, that's fine! You have to do what is best for you guys. It's been lovely that you haven't just whipped them off without a bye or leave. I tell you what, I'll round up the rest of the children and they can say goodbye to them, is that OK?" Sandra said.

"That would be great, thank you, Sandra."

Bet returned to the living room and told Bruce what Sandra was going to do.

"Alison, Tom, we are going to have to make a move soon," Bet said.

"Yes of course, thank you for letting us stay to be with our friends for the last time at Craven House," Tom said.

"Yes, you'll see them next summer when they come down to Margate for their week's holiday," Bet replied.

"Bruce, would you like a hand putting their luggage in the car?" George asked.

"Oh, would you, George? That would be great, thank you," Bruce said.

Bruce followed George into the staffroom where their stuff was. He took the keys out from his pocket and went down to the car. When he returned to the living room it was full of kids saying goodbye and hugging Alison and Tom. Bruce couldn't even see Bet, under the sea of children and staff.

When everyone had hugged and said goodbye, Bet, Alison and Tom made their way to the doors entrance.

"Thank you all of you for everything you've done for Alison and Tom and for us, we will never forget it," Bet said, in tears. Sandra and George followed them down to the car, while all of the children were at the windows waving and cheering.

Alison and Tom gave Sandra and George big hugs then Bruce opened the door to the car. They got in the back. Bet hugged Sandra and George and Bruce shook George's hand and gave Sandra a big hug.

"Now I know we will see you in the summer next year, but if you ever want to come and see us all you're more than welcome; our door is always open to you. Even if you just turn up, it will be fine and if you want, we can get the children to call you once in a while, say every couple of weeks, just so you know that they're fine. We don't mind. They have always looked at Craven House as their home and that's never going to change in my book. If you want to call to talk to them, you can," Bruce said.

Bet and Bruce got into the car and Bruce turned on the engine. Bet waved frantically, as did Alison and Tom, until they were out of sight. That feeling that Sandra had last time hadn't come. She was awash with emotions, feeling happy and sad all at the same time, but this time, she knew it was the right thing to do.

***

"So, who's for fish and chips on the way home, because by the time we get home, we will be too tired to eat it," Bruce said.

He stopped off before he got onto the motorway and got everyone fish and chips.

"Did anyone need the toilet before we drive off again?" Bet asked.

"Yes please!" Tom said. "I don't think I can hold on until we get home."

Bet smiled to herself, he's calling it home already. She was so chuffed and knew they had done the right thing, for them all.

They all got back into the car and Bruce threw the rubbish in the nearest bin he could find.

"Everyone happy now they have full tummies?" He laughed.

It didn't take too long for them to get back. They'd missed rush-hour, so there wasn't much traffic on the roads. They got in at eight o'clock and Bruce emptied the boot of their luggage and took it upstairs to their bedrooms.

"Do you want to go and change, and we can unpack your things in the morning?" Bet asked.

"Bet, our things are in the cases and bags," Alison said.

"Yes, I know, Honey, but I got you some new things yesterday. I knew you would be too tired to do it, so there's some night things and an outfit each for tomorrow, if that's OK? Then we can sort out your stuff tomorrow, we can put the TV on and watch a bit before you go to bed if you want?" Bet suggested.

"That sounds lovely, thank you, Bet," Alison smiled.

"Your new things are on your beds. Put your new outfits on your chairs and we can sort it all out in the morning," Bet added.

"OK," Alison said as she yawned.

"Or do you want to go straight to bed?" Bet could see how tired she was all of a sudden. Tom had that same look.

They both went upstairs with Bet and Bruce had just come down and gone to lock the car up.

When he came back in, there wasn't anyone downstairs. Bet was coming down the stairs again on her own.

"Aren't they coming down?" Bruce asked.

"They're shattered. See them. As soon as their heads hit the pillow, they were both fast asleep," she said.

"Maybe we should go as well. I'm feeling rather tired, with that fish and chips and that drive home," Bruce said.

He went upstairs to look in on them both. Just as Bet had said they were both fast asleep. They'd a busy and hectic day. They had the rest of their lives to decide for their futures. Bruce had just come out of their rooms when he noticed Bet, he made his way back down to their bedroom. Bet was already in her night things.

"It's contagious this travelling, Bruce!" Bet said.

Bruce changed into his pyjamas and got into bed. The couple was asleep within minutes.

**

The following morning, Alison woke up and even though it was nearly late October it was still very bright. She looked around the room. She had forgotten where she was for a moment, then she blinked, once, twice…yep they were at Bet and Bruce's.

She looked at her new alarm clock on her bedside cabinet: 8 o'clock.

She hadn't realised she was in her bed in her new pyjamas, and it took a few minutes for it all to sink in.

There was a knock at the door, it was Bet.

"Good morning! I just brought you a cup of tea," Bet said.

"Oh, yes, thank you, Bet."

Alison sat up in bed and then Bet handed her the mug of tea.

"I have one for Tom, be back in a jiffy," Bet said.

When Bet returned, they both looked at the suitcase sitting under the window.

"I tell you what, let's have some breakfast and then we can tackle your things, that OK?" Bet said.

"Yes, that would be great," Alison replied.

"So, what would you like to do today once we have your belongings unpacked and put away? You can have a shower or bath and if you want, we can go into town and see if there's anything you both need, what do you think?" Bet asked.

"Yes, that would be lovely. Do you need a hand with anything Bet?" Alison asked.

"No, not that I can think of. We can have a sit down later on and decide on what little jobs you can both do. Nothing much, but if we all pull together it won't take so long as if left to one person," Bet said.

Alison drunk the last of her tea, put her mug down on the bedside cabinet and then threw the quilt off her. She pulled the covers back over, tidied the bed, grabbed the mug, and followed Bet out of the room.

Bet knocked on Tom's door to see if he had finished his tea. He had and was also just getting out of bed.

"Morning, Tom," Alison said.

"Morning, Al," Tom replied.

They both went downstairs.

"Tom, once we have had some breakfast, we can unpack your clothes and see if there's anything you need and we can pop into town and buy it, is that alright?" Bet asked.

"Err yes, that would be great. When we've unpacked, can I sort out my trucks and cars?" Tom asked.

"Will that take a long time, or do you want to wait until we come back from town, I just don't want us to be out all day, if that's OK?" Bet asked.

"Yes, that would be fine. Bruce, would you like to help me with my trucks and cars later on then?" Tom asked, hoping he would say yes.

"Of course, trucks and cars are very important, but as Bet said, we wanted to pop into town and see what we can get for you," Bruce said.

"Bet, can I ask you something?" Alison suddenly asked.

"Yes, Honey."

"Do we have a school to go to next week?"

"Well, we didn't want to rush you both. You'll have to go to school, but we wanted to discuss it with you first. We have the school prospectus with lots of information on them," Bet said. She could see both of the kids looked confused.

"Once we've all had a look, we can make enquiries, and see if they have a place for you and see when you can start. Then we can sort out your uniform and shoes. Is that all right?" Bet asked.

Both of the children were astonished. The Coopers couldn't wait to get them into school. Bet and Bruce wanted them to take it slowly and choose the school they wanted, not push them into the first school they came across.

Alison went over to Bet, and Tom went over to Bruce and they both hugged them.

"Thank you, both," Alison said.

"What for?" Bruce asked.

"Because you're not rushing us into school just to get rid of us. It means such a lot; we can't thank you enough," Alison smiled.

"We want you to settle in before anything else. We both want to make sure you're going to be happy living here and we wouldn't think for a second of shoving you somewhere because it was convenient for us," Bet said. "So, once we have sorted out your clothes, see if there's anything that no longer fits or you want some new shoes, just because you can, that's what we will get. Oh, before we forget, there's something else," Bet said.

"What's that?" Alison asked.

"Well, we want to start giving you pocket money, but we would like you to put some of it away in a bank account which we will open on Monday, if that's alright with you both?" Bet asked.

"Why wouldn't it be alright with us?" Tom said.

"We wanted to give you both twenty pounds each week, but for you to put ten pounds away. It will get you used to saving money and then you can put that towards something when you're a little older, like a car or something?" Bruce said.

Both of the kids eyes were like saucers; they couldn't believe what they were hearing. Again, they both went to the other one and hugged them.

"Right, we're not going to get a lot done if we keep hugging, we love it, of course, but let's get your unpacking done and Bruce can make breakfast. What do you want to eat?" Bet asked.

"Boiled eggs and soldiers, please?" Tom said.

Alison nodded also.

Bet went back upstairs with both of them to start unpacking their things. Alison opened up her wardrobe and her chest of drawers.

"Oh, I forgot, our things from yesterday and our party on Thursday, Bet! Are they in our overnight bags?" Alison asked.

"Oh, that's all right. Just put it in your laundry bin and I'll wash it later," Bet said.

When they were finished, Bet put the suitcase in the cupboard in the hallway.

"Shall we go and see if Tom wants a hand?" Bet asked.

When they got into Tom's room, he had made a start on his underwear and socks, so it was just his hanging up stuff left to be done.

"Well done, Tom! You have put away a lot already!" Bet said.

Alison took away Tom's suitcase and put it in the hallway cupboard.

Bruce shouted up that breakfast was ready.

"Perfect timing, as always!" Bet laughed.

Once breakfast was finished, Bruce and Bet cleared away and told Alison and Tom to go up and get ready. They were both down a few minutes later and both had their duffle coats with them.

"Ready?" Bruce asked.

Bruce locked up behind them and then opened the car so they could all get in. Once they were in, it didn't take long to go to town. They didn't want the children to walk, so they parked up paid the parking meter and had a wander around the town.

They went into various shops. There were some new boutiques that Bet thought Alison would like to look around in. They were in there for a little while and came out with a couple of carrier bags.

Alison got a couple of tops and a pair of trousers. She thanked Bet and then they went along to the next shop, which was Marks and Spencer. Bet wanted to get Tom some trousers and some tops, but if he saw something else, he liked then he could get it. They got him four tops that he liked and two pairs of trousers and some new underwear.

Alison also got some lovely underwear and some thick tights for the winter months.

"If you like them, then we can get you some more, just want to see really what they wash up like," Bet said.

They went along to Curtess Shoes to see what they had. They still had some wear in their school shoes, but Bet said they would return once they have their schools sorted out. But she wanted to make sure they had slippers and a pair of shoes each, even if they were for when they go out casually.

"But Bet, you got us some comfortable shoes yesterday for us with the new outfit that we didn't get a chance to wear yet!" Alison said.

"I know, but a lady can never have too many shoes, Alison," Bet laughed.

They only seemed to have black shoes for school, so Bet looked around a bit.

"No, you don't want them, they look like old ladies' shoes, we want something for a younger person," Bet said.

"That's more like it!" she said when she found some canvas shoes in a navy blue, with a canvas wedge heel.

"Can we try a pair of those in a size three please?" Bet asked the sales assistant.

Alison tried them on, and they fit like a dream.

"Do you want them, Sweetheart?" Bet asked.

"Yes please, they are so comfortable, Bet!" Alison said.

"Are they?"

"You should try a pair!" Alison said.

"Are you sure, you don't mind me having the same as you?" Bet said.

"Of course not, they would look lovely on you!" Alison said.

"In that case, could you bring me a size five please then, lovie?" Bet asked the assistant.

The assistant disappeared again and came back with the shoes.

"I'm afraid they only have them in red or black in a five, they have been very popular." The assistant said when she returned.

"Bring them both and I will see what looks better on, if that's OK?" Bet said.

Bet tried them on, but she decided on the black.

"You both look lovely in them," Bruce said.

"Is there anything else?" The assistant asked.

"Yes, we have to find something for Tom," Bet said as she looked around the boys' section.

She spotted some other flat canvas shoes.

"Tom, do you like these? They look like sailors shoes, blue and white stripes, do you think you would wear them?" Bet asked.

"Yeah, they look alright," Tom said.

"Now don't forget, this is just a pair of fun shoes, we will get you boots and that for the winter and definitely school shoes. Can we have these in a size twelve please?" Bet asked.

Shoe shopping done, Bet and Bruce thanked the assistant for her help, and they left the shop.

"Now your coats are lovely, but would you like to get new ones today, or do you want to wait a little while?" Bet asked.

"Whatever you think, Bet. We don't want you to think we're being greedy," Alison said.

"Now that is something I know isn't true. It's just it doesn't look like they will fit you both for much longer. Do you want to both go back into Marks and Spencer and we can see if we can get you the same coats?" Bet asked.

She was enjoying shopping with the kids and Bruce could see she was enjoying herself. They went back into Marks and Spencer and had a look at the coats.

Once Alison and Tom had chosen their coats, Bruce went to pay for them.

"Bet, is there anything else we need to get today?"

"No, I think that's if for now," Bet said.

"Well, I was going to say, what if we put this lot in the boot, we can go and have a bite to eat and a cup of tea; all of this shopping has given me a bit of an appetite and it's been two hours since we had a cuppa, I'm parched!" Bruce laughed.

"OK, that sounds like a good idea," Bet said.

The family decided to go to Molly's Tea Shop again.

They walked back to town.

Molly noticed them when they opened the door and gave them all a big smile.

"Hello again!" Molly welcomed them and showed them to a table. She returned with menus for everyone.

They all had a look at the menu and Bet asked Bruce what he wanted and then the children. "What if we have the set menu for sandwiches and then have a look at the sweet trolley?" Bruce suggested, winking at both Alison and Tom.

"Yes, that sounds like a good idea!" Tom winked back.

Molly left the table with their order and returned with their drinks. She then returned with the tiered plate of sandwiches for them, which they tucked into happily. Molly smiled over at the family. She could sense a completely different vibe and atmosphere with this family than when Alison and Tom were with the Coopers.

She never said anything about it, but Bet was right in what she had said about the Coopers. It was good to see the children happy and settled now.

When they had cleared their plates, she took them away and brought over clean plates and cutlery and then the sweet trolley. Bruce had a look. They had strawberry cheesecake, chocolate gateau, Rum baba's fresh cream slices, strawberry tarts with cream on top, chocolate eclairs, and chocolate choux buns, fresh cream doughnuts, and many more.

Bruce couldn't choose. It was between a chocolate choux bun or a strawberry tart. Bet chose a slice of strawberry cheesecake and Alison already chose a chocolate éclair and Tom wanted one too. Bruce finally decided on a chocolate choux bun. Molly served them up.

"Molly, could you tell me, do you do take away boxes?" Bruce asked.

"Yes, Sir, we certainly do!" Molly smiled.

"I just wanted to know because if we want to get some more to take home for tomorrow, as long as they are in the fridge," Bruce said.

They tucked into their sweets, and the look of satisfaction on all of their faces, they were definitely enjoying the cakes.

Once they had finished their cakes and then had the rest of their tea, Bruce went back over to the trolley and then over to the till.

"Could I order some cakes to take away with us, please?" Bruce asked.

"Yes, sir, what cakes would you like?" The waitress asked.

"Can I order four chocolate eclairs and four strawberry tarts please?"

"Certainly, Sir," the waitress said.

She returned a moment later with the cakes in the box. She closed it up and tied it with a golden ribbon. Bruce paid the bill and returned to the table.

"Ready then?" He asked.

They already had their coats on and were ready to go.

They all said goodbye to Molly and her staff and Bruce left a tip on their box on the counter.

"Bet, as it's coming up to Christmas, we should have a look and see what sort of treats they do and we can get for home, what do you think?" Bruce said.

"I think if we are not careful, Bruce, you will end up with a very big belly and a heart attack if you keep eating all of those cakes!" Bet laughed.

When they got home, Bruce emptied the boot and gave Alison and Tom their things and he took the rest inside for them. The children took their stuff upstairs and Bet went into the kitchen to put the kettle on and put the cakes in the fridge.

Bet then went upstairs to see if they needed help to put away their stuff.

"Next time we go out, we can get you both boots for the winter. It can get cold down here by the sea. We can get your school shoes and anything else you need on Saturday. Come down when you're done. I've just put the kettle on, and I feel a bit cold," Bet said.

"OK, Bet, see you in a few minutes," Alison said.

When Alison had finished, she went into Tom to see if he needed help. He couldn't put his new coat on the hanger in the wardrobe; it was too heavy.

"Tom, do you like your new things?" Alison asked.

"Yes, I do! They're great, aren't they! Bet and Bruce are so nice and kind and not at all like that other family," Tom said.

Neither of them could bring themselves to say the Coopers; it was always that other family. But they weren't worried about it anymore, they both knew they were going to be OK now.

"Come on Al, Bet's making tea!" Tom said.

They had both changed into their slippers, so they headed off back downstairs.

Bet and Bruce were already sitting down in the living room. When Alison and Tom had sat down, Bruce stood up.

"We said we were giving you some pocket money every week, what if we give it to you on a Saturday sometime before lunchtime? That way you can put it away in your room and you can give it to Bet so she can put it in the bank for you," Bruce said, four ten-pound notes out of his pocket.

"So, there's ten for you to spend, and ten to put away, is that OK?" Bet said.

Alison handed back her twenty pounds.

"Here Bruce, you can have this back," Alison said, returning the money to him.

Bet and Bruce looked at her, puzzled.

"You have spent plenty of money on us today, and we are grateful, but we don't want you to think we are greedy," she added.

"Alison, Tom, I am really chuffed that you recognise that we bought you stuff today, but that's stuff you would have bought anyway, so you keep this. It's your pocket money. It's for you to spend and save. If you put it away for now, then on Monday when we go to the bank and use ten pounds to open your accounts. OK?" Bruce smiled.

"Thank you, Bruce, and you too Bet, apart from Craven House and Rose and Henry, we haven't seen such kindness. Thank you for choosing me and Tom," Alison said.

Bet had welled up again.

"You two are the loveliest children we have ever met and yes we are so glad we chose you, both of you. You are part of our family now, and we will give you the happiest times we possibly can," Bet said. "Now let me make this tea before it goes cold."

"Oh, before we forget, Alison, Tom, Bruce finally decorated the top room. It looks lovely! When we get a minute, we'll take you up there. It already has a seagrass carpet and the walls are done, but would you like to help to choose some furniture for it?" Bet asked.

"Yes, please! Thank you for asking us," Tom said. "Bruce, after we have tea, would you like to help me sort out my trucks and cars?"

"That would be great, Tom," Bruce said.

The rest of the day was just as chilled as Bet and Bruce were, they had all had a good day. Bet had asked them if they could keep their rooms tidy and they would strip the beds and tidy and hoover on a Saturday and sort out the bathroom, but that would be it. Except for in the summer, it would be different, but they hadn't sorted that out yet, that would be when they worked for Rose and Henry throughout the summer holidays when the children's home were down for a week each.

Tom and Alison said they would help too, as they knew the kids from Craven House, but some from Benson House too.

They had a nice weekend with a lovely roast dinner on Sunday and they popped in to see Rose and Henry.

***

On Monday they went down to town and opened up a bank account for both children, and Bet kept their account books in a drawer for safe keeping.

They had decided on a school each: Deveraux Ladies for Alison, which was a very good secondary school, and Bolton Abbey Primary for Tom.

Bet and Bruce took them to town again once they had their place and the list of uniform needed.

Alison and Tom had a tour of their new schools and liked them very much. They also got new school shoes each and they popped into Molly's again. They were becoming quite regulars there and Molly always had a smile for them.

Molly had become quite friendly with Bet, and always popped in an extra cake or didn't charge them for the odd cake.

Mr Prowse had popped down for his visit as promised and was delighted that they had settled in so well. He went back to Craven House with a glowing report, telling the staff that the children had put on a little weight but looked good for it. It was all of the sea air that helped.

Sandra and George were really pleased as they hadn't really heard much from them, only once that first weekend. The children had called and Sandra and George were so pleased to hear from them.

They sounded so happy, like home from home.

They had settled in well, Bet and Bruce and were really happy and delighted that their dreams of a family had come true.

Chapter 22

"Morning, are you ready for your first day of school, Alison?" Bet asked as she handed her a cup of tea.

Bet always brought them both a cup of tea in bed in the morning, just to help wake them up. Then they would get up, have their breakfast, then get washed or showered if they had time.

Alison got up and made her way downstairs to breakfast with her empty cup.

"Morning Bruce, did you sleep well?" Alison asked.

"Yes, I did, Alison, did you?"

"Like a baby!" Alison replied.

"Are you all set for your first day at school today?" Bruce asked.

Tom then came down.

"Morning Tom, did you sleep well?" Bruce asked.

"Yes, I did Bruce, thank you," Tom said.

"Are you all set for your first day at school today?" Bruce asked.

"Yes, I am, and it's bonfire night on Saturday, so that will be fun," Tom said.

Once Tom and Alison had had their breakfast, they went upstairs to get ready for school. They got their new uniform the week before in town and Bet got them some school shoes each and some new underwear and socks. They came down the stairs in their new uniforms. Bet had her new camera out ready.

"Alison come over here. Stand by the wall and I'll take your photo, then Tom come over and I'll get one of both of you, then one of Tom on his own," Bet said.

"Yes, then we can take some of us altogether," Bruce said.

After the photographs, they picked up their school bags. Bruce was taking Tom to school on his first day. It wasn't as close as Alison's school.

"Now you two have a great day at your new school, do you have enough money on you?" Bet asked.

They both nodded. Tom followed Bruce to the car.

"Are you sure we can't take you some of the way, Alison?" Bruce asked.

"No, I'll be fine. We're getting to know Margate now, so it should be fine, thanks anyway, Bruce," Alison said.

When she left the house, she went left away from the seafront, to the top of the road then a right, straight down the bottom of that road, then a left and her school was about halfway down the road. She bent down to pull her socks up; one of them had fallen down. A young man in a hurry bumped into her.

"Sorry!" he apologised.

He was gone before Alison had a chance to reply or even say hello. Mind you, from what she did see, he looked very nice, she thought. He ran across the road, so he wasn't going to her school, but the one opposite: Harlequin Boys' School. She made a mental note of it then went through her school gates.

There were a couple of teachers at the main gate. Alison knew her way to reception, but she would have to be told where to go after that. She was in the second year of secondary school, so she would have at least three more years at school, unless she wanted to go onto college after that. She hadn't even thought about university. That was a long way off and at least ten years away.

Alison found her classroom. The door was already open. She saw the teacher who directed her to an empty seat.

"Hello, I'm Stacey." The ginger girl, sitting on her own, said.

"Hello, Stacey, I'm Alison," she replied.

"Nice to meet you, Alison," Stacey said.

Alison put her bag on the back of her seat. Her teacher, Miss Clarke began registration. She handed Alison a timetable and asked Stacey to help her fill it in. Stacey had already started just after the new school year, but she was sure she was going to catch up in all of her subjects.

The bell rang and it was her first lesson: double English on a Monday morning, great!

Once English was over it was break-time. The main gates were closed, but the girls stayed in the playground. There was tuck shop run by some other girls available at break-time. They grabbed a bag of crisps each and a drink and stood over by the main gate. Alison saw the young man who had bumped into her earlier that morning. He also noticed her and smiled. She blushed a bit and turned away.

He was lovely looking, he had dark wavy hair and dark brown eyes. Even though he was across the road, she could take in quite a lot of detail. He wore a grey uniform and a burgundy and grey tie. The uniform wasn't dissimilar to hers.

426

Break time was only for twenty minutes. Alison then had Maths and then science after that, followed by cooking. The lessons went really quickly. Alison knew it wouldn't take her long to catch up, she knew some of it already.

Before she knew it, the day was over. She came out of the gates and said goodbye to her new friends, who went the other direction.

As she made her way home, Alison heard footsteps behind her, and she quickly turned around. It was the boy who she saw this morning. He was walking behind her.

"Hey up!" He said.

Alison stopped and looked behind her.

"I'm sorry I didn't catch your name this morning?" He smiled.

"That's because I didn't throw it," Alison smiled back.

"Oh, a smart Alec!" The boy laughed.

"My name is Alison," she told him.

"I'm Robert; everyone calls me Rob. Nice to meet you, Alison. I'm sorry about this morning, I was rather late. I didn't mean to bump into you, literally," Rob said.

"It's OK, no harm done. Nice to meet you too, Rob," Alison replied.

"Have you just started school today? I haven't seen you here before?" Rob asked.

"Yes, I started today," Alison replied, as they walked along the road together.

"How do you like it so far?"

"It's OK. I made some new friends. I enjoyed the lessons, so a good day all around, I suppose," she added.

"And now you've have met me too! Could the day get any better?" Rob said.

"Oh, a big head, I see!" Alison laughed.

"Very funny!" Rob smirked.

They had talked for most of the way and Alison didn't realise she was nearly home.

"What time do you leave in the mornings?" Rob asked.

"Well, I left at 8.30 this morning, so probably the same time again tomorrow," Alison said.

"OK, so what if I meet you in the morning at 8.30 and we can walk to together? That way I won't bump into you again and nearly knock you flying! That OK with you?" Rob smiled.

"Yes, I'd like that," Alison said.

"Until then, future Mrs Freeman, I'll see you in the morning," Rob said.

Alison shook her head and waved her hand behind her. They were already outside her house.

Bet was at the window and spotted the two of them together.

"Hi Bet, I'm home!" Alison said.

"Hi darling, did you have a good day? And who was the boy you were talking to?" Bet asked, smiling.

"Oh, that's Rob. He nearly knocked me over this morning on my way to school," Alison said.

"He's allowed to drive then?" Bet asked. She thought he didn't look old enough. Alison laughed.

"Oh no, he was running as he was going to be late and ran into me. Don't worry, nothing's broken," Alison said. "Do you mind if I go up and change out of my uniform?"

"Oh yes, Honey, go up and put your blouse in the dirty laundry and I'll wash it in the morning," Bet said.

"Bet, it's clean on!" Alison replied.

"That's alright, Honey, there are plenty more in the wardrobe," Bet smiled.

Alison went up to her bedroom. The door opened and it was Tom and Bruce.

"Hi! We're home!" Bruce called out.

Tom came in and dumped his bag and took off his coat and hung it on the hooks in the hallway.

"How was your day, Tom?" Bet asked.

"Oh, Bet! It was great! I've got three new friends: Tommy, Antony and Lee. They're great and they all like trucks and cars too! I am so glad," Tom said.

"I'm so glad you had a good day, how were the lessons?" Bet asked.

"Oh, they were OK. We did math and English and we have PE tomorrow, so I need to put my kit in my bag," Tom said.

"Did Alison have a good day?"

"Yes, she did. She's upstairs getting changed, do you want to do the same. The kettle's on and I have snacks before I make a start on dinner," Bet said.

Tom went upstairs.

"Bruce, when Alison came home, she was with a young boy," Bet said.

"Oh?" Bruce said, a bit startled.

"Yes, I think he walked her home, or they just walked the same way I suppose."

"Oh well, if she's made another friend, that's a good thing, Bet," Bruce said.

"Hmm," Bet said, he didn't see the way he looked at her!

Alison and Tom were talking in their bedrooms comparing notes from their day. They both went downstairs. They had got used to Bet making them tea, and she made a great cuppa. They both asked how their days went and they both enjoyed them.

Alison was quite looking forward to going in the morning, she felt rather excited. After they had their dinner, they all watched a bit of TV. Bet knew they wouldn't have any homework yet and they needed to get an early night. They both said goodnight and kissed Bet and Bruce on the cheek and went up to bed.

Alison couldn't wait to get into bed, and she snuggled under the covers.

The next morning, she was ready and out of the door just before 8.30 am. She saw Rob walking towards her.

"Morning Alison, how are you this fine November morning?" Rob asked.

"I'm fine, Rob. How are you this fine morning?" Alison laughed.

They had walked a little way up the road Bruce's car drove by. He tooted to them both and Alison waved at him and Tom.

"Who's that?" Rob asked.

"That's Bruce, my foster father, and Tom, my brother," Alison said.

She looked closely at Rob; he didn't say anything even about Bruce, her foster father. He just smiled.

They walked to school, chatting about everything and anything. Alison found out that Rob was two years older than her and wanted to be a plumber; that's what his dad did and his dad before him. He asked Alison what she wanted to do when she left school.

"To be honest, Rob, I have no idea. But I'm sure that will change later on," she replied.

They were at the school gates, Rob crossed the road, he just made it in time. Alison made her way to class and took her seat next to Stacey.

They started their lessons and even though Alison was enjoying her new school, she kept thinking about Rob.

Once the day was over and the final bell went, she was glad to be going home with him. They talked constantly about all sorts of stuff. Rob left Alison at her front door again. Bet was looking out of the window again.

Alison let herself in.

"Hi Bet, I'm home," she said.

Bet was sitting down on the sofa when she walked into the living room.

"Alison, who is that dish you were with again this afternoon?" Bet asked.

"Dish?" Alison laughed. "Oh, that's Rob. He's the one who bumped into me on Monday. We go the same way; he lives just down the bottom and around the corner. We're the only ones who come and go this way. Is it OK I walk back with him?" Alison asked.

"Of course, Honey! It's nice that you have someone to walk with to and from school, it can be quite lonely otherwise," Bet said.

"I'll just go up and get changed," Alison said.

Tom and Bruce came in and Tom followed Alison and went up and got changed.

They were getting used to their routine and had another lovely evening and an early night again. That was going to be their regular routine.

The rest of the week went really fast. Alison was enjoying the company to and from school each day and she and Rob were getting to know one another. On Friday morning, on their way to school, Rob wanted to ask her something.

"Alison, there's a big firework display over the other side of town tomorrow night, I was wondering if you would like to come with me?" He asked.

"Erm, I would love to, but I have to ask Bet and Bruce first. How about when we walk home this afternoon, we can ask Bet? Bruce isn't normally too far behind me when I get in, would that be all right?" She said.

"Yes, that would be great!" Rob said. "Right, I'd better go now, see you later on," he said as he crossed the road to go through the school gates.

The school day went really quickly and when Alison had walked through the gates, Rob was already waiting there for her. She waved goodbye to her friends and walked home with Rob. Alison was quite surprised that during her first week, she'd had no homework set.

"Oh, don't worry about that, they'll make up for it next week. They always give you a week to settle in," Rob assured her.

They were already outside her door.

"Come on in then, we can wait for Bruce to come and ask both of them at the same time," Alison said. "Hi Bet, we're home." Alison called out.

She came in from the kitchen and saw Alison and Rob.

"Bet, this is Rob, who I've been walking to and from school with," Alison introduced Rob.

"Hello, young man," Bet said, holding out her hand to shake it.

"Hello…Mrs…sorry, Bet," Rob said.

"How were your days at school?" Bet asked.

"Fine, busy," Rob said.

"Same here!" Bet replied.

"Hi we're home, Bet!" Bruce said as he and Tom came through the front door.

Tom took off his coat and hung it up as normal and Bruce went into the living room.

"Oh, and who's this?" Bruce smiled.

"Bruce this is Rob, he's been walking me to and from school every day," Alison said.

"Nice to meet you, Rob," Bruce said.

"Nice to meet you too, Sir," Rob held out his hand and shook Bruce's.

"This is Tom, Alison's brother," Bruce said.

Rob said hello to Tom.

Now that was over, Rob could relax.

"There's a firework display over the other side of town tomorrow evening and I was wondering if I could take Alison?" Rob asked.

"Well, that sounds a good idea, Rob, but as you know Alison is only twelve and I think that's a bit young to be going to a firework display without an adult. Would you mind if we came along as well, don't worry, we won't be in the way, but we want to sure you will be both safe," Bruce said.

"That's fine, Bruce. It starts at 6 pm, can I call on you all then?" Rob asked.

"If you want, or we could collect you in the car, save you walking?" Bruce suggested.

Alison nodded to Rob.

"OK, that will be lovely. I only live around the corner, are you sure it wouldn't be any trouble?" Rob asked.

"No, it would be our pleasure, so see you around 5.30 pm?" Bruce said.

"Bye Rob, see you tomorrow."

"What a nice lad!" Bruce said. Bet nodded.

Well, that went well, Alison thought. Both of the kids went upstairs to change into their other clothes.

"Bruce, she's only been there a week and she's already met a boy!" Bet panicked.

"Bet, it's fine! He seems a nice lad, we can just keep an eye on the two of them, but I have no worries about it, and neither should you, stick the kettle on, will you?" Bruce smiled.

***

Saturday went by quite quickly. Alison picked out some new jeans, her ankle boots and a Jumper. The weather was starting to get a bit chilly. Tom had some new things on also. It was time to go and meet Rob. Alison and Tom had some of their pocket money with them. They had already opened their bank accounts and had started saving some money.

They all got into the car, drove down the bottom of the road, and turned right. Rob was coming out of his house and his mother was at the door waving him off. Bruce pulled over so he could get in, Rob's mum came over.

"Hello, I'm Dorothy, Rob's mum. Thank you for taking him and bringing him back tonight, he has money, have a great time everyone," Dorothy said.

Bruce introduced himself and Bet and shook her hand out of the window.

"Don't worry, Dorothy, we won't be back late," Bruce said.

"Have fun all of you!" Dorothy said as they drove off and made their way to the firework display.

It didn't take long to get there, and it wasn't too busy at this time. Bruce parked up and locked the car. They made their way to the big bonfire. This was the first time the kids had been to an organised display, so, Bruce told both of them about the dangers of fireworks; not to pick one up, if it doesn't go at first, just wait because sometimes they don't always work straight away. And never pick up a sparkler once it's gone out; it will still be hot.

With this knowledge, the children felt confident about the fireworks. There was a burger van and candy floss and toffee apple stand, also, tea and coffee. Bruce looked around, yes, he could see the toilets if they needed to go. Bruce paid a donation of five pounds to the event organiser and they all made their way to the tea and coffee stand.

It was starting to get a bit colder, so they were pleased with the hot drink. it didn't take long for things to get started. They stood around the edge of the area. The organisers started the fireworks up. Thankfully, it was dark by now, so they could be seen from a distance. There were lots of ooohs and aaahhhss with all of the lovely fireworks, even though they were loud, they were lovely and made lots of pretty patterns.

Rob and Alison were enjoying themselves. They included Tom in their group and Bruce and Bet stood behind a little way but loved watching the children enjoying themselves.

The fireworks and bonfire finished at 8.30pm and they all headed off towards the car, when Tom said to Bruce.

"Bruce, Rob likes cars and trucks also, even though he said he wants to be a plumber when he gets older, he likes cars and trucks, isn't that great?" Tom said.

"Yes, Tom, that's great. So, if Rob wants to come again and we haven't scared him off, and he wants to, he can play cars with you, if that's OK with Rob?" Bruce suggested.

"Of course! I'd love to play cars and trucks. I had some cool ones when I was younger, I can have a look for you if you want?" Rob said.

That was it; Tom was over the moon.

"Yes, please, Rob! I'm glad Alison met you!" he added. Everyone burst out laughing.

They pulled over outside Rob's house.

"Thank you, Bruce and Bet, for a lovely time this evening and for dropping me home. I'll see you again on Monday, you too Alison and of course Tom. Night!" Rob said, waving to the family.

"Night!" They all called back.

Bruce then drove off and parked outside their home.

"Everyone out and inside, it's getting cold out here, brrrr!" Bruce said, feeling the cold around him.

They all went inside, and Alison and Tom went upstairs to put on their night things. They came back down to a hot drink and the TV on.

"That was a good night, did you all enjoy yourselves?" Bruce asked.

"Yes, it was great, thanks for picking up and taking Rob home, Bruce" Alison said.

Once they had drunk their drinks, Alison and Tom made their way up to bed; at least they could have a lie-in in the morning. Alison just wanted to get snuggled under her quilt.

"Well, do you know what, Bet?" Bruce said. "I think we have a little romance on our hands. I think Rob and Alison are made for each other and he didn't leave Tom out once," Bruce smiled.

"Yes, I did! Now don't go making plans just yet! I don't intend on buying a hat yet, you know, also we have to adopt them first, remember?" Bet said.

"Don't worry, but I can feel it, Bet, he's a keeper for our Alison. You'll see," Bruce laughed.

"Whatever you say, Bruce!" She laughed.

***

"Bet! Bet! Where are you?" Bruce shouted up the stairs.

"Hold on, Bruce, I'm just in Alison's room stripping her bed, I'll be down in a minute," she told him. "What's wrong?"

"I thought Alison strips her bed on a Saturday, today is Wednesday?" Bruce said.

"I know, but we didn't get chance to do it on Saturday and I said I would do it today. With all of that shopping on Saturday, I didn't think it fair for her to do that as well, and we just haven't had the chance until now. So, what did you want?" Bet asked.

"When?" Bruce said.

"When you just shouted up to me just now?"

"Oh, that! I wanted to know what we were doing for presents for the kids' for Christmas. It's nearly the end of November and I don't know what we are doing for them," Bruce said.

"Bruce, you worry too much, I have it all in hand," Bet said.

But Bruce interrupted her.

"Have you bought anything yet then?" He asked.

"Yes, I've picked up some small things, like hankies, bath cube sets, similar for Tom, new socks, and a new hat and scarf set, but I wanted to ask you about the bigger things," Bet said.

"Well, I thought we could get Tom an Action Man and some accessories, and I wanted to know if you thought it would be OK to get him a bike? I don't think he has ever had one. I know he likes his cars and trucks and we can get him some more, but I've also seen a garage I think he would love?" Bruce said.

"I was wondering as well, what else can we get Alison? I mean, it's difficult with girls," Bruce said.

"No, it's not, Bruce. Boys are harder to buy for," Bet laughed.

Bruce looked at her.

"Can you remember, this time last year, who would have thought we would be buying Christmas presents for our own kids; well, nearly our own," Bruce added.

"I know, it's worth all of the hard work. I'm glad our meeting with Mr Taylor went well, he seemed really pleased and we got another letter from Mr Prowse, did you see it?" Bet asked.

"Yes, I did, it looks like it's going really well and hopefully we can start the adoption process if you want?" Bruce said.

They both couldn't wait to make it official. That these two young people were going to be their children, was a dream come true.

"Bruce, are you busy tomorrow?" Bet asked.

"I don't think so, why?"

"Well, I thought once the kids go off to school, we can go and get that bike and garage for Tom and I can have a look around for Alison," Bet said.

"I think that's a great idea!" Bruce said.

Bet put the kettle on and had a look through the Argos catalogue to see what they had for Alison. After a while, she already had half a dozen items for Alison and a few for Tom. They knew they had to keep track, so they had the same amount of presents and the same money spent on them.

***

Alison couldn't believe how quick it had taken her and Tom to fit in with Bet and Bruce, and with her new school and friends. It was like they were always in their lives. She really liked Rob and he had finally asked her to be his girlfriend.

She was trying to sort out what to get him for Christmas. Rob liked books but he also liked music. She didn't know what to get; she would wait another week and try and ask him what he would like.

Alison knew what she was getting Tom for Christmas. He had seen some new cars in town that he really liked, so she went straight from school one day and bought them for him. She didn't know where to hide them, so she asked Bet. Bet told her to put them in the spare room upstairs; but the other one to where they were storing their presents.

Bet had a look at what Alison had bought him.

"I've seen a wicked book on cars that I think he would like. I saw it in town in a book shop, so will go again later on in the week or next week. I don't want it to get sold," she told Bet.

That was Tom sorted out then.

Alison thought she would get Bet some perfume. There were some lovely ones in the department store, and she had noticed Bet looking at some when they were on a recent shopping trip. Alison was just trying to decide what to get Bruce. She asked Bet for his size. She told her that he was a large size, thanks to all the cakes he'd been eating from Molly's.

"I'm going to have to put him on a diet if he's not careful. Why do you want to know his size, love?"

"I wanted to get him a jumper for Christmas," Alison smiled.

Alison thought she would kill two birds with one stone and get them both at the same time, but she was going to ask Tom if he wanted to come along and get their presents from him at the same time. Tom was definitely agreeable for them to do their shopping for presents at the same time.

Tom wasn't sure what to get either of them, so he asked Alison what she was getting; she told him.

"Oh, I could have gotten those," Tom said disappointedly.

"Don't worry, Tom, I'll help you when we go shopping," Alison said.

The following Saturday the children went to buy their presents.

"I want to get Alison her present for Christmas and I want to pick up something for Rob as well; he's a great buddy. Don't you think Bet?" Tom asked.

"Yes, he is, I should get him something too, we can look together, that alright?" Bet said as they got ready to go to town.

Once all of their shopping was done, they made their way home. Alison was up in her room finishing off her homework.

"Bet, where can I put these?" Tom asked, pointing at the bags with his gifts in.

"Give them to me. I'll hide them for you," Bet winked at Tom.

"Bet, when are we putting the decorations up for Christmas?" Bruce asked.

"Not until 13 December; it's unlucky otherwise," Bet shouted from upstairs.

"I'll need to get into the loft then, I suppose, to get the tree down and the decs," Bruce said.

Bet came back downstairs.

"Yes, but not yet, Bruce; it's only 6 December. Tom, have you written your Christmas cards yet?" Bet asked.

"No, I haven't; I haven't bought any," Tom said.

"Well, I got some the other day. Would you like to have a look through? I suggest you write your list first, so you know who you're going to send them to, including your school friends," Bet said.

"That's a good idea. Do you have a notepad I can borrow?" Tom asked.

"Yes, there's one in the cupboard. I'll get you a pen," Bet said.

Tom took out the pad and started making his list. Alison came down and asked Tom what he was doing, he told her, and she pulled a chair so she could sit next to him.

"Are these all for your school friends, Tom?" Alison asked.

"No, I have put one for the children and staff at Craven House. We'll be seeing them all soon, and I do miss them. I love it here with you, Bet and Bruce, but I do miss Freddie, Charlie and the others." He said.

"Are you writing your list as well?" Tom asked.

"I will when you've finished yours, if that's alright?" Alison said.

Tom had his list all completed, and Alison was making a start on hers. She was getting Rob a special card and Bet and Bruce as well. Also Rose and Henry, because they were like family, but the rest of her list would be out of a box.

"Al, have you got anything for Rob yet?" Bet asked.

"No, not yet Bet. I don't know what to get him. I was trying to hint to him about what he wanted. I know he likes books and music but doesn't talk about them much," Alison said. "I could get him a jumper or something?"

"That's a good idea. When we go out next, we can have a look around, if you want?" Bet said.

"Yes, that would be great!" Alison said.

Bet was going food shopping every weekend and putting some extras in for Christmas. The shops were getting busy, so she ordered her turkey early from the butchers. She got her fresh stuff the last couple of shopping days, but the tinned and jar stuff, early.

Bet and Bruce had asked Rose and Henry to join them for Christmas day. They worked so hard and they wanted to wait on hand and foot for them both. Christmas was getting closer. The shops were busier than ever with everyone rushing around.

Bruce got the Christmas stuff out of the loft, so they could all put everything up together.

They put some Christmas songs on which put them in the Christmas mood. It was a lovely day and they had all finished their Christmas shopping, so they could relax now.

Alison bought Rob a Sherlock Holmes hat and a magnifying glass. He had mentioned that he loved anything to do with Sherlock Holmes, but he didn't have a hat or a magnifying glass. He loved it.

Tom bought him a book on cars from the bookshop in town and wanted to get himself one, but when he went back, the book he wanted had gone. Unbeknown to him, Alison had already got it for him for Christmas.

Bet was glad she got the kids some boots, as it was really cold now. They both had wellington boots, but they were for the rain and the snow. The boots they got them had fur in the bottom, so their feet were always warm even when it was freezing.

***

On Christmas Eve, Bruce had already picked up the turkey, and Bet had got the last of the fresh stuff the day before. They had Christmas Cake, pudding, brandy sauce, brandy butter, brandy snaps, custard, pickles, Branston Pickle, red cabbage, pickled onions; they didn't miss a thing.

The fruit bowls were full, the fridge and freezer were both full and the cupboards and pantry was bulging. They also had plenty of drinks too; soft drinks, mixers, Champagne, to have with Christmas dinner, snowballs, Babycham, port, brandy and whisky.

They didn't need to buy anything else.

"Bruce, I have to pop into town; Al, would you come with me? I forgot to get some mint sauce and gravy and I want to make sure there's nothing else we need," Bet asked.

"Yes, of course. It looks a bit wild out there, Bet, I'll just get my boots on, give me a minute," Alison said.

The two of them headed towards town.

"What do we need again?" Alison asked.

"Erm well, I wanted to pick up a couple of bits from the supermarket, but I wanted to go into Molly's and pick up some of those nice cakes for a treat for

Bruce and us for later on when we're watching the TV. What do you think? A bit naughty, eh?" Bet giggled.

"Yes, but why not, Bet, it is Christmas after all!" Alison laughed.

Once Bet picked up the last of the things she had forgotten, she and Alison went into Molly's. "Do you fancy a cup of tea and maybe a small cake or mince pie?" Bet asked.

"Go on then, we may as well, it's bitter out there, and we won't be long," Alison said.

Molly showed them to a table next to the fire.

"Two cups of tea please, Molly," Bet asked her once they were seated.

"Anything else?" She asked.

"I tell you what, what about two slices of hot apple pie with custard? That will warm us both up," Bet said, looking at Alison who nodded her approval.

They were drinking their tea, then Molly brought over their desserts.

Alison was tucking in and she looked up. She noticed a lady who looked familiar, but she couldn't remember where from. Alison had a sip of her tea. It was bugging her now. Where did she know the woman from?

She thought maybe she knew her from school; maybe she was a supply teacher who came to help out? Alison tried to put it out of her head.

Alison and Bet had had a nice time out, getting the last of the food shopping and coming out for this treat, but this was now annoying her. She was trying to think where she had seen her before.

They had finished and were waiting for the bill. Even though it was Christmas Eve, Molly's was really busy. People had done the same as them; gone out for their last-minute items and then popped into Molly's to have something warm to eat or drink.

When a man went over to the table with the woman sitting there, Alison suddenly stood up.

"Ruth?" Alison shouted.

Ruth and Harry nearly jumped out of their skins when they saw Alison. They were on their own, no Hannah with them. Bet looked at Molly, who nodded and quickly went out to the back of the kitchen.

There were a lot of people in the tea shop, but nobody knew what was going on.

Harry could see that Molly was on the phone to someone. He realised he wouldn't be able to get out through the front door, but he had been to the loo and found a quick way out.

He grabbed his wife's arm and pulled her up and out through the backdoor.

Alison stood frozen; she couldn't move. Harry and Ruth had gotten clean away again. Molly was talking to a police officer who had appeared at the front of the tea rooms. She pointed to Alison and the officer walked over to her, notepad in his hand.

The police had been looking for Harry and Ruth ever since Social Services had reported them. "Had they paid their bill, Molly?" Another officer asked.

"No, they just shot off out the back door, why?" She asked.

"Don't worry. They won't get far." The officer said, as he got his radio out.

"They will be long gone now, Sir," Alison said, "that man is so slippery, he's like an eel. They have a daughter, Hannah. She's about nine now," Alison said.

"Was she with them?" The officer asked.

"No, they probably left her at home like they used to with me and my brother, when we were in their care," Alison said.

Most of the customers in the tea shop overheard her.

Once the police had asked Alison the questions they needed, they said she could go. They would be in touch if they caught up with them. Alison knew that would be very unlikely.

Molly made up their order and threw in a few more cakes.

"I'm so sorry, Bet, I didn't realise they were the couple who had fostered Alison and Tom," Molly said.

Bet and Molly had become good friends and Bet had confided in her about the awful time the children had endured whilst in the Coopers' care.

Bet and Alison thanked Molly for her help and their lovely dessert and left.

"Come on Al, let's get a taxi," Bet said.

"But Bet, it's not far away," Alison replied.

"Yes, I know, but I'm getting cold again and you've had a bit of a shock today," Bet told her.

They got a taxi pretty quickly. Bet really wanted to get Alison out off the streets just in case Harry and Ruth follow them. Not that they had any reason to, but she wasn't taking any chances. As soon as she got in, she was going to see Rose and call Craven House and let them know what had happened in Molly's.

"Bet, I don't mind telling Bruce, but I don't want to worry Tom, can you tell him later on when we are out of the way, when you're sorting presents or something?" Alison asked.

"Yes, of course, Sweetheart. I don't want to worry Tom either. Look, when we get in, we can put away the shopping and I'll pop down to Rose's and call Craven House. They will have to be notified, OK love?" Bet said. "But if Tom asks, just say I had to pop in to see Rose about something," Bet added.

Alison nodded.

Bet paid the taxi and they got out of the car and went indoors. Alison put the shopping in the cupboard and Bet went to see Rose. She took the phone number with her.

***

"Yes, that's right, Sandra. I thought you would need to know straight away…yes, the police came, and Alison was so brave. She shouted Ruth's name out at the top of her voice. They were so embarrassed, but they ran off through the back of the café…Oh and they didn't have their little girl with them either…Yes, it seems so…That's OK, it's just if the police call, you know why," Bet explained.

"Yes, she's a little shaken. She said that she couldn't remember where she had seen the lady, then it all fell into place…Yes, we got a cab home, I wasn't going to take any chances…No, I think they are long gone by now. If you could tell Mr Prowse and I'll let Mr Taylor know once the holiday is over…Yes, if anything else happens, I'll let you know," Bet said. She put the receiver down.

"Bet, do you want a cuppa?" Rose asked.

"Better not, Rose. I've got to tell Bruce about what happened. I don't want Tom to find out just yet though," Bet said.

"OK, Love, you go home and talk to Bruce and we'll see you in the morning," Rose hugged her.

Bet went back indoors. Bruce was looking confused.

"Bet, I've put the stuff away but left the box on the side, I'm heading up to see Tom," Alison said. She went up to Tom's room.

Alison and Tom had never heard Bet and Bruce ever argue, but there were some loud voices coming from downstairs. Bruce was fuming.

"Bet! Why didn't you call me? I would have come up," Bruce said.

441

"By the time you would have got there Bruce they had already left," Bet said.

"How's Alison?" He asked.

"She was rather quiet when she came in, and I didn't know what was going on," Bruce said.

Bet explained what had happened in the tea shop and how brave Alison was.

"The police arrived and took a statement from Alison. She gave them a good description; she has a good memory," Bet said.

"Well, hopefully they will catch up with them soon. Let's not let this spoil our Christmas," Bruce said, hugging his wife.

"Let's have a Chinese for a change tonight," Bet said.

That evening, the four of them tucked into a cake each while watching TV. Alison went upstairs to have a bath and get into her night things, then back downstairs to relax. They had a hot chocolate. She'd had quite an eventual Christmas Eve!

***

The following day, the family got up early and opened their presents. They were placed in piles and Tom and Alison's were huge!

Both of the children sat in front of their presents.

"Go!" Bruce said, and they started unwrapping their gifts.

Tom got his bike, along with some books, cars, trucks, a new garage, a hat and scarf set, some colouring books with cars in them, some coloured pencils…the list went on. Rob had bought Tom a monster dump truck, which was bright red. Tom didn't have anything like it and he loved it.

Alison got a 'Learn about Beauty' set, which had cleanser, toner, etc. in it. She also got a Girls World head, with make-up.

"I know you like doing hairstyles, so I thought you might like to do more practising on someone else, just in case you wanted to go into hairdressing later on or become a make-up artist or something," Bet said.

Alison got a new gold Figaro necklace. It was lovely. She also received some bath gift sets, which she was chuffed with.

Tom got Alison a jumper, in a lovely red colour. It was Shetland wool and would keep her warm in the winter. The children were both thrilled with their presents; they had never been this spoilt before.

Bet and Bruce opened their gifts and Alison and Tom both stopped what they were doing, so they could see their expressions.

Bet loved her jumper and perfume and Bruce loved his aftershave and his new jumper.

"Hey! It's a large! I'm a medium!" Bruce protested.

"Not since we have been eating cakes from Molly's!" Bet laughed.

They continued opening their presents.

"Oh, we forgot, these came for both of you," Bet said, handing them both a huge wrapped gift.

When they opened the boxes, there were lots of little gifts inside.

"It came the day before Christmas Eve," Bet said.

"It's from Craven House, Al! They didn't forget us!" Tom said excitedly. "Look, there's a truck from Charlie and a huge car from Freddie!" tom said.

"Oh, look Tom, Emily, Lisa and Susie got me some nail polishes and some make-up," Alison said, "and some new tights, those will do well for school," Alison laughed.

Bet got up to get a black bag to throw the wrapping paper in the bin. Alison gave her a hand. "Bet, can we use the phone soon, so we can say thank you to everyone at Craven House?" Alison asked.

"Of course, you can," Bet said. "Right, bacon sandwich, anyone?"

Soon enough Rose and Henry arrived. They exchanged gifts with each other.

Rose and Henry didn't know what to get the kids, so they gave them both twenty pounds, to buy something they wanted.

Alison and Tom had a surprise for Bet and Bruce, but they would do that later on, once they'd had their dinner. They wanted to give it to them in front of Rose and Henry.

Rose gave Bet a hand in the kitchen. Bet wanted to give Rose a break, but Rose was bored with the men talking about sport, so she watched while Bet prepared and cooked the dinner.

They spoke quietly in the kitchen about the day before. Alison hadn't mentioned anything about it and Bet and Bruce decided not to mention it again.

Christmas lunch seemed to be made quicker than last year. Everyone sat down at the table, which Tom and Alison had dressed before Rose and Henry came over. Bet and Rose brought in the platefuls of lunch; there was so much food, but the kids had big appetites.

"Anyone for dessert yet?" Bet asked as she cleared away the dinner plates.

"Oh, not yet, Bet! Let's let that go down first!" Bruce said, patting his full tummy.

Alison and Tom went upstairs, they had a little chat and came back down with an envelope. Alison asked for a little bit of quiet, as she and Tom had something they wanted to say. She cleared her throat and began.

"Bet, Bruce, Rose and Henry, this is the best Christmas we have had, and we love being part of your family, so this is for you Bet and Bruce. We hope you like it," Alison said, handing over the envelope to Bruce.

Bruce undid the envelope, and pulled out a letter…

'Dear Bet and Bruce, we couldn't have been made happier than living with you both, we want you to know that, even though we are on a six-month foster placement, we would, with your blessing, like to go ahead with the adoption process. From your loving children, Alison and Tom.'

Bet burst into tears, and Bruce had welled up; they were both in shock.

"We know we got you gifts to open for Christmas, but we think we can't give you anything better than a permanent family," Alison said. Tom nodded too.

Bet got up and hugged both of the children.

"Are you sure?" she asked.

They both nodded.

Bruce came over and joined in the hug; so did Rose and Henry.

That had made Bet and Bruce's Christmas.

The rest of the day became a bit of a blur, but everyone enjoyed themselves. Rose and Henry went back home about ten o'clock and both of the kids went up to bed not long after. It had been a long day. Rob was popping over tomorrow, Boxing Day.

***

Before they knew it, the Christmas holidays were over, and they were back at school. The time had flown by. Tom's birthday came and went; he mainly got money for his birthday because he'd had so much at Christmas, no one knew what else to get him.

Alison was doing her mock exams, which would be good practise for the following year when she would have to choose her options for the next two years at school. She was coming up to thirteen her next birthday, so this time was crucial for her education.

She had been using the Girls World head to make loads of styles, and she tried experimenting with the colours for the make-up, which was going well. Rob had already sorted out his options. He still wanted to be a plumber, so when he finished school, he would go to college to study for his City and Guilds. Hopefully, three years after that he would follow in his father's footsteps and he couldn't wait.

Alison's birthday was soon upon them. She was now going to be a teenager!

Bet and Bruce asked her what she wanted to do for her birthday. She asked if her, her three friends and Tom and Rob could all go to the Wimpy in town and then have a cake later on at home. It was a far cry from the birthday she'd had with the Coopers.

Alison never did tell Tom about seeing Ruth and Harry in Molly's. She didn't want him to worry and they never heard any more about the Coopers once Christmas was over.

Bruce asked Alison if she wanted them to come along, she said yes, but Bet said they would have a tea at home with Tom and Rob when they returned from town. She thought it would be better for Alison and her friends to have time together and that she and Bruce would just feel as if they were in the way.

They all had a good time out at the Wimpy and Tom enjoyed the birthday cake at home.

They had to start thinking about working over the holidays. Before they knew it, it was upon them and Alison and Tom couldn't wait. They were going to help out with Rose and Henry with Bet and Bruce, even if it meant taking orders for the evening meal or stripping the beds.

July was here and August was soon approaching.

Jo was still at Benson House and she loved it, but she couldn't wait to see Tom and Alison. The same thing happened every year: the older children came first, then Craven House, then Benson House and finally, Denham house.

All of the children were delighted to see Alison and Tom, especially Craven House.

Bet and Bruce had already applied to adopt Alison and Tom They had lots of meetings with Mr Taylor and Mr Prowse came down every so often to see how things were going.

They had all got used to it by now.

Jo was saying to Alison that she would have to make up her mind soon as she would have to decide on her options. She said there was some hiccups at school about it, but it was sorted out now. She wanted to learn about book-keeping and how to keep accounts, which would be a good job to have.

Alison and Tom took some of them out to various new places they had been to, which everyone enjoyed. Alison and Tom had gained more confidence over the past year. Rob would come around and give rose and Henry a hand too. He didn't have to work through the holidays, but occasionally his dad would take him on jobs with him, which gave him a bit of money.

The summer holidays went so quickly. When they weren't helping out with Rose and Henry, Alison and Tom relaxed with their friends. Bet and Bruce took them out sometimes to different places.

"You could be a travel guide, you know so much about the area now, Tom," Bruce said.

Tom liked the idea of being a travel guide.

"I thought that meant I had to go on aeroplanes!" Tom laughed.

***

Autumn was starting to show itself, with the leaves changing colour and the town and seaside was starting to empty from holidaymakers. Alison had already started her third year of secondary school; she was the youngest person in her class. Tom had this school year and then the next which would be his last year in primary school. He was looking at going to Harlequin Boys' School, like Rob did and he would be opposite Alison for a little while.

"Bruce, Bruce, can you come down a minute?" Bet shouted to her husband.

It was the beginning of December and they were starting to think about Christmas again.

"What's up, Bet, I was just looking in the loft, I think we need to get new ones; those paper ones, love, aren't very nice. I've seen some metallic ones in Woolworths," Bruce said as he made his way down the stairs.

"Bruce, shh, come and have a look at this!" Bet whispered.

"What is it? Didn't you hear me, about the decs, Bet?"

Bet handed Bruce a letter.

446

Dear Mr and Mrs Linton,

We are happy to announce that the adoption for Miss Alison Davis and Master Tom Davis has now been completed. Congratulations, you are now the legal guardians for the said children.

I hope you will be very happy as a family and wish you all of the best for your futures.

Yours Sincerely,
Mr Simon Prowse
Mr Alan Taylor
Mr John Dunn Commissioner of Children's Services.

"Oh, my goodness!" Bruce gasped. "We did it, Bet! They are our children now! I can't believe it! All those meetings and checking us out at home...we finally have our own little family! We need to celebrate, what should we do, Bet?" Bruce was jumping up and down.

Bet had tears rolling down her face. She was ecstatic.

"Should we have a party, book a holiday or what do you think?" Bruce said.

Bet was silent; she couldn't believe it. She was smiling from ear to ear.

"What Bruce, what did you say? A party? Yes, why not! I think that's a great idea!" Bet replied. "I'm just going to sit down for a minute. I need to process this."

Once Bet and Bruce had a moment to take the news in, they went to tell Rose and Henry the good news.

Rose and Henry looked at each other then back at them. Bet couldn't contain her excitement anymore.

"We've been granted adoption for Alison and Tom!" she screamed. "The paperwork has just arrived!"

"Oh Bet, Bruce! That's wonderful news!" Rose said, hugging them both.

"We can't believe it, Rose!" Bet said.

"Why not? It's what you have always wanted! Of course, they were going to let you have those kids. I have never seen them happier than when living with you!" Rose said.

"I'm so pleased for both of you!" She added.

"Have you told Alison and Tom yet?" Henry asked.

"No not yet, they're still at school, but we felt we wanted to tell you two first because if it wasn't for you both, we would never have met them or got into fostering in the first place. So, thank you to both of you," Bruce said.

"No, thank you!" Rose said. "Because without you two, those two may never have found love in a proper home with a family. They could have easily been passed over and ended up in the care system for the rest of their childhoods."

"Well, this is the best Christmas present we could ever have!" Bet said.

"Time for a quick glass of something to celebrate?" Henry asked.

"Yes, why not, just the one though, don't want to be drunk when they get in from school!" Bet laughed.

"Oh Rose, we were thinking of having a party to celebrate, what do you think? We have to ask them first, but we thought it would be our way of sealing our deal with them as a proper family, what do you think?" Bet added.

"I think it's a wonderful idea, but talk to them first, then you can arrange it all together. If you want any help, you know where I am," Rose said.

***

Alison got in at her usual time and Tom was in not long after. He had started to use his bike he got for Christmas to get to school. It was a BMX bike and he loved it.

"Alison, Tom, can you come in here please?" Bruce asked. Bruce very rarely called them both in together, they hadn't done anything wrong, so they were a bit surprised by the call.

"What's up, Bruce?" Alison asked.

"Nothing's up, Al, we just have some news for you. Would you both sit down?" Bruce said.

Bet and Bruce looked excited, but Tom and Alison looked nervous.

"Hey, you haven't done anything wrong, either of you. It's just we got some paperwork today," Bruce said.

Alison and Tom looked at each other.

"Well, it looks like you now have a new mum and dad!" Bruce said.

"Huh?" They both said at the same time.

"Does that mean we are going away then?" Tom asked.

"No, Tom, Alison, we have the final paperwork for the adoption, it went through, we are now your legal guardians, your parents!" Bruce said.

Alison and Tom both jumped up and hugged their new mum and dad. They were all crying.

"I thought you were going to send us away!" Tom said, through tears.

"No chance! We would have fought tooth and nail to make sure you stayed with us. You're happy here with us, aren't you?" Bruce said.

"Yes, yes, we are, Dad!" Alison laughed.

Bruce beamed a big smile. He liked hearing that word, so did Bet.

Alison went over to Bet and gave her a big hug.

"And you too, Mum!" She said.

"Now there is something else we want to talk to you about, we know that your surname is Davis and we don't want you to give that up just yet, because it's who you both are, but what if we call you Davis-Linton for now until you get used to the idea, is that alright?" Bruce suggested.

Bruce and Bet had already spoken about it when they got back from Rose and Henry's.

"What do you think?" Bet asked.

"I think it's a great idea, Mum," Alison said, and Tom nodded.

"Oh yes, we wanted to tell you first, but we also told Rose and Henry today, because if it wasn't for them, we wouldn't have got to meet you, we hope that was OK?" Bet said.

"Of course, it was! As you said, if it wasn't for Rose and Henry, you wouldn't even know us!" Alison said.

"Mum! What's for dinner? I'm starving!" Tom said.

Bet laughed. For so long, she had wanted to be called Mum.

"Oh, well, Rose and Henry have invited us over there for dinner tonight. They're having roast pork," Bet said.

"Yes! I love roast pork!" Tom said. "And dessert?" he added.

"No idea yet," Bet laughed. "Oh, but we wanted to ask you something else. Celebrating the adoption going through, would you like to have a party?"

"Oh yes, that would be great, Mum, who can we invite?" Tom asked.

"We wanted to ask you first before making any decisions. What about asking your friends from Craven House and Jo?" Bet said, looking at Alison.

"That's a great idea!" Tom said. "But can we go and have dinner and then talk about this later on?"

Bruce looked at the clock, it was just gone 5 pm.

"It's a little early, Tom. Do you have any homework, and don't you want to change out of your uniform before going next door?" Bruce said.

"Sorry, I forgot with all of the excitement!" Tom said.

"Al, do you have any homework?" Bruce asked.

"I have some French and a bit of Math I didn't finish in class. Can I have a cup of tea please?" She asked.

"'Course you can. I'll bring it up in a minute, give you a chance to get changed," Bet said.

Alison went up to her bedroom; Tom had already gone up to his to get changed and do his homework.

Bet came up with a cup of tea for both of them, they both had their heads stuck in their books.

"I'll give you a shout when it's nearly time to go to Rose's, that OK?" Bet said.

"Yes, OK," Alison replied, not looking up from her book.

A while later they all went next door to Rose and Henry's.

"Dinner is nearly ready. Go downstairs to the dining room, Rose is just starting to dish up." Henry told them.

They made their way downstairs. When they were all seated, Henry brought the plates in all ready and smelling heavenly.

"So, what do you think of the good news then?" Rose asked.

"We're delighted, aren't we, Al?" Tom said. "It's lovely to have a mum and dad again."

Rose and Henry were a little shocked to hear them refer to Bet and Bruce as mum and dad so quick, but Bet and Bruce were beaming again.

"Come on everyone, tuck in, before it gets cold!" Rose said.

When everyone had finished their dinner, Henry cleared the table and then went back upstairs. He returned with a huge bottle of champagne.

"We put this on ice after you left earlier, to celebrate!" He said.

Everyone cheered.

"Rose, we're going to have a party, but will sort it out at the weekend," Bet said.

"Bruce, can I give them a small glass, just so we can toast?" Henry asked, nodding to Tom and Alison.

"Why not, this is a huge celebration!" Bruce said.

Henry poured two very small glasses and filled the other's glasses.

"To the Lintons and their family!" He toasted.

Everyone else copied, "To the Lintons" and then they all had a sip of champagne.

Alison thought it was very bubbly, but Tom downed his in one.

"It's like lemonade, Al!" Tom said. Everyone laughed.

Rose left the table and returned with a giant chocolate cake. Both Tom and Bruce's eyes lit up. Rose had a little chuckle as everyone tucked into their cake and Bruce and Tom were very much enjoying theirs with the noises they were making.

The evening had gone very well, and they thanked Rose and Henry and hugged before going back home. Tom felt like his tummy would explode. When they got in, they all went straight upstairs, so they could change into their night things and go to bed. That Champagne had gone to their heads and they were all tired all of a sudden.

When they all said goodnight, Bet climbed into bed.

"I think we may need to get a hall for this party," Bet said.

"A hall?" Bruce said, looking at Bet, but she was already asleep.

***

"Bruce, do you know if the Bulls Head let out their function room at this time of year?" Bet asked.

"I have no idea, Bet, I think they may do. I'll pop along and check. When were you thinking of having the party?" Bruce asked.

"Well, the thing is, it's quite short notice, but I want to do it just before Christmas. That way we have something else to look forward to before Christmas, what do you think?"

"I'll go and ask Eric; I think he's still in charge. Then we can sort that out, they have a bar, so it's just really food and invitations to do. Actually Bet, if you want, we could go now? The kids are at school and we might be able to organise it today if you want?" Bruce said.

"Bruce, that's a good idea, it's only eleven o'clock, so they should be open and yes, I think if we can get that side of it sorted, we can get invitations out before the end of the week," Bet said.

They set off down to the pub. Eric said they could have the function room on the 18th December. They could get in about four pm to decorate the hall and bring the food down by seven pm. When Bet and Bruce got home Bet grabbed a pen and started writing down some ideas for food. Bet would ask Rose if she would give her a hand with the food and as Bruce had the car, he could ferry back and forth with the food on trays.

"Hello, can I speak to Sandra, please?" Bet said into the phone.

"Hello Sandra, it's me, Bet, from down in Margate…yes, how are you?"

Bet explained to Sandra all about the party she was planning.

"I'll put an invitation in the post, but wanted to give you the date, just in case you needed to arrange for a coach," she added.

After calling Sandra, Bet popped along to Rose's and wanted to ask her if she would be able to help with the food.

Bet was telling Rose about the upcoming event.

"What do you think, Rose? Rose? Are you OK?" Bet asked.

"Sorry? Oh, yes, I'm fine; just a bit tired. It's starting to get a bit hard now doing this job. Perhaps running a bed and breakfast is getting a bit tough for us old birds!" Rose said.

"Maybe you should take it a bit easier, Rose. I know you and Henry are a great team, but maybe it should be time you think about retiring?" Bet suggested.

"Nah, I think I am just having a moan, take no notice of me, Bet," Rose said, trying to throw Bet off.

"Rose, if it's too much for this party, let me know and I'll do it," Bet said.

"Don't you dare! I would love to help, especially as it's such a special occasion," Rose said.

Bet thanked Rose and told her to take it a bit easy if she could. She went home, so she could tell Bruce and they could start planning, and at least write a list of who to invite.

When Tom and Alison came home from school Bet and Bruce told them both that they were having a party on 18th December and did they want to make a start on their list of who they want to invite, but only once they did their homework.

"Oh, I have already spoken to Sandra at Craven House, so she has the date and they can arrange for a coach, but we will send them an invitation," Bet said, "Oh, and Alison, I have asked if Jo and the other girls you got on with who have left Craven House if they can come too? Yes, Tom, Freddie and Charlie will be here too," Bet laughed.

"Lisa, Kim, Stacey, Rob," Alison said aloud. "Mum, I can't think of who else to invite."

"What about Rob's parents? Rose and Henry will be there, and we were going to ask a few friends, is that OK?" Bet said.

"Of course, it is. It's for you and Dad as much as me and Tom," Alison said.

Bet only had one sister and Bruce had one brother and one sister, but they were family. Bet didn't really see her mum and dad very often, but thought they would like to come, so she put them on the list. Bruce's mum was a widow, but he put her also on the list. By the time they had all written their lists, it was just under a hundred people.

Bruce and Bet were very busy with preparations for the party, but she still had time to go out and get them both something nice to wear for the party. They all went out the week before to town to see what was available. Because it was nearly Christmas, there were some lovely party clothes in the shops.

They went into a boutique and saw some lovely dresses, but Bruce shook his head.

"I know she's a teenager, Bet, but some of these things are way too old for her!" Bruce said. Alison took one look at what Bruce was looking at and she shook her head.

"Dad, I wouldn't be seen dead wearing any of that stuff!" she said.

Alison headed toward the back of the shop, she shook her head, she left the shop and they all followed.

"I know it's not always cool, but what about Marks and Spencer? They do some nice stuff, maybe they will have some seasonal party wear?" Bet said.

When they walked in, there were some lovely things and Alison found a lovely deep red sparkly dress, with a crossbody occasion bag over one shoulder.

"Oh, I like that, Mum!" She said, checking they had it in a size 10.

"That's much better than that other shop we just left," Bruce laughed.

Alison went to the changing room and tried on the dress. When she came out of the dressing room, Bet looked stunned.

"Oh my! You look beautiful, darling! If we get you some cream-coloured tights, and then maybe see if we can get burgundy shoes to match. Definitely get it!" Bet said.

Alison went back to the changing room to take off the dress. She soon found some shoes to complement it.

"Right, Tom's turn next! Let's head over to the boy's section," Bet said.

Bet had a look at the rails and found some lovely bottle green corduroy trousers, and a lovely shirt, they had it in cream as well as white, so she put both up against the trousers, the cream looked better. She then found a lovely V-neck, green jumper, which looked lovely with the cords.

"Tom, do you like this colour? Let me put it up against you and see what you think?" Bet asked.

Bruce went into the boys' changing room with Tom, while Bet found some new shoes to match Tom's outfit.

She headed back to the changing room, called Bruce, and handed him the shoes. Tom came out and he looked so lovely. Both children had grown a couple of inches in the past year.

After finding a tie to match Tom's outfit and some new underwear for them both, they headed home.

When they got home, they took their clothes upstairs and hung them up on the front of their wardrobes. Even though it was a week to their party, Bet and Bruce had been buying presents for the kids. Bet and Bruce were still hiding presents up on the top floor rooms. Thankfully, Alison and Tom were still not aware of it. They had already stocked up a few more presents for them just the day before.

The following week came around really quickly. Everyone from Craven House had gladly accepted the invitation and Jo and the other girls were also coming. Rose and Henry said that they could stay there for the night, including the coach driver, so he could take them back the following day.

Bet and Bruce had been busy all day and Alison and Tom had been helping since early that morning. Rob had popped by to see if they needed any help and he got a couple of his mates from school to help with the decorations and Rob's mum helped out as well. The boys got an invitation to the party too, which they gladly accepted.

It didn't take as long to get it all done in time. Rose had been cooking all day and they were almost ready to start the party.

It didn't take long for the children to get ready. Alison wanted to put a little make-up on. She had been practising with her Girls' World model for a while now, but she had already bought some new make-up recently.

She looked lovely! She had curled her hair, which was now flowing down her back in long, blonde trestles. She looked stunning.

Tom came out of his room, having a problem tying his tie. Alison bent down to help him, she looked at him and he looked at her; they smiled at each other. They had a quick hug; this was their night all four of them.

When they went downstairs, Bet was struggling with her shoes.

"Mum, what's wrong?" Alison asked.

"I can't decide what shoes to wear, what do you think? The higher ones or the slightly lower ones?"

"The slightly lower ones look a bit better, otherwise you look like you're going to a cocktail party!" Alison said.

Bet took one look at both of them. They had both grown up since the first time she met them. She had slight tears in her eyes. She swallowed and cleared her throat.

"I think we all look rather dashing, don't you?"

"Dashing?" Tom asked.

"Well, rather stunning, if you ask me," Bet laughed. "Now, let's get to this party and start having some fun!"

Bruce then opened the door and all three of them went downstairs.

"Wow! Don't you all look lovely, are you nearly ready? I just have to nip upstairs," Bruce said. He was down a few minutes later in his suit. He looked so handsome, even though he was in his early 40s, he still looked great.

"Right, let's get this show on the road!" Bruce said.

"Dad, did you pick up Rob's mum earlier?" Alison asked.

"Yes, and dropped her home again. She said she would see us there, I think she still had a couple of things to do to get ready."

Bruce parked up the car, and they all got out. It was a cold evening, but they would soon warm up when they got inside. Once they got inside, some people had already arrived, but the Craven House lot hadn't arrived yet. Rob's friends were there, and Bet's sister, Sue, arrived with her new boyfriend.

They went to the bar and then found somewhere to sit down and enjoy her drink.

"Rose, thank you so much for all of your help with this. Now, you have to have a good time, you're not here to look after everyone else tonight!" Bet said.

Rose laughed and went to the bar with Henry.

The coach had pulled up and there was the noise of footsteps coming up the stairs. Freddie and Charlie were at the front with Sandra and George, Jo followed behind, with the older girls and then everyone else. They were so pleased to see Alison and Tom.

The children hugged Bet and Bruce and then Rose and Henry. It was crazy with loads of kids everywhere!

When they settled down and found tables, Sue looked like she was in a horror film with kids everywhere. Once the kids had a drink each and Bet opened up the food. They had brought the cakes they ordered from Molly's for the kids for later on but Bet asked Molly to make a huge cake with.

'Welcome to the family, love Mum and Dad' written on it.

Rob and his parents arrived then Kim, Lisa and Stacey came all together, and Tommy, Antony and Lee came with their parents. Bet and Bruce had organised a disco as well, so everyone was up on the dance floor. Bruce's mum came for a little while. She hadn't met Alison and Tom before tonight, but they had arranged for her to come for Christmas, so she could get to know them properly.

Rose disappeared from the party for a little while. When she returned, Henry asked her where she'd been.

"Well, I had to let the coach driver in and give him his meal I made, he was chuffed to bits, said he would have a cuppa then go to bed," she told Henry.

The party was in full swing, and about 9 pm, Bruce and Bet asked for a little bit of quiet, they wanted to make a little speech.

"First of all, we would like to thank you all for coming this evening on this cold December night. We know some of you have come a long way, but we wanted you all to be here tonight so we can celebrate welcoming Alison and Tom to our family permanently and to let you all know that adoption has finally gone through. So, if you could all raise your glasses and say "Welcome to the family Alison and Tom"," Bruce said.

Everyone clinked their glasses. Rose brought out the huge cake. They had placed four candles on it: one for each of them. Bruce lit them and they all blew them out together.

Sandra and George and the staff started clapping. They went over to the children and Bet and Bruce and hugged them.

"Bruce, can I say a few words?" Sandra asked.

"Yes of course, you can. Everyone, can he have a little hush for a couple more minutes, thank you," Bruce said.

Sandra stood looking at everyone.

"Hello everyone, my name is Sandra and we work at the children's home where Alison and Tom lived with us for six years. It was wonderful having those years with the children, but we want to also say, there are people who want to foster or adopt children that have come from the care system, and like this family now, there are success stories. I would like to thank Alison and Tom for staying with us and we wish them well on their new chapter with their new family. Thank you, Betty and Bruce, and also Alison and Tom," Sandra said.

Everyone in the room clapped and cheered. Bruce and Bet, Alison, and Tom, stood around the cake and started to cut it. Bruce and Bet took the cake out into the kitchen to cut it up for everyone. The DJ put the music back on and the party was in full swing.

Rob had come over to Alison to ask her for a dance.

When Bet came back in, Sandra went over to her.

"Hey Bet, when did that happen?" Sandra nodded to Alison and Rob.

"Alison met Rob, the first day of school, so not long after they got here and he is a lovely boy, he gets on well with Tom too," Bet said.

"Wow, who knew?" Sandra smiled, thinking how grown up Alison looked now.

Everyone enjoyed themselves and before long it was time to wind up the party. Freddie and Charlie were so glad to see Tom and Alison and so was Jo and the other girls. Thankfully, they were staying with Rose and Henry, so they could see them in the morning before they left.

Everyone had a great time and Alison had her first kiss outside. Sandra, George, and the other staff had rounded up the kids and walked them back to Rose's. Bruce and Bet thanked everyone again as they were leaving.

When they got in, Tom was already half asleep. Bruce put the cake in the kitchen and then they all went upstairs to go to bed.

"Don't forget, everyone, we have to give Rose and Henry a hand in the morning," Bruce said.

They both said goodnight to Bruce and Bet. They'd all had a lovely time, but sleep had now taken over.

Chapter 23

Christmas was here the following week after the party and everyone was excited. Bruce's mum was being picked up on Christmas Eve and Sue, Bet's sister was coming over for a few hours on Boxing Day. Bruce left about 10 am to collect his mum. She was a sweet old lady and had a good life. She had three children but didn't see much of them as they all had their own lives.

Thankfully, they had space for her to stay. She would have to go to the top floor, but that was OK. She had a stick and didn't like people trying to do things for her. She was very independent.

Bet, Alison and Tom had been running around like headless chickens since the party trying to get everything done. Bet didn't want to go out this time on Christmas eve, like they did this last year and the disaster that happened at Molly's, bumping into Ruth, so they all stayed home instead.

The new decorations were up and looked rather lovely. They had a big tree in the window, and it looked all festive.

Christmas eve went really quickly and so did Christmas day and then Boxing day. It was lovely for Sue to meet Alison and Tom properly this time. She had asked Bet for their ages and bought them the appropriate gifts.

They had a lovely lunch and then Rob and his parents came over in the evening. Rob had bought Alison and Tom a gift each. Alison got a pair of gold earrings and she loved them. Tom got some boxing gloves and a punch-bag, as he was starting to like watching the boxing on TV with Bruce. Bruce got him some punch pads so he could train, but he gave them to Tom once Rob had given him his gift. Tom was delighted. If they thought they got spoilt the last Christmas, it was nothing to this one!

But it was a special one as this was their first one as a proper family. Everyone enjoyed themselves. Tom and Alison had finished all of their homework as soon as they broke up from school; they didn't want it to get in the way of the celebrations and festivities.

Once Christmas was over and they were waiting for the New Year, they had lots of time to chill out but also help around the house. They went in every couple of days to see if Rose and Henry were OK. They'd had Christmas at home this time, saying they wanted to give Bet, Bruce and their family some quality time together.

***

Two more years had passed, and Alison was coming up to sixteen. Tom was almost thirteen.

Alison was on her last year at school and Rob had already left school and was now on his third and final year of City and Guilds to become a plumber. He enjoyed what he did and was looking forward to becoming a fully-fledged plumber, just like his dad. Plumbers were in his family, so it was in his blood.

Alison, on the other hand, had already been doing typing at school, but she wanted to perfect it. She was applying for a Pitman course for when she finished school.

Alison had been wondering what she should do for a job. She wanted to be a secretary but found that she could further her typing and also do a dictation and audio course as well. She wasn't sure about shorthand just yet. Having decided on her career path, she knuckled down at school and did just that. The school years were going very quick now and time seemed to be going so fast!

Tom was now at Harlequin Boys' School, opposite Alison's school. He liked seeing his sister at lunchtime.

Once in a while, Rob would finish early from his course and wait for both of them, so they could all walk home together.

Alison and Rob had been a couple now for four years. They were very happy with each other's company and spent a lot of time together. Rob knew a lot about plumbing before he got started on his course, so it was easy for him when he had to revise for his exams when the time came in May.

Alison started studying early too. She had worked hard for this and she wanted it to pay off. Tom was Tom and he did what he wanted. Bet and Bruce were proud of their children and supported them with everything they wanted to do.

Another Christmas came and went, and Tom's birthday was celebrated with a trip out to town with his friends, Alison, and Rob. Even though it was January, everywhere was still open for the residents of Margate. They popped along with Tom and his friends and Bet, and Bruce had given him money for his birthday, so he could buy what he wanted.

Tom was getting to the age where he was taking more notice of his appearance and Alison couldn't always get into the bathroom as Tom was always in there. He had also noticed a girl at Alison's school, Debbie, who he liked rather a lot. She was in the same year as him and he would notice her at break time.

She was the prettiest girl he had ever seen. She had dark hair cut into a shoulder length bob and big brown eyes. Alison chuckled, as she could see Tom looking at Debbie how Rob used to look at her.

When it came for him to spend his birthday money, he was looking at clothes, instead of cars and trucks. He felt a bit old for them now and had put them away in the cupboard in his bedroom.

Now he was looking at proper and real cars. Bruce also loved cars and had bought him a couple of magazines with lovely posters inside, which he had put up on his bedroom wall.

***

It was already February and Alison only had until May for her final exams. They were doing mock exams in April, but the main ones would be taken in May. As she and Rob were both at crucial times in their learning, they both decided to not see each other until their exams were completely finished. Bet, and Bruce were pleased with that decision. They didn't want anything to ruin Alison's chances of getting the grades she needed for her secretarial course.

Day one of Alison's exams came and she had maths in the morning and then biology in the afternoon.

She had revised a lot over both subjects and was pleased with how they both went. After a few more days of exams, Alison had her typing test. Bruce had bought her a typewriter for her to practice at home.

After five days of non-stop exams, Alison was delighted when they had finished. She finished school early and Tom said he was going to make his own way home. He wanted to walk home with Debbie.

Alison was relieved when she finished at school the following week. They would have their final assembly, but they wouldn't get their exam results until the summer holidays.

"Hi Mum, I'm home!" Alison called out.

"Hi Love, how did it go today?" Bet asked.

"Better than I expected, but I'm so glad I've finished now! What's for tea?" Alison asked.

"Did you see Tom when you left?" Bet asked her.

"No, he isn't finished just yet. He'll probably be walking Debbie home anyway," Alison laughed.

Bet brought in a cup of tea for both of them and some chocolate digestives.

"I was going to do steak and chips for dinner, that OK?" Bet asked.

"Mum, that sounds delicious! Where's Dad is he out?" Alison asked.

"Yes, he popped down to see Henry," Bet told her.

They were enjoying their tea and biscuits.

"Are you seeing Rob later on?"

"No, not yet, he still has a couple of days of exams. He has to do practical ones as well as written, just to show he knows how to unblock a sink and to install a washing machine and try and find leaks and stuff, but he's doing that next week," Alison said.

"Have you thought about what you want to do once you finish school next week?" Bet asked.

"Well, I was thinking of having a week off, if that's all right? But I was going to have a word with Rose and Henry to see if they need a hand with anything. Even if it's stripping the beds, or helping out the meals? Would you mind?" Alison said.

"Not at all, it shows initiative! Plus, once you have finished secretarial college and are working you won't be able to do it. A company won't give you that much time off over the summer. Have a word and see what they both say," Bet said.

"I can help out up until the end of August and at least it means I can help when the homes come for their week. I'm really looking forward to seeing Jo again and Freddie and Charlie; they're getting so big!" Alison said.

***

Alison and Tom had been with Bet and Bruce now for over four years; one as their foster children and three as adopted. Bet and Bruce had been discussing what they wanted to do next. Bruce had been doing bits and pieces to keep him occupied, but as Tom and Alison were growing up, they had talked about fostering again.

They still had plenty of room and they had made a couple of decisions. They wanted to talk to Sandra again. They knew how well Tom, Freddie and Charlie got on, and they wanted to see if they could foster both of the boys.

Bet knew from the previous years that they had already left Craven House and were now living at Benson House, where Jo went when she left. They had to talk to a different member of staff, but they all knew Bet and Bruce. They wanted to talk to the kids about it before they came down for their week away.

They had already spoken with Sandra but wanted to ask the kids tonight.

Alison and Bet heard the key in the door; it was Tom. He had already walked Debbie home. They were getting on really well and he had a big smile on his face when he walked in the door.

"Hi Mum, hi Al, how are you today? Oh Al, how did the last of your exams go?" Tom asked.

"They went rather well; I'm pleased. You're a little late today?" Alison smiled.

"Err, yes, I walked Debbie home," Tom said, going a bit red.

"Tom, there's tea in the pot and also chocolate biscuits, your dad will be in soon," Bet said.

"Where is he?" Tom asked.

"He popped down to see Henry just before Alison got in," Bet said.

Tom grabbed himself a cup and looked for the biscuits. He took his cup into the living room and sat down, with Alison and his mum. Tom had a big gulp of tea when the key went in the door again.

"Ah, that will be your dad. Bruce? Is that you?" Bet asked.

"Yep, why, who else were you expecting?" Bruce laughed.

"No-one, just wanted to make sure you hadn't been kidnapped on your way home," Bet said.

"Bet I was only three doors away!" Bruce laughed.

"You never know these days!" Bet said.

Bet left the living room and fetched a cup for Bruce.

"Ahh lovely, thanks, Bet," Bruce said.

Tom had finished his tea and went in to the kitchen to get another cup for himself.

"Now, I'm glad you're both in. Me and your mum wanted to discuss something with you," Bruce said, as Tom came back into the living room.

Alison and Tom sat up in their chairs. They didn't have big discussions often, but when they did, it was always important.

"Dad, what's up?" Alison asked.

"Nothing's up, Al. Right, me and your mum have been talking. As you know, this is a big house for just four of us. We were wondering if you thought it would be OK for us to foster another child or two?" Bruce began. "Obviously, if you don't want us to, we won't. We want you two to both be happy about this, otherwise we will scrap the whole idea," Bruce added.

"It depends who it is, doesn't it really?" Tom said.

Bet and Bruce both looked at Al.

"Well, you both took us on and that's worked out OK, so why not?" Alison shrugged. "How young are we talking though?"

"We were thinking about ten or twelve, what do you think?" Bruce said.

"Yes, we could give it a go. Do you have anyone in particular in mind then?" Alison asked.

"Well yes, we do actually, but we have to check it out first," Bet smiled.

"Come on then, who do you have in mind?" Tom said.

"Well, there are two boys who we thought about?" Bet said.

Bruce and Bet smiled over at him.

"Freddie and Charlie," Bruce said.

Tom's eyes lit up.

"You mean our Freddie and Charlie, from Craven House?" He said.

"Yes, that's exactly who we thought about. Would you still like us to try and see if we can foster them?" Bruce asked.

"Yes! Definitely! Double definitely!" Tom punched the air. "What do we have to do? Who do we need to talk to about it and do they know yet? Oh, Al, I can't wait!" Tom said, excitedly.

"First, we have to talk to Sandra, but we have done that, but we had to see you both first and see what you thought. Second, we wanted to apply but wanted your blessing for that, and I think I can say that we have that? Third, they don't know yet. We didn't want to build their hopes up in case it couldn't happen," Bruce said.

463

"So now, we know you're both in agreement, we can start the procedure. But they've already left Craven House and are at Benson House," Bet said.

"Where Jo is?" Tom said.

"No Tom, she's now at Denham House."

"Oh, I didn't realise."

"Yes, she doesn't have long there. She'll be leaving next year," Bruce explained.

"Oh, where does she go from there then?" Tom asked.

"She will be given help to get somewhere to live and help to stay in education if she wants: college or get a job or an apprenticeship," Bet said. "When we first saw all of the children that first summer, we got to know the system a bit and that's what we were told would happen."

Alison thought for a moment.

"So, it's Friday now, can we call them today or do we have to wait until Monday?" She asked.

"Well, Al, as it's still only just gone four o'clock, we may catch them at the office. Now, are you both sure about this?" Bruce asked.

"Yes, we are, Dad. I think it would be great!" Alison said.

"OK, so you two go upstairs and get changed and I'll call Sandra and tell her we want to go ahead," Bruce said.

"Dad, why do you have to call Sandra? She's at Craven House," Tom asked.

"She's the boss now, Tom. She's in charge," Bet said.

"How come, Mum?" Alison asked.

"Well, there has been a lot going on before and after you were there and it was how she dealt with it, like a dream. Mr Dunn retired last year, Mr Duffy wanted to stay at Craven House, so he put Sandra forward for it and she got the job. She's actually very good at it. Right, off you go upstairs and come back down once you've both showered," Bruce laughed.

Alison took off her uniform; it needed to be washed and next week she could wear her own clothes as she had technically finished school. She jumped in the shower, while Tom was admiring some cars in his new magazine.

Once Alison had finished in the bathroom, Tom went in. They didn't have any rules about the bathroom, but as they were getting older, they both wanted their privacy. Bet and Bruce understood that and gave them their space.

They weren't going out at all, so they both got their night things on.

They both came down with their dressing gowns on. Bruce had just put down the phone to Sandra.

"Well?" Tom asked. "What did Sandra say?"

Bruce didn't look very happy or excited.

"Oh, have we missed our chance then?" Tom said, looking a little forlorn.

Bruce broke into the biggest smile ever!

"No Tom, we didn't miss our chance. We can see both the boys next weekend! Do you want to come with us?"

Everyone cheered and started hugging each other.

"We really can foster Freddie and Charlie? I can't believe it! So, what happens now then?" Tom asked.

"Well, once we go down to see them both, we have a few meetings and see the boys, see they are happy with everything: the same as you two really. That wasn't too hard was it?" Bruce said.

"No, it was great. Do they know yet?" Alison asked.

"No, not yet. They will be told over the weekend that a family want to meet them, and then we pop down there and say Surprise!" Bruce said.

"I like the idea of that, Dad, and they will love it too!" Tom said.

"The only thing I am worried about is Alison," Tom said.

"Me, why me?" Alison said.

"Because you're going to have three boys in the house and Dad too! We're going to drive you crazy!" They all laughed.

***

After the weekend, Alison popped down to see if Rose and Henry needed some help before the summer holidays started. They were struggling a bit more than they had before, so they both welcomed the extra help.

"That's settled then. You can start after next weekend. Is that OK, Alison?" Rose asked.

"Perfect. Thank, Rose. I can only work until the end of August," Alison replied.

"That's fine, Al. We don't have as much as we used to after the holidays. It settles down then and then we start thinking about the winter," Rose replied. "Enjoy your weeks' break before you start. Rose said.

"Did Mum tell you where we are going next weekend?" Alison asked.

"Yes, she did! I bet you're all excited?" Rose Said.

"Yes, you should see Tom, he can't wait especially as they don't know it's us coming," Alison said.

"They haven't been told; they want us to surprise them. I had better get back, thank you, Rose," she added.

***

The following week came around quickly. Alison had her final week at school. She had a great time with her friends, Stacey, Lisa, and Kim. Stacey was going to do her Pitman Course, the same as Alison, Kim was starting an apprenticeship to become a seamstress, and Lisa was starting a job at Woolworths, until her results came back, then she would make a decision after that.

"Mum, what time are we setting off?" Tom asked.

"We're going in about ten minutes, I hope you're ready?" Bet asked.

"Yes, I have been ready for ages!" Tom replied.

"Alison are you nearly ready?" Bet asked.

"Yes, Mum, just coming. I wanted to grab a couple of magazines to read on the way down," Alison said.

Ten minutes later they were in the car, on their way down to Benson House. It wasn't far away from Craven House. As always, it didn't take too long to get there as Tom was talking all the time and Alison was reading her magazines and Bet was humming along to the radio.

When they pulled up outside Benson House, Sandra was already there waiting for them.

"Do they know yet, Sandra?" Bet asked.

"No, we have kept it quiet since we told them, so they will be surprised to see you all," Sandra said.

Benson House wasn't as big as Craven House. It didn't take as many children or young people. They made their way inside the building, and Sandra was welcomed by Tina, who had worked there for a while and had met Bet, Bruce, Alison, and Tom.

Tina showed them into the living room where Freddie and Charlie were already seated in their best clothes.

466

They first saw Bet and Bruce and looked a bit confused, thinking they were just visiting someone. Then Tom popped his head around the door and then Alison.

"Hi, remember us?" Tom smiled.

"Tom, Alison, Betty and Bruce, yes, what are you doing here?" Freddie said.

"Surprise! We're here to see you two!" Tom said.

Freddie and Charlie both looked at Sandra and she nodded her head. They ran over to Tom and jumped on him.

"Oh, Tom! It's you coming to see us! We thought we would have a nightmare family, like you…" He trailed off. He didn't want to remind them of that horrible family. They went up to Alison and hugged her, then Bet and Bruce.

"We can't believe it! So, what happens now?" Freddie said.

"Well, if there isn't any tea here, what if we all go out and have something to eat and drink, what about Wimpy?" Bruce said.

"Yes!" All three boys shouted.

Sandra and Roger went out with them. When Roger saw how big Alison and Tom had gotten, they knew that they had made the right choice letting them go with Bet and Bruce. You could see that they were both happy; a lovely family unit and now they were hoping to expand it.

They went along to town. Alison had completely forgotten about town; they were so used to Margate, it felt like they had never lived anywhere else. They went along to Wimpy. Tom was in his element, with his friends and Bruce was enjoying some more male company and they started talking about cars.

Bet, Alison and Sandra sat in the booth behind them.

They ordered their food and drinks and were still chatting.

"Alison, what are you doing for your birthday this year? You're going to be seventeen," Sandra said.

"Oh, I have no idea yet, I've just finished my exams, so I don't know yet," Alison replied.

"What do you want to do, once you get your results?"

"I'm hopefully going onto secretarial college in September, but now school is finished, I'm having next week off, then I'm starting work for the summer with Rose and Henry, at the guest house," Alison said.

"Oh, that will be good, so we will see you when we come down?" Sandra said.

"Will you be coming down now that you're the boss?" Alison asked.

"Oh yes, because I still like to see the children having a good time," Sandra said.

Their drinks arrived.

"So, what happens after today, once this first visit is done?" Alison asked.

"Well, there will be another couple of visits here first, then they come down for a day to visit and then…"

"An overnight?" Alison laughed; she knew the system.

"Yes, and if it's successful, or anyone want to do another overnight, they can. Then we go for the placement and take it from there," Sandra said.

"You and Tom both look happy. Are you still seeing that young man I saw you with at your party?" Sandra asked.

Alison blushed.

"Rob? Yes. He's training to be a plumber. He's finished the last of his exams and practical tests this week, so like me, he now has to wait until he gets his results," Alison said. "And if he does, he already has a job lined up with his dad," she added.

"That sounds like a good job to have. People will always need plumbers," Sandra said.

Once they had all finished their food and drinks, Sandra suggested that they have a look around town and then head back to Benson House. The boys wanted to show Bet and Bruce their bedroom now that Tom and Alison had left the home. They made their way back.

Freddie and Charlie were excited to show them their bedroom; they had bunked beds again and their room was decorated differently to Craven House. It was a darker blue and there were plain curtains in their room, to match the carpet.

Bruce had gone to unlock the boot and took out two carrier bags. They'd brought presents for Freddie and Charlie. Tom gave them their bags. He'd remembered how much they both liked cars and trucks too, but like him, they were growing up, so Tom had chosen a classic car for each of them. One had a Jaguar and the other had a Rolls Royce.

They both received a T-shirt and a pair of shorts, and a pair of pumps each.

Alison could remember what it was like when Bet and Bruce had come to see them. They had showered them with gifts and lot of love. She was glad Mum and Dad were doing this. They had a house big enough for everyone and to make two more children part of a family and a happy life, she couldn't think of nicer parents for a child to have.

Bet had bought Alison and Tom some clothes and Freddie and Charlie some sketch pads and art materials. Freddie got up and showed them all a pad of what he had drawn, cars, trucks, trains; he had a real talent for it. Charlie liked to draw as well, but he did more still life, like a bowl of fruit or a cup and saucer.

"So, we have two budding artists on our hands, do we?" Bruce asked, admiring their artwork.

Sadly, it was getting to the time that they would have to leave.

"But you're coming again, aren't you?" Freddie asked.

"Of course, we are, you try keeping us away!" Tom said. "We're going to be like proper brothers!"

"Of course, we're coming back. Just try to stop us!" Bruce laughed.

Bet went over to them and hugged them.

"Come on, Tom, you're going to see us again soon," Freddie said.

"See you in two weeks?" Bruce asked.

Sandra nodded. "Yes, see you in two weeks," she smiled.

Tom was full of chatter on the way home. He was so excited to see his friends again.

***

The next time they went down there, Alison had already started with Rose and Henry and she couldn't leave them in the lurch, so the three of them went.

Freddie and Charlie were a little worried that Alison didn't want to see them, but Bet assured them that it was only because Alison was working and that they would see her again soon.

"We've made lunch for you this time." Freddie said, producing some fairy cakes. "I hope you like them."

"I'm sure we will, Freddie and Charlie," Bet smiled.

Tina and Roger were busy sorting things out. Sandra was only there the time before so that she could surprise the boys and see Alison and Tom and wanted to catch up with how they were doing.

They had made them a selection of sandwiches and tea or squash to for lunch.

When they had finished, tina brought in the fairy cakes and a big chocolate cake. Both Tom and Bruce's eyes lit up wherever cake was.

They sat down with another cup of tea and the fairy cakes.

469

"These are very good, boys! You're very good cooks! You must show me how you made them when you come to see us at home," Bet said.

The boys had big beaming smiles.

They'd all had another promising visit and Roger and Tina were pleased how it went.

"We were wondering if you wanted us to bring the boys down to you next time?" Tina asked.

"Yes, that would be great. In two weeks' time again?" Bruce said.

"Yes, that would be fine. And don't forget they will be coming down for a holiday anyway with all of you in the summer. So, we can see them again then," Bruce added.

"Well, actually, it may be before that." Tina said.

"What do you mean, Tina?" Bet asked.

"Well, as this is your second time down and if they come down in two weeks' time, the next visit will be two weeks later, if all goes well, you would normally have your meeting that following week and then the boys can come back with you, so you may see them before the summer holidays, but only for a week or so?" Tina said.

Bruce and Bet looked at each other. They couldn't believe it.

"That quick!" Bruce said.

"Yes, Mr Taylor will see you next week before the kids come down and then we have a meeting with Mr Prowse and then take it from there."

"Oh my gosh, I didn't think it would be that quick!" Bet said.

"It's not a problem, is it, Bet?" Tina asked.

"No, of course not, but we had better get their rooms ready! It still needs decorating. I know what you will be doing for the next two weeks, Bruce!" Bet laughed.

The boys had been playing in their bedroom with Tom, showing him their new things. They decided to tell him and Alison when they got home. It was already four o'clock, so they said goodbye to everyone and hugged the boys and left.

***

"Hi everyone, how did it go today?" Alison asked when she got in from work.

470

"It went really well Al. Freddie and Charlie look so happy when we get there," Tom said.

"Alison, Tom, we need to talk to you," Bruce said.

They both sat down on the sofa and waited for Bruce to speak.

"So, it looks like we could have Freddie and Charlie a little earlier than we expected, it's fine though, it just means we have to get their rooms ready," Bruce said.

"Dad, that's OK, we can help, can't we, Al?" Tom said.

"You don't mind?" Bet said.

"No, of course not. How early are we talking?" Alison asked.

"Six weeks! They'll be coming down for the day in two weeks, then the following two weeks, they will stay overnight and then two weeks later on. Just like you two did. Then, hopefully, we will have a meeting at the home, sign all of the paperwork and hey presto, they will be part of our family!" Bruce said, smiling.

"So, are you two OK with this? We can look at paper and paint on Monday, but what if we just have a look at the rooms and see what we can do now?" Bet said.

"We can clean the rooms up before you get paint and paper, so that's a start. Let's have a look now Dad, then we can make a start tomorrow," Alison suggested.

They all went upstairs. It was a bit untidy and the windows needed cleaning, a fresh coat of paint and wallpaper, curtains, and new carpets for both rooms.

"Al, are you working tomorrow at Rose's?" Bet asked.

"Yes, but I think I'm finishing after the dinners have been done, so I can come and give you a hand," she added.

They all got up extra early the following day. Alison had to be at Rose's for 7 am to get the breakfasts started. They didn't have any new arrivals coming until Monday, so Rose let Alison go once breakfast was all finished.

She got in and everyone was upstairs, stripping the wallpaper off the walls.

"Al, I thought you weren't finishing until this evening?" Bet asked.

"Rose let me go early. They haven't any new guests until tomorrow and she said that there wasn't anything to do until dinners, so I'm here to give you a hand," she said.

They had finished stripping the bedroom walls to one of the rooms; with four hands it didn't take too long. Tom followed Bruce with a black bag, picking up all the old wallpaper and sticky paste and throwing it in the bin.

When they cleared that room, they made a start on the next one.

Alison could hear the phone ringing downstairs. Bruce was up the ladder and Bet was below him, peeling paper off the wall.

"I'll get it!" Alison called out.

"Dad! Dad! Come quick!" Alison screamed.

Bruce was down the stairs in no time.

"Al, what's up?" Bruce said.

"Dad, it's Henry, he's collapsed! Rose, she's called for an ambulance, but she sounds terrified," Alison told him.

"Right, everyone, down tools!" Bruce said.

Bet grabbed the keys and they ran out the door. They got to Rose's and pushed the door open.

"Rose? Rose, where are you?" Bruce called out.

"I'm downstairs in the dining room!" Rose called back. "It's OK, Henry, love, the ambulance is coming," Rose said, rather shaken.

"Rose, what happened?" Bruce asked. Henry was lying, face down on the floor with a blanket over him to keep him warm.

"Henry, Henry mate, can you hear me?" Bruce asked.

Bet had come downstairs with the kids. They didn't know what to do; Henry wasn't moving.

"I'll wait upstairs for when the ambulance comes and show them where to go," Alison said.

"Good girl," Bet said. "Rose, do you want anything? Tea? Brandy?"

"No, I just want to make sure Henry's OK," Rose replied.

Then two paramedics came down the stairs with a stretcher. They looked at Henry and moved the blanket slightly so they can do the relevant checks.

"What's his name?" The paramedic asked.

"Henry," Rose said.

"Henry? Can you hear me, Henry?" One of the paramedics asked. "No response, but he has a pulse. We'll have to take him to the hospital. Is anyone coming with us?" He asked Rose.

"Yes, I'm his partner," Rose replied.

"Rose, don't worry, we'll stay here, you go with Henry," Bruce said, hugging her tightly.

The ambulance drove away.

"Alison, do you know what was for dinner this evening?" Bet asked.

"It was going to be shepherd's pie and veg. I think Rose has already made it; she was starting it when I was leaving. It's more than likely in the fridge," Alison said.

Bet opened the fridge. There were two shepherd's pies and a trifle.

"Right, that's dinner for the guests and dessert, so we can do that for her," Bet said. Bet looked at the time. "I think we need to make a start on cooking these pies Al, and start on the veg, what do you think?" Bet asked.

"Yes, we may as well make a start, time's getting on and it will give us something to do," Alison said.

They prepared the vegetables and the phone rang.

"That's the phone, it might be the hospital," Bet said to Bruce.

"Hello? Rose...yes, how is he? OK, I'm on my way, hold on tight," Bruce said and hung up.

"How's Henry?" Bet asked.

"He had a mild heart attack. When he was on the floor he fainted with the shock, but he's doing all right. Rose needs us to get his pyjamas and some other stuff. He's come around but was a little disorientated waking up in hospital. She says he has to stay in for a few days. I'm going to get Rose now, are you three OK here?" Bruce said.

It didn't' take long to collect Rose from the hospital. Bruce brought her downstairs to Bet and Alison. Tom was helping with the drinks.

"Hey Rose, how is he?" Alison asked.

"I think he's more shocked than anything Al. He didn't realise he hit the deck. He thought he just fainted, so he was surprised to wake up in hospital! I just need to get his stuff," Rose said.

"Rose, please sit down and have a cup of tea, just for a few minutes. Bruce can get his pyjamas, can't you Bruce?" Bet said.

Bruce shot off to their bedroom and packed up a bag with what he thought Henry would need. knew where their bedroom was, so he went and.

"You don't mind taking me back to the hospital, do you, Bruce? Oh, I forgot we have guests!" Rose said.

"Don't worry about that Rose, me and Alison have it all under control. Shepherd's pie in the fridge and trifle," Bet said. Rose nodded.

"Have you finished your tea? Do you want to make a move then Rose?" Bruce said.

"Dad, can I come too?" Tom asked. Bruce looked at Rose and she nodded.

"Henry will be pleased to see him," she said.

They all left, and Alison and Bet continued to get the dinner ready. The guests would be here in a few minutes. Alison put the kettle on to fill up the teapots and Bet started to dish up dinner.

The first couple of people came down for dinner.

"Is everything OK? We saw an ambulance pull up outside?" A lady said.

"Yes, the boss was taken to hospital but he's going to be OK," Bet said. "Please, take your seats, dinner will be served in a moment," Bet said.

Alison brought in their dinners and Bet brought in their teapots. The next couple came down. They hadn't noticed anything, but their eyes were like saucers when they saw their dinner. Rose gave generous portions for her meals and Alison and Bet did the same. It meant that people would come back if they enjoyed the food.

***

"Hi Henry, how are you feeling, love?" Rose asked.

"I feel OK, Rose. I don't know what I'm doing here though." Henry said. "Bruce, Tom, it's good to see you!" He added.

He looked at Rose and realised they must have bought her to see him.

"Thanks, Bruce." He smiled, shaking him by the hand.

"How do you feel, Henry?" Bruce asked.

"I feel fine, honestly. Can I get out of here now then?"

"No, Love, you have to stay in for a couple of days," Rose said.

"A couple of days? But I feel fine Rose!" Henry said.

"Henry, you had a mild heart attack. You have to stay in for a couple of days; they want to keep an eye on your blood pressure for a bit longer," Rose said.

"A mild heart attack? I thought I'd just fainted! I didn't realise, Rose, I'm so sorry," Henry said.

"What are you sorry for, you silly sod?" Rose laughed.

"Sorry because I can't help out at home," Henry said.

"Oh, don't worry about that! We have that covered," Bruce assured him. "Bet and Al are doing dinners and we will be there in the morning to help with breakfast and stripping beds and that, so don't worry, OK?"

"But Al said you have another couple of kids coming in a few weeks," Henry said.

"Yes, we do, but we have done lots already today, so it's not a problem and when you're feeling better and fighting fit, you can give us a hand. We have two lads coming and I think I need some moral support," Bruce said, winking at Henry. "I think we are going to have our hands full, but we wouldn't have it any other way," he added, tousling Tom's hair.

"That gives you a good incentive to get better and get out of here, but only when the doc gives the go ahead, OK?" Bruce said.

Rose was thankful and gave Bruce a little smile. It meant that Henry had more than one reason to live for.

Henry was only in hospital for a couple more days and Bruce and Rose went to collect him. Henry was delighted to be going home. As soon as they got in the door, Henry breathed a sigh of relief.

"When you're in those places, you don't think you're ever going to come out again!" he said.

He saw the look of shock on Rose's face.

"I'm only joking, Rose! I'm so glad to be home though and getting stuck back in," he added.

"Oh no, you're not!" Bruce said. "You have to take it easy or you'll be straight back to hospital, get it?" Bruce said sternly.

"OK, OK, I get it! So, am I going to have to stay in bed then?" Henry asked.

"No, you can rest in the dayroom and you'll be waited on hand and foot until the doctor says different," Bruce said.

"But Rose, we have the summer hols upon us!" Henry suddenly remembered.

"Yes, we do, and we have that all covered. Bruce and Bet will be here as always and Alison and Tom, the two new kiddies are going to help out and Rob and his mum are coming into help, so you're not doing anything, is that clear?" Rose said.

"OK, I know when I'm beat." Henry laughed. "So, I will go up to the dayroom and…" Henry cut off. Bet and Alison came in to see how he was.

"Better for seeing some friendly faces, not telling me what to do!" Henry laughed.

"Oh, don't think you're getting around us; we're all with Rose and you won't get her or us to do otherwise until the doc gives you the all-clear," Bet said.

"Well, that's me told then!" Henry said.

Bet and Alison gave him a hug.

"Right, we have to crack on, so see you later, Henry," Bruce said.

* * *

Bruce and Tom were still sorting out the bedrooms and Rob and his mum were helping out at the guest house. Even though they had Freddie and Charlie coming, they didn't want anything to spoil it for them. They had been helping out at Rose's and then heading back home and doing what they could at night to get the rooms finished.

It had all been hectic but definitely worth it.

Saturday arrived and Tina and Roger were already on their way. Alison was at Rose's from early morning until gone 8 pm every day. Once they knew the guests had gone, she and Rose would go up and strip the beds, clean the room, hoover, clean the bathroom, and then remake the beds with fresh bedding. It didn't take long, but she was shattered.

When she knew that Tina and Roger would be there, Rose let her pop off for an hour or so to spend some time with them. Bet and Bruce had told Tina and Roger what happened to Henry, and that all hands were on deck. But that didn't stop Tom taking the boys up to his bedroom and then Bet and Bruce took them all up to see their new bedrooms, which hadn't quite been finished.

Bet looked a little worried.

"But they're coming back in two weeks, so that gives you plenty of time, if it doesn't get done, Bet, don't worry, you do have a lot on your plate. Please stop worrying," Roger told her.

Both he and Tina smiled at them both.

It was like they were back to square one with Tom and Alison again and all the nerves came back.

"Mum, it will be fine! You know we will all muck in," Tom said.

"Hi, I'm home!" Alison shouted out.

Tom, Freddie and Charlie all came running down the stairs.

"Hey, be careful, boys, we don't want anyone to hurt themselves!" Bet said.

"Hi Alison!" Freddie said, running up to her and hugging her hard. Charlie followed suit.

"Hey! Look at how tall you've both gotten! I can't believe it! It must be all of those greens you're eating, like Popeye!" Alison laughed.

They were both so pleased to see her.

"I'm sorry I wasn't here when you arrived, but I have had to…"

"Yes, we know. How is Henry?" Freddie asked.

"He's on the mend, but he still can't do anything too strenuous, but he'll get there. So, what are you doing today then?" Alison asked.

"Well apart from having something to eat, we were going to take a walk down to the beach and see where we end up, if that's OK, Boys?" Bet said.

Both of the boys nodded.

Alison had a bite to eat and a cup of tea.

"I have to go, I'm afraid. I've got to get back to help Rose. It was lovely seeing you all and I'll see you two in two weeks' time; hopefully, we'll have your rooms ready by then. Oh, I forgot to ask, do you like the colours of your bedrooms? Me and Tom chose them, as you're not little kids anymore, we thought you may like a bit more of a grown look," Alison said.

"We love them! And the colours are great!" Freddie and Charlie said.

"Well, we can get you some posters if you want to decorate and put your own mark on them. See you later everyone," Alison said and then left to return to work.

***

The visit went well, and everyone was pleased with how it went. Between working at the guest house and sorting out the boy's bedrooms the boys' were coming for their overnight stay. Thankfully, everything had been finished. They were all shattered but delighted they had it all finished and complete.

Tom went with Bet and Bruce to collect the boys, who were really excited. Thank goodness for Dorothy and Rob helping out with the guest house, otherwise they would never had managed it all.

The boys were going to visit Rose and Henry the following day and everyone was excited, even Henry. He had been cooped up indoors and was getting bored. Rose let him sit in the garden, otherwise he would start trying to do things.

The boys' visit went extremely well, and Tina and Roger were both happy how it was all going. On Friday they would be back at Benson House to have their meeting. The next meeting went as good as expected and they had all of the paperwork, signed, and sealed. They asked Freddie and Charlie if they wanted to stay for a little while, like Tom and Alison had done, but they wanted to say goodbye and leave pretty much straight away.

They had only been at Benson House for just over a year or so, but they didn't get upset like they did when they left Craven House.

They said their goodbyes and Bruce took their belongings and put them in the boot. Tom, Freddie and Charlie sat in the back of the car and chatted all the way back home.

The boy's settled in well. They didn't have much time to do much because in a week, the children from the home would be coming down to Margate.

Tom, Freddie and Charlie would go out on trips with the staff and kids to let them know the best places to go were. Freddie and Charlie loved what they were doing. They had seen Tom numerous times since he moved down to Margate, and they felt amazing that they were now going to be part of that.

***

The first home that was visiting Margate was Acorn, followed by Denham, and then Craven house and finally Benson. Jo who was now at Acorn House and would be the first one they saw. They were all excited about the kids coming down and extra excited to see Jo. She did know that Freddie and Charlie were now living with Alison and Tom.

Saturday was here and Rose had been running around like a headless chicken, as had Bet and Bruce. Henry was still out of action, but they all got stuck in to do what needed to be done.

The coach pulled up and Alison, Tom, Freddie and Charlie were waiting at the front door.

Jo was the first one off the coach and her face lit up. She was so excited to be back! It was going to be her last time there, that summer.

Alison and Jo hugged, then she grabbed the boys and was so happy to see Bet, Bruce and Rose.

478

They went inside and opened up the doors so they could all go into their allocated rooms. Jo was surprised to see Alison helping out in the kitchen; she wanted to help out too.

"But Elaine, I'm bored on my own. If I ask Rose and Bet and if they say yes, can I help out?" Jo asked.

"But Jo, you're on your holiday, why would you want to help us out? You should be enjoying yourself!" Rose said.

"Since I left Craven House, I have felt lost since Alison and Tom left."

"Oh, I'm sorry, Jo," Alison said.

"Al, it's not your fault; you were able to move on and have a family and I am so happy for you, but this year is my last in care. I've started doing this bookkeeping course and I'm really not getting on with it. I can do the basics and accounts a bit. My math is good, I just don't understand it. So, if I at least do something for a week that has nothing to do with numbers, then it's all the break I need." Jo laughed.

"OK, Jo, I tell you what I will do, we can try you out for a couple of days and if it's too much, you stop and continue with your holiday. What do you think?" Rose asked.

"Deal!" Jo said, shaking Rose's hand.

Jo got stuck in with the stripping off the beds. If a child wet the bed, she stripped and cleaned it and left it to dry. She was so good with the kids, they liked her, she was like a big sister. Jo worked well at the guest house and seemed to enjoy it.

Elaine pulled Rose and Bet to one side.

"Do you know what? Jo hasn't been herself until she has come here and seen the other kids. I haven't seen her this happy at all since she came to Acorn House," Elaine said.

Bet and Rose went into the kitchen to have a chat.

"Do you know what, Bet, I think Jo has adapted really well. Me and Henry were talking last night about it. What do you think about if we had Jo work for us permanently and became part of our family? What do you think?" Rose asked.

"Well, it's not difficult to see that this place is too much for just the two of you to do on your own anymore, Rose. If you get Jo in to help on a day to day basis, we can always help in the holidays as we have done. I think it would be a brilliant idea. You'll need to talk to Elaine and Sandra first though, to see if they will let her go just yet and you need to make sure she definitely doesn't want to continue this course," Bet said.

"Bet, you have seen how good she is with the kids, what if we do a trial run, let her stay for the whole four weeks and then at the end of it, if she wants to go back, then we can take her back. If we propose that to Elaine and Sandra, they may go with it?" Rose suggested.

Jo continued to work all week at Whelk Combe, and she loved it; she was a natural. Rose had a quick word with Elaine about her proposal. Elaine spoke to Sandra and see what she thought. They all agreed if this is what Jo wanted, then she could try out for the month and then take it from there once the month was over.

The night before they were due to leave, Elaine, Rose and Bet spoke with Jo in the dining room. They told her their plans for the next month and asked if she would be interested in staying on for the rest of the month.

"Really? I can stay the rest of the month to see how it goes. Yes! I would love to, thank you," Jo said. "I can't believe it, that's fantastic!" she said, hugging Rose, Bet and then Elaine.

"But if at the end of the month, you don't want to continue, Benson House will bring you back to Acorn House, is that OK?" Elaine said.

"Yes, that's fine," Jo replied, absolutely ecstatic.

She knew she wouldn't be going back, only to get her stuff.

Jo excelled in the weeks that followed. She loved it; she was back to her normal self. The other homes noticed it as well. George and Celia from Craven House noticed a huge change in her, and they had only seen her a few weeks before the holidays started.

In the last week, Sandra came down and saw for herself the change in Jo. She had arranged a meeting with Rose and Henry sat in on the meeting, along with Bet. They had all noticed a huge change in Jo's behaviour; not that she was ever any trouble, she just seemed more alive than she had been in a long time.

Sandra had had a meeting with Elaine before she came down to Margate and asked her thoughts on it. She had agreed with everyone else. This was a great setting for her. She just wanted to hear Rose and Henry's thoughts on it and could they give her a home and a job all in one. What if it didn't work out?

"Sandra, Jo has been a breath of fresh air, she has lifted the kids' spirits no end and Alison said that she is the same Jo she has always known and loved."

480

"We would love to offer Jo a full-time position and a home, and a family life. It's a busy one and although it's quieter in the winter months, there are always things to do. We know she's not eighteen yet, but hopefully that won't really matter?" Rose asked.

"Can I add something to that?" Henry asked.

"As you know, I had mild heart attack not that long ago and I have been completely out of action ever since. We have Alison and Bet," Henry looked at Bet, "And yes the kids get involved too, but as Rose has said, Jo has been a breath of fresh air, so if it's possible we would like her to stay. We know she will have to collect her things and say her goodbyes. But we really would like to offer her a chance, as this is what these kids have had; a chance and my goodness they have really flourished and blossomed. Well that's it really." Henry said.

Sandra knew what Henry said was true. Alison and Tom had really blossomed, and she knew Freddie and Charlie would too. She was going to let Jo have a chance of a happy family life.

"I agree with all that you say, so what if we get Jo in and ask her?" Sandra suggested.

Alison got up to find Jo. She was upstairs helping out with the kids; she loved doing that.

"Jo, can you come downstairs for a minute?" Alison asked.

"Al, is there anything wrong?" Jo asked.

"No, but can you come down with me?" Alison said.

Jo swallowed hard, *oh hell, what had she done wrong?* she thought.

"Jo, please sit down," Sandra said.

"Have I done anything wrong?" Jo asked.

"No, not at all, we want to have a word with you, that's all," Sandra said. "Jo, how have you enjoyed these last four weeks here at the guest house?"

"I have really enjoyed it! The work, seeing the kids' faces, who have never been to the seaside before! I've loved every minute of it!" she added.

"Well, Rose and Henry want to talk to you about something," Sandra nodded to Rose and Henry.

Jo looked at them both.

"Jo, you have been a breath of fresh air these last few weeks and we would like to offer you a job and a home for you permanently, if you're interested?" Rose asked.

Jo had a look of surprise on her face; she couldn't believe it.

"Oh my God! Yes! Yes! I would love that, that would be fantastic!" She replied and ran over to Rose and Henry and hugged both of them. She then hugged Alison and Bet and then Sandra.

"You're really sure I can stay?" Jo asked Sandra. "I'm not eighteen yet."

"Yes, but sometimes there are extraordinary circumstances and even though I know everyone at Acorn House will miss you, I think Rose and Henry need you much more," Sandra smiled.

Jo gave Sandra an extra hug.

"But what about my things at Acorn House?" she asked.

"Well…I guessed what your answer would be, so I've sorted that—they're in the boot of my car. I brought them down just in case and everyone knows how much you love it down here and you will see them all again next summer," Sandra said.

Jo was so happy.

"Come on, Jo, I'll show you where your bedroom is!" Rose said. Jo was delighted with this news. She could hardly contain herself.

When she put her things away, she collected the stuff she had in the bedroom she was sharing with the other girls and put them into her new bedroom.

That evening went rather quick and breakfast time was here already. When everyone had eaten, they were getting ready to leave. Jo had helped the other kids pack up their stuff to go back to Benson House and Freddie and Charlie, said their goodbyes to their friends who were getting on the coach.

When the coach drove out of sight, they all went back inside. Rose had put the kettle on, and they all had a cup of tea. They all flaked out on the chairs in the dining room. After they had their tea, they had to go and strip all of the beds and then do all of the washing.

"Jo, are you sure you have made the right decision? You may change your mind once we have done all of the cleaning today!" Alison laughed.

"I have definitely made the right decision and I'm not afraid of hard work," she said.

"Good, because we are all going to be working hard today," Rose said. "Once we get all of the beds stripped and the bedding washed and dried in the garden and in the drier, then it will all need ironing, which will be done tomorrow."

"This is the work not seen by the guests," Alison said.

"But believe me, it's all worth it," Rose said.

When they had finished all of their chores for the day, Alison said goodbye to Rose, Henry and Jo. Alison was coming back tomorrow to iron the duvet covers with Jo, then it was all done until it was needed next time.

"I'm off now, see you in the morning!" Alison said.

She had enjoyed working at the guest house but was glad the summer holidays were now coming to an end.

She opened the door and Bruce and the boys were in.

"Hey Al, we're off to get fish and chips, what do you want?" Bruce asked.

"Oh, cod and chips please, Dad," she replied.

"Oh, Al, there's a letter over there for you; it came this morning," Bruce told her.

"OK, thanks. I wonder who can be writing to me? Oh, Dad, it could be my results from my exams," Alison said.

"You had better open it then and see how you've done!" Bruce said.

"Well, I should really wait for Mum," Alison said.

"Tom, go and see if your mum is finished with Rose and Henry," Bruce asked.

By the time Tom got to the door, Bet was just opening it with her key.

"Oh, sorry Tom, did I catch you?" Bet asked.

"No Mum, Dad asked me to come and get you," Tom said.

"Oh, is anything wrong?" Bet asked.

"No, Alison has gotten her results and she didn't want to open them without you being there."

"Go on then, love, open them up," Bet said to Alison.

Freddie and Charlie had both come into the room as well now and everyone was waiting with bated breath.

Alison opened up the envelope and read the letter.

"Oh, my goodness! I got four A+, one A, four B and a C. I've passed! I can't believe it!" Alison said.

"Why not, Alison? You've studied so much. We hardly saw anything of you and neither did Rob. So, well done, Al. Well done!" Bruce said.

"Congratulations Al, you have done amazing, did you get the grades you needed for typing college?" Bet asked.

"Yes mum, I got an A+, that's what I needed. I got the other A+'s for Math, English, Typing and Home Economics, that's what I needed, I am so chuffed," Alison said.

Bruce and Bet looked at each other and then at Alison.

"Al, we have something to tell you…" Bet said, "we know we didn't get chance really to celebrate your birthday this year, because of what happened with Henry and all hands on deck to help out at the guesthouse, so this is for you," Bruce said.

He left the room and came back with an envelope. He handed it to Alison, inside was a letter saying that there had been twenty driving lessons all paid for with a local driving school.

"I don't know what to say, Mum, Dad," Alison said. She had wanted to drive and now she was seventeen, she could take lessons.

"They are to start whenever you want to, so do you want us to arrange it for you or do you want to sort it out yourself? But don't forget, Al, you have to apply for your provisional licence first though," Bruce said.

"Erm, can I apply for my licence first then I can arrange for the lessons?" Alison said.

"Of course, darling!" Bruce said.

"Mum, I know it's the weekend, are you busy on Monday? Would you come with me in to town, so I can get some office clothes, so at least I will look the part," Alison said.

"Of course, after what we have been doing for the last few weeks, we need some retail therapy, so yes, count me in. Your dad can stay indoors with your brothers," Bet said.

Alison told Rob later on in the evening about her results and Rob came around a couple of days later and told her that he got his results for his exams to be a plumber and he got a distinction. They were both thrilled.

When they went shopping, Alison looked at the suits and found some nice ones in Marks and Spencer. She decided on a few separates and picked up a cream skirt and a brown jacket, a deep lilac jacket and a beige jacket.

By the time she had finished, she had spent a small fortune on new clothes. Bet had a look around, and picked up a couple of items she needed, then she suggested that they get something to eat.

"Molly's?" Alison suggested.

"Where else?" Bet replied with a smile.

They went inside and it wasn't very busy as it was a weekday and lunchtime had already been and gone. They had some sandwiches and then they had a cake each.

"Should we take some back home, for your dad and the boys?" Bet asked.

"I think they may be a bit hurt if we don't take anything back, Mum, especially Dad!" Alison laughed.

They chose some cakes for the boys, then Bet hailed down a mini cab. They had too much to carry to get the bus.

As Bet put her key in the door, she heard Bruce put the phone down.

"Hi Bruce, who was that?" Bet asked.

"It was Stacey for Al, she's left her number and I wrote in on the pad for her," Bruce said. "Ooh, I see a Molly's box?" Bruce asked.

"Yes, but for after dinner!" Bet said.

"I'll take this lot upstairs then I'll give Stacey a call," Alison said.

"Hi Stacey, you OK?" Alison asked when Stacey picked up the phone.

"Yes, yes, that's great! Are you excited? I'm so excited for you, yes, see you on Monday…that's why I wasn't in when you called, I was shopping for some stuff for college…Yes, bye!" Alison said, putting down the receiver.

"What did Stacey want?" Bet asked.

"She only just got her results in as she had been away and wanted to let me know and yes, she's happy to be going to college like me. She asked me if I have got any new office clothes, I told her I was out doing that today. She wants me to go out with her on Thursday, do you mind if I go, Mum?" Alison asked.

"Of course! I think it would be good to catch up with Stacey before you get started and you might see something else you didn't see today," Bet said. Bruce nodded his head in agreement.

Alison had a couple of days of not doing too much, which she needed after all of the holidays helping out with Rose and Henry. The money came in handy and she was still getting pocket money. Bruce had said until Alison was earning her own money, they would still help her out financially. What she didn't know was Bet and Bruce had already seen a car for her.

***

Thursday came around and Alison and Stacey met up in town and chose some new things. Alison had picked up a couple of blouses she had missed on Monday. Stacey wanted to get quite a lot. They popped into Wimpy for lunch.

Alison picked up some underwear when they went into Marks and Spencer, then diverted into the sexy underwear section.

485

"What are you doing over this side for, Stace?" Alison asked.

"Well, I wanted to get some nice stuff; you know, the silky stuff," Stacey replied.

"Why?" Alison asked.

"I've got a new bloke and I think it's nice to have some nice underwear on when you go out with him," Stacey said as she looked at the lingerie.

"Oh yes, who is this new bloke then, Stace?" Alison asked.

"His name's Mike and I met him in the local fish shop. He's lovely Al! He's tall, dark, and very handsome! He works over at that construction company as a carpenter, he does repair work. Oh, Al, you will love him! You can meet him in a bit, he's picking us up from here and we'll drop you off," Stacey said.

"Oh, OK, thanks. It'll be nice to meet your new man," Alison said.

They finished their lunch and then popped over to the shoe shop. Stacey picked up four or five pairs of shoes. Alison lost count in the end. Thankfully she and Stacey had slightly different taste, so they didn't have anything the same.

"Mike should be here soon, I told him to pick us up at four outside Curtess Shoes. Oh, there he is over there, in the Blue Ford Escort," Stacey said, waving over to a nice tall guy.

They walked over to him standing outside his car. Stacey introduced Alison to Mike.

"Are you heading home now, Stace?" Mike asked.

"Yes, but can we drop Alison home first? She only lives around the corner from town, but I don't think it's fair making her walk home," Stacey said.

"It's fine," Mike said.

They all got into the car.

When they pulled up to Alison's house, she thanked Mike and got out of the car.

Bruce was in the window and noticed Alison getting out of a strange car.

"Hi, I'm home!" Alison said.

"Hi Honey, who was that you were with?" Bruce asked.

"I was with Stacey and her new boyfriend picked us up," Alison said. "He seems a nice enough bloke, Dad, he works over at that construction company, he's a carpenter."

"Wow! He told you a lot about himself," Bruce said.

"He didn't; Stacey told me all about him. She met him in the local fish shop, apparently. Right, I'm just going to put this upstairs, I'll be back in a minute."

With that, Alison headed upstairs, leaving Bruce looking bemused.

Chapter 24

Alison took another look in the mirror; she was ready. She brushed herself down and then left her bedroom and made her way downstairs.

She had already had her breakfast and was leaving a little early to get the bus. She knew where the college was; she and Stacey had gone past it the week before while they were out shopping.

Tom, Freddie and Charlie had already left for school. Charlie was at Bolton Abbey Primary school and Tom and Freddie were at Harlequin boys school.

"Mum, I'm off now, I will see you later!" Alison said.

"Do you have everything, what about lunch money?" Bet asked.

"Yes, I have everything. Once I do today, I'll let you know how the land lies. I'll see you later," Alison said, giving her mum a kiss on the cheek.

It didn't take long to get there once on the bus. She got there just before nine am. Stacey was walking up at the same time as Alison. They went into the building together.

There was a huge noticeboard in reception.

"Ah here it is, we have to go the second floor, Stace, come on, otherwise we're going to be late," Alison said.

They both ran up the stairs and were out of breath when they got to their classroom. There were another ten girls doing the same course as them.

The door opened and a tall thin lady stepped out of the classroom and ushered everyone in.

The desks were all full of typewriters and in and out trays either side of them.

"I'm Miss Snodgrass and I'll be your teacher for this lesson for the whole of your two-year course. I do not tolerate lateness and bad punctuality, so if you do want to be late or not attend my class, you will get a de-merit and after three, you will be kicked out. There are plenty of others who do want to do this course. Is that understood?" she said. "I'm waiting!"

"Yes Miss." The class all replied.

"It's Miss Snodgrass when you want to address me, so let's try again, shall we?" she said.

"Yes, Miss Snodgrass." The girls replied.

Oh wow, Alison thought, *what a miserable old bag this lady is*.

They all found their desks.

"Now you have chosen your seats and desks, this is where you will sit every time for this lesson," Miss Snodgrass added.

They were all given their work to complete and a timetable at the beginning of the day, which was to be filled in. When they weren't in this lesson, they had audio dictation in a classroom down the other end of the hall. Thankfully, they didn't have Miss Snodgrass. They would have a lovely lady called Mrs Miller. She was a little older but had a softer side to her that Miss Snodgrass would never have.

They would have typing skills in the morning and audio dictation in the afternoon. The rest of the time, it would be written work, the same as school really.

When the girls had finished their first day, Stacey and Alison went in different directions home, so they would stand outside talking for a few minutes before heading home.

"So, Al, how did you find it today?" Stacey asked.

"Oh, it was OK, I suppose. I think once we find our bearings it won't be so bad and before we know it, we will have completed our first year," Alison said. "Anyway, I have to go. See you tomorrow, Stace," Alison said.

"Yeah, bye!" Stacey replied.

Alison caught the bus, then walked a little of the way. It was almost five when she got home.

"Hi Al, is that you?" Bet called out from the kitchen.

"Yes, hi Mum!" Alison replied Alison.

"How was your day? How was secretarial college?"

"It was OK. We have a right battle-axe for our typing teacher, but a lovely lady who we do audio dictation with," Alison replied.

"Oh well, as long as you had a good time. Now I wanted to ask you something," Bet said.

"Go on," Alison said.

"Well, you know we got the boys in July, how have you found it with them?" Bet asked.

"Mum, it's been a bit difficult," Alison said.

"Oh, don't you like them being here, love?"

"Oh no, Mum. I meant it's been difficult because I haven't really had the chance to spend any time with them, like Tom has. With working at the guest house with Rose and Henry for the summer, I didn't get much time to see any of you. But it's fine because Tom's happy and that's the most important thing. I love having the boys around. Why do you ask anyway?" Alison asked.

"Well, me and your dad wanted to know if you think it's too early to apply for adoption for them, like we did with you two," Bet said.

"If that's what you and Dad want, I'm fine with it. I know it's what Tom, Freddie and Charlie will want. They get to become part of a proper family and it gives them security like it did us," Alison smiled.

Bet was relieved and smiled at her daughter.

"We opened a bank account for each of them, like we did for you and Tom," Bet said, looking at Alison for approval.

"Mum, you and Dad are wonderful people and you wouldn't have been given any of us if you weren't, so I suggest if you want to talk about it with the boys, how about we do at dinner time? Tell the boys what you want to do and see what they say," Alison said with a beaming smile and then she gave Bet a huge hug.

Bet spoke to Bruce in the kitchen, then the doorbell went.

"I'll get it, Mum!" Alison called out.

It was Rob, coming to see how Alison got on her first day at college.

"It was great! Our typing teacher isn't much to write home about, but that's not what I am there for. How was your day, Rob?"

Rob had already started working with his dad and he loved it.

"Alison, do you fancy coming out on Saturday night?" Rob asked.

"What did you have in mind?" Alison asked.

"No idea as yet, I was thinking of maybe going to the local pub. There's a live band on and we can go and watch them if you want?"

"Yes, that sounds great. Let me know what time," Alison said.

"What about seven-thirty, I can pick you up," Rob said.

"OK, see you then if not before," Alison said.

Rob said his goodbyes and left. Alison closed the door and told Bet about Saturday night.

"That's fine, will he pick you up and bring you home?" Bruce said.

"Of course, Dad. Rob is a gentleman," Alison smiled.

"He's a good boy, Bruce—and he works hard," Bet assured her worried husband.

They had their dinner and spoke about wanting to put the adoption through, but they wanted to hear what Freddie and Charlie said about it. They were both delighted and started all hugging each other.

***

Alison had worked hard all week. On Friday Stacey asked her what she was doing at the weekend, she told her that she and Rob were going to see a live band at the local pub. Alison was only seventeen, but she could have a soft drink in there.

Saturday was soon here, and Alison didn't know whether or not to dress up, so she chose a pair of jeans with a nice top, flat shoes, and her lightweight jacket. It was still September and quite warm in the evenings still.

Rob picked her up at seven thirty on the dot. Alison picked up her jacket, said goodnight and left with Rob. The pub wasn't very far away, so they could walk there.

Once they had found seats, Rob got them both a drink, he was drinking lager shandy and Alison had a coke.

They were talking and Alison mentioned that Stacey wanted to know if they could go out on a double date later on. Rob said that was fine. Alison thought that Rob and Mike would get along as they were both in the building trade. Rob suggested the next time Stacey offered they go with them they could.

They didn't have to wait too long; Stacey asked the following Friday for Saturday night. Alison asked where they were going. She told her that they were going for a meal, maybe Chinese.

Rob could be a bit shy when you first met him, but he soon got more confident once he got to know Stacey and Mike. This new arrangement became quite a regular thing on a Saturday night.

***

Alison had started taking her driving lessons in the day and then going out in the night time with her friends. Bet and Bruce were delighted that things were going well for her. Especially as she was the only girl in the house.

491

Before they knew it, Christmas was upon them and Bet and Bruce had arranged some lovely things for them to do and they had totally spoilt all of the kids.

Bet and Bruce had applied for the adoption of Freddie and Charlie and were waiting for confirmation to complete their family.

Every Christmas eve, Bet and Alison went to town for shopping and to Molly's. They had never seen the Coopers again. This year, Bet's sister Sue didn't come, she was away abroad with her partner and Bruce's mum was going to his other sisters for Christmas, so it was just going to be the six of them.

When Bet and Alison got back it was nearly 6 pm. They didn't buy as much as they usually did on Christmas Eve, because Bet had already bought everything they needed.

Rob was sitting down with Bruce and the boys. Alison and Bet looked a bewildered to see Rob there. Bet took the bags from Alison once they took their coats off, Rob cleared his throat. What Bet didn't realise was that Rob's parents, Dorothy and Ernest, were in the kitchen.

Dorothy had her finger up to her lips. They all entered the sitting room quietly.

Suddenly, Rob got down on one knee and looked at Alison.

"Umm…Alison, from the moment I accidentally bumped into you on the way to school, I knew you were the girl for me…"

Alison looked startled and blushed.

"I love you so much, Al, and I know that we're are young still, but would you give me the pleasure of being my wife? Will you marry me?" Rob said.

Alison didn't know what was happening. One minute she was shopping with Bet and the next Rob was down on one knee asking for her hand in marriage! Rob looked very nervous, waiting for her reply. Alison didn't hesitate.

"Yes of course, I will marry you!" she screamed.

Rob's shoulders dropped with relief. He stood up and hugged her then kissed her on the lips.

"Woooo!" The boys mocked.

Rob told Alison to hold her left hand out and he brought out a small box containing an engagement ring, which he'd bought her with his first two weeks' wages. It was a solitaire diamond set in a 9ct gold band. Alison loved it.

Dorothy, Ernest, Bet and Bruce all clapped and cheered. Alison turned around. She didn't realise she had an audience.

"I know we are just starting out; you with college and me just starting work, but we can get married in a few years, if that's OK with you? That way it gives us time to save up," Rob asked.

"Yes of course! There's still stuff we have to do, like me getting a job, once I finish college, which is only eighteen months or so away. Then set a date maybe after that, what do you think?" Alison was beyond excited.

Bet returned from the kitchen with a bottle of champagne.

"Well, we won't forget this Christmas Eve, will we?" She laughed.

Alison looked down at the ring with tears in her eyes. She had never felt so happy.

"Congratulations, son, and welcome to our family," Bruce said.

"Does that mean I can have Alison's room when she's gone then?" Tom asked.

"You cheeky devil!" Alison laughed. "I'm not going anywhere just yet!"

Rob asked Alison if he could have a quiet word with her outside. They sat on the swing together.

"When did all of this happen?" Alison smiled.

"Well, I asked your dad a little while ago, he said he would rather I waited until you were eighteen, but as we won't be getting married just yet, then it was OK with him," Rob smiled. "Is your ring OK? We can change it if you don't like it?" Rob added, nervously.

"I absolutely love it! It's beautiful, thank you," she said, kissing him on the cheek. "Well, this is definitely something to tell Stacey when I go back to college!" Alison laughed. They went back inside to join the others.

"That will be OK, won't it, Rob?" Bet asked.

"What's that, Bet?"

"You, mum and dad come over for dinner on Boxing Day?" Bet said. Rob looked at his mum, she had a big smile on her face.

"Yes, that will be lovely, Bet, thank you. Right, I think we had better go now though, Mum, they haven't had their dinner yet," Rob said.

Once they had eaten, Bet and Alison sat on the sofa while Bruce washed up the dinner things and the boys went upstairs to have their showers and to get ready for bed.

Bet and Alison were both admiring Alison's new engagement ring. It was beautiful and with the fairy lights on the tree, it shimmered in the light. All of a sudden, Alison was tired, it had become quite a hectic day and evening but for the right reasons. She said her goodnights, then jumped into the bath. The three boys were in Tom's room playing and didn't notice her go into the bathroom. She had a lovely soak still admiring her new ring. Once she finished her bath, she got into her night things and got into bed, laying there just looking at her new ring and smiling to herself.

***

The following morning was Christmas day and Rose, Henry and Jo were coming over for Christmas lunch. Everyone was up early, and they were all excited for their presents. Alison couldn't stop looking at her new engagement ring on her hand and smiling.

Bet and Bruce had bought the children lots of gifts: they got games, roller skates, new pyjamas and dressing gown, which they all got every year for the winter. Alison had got a new gold bracelet and necklace set with matching earrings and some new clothes. They all received money as well.

Once all the presents were opened, Bet and Bruce cleared away all of the wrapping paper. The boys hadn't noticed that there were three huge unopened gifts in the kitchen. Bruce brought them all in and told them to sit on the sofa until they were all in.

Tom, Freddie and Charlie were excited when they saw their names on the tags. Tom and Freddie's bikes were the same size Charlie's was a little smaller. They started ripping the paper off. They all got a BMX bike! Charlie had a yellow one, Freddie got an orange one and Tom got a green one.

Bruce looked at Alison and handed her a small box.

"You don't think we forgot you, do you?" He laughed. Bet was smiling at Alison, she opened up the box and saw a set of keys.

"Mum, Dad, what are these for?"

"Take a look out the window," Bet smiled.

Alison got up and looked out of the window. There, outside the window, was a brand new, navy blue Renault Fiat.

"A car? Oh, my goodness, is that mine?" Alison screamed.

"Yes, it is! We wanted to get it for your birthday with your driving lessons, but there was so much going on, we just didn't get chance, are you pleased with it? We know you haven't passed your test yet, but it's more on an incentive to pass it now. It's taxed and insured, and we have some learner plates, so we can

494

go out in it later on or tomorrow and have a drive, if you like," Bruce said, beaming a big smile.

Alison ran over to her mum and dad and hugged them both tightly. She didn't know what to say apart from thank you.

Once breakfast was over, Alison, Bruce and Bet went outside to have a proper look at the car, Alison was so happy. So much had happened in less than twenty-four hours. She had gotten engaged, she had lots of lovely presents and now a car!

Her lessons were going well, but she wasn't sure to put in for her test just yet, but now with her own car, she was able to get extra practice in.

Rose, Henry and Jo came over at lunchtime, wishing everyone a happy Christmas. Alison showed them her ring. They exchanged presents and everyone was delighted with what they got. Rose was delighted to see Alison's ring.

"I like the way it sparkles in the light, Al," Jo said.

Jo was also very happy. She had settled in well with Rose and Henry. She had fitted in well and loved living at the guest house.

They all had a great day. Christmas lunch was delicious, and a good time was had by all. Boxing day had gone just as good and it was as if Alison had blinked and she was back at college again.

***

Alison was able to help out again at Rose's for the summer, which Jo was pleased with.

Henry could still only do light duties and they didn't want him taking any chances. When the home children started to come down for their week, Sandra had come down with the Craven House lot and she was pleased that things were working out for Jo. She also noticed the ring on Alison's left hand and her driving around in a new car. She was so pleased to see how she had blossomed.

Alison passed her test first time when she took it at Easter. Now she could drive herself to college. Miss Snodgrass would always turn her nose up whenever she saw Alison and couldn't help herself making comments about her being engaged whilst being at college. I didn't bother Alison; as long as she got on with her college work, Miss Snodgrass had no cause to complain about her.

In fact, Miss Snodgrass quietly admired Alison, because she got on with her work but wouldn't let anyone take liberties, even her sometimes. But she would never let on. Stacey worked well, but not as well as Alison.

As Easter had approached, the adoption letter for Freddie and Charlie came through and they held another party for them.

The Lintons were now a family of six and everyone was delighted. Sandra was very pleased because it meant four of the children who were under her care had found families and happiness all under one roof.

Alison and Rob, Stacey and Mike were still double dating and once Alison and Rob got engaged, Stacey and Mike followed suit that summer. But they had a big party, and Stacey asked if she and Rob had named the date yet.

"Not yet, Stace, I want to get college done first before I even think about it. What about you and Mike?" Alison asked.

"Well, we have named the date: October 29th!" Stacey said, excitedly.

"Oh, that's good! That gives you some time to save and sort out your dress and your venue," Alison laughed.

"No Al, you've got it wrong! We're getting married on October 29th—this year!" Stacey said, patting her tummy lightly.

"Oh, my God, Stace! Sorry I didn't realise!" Alison said. "Are you happy?"

Stacey beamed a smile. "Over the moon! It was a bit of a shock for both of us! But my parents are coming around to it, so we have to sort out the wedding as soon as possible!" Stacey laughed.

"Have you sorted it out then yet?" Alison asked.

"Yes, we're having the Grand on the front; a sit-down meal. I have to get my dress and that…I was wondering, Al, would you be my maid of honour?"

"Oh, I would love to, Stace!" Alison smiled. "Do you want any help with planning anything?"

"No, Mum and Dad and my aunty Vera are sorting that out. You could come with me and find a suitable outfit though? Mum says I can't wear white, but I was thinking a cream or ivory, what do you think?" Stacey asked.

"Yes, I will come with you, but what about your mum, she will want to come as well?"

"Yes, she does, but I want you to come too, that way you can give a younger perspective," Stacey said.

A couple of weeks later, the two girls went to look at some bridal shops. Stacey wasn't too bothered about what she got, but she didn't want to look too frumpy or pregnant.

"So, Stace, will you be leaving the course then?" Alison asked as they looked at racks of wedding dresses.

"Yes, I have to. I can't have Miss Snodgrass looking down her nose at me all the time and also I don't know how long I will fit behind the desk with the typewriter and my growing tummy," Stacey laughed.

The girls had invited Bet to come along too.

"I love weddings and I thought your mum may need some moral support with you two!" Bet winked at Stacey's mum.

They went inside another shop where there were plenty of dresses. Stacey was looking at them, and it was very overwhelming for her.

"Do you have anything in a cream or ivory?" She asked the shop assistant.

The assistant looked at Stacey and then at her tummy and gave a smirk and a small laugh.

"Excuse me young lady, but my daughter asked you a question! You don't have to smirk at her like that! Do you have any dresses in the colour that she has asked for? Of course, if it's too much trouble for you, I am sure we can find a dress somewhere else!" Stacey's mum said. Stacey smiled at her mum as a thank you.

Another lady came through the curtain.

"I'm sorry is there anything I can help you with?" she asked.

"Yes please, could you tell me if you have either cream or ivory dresses please?" Stacey asked again.

"Yes, we do, if you bear with me for a moment, I'll be right back." The second assistant said, giving the first member of staff a stern look.

The staff member recoiled and went back to dusting the shelves.

The lady returned with quite a few dresses, which she hung up on the hook. There was lace, satin, taffeta and tulle. Stacey looked at all of them. The assistant opened up the changing room and Stacey followed her in. Stacey's mum, Bet, and Alison were excited to see what she was going to look like in the dress.

Stacey came out shortly after in a cream lace, long-sleeved full-skirted dress.

"Oh, I don't know, Stace, have a look in the mirror." Her mum pulled a face.

Stacey looked at herself in the mirror.

"No, I don't like it now I've seen it on, can I try on another one please?" she asked.

"Don't forget, Stacey, it may not be very warm in October." Her mum called out.

Stacey came out in another dress. It was too low cut and you could see her cleavage.

"No, definitely not!" Stacey said.

"Erm, when do you need the dress for, Miss?" The assistant asked.

"I need it for October."

"Next year?"

"No, this year," Stacey replied.

"Well, then none of these dresses will be able to be ready by then. Hang on, we do have a couple I could show you that you could take with you today if you like," the sales assistant said.

She disappeared into the stock room and came back with two dresses. One had long sleeves and the other was strapless.

The long sleeve one was too tight, but the strapless had a lovely flowy skirt.

"But it might be freezing!" Stacey said.

The assistant disappeared again and returned with a fake fur looking bolero. It would cover her shoulders and her arms down to the elbows.

The assistant put it on her over the dress.

Stacey looked in the mirror and tears started to trickle down hers, her mum's, Bet's and Alison's faces.

"That's the one then!" Stacey's mum laughed through tears. Stacey nodded. She looked beautiful.

She asked the assistant to wrap it up whilst Stacey looked at the other accessories.

"Stacey, do you want a veil, or would you like to try on maybe a hat or something?" Alison asked.

"Oh, a hat might be a nice change rather than a veil, what do you think, mum?"

"Let's see what they have, oh, Stace this one is lovely!"

It was a nice size hat, with a little veil attached to the back. Her mum pulled it over her face, it was simple but very pretty. They all started tearing up again.

"Yes, we will take that as well," Stacey's mum said.

Stacey was delighted with what she had got that day, she didn't think she would get anything, as her tummy was starting to grow. She was already three months pregnant and her tummy would continue to grow.

"Thank you for all your help today," Stacey said to the nice assistant before they left the shop. The lady smiled at Stacey and her mum and the party with her. She then turned to her assistant.

"I do not appreciate you looking down your nose at any of my clients. It doesn't matter who they are; it's none of our business! They want to feel like a million dollars and that's our job, if I hear that sort of behaviour from you again, you can look for another job, do you understand?" She snapped.

"Alison, I was going to look for a dress for you in there, but that lady was so rude before, but what if we have a look in Marks or something?" Stacey said after they had left the shop.

"What if we go to Molly's, then go to Marks?" Alison said.

They all headed off to Molly's. After refreshments, they went to Marks and picked up a pair lovely burgundy dress and shoes. Alison looked lovely in that colour and they managed to get some nice cream ballerina pumps for Stacey.

Once they finished shopping, Alison offered to give them all a lift home.

When Alison and Bet got home, they were talking about the bridal shop and the service by the first assistant.

"When you get married, Al, we can go into Ramsgate or anywhere else, even London if you want, but I'm not taking you in there for your wedding dress!" Bet said, kissing Alison on the forehead.

"Don't worry, mum. Poor Stace though; I'm glad we got her something in the end. Anyway, I won't be getting married for a little while, so we don't have to worry about it yet," she added.

***

The wedding day was here, and Stacey looked amazing! Her cousin had done her hair and make-up. Her dress, the shoes, everything looked lovely.

"Stace, where are you going to be living?" Alison asked.

"With Mum and Dad for now. We're saving for our own house, but with only Mike's money coming in, it's a bit hard, but we'll manage," Stacey said.

The wedding ceremony was lovely and there were lots of photos taken to remember the day. Everyone ate and drank too much. Rob enjoyed himself, but like Alison, they weren't in a rush to get married just yet. He had been saving so they could start putting money away for somewhere to live.

Stacey and Mike were going away for a few days, then it was back to normal life.

***

Alison had already started back at college and was already missing Stacey. Even though she had already dropped out before September, it was still strange going there on her own. Miss Snodgrass didn't seem bothered that Stacey had dropped out. It made no difference to Alison, they didn't live far away so it wasn't as if she wouldn't see her again.

The year had flown by and once the wedding was over, Christmas was around the corner again.

Rob had been in his job for over a year now and was loving it. He was getting paid well and they had decided that when Alison had finished college, she could get a job and contribute to Rob's savings. She still had her own bank account, which she was still putting money into. She was going to talk to Bet and Bruce about it when the boys were out.

"Mum, Dad, I was thinking about something," she broached the subject one evening when the boys weren't around.

"What's that, Honey?" Bruce said.

"Well, you know I've been saving in my bank account since we moved here. Well, I was thinking that money was to get a car or something," Alison said, "but since you got me a car last Christmas, I haven't spoken about a wedding at all, But Rob is saving like mad, for us, for somewhere to live, I was wondering if you wouldn't mind if I gave him some of it towards my share for somewhere to live, what do you think?"

"Well, as you said, we got you the car and I know that you haven't decided about getting married yet, but we want to pay for that for you, but yes, if you want to contribute, why don't you take a chunk out? You can keep putting more in. How much do you have at the moment?" Bruce asked.

"I've got just over three and a half thousand pounds," Alison said.

"Well, what if you give Rob two thousand pounds and you just keep adding to your money, that way you're helping out and you still have a little money of your own. Once you get a job, you'll be paying towards your keep, but that's not yet," Bet said.

When Alison saw Rob next, she gave him an envelope.

"What's this?"

"My contribution towards saving for a home," Alison smiled at him.

"Al, you don't have to put this much away!" Rob said.

"How much do we have already?" Alison asked.

"Two thousand, with this it's four thousand! Almost enough for a deposit!" Rob said.

The happy couple hugged each other. They were so in love.

***

Christmas had come and gone, and Stacey was getting really big with her pregnancy. At least she didn't have to deal with the heat from the last summer.

Alison had just got in when the phone rang, Bet answered it; it was Mike.

"Al, Stacey has had the baby! A little girl, 6lbs 40z and she has tons of black hair and she's lovely!" The proud father told Alison. "She'll be in hospital for a couple of days, just to check she's OK; her blood pressure was playing up a bit. I'll tell her you'll come up tomorrow, OK?" Mike said. "I'd better go."

Alison put down the phone and told Bet and Bruce the good news.

Alison went to see Stacey and her new baby daughter, who she called Emma. Alison thought she was absolutely beautiful, but she wasn't feeling broody at all. She was still focused on getting her exams finished and getting a job, so that she and Rob could get married and then maybe start a family.

It was the Easter holidays again and Alison was helping out a little at Rose and Henry's as Jo was there and doing the lion's share of the work. Henry was able to do a bit more, but he was still on light duties.

Alison and Jo still hung out with each other as much as they could, but the holiday times were always busy for Jo.

Jo had slotted into seaside life and she had loved it and she loved seeing Tom, Freddie, and Charlie. It was like they were still at the home, but in a family environment. Alison was knuckling down with her work and she was having to start studying for her exams as they weren't that far away now. Rob was also really busy with work, so they were able to save lots of money for their own home.

Alison only had three exams, but they were important ones. She had an exam every other day, which made it easier to concentrate on the subjects. Once her exams were over, which was in late June, she was able to leave. She wouldn't hopefully have to do another year, but if she did, she could enrol before the end of the holidays.

On the last day of college, Alison had made some lovely friends. They would be holding a graduation ceremony, so she would see them there and her family could attend and watch her get her certificates. She had already applied for a couple of jobs: one was for an accountant's firm and the other for a construction repair company. Both were local, so she was pleased with that.

She had a week off before her interviews, just so she could have a break. Having a couple of lie-ins and just plodding around the house, seeing Rob in the evenings, as she didn't have to get up too early for college or revise for exams. Rob was glad he had finished that a long time ago.

***

Just before her nineteenth birthday, Alison had her first interview. She certainly looked the part for the accountants.

She got there early, and the receptionist showed her to the waiting room and said someone would be with her soon. She sat down on one of the comfy chairs.

A gentleman came in and called her name. His name was Mr Andrews and he showed her into an office on the second floor and invited her to sit down. He already had her curriculum vitae in front of him.

Despite not having received her exam results yet, he wanted to test her typing skills, so he handed her a sheet of paper with writing on it and asked her to type it up on the typewriter in front of her, while he timed her with a stop-watch.

When she had finished, he stopped the watch. She could now type 80 words per minute, was good going.

Alison answered all of his questions very well and once he'd finished, he stood up and shook her hand and told Alison that he would be in touch with her as soon as possible. He had a few other people to interview first.

Alison thanked Mr Andrews and left.

Alison's next interview was on Friday and she was looking forward to it. She asked Bet if she wanted to pop into town the following day, so they could have some time together. Bet was delighted; she didn't get as much time to spend with

Alison as she had wanted, and she wanted to make the most of the time she had off before she went to full time work.

"Don't you want to look for other jobs yet, Al?" Bruce asked.

"Not yet, Dad. Let's see how this one goes on Friday first," she said.

Alison and Bet had a lovely time in town. Bruce was excited for them to go – it meant they would go into Molly's and bring back cakes. But he had a shock this time; Bet didn't bring any back for him.

"I'm sorry, Love, but I don't want you having a heart attack like Henry!" she said.

Alison wore the cream skirt and the lilac jacket with a little camisole top underneath for the interview. She looked lovely and she'd put a little make-up on. Having had experience of being interviewed, her confidence had increased and she felt she was better prepared this time.

Shortly after arriving, a lady called Sue met her in the reception.

Sue took her up in the lift. They reached the first floor and Sue showed her into a lovely side office, she asked Alison if she wanted a drink. Alison declined; she was nervous enough without spilling tea or coffee on her cream skirt.

Mr Robinson came into the room.

"I'm sorry to keep you waiting," he said, offering his hand out to shake Alison's.

She shook his hand. He seemed nicer than the one at the accountants.

Mr Robinson had her CV in front of him and asked her about her typing skills. Alison explained that she was still waiting for her results.

"I expect you to have done well with those, judging by your CV. You have excellent typing skills, Miss Davis-Linton," Mr Robinson said. "Do you have any other interviews lined up?"

Alison thought it was a strange question.

"No Mr Robinson, I had one already on Tuesday, but I wanted to see how this one went first," she said, then regretted saying that.

"It's OK, Alison, everyone gets a little nervous at interviews. I just wondered because I wanted to offer you the job," Mr Robinson said.

"Pardon?" Alison stuttered. She looked shocked.

"Yes, I think you would be a real asset to this company and I don't want to see anyone else, so if you think you might like to work here, Welcome to Cedarways Construction!" Mr Robinson smiled and reached over to Alison once again to shake her hand.

"Would you be able to start on Monday?" he asked her.

"Err…Umm…I mean, yes! Yes, I would, thank you so much, Mr Robinson. You won't regret it."

He knew he wouldn't. Alison had such great skills.

"Oh, before you go, Miss Davis-Linton—" he said.

"Oh, please call me Alison."

"Alison, do you know when your certificates will come through?" He asked.

"Well, once I get my letter, I should know. Do you need them?" Alison asked her new boss.

"No, it's just I know you will want the day off to collect them and then you can add them to your CV. Just let me know and I'll arrange for your day off. Our personnel department will deal with holidays and salaries and all that…Sorry, Alison, I'm assuming you know the salary for this position?" Mr Robinson said.

"It said in the paper that it was ten thousand per annum?" Alison said.

"Ah, I'm sorry, that was a misprint…it actually should have read twelve thousand." He smiled at her.

"Oh, brilliant! I mean, thank you, Mr Robinson!" Alison said.

Mr Robinson laughed.

"Well, thank you and well done. Have a great weekend and see you bright and early on Monday, it's an 8.30 am start," her new boss said.

Alison was delighted! She hadn't expected to be offered the job on the spot. She had a spring in her step when she left the building.

"Hi Al, how did it go?" Bet asked as soon as she walked in.

Alison smiled.

"Come on, Love, how did you get on?" Bruce said.

"I got the job!" Alison screamed with joy.

"No? They offered it to you straight away?" Bet said.

"Yes, the boss had asked about my certificates, but said he would take me on with what I already had, and I can have the day off to get them," she added.

Everyone was jumping up and down in the kitchen.

"Did he tell you the salary?" Bruce asked.

"Yes, apparently there was a misprint in the paper, Dad, and it's increased by two thousand pounds per year!" Alison said.

"That's amazing, Love! Well done!" Bruce scooped Alison up and swung her around the kitchen.

"Put me down, Dad!" Alison laughed. "I want to tell Jo, Rose and Henry," she said.

Alison ran over to Rose and Henry's and told them her good news. They all clapped their hands in delight.

"I start Monday!" Alison said. "Oh Rose, Henry, it's a lovely place and everyone is friendly, not like that accountants I tried on Monday, what a difference," she said.

Alison shared the good news with Rob that night.

"Now, I can start helping with the saving for a home for us!" She told him.

"Hang on a minute," Rob said.

"Why, don't you want me to start saving with you?" Alison said.

"No, I don't mean that, but don't you want to splash out on your first wage packet before you start saving?" Rob smiled.

"Are you sure you don't want me to help straight away?"

"I want you to enjoy your first and second wage packet, then we can both start saving. We have a good bit saved. If you want at the end of the year, we can tally up what we have and see how much we may need for a mortgage. What do you think?" Rob said.

"That sounds perfect!" Alison gave him a kiss.

***

Alison drove herself to work and arrived at 8 am, half an hour early. The receptionist, Sharon was already in and she let her in the building.

"Do you want to go on up, Alison and I'll see you later. Sue will give you a tour of the building when she gets in." Sharon said.

Alison took the lift, until she knew where the stairs led to. She sat at her desk and Sue arrived shortly after.

"Come on Al, let's show you the staff room. You can bring sandwiches in or go out for lunch. We always make a hot drink in the morning before we start, so we may see the others in there already," she said.

They walked along to the staffroom, which was on their floor. There were a few more ladies and a couple of men there as well. Mr Robinson was already in his office, but Sue introduced Alison to everyone.

"Don't worry, you will soon pick it up." Sue said, sensing Alison was nervous. "We can leave your drink at your desk, then we can see Mr Robinson; Mike, and see if he wants a drink then I'll show you the ropes."

Sue knocked on Mike's door.

"Morning Mike, would you like a tea?" Sue asked.

"No, I'm OK, thanks Sue. Oh, hello Alison, is Sue showing you the ropes then? Good, see you later then." Mike smiled and picked up the phone to make a call.

Alison was introduced to everyone as they continued their tour of the building. Sue showed Alison where the personnel department was, which was just down the hall from her office and there were two sweet ladies working there: Joan and Doris. They dealt with the wages and staff holidays.

Alison had twenty days holidays a year, from January to December, but as it was now the beginning of August, she had about a week to take before Christmas. There would be skeleton staff over the Christmas holidays, as it was dealing with repairs. Alison would see how she went. She didn't mind working between Christmas and New year, as Rob normally did anyway.

Her first week went really quickly and she loved it. Her duties were to type up the tenders for up and coming work.

She had been at work for a couple of weeks when her results came in from her college. The letter had come while she was at work. Everyone waited for her to get home to open it.

Alison opened up the envelope, she pulled out the paper and had a big smile on her face.

"Distinction for both subjects!" She said.

Everyone cheered. She had done it! She'd got the highest possible grade. She was over the moon.

When she went back to work, she took her letter to show Mike and he told her to speak to Joan or Doris to arrange for her to have the day off.

Stacey was delighted for her. Emma was getting big now and was nearly six months old. She wanted to come to see her, but she thought the baby might make too much noise, so she asked if they could go out the following weekend. Her mum would babysit, and Mike would also enjoy a night out. Alison said yes as she thought it would be a great excuse to go out.

Graduation day arrived and everyone got dressed in their best clothes.

Miss Snodgrass would be presenting students with their certificates and Mrs Miller would be there too.

Bruce took his camera; he wanted to capture everything he could for this day, they were all so proud of her. Rose, Henry, and Jo came as well.

They all sat in the college hall and the candidates sat on chairs up on the stage. They had a podium and Miss Snodgrass, Mrs Miller and the Head of the College were all there. Bruce took a few photos. Even Miss Snodgrass cracked a smile when Alison stood up to accept her certificates.

Bruce suggested they go to one of the lovely restaurants in town to celebrate.

Alison took her car and Bruce took the family car, so everyone could get a lift. Once there, Bruce ordered champagne.

"Dad, I don't think we should, we're both driving," Alison said.

"Honey, just one glass to toast to you, then on coffee, yes?" Bruce said. He was so proud of his daughter.

They all had a lovely meal and by the time they left the restaurant, it was already gone five o'clock.

Alison was worn out.

"Thanks everyone for coming today and making it extra special," Alison said before going up to bed. Tom, Freddie and Charlie all hugged her at once. She kissed Bet on the cheek and Bruce on the head and went upstairs to bed.

***

The kids had come up for the summer holidays as usual and it was all hands-on deck. Everyone was used to doing it all now and it was the first time that Alison couldn't join in.

She had the weekends off work, but she started seeing Rob on a Friday and Saturday night. Now she was earning her own money, she gave Bet some housekeeping money every week, then she put some away to save for their new home.

They still had Christmas at their own homes, but Rob was keen to start looking at houses in the area.

Alison had suggested to Rob that they wait until the summer and start looking, then she would be twenty and once they find a house, they could then start thinking of getting married. They had known each other seven years now and had been engaged for two.

Bruce, Bet, Dorothy and Ernest had already started looking out for properties in the local area that were coming up for sale. It gave them all a bit more of a purpose and an excuse to continue to be in their lives.

A few months after they had started looking, they were on their way back from the shops when they noticed a house on the corner at the top of their road.

"Al, the estate agents are only up the road, let's take down the door number and go and enquire, what do you think?" Rob said.

"OK, you never know, it may be just what we need!" Alison said excitedly.

They went to the estate agents and asked about the house. It was still on the market and the sellers hadn't had a lot of interest in the property. As they had the keys, they said one of their agents could show them around.

They stood outside the house, while the lady opened the front door.

The property used to be a bed and breakfast and was rather large. It was a similar layout to Rose and Henry's, but as they wanted it as a home, they asked if they would be able to convert it back to just a house. The agent said she couldn't see why not.

Alison wanted Bet to see the property, so asked Rob to stay with the agent and quickly ran home.

"Mum, Mum are you in?" Alison shouted as she opened the front door.

"Yes, yes, I am, what's wrong?" Bet asked.

"Nothing, it's just me and Rob have just looked at a house at the top of the road, Rob is still with the lady, do you want to come and have a look at it?" Alison said, out of breath. "Oh Dad! You have to come too! There's a house—"

"I heard you!" Bruce laughed. "Come on then!"

Rob was still standing with the lady talking about the house when Alison, Bruce and Bet arrived.

"Hello again, I was just wondering if we could have another look inside? My mum and dad want to see it, is that all right?" Alison asked.

"Yes of course, but I can't be long, as I need to get back to the office." The lady said.

They all went inside the house and had a look.

"It's so big without any furniture inside, isn't it!" Bet said.

They looked on all the floors.

"Dad, the only thing is, if we want to turn it back into a house, like bring the kitchen back upstairs like you have and the same with the bedrooms, would that be possible?" Alison asked.

"Well, if you want the house and you get a surveyor to have a look at it, they can tell you if it can be done, and don't forget who you're with!" Bruce smiled, nodding to Rob. "Al, you're marrying a plumber and between Rob and Mike, I am sure you can get it done," Bruce laughed.

Once they had finished having a look around, Rob spoke to the lady.

"Do you have anyone else interested in the house?"

"Not at the moment. You're only the second viewers."

"So, can we think about it and let you know in a couple of days or so, is that alright?" Rob said.

"Yes, that's fine, but if I can have a contact number for you, Mr Freeman, just in case we do get any other interested parties," she asked.

Rob gave her his number and she put it in her bag.

"I will put it in the diary and it's there if I need to contact you," she said with a smile.

"Rob, that house is priced really well, at eighty thousand pounds, do you have a good deposit and when would you move in?" Bruce asked.

Rob looked at Alison.

"We have just over ten thousand pounds and me and Alison want to get married, so it's just a matter of sorting it all out." Said Rob.

"Getting married? When?" Bruce said.

Alison shook her head.

"Dad, we agreed. If we buy a house like this one, it will need doing up, but we wanted to get married before we move in," Alison said.

"Yes, I gathered that, but what I wanted to say was, you're our only daughter, Alison, and we want to pay for your wedding—as long as it's a registry office and a bacon roll and a cuppa afterwards!" Bruce said, smiling. "I'm only joking!" he said, looking at the horror on her face. "If you want that house, then put down your deposit before someone else gets in there!" He added, "Me and your Mum will sort your wedding out."

Alison didn't know what to say.

"Come on, no time like the present! Let's go up to the estate agents again, ask what you need to and then start the ball rolling. Now, about this wedding, have you set a date yet?" Bruce asked once he stopped for a breather.

"Well, we were thinking about next September. Once the summer season is nearly over and the summer holidays have been and gone," Alison said.

Bet pulled out her diary.

"What about 23 September?" Rob said, looking at Alison. She thought about it for a moment.

"Yes, that would be great! That's just under a year. Reckon we can get a wedding arranged in a year?" She laughed, looking at her mum.

"Of course, we can!" Bet laughed.

Rob popped home to tell his parents what was happening.

Within half an hour, both families were standing outside the property with the estate agent.

Bruce and Ernest had a look around and agreed that moving the kitchen would be a relatively simple job. Sarah, the estate agent was talking to Bet and Alison was having a further look again over the house.

"What are you thinking about"? Rob asked Alison.

"I love it, Rob! I knew that when we first walked in; before Mum and Dad came around and now your mum and dad. Can we afford it though?

"Yes, we can and now we know your mum and dad will pay for the wedding, it means we can put everything into the house," Rob said.

"Are you going to put an offer in then?" Bruce asked.

"Yes, I think it's a bargain! If we don't Bruce, someone else will snap it up, so I think me and Alison can go back up to the office and start the ball rolling," Rob said.

They told Sarah they wanted to put in an offer. She said she would call the vendors as soon as she got back to the office.

***

On Monday, Alison had a word with Mike the boss and asked him if one of the surveyors at the company could have a look at the house she was buying. He knew just the guy, Doug; he had been with the company for years and knew his stuff.

"Mike, how much do I have to pay for Doug's time and his service?" Alison asked.

"Oh, don't worry about it; it's a perk of the job! It's not often people move, so once in a while, they need it checked over and here we are very thorough." Mike smiled.

Doug, one of the company's surveyors, had completed the survey at the house and when he returned back to the office, he had a quick word with Alison.

"Al, the house is as sound as a bell, and yes, you can bring the kitchen upstairs. There's plenty of room and it's a good price. I can't get you to type up my report though; conflict of interest, but I can get one of the other girls to do it. I will give it to you later, but I will also run off a couple of copies just in case you need to apply to more than one place," Doug said.

"Thank you, Doug! That's great, now we can start the ball rolling!"

Rob called Alison at the office at lunchtime and she told him what Doug had said. She suggested he start looking at the bank and mortgages, as she would have the report at the end of the day. They were both delighted. Rob had contacted two banks by the time he had got to see her that evening.

Rob had an appointment with the bank manager the following morning and after discussing his and Alison's salaries, he offered him a 100% mortgage, suggesting that they use their deposit money for the renovations.

Rob was delighted, he kicked his legs up in the air together as soon as he got outside the building. He went straight over to Alison's office and told her.

When she saw Rob, he told her about the mortgage, Alison was over the moon. He'd signed all the paperwork and just needed to sort out a solicitor.

When she got home that evening, everyone was so excited for her. Things had turned out really well for her and Tom since they met Bet and Bruce.

It took a couple of months to get everything sorted out and exchanging contracts, so it was just after bonfire night before they got their keys. Bet, Bruce, Dorothy, and Ernest were starting to get ideas about the wedding.

There was a church three roads away. It was a beautiful old church and they thought it was perfect for them. They had seen the vicar and he put the date in his diary; 23 September, at 2 pm. They had already enquired about the venue for afterwards; they had thought of Botany Bay Hotel. Bruce booked it up.

***

Once they got the keys for the house, apart from sorting out the kitchen and decorating there wasn't much else to do. There was a lot of decorating, but that was just general maintenance.

Rob, his dad, and Bruce were sorting out the house; Bet, Dorothy, and Alison were choosing bridesmaid dresses, flowers, wedding cakes and curtains and colour schemes for each room.

It was a crazy time, but they were getting it done. Rob had a couple of cousins he wanted to ask, and Alison had asked Jo and Stacey and also little Emma to be her flower girl.

It was all coming together nicely.

"Alison, we need to sort out where you want to look for your wedding dress. Would you like to go to London for the day and we could ask Dorothy if she would like to come along unless you have other ideas?" Bet said.

"That sounds great, Mum," Alison said, "and I think Dorothy would love to come to look at wedding dresses. Are you sure you want to go to London though?" Alison asked.

"Yes, because if we can't find anything in London, then I don't know where else we can look!" Bet laughed.

"We just need to know when. I can't really take any time off in the week, so it will have to be a Saturday," Alison said.

"That's fine, we can leave early in the morning and get the train. Your dad will be busy with the boys on a Saturday, unless he's helping Henry," Bet said.

They arranged to go the following week, which was going to be Valentine's day, but they had to get a move on.

Alison had only agreed to look in London, because she had been looking in her lunch break for the last few weeks and hadn't found anything she liked.

***

Saturday was here and Alison had asked Dorothy, Jo, Stacey, and little Emma, if they fancied a day in London.

They got the nine o'clock train to London Victoria, which was about an hour and forty-five minutes, and they all headed straight to Oxford Street.

They were all so excited; especially Bet, this would be her one and only chance to go wedding dress shopping and she loved London.

When they arrived at Marble Arch, they jumped off the bus and bundled Emma back into her buggy.

The first store they came to was Selfridges. It had some lovely window dressings. They found their way to the lifts and went along to the bridal department. It was on the fourth floor and there were some lovely gowns, but Alison didn't see anything she liked. They looked at the bridesmaids' dresses, but there was nothing there, either.

"Come on, let's try the next store," Bet said.

"Dot, didn't Rob want his two cousins to be bridesmaids?" Alison asked as they negotiated the busy traffic.

"Oh no, dear, you have enough on and they're only distant cousins, when all said and done," Dot replied.

"If you're sure? We can always squeeze another couple in!" Alison laughed.

"No, I'm sure." Dot smiled.

They crossed the road, walked up a bit and saw DH Evans' department store. When they walked in and entered the perfume department.

"This way everyone, it's on the second floor," Bet said.

They got the lift up, as they couldn't take the buggy on the escalator and came out at the ladies' wear department.

"Over there, Bet, Alison?" Dorothy pointed to the wedding department.

There were some lovely dresses on display: lace, satin, taffeta, tulle, white, ivory and cream.

They didn't know where to look first.

"Come on everyone, let's have a look around!" Bet said, excitedly."

Jo and Stacey were looking at the satin dresses, but Alison was drawn to the lace. The assistant came over and asked who the bride was; Alison put up her hand. She asked her when the wedding was.

"Do you have any idea what style you would like or what material?" The assistant asked.

"Well, not really, I do like the lace though," Alison replied.

"Would you like sleeves or strapless?"

"Oh, I hadn't thought, why not try them both and then once I have one on, I can decide from there?" Alison said.

The sales assistant took Alison into a changing room and brought in two dresses for her to try on. She slipped it over Alison's head.

The assistant was doing up the zip. It was a long-sleeved dress, with a bit of lace, on the sleeves and the bottom of the dress. Alison wasn't very impressed with it. She looked in the mirror and thought no.

"Mum, are you sitting down? I'm coming out," Alison said to her mum.

Bet and the others had big smiles on their faces, until Alison walked out of the changing room and their smiles dropped to the floor.

"Al, is that the one you really want?" Bet asked.

"No, I just thought you would want to see it and I'm glad you don't like it either," she laughed.

They all burst out laughing.

She went back into the changing room. Alison had picked up a couple of clips from home, so she could put her hair up. It may make a difference to the style of the dress. The lady put the dress away and got the next one ready. This one was white lace and off the shoulder, with a delicate bow at the top. The skirt had two delicate pick-ups, with another little bow at the top of it and a huge one at the back, but it looked so lovely. On either sleeve, it had a lace trim with a tiny bow on each.

This time Alison put her hair up but left some delicately hanging down. She emerged from the changing room and Bet gasped, so did the others. Alison looked like an angel, especially with the blonde hair with delicate curls. Bet had tears in her eyes and so did all of the others, except Emma.

"Pretty Alison!" Emma said, clapping her hands.

The assistant went over to the accessories stand and picked up a headpiece and a tiara and a couple of veils. She tried the head piece and a short veil. They looked lovely, but then she changed it over to the tiara and the long veil and Bet, burst into tears.

"Al, that's it, darling! You look so beautiful. Do you like it?" Bet asked.

Alison was still looking at herself in the mirror.

"Yes, I love it, Mum! What do you all think?" She asked the rest of the girls.

She took one look at them and realised they were all crying.

"I think this is the one then." She laughed. "What do you think about the tiara and the long veil or should I try the short veil again?"

"No, leave it how it is, Alison, it's all beautiful!" Jo said.

"Now, what about shoes?" The assistant said.

"Oh, I hadn't thought about shoes! I need a small heel, not a high heel, in a size five," Alison said.

The lady disappeared and came back with three shoe boxes. Alison had already taken off her shoes. The lady put a pair on her.

Alison lifted up the dress to have a look and then in the mirror; she wasn't sure. She tried on the next pair and then the next. She tried the second pair on again, then put two different shoes on and then settled on her favourite.

"Stacey, Jo, have you seen anything in the bridesmaid section?" Alison asked.

"No, we were looking at your choices, we'll have a look now," Stacey said.

Both of them went over to look at the dresses.

"Mum, do you really like the dress?" Alison asked, as her friends looked through the racks of bridesmaid dresses.

"Alison, I love it and all of the accessories and shoes, everything. If we can get the girls sorted out today, then that's another thing done," Bet said. "Excuse me, do you have another of these dresses or is this the only one?" Bet asked.

"There is another one in stock in her size, this one is only a sample dress. I'll get it for her," the assistant said. "On the day of the wedding, the best thing for the veil is to steam it from the kettle, don't iron it, it will ruin it," she added.

"Can I leave this with you for a few minutes, Mum, so I can go and have a look with the girls and see if there's anything we all like?" Alison asked.

"Go ahead, we aren't going anywhere," Bet said.

Alison went over to the dresses; there were lots of colours.

"Al, are you thinking of a particular colour?" Jo asked.

"Well, I was thinking of a nice peach and maybe put Emma in a cream?" Alison said.

They found two different dresses, which they all liked, and the girls tried them on.

"I think I like Stacey's better," Bet said, as the girls came out of the changing room.

"So do I," Dorothy said.

"Do you have another of these dresses in a size 12?" Alison asked the sales assistant.

"I'll have a look for you," she said.

Once the sales assistant had found the matching bridesmaid dresses, she went over to the infant flower girl dresses and found a cream dress with a touch of lace but had a peach coloured sash around the middle. Stacey put it on her quickly and she stood next to them, they looked a picture.

"Yes, to all three dresses, Mum?" Alison asked.

"I agree; Dot?" Bet asked.

"Most definitely!" Dot said.

The lady asked them their size shoes, and she bought out the same as Alison's. They tried them on, and they all looked perfect.

They took everything over to the till, so they could look for the headwear, but they didn't really see much else.

"There is British Home Stores up the road, if you want to have a look in there, but I shouldn't really be telling you," the assistant whispered and smiled.

"Thank you, love," Bet whispered back.

Bet paid the bill, and the assistant boxed up Alison's dress and bagged up her shoe box and tiara box. She needed the hoop as well otherwise the dress would be rather flat. That went in another box. The veil went in with the shoes and tiara. Then she bagged up the girl's dresses and shoes.

"When you get home, put the dresses up on their hangers. I know you didn't want the hoop under the dresses, but if you put them up under each one for a time, it will fill the dress out and it won't need ironing or anything," she told them.

They went along to British Home Stores to look for some headwear for Emma, Stacey and Jo and some shoes for Emma.

"Do you sell bridesmaid shoes for little tots?" Alison asked a shop assistant.

"Yes, we do, right this way," the member of staff said.

Dot found a seat, so she sat down, and they left the bags and boxes with her, so they could have a look at what shoes they had. Stacey told the lady the size for Emma and she returned with some lovely flat shoes for her. Some had a strap across with a buckle with little diamantes on them. Emma tried them on. They were soft and she could practise ballet once the wedding was over.

Next, they looked at the headwear. They chose flowered clips for Stacey and Jo and a ring of flowers for Emma.

Bet paid the bill at the till, thanked the lady and they went to find Dot, who looked like she was about to fall asleep.

"It's so hot in here!" Dot said, fanning herself with a brochure she had found.

"It's OK, Dot, we're done now. Come on, let's go," Bet said.

They finally found their way to the lifts and left the store.

"Now, who's for something to eat and drink? All this shopping is exhausting!" Bet said.

"Yes, but where Mum?" Alison said.

"Look, there's a Pizza Place, if we get a big enough table inside, we can put the bags down for a few minutes," Bet suggested.

They went across the road and then made their way to the Pizza Place.

Stacey took Emma to the toilet, and they all sat down and ordered their drinks while they chose their food.

Bet looked at her watch, it almost three o'clock.

"I can't believe the time! Once we have had something to eat and it goes down, I think we will need to make a move back home, otherwise we will be going back when all of the revellers will be going out," Bet said.

Stacey came back with Emma.

"Who's going out?" Stacey asked.

"Stace, I was just saying when we finish here, we should start thinking about heading back home, otherwise we will get caught up with the revellers going out for the night, what do you think?" Bet asked.

"I agree, it's getting rather busy," Stacey said.

After their food, they hailed two cabs back to the station. They only had to wait about ten minutes for the train to arrive.

"Don't forget it's Valentine's Day today, are you going out tonight?" Bet asked the girls.

"Rob's taking me out for dinner, providing we get back in time," Alison said.

"Me and Mike are going for a drink and we'll see after that. Mum said she would babysit Emma," Stacey said.

"I'm staying in, I'm bloody shattered! I'm going to have a lovely hot bath then relax in front of the telly!" Jo said.

"Is Tom going out with Debbie tonight, Mum?" Alison asked.

"I think so. Freddie and Charlie are home tonight though. We may get a takeaway; see how we feel when we get in," Bet said.

They got on the train and were talking about the day and how lucky there were getting everything sorted out already.

"Bet, what are you wearing for the wedding?" Dot asked.

"Do you know, Dot, I haven't even thought about it! I'll let you know, but if you get your outfit before me, let me know the colour!" Bet said, "We don't want to turn up wearing the same outfit!" Bet laughed.

They pulled in to Margate train station and Bruce picked them up. Stacey's husband Mike met her and Emma, so they went home together, and Bruce took everyone else.

"Thank you, Bet for a lovely day." Dot said, "and you, my dear, are going to be a stunning bride!" She said to Alison.

Bruce dropped Dot off, then parked up outside their house.

"Rob called a little while ago, I said you weren't back from London yet, but as we have just dropped his mum off, he will know your nearly home," Bruce said.

"Are you going out tonight, Al?" Her dad asked.

"We are supposed to, but see how I feel when we get in, Dad," Alison replied.

After dropping Jo off to Rose and Henry's, Bet, Bruce and Alison headed home.

It had been a long and exhausting day.

Chapter 25

It was a bright, sunny morning and Alison woke up early. She looked over at her alarm clock and it already said seven thirty. This was too early to be up today, but she couldn't sleep anymore; she was far too excited.

Today, this day was going to be the day she would become Mrs Robert Freeman! Who would have thought on that first day at secondary school she would meet the love of her life? He had literally knocked her over when she was pulling up her sock and they had been together ever since.

She looked over at the gown on the front of her wardrobe. It was a bright white and she would look stunning in it. There was a gentle knock on the door.

"Come in," Alison said.

It was her mum with a cup of tea for her.

"Morning, how are you feeling this morning? Nervous?" Bet asked.

"No, not at all, I just wish it wasn't so bright, then I may have had a chance to lie in for half an hour more!" Alison said.

Bet hugged her daughter; they were both excited. As Alison had chosen peach for her colour theme, Bet chose a soft pink outfit with matching hat and clutch bag. She would look coordinated with her whole outfit.

Alison sat up in her bed drinking her tea, with her mother sitting on her bed.

"What would you like for breakfast? Egg on toast? Fry up? Smoked salmon and scrambled eggs?" Bet asked.

"Can I have smoked salmon and scrambled eggs? That way if I don't feel too well later on, the sunny side ups won't come back up!" Alison laughed.

Bet took her cup and Alison got out of bed, and walked over to her dress, and touched it lightly. She loved it!

"Here comes the blushing bride!" Bruce shouted as Alison came down the stairs for breakfast.

"Here, Honey," he said, pulling out a chair for her to sit down. Bet had already made most of the breakfast, then Tom, Freddie and Charlie came running downstairs.

"Morning Al, ready for the big day?" Tom asked, giving her a kiss on the cheek. The other two followed suit.

"Boys, where are your suits?" Bet asked, as she came in with their breakfasts.

"They're up in the top room, Mum, so we can get ready up there out of the way," Tom said.

"Right, good. What time are Jo, Stacey and Emma coming over to get ready?" Bet asked.

"The plan is they get here about twelve, that way we can have our make-up and hair done at the same time," Alison said.

"OK, that's fine," Bet said, handing Alison her breakfast.

Bruce had been put on a diet by Bet a while ago and he had stuck to it very well, but occasionally she let him have a treat.

"Here you are, my love," Bet said handing Bruce his breakfast. He had the same as Alison.

"Why have I got smoked salmon and scrambled eggs, Bet?" He asked.

"I'm sorry Bruce, but you can't have a fry up today. With all of the rich food you're going to be eating today!" Bet said.

"Bet, darling I haven't had a fry up in a long time! I thought this once, you would allow me!" Bruce said, pulling a sulky face.

"No, Bruce, anyway, I thought you would like to eat the same as the bride," Bet smiled at her husband.

He looked at Alison's breakfast and a huge smile came across his face. He shut up and started to eat.

"Now, once you've all eaten your breakfasts, I want you boys in the shower as there are three of you and it takes you time to get you all sorted out. I'll go and sort out your underwear and shoes, so once you've had breakfast, go upstairs; unless you want your hair done by the hairdressers?" Bet said.

"Eww, no thanks!" The boys all said.

When they had all finished, Bet chased the boys upstairs. She was nothing if not organised.

"Al, are you having a bath or shower?" Bet asked.

"As it's only just gone nine, I thought I might have a bubble bath soak, what do you think?" Alison said.

"Al, you have plenty of time, go and have a soak and relax," Bet said.

They had been rushing around for days, making sure the last-minute things were all ready for the big day.

"Bruce, where's your suit?" Bet asked.

"Same as the boys; in front of the wardrobe, just beside your beautiful outfit," Bruce replied. Bet smiled, she went back into the kitchen and finished washing up. Bruce grabbed a tea towel and started to dry up.

Alison went back upstairs to run her bath. The hairdressers and make-up girls were coming about eleven, so she wanted to be ready in her underwear by the time they arrived.

She put a luxurious bubble bath in that Rob had bought her for Christmas.

They had just finished doing the renovations on the house, which they were all delighted with.

The doorbell rang and Bet answered it.

"Al, the flowers have arrived! Bet shouted up the stairs.

Despite her mother rushing around like a headless chicken, Alison was as calm as a cucumber.

She smiled and took off her robe and stepped into the bath.

While lying there, she imaged what the day would be like. She dipped under the water to rinse her hair, before shampooing it. This would really be the only time to herself today and she was going to make the most of it.

When she got out of the bath, she put her slippers and robe on and then went to her bedroom. The wedding presents were going back to her mum and dads and they would put them in their new home when they returned from their honeymoon.

Bet knocked on the door.

"Honey, would you like another cuppa?" She asked.

"I better not, Mum; I don't want to be on the loo all morning!" Alison laughed.

The doorbell rang again, and Tom answered it and called up to Alison.

"Al, there are two ladies here; very pretty ones at that!" He said cheekily.

"Send them up, Tom! It'll be the stylists," Alison shouted back down.

Tom let them in and showed them where to go upstairs.

"Oh good, you kept your hair in a towel." Maxine, the hairdresser said.

Maxine took the towel off Alison's head and her hair was still a bit damp, damp enough to make a lovely hairstyle for her.

521

Bet knocked on the door.

"I just brought this in for you, girls," she said, holding a bottle of champagne and some glasses.

"Oh, thank you, Mrs Linton," Maxine said.

Stacey the make-up artist took a glass as well.

"Mrs Linton, are you having your hair done too?" Maxine asked.

"I'm not sure. We still have the bridesmaids and a lovely little flower girl to be done first, but if we have time, that would be lovely," Bet said.

Maxine made a start on Alison's hair.

"Now Alison, did you want your hair up or down?" She asked.

"Up, please, I have natural wavy curls, so I would like them to cascade down, but mostly up, if that's all right?" Alison said. She was looking forward to having her hair done, she didn't normally go to the hairdressers, only for a trim. Maxine set to work.

By the time everyone else arrived to have their hair and makeup done, Alison's room was getting full up. Bet left the room to get some more glasses for the champagne. She returned minutes later, with a glass each for Stacey and Jo.

Bet had brought their dresses down to Tom's room as the boys were using upstairs to get ready and Bruce was getting ready in his room.

"Oh, sorry Jo, I forgot to ask, how's Rose?" Alison asked as Jo was having her hair styled.

"Oh, she's OK. She'll be over in a little while," Jo said.

"Of course, she's family," Alison said.

Bet smiled to herself and shed a little tear, she wiped her eyes dry.

"Are you OK, Mrs Linton?" Maxine asked her.

"Sorry, yes, yes, I'm fine. It's just we had some bad news a couple of days ago," Bet said.

"We lost a dear person to us on Wednesday who was as important to us as Mum and Dad," Alison explained, giving her mum a hug.

Henry had always taken it easy since his heart attack a few years ago, but recently, he was so excited and happy about the wedding and he tried to do a bit more than he should have. He collapsed and was taken to hospital again—this time, he didn't make it and died on the way there.

Rose was still in a state of shock, but she still wanted to come today and celebrate with Alison and Rob and be with the family for happy times. The only thing was that Alison wouldn't be able to attend the funeral as it would be while they were away, and they were going to Greece for their honeymoon. But she would go with mum and dad and Rose to the grave on her return.

Everyone in the room had teared up. Bruce had knocked on the door and was surprised to see the women in tears.

"Cheer up! It's supposed to be a happy day!" He said.

"We were just talking about Henry, Dad," Alison said.

"Oh, OK. I'll go back downstairs. Does anyone want a cuppa?" Bruce asked.

"No, I think we're all fine with the champagne, thanks love," Bet said.

Bruce left the room and then called up.

"Bet?" He called.

When she got downstairs, Rose was in the hall, looking a million dollars.

"Rose! How are you, darling?" Bet said, hugging her.

"Not too bad, how's my girl? All excited?" Rose asked.

"Why don't you come up and see her, she's not in her dress yet, she's still getting sorted out with her make-up. Come on up," Bet said, leading her up the stairs.

"Hello everyone!" Rose said.

"Hello Rose!" Everyone said.

Emma was just having the last of her curls done and then it was time for Bet to have her hair done.

Stacey was having her make-up done, Jo had just finished. Jo went over to Rose, who looked at her face, she had tears welling up, as did Jo. Jo hugged Rose and then Alison hugged Rose and Jo.

"That's all I need, girls, for my make-up to run," Bet said with a smile. She wiped her eyes.

"Not to worry, Bet, I'll touch it up for you," Stacey said.

"Well, I think we need to go and get these dresses on," Stacey said, as she took Emma into Tom's room and picked up her dress.

Maxine and Stacey left the room, so Alison could put on her dress and then came back in when she had got it on.

"Oh Alison, sorry I forgot, I bought you a blue garter!" Stacey said.

Emma handed it to her, and she pulled up her dress and put it on her left leg.

Alison was ready: she looked absolutely stunning.

Bruce knocked on the door and opened it, he stood there just staring at Alison, his breath taken away.

"Oh, sorry everyone," Bruce said, "the photographer just turned up."

They thanked Maxine and Stacey for their hair and make-up and then went downstairs. He had already been to see Rob and his best man, his cousin Garry. Alison took her time down the stairs, she had two floors to come down, thankfully everywhere else would be on the ground floor.

The photographer placed them all where he wanted them to stand. Rose was in a couple of the photos with Alison and with Bet and Bruce as well. The boys looked lovely in their suits and the photographer was great putting them all at ease.

Alison and her mum were at the window, looking out, and saw the wedding cars pull up—two beautiful white Rolls Royce.

Bet went with the bridesmaids and Rose. Bruce waited with Alison for a few minutes.

"You look absolutely beautiful, Alison. I am so proud of you!" he said as he kissed her on the forehead. "Come on, we had better go, you're nearly late for your own wedding!"

Alison held her flowers on her lap; they set off. The church was only a little way away and when they got there, the photographer was taking photos of the bridesmaids at the church with Bet and Rose.

When Alison and Bruce pulled up, he positioned his tripod ready to take more photos of them, then they all got ready to go into church.

The wedding march started, and Alison and Bruce moved inside the church. Alison stood on her father's right and then they walked down the aisle with Emma behind them, followed by Stacey and Jo behind her.

Alison met Rob at the alter and he looked astounded at how beautiful she looked. They started to sing their hymns and then the vicar started the marriage ceremony. After another hymn, they exchanged their vows and wedding rings.

When it came to signing and witnessing the marriage, Alison asked her mum and Rob asked his mum if they would be the witnesses. They both felt so proud. Their little ones were all grown up and taking the next step to their lives together.

The wedding tune started up on the organ and it was time to leave the church. The flowers in the church looked lovely. Alison hadn't had a chance to look on the way in.

Alison was so pleased to see Sandra, George, Roger and Celia had come. They threw confetti over her and Rob when they came out of the church.

They got back into their cars, Alison and Rob drove off to the reception. Bruce, Bet, Rose and the bridesmaids and the boys all just about managed to get in the other car.

The hotel on the front looked lovely and they were all greeted by a member of staff standing in the foyer with a tray of champagne on it. They were then ushered into their room for the reception.

The room had been decorated lovely, with peach and cream balloons strung up in a rainbow shape over the top table. The tables had either balloons on them or a flower arrangement. The cake was a beautiful heart shape; four tiers and a little mini Alison and Rob on the top of the cake. Bet and Bruce had done them proud.

The happy couple had a few moments to themselves before everyone came in and the photographer took a few photos of them cutting the cake.

Once everyone was greeted and had a glass of champagne, they all found their seats. Rose was on the top table with Bet and Bruce, but also sitting next to Jo, which she was pleased about. The food was served, which was either clear soup or prawn cocktail, there was wine on the table, the main course was beef with seasonal vegetables and a choice of potatoes.

When the table was cleared, dessert followed: profiteroles, lemon sorbet or chocolate gateau. Tom and Bruce licked their lips.

Once dessert had finished and the tables were being cleared, Bruce got up from his chair and clinked on his glass for a little hush. He thanked everyone for coming, said the bridesmaids and flower girls looked lovely and then held his glass up for everyone to toast the bride and groom.

Once Bruce finished his speech, Garry stood up and said his piece about the bridesmaids and how lovely they all look and wasn't it nice to dress up once in a while. Everyone howled with laughter. He said a few comical things about Rob, then toasted the bride and groom.

Then it was Rob's turn. He thanked Bet and Bruce for all of their help with the wedding and their house, thanked the bridesmaids and gave them their gifts. He then gave his mum and Bet a huge bouquet of flowers each and his best man, a tankard. Then he came to Alison.

"I would like to thank Alison for agreeing to being my wife today. She has made me the happiest man alive and she looks absolutely stunning! I would like you to all raise a glass to my new wife and bride, Alison!" Rob cheered.

"Oh, before I forget, there is a very special lady here today who we all want to thank…" Rob said. He picked up another bouquet of flowers and handed them to Rose.

"These are for you, Rose, because without you, I would never have met this beautiful lady!" He bent down and gave Rose a kiss on the cheek.

Rose went back to her seat, with tears in her eyes again.

Garry the best man stood up again.

"Is that the speeches done now then? Right, let's get drinking and dancing!" He said.

There was still wine on the tables, the staff came over and moved the tables further back so there would be more room for dancing. Bruce went up to the bar. He and Bet had paid for a free bar, so everyone could enjoy themselves.

The evening was soon here. Alison went over and had a chat with Sandra and the other staff. This was the best outcome they could have wished for Alison and Tom. Alison was starting a new life, Tom and his brothers were all together and Debbie, Tom's girlfriend came along as well, and they looked as happy as Rob and Alison.

"We are so pleased, Alison, that things have worked out so well for you!" Sandra said.

"Yes, I still can't believe it!" Alison beamed. "Did you hear about Henry?"

"Yes, your mum called and told us, knowing we would be seeing Rose, we didn't want to say anything, you know, to upset her," George said.

The disco was starting to get ready, he already knew what Alison and Rob wanted for their first dance, it was a little early, but there were a few children who wanted to dance, so they decided to go ahead.

"Well, it's now that time of the evening, when Mr and Mrs Freeman have their first dance!" the DJ said, as *We've Only Just Begun* by The Carpenters came on. It was one of Alison's favourite songs, and very appropriate for the events of the day. Rob and Alison danced in a circle as people took photos of them as man and wife.

When it finished, Rob and Alison left the dancefloor to get a drink. The DJ started playing some lively music, so when they got their drinks they were back on the dancefloor. Tom had a couple of dances with Debbie and the night flew by.

Alison and Rob were staying at the hotel for the night, their stuff was already there, from the day before, so when they had had enough dancing and ready said goodbye to their guests, they said goodnight and went upstairs to their beds.

Alison and Rob were due to fly out to Greece the following lunchtime, so they had to leave by eleven. Bruce was going to take them to the airport, but take Alison's dress and stuff back after they dropped them off.

Alison and Rob looked so happy as they headed off to Gatwick airport.

***

The car pulled up; it was big, long, and black. Bet, Bruce, and the boys were standing inside and were worried they were going to be late. They left home and walked down towards Rose's house. The hearse was right outside the house. The car following was for Rose and Jo, but Rose wanted Bet, Bruce, and the boys to come with her. There were only a couple more people behind; people Henry knew from the local club he used to go to.

The undertaker took the flower tributes from Bruce and Tom. Rose and Jo got in the car and sat in the back. Bet sat with them and the boys sat in the seat in front of them. Bruce sat in the front with the driver.

The funeral director walked in front of the hearse with the coffin in. Henry was having his service in the same church that Alison and Rob had just got married in. It felt funny to have been there a few days ago celebrating.

The vicar told the congregation all about Henry: he had been a soldier and had fought in the Second World War, where he had got injured. He continued, saying how he had met Rose and how they had set up the guest house together.

Rose smiled occasionally.

When they had finished, they left the church and went back to the cars. Henry was now going to be laid to rest at Margate Cemetery. It didn't take too long at the graveside and Bet and Jo were crying a lot. Rose had wet tears, but no sound came from her. She knew she had had a good life with Henry, and they had both been happy and she was grateful for that. She had such good memories of him and that was how she wanted to remember Henry.

She threw a single, red rose onto his coffin as it was lowered into the ground and she stood there for a little while and told Henry she loved him.

Rose had arranged for the wake to be held in the local club, where Henry used to go and play darts. She couldn't face doing the food herself.

It had been a couple of eventful days they'd all had, but Henry had had a lovely send off.

"What a funny day," Tom said to his dad.

"What do you mean, Son?" Bruce said when they were back home.

"I didn't mean funny ha-ha, Dad. It's just we were at the church on Saturday for Alison and Rob's wedding and then back today to say goodbye to Henry," Tom mused.

"I know, Son," Bruce nodded. "Right, everyone into your night things; you still have school and college tomorrow," Bruce said.

***

Two weeks came and went, and Alison and Rob were home and standing outside their new house. They went up the steps to their newly finished house. Rob opened the front door and then picked Alison up and carried her over the threshold. They were both laughing.

"Rob, our luggage is still outside!" she told him.

"I know, but I wanted to be a bit traditional!" He laughed.

He went back outside and grabbed their bags and cases.

Alison closed the door behind him, she helped him take their stuff upstairs to their bedroom. The dinning-room table was covered with their wedding gifts.

When they had finished unpacking, they went down to the kitchen. There was already milk in the fridge and something for a snack.

"Mum?" Alison laughed.

"Yep, I bet!" Rob laughed.

After a quick cup of tea and a sandwich, then thought they had better see both sets of parents. Everyone was so pleased to see them.

"Did you have a good time? You both have lovely colours! Did you get chance to sunbathe or was it too hot?" Bet bombarded them with questions. She had missed them so much.

"Oh. how did it go for Henry?" Alison asked,

"It went as well as to be expected," Bruce smiled. He was glad to have them back too.

"How's Rose?"

"You know Rose; she just plods on, she gave him a good send off and she said she has her memories and that's how she wants to remember him, not stuck in the ground," Bet said.

Alison and Rob popped in to see Rose and Jo once they had seen Rob's mum. Rose was delighted to see them. They told her they would come with her on Saturday to the cemetery as they both had to return to work the following day.

They said their goodbyes to everyone and headed back to their own home.

***

Alison woke early the next day to go to work. It was as if she hadn't even been away, and everyone was glad to see her back and they all said how much they enjoyed the wedding. She was quickly back into the swing of things and married life was working out well for both of them. They were so happy and so much in love.

***

Rob and Alison went to Bet and Bruce's for their first Christmas. Dot and Ernie were invited too, as well as Rose and Jo. Rose was still grieving for Henry, but he would have wanted her to enjoy herself even though he was no longer around.

After New Year, it was Tom's eighteenth birthday. He wanted a car and got one. He had been having lessons and was definitely following in Alison's footsteps.

In the summer, it was all hands on deck with the guest house. Rose had employed more local people to help out because Alison and Rob had full time jobs and could no longer work there, but Rob was always on hand if Rose needed a plumber.

Just as Alison and Rob were about to celebrate their second wedding anniversary, Alison was starting to feel a bit more tired than normal, and she was constantly hungry! When she was at home, she would be watching TV and if the adverts featured anything with fish in them, she would feel sick. She had no idea why.

She only saw her family at the weekend because she was exhausted when she got in from work, so she made an appointment with the doctor.

Alison was given a urine sample bottle to pee in by the receptionist.

"Mrs Freeman?" The nurse called her name.

Alison got up from her seat and went to the nurse's room.

"So, what's wrong then?" The nurse asked her.

"I don't know really. I am really tired at night and I'm struggling to get up in the morning…I'm eating more, my clothes are getting really tight and I have this really horrible taste in my mouth," Alison said.

The nurse smiled at her and nodded.

"Sounds to me as though you're pregnant, Mrs Freeman," she smiled.

"Pardon?" Alison said.

"You're pregnant, love. When was your last period?"

"20th July, I think…Oh, we're now in September! Oh, my goodness! I didn't realise! Oh my God, I'm pregnant!" Alison squealed.

"Just over eight weeks by my calculations. Are you pleased?" The nurse asked.

"Shocked is better the word!" Alison laughed.

The nurse completed a pregnancy test, which confirmed that Alison was indeed expecting a child.

"Now, we have a maternity clinic and a baby clinic on a Monday. You need to see the doctor, then she can sort you out for what you need, what to take. Oh, and you need to take Folic Acid; it helps during pregnancy, you can pick some up when you go to the chemist." The nurse smiled.

"Make an appointment with the doctor for tomorrow. The maternity clinic is on a Wednesday afternoon." The nurse added, "Congratulations, Mrs Freeman, and see you soon."

Alison's head was still spinning when she left the surgery. Pregnant? She would have to tell Rob before she told anyone else; mind you all she wanted to do was go home. Which she did.

Alison didn't hear Rob come in; she was on the bed fast asleep.

"Al, you OK?" Rob sat by her side on the bed.

"Erm what?" she murmured.

"Al, you OK?" he asked again.

"What? Yes." She sat up on the bed. "Rob, I have something to tell you. I'm pregnant…about eight weeks," Alison said.

"Pregnant? Are you sure?" Rob looked stunned.

"Yes, I am. At least now I know why I've been feeling so run down…are you OK?" she asked worryingly.

"OK? I'm bloody over the moon!" Rob said, grinning from ear to ear, and kissed her. "Shall we tell our parents?"

"I know we should, but I'm so tired," Alison said.

"How about I call them all around now and we can tell them and if you still feel unwell, you can get some rest, but I think they need to know as soon as possible Al, what do you think? Al?" Alison had fallen back to sleep.

Rob called Bet and Bruce and his parents to come over and they let themselves in.

Rob showed them into the sitting room and asked them to sit down. He went back upstairs to Alison who had just come out of the bathroom. Alison followed him downstairs. Everyone looked worried. They looked at Alison; Bet and Dot both knew.

"Hi everyone, sorry to worry you!" she said. "It's just me and Rob have something to tell you…we're going to have a baby; I'm just over eight weeks…and I feel awful!" Alison laughed.

Everyone cheered.

"Oh, this is wonderful news, Al!" Bet and Bruce said, hugging her.

Alison sat down on the sofa.

"Al, do you want to go back up to bed, we can go, I know it's great news, but you look like you need to go back to bed," Bruce said.

"Dad, I'm fine, I think I am just in shock. I've been asleep for a few hours and didn't hear Rob come in and I was just sick before you got here. But I will go back up to bed, if you don't mind, but I have to go to the doctor's tomorrow afternoon just to get checked in and the pregnancy detailed for the hospital. Sorry, I have to go back up!" Alison said and quickly left the room.

Alison went straight off to sleep again. Everyone was so happy with the news, as she and Rob were, but she wasn't feeling well at the moment.

The following day Alison went to work and explained to Mike that she needed the afternoon off. She had to go back to see the doctor and have her first check up for her pregnancy and have it registered with the hospital. Mike was fine with that. He had two daughters, one who was heavily pregnant at the moment, so he could empathise.

"Just let me know when you're going to be off and don't forget to tell Doris and Joan, so they can keep up with everything for you," he said.

Alison went back to her office, then went to see both of the ladies and told them about her being pregnant. It wasn't a secret, but she hadn't had time to tell anyone, with just finding out the day before.

They congratulated her and Rob and she went back to her desk to finish what needed doing before she went at lunchtime.

The doctor called her in and spoke to her for a while, and then asked her what hospital Alison would like to have her baby. Alison asked for Queen Elizabeth The Queen Mother Hospital. The doctor gave her a referral letter and asked her to make an appointment. Her due date was 12 April. The doctor took her blood pressure, weighed her and asked her to bring a sample with her every time she attended an appointment.

The doctor wanted to see her again in a few weeks' time and she should have had her appointment at the hospital by then.

Alison left and made her way home but called into Bet and Bruce first.

"Hi," Alison said.

"Hi Al, how are you doing?" Bet asked.

"Mum, I'm fine. Just had my first doctor's appointment for the pregnancy," Alison said and told Bet and her dad all about it.

"Al, it's only like this for a little while longer," her mum said.

"You were pregnant?" Alison asked.

"Well, before me and your dad went down the fostering route, we had been trying to have a family for years, and a couple of times, we got lucky, but I couldn't ever carry past three months. I shouldn't even be telling you this, it's not fair on you. Anyway, after about the third time, I couldn't take anymore and we gave up trying," Bet said.

"Is that why you decided to foster kids then?" Alison said.

"Oh no, we had already given up and resided to the fact that we would be childless. Until we met you and Tom, that is," Bet smiled at the memory. "When we saw you again, when you had run away, that determined our decision. We didn't want any other child to be treated how you and Tom had been treated and we had fallen in love with you both. That's when we made our mind up to start the ball rolling and look how it turned out—we don't have just have two wonderful children but four wonderful children, and Jo is just down the road. It has worked out perfectly," Bet said, hugging Alison.

"Now, you have had your tea, go along home, have something to eat and put your feet up, but don't forget to call the hospital," Bet told her daughter.

Alison did as she was told.

Her first hospital visit had been arranged for 30 September; a week after their anniversary. She told Rob when he got in and he said he wanted to come with her and she told him the due date as well, he was delighted.

Three weeks later, Alison had her first scan. It was a surreal moment seeing their baby for the first time on the monitor.

"There we have it! Here is your little bubba!" The sonographer said, pointing out the small baby on the screen. Alison and Rob were mesmerised; they couldn't stop looking at their baby.

"Can you see what it is yet?" Rob asked.

"Not yet, Sir, but you should do at the twenty-week-scan in about nine weeks' time. Would you like a photograph?"

"Oh, yes please, how much are they?" Alison asked.

"Oh, the first one is free. If you want any more, you have to pay, I'm afraid," she told them.

"Can we have two then, one each?" Rob asked, with a huge beaming smile on his face.

"Of course, hold on a sec."

The lady handed both of them an envelope with the scan photo of their baby. Alison wiped the gel off her tummy and pulled her trousers back up.

"Don't forget to make your next appointment at the desk to see the doctor," the sonographer told her.

"We will, thank you!" Alison said.

They went home and showed their families their scan photos.

"Bubs is so small!" Bruce said, smiling at the photo.

"Yes, but he or she will grow, Dad, don't worry, everything is fine," Alison reassured him.

***

The following week Alison was already twelve weeks pregnant. She was starting to get a little belly on her. She noticed it when she got out of the bath. She and Rob had spoken about her carrying on with work as it wasn't too taxing a job and she said she would continue until she felt it was getting too much.

The months were flying by. Rob wanted to decorate the room next to theirs as a nursery and he and Alison were starting to choose colours schemes. she had only a week until her twenty-week scan, and they wanted to see what they were having before choosing the final details for the baby's room.

"Hello again, you're here for the twenty-week scan," the sonographer said. "Did you want to know the sex of the baby today?"

"Yes please!" Both Rob and Alison said at the same time.

They all looked at the screen again, mesmerised by how big their baby had grown in those last few weeks.

"Nurse, can you see what the baby is yet?" Rob asked.

"Err, yes, I can. Positive you want to know?"

They both nodded.

"You're having a little boy!" the lady said.

"A boy! Are you sure?" Rob asked.

"Yes...there's a sure sign! He's definitely a boy!" She laughed, pointing at the screen.

They were both beaming at the thought of having a boy.

"Right, well, everything seems fine. He's a good size and for his age, so I'm happy with your scan, good luck with everything."

Alison sorted herself out and they left the room with yet another photo each of their boy. "Right, we have to start thinking about names!" Rob said.

"I have been thinking a bit about names, but now we know it's a boy, do you have anything in mind?" Alison asked.

"Not really, Al, what about you?" He asked.

"Well, yes, what do you think about Henry? Henry Freeman?" Alison asked him.

"I love it and Rose will love it and Henry would have been chuffed to bits, what about a middle name?" Rob said.

"If we start using our dad's names he will sound like an accountant! What about Henry Thomas Freeman? I know there are Charlie and Freddie, Dad and your dad, but then it gets crazy," added Alison.

"Do you know what, I think it's excellent and the boys won't mind too much, and if we have a girl later on, we can call her Charley Frederica or something like that, what do you say?" Rob laughed. They left the hospital and went home.

***

It was only a couple of weeks until Christmas. Bet, Bruce, and the boys were all helping out. Tom had already got his new car and he was working with Rob and his dad, which he loved. Rob and Alison thought they would surprise everyone at Christmas and reveal the baby's name they had decided on.

They arrived at Bet and Bruce's on Christmas Eve and everyone was running around, getting last minute things. It had been snowing and Bet and Bruce didn't want Alison going anywhere she didn't need to, so they were running errands for her. They ordered the crib and the cot, they had seen some lovely wallpaper and borders for his bedroom and Alison had seen a beautiful rocking chair in a white, so Rob bought it for the nursery.

Rob had finished decorating the nursery the day before Christmas Eve. As he worked in the building trade, they would shut down for two weeks, and only do emergencies. He had put the cot together and the crib was going into their room for when they both came home from the hospital.

When they went to Bet and Bruce's it had already been finished. Rob carried their presents then went back for their bags. They were staying for Christmas then going home for a couple of days, then returning for New Year. Bet stayed home while Bruce went out to town. It was now a tradition of theirs to get cakes from Molly's on Christmas Eve for everyone to have later on in the day.

Alison was now blossoming into a heavily six-month pregnant mum-to-be. She hadn't put on a lot of weight, she was all baby, but was always so slim, so she seemed to waddle when she walked. Bet wouldn't let her do anything though.

Tom went out later on with Debbie and came back rather late, they were both laughing, and Debbie kept raising her left hand. It took a while to sink in, then Alison suddenly noticed the huge diamond on her wedding ring finger.

"Oh my God! Congratulations, you two!" she shouted.

Bet and Bruce turned around.

"Oh, my goodness! Tom, Debbie. Congratulations, this is fantastic!" Bet said.

Bruce picked up the bottle of champagne that was chilling in the fridge and everyone jumped up to wish them congratulations.

"Thank you, I can't believe it!" Debbie said. "Tom took me to the end of the promenade and asked me to marry him. Just the two of us. You're not angry, are you, that we did it first?" she added.

"No of course not, you do it how you want to," Alison said, hugging them both.

Bruce poured out the champagne and offered everyone a glass.

"Oh, Debbie, what about your mum and dad, do they know?" Bet asked.

"Yes, we popped over there first. Tom wanted to ask for my hand in marriage, but considering he had already given me the ring, it didn't make much difference," she added.

After everyone had had their champagne, Debbie and Tom went out for the evening. There was something nice about being along the seafront in the winter, especially at Christmas.

By the time Tom got back, most of the group had gone to bed. Bet and Bruce stayed up, but Alison was shattered. The extra weight she was carrying was wearing her out.

"Rob, when do you want to reveal about the baby?" Alison asked him.

"What about after dinner?" Rob said sleepily.

They both fell asleep.

Bet woke them up at nine and gave them both a cup of tea. The boys were still in bed. It was funny, when they were little, they were up at the crack of dawn on Christmas Day. Now they were older, they wanted to stay in bed for a little while longer.

Soon everyone was up, with a bacon sandwich and cup of tea and they started opening their gifts. They were all pleased with what they got.

Alison mostly got stuff for herself and a few things for the new baby. Rose and Jo turned up about an hour later with their gifts.

Bet was in and out of the kitchen, sorting out the dinner. Rose went in and gave her a hand.

Soon it was lunchtime, and everyone sat down.

After they had eaten, Rob cleared his throat.

"Erm, I have, well, we have a few words to say, if you don't mind? Al and I are going to have a baby boy in April, and we wanted you all to be the first to know. We've decided to call him Henry." Rob smiled at Rose.

"You don't mind, do you, Rose?" Alison asked.

"No, I don't, love; Henry would have been chuffed to bits!" she said.

"He's going to be Henry Thomas," Alison added, winking at her brother.

Everyone looked at Tom, then Freddie and Charlie.

"Don't worry, boys, if we have a girl, she will be called Charley Frederica," Rob laughed.

Everyone laughed and Rose came over to Alison and Rob and hugged both of them.

"Henry would have been so pleased and so proud at how you two have turned out. You're so lovely, all of you," she said.

It had been an emotional couple of days. Rob's parents came over and Rob told them; they were both delighted. They all enjoyed Christmas and the New Year celebrations.

Tom saw a lot of Debbie over the holidays. She was working at the local hairdressers and she loved it. She didn't earn very much, but like Bet and Bruce, her parents were going to pay for their June wedding.

Alison kept on working up to the end of February. She was going onto maternity leave, but she didn't know if she was coming back or not yet.

She was called into Mike's office and she waddled down there. When she got to the main office and there were balloons up and congratulations banners in blue and white, along with a huge pile of gifts. Alison didn't know what to think, Mike broke out the Champagne so everyone except Alison had a glass. They had a small celebration and had laid on some sandwiches, biscuits and they got some lovely cakes from Molly's.

Before Alison left, Mike called her into his office and thanked her for all her hard work and assured her she would always have a job there if she wanted it. He handed her an envelope but told her to open it when she got home.

"Good luck with everything, Alison. I think I spot your husband waiting for you." Mike nodded in Rob's direction."

"Mike, thank you so much for everything, I really appreciate it. I will come back with the baby to show him off," Alison said.

Rob was waiting for her, he helped her take the stuff downstairs. "What if we take it down, leave it in reception and come back for the next lot?" Rob said.

Alison turned off her computer and typewriter and checked her desk was tidy. She was going to miss her office. She said goodbye to Doris and Joan and left the building.

When they got home with lots of gifts, Rob helped Alison out of the car, opened the front door and then emptied the very full car of gifts. Bet came running up the road, she saw them in the car with lots of stuff.

"Oh, my goodness, Rob! Where did all of this stuff come from?"

"Alison's work colleagues bought us all of this for the baby." He smiled.

"Need any help?" Bet asked.

"Err maybe upstairs, yes Bet, thank you."

Bet loved being around all of the baby stuff.

***

Alison was in bed one night. Just before her due date, she started to get pains in her back, which were quite strong. She never had pains like this; even her Braxton Hicks weren't this bad. She woke Rob up.

"Rob, Rob, wake up! I'm getting pains!" Alison said.

"Pains?" he asked half asleep, then he realised. "Pains? Al?"

"Yes, I think you'd better call an ambulance and mum and dad, and yours too," she added.

Rob jumped out of bed.

Thankfully, Alison had her bag ready to go to the hospital. Rob ran downstairs and made the relevant calls. Alison had managed to get out of bed but was huddled over the bed now. She was trying to find her flat shoes. She had one on, the other must have gone under the bed.

Rob came back in.

"Everyone's been called, and the ambulance should be here in a few minutes, are you OK?"

"Found it!" Alison said through gritted teeth.

She had put on a maternity dress when Bet and Bruce burst in.

"Al, you OK?" Bet asked.

"Yes, just getting ready for the hospital, but these pains! Argh!" She shouted.

Bet grabbed hold of her and told her to hold on tight to her and squeeze her hand if it hurt. The pain left as quick as it came.

The ambulance men turned up and Bruce let them in. They asked the relevant questions, which Alison answered in between pains and they asked if she had her bag ready. She pointed to it, then they said they had better leave.

Bet and Bruce followed in their car and Dot and Ernie went with them.

Alison and Rob were whisked away in the ambulance where she was taken straight up to the labour ward.

Alison was still having pains in her back; she had been having them since about eleven o'clock, it was now just after twelve thirty in the morning.

Rob went out to see the parents and just update them, there wasn't much going on, but they wanted to keep a check on her.

"Go back inside with her, Rob," his dad told him.

Rob went back in to be with his wife, who seemed to be struggling with the pain. They gave her gas and air, but it didn't seem to be enough. The midwife came back in and examined Alison, who nearly hit the ceiling when she examined her.

Another midwife came in and spoke to the first one. They looked at the readout from the monitor and called for a doctor to have a look.

"Alison isn't dilated enough for her to give birth yet, Doctor. She's in a lot of pain, can we give her an epidural? She's only dilated 5cms," the first midwife said.

"Yes, I think that's a good idea, otherwise we may be too late with administering it," the doctor said.

They helped Alison onto her side, bringing her knees up to her chest, which was nigh on impossible. Rob was encouraging her to do it, which she did eventually. An anaesthetist administered the epidural, then the doctor returned to take a look at how mother and baby were doing.

Alison wasn't feeling any pain now, but she still wasn't any further dilated. The doctor made a decision.

"Right, this baby is going to be in distress if he's not delivered soon, so I suggest we call theatre and ask them to prepare for a caesarean section," he ordered.

Everything happened so quickly after that. Rob was given a gown and mask and shown how to scrub up. The family waiting outside asked what was going on. Rob explained that Alison had to have a caesarean and was going up to theatre.

After a few minutes on being in theatre, the doctor had begun the procedure. Alison couldn't feel anything, but she was feeling anxious that their baby would be OK.

The next thing Alison heard was a loud cry.

Her baby had been born!

The midwife placed the baby in Alison's arms; he was huge, weighing in at just over nine pounds. He had tufts of dark hair, just like his dad. Alison couldn't believe it. He was here. Henry was really here!

Rob kissed Alison and his son and went to tell the family the news.

"Thank goodness that doctor suggested a c-section, Bruce!" Bet said, with a worried look on her face.

"Bet, she's fine, that's the main thing and the baby is here safely," Bruce said.

Bet nodded. she knew Bruce was right, but she had been so worried for Alison and the baby.

It took a while to stitch Alison up. They then moved her into the recovery ward.

"Oh, Al, how are you doing?" Bet asked.

"Yes, fine, Mum," Alison said.

"He's beautiful," Bet said, picking him up from Alison and cuddling her first grandchild.

***

They had all been there all night, and it was now gone six in the morning. Alison looked tired, but she was happy and relieved that Henry was finally here.

The midwife came over and took her blood pressure.

Bruce and Ernie had seen the baby and wanted to get a cuppa. Bet and Dot stayed a while. Alison would be in recovery for a couple of hours.

The men returned to Alison's bedside. Rob looked exhausted, so Alison sent him home. Bet brought Alison a cup of tea.

"Mrs Linton, they'll be taking Alison down to the mother and baby ward soon, do you want to come with her to get her settled, then I suggest you go home. Alison and the baby need their rest," a nurse said to Bet.

"Yes, certainly, thank you," Bet said.

Two porters came over and took Alison and Henry down to the ward on the first floor and got her settled in her space and the nurse looked at Bet.

"Darling, I will be back later. Get some sleep, both of you." Bet kissed both of them on the head.

Alison slept for a couple of hours and was woken when a nurse brought her a cup of tea.

"Hello." The nurse smiled.

"Oh, hello," Alison replied.

She felt down to her tummy and felt it flat. She then looked over in the crib to her sleeping baby.

"I thought I had dreamt it," Alison smiled.

"Don't worry, Alison, they all do at first."

Alison drank her tea down.

***

When Bruce and Rob got back, Rob fell asleep on the sofa, so when the boys came down to have breakfast, they were shocked to see him asleep. Bruce made the breakfast for the boys.

"Dad, why is Rob fast asleep on the sofa?" Freddie asked.

"Oh, because Alison had the baby at 5.20 am this morning and I brought Rob back with me. He's been up since eleven last night. What do you want for breakfast?" Bruce asked.

"Al's had the baby?" Tom said, surprised.

"She has, Tom. Don't worry, she's fine and in safe hands and Baby Henry is a healthy nine pounds in weight, tons of black hair," Bruce assured her brother. "Alison is going to be very sore and uncomfortable for some time, so if we can help her, we do, OK boys?" Bruce said.

"Yes of course, Dad." The boys replied.

"Alison, would you like to have a wash?" Mariette, Alison's nurse, asked.

"How?" Alison asked.

"Well, if you wash the bits you can do; you know, face, underarms, we will do the bottom half when we take your catheter out, then you have to use the loo." Mariette smiled.

Rob returned to the hospital in the afternoon. He looked in at his son in awe. Alison was fast asleep and looked so peaceful. Rob brought Alison flowers and a nurse put them in a vase by the side of her bed.

Shortly after, Alison woke.

"Hi Beautiful," Rob smiled at his brave wife, "how are you both? Have you changed him yet?"

"I did the second one; the nurses did the first change," Alison smiled, "he's such a good baby."

Soon, the rest of the family arrived to visit Alison and the baby.

"I should be able to get up soon," Alison told Bet and Dot.

"What did you have for lunch?" Dot asked.

"A ham salad sandwich," Alison pulled a face.

"Well, that's not enough, so thank goodness we bought you this." Dot handed Alison a bag of food. "I'll put it in your little cupboard."

541

Bruce looked at his watch.

"Bet, we should make a move, we have to get back for the boys' dinner," he said.

The family left Alison and Rob to have some quiet time with their new baby.

Rob stayed until 8 pm when visiting hours were over.

"Darling, I will see you both tomorrow; I'll come in the morning," Rob said, kissing her on her forehead.

Alison nodded; she was tired and was drifting off to sleep again.

After a good sleep, Alison felt like a new woman. She was able to get washed and out of bed and put some underwear on. She had her dinner, but Mariette was a little worried as she hadn't really had more than a sandwich, so she went to the kitchen and came back with a cup of tea and some hot buttered toast.

Alison had never enjoyed either so much before. Henry had been fed and changed and was in a fresh, blue Babygro.

"I feel like an invalid!" Alison said, as she tried to get out of bed when Henry cried.

"You're bound to, love, you've had major abdominal surgery; it will be a while before you can do what you did before you got pregnant, so take it easy please. Obviously, you have to move around but take care," Mariette told her.

Alison was now able to feed and change her son without any problems and was feeling better every day. The ward was noisy whether it was day or night and she couldn't wait to get home.

Henry didn't wake up until about six the following morning. Alison gave him another bottle, which he guzzled down. He was one hungry baby! Once he had his feed, he went back to sleep.

The tea lady came around to the ward again. Alison was grateful to have a cup of tea. Alison had had some sleep, but not as much as she had hoped for.

Henry was stirring, so she got him out of his crib and cuddled him.

It was now ten o'clock and the fathers' visiting hours had begun, so the ward was getting busy again. Alison looked at her bundle of joy. She still couldn't believe he was hers. She looked up and saw a lady at the door. She walked with a stick. Alison didn't think she was staff because she was in normal clothes.

Alison looked at the lady again; she recognised her from somewhere, but couldn't remember where from.

Then it suddenly hit her!

Tears started rolling down her face.

Rob was standing behind the lady with the stick, encouraging her forwards. She looked the same, but older, and her hair, even though blonde, was starting to grey a little.

"Mum? Mum?" Alison whispered, with tears in her eyes.

The lady edged over a little more; she looked at her grandson and then at her only daughter and then hugged them both.

The End